To Marlene —
A very friendly librarian in Fraser, Colorado. Thanks also for being a good listener to my story on my special TEST M train-sighting day!

Enjoy your small-town benefits, and your important service career.

Hope you like this read!

Burton
6/28/21

T.E.J.T.M.

The End Justifies The Means

by Burton Mitchell

www.BurtonMitchell.com

7/23

T.E.J.T.M. is distributed and available through BookMasters, Inc.
30 Amberwood Parkway, P.O.Box 388, Ashland, Ohio 44805
800-537-6727   419-281-5100   Fax: 419-281-0200
Ordering Number 1-800-247-6553.
order@bookmasters.com   www.bookmasters.com

This book is a work of fiction.

Design and Production by VisionServer LLC
info@VisionServer.net
www.Design.VisionServer.net/

Published by Mitchbook Publications, LLC
www.burtonmitchell.com
First printing, 2009

Library of Congress Control Number: 2009942412

ISBN: 978-0-615-32210-0

Cover Design by Russell Anderson, Layout by VisionServer LLC

Printed in the United States of America

Early Note To Readers:

Two sections which may prove helpful are placed after the story--

1- "Chapter of Contents" begins on page 471
2- "Character Reminders" begins on page 479

"About The Author" and "Celebration Page" conclude these printed pages, but hopefully our time together will continue in the future.

Acknowledgments

I am deeply grateful to my lovely wife Kathryn, who has patiently watched my dreams of peacemaking take many turns during our forty-six years of marriage. The idea of a national Peace Academy goes back for thirty-three of those years, while we were busy working and raising our wonderful children Jim and Cindy, and enjoying our new in-laws and five neat grandsons. There have been at least a dozen revisions of this story in manuscript form--just imagine how much time that has taken away from my helping with housekeeping chores and just enjoying being together! She's a doll for putting up with me, and I love her dearly.

Thanks also to my good longtime friend Dick Parker, who read various segments over and over for technical accuracy in areas not my expertise, and answered a hundred questions to keep me current. He and Mary Ellen McGinnis have provided an excellent support system, and lots of fun times watching movies together to relieve stress. I offer special thanks to John Richardson for his valued friendship and good advice; he made this publication finally possible. And much appreciation goes to Russell Anderson, a talented graphic artist, and his wife Terri, a skilled computer whiz, fine friends and nice relatives who helped us pull the logistics together to get this ready for the printer.

I believe the writing has some areas of inspiration that came out better than I could have written relying only on my own skills. And then there is the cumulative brainpower generated by the writers' group at *Marharbour*, offering early critiques as ideas poured onto paper: Bill, Susan, Nick, Janet, Max, Sylvia, and Mary Marr--our absolutely incredible hostess, gentle mentor, formidable writer, and forever-remembered friend. Ah, if only everyone were like her in even small ways…

Which takes me back even further--to Olympus High School in Salt Lake City and Estelle Tucker, my English teacher as a senior, who told me that I had a special talent and mind, and that she felt she had not met the challenge--wow! And Dr. Clarence J. Simpson, my astonishing English professor at Whitworth College in Spokane, Washington, who had the most compelling speaking voice and precise presentation. Oh, how I admired that man and his knowledge and skill--so getting A's in his class made me feel I could accomplish anything!

Lots of peacemakers provided blessings and challenges: John Heidbrink, with Fellowship of Reconciliation; the Peace and Justice Task Force at Montview Presbyterian in Denver, with materials from the Presbyterian Peacemaking Program; American Friends Service Committee, in peaceful protests and positive programs; Armand Hammer United World College, opening my eyes to the power of mediation; Colorado Council of Mediators, broadening my mediation skills; and retreats with Sister Mary Luke Tobin of the Sisters of Loretto, and Dr. Allen Maruyama at Ghost Ranch, for deepening inner peace.

There are so many others to thank, certainly, too many to mention--but all had a part in the completion of this project long in the making. Hooray to all of us!

Introduction

T.E.J.T.M.
The End Justifies The Means

The twenty-first century was struggling through its early teens. The world had survived the worst years of the economic crisis, and was slowly rebuilding in the areas of financial ruin. But poverty in the Third World remained a catastrophe, with more people starving to death each year than the year before.

As the richest nation, America had been hit hardest, especially in the middle class. Many who had lost homes and businesses were still collecting welfare checks; some jobs were coming back. Government grew in its caretaker role to help people survive, but trust in the wisdom of its leaders had been shaken to its roots. So voters changed Administrations every four years, blaming those in office for the continuing problems.

The weather had been farmer-friendly for several years, providing a time of plentiful food. However, many small farmers had disappeared on paper into large co-operatives during the economic downturn. People now saved their money, and left food on the store shelves except for weekly specials. A government afraid of terrorist attack and unpredictable weather cycles was storing surplus to insure food supply, but in atrocious quantities.

The peaceful balance of life was upset. The deterioration of the economy fed a rising tide of political extremism and violence. Liberals became disaffected with a government they saw as increasingly uncaring and unresponsive. Conservatives saw the justice system going soft on criminals and dissidents. As one group would rise to champion a cause, activists would grow at the other end of the political spectrum to challenge them. Their confrontations with the system became increasingly violent. The challenge to law enforcement was enormous, calling for new tactics, but should they be harsher? Or more understanding, since no one in authority seemed to care enough to even listen to radicals?

The old tough questions came up again and again: Is it right to break one rule in order to obey another that is considered more important? Is it okay to run a red light when driving a person having a heart attack to the hospital? Is it better to steal food to give a hungry child, rather than to let them starve? Does the law have the right to do whatever it deems necessary, even lie and murder, to protect its citizens from terrorist threats?

Does the end always justify the means? Well, does it or not? And whose decision is it to make anyway? Can all sides be right, even while disagreeing vehemently and violently? And if so, what in the world happens then??? The story of *T.E.J.T.M.* here begins…

Chapter 1

The Salt Lake City bus depot was like any other in a large U.S. city, looking twice its age from hard use by hard people. Ardis Borgeba stood impatiently in line for her luggage. Her olive-colored skin oddly averaged out the various shades of those milling around her, and she was younger than many fellow travelers. America's melting pot, she mused in her sloppy sweatshirt, faded jeans, and Nike runners. She blended in, and was as uninviting and uninteresting as she intended.

Ardis finally reached the counter, where the clerk exchanged a mid-sized imitation leather suitcase for her magic number. At least this bureaucracy was still responsive, even if the government wasn't, she consoled herself. She gave the bag attendant neither smile nor thanks.

The far wall of metal lockers by the front entrance was her immediate destination, but she slowed her stride as a uniformed policeman walked in the door. Ardis made a casual turn to her right, toward the rows of hard plastic seats. Picking up a magazine, she sat down tiredly, putting her bag by her feet. She opened the magazine, and began counting.

When she reached ten, she turned the page to count to twelve, then turned the next page. Only then did she look up, and only to her right.

There were two lines of people waiting early for boarding announcements. The clock above the dock doors showed nine minutes past midnight, and she had confirmed that her bus was scheduled to leave in twenty minutes. She forced her dark eyes to point again at the tattered magazine, and counted. Two pages later, she brushed her unwashed hair back away from her face and over one shoulder. Only then did she casually look up in front of her, toward the lockers and the front door. There was no sign of the policeman there. She saw only a young couple, a derelict, and three teenage black boys.

Next came the easy look to her left. There was still no uniform. A full survey showed none in front, and none to her right. He must have gone behind her.

It was thirteen minutes after twelve. Ardis needed to leave her bag in one of those lockers before the announcement of her bus. That was her task as munitions courier for the Denver Shakespeare Group.

She stood stiffly, stretched to pivot a half turn, and glanced over her shoulder. The uniform was visiting with a pretty clerk at the counter, and paid absolutely no attention to the average-looking lady who leaned down to pick up her ordinary brown suitcase. Ardis moved slowly along the row of chairs toward the lockers, aware of who was everywhere and inattentive.

Randomly, she picked locker fifty-four. Opening the door, she carefully slid the suitcase into the empty space. She took three quarters from her purse and pushed them in the small slot, turned the key, and pulled it out. She pushed and twisted on the handle quietly. It stayed firmly locked. Taking a tissue from her purse, she wrapped key 54 carefully. On a small pad, she wrote "54-U," just below the other notations: "82-W," "103-O," and "77-I."

Speakers on the wall announced her departure: "Now boarding for Cheyenne, Wyoming at door seven. Passengers continuing to Denver and Omaha, now boarding at door seven."

Ardis stepped away from the bank of lockers to meander in the direction of the loading docks. She was leaving her last brown suitcase, and would be home by mid-morning. Three other major cities on her cross-country bus trip also had matching suitcases now in storage, each with sufficient explosives to level the depot buildings, which so dutifully housed them.

*   *   *

Peter Wayman and four close college friends listened intently as Colorado Senator Stuart Frye calmly lectured the neatly dressed students on political reality. The senator was a picture of hard work on this early Wednesday morning. His long white shirtsleeves were twice rolled, and he had loosened his collar and blue tie. The desk was tidy, and of course his bookcases were filled with law books and career mementoes. The new president had posed with him for the obligatory autographed picture, proudly centered on the back wall of his Denver office.

"People, the farm surplus issue is just too complex to resolve in one term. Change in a new Administration takes time--studying what's working and what's not, how one policy impacts another, and so on. I have been in touch with numerous other senators, and several studies are now underway. I have also proposed a special subcommittee--"

"We are not just 'people,' we have names!" Peter spoke sharply. "You promised in your campaign, and right here to us, to sell much more Colorado grain, not store it."

"Oh, I do know your name, Mr. Wayman. 'People' was merely Washington slang. Your group has picketed enough in Colorado that you're certainly familiar. And I assure you that I've been trying to open more markets for us. We have continued our 'Always Buy Colorado' program here at home. Our ski industry--"

Peter interrupted. "Focus on grain, Senator. More small farmers have been ruined since you took office. And forty percent of the big corn growers are hoarding it until the price of beef goes up. Surplus wheat is rotting in the elevators, just because your agriculture secretary is worried about shortages of irrigation water next year." The other four voiced noisy agreement.

"You got your facts out of a cocked hat," Senator Frye countered.

"So you're a liar, as well as a weak--," Peter blurted out.

"None of that, Wayman," the senator cut in sharply. "I agreed to this ridiculous 8 A.M. meeting because you've made some valid suggestions in the past. Now I'm trying to report some progress, so if you all will calm down--"

"We waited two months to get any meeting time," Peter said angrily, "and we came here mad, not calm. Didn't you see that TV special last week? Those people in India are starving right this minute! And it used to be that helping neighbors was a virtue in America!"

"Now this has nothing--"

The senator started to speak, but the lanky young man stood and shouted him down. "Can't you see? We've got the surplus grains right here to feed them. All you have to do is ship it there!"

Peter moved forward, agitated, speaking fast. "Senator, let's not mince words. You know that last year's wheat crop in Colorado was up from thirty bushels an acre to forty, with the weather perfect. We had more than two million acres planted and harvested. World demand sent bushel prices skyrocketing up from four to more than seven dollars--even ten, like it did back in '07 and '08. That's $600 million bucks generated. So the rich decide to get richer, plant more than ever, then stick it into surplus grain elevators to keep the prices up. Now the spring wheat is ripening, killing the futures market. With the coming glut, they'll be letting the grain rot in the fields before long!"

"Oh, let's not get carried away with textbook statistics and projections, college boy. The farm community knows what it's doing."

"My ass! Those mega-farm owners sailing their yachts and driving their golf carts only see sales going up and say, 'Plant more!' Colorado has surplus enough to help save starving kids right now, with lots more growing. But you have to change the export regs and lower prices to get it moving!"

"I don't have that power. I'm one person out of a thousand in that decision-making chain."

"And you're the weakest link, that's for sure," Peter shot back.

Senator Frye stood, trying to regain control. But as he did, so did the other youthful activists. The senator spoke very firmly, but hissingly quiet. He pointed his finger directly at Peter. "Mr. Wayman, have you gone crazy? How dare you speak to me in those tones? I insist that all of you leave."

"So that's your final answer?" Peter asked in disbelief. "What if your own family was wasting away? Senator, please, for God's sake--"

Senator Frye pushed a button on the phone console. "Mrs. Johnson, call security."

One of Peter's friends pounded his fist on the desk in frustration. "No, man, this is your chance to do something real. Just send our surplus--"

"There's no money to do that, and there won't be. Never for radicals the likes of you. Get out of here before I have you arrested!"

Peter stood ramrod straight, pointing a long arm and finger at the senator's face. "You are a murderer, but you won't have the last word."

The secretary walked in just then, with two armed officers behind her. Peter and his Shakespeare Group left without a further word.

Back at their car, they stopped to talk. "Well, we blew it with the government, didn't we?"

"Or they blew it with us."

The five dreamers grew silent, thinking of what might have been, and what was going to be. Saving lives was now up to them.

*   *   *

Monty forced his foot to accelerate the '88 Dodge again to fifty. Every passing mile hardened the burning knot in his stomach. He pictured his pretty Felicia--his Mrs. Montropovich for twenty-seven years. This morning he had said her hot apple crisp was the world's best, and so was she.

"Why so mushy?" she had asked.

"Because our marriage is forever." He surely couldn't tell her they might never share another meal.

But it is right to be leaving those I love, he thought as he watched fields pass by this Wednesday morning. He was many miles closer to his Denver destination now than to his home in Wray, Colorado. His granddaughters, Caroline and Joannie, needed to be able to count on his aging generation to be wise and strong. He had to do the right thing, though it meant sacrificing himself. So many children were suffering each day, and that couldn't go on, not since his friend Peter could stop it. And in Peter Wayman's plan to end starvation, Monty held the key.

Traffic passed him as his mind grappled with consequences. This hijacking of a grain train would put the railroad bosses right behind the eight-ball, where they belonged. Monty had never forgiven them for firing him. Substance abuse tests--how valid were they in testing a man's real competence? But no other rail line would hire him after that. His skill as a top-notch train engineer didn't help get regular work back in Wray. He had failed at his try for a Master's degree, so he settled into odd jobs as a garage mechanic, handyman, then tenant farmer.

Monty's thoughts raced by faster than the phone poles. Peter had worried about the National Peace Academy finding out too soon, figuring they would try to prevent violence by stopping the train plot before it even got started. Monty had agreed his NPA friends wouldn't hear it from him. He hadn't even given his Felicia a clue to his life-changing decision. He lied instead, and cursed himself again for that.

It hurt too much. He had to put thoughts of her away, along with their loving home. He focused on Peter's bigger ideas from Bible pages--love your neighbors, even around the world. Another trainload of surplus grain would soon be leaving the Dakotas, bound for Gulf Coast storage. He knew it was due to be detoured by devotion. Their farmer friends and Peter's college crowd would make sure of that.

Monty took one last look in the rear view mirror, then prepared to exit Interstate 76 for the North Denver Motel. The tall steam stack of the Xcel Energy power plant dominated his view to the west. At that spot, the grain train would be moving slowly after crossing the Platte River, rounding a sharp curve. That's where they would stop it. That's where he would immediately become an engineer again. From that point, it was only a mile further to the almost deserted rail siding, where six empty boxcars would have been turned into temporary homes for farmers in protest.

After registering in at the motel, Monty went looking for Peter. He and his visionary friend had met seven years ago, when Peter came to Wray on a typical summer visit. Peter's grandparents owned a large farm east of town, and were longtime friends with the Montropovich family. Monty had taken to the lad right off, and a pleasant father-son bond formed during those vacations. Hopes and disappointments were shared in the shade during lazy lemonade hours.

Monty found him behind the office, near one lonesome line of tracks. Just then, the crossing whistle of an approaching train sounded--two long tones, one short, and one final long tone. The compadres tensed, looked for a moment at one another, and then turned to watch three green Mid-Western Pacific engines come rapidly toward them, pulling empty coal cars. Both men comfortably stood their ground only ten feet from the tracks, waving back when the engineer threw them a jaunty salute.

The whine of the huge passing diesels was almost deafening. Then the rhythmic clanking of the eight steel wheels on a hundred cars crossing the rail-ends held the two transfixed, each thinking of how this week would change their lives, and their world.

The train ended, and the moment of reverie. Back in the motel room, Peter called Harran Winfree, and chatted briefly. This was the rail yard dispatcher Peter targeted three months ago for quick friendship and unsuspecting answers on train movements. Harran, the unwitting henchman, confirmed he would be working the late shift tonight in the Denver yard tower of the Mid-Western Pacific Railroad.

Monty and Peter left their motel operational base, getting into the Chevrolet Corsica that Peter had bought used three years before. His teal T-shirt matched the car's exterior perfectly. With his dark hair and tanned skin, Peter liked making a statement.

There were many expedition errands to fill this last day of normal life. Peter drove, excitedly filling Monty in on many details he didn't need to know. The larger man just nodded his understanding, until one critical part of their plan seemed to hit a snag. "All this planning, then you spill your guts to some punk woman obit reporter you just met? And she still hasn't agreed to go with us?"

"It's too late now to make any changes, Monty!" Peter's face flushed a shade redder as he again lashed back at criticism. Senator Frye's earlier rebuffs were still stinging. "She will say yes when I call her tonight."

"And if she doesn't? What if she's out on a date? You said you'd have a media type lined up to ride along so we'd get into the news early." Monty thumped the dashboard angrily with his fingers. "It's a damn shame you didn't come up with more choices."

The comment hurt. Peter flashed a look of utter impatience as he turned sharply into a parking lot space and stopped. He started to shout a response, but held it back. He knew Monty was right. He had left a question mark, and was worried.

When Peter opened the door and slid out from behind the steering wheel, he only slightly slammed the door behind him. He calmed his outward appearance further as he walked into the Denver Metropolitan Credit Union.

Three loan officers were busy at their desks with phone calls, as was the receptionist, but he took a moment anyway to smile at each one who looked up, as he always did. He sauntered into a teller's line. His turn came soon, and a woman motioned him forward.

"Time for a really big family vacation," Peter said excitedly, pushing a VISA cash advance draft toward her for three thousand dollars.

"Wow, I'll say! In Traveler's Cheques?" she asked.

"No, break it down, please--sorry to say. Hundreds, fifties, twenties. We're going to be fairly remote." He chose his words carefully, knowing that tomorrow this woman would be trying to quote their conversation verbatim to FBI questioners. They would also find out that two days before, Peter had cashed in his last $5,000 CD. His dad had been left a family inheritance, and the rest of Peter's share had gone for his schooling.

Transaction completed, the partners in future crime tried to talk out their frustrations on the limited options in other areas as they drove to the Auraria Higher Education Campus near downtown Denver. For some, there would just be no certainty. But arrival on campus rejuvenated Peter's hope, for this was the hotbed of his rebellious support. Six students had banded with Peter to hatch the scheme, first philosophically, then gradually becoming more real-world challenging, each adding ideas and solving projected dilemmas as they allowed themselves more commitment. Peter remained point man from the first, set up for highest risk and profile. However, it was plain that each of them could be arrested and prosecuted as co-conspirators. They held utmost confidence in the *lesser of the evils* courtroom defense strategy. It had been upheld in several recent abortion clinic bombings in which no one had been injured. And they planned no injuries right from the start. But they realized the risk of arrest was real, recalling the environmental activists who had burned the ski lodge at the top of Vail Mountain to protest expansion, and were hunted down viciously then sentenced to long jail terms. Colorado lawyers routinely plea-bargained students who broke minor laws while trying to call attention to a greater injustice, and no protesters had been jailed from the skirmishes at the Democratic National

Convention in 2008.

The group had named themselves after Shakespeare as a cover for meeting openly to plan clandestinely. Tom Buchanan was Peter's second-in-charge. On his faculty advisor's timetable, Tom would graduate *magna cum laude* in December. Stanford's graduate school was romancing him and his macro-revitalization thesis for doubling grain production in arid regions.

Being on time was another of Tom Buchanan's admirable qualities, and he was now waiting for Peter in the school library's parking lot. He climbed into the back seat to meet their train engineer for the first time. The handshake was one of sincere respect for an occupation that helped keep commerce flowing. Tom quickly confirmed that Ardis was back in Denver from stashing the Composite-4 plastique explosive in bus terminal lockers. Nobody had blinked an eye at her or her luggage, so the trip had revved up her craving for the use of force in effecting change. She was anxious to leave for her assigned city.

"I only wish there was a peaceful way," Peter conceded. "Did everyone get their e-tickets confirmed for flights tonight?"

Tom said yes, and that they would have picked up and placed their bombs before dawn tomorrow. Peter gave Tom four envelopes with $1,000 in each, for food, lodging, cars, and emergencies in the four target cities during their brief stays. The fifth envelope held $2,000 for Ruth, to cover heavy cabfare delivery around the Denver metro area.

Then the three exchanged heartfelt wishes, for success and safety. Tom left to distribute cash, and tie up a dozen loose ends.

They drove through the busy downtown. Monty inquired how Peter's *righteous cause* chat with his father turned out the night before.

"Stubborn ass, like me," Peter answered. "Only one way to do things, the right way--his way. I tried telling our story like it was a morality play our Shakespeare Group was putting on. You know, folks take a shipment of stuff that isn't theirs anymore, but used to be, and truck it a thousand miles to get it to the people who need it the most. They take a hostage, threaten to blow up buildings, all for a really good cause."

"And his comment?"

Peter lowered his voice even more for the quote. "'Young man, don't whitewash internal terrorism. In your play, good guys doing hijacking, grand theft, interstate trafficking, and extortion, become the bad guys.' Then he asked who was going to play the FBI lead, and even laughed. I told him he had the inside track if he had some free nights for rehearsal."

Monty chuckled. "Frank probably said he didn't need any practice, because he's already pretty good at cops and robbers."

"Right. But he said something about odd timing for me to ask, and that he'd like to hear more about the characters and plot. That's when we got into the old argument over whether the end justifies the means. We both said yes, but still totally disagreed. He said justice is blind, and applies to everyone equally. I said it's more than equal to those who can afford the best lawyer, and to CIA contract hits for national security. Then he soared off into supporting the Constitution and Supreme Court decisions. He said his career should have taught me to respect the law. I sort of screamed that there could be a higher moral law. And that's when we called a truce and said goodnight."

"Do you think Frank suspects anything?"

Peter stayed silent a moment. "Nah, he doesn't really listen."

They drove north twenty miles, then backtracked, following a train from Brighton toward the switching yards. Four miles before Denver's centralized traffic control tower, they passed the row of six boxcars standing idle on a siding, targeted for the farmers. Then the two friends tagged another train going west up into the foothills, until it left its parallel highway run and began the climb up into the narrow canyon. The enormity and immediacy of the hijacking occupied their total conversation. Peter replayed the cell phone messages he had been receiving: "11:30 A.M.--Mr. Bowman running hour late for meeting." Then, "3:05 P.M.--'The Spearfish' needs extra half-hour." Next, "4:57 P.M.--Mrs. Newcastle's on schedule, good luck." The cryptic messages told them the grain train from North Dakota was back on schedule, and headed south in Wyoming, right toward his Denver ambush.

It was late afternoon when the two men arrived at Peter's home. The spicy simmering of Italian sausage, onions, garlic, anise, black olives, mushrooms, oregano, tomatoes, and hamburger filled the house. Peter beelined for the kitchen.

"Mom, the spaghetti sauce smells delish! It's perfect for tonight. You're a doll for taking time off to make it." He kissed her cheek.

"Thank you," the attractive woman curtsied slightly. Even in a blue housedress, Marion Wayman looked the part of a lady executive, carving out time for family. "A day away from the office also helped me get caught up around here, and get a few charity chores done. Does your good will extend to dishwasher duty afterwards?"

"I'd like to, really, but I leave right after dinner to drop Monty off, then pick up Janet and head for Colorado Springs. There's a great group playing down there tonight. Give you a rain check?"

Somehow that seemed expected. She next asked how late he'd be.

"They'll go until two o'clock, so I might sleep over on Janet's couch."

"No classes tomorrow?"

"First class on Thursdays is afternoon--as always, Mom." Peter left the kitchen quickly. He was upset with his untruths, and was thinking about finalities all around him. This might be the last spaghetti he'd have at home for a long while, and maybe he'd washed his last dish and gone to his final summer class. He didn't want to get mad again at her forgetting his class schedule. She was thinking about dinner, and they did have a good talk last night, patching up some old hurt feelings.

Frank Wayman occupied a patio lounge chair, studying papers as middle-aged workaholics do at home. Peter's sister, Candice, idled on the pool's edge, dangling her bare feet in the water while telling Monty of her tribulations as a college junior.

Peter pulled up a chair beside his father, who didn't look up. "Howdy, Dad," he said. He wanted these last hours to count.

"I really don't have time to be chatty, son. I need to finish this farm brief."

"Farm problems? Will Grandpa be affected?"

Frank had slipped up, for now he'd have to spend time calming concerns over the revered octogenarian. Dinner was almost ready, so he laid his work aside. "No, Pete, Grandpa's not involved." He began a cursory explanation, but Peter interrupted. Frank tried again, only to receive a caustic barb.

"Kind of hard to finish a sentence with such an expert around." Frank looked perturbed. Peter looked away, and heaved a sigh.

"How about a hand in serving?" Marion called, ending the stalemate.

Peter put a hand on his father's knee. "We'll finish later," he said, and headed for the kitchen, following his sister's wet footprints.

Dinner was delightful in the cool evening air at the picnic table. Conversation ranged from the Denver Bronco's new defensive coach and the C.U. Shakespeare Festival to global warming and farm town parades.

"Speaking of farmers, there's a TV special tomorrow night on food shortages and farm surpluses. Maybe some new solutions," Monty said.

"Mom, will you tape it for me if I'm not here?" Peter asked.

"I'll try to remember. Doesn't the spaghetti suit you?" She gestured at his plate. "You've hardly made a dent in the pile."

"I've got a little stomach ache. It'll go away."

Frank abruptly excused himself, to finish working on tomorrow's meeting.

He walked past Marion's frown, inside to his office, and closed the door. At the desk computer, he picked up the security phone and dialed the special D.C. number for the National Crime Information Center network. The green light on the phone line modem glowed steadily. When he slid his FBI card through the reader and put his palm on the screen, nothing happened. The security check processed in private, the program opened.

He skimmed through menu selections to get Master Addresses and began typing: *montropovich,monty/wray/co/railroad engineer,* and pressed Enter. The little stick figure began running in the lower right corner as a huge mainframe began searching the international database. Peter's earlier questions about lawbreaking, his upset stomach, Monty's visit, plus his own suspicious nature had all stimulated Frank's interest.

A page of print appeared on the screen, spelling out a human being:

"MONTROPOVICH, IVAN KLAUSE / AKA: MONTY
RACE: CAUC; DOB: 11/7/1953;
PLACE OF BIRTH: CHICAGO, IL
HT: 6'4" ; WT: 295 LB; HAIR: DK BRN/GRAY"

Frank scanned down through the profile, to the educational section.

"--M.A. STUDY: NATIONAL PEACE ACADEMY, 9/2011 - 12/2012
WORK: ODD JOBS, TENANT FARM 3/2008 - CURRENT
RAILROAD (MID-WESTERN PACIFIC):
    ENGINEER, 1998 - 3/2008 (FIRED, DRUNK)
ODD JOBS, 1987-96;
FARMER (SELF-EMPLOYED), 1975-87
    CAUTION: TEMPER; WATCH OUT FOR POSSIBLE RETRIBUTION AGAINST RAILROAD"

Frank printed the report and studied it, debating each item in his mind: *Description fits...intelligent, shouldn't normally be a lawbreaker...schooled in non-violence at the Peace Academy, could be an activist...farmer, family man, nothing there...engineer--probably able to drive an eighteen-wheeler...fired, so bitter about loss of longtime career, ruined reputation... hmmm, drinker and temper, bad combination...retribution.*

"Just might be the man in Pete's hijacking story last night," Frank muttered quietly. "His old farmer friend and peace buddy got the shaft. But if that's my radical son's idea of a righteous cause, he's in trouble. No, we're all in trouble."

Frank's words were barely audible as he rocked back in his chair, his fingers building steeples then collapsing them. "Now let's say Pete has flipped. Those two couldn't pull off a big stunt alone. He mentioned a group wanting answers, what group? Church? No. College? That Shakespeare bunch may be fringe enough. Neighbors, farm friends? Hmmm. Janet would know. Damn, I hate messing around in Pete's life."

Frank began pacing, wanting to doubt suspicion, but logic hounded him. Mentally, he listed things to do: ID checks, arrest records, associates. He wondered how much time he had as he left the room for a casual, targeted conversation.

"Oh, Dad, I came to say goodnight." Peter was in the hallway.

"Well, I was hoping you and Monty would have time for an after-dinner drink, if you're feeling better. We could visit a while."

"That's an unusual...ly nice offer, but we can't. Got to leave for the Springs concert right away."

"Uh, who are *The Springs*?"

Peter laughed. "No, Pop, Colorado Springs. I think I lost you on the curve. Mom knows all about it." He hugged his father. "I love you a lot."

"Uh, thanks, kid," Frank said, surprised. He hugged back. Things were happening too fast. "Now, is Monty going or staying?"

"I'm dropping him off, and picking up Janet," Peter said over his shoulder. He took his jacket from the hall closet.

"When are you due back?" Frank was desperately piecing together how to intervene.

"Late, so I'll see ya tomorrow night, Pop. Thanks for everything." He smiled. "See ya, Mom," he hollered into the house. "See ya, Sis. I love you both." He started out the door.

"Thanks again, Marion. Bye, Candice," Monty said loudly. He stuck out his hand to Frank. "You have a fine family, Frank, and a beautiful home. Thanks for the hospitality."

Frank shook his hand, noting the strength of the man. They looked for a long moment, eye to eye. With much left unsaid in the home, Monty and Peter walked into the night. The door closed behind them, and the house was silent.

*   *   *

Far on the other side of Denver, Jeremy and Manuel easily cut the old chain link fence. They crawled through the flap and replaced it, tying it with thin wire. Trees and bushes on the banks of Sand Creek shielded them completely for the moment.

The two men checked each other's backpacks for tightness, never saying a word. Actions were well rehearsed at Peter's insistence, a stickler for details. No cloud covered the quarter-moon. Only the city's pollution cloud dimmed its shine, which reflected off the slow shallow river at their feet. No security guards patrolled here.

Cold water filled Jeremy Downing's canvas shoes, creeping up his legs as he began wading the creek. His guess had been only knee-deep, but he soon stood in a channel up to his crotch, wondering whether to take another step forward or turn back. Manuel Gomez saw the predicament, and left him, to move upstream fifty feet to make his crossing.

Jeremy watched, aggravated but relieved, as Manuel negotiated the river at a minimum depth. Jeremy turned and backtracked, then headed upstream, avoiding any risk of getting his pack wet. He quickly walked across, marking his entrance and exit spots by stacking several large stones.

The two backpackers sloshed across a sandbar, and started climbing the steel net holding up a wall of boulders back from the shoreline. The wall had been constructed for channel control after the big flood in 1965. Jeremy idly wondered what it would take to pull the old net loose, shuddering at the thought of rocks crushing onto his body. Then he was over the top, and crouched low as he ran toward the nearest white tank. It was isolated from the others, marked with a large black number 79. Manuel had already reached it, and was hidden from any wandering eyes from the elevated highway traffic zipping by several blocks away.

They quickly accomplished their tasks. Jeremy tapped the tank with a rock he carried up from the streambed, to make certain gasoline was inside. It was not an empty echo. A friend had once shown him around a tank yard, explaining piping network and volume checks. This history instantly made him the Shakespeare Group's expert.

Manuel placed the block of C-4, blasting cap, and its wired box next to the tank, directly under the pipe connection and valve wheel, at ground level. Ardis Borgeba, their fellow adventurer, had told him clearly how to set all sorts of explosives, and this was his exciting chance to finally try his skill. He had brought a tumbleweed from the riverbank to hide the bomb, and now anchored it with Jeremy's stone. No one would guess, if anyone even looked. And it only needed to remain undetected for seven hours.

"Hey, friend, get way back from me while I plug this in and set the clock. I'm sure it's rigged right, but just in case--"

"Jeez, Manuel, I hope you know how to build bombs better than you build a guy's confidence. Be cool down there."

Manuel squinted one eye almost shut as he barely touched the blasting cap wire to the ticking alarm clock.

Nothing happened.

He smiled, and attached the wires carefully as in the picture Ardis had shown. He placed the clock with the C-4 under the weed, and anchored it with a rock. The alarm was set for 3:30.

Peter's pair of student commandos ran back toward the marked river crossing. A mile to the west, the huge steam towers and tall stacks of the Xcel Energy power plant loomed above the treetops, flashing their red warning lights at passing air traffic. The two men had one more bomb to place before they left from Denver International Airport. Ardis was already gone. Tom was working on the boxcars with Ruth. Shakespeare was scattering.

*   *   *

Chapter Two

Peter and Monty stayed quiet during their drive after dinner to the home of Janet Binghamton. Peter thought back to when his sister Candice introduced her class vice-president to him last spring, and the urgent magnetism began. The two swam frequently in the Wayman pool, and traveled to the Wray farm to visit his grandparents. However, it was their Wray trip last weekend that haunted this evening's drive, leaving Peter wondering whether Janet would even speak to him tonight. He remembered last Saturday morning, reliving it minute by minute.

. . . LAST SATURDAY, AUGUST 6 . . .

The haymow was high in the east end of the barn, firmly supported up in the rafters. Bales were stacked three deep, shoulder-high, forming a U-shape hideaway facing the open loft door. Janet sat there with her eyes closed, melting in the August heat. She wiped away a trickle of sweat from her cheek as Peter approached.

He sat down quietly on the floor facing her. She was leaning back against the stack behind her, still with her eyes shut. She was on the third button down her yellow blouse, unfastening them very slowly. He was immediately aroused by the prospect.

Peter had seen the firm outline of her very womanly figure in a swimsuit, but the real thing was beginning to show now. He sat very still, watching the unveiling. She undid the bottom button and let the garment fall open to both sides. The cups of her lacy white bra seemed very full, creating considerable cleavage. He knew the darker circle in the center of each cup was not a blemish in the material.

Janet opened her eyes sometime while he was looking at her chest, embarrassing him when he got caught looking. She smiled and sat up, then took off the blouse and laid it on the floor. She leaned over, picked up the towel she had brought from the house, and spread it lengthwise on the bale next to her.

Unmoving, Peter watched the slender girl's movements as she worked. The black-haired beauty leaned back again, and unzipped her jeans. His heart raced faster. His own jeans had grown uncomfortably tight in the crotch. *What's going to happen here,* he wondered. *What cannot happen here?*

"Janet, we must wait."

"I know, not to worry." She raised her hips, slipped her thumbs into the waistband, and pulled her jeans down, revealing yellow bikini underwear. The jeans dropped below her knees, over her yellow and red boat shoes. She stood up and stepped out of the pile of clothes, then picked up her jeans to shake out the hay and dust. Her black ponytail flicked as she moved, but it was her hourglass figure that held his gaze. Her waist was small, her stomach very flat, and her hips nicely broad.

While she busied herself, he reached down and quickly tugged at his crotch, loosening the two layers of material to give himself room to grow. She turned toward him to lay her pants out lengthwise on another bale. He looked up at the darkness of the bikini area between her legs, and then back at her rounded rump. His manhood pushed longer in response to her actions and his thoughts.

"You're a beautiful girl, Jan," he said in soft admiration.

"Thank you, my handsome Petey," she responded, smiling down. She knelt on the pants bale and bent over close to him to straighten her blouse. But it didn't need straightening. Peter knew it was to allow him to study the curves of her breasts as they fell slightly away from her chest, gravity pulling against the thin material and outlining her nipples. What a temptress, he thought.

Then she lay face down on the towel bale, shut her eyes, and started soaking up the hot sun streaming in. Her tan was already a rich brown. "There's a bottle of lotion down on the floor by my feet," she offered, without opening an eye.

"I hoped you'd say that," he said, peeling off his own shirt to take advantage of the rays, and to keep it from getting soaked with sweat. He squirted some lotion into his palm, rubbed his hands together, and began spreading it across her shoulders. Her skin was sun-warmed, and smooth as a ripe tomato. He massaged the white film in deeply, slowly erasing contrasting colors, loving each stroke.

"Say, sport," he said softly, "since when did you start using *Petey* for me.

That little boy nickname is reserved only for private use by grandparents, you know."

"I think it's cute. It's you when you're all wet in the pool."

"That right? Well, remind me not to invite any reporters in for a swim with you if I do get into politics. I don't know any *Petey* who ever got elected. Besides, you're a faster swimmer than I am."

"Gotcha, Rep. Don't stop rubbing, it's just getting interesting."

He poured out another glob and moved to her lower back. She purred a little, then continued. "I just feel that if your *Rude* campus group--what's that name stand for again?"

"That's 'Republicans United With Democrats,' and it isn't intended as an acronym, thank you," he chided her.

"Right. If the *Rudes* think you're good enough to have been chairman this year, and are already planning your campaign for when you turn twenty-five, then they've obviously decided your name's okay. Could you unsnap my bra, so I don't get a line?"

Peter hesitated a moment, then took the next small step toward intimacy, knowing he could and would stop at the right time. He laid the ends of the straps out to either side on the hay bale. With his moistened fingertips, he traced tiny circles all around her nude back.

"Oh, will you pull my bikini down a little more? I usually wear them pretty low when I tan."

"Uhh--" Was he made of sterling, or clay--or much of both? "Sure." Peter enjoyed being with this girl more than any other with whom he had gotten close. However, he had drawn a firm line in his mind, which he would not cross over on this trip. Seeing just a bit more skin is within limits, he rationalized.

He hesitated to touch the material with his oily fingers. Simply pushing down on the elastic edges didn't budge it. He debated about where to put his fingers under the waistband--at her back, or on her sides?

Finally he decided to tug gently on both sides of the yellow material just below the waistband, and she raised her hips to oblige. He pulled down one inch. The skin was still tanned with no sign of white. A mite more, and her cleavage began to show, making him wonder if there was an end to her tan line. He raised the elastic up a little and looked to see. The firm rod between his legs surged once, but he was still in control. He let the underwear softly cover her again.

"You'd make an exciting centerfold, m'love," he told her.

"More to be seen than yet meets the eye," she teased.

He grinned. "But not today, love." Peter gingerly massaged the backs of her arms and legs. Eventually, he left her to the mercy of the sun, with a kiss and a whisper, "Love feels good."

He wiped at the trickling sweat on his face and chest, and in the creases where his elbows bent. He spread out his shirt, and lay down on the dusty floor very near her. His mind was alternating between thoughts of pleasure and the rigors of next week, the second week in August, his Genesis week.

After a few minutes, Janet whispered, "Tell me more about this man I'm in the hay with. My momma said I couldn't be too careful about the company I keep." She traced a finger through his hair as he lay on the floor, circling his ear, along his sinewy neck and shoulder. She moved her face to look deeply into his eyes, seeing the same rich brown shade as his hair.

Peter began reciting his life, glad to have someone really caring. He mentioned awards and camping trips in scouting, and stories from Central Africa four years before in the Student Exchange Program.

Janet asked, "Is that where you met, uh, Mubgammy, that missionary who stayed in your home last year?"

Peter chuckled. "Mumbabwe. No, he's one of the missionaries we sponsor now at Faith Temple. He had so many tragic stories to tell. A mother brought her starving nine-year-old daughter to their clinic in Nganta, almost dead. He carried her to the hospital to help the mother get her admitted. They were too poor for a room, and nurses were too busy to check her until morning, but the hospital let her rest on a hallway mat since her mother stayed with her.

"A janitor walked by and spoke to her. He came back with a bread crust and a cup of water, and knelt down to make a sign of the cross on her forehead. Mumbabwe took the cross from around his neck, and the janitor took it in his hand and kissed it. So there's a Catholic janitor, an evangelical, and a bush native, kneeling in an open hallway giving communion to a little soul who didn't make it through the night.

"That missionary program is the big reason I go to Faith Temple instead of the folks' church. My tithe actually pays for food and health and farm programs."

Janet had waited for him to finish his story before expressing her question. "You'd rather be a missionary then?"

He knew there were a hundred questions behind her one. "Jan, last week the Church Board asked me to serve a two year mission in Africa."

She hesitated, composing her thoughts, speaking slowly. "But, you just have twelve more credits to finish your double major and graduate. Then we had talked of you joining Colorado's International Trade Development Office, and right into politics."

"I haven't decided anything yet, Jan. I don't have to right away. Besides, things are coming up that may make a huge difference. The only thing I'm sure of is that people are starving to death today, and more will tomorrow, and I should be preventing that."

"Were you planning to talk these things over with me?"

"You're the first I've told about the Board's offer."

"The first? You have other women to tell, Peter?"

Females, Peter judged. Possessive, jealous females. He looked into her face, but her eyes were closed. He studied her smooth side, round rump, long leg. Hard to think of living with, or living without. "I'm still getting to know you, Jan," he whispered. "I'm starting to love you, and it's a stronger feeling every time we're together, and even when we're apart. There's no other girl in my life now." Why, oh, why had he chosen to end with that stupid word? He waited for a head-banger comeback.

"Big decisions, babe," was all she said.

If only she knew, he thought, how big some of them really are, threatening life, forcing everything onto hold. He turned their talk to the farm, and city life, of places they'd both like to visit, and people they admired and hated. She warned him again about his bitterness, and being so quickly outspoken that he stepped on toes.

Thirty minutes had passed. Janet raised up slightly, reaching one arm across her chest to hold her bra mostly in place. Then she sat up to sip the cool tea Peter poured from the thermos.

"Feel like pouring the rest over your head?" he asked, grinning.

"Yes, indeed. That water tank outside is looking more inviting all the time. But I have a whole front half to tan yet. How are you doing?"

"Hot. Enjoying you," he said, leisurely reclining to face her.

"I like being with you, too," she said, letting her eyes roam across his body. His arm and chest muscles were built up from summers on the farm and exercising in his workout room at home. His chest hair glistened in the morning sun, curling over skin tanned from running on the school's track at noontime. She had been there watching the twenty-two year old senior, the tall two-hundred pounder in red and white gym shorts. Somehow his styled hair always stayed right in place there, as if he was expecting a photographer to be waiting. But here there was hay in his hair, sweat on his tight stomach, and a prominent bulge in the front of his jeans.

She carefully lay down on her back, still clutching material to her chest with one arm as she re-positioned herself to avoid shadows. She straightened the thin top, putting the strap ends up onto cup fabric, then stretched each arm back over her head in rest.

From his vantage point on the floor beside her bale, the rounded edge of a breast came fully in view under her loose top. *That's it*, he thought. *She's some woman, and I'm getting too close to taking her. Man, I want her, but it just wouldn't be fair--not now.* He took a long last look, then turned over and stared outside. What a perfect package she offered--all the beauty and brains in the world, four-point grades, class leader, on the State debate team, ambitious to always be best. He tried changing his thoughts to the train plans, but his mind kept slipping back to the offer his sunshine girl was silently making. In absolute frustration he finally said, "Well, I'd better go see if Grandmom needs help with lunch."

"Oh, before you go, my legs are a little sore from our hike yesterday. Some rubbing sure would help, along with some lotion." Her tone was a plea.

"Listen, babe, your beautiful bod is turning me on like crazy. I'd better leave while I can, as much as I'd love to stay."

"Legs are just legs, jock. I promise not to move."

He looked at her prone figure, and her smile. "Well, for a minute or two." Despite efforts at control, his insides did a flip-flop in anticipation. He adjusted his crotch again for comfort as he got up on his knees beside her hay bale. The air was totally warm.

Starting with her feet, he massaged deeply, then lotioned her left leg, then her right. She lay contentedly as his fingers plied the long muscles. Her national college swim-meet competitions had rewarded her the trim firmness of a gold medallist. He doggedly kept his fingertips an inch distant from her underwear, but his eyes kept rummaging over the covered mound between her legs.

"How's that?" Peter broke the silence of their thoughts.

"Marvelous," she cooed. "I'm thinking about keeping you on permanently as my masseur." Her eyes spoke sweetness into his. "Would you take just a minute more to do my stomach, if you have time."

He looked at his watch instinctively with her question. It was after eleven. His inner warnings kept rising, but he shut them off and said, "Three minutes, no more. I promised to meet Granddad at the grain elevator."

She accepted his compromise, as he squeezed lotion from the bottle again, and began deep clockwise circling motions on her flat abdomen. Her yellow briefs were very low from when he had pulled them down in the back. He was careful not to apply too much pressure on her relaxed body. When he came to her pelvic curves, he curved his hands to fit. She was as pliable as cookie dough.

"You're really good at that."

"I enjoy doing it. I enjoy you."

He poured a dab of lotion and made several quick passes up onto her rib cage, carefully staying just below the limp bra, but thinking what it would feel like to push up under it and cup her with his hands.

"I've been watching your eyes, Petey," Janet said softly. He looked up to her face, then stroked her cheek with his fingers. She brought one arm down and her hand clasped his. She whispered, "Why stop when you're so close to finishing the job?"

"What?" he asked, barely hearing her.

Instead of saying anything more, she brought her other hand down to her loose top. She started lifting it, fully exposing one pretty breast to him.

He grabbed her hand and pushed it down, startling her.

"What are you doing?" she asked, puzzled.

"What are you doing?" he shot back.

"Just--there's no reason for stopping," she said haltingly.

"For stopping? We were just enjoying each other, Jan."

"But I felt like you wanted--"

"I do! Of course I want you! But after we're engaged. That's what we decided."

Janet's eyes filled with tears of rejection and frustration. "I know what we said, but I don't want to wait. Let's go ahead now. Ask me now!"

"No," Peter said flatly. "I can't."

"Why not? That stupid secret trip of yours?"

"Yes! Look, it's only until I get back. I'll know a lot more about our future then."

"Will you tell me where you're going? Please. Especially if it's so vital to us. Pete, I want to help you and be with you."

"Jan, I just can't. I'm sorry."

"Thanks for all this loving trust, fella." She flung the words at him. Sitting up abruptly, she covered her chest tightly with one arm, and with the other hand slapped his face hard. She quickly stood, pushing his hand away as he reached out to her. Getting dressed took her less than a minute.

"I think I've had enough sun for today," she said, flashing a curt smile at him, tears running down her cheeks. She walked around the bales and toward the stairs.

"Be careful going down," Peter said quietly. "I'm sorry." He plopped down in the sun, and leaned back against one of her bales. All he could think of was her going...and his making her leave. The smell of straw and sweat and lotion was terribly bittersweet.

*

Peter glanced at Monty in the dark car as they drove to Janet's home. Monty was staring straight ahead, unaware of Peter's upsetting memories, content with silence for the moment. Peter's drive back from Wray last Sunday with Janet had been silent also, and icy cold right from that same passenger seat. But she had changed by the very next night.

Peter remembered driving last Monday to the old Brighton Grange Hall for a speech to the Serv-U.S. Club. He was surprised to see her blue Honda in the parking lot, complete with colored ribbons adorning the antenna and Auraria decals plastered on the rear bumper. Thinking of confronting her made him more nervous than the speaking prospect, for he had given countless talks as a college expert on farming problems.

His host, Al Federson, had greeted him, then introduced everyone all the way to the head table. Peter recalled only looking for one person until he spotted the back of her hair and a pretty blue dress at the far side of the room. He visualized the scene clearly.

. . . LAST MONDAY, AUGUST 8 . . .

The dinner and speech and applause were over when a gavel rapped for order. A surprise waited. The Brighton Serv-U.S. Club President, Harold Swenson, owner of Main Street Drug and Emporium, pounded his gavel for attention. "A fine speech, Pete. Now you're still a young man, pursuing a college career, but you also spend remarkable energy and enthusiasm in trying to make things better for those of us in the farming community.

"We've read your numerous letters to editors, here and around the country. We've signed your petitions. We went with you to plead our case with the Department of Agriculture and elected officials. Ha, and we all got hauled off to jail together for our peaceful protest at town hall. We know you're involved with church and missions and charitable hunger programs, and the list just goes on.

"Now we Serv-U.S.'ers are hard workers, as you just said, and we want to give you a token of appreciation for your working hard for us. So here's a framed certificate." Mr. Swenson opened a box and held up the shiny glass gift. "It says, 'Serv-U.S. Club Citizen's Honor: Peter Wayman, in recognition of your dedication and service to a very worthy cause.' Congratulations, Pete!"

Peter was shaken up by the crowd's raucous applause. It seemed so personal. He spoke haltingly to the grinning crowd. "Well now, this is surely a surprise." Peter looked toward Janet, and she gave him a quick thumbs-up gesture. "See, I never thought I'd get any awards..." His voice broke, and everyone laughed and clapped. Then he firmly said, "But, friends, you ain't seen nothin' yet!" They cheered their new hero for his hopeful words.

Peter shook many hands of congratulations after the meeting. Several said they'd wait to see him after the crowd cleared out. At last Janet came, extending her right hand. She looked stunning in blue. Her hair shone in lazy curls over her shoulders. Peter's impulse was to hug the smiling woman hungrily, but he merely grasped her hand tightly with both of his.

"Jan, I'm so glad to see you." He tried to put his feelings into the plain words.

"Oh, you know each other," Al noted. "Say, they sure grow them pretty at Auraria, eh, Pete?" He poked his guest's ribs for emphasis.

Peter didn't flinch, but kept his locked gaze as he agreed. "Exceptionally."

"Thank you," Janet said, with no trace of a blush. She left her hand in his grip. "I wouldn't have missed hearing your opinions."

He tried analyzing her tone of voice and message. It was too complicated.

"Thanks for inviting me, Mr. Federson," she said to the host.

"Pleasure's all ours, Miss Binghamton," Al said. He winked at Peter, confiding, "She saw the date in her Dad's Serv-U.S. newsletter, and called me a month ago. I think you have a fan here, Pete."

"Can you stay awhile?" Peter asked her.

"Oh, no, it's late, and I know you have others waiting to see you. Maybe we can talk after our two o'clock class tomorrow."

"I'm missing class. I have a meeting, but I'll call you." He held onto her hand until she moved more than an arm's length away as she left.

When the assembly room was all but deserted, the three men who stayed behind asked Peter to seriously consider a run for the state representative's seat in four years. With their support and grooming, they felt he had a good shot at winning, where he could make changes from the inside. He said he was honored by their interest, and would be in touch. Then they all said goodnight, with the last man turning off the lights as they left. Her blue Honda was gone.

On the lonely drive home, Peter reflected on the strange tangling of events. His life changed daily. His troubled relationship with Janet was keeping him off balance emotionally. Why had she driven so far and then not waited so they could talk--and touch? The silent voices of starving children were also shouting ever more loudly at him.

He had noticed his shorter patience and temper flares. His nerves were right on the edge. Thoughts of the changes he could make as a successful politician, or the help he could bring as a missionary--all were now in jeopardy. And the system had just given him a traditional reward for waging a polite battle in a war of words. How ironic, he mused, that his plaque of appreciation could overnight become his tombstone.

*

Peter slowly drove the curved streets of the upscale sub-division, with Monty still quietly in thought also. He pulled over to the curb and parked in front of the nicely landscaped Binghamton house. Memories of haylofts and civic speeches weren't enough. He had debated this with himself, and talked it over again with Monty. Finally he reached in his pocket for a coin and flipped it. It came up wrong, of course. He had decided to see his love one more time.

The eager young man ran up to ring the bell. Janet opened the door, and forgot to breathe. He smiled, and motioned for her to turn off the porch light and come outside into the dark night.

"You're so beautiful," Peter said, and urgently drew her close.

"I so hoped you'd come," she whispered. "Are you still leaving?" She held him tightly in his silence. "I know you must. Will you come back?"

"Soon as I can." He pushed his fingers into her black hair and combed the long tresses. She tilted her head back, savoring the feeling. He softly kissed the side of her neck, then around her face.

"Dreamers can be a real pain," she murmured, her cheek next to his.

"They're working on a cure," he said. "It's called *Dream Come True*. I'm conducting research on that subject over the next few days."

Suddenly she seemed as delicate as a dandelion's white puffball, covered with small umbrella seeds, each to be a full vibrant expression of life if it blew away to grow. He loosened his amorous hold, fearful the fragile orb might fly apart from his breath. Then he tightened against her again, as she became a sturdy yellow-petaled dandelion in full flower. Love plays such tricks in the young mind.

"I think I love you," he said softly.

"I think I love you too," she confided. "Help me understand."

They moved slowly apart. "That's a promise, for we are a promise," he said, smiling and touching her hair, her cheek, the tip of her nose. "Soon." Then he was out of reach. "Bye, babe."

"Be careful, Petey," she said, half-aloud, as much to herself as to him. Touching her cheek, she sadly watched him leave for his mystery rendezvous.

Monty had moved to the driver's seat, so Peter could just sit as they drove. The absence of words in the car was a kindness. Monty's tears of leaving had fallen earlier this morning, and he knew it was now Peter's turn to feel his farewells. Monty turned on the CD they had been listening to, and the soft music of Bach replaced the silence. Peter sighed deeply, closing his eyes and bowing his head at the emotions welling up and washing over him yet one more time.

... EARLIER THAT SUMMER, ONE SATURDAY AFTERNOON ...

Peter was in the worship sanctuary with the vaulted ceiling where he and his grandparents attended church when he visited Wray. Here he felt welcome and peace and God. He was seated in a rear pew, silently praying. The organist was practicing Bach's gentle melody of the Gentle Shepherd, "Sheep May Safely Graze," filling Peter's heart with purest praise. Then the organist missed notes in a run and stopped, bringing Peter back to the reality of their human imperfection. The two moods tripped in and out of this bit of church paradise.

The organ began again, and Peter sat moving in slow half-time swaying motion, his mediation deepening. *Thank you, God, for preserving this beautiful music for my ears,* he prayed in his mind. *And thank you for the fingers and feet that bring it to me now, and for the craftsmen's hands who built the marvelous instrument, and for those who donated money to buy it...who could have spent the money to print Bibles or feed the starving...*

He was brought up short by his dichotomy of feelings. Always an overlap: thanks and guilt, joy and sadness. Simpler emotions were only a luxury of earlier days. He was grateful when the organist's resounding chords came barging into his rampaging mind, quieting his own thoughts. He simply absorbed the melody for a while until the organist paused again to correct a tempo problem, murmuring dissatisfactions softly.

Great God, why did you make me an instrument, yet unable to play your music? Peter formed the thought so forcefully he wondered if it had been heard. *Make me an instrument of your peace...but you cry peace, peace, and yet there is no peace.* It had begun again. Arguing inside of him. Who, and what was the argument really about? How would the incessant bickering be resolved? The music drew out his inner division: loud passage followed by soft echo, then again two voices, alternating dominance. He yielded to emotion, and felt his spirit-self soar around the high vaulted ceiling. Was it seeking the source of the music--the pipes or the organ, or trying to escape it? Or just enjoying the amorphous waves filling the air in this beautiful passage? Part of him seemed to want to be a butterfly in the treble clef, fluttering lightly, brightly, higher, with the other side trapped in the bass clef, a troll swooping into the abyss, struggling to rise.

Peter was driven to his knees in the sanctuary, desperately repeating the Lord's Prayer in hushed fervor, fearful to release the spirit and return to his own mind, where he must finally decide his *raison d'etre*. The boy in him wanted to cry, but the man in him wouldn't permit it.

*

Monty stopped the car at his motel. Suddenly Peter's reverie was over. The time for goodbyes had passed, and present reality flooded in around him. The finality of the final decision now rested squarely on his shoulders, and he accepted that.

Peter's mind began organizing again. His first task was to call Wilma Fletcher, a reporter for the *Rocky Mountain Herald*. Young, enterprising, frustrated with few assignments beyond neighborhood events and obituaries, needing a lucky break--that's how Ruth Fitzwater had described Wilma to the Shakespeare Group after a visiting lecture in her journalism class at Auraria. Wilma's credentials and honors from school papers had all led Peter to his earlier interview with her about a hypothetical train hijacking.

Peter punched his cell phone memory key after Monty went inside the room. He would need time and space before facing Monty if Wilma said no. He pictured the pert lady who would answer. Her skin was like pure ebony. Tight beaded ringlets in her hair with rose-colored beads, manicured fingernails, and pretty lips also colored rose had made a lasting impression.

Her carefully crafted sample articles and lofty career goals rounded out the image at their first meeting. He wanted her to be their reporter.

The phone had rung five times, and Peter moved the phone to his left ear. There was no reason to worry yet. Their conversation over iced tea at the Denver Art Museum had included the agreement that the make-believe event would be a great opportunity for an inside scoop. She'd be in on lawbreaking, but not as an actual accomplice. Courts were lenient on the reporter standing next to the criminal embarked on a good cause--like Robin Hood's merry band including a *Fast Quill*, she said. They had laughed together, and hit if off. When they parted, she had said only that she would seriously consider accompanying *a man a lot like* Peter, and asked what this *Pulitzer* was that he mentioned?

He clicked off and re-dialed, checking the number she gave him. "Wilma, this is Peter," he spoke with quiet relief when she answered.

"Nine o'clock on the dot. You keep your appointments. What's up?"

"Time to drop hypothetical talk. You ready to ride to a big story?" The phone was silent. "Hello? Turning on your tape recorder?"

"No, Peter, deciding how to react now that the moment is really here."

"We desperately need a good reporter--we need you. We have no backup if you turn us down. We leave early tomorrow."

"What a jokester. I'd have a hundred things to do to get ready. Places are closed for the night. There's no way. Is this really life and death stuff you're dealing with, or just flashy headlines?"

It was Peter's turn to be quiet. Then he said, "I'm disappointed. I thought we covered this ground well enough to convince you of the seriousness of starvation--and the promise that surplus American grain holds."

"Hypothetical stays gray. You're getting into black and white now."

They talked of clothes for the trip, food, numbers of people, facilities, and her insurance, with its exclusions for criminal activities. Peter went through his plan carefully. "About three hours from now. You need to drive to a bar and meet us at 12:30 A.M. Speak carefully, so if you want to be *kidnapped*, you could make it sound convincing later. Go in the Union Station Hotel on Fourteenth and Wynkoop. Get known by at least the bartender. Then come outside and we'll be waiting. Got it?"

"So I go to the worst part of downtown, after midnight," she recapped. "Have drinks and be a chummy come-on, then get kidnapped. Not a bad night's assignment, for a lunatic. Are you crazy, Peter? Am I?" They fussed a few more minutes before working out the remaining details and hanging up.

"Wilma is going! Our own public relations pro!" Peter was elated entering Monty's motel room. "I told you not to worry."

"That's great." The big man turned back toward the TV. A perturbed Peter asked when the show ended so they could leave to pick up Fork.

"Show's over at ten, and don't be a grouch. We're not picking him up. He's meeting us here at ten-thirty. I figured you'd want to catch the news."

"Man, I love changes." Peter was nervous again. They had to have a backup engineer, but Monty's trusted friend Fork was another unknown factor.

The program ended, and the news and weather proved uneventful. Sports just started when Fork arrived and blurted out, "Two's company, three's a hijacking!" He immediately headed for the bathroom, declaring, "But first things first." The man was as small and skinny as Monty was tall and heavy. The way the new arrival had raised his arms straight up and spread his fingers when he saw his friend reminded Peter of fork tines, so he didn't need to ask why the strange nickname. Fork hadn't shaved for days. His stubble was salt and pepper mix, and looked strange with his ketchup colored hair. He moved oddly, like jockeying a horse through a rainstorm.

Fork had left the bathroom door open and kept talking. "Pretty classy place--enough towels for everybody. Bronson movie at eleven, Monty. Got chips?"

Peter stood in disbelief, shaking his head at his peculiar new ally. He reached for his phone to call a boxcar in this strange new world he was creating.

. . . TWO HOURS EARLIER, WEDNESDAY NIGHT, AUGUST 10 . . .

A rented moving van bounced across the railroad tracks and jerked to a stop. The driver walked around back, pulled the metal ramp down, and swung open the back doors. Twelve people climbed out, grumbling and joking about the rough ride. They spoke in hushed voices while unloading ladders, boxes, and other tools. It looked like any construction crew coming to work--secretly and late at night.

They moved quickly, like ants hurrying from bread crust to anthill, and back. Their path was beside the row of six boxcars standing on the isolated rail siding where the truck had parked. The crew laid materials west of the huge cars, shadowed from the moon's sliver.

"Done with this load, Stan. Hustle back with the rest, and don't get caught!" Ben Cody winked at the driver. The truck bumped away into the night. Ben was a husky six-footer, weathered by a lifetime of farming, hands gnarled now by arthritis. The Wray farmers had designated him as their leader.

"Time to get this stuff hidden, Tom?" Ben asked.

The young man from the Shakespeare Group was directing the busy traffic of movers. Tom Buchanan was several inches shorter than Ben, and plumper. Tom's excessive time in the college library showed in more than his grades. He nodded, and waved his flashlight beam down along the string of cars, motioning the others to come gather around. Then he aimed the light on the heavy metal latch securing the first boxcar door.

"This is all there is to it, for you newcomers," Ben said, stepping up and pulling at the handle. He tugged again, then reversed his position and pushed up hard. His face registered the pain in his hands. The latch barely moved.

"Let us help, Ben," some others said, but he waved them away. "Just get me that crowbar." He put the bar into place under the latch and strained to pry it open. "Hand me a hammer, Larry."

"No, Ben," Tom said in a whisper. "We don't want to telegraph rail security that we're commandeering their train."

Two people leveraged crowbars, and the rusted latch arm finally released, clanging open. "Be sure and hit that latch with some bear grease," Ben said, as he reached up and began pushing on the tall steel edge of the door, straining, then his rough voice called out, "Okay, how about some help with this?"

Feet shuffled across the gravel next to the tracks. Ben's two hands became four, and the same number grabbed hold on the other end of the boxcar door. Somebody spoke up nervously in the darkness. "We are sure these cars are empty, aren't we?" A few laughed half-heartedly.

The huge metal slab slid open reluctantly, scraping noisily through the accumulated dirt in the door track. Flashlights played anxiously all around the inky interior. Tom quickly gave firm orders. "Only open this side on every other car, third and fifth on this east side. Cars two, four, and six open over on the west side only. Stay close to the train. If a car comes along the road, duck under and lie flat. We just have two crowbars, so work fast when you have them. Let's beat that deadline! Go!"

The little group scattered down the motionless row of rail cars. Ben leaned a ladder up against the closed side of car two, climbed it, and began working with the cordless drill. The short sound bursts seemed to shatter all hopes for secrecy. It was worth it, Tom had reasoned, to get those eyebolts in place fast. The lines through those two rows of bolts would hold their banners tightly.

"Tarnation! All I'm doing is grinding the tip off this bit," Ben called down. "It's too soft. What we need is a torch."

"Not so loud," Tom warned again, then mumbled something to himself. "A bolt wouldn't hold in a burn hole, would it, Ben?"

"Not one any of us made. How about spray painting some messages?"

Tom grimaced in the darkness at the thought of sloppy lettering and runny paint being telecast nationwide. His shoulders slumped, and he disappeared between cars, headed for a crisis conference. In a short time he was back at the ladder. "Ben, here's what we've decided to do for now." He explained the revised plan.

Twenty minutes later, Ben said, "Ropes all in place on number two." Heavy clothesline cord had been tied to the ladder on one end of the boxcar, run along the closed side, cut, and tied to the ladder at the other end, one high and one low. Strong snap hooks were spaced along it and tied. "By the way," Ben continued, "some end ladders only go halfway up, so the banners are going to be pretty low. We may have to cut them off."

Tom knew this would upset Peter, since it wasn't part of their carefully structured plan. Still, it met the publicity goal. They would do the best they could. Anyway, somebody should have known about the steel before tonight. "Stop arguing with yourself," he muttered aloud.

Others brought a second ladder, and began fastening a large banner in place between the two clotheslines. Another fellow was trying to help them center it by eyeballing from a distance and sending flashlight signals instead of shouting. The banner words were so large, though, they seemed to shout at him along the length of the boxcar: "U. S. GRAIN FOR THE HUNGRY."

Suddenly, headlights appeared. They were far down the road, which ran parallel, and east of the track spur. The watcher on top of the train blew twice on a small whistle. Ben climbed down hurriedly, laid the ladder on gravel, and stood behind the wheels with other men on the west side. The streetside workers flung down their ladders in a panic, narrowly missing heads, and scurried underneath between rails. They waited...seven seconds...nine...

The car passed without slowing, and the taillights faded away. One whistle, and work commenced quickly, minus one extension ladder that bent when it hit the ground.

After an hour, the van returned. Its overhead flashers stayed on to identify it at a distance, so the crew kept working as it bounced through weeds toward them. Ben and others rushed to unload carefully counted stacks of bedding, food, and boxes with numbers marked on the outside.

A workman ambled up to Ben. "Say, nothing is here for cars five or six."

"Larry, remember what Peter told us out at the ranch last weekend? Since only eight of us are going, and there's two in each car, that's only four cars with men. We just have two spare boxcars for company on the trip. But I'm glad you're looking out for trouble spots."

Larry Shafner was a wrangler for the Birdwhistle Ranch. In 2003, he had suffered a bad fall from a horse. It hadn't hurt his good heartedness, just jumbled his head. The Wray group and Peter had made certain several times that Larry understood he could get hurt real bad on this trip, but he kept saying if they were going to save little kids' lives, then he just had to go. Now he remembered about the boxcars. "Oh, yeah, thanks, Ben. We're doing pretty good for a bunch of hick farmers in the big city, ain't we, Ben?"

"You bet we are. Better hustle with that stuff now."

The warm thick air muffled the sounds of moonlit remodeling and packing. The crew worked without talking, except for an occasional curse when someone stumbled in the darkness.

Ben and Tom tested the eyebolts now screwed into place around the wooden walls inside each boxcar, about three feet off the floor. Rope would be pulled through the eyebolts and tied, making a complete safety loop to hold onto. This was especially necessary across the open doors on one side, once all was loaded.

They walked back toward the parked truck. From the shadows, a young woman's voice surprised them. "Tom! Where the devil are the port-a-johns? The train can't leave without *them*!"

"Now just relax," he soothed. Ruth Fitzwater's dark hair and eyes seemed part of the night as he looked at his collaborator. Her familiar presence and down-to-earth question took a little edge off their lawbreaking. "I called on my cell, and they're on the way," Tom told her. "Probably forty minutes. Is the stuff for the engine loaded? Got the hand-held radios?"

"Yep, all here in the first car. It's already half-past ten. Peter just called to say Fork got in to the motel, and they're on schedule. Shall we hoist the banners on the street side?"

"Better wait 'til after midnight," Tom said. Ben nodded in agreement. "We'll get everything else on board and the men out of sight in their boxcars."

The three talkers stood close together, as friends will do in the night. They looked down along the rail line. The six huge boxcars stretched out longer than a football field. Active sounds floated back to them--of metal attacking wood, and of boots scuffing on ladders and loose rock.

"Tom, your bags are in your car, and your plane leaves in three hours. It's time for you to turn this part of the operation over to us," Ruth said softly. Tom looked at her and screwed his face up in a look of reluctance. "So get outa here, and God speed," she finished strongly.

Tom nodded, and hugged her hard, and long. He took Ben's hand, clasped his elbow, and held on firmly. "God speed," he said to them, then quickly turned to leave for Denver International.

Another set of headlights turned onto the road approaching the train. It was a truck. The clearance lights on the trailer flashed twice, but then stayed on instead of continuing to flash. Ruth frowned, the whistle resting in her hand. Was it an unexpected intruder? The crew kept working, trusting her to warn them of strangers.

*   *   *

The freighter's dark hulk remained motionless as Pacific waves swirled past. Water around the ship was frothy white from beating against the flat stern. Rain poured in silvered sheets, shining in the lightning. Even thunderclaps could scarcely be heard above the roaring gale.

Inside the high afterdeck cabin above the stern, the captain shouted in Hindi to the man standing near the wheel. "Kasir, you've gotten us into quite a predicament!" The captain's uniform was crisp, despite the soggy weather, and he held his back very straight. Light brown skin, jet-black hair and mustache, and a rather sharp nose confirmed the lineage of India.

"But, Captain, there's no sandbar within twenty kilometers on this chart."

"What is the date on that fax?"

"July twenty-fifth, sir."

"You were to get updated coastal flow maps, Third Officer."

"But, sir, this is barely three weeks old." The younger man shouted back over the storm, obviously upset at grounding the ship. Their nationality was the same, but their resemblance ended there, for he was utterly disheveled.

"The Columbia estuary channels shift unmercifully, especially during storms. I shall give you just that, Third Officer, no mercy, if we are late making port to reload!" Surging winds abbreviated the captain's next words. "...people depending...crucial timing--"

"…make…lost time," the steering mate shouted. He repeated it when the captain cupped his ear. "We'll be there Friday."

The man in charge turned to watch the downpour. He counted on vigorous waves freeing his light draft ship undamaged. Then he would anchor until dawn.

"Sheefah," he radioed below. "Check those hull plates in the empty Sirai grain hold. Stay in there. The least leak could spoil it all now."

*   *   *

Chapter Three

Denver was calling an end to the day. Frank Wayman turned over in bed, still perturbed over his encounter with Monty four hours earlier. Across town, FBI Regional Director Brody turned on Bill Pierce's "Nightsounds" Chicago re-broadcast to lull him to sleep. Janet Binghamton cried quietly into her pillow. Traffic diminished as garage doors opened then closed their mouths on signal, taking their evening meal in one or two gulps.

There were exceptions. Interstates still bisected and encircled the metropolitan area with thousands of headlight beams shining every direction. Shafts of light oscillated crazily through gulches of rail yard steel.

A few cars still prowled the quiet downtown streets after midnight. One of them belonged to Peter Wayman.

"There's a woman up at the corner. Is that Wilma?" Monty asked.

"Can't tell yet," Peter said, slowly driving toward the intersection.

"Uh, oh, check out the dudes walking up to her."

Fork snickered. "Expect a woman to stay alone long at this hour?"

"Right. I put her at risk here." Peter stopped for the light. Wilma's gestures were clear, brushing their hands away from her arms, and pointing the two men back in the direction of the hotel bar.

"Look legit, or set up?" Peter asked as they watched. The light turned green. "It's time," Peter decided. "We'll take off if it's a trap." He pulled just past the corner where the three people stood, then stopped to open his door and step out.

"Hey, lady, you look familiar. What's your name?" he hollered shakily.

She turned abruptly toward him. "Wilma Fletcher, what's yours?"

"Right, the lady from the *Herald*. My name is Peter. We met at today's tournament. How about a lift to your car?" She hesitated, playing it to the hilt, Peter thought. "Rather have your two friends there take you?"

Wilma took steps toward Peter's car. One of the men reached out and grabbed her sleeve. "Not so fast. We were just getting close."

Peter yelled loudly, his voice becoming fully resonant. "Hey, fella, my friend and I want you to let the lady go--right now." Monty slowly stepped out of the car, his massive frame hulking in the shadows of the streetlights. The two men pestering Wilma began backing away toward the bar.

"Miss Fletcher, your limousine is waiting." Peter held the back door open for her to slide in next to Fork. Quick introductions were made.

"Your bags in your car?" Peter asked as they drove away.

"One block right, one left," she said. "I'll bet you men wondered if those were cops with me," she offered, reading their coolness.

"Well..." Peter mumbled, and Fork finished, "...yep."

"Convinced they weren't?" Wilma prodded her trio of comrades.

"Well..." Monty said, and Fork finished, "...nope."

"Fork," she laughed, "you be Frank, and I'll be Earnest." The ice melted a little, and she kept up the thawing process. "See, no headlights following."

"Don't need none downtown," her back seat companion said.

"You're right," Wilma said. "I hadn't thought of that before now."

"Me neither," Fork admitted, and they shared another laugh. Peter felt a twinge of jealousy, which he promptly dismissed as childish.

She was disappointed when Peter drove past her car after she pointed it out. After two more blocks, Wilma grew petulant.

"Listen, guys, if you can't trust me, I don't want any part of this caper. No need to transfer bags when we finally get back to my car."

Peter braked his car. "Too much is at stake here not to be suspicious."

"Suspicious, sm--ush--spicious," she stammered out, trying hard to sound mad, but snickered at the mushy sound, along with those around her.

"You win. Anybody with a mouth like that has got to be all right," Peter said, looking out the back window down the vacant street. He made a quick U-turn and headed back toward her car.

After loading Wilma's two suitcases, blanket, and pillow, and commenting on luxury cruises, they headed to change to an old rental car. Peter parked his teal Chevrolet Corsica, and bid it a fond adieu--until they met again at the impound lot. He called the boxcars, and they reported the banner sign snafu. "Well, can you find some way to hang them up so the world can read them, even if they're low?" Peter asked Ruth over the phone.

"Guess I shouldn't vote on that, since I can't read," Fork volunteered quietly from the back seat.

"I shouldn't vote either," Wilma added under her breath, "since I can't write."

"Just what we needed," Monty said, "a team of comedians traveling with us for three days." Peter punched Monty's leg as a warning.

Wilma catalogued the three-day information tidbit for later calculation, but kept up the easy banter. "Did you bring a knife, Fork? I've got a pie."

"Hope the wit holds out," Peter said over his shoulder.

"Sure it will," Wilma threw in, "because I know how to knit."

"And that's why they call you such a..." Monty fed her the line.

"...knit wit," she announced exuberantly.

"Sorry, I only caught half of that," Fork said.

The onslaught of one-liners continued as they drove northward, leaving the lighted checkerboards of skyscrapers a mile behind, then two.

Peter followed rail line 96, then exited on a dirt road and stopped. The two odd couples sat parked in the old clunker near the tracks, concealed in heavy bushes. One window was down to listen for train whistles, and apparently also to attract mosquitoes. Several trains rumbled past, one carrying coal, the other flatbeds and new cars. It was after one-thirty as they monitored the train frequency.

"You sure the 9039 is the only one coming in on this track at two o'clock? Their radio code seems like a lot of gibberish," Wilma confessed. Fork began interpreting.

"Hey, you two, quiet!" the man in the driver's seat said sharply. The twosome in the back seat leaned up to listen.

"Go ahead, 9039," the dispatcher radioed from the switching yards four miles south. Peter gratefully nodded at the sound of Harran's voice.

The background noise was clearly from a train moving fast. "Passing the new Silverleaf. The dogs must have finished early tonight, place is deserted."

"Yeah," Harran answered. "All the new millionaires are home planning how to spend tomorrow. Just like those who went bust. See ya in twenty minutes. Out." The radio lapsed silent.

"Okay, Fork, it's time." Peter laid it out. "Walk a hundred yards up the track, climb that hill to get a clear view of us and the track for at least a half-mile north. Verify our train with the binoculars, then flash your light every three seconds until I flash our headlights. Hide down close to the tracks. It's up to you to get behind the engineers and make sure they don't start again or radio for help, once they stop."

"Got your gun?" Monty asked.

"Hold on one minute, mister," Wilma butted in. "You said non-violent to persons all the way."

Peter turned to face her. "The guns aren't loaded. We need the threat to keep the engineers from resisting and maybe getting hurt."

"Makes the crime worse," she rejoined.

"What's one more count on top of dozens?" Peter asked. "Fork, flash us when you get into position and I'll flash you back."

"If that's what you wanted, Peter, we should've done it at the motel," Fork grinned. "There was a lot more light."

Monty snickered, and after a moment to catch on, Peter laughed too, then Wilma. Fork opened the door and said, "See ya soon."

"Be careful jumping on," Monty cautioned.

"And Fork," Peter added, "if it's the wrong train, wave a solid, right?"

"I remember the plan, boss." Fork disappeared.

It was a long five minutes before a light flashed once from halfway up the dark hillside. "Got him spotted, Monty?" Peter asked. Monty and Wilma both said yes.

Peter flashed the headlights, noting Fork's dot of light in front of them, just left of the rearview mirror. Then he turned to Wilma. "This would be a good time to mark up my drafts. The broadcasts need to be in your words, now that you have facts. You'll make the first recording on the way to the boxcar hookup, to get the train in the background sound. We'll give the chip to the courier there to make dupes for delivery."

"Dupes? Another surprise, Peter? I thought this was to be a scoop--you know, as in one paper and one national network."

"It'll be a scoop, for the papers and stations that use it," Peter said, still watching the hillside. "We can't afford to play life and death games, so we need to make sure your recording is broadcast at once. A single network exec might be forced by the Feds to delay. We'd be sunk without public awareness right from the start. Then we need to grow their support."

Wilma thought of her boss. *Serves that honky Hargrave right. He's too dumb to see a scoop even when his own reporter is trapped on the train.* She nodded in the dark and said, "I follow you. I'm just wondering how many other not-quite-whole truths you've laid on me. It makes this seem all the more tentative for me."

"Sorry you're doubting, since you're our key." Peter turned to look at her.

"Yeah," Monty said. "You know how to make things happen that we wouldn't even think of." He also turned to face her from the front seat.

"Monty, we can't both look at this beautiful and talented lady, or no one will see Fork's signal," Peter warned by compliment.

Wilma smiled. "If you trust me as a partner to watch for Fork's light, you can both fill me in on more of what's going on."

They both agreed. Wilma asked, "Won't they jam our cell phone broadcasts from the train?"

"They'll try, but we have fairly sophisticated gear." Peter noted her first use of that critical word *our*.

"And quick as they block one frequency, we'll switch to another," Monty added. "That way, we can buy more time before we have to carry out our threats."

"We hope to be doing live broadcasts before noon, and from then on-- with public pressure," Peter shared.

"Why do you think you'll even get as far as Salt Lake City?" Wilma asked.

She's fishing for a destination, guessing the West Coast, Peter reasoned. Monty blurted out, "How did you know--"

Peter spoke up, hitting Monty's leg again. "How did you know that's the first question we asked? What leverage do we have? Threats--that's what. We're not going to give them any reason to doubt we'll carry out our threats to bomb power supply stations. We're betting that our one train can't be worth crippling any cities."

"I don't know, guys. Sounds like you already plan more violence. And violence begets violence--they could vaporize this train before any signal got out."

"Yes, they have all the power and authority--except the power of the American people," Peter assured her.

"You must convince the people to insist on our getting through," Monty added.

"Through to where, Monty?" she queried at once.

The silence of the outside world descended into the car. Monty turned to face the front again, looking up at the barely discernible hillside, leaving the answer to Peter.

"I'm your key, huh? You two are pathetic," Wilma said disgustedly.

"We can't give you that information," Peter tried explaining. "It might slip out, inadvertently, in a broadcast. Then we'd have the whole cavalry lined up against us, instead of one city and state at a time."

"But every city you go through will limit your possible--"

"Right. Limit! And secrecy is for your own protection, too. You'll never become a full accomplice."

"Then why do I feel like I'm wearing a bandana right now?" Wilma sighed, chuckling softly, reaching for her penlight. "I've got a script to write, boys."

Five minutes passed like years. Each person was thinking private thoughts of momentous changes, each becoming dependent on the other.

Then another five-minute eternity crept by.

The narrow beam of light shining from the hillside was barely enough to penetrate the clouded blackness surrounding them.

"Pete?"

"I see it." Wilma suddenly became alert in the back seat.

"Again, and there again. Our first moment of truth is upon us." The words just formed themselves as they slipped from Peter. They felt right, and he wondered if their reporter would record actual words along the way.

Peter signaled back with the headlights. "Wilma, you're as trusted now as you ever will be by anyone. I want you to get out of the car and wait right here in these bushes for us. I don't want you to be seen, or put in any extra danger. And I don't want to jeopardize your chances to escape charges. If something happens to us and this goes haywire now, just make the most of a headline story about lofty schemers."

She gathered up her things quietly, and reached for the door handle. Her silence bothered Monty. "Wilma, don't run away now. We need you. We do need you to be right here when we come back. You with us?"

The whistle sounded from the invisible train.

"With you to the end," Wilma said in hasty departure.

Peter and Monty grasped right hands in a comrades' salute. Peter started the motor, put the old clunker in gear, and drove slowly ahead, bumping over the rails with the front tires, then stopping the car when it directly straddled the tracks. He turned off the motor, turned on the interior lights, left the headlights shining into nowhere, and shifted into neutral.

There was no sound inside the car as both men held their breath, watching for the first sign of the light from Engine Number 9039. A minute had not passed before they saw the trees brightening far up the track. They got out quickly, Monty moving behind the car ready to push, Peter going to the front and raising the hood.

Suddenly they and the clunker were bathed in the oscillating glare of a train's very bright headlight. Shrill blasts of an air horn hit their ears.

Peter looked up from under the hood, directly into the headlight, judging the distance and speed. He paused for a moment, then ran around to the back of the car where Monty was motioning furiously for help.

Brakes squealed as metal discs strained to slow hundreds of tons of metal hurtling forward at five yards a second. The air horn became a solid sheet of warning sound. As the two men leaned into pushing the car forward, Peter thought of the engineer in the approaching train radioing their crisis to the dispatcher. Timing was everything.

"Front!" Peter yelled, and they raced to the front of the car and started pushing. The train was three hundred yards away, and closing.

"That damn train better be able to stop!" Monty shouted as they pushed the car backwards until the front tires stopped against the track.

"Yeah, it won't do us any good if it's wrecked," Peter shouted back over the air horn and brakes. The engine was within one hundred yards, but slowing fast. Peter ran to jump in behind the wheel and start the motor. That engineer is calling for a tow truck to haul us off the tracks now, he thought, putting the car into reverse and spinning his back tires into a cloud of dust. Monty ran toward the train, waving his arms wildly.

Now they're telling dispatch we've got it started, Peter reasoned, as he shifted into low and eased the car's rear tires up over the first track, then the second, while looking desperately into the bright headlight of the now stationary train. They'll radio that the track is clear again, no need for a tow truck. Now, Fork, now, up into the cab, Peter said to himself. He got out, a foolish grin plastered on his face. A roll of wide strapping tape hung around his wrist, and his gun was pushing against his spine where he had it tucked in his belt.

Monty was now abreast of the first of four huge diesel engines, on the left side. The engineers' cab was in the front, with ten feet of steep steps to climb to force open a door for an involuntary entry. Both engineers were leaning out of their high left window talking with Monty as Peter reached his side.

Suddenly a shout came from inside the cab. Fork was at their backs. Monty leaped up the front steps, clambering toward the door.

"Put your hands way up!" Peter shouted, pointing the empty gun straight at one engineer's frightened face. Peter felt queasy, like a hundred eyes were behind him, watching his crime.

Monty pulled open the narrow door. Both engineers had their hands raised, with Fork inside pointing his gun at them. It was hot and stuffy, even with the windows open, instantly returning Monty to years past. He leaned back out the door to catch the tape Peter pitched, relieved that he didn't recognize the two engineers. He taped their hands tightly behind them, and took their ID cards. Fork marched them out along the catwalk behind the cab, his gun still very evident.

"Turn around and step down backwards--real slow," Fork commanded. Peter steadied them as they awkwardly climbed down using no hands.

It was over, without a scratch to either body or equipment. The train had a new crew.

Monty stayed in the cab, checking all the gauges to determine operating conditions. With the two ID's in hand, he radioed a lie to the dispatcher. "9039 about ready to roll. Traffic okay?"

"Roger," Harran replied, "slowed down for you. Get humping!"

"Clear," Monty responded, minimizing words.

Peter and Fork marched the two engineers with taped hands and gags in their mouths back toward the old clunker. They sandwiched both men inside the big trunk space--a *must* feature when Peter rented the car. Peter motioned with his head for Fork to go get Wilma. Fork handed him the gun, and jogged across the tracks.

"Listen up," Peter said to the two cramped engineers. "This lid has lots of air holes in it, so you won't suffocate. See? Look up!" He shone his flashlight onto the holes in the trunk lid. "And these guns were not loaded, see?" He pulled back the slide on the first one and locked it open, with no shell ejecting. Then he popped out the empty cartridge clip and showed them, repeating the same procedure with each handgun. "And I'm leaving the guns here in the trunk with you. So we are now unarmed. Got that?" The men nodded when the light hit their faces. Peter put the handguns on top of the trussed men.

"Now, I'm going to take the gags off, so if you throw up you won't choke to death. In return, I need a promise from each of you: Don't make a sound. We'll notify people to come get you in three hours, before sunup. Your promise?" The flashlight again recorded their vigorous yes. Peter removed the gags, closed the lid, and locked it on two very shaken and helpless engineers. He left the key in the ignition, and scanned the bushy landscape for movement.

What if Fork hadn't found their reporter? What if she ran?

He started breathing normally again when he saw three heads moving in the lighted cab of the waiting engine. He ran toward the back steps, charged up them, and along the catwalk. As Peter slammed the narrow door behind him, Monty inched the train into motion with a great whining of diesel power. An endless series of clanking sounds followed behind them, as couplers grabbed car after car and pulled it obediently forward. Their hijacked grain train was finally underway.

*   *   *

Interstate Highways 70 and 25 intertwined in north Denver with endless loops and overpasses, at a place nicknamed the *Mousetrap*. Two miles north, Police Cruiser 406 moved along a deserted street, paralleling the railroad track that serviced the industrial warehouses. The officer glanced again at the helicopters lasering the night sky with searchlights while he listened to the radio traffic. Help was being pulled from all over the metro area to round up thirty head of cattle in and around that Mousetrap .

The herd scrambled loose when a cattle truck jackknifed along a curve past a poorly-marked painting crew. Animals were everywhere, either dead or running wildly.

A row of boxcars parked at Nye Siding casually drew his attention. Suddenly, his mind caught the outlines of movement behind one boxcar.

The lone officer in 406 adjusted his right spotlight. Coasting slowly, he played the beam back and forth under the boxcar. Nothing. Up across the side of the long car. Door open--not unusual. Nobody between cars.

He jammed on the brakes. A banner had been strung along the whole lower half of the next boxcar: "LET'S BE GENEROUS." He aimed his light along the top of the boxcar, then under it, and dropped the beam lower, along the gravel slope of track bed. The bright egg shape of light reflected off an aluminum extension ladder, bent at the middle joint. He moved the light quickly along the ground by the other five cars, revealing more clumps of things that could be graffiti materials.

Abruptly, he adjusted the light back to the door of the first open boxcar, and was certain two heads ducked out of sight. Hobos. The light picked out boxes stacked in the far corner. It should have been empty.

The officer in cruiser 406 became suddenly aware of the darkness surrounding him, and his aloneness, and wished his partner wasn't on sick leave. How many persons were in, or around this train? Why?

He activated his shoulder mike: "Dispatch, this is 406. I have a big graffiti here, on Powell Road, north 10800. Suspicious activity around a six-car train on Nye Siding, two unknown parties sighted. Banners have been strung--"

Dispatch interrupted. "406, ignore the graffiti, unless actually in progress. Report to Mousetrap command to help in cleanup. Do you copy?"

"Copy." The officer logged in the order. "Please notify Mid-Western

Pacific to send their railway security to this location. 406 clear." The officer flung the light beam once more along the row of boxcars. He sent his other spotlight out randomly through the fields on his left, like a hunting dog rooting through weeds for a game scent. Nothing.

He checked his rear view mirror for traffic, and turned on the cruiser's bright flasher bar. Red, blue, and white light dramatically flashed all around the area as he punched the accelerator to the floor.

"Well, I do have new orders" he consoled himself aloud, tires still screeching to catch up with his engine. "How much damage could anyone do to a bunch of boxcars--or with them? Probably kids in some kind of protest, and not as bad as real graffiti artists anyway."

He turned right, ignoring the stop sign, then glanced both directions just before bouncing across the railroad tracks. There was a train coming, its torch headlight about a half-mile away near the Xcel Energy Company. The officer was glad he wouldn't be stuck waiting for it to pass.

*   *   *

Wilma sat on one of the two padded footlockers that had been brought into the engine cab. Her cell phone recorder was turned on, and her penlight was focused on the paper as she carefully read the script that she had quickly modified in the car's back seat. She hoped the new cell phone device the salesman called *cpd* was picking up her words over the important background sounds of the working diesels.

"This is Wilma Fletcher, reporter for the *Rocky Mountain Herald* in Denver, Colorado. It is 3:00 A.M., Thursday morning, and I'm in the noisy cab of an engine pulling a train--which is this very moment being hijacked." She paused to let that sink in. "I am a volunteer hostage."

She took a deep breath, looking around at the three men looking at her. She had asked Peter before starting the recording whether he wanted to look at the script she had rewritten. He had told her that she was the reporter. But now they had looks of concern at her choice of words, so she hurriedly continued.

"I do not feel at all threatened by these train hijackers, for they claim to be non-violent. But I am in jeopardy simply by being an observer on board. I don't know how the authorities will deal with this situation. If they choose violence, then I am in danger.

"The hijackers call this the *Grain Train*. Indeed, it is pulling car after car full of grains of wheat. This surplus wheat was on its way to a storage yard full of already overstuffed federal grain elevators. The hijackers have *borrowed* the train, and six boxcars. Those boxcars were empty on a siding a few hours ago, but are now carrying farmers, angry farmers, who are losing their farms due to a lot of old accumulated government policies which they consider wrong.

"These men are humanitarians. They make the points that the grain was going to rot if not used, and that they will return the train undamaged, if they are permitted to, after the cargo is unloaded and given to feed the hungry. For now, we are headed toward an undisclosed location."

She monitored the undulation bars as she read from her notes, holding the cpd close to her lips to reduce the interference from the background noise. "I don't consider myself an accomplice to a crime, if indeed a crime has been, or is being committed. Rather, I find myself forming a link in a communication chain, here to help us as Americans focus on a national problem. We hoard our food surplus, and our farmers and their fertile lands stand idle, while hundreds die each day from starvation outside our blessed homeland."

Wilma paused to reword her involvement. "I'm done for a minute," she hollered to the big shadow of a man at the right console of engine controls in front of her.

Monty nodded, and picked up the hand mike of the radio. "CTC, this is 9039, over."

"Dispatch, over."

"We're experiencing some possible air brake loss. Need to pull off on the next siding to run some checks."

"This isn't your night, 9039. Let's see, Nye Siding is next, mile post six dot two, three empty tracks, and number four has some cars on it. Take number two. You've got seventy-four in your string?"

"Affirmative," Monty stated, but formed a question with his hands to the others.

"Plenty of room. I'm switching for you now, so cut your speed to about five."

"Thanks, dispatch. Who's behind us?"

"311, forty minutes back. Don't rush it. We'll work you back in, clear."

"Appreciated, clear." Monty replaced the mike.

Wilma began recording again. She was accustomed to working under pressure with interruptions. "I agreed to travel with this strange small band, and to give them a louder voice through this radio network. I'll be back in an hour, God willing, with more news. This is Wilma Fletcher, with the

Rocky Mountain Herald, riding the Grain Train."

She clicked to restart and played it back from the chip very loudly. Peter, Monty, and Fork clapped and stomped when it finished.

"Now that's the ticket!" Monty said.

"That's Wilma's ticket," Peter followed up, full of smiles. They all agreed.

And maybe our ticket home safely, Peter thought. He gazed out of the cab into the pale moonlight.

Within minutes, the engines pulled their long load of grain cars onto the Nye Siding to the right of the main track. Their bright headlight picked up six hulking boxcars waiting on a parallel track further to the right. Every other car had either an open door or a big-lettered banner. Not a person was in sight.

The horn of the hijacked train blew four short blasts, as agreed. Monty tested the air brakes hard while noisily stopping. Peter and Wilma climbed off and moved toward the boxcars through the weeds and darkness. Wilma's heart was thumping wildly.

Fork climbed down from the left side, Monty from the right, to run back past their four tandem engines. They each chocked a wheel on the first three grain cars to anchor the long string, and even wrapped chains around wheel contact with rails on two wheels, because of the uncertain grade. Fork unfastened air hoses, turned the angle cock, and released the coupling to the first grain car with the pin lifter. Then he climbed the fourth engine's steps and radioed Monty, who had returned to the 9039. The engines were free of the string.

On track four, Ruth Fitzwater and the farmers waited and listened in dark seclusion inside one boxcar. The police car had been gone only two minutes, and they had debated whether to abandon the whole project before the suspicious officer returned with reinforcements. Ruth wasn't certain that this man coming toward them was the leader they were expecting, and who was the other person?

On track two, the four engines lurched slowly forward again. Fork jumped off to the left as they passed the switching stand and radioed when all engines were clear.

Peter reached the row of tall silent boxcars on track four. What if this had become a trap? He hesitated, tensed, and then realized he had no choice. He called out, "Ruth? Ben?" The sound of his familiar strong voice was all it took for the farmers to let out whoops and hollers of relief. Their first trial period was over. "Shhh!" Peter entreated, as the other farmers were rushing up to him. The ruckus quickly quieted.

Fork had unlocked the ground switch and levered the curved rails into alignment with siding track four. He stepped across them, double-checking, and then locked them securely and radioed Monty. The engines began whining, winding backward toward the boxcars.

Peter watched appreciatively as Wilma got a warm welcome. He decided to tie the wider banners to those grain cars that would be nearest the boxcars. Grain cars had end ladders reaching from bottom to top, unlike the stubby boxcar ladders. This would take a few more minutes, but the extra media coverage it afforded made the risk worth taking, Peter and Wilma agreed. "Move fast! Take two banners, four people to each one, on this side. Go!"

Fork had jumped on the rear engine, radio in hand, feeding distances to Monty. He watched the shadowy boxcar end getting closer. Thirty feet away, he jumped gingerly off. "Stand clear!" he hollered. Twenty feet... ten...clang! Two train sections coupled solidly, bumping each car into the next. Fork checked the connection, locked air hoses together with the *glad-hand* device, jumped on the first boxcar ladder, and radioed.

They continued backing up on track four, with Fork counting on the radio all the way back to grain car number fifty of the string of seventy-four on track two. The engines stopped and Fork jumped off to repeat setting chocks from the engine compartment and wrapping chains to anchor cars fifty-one and fifty-two. Then he unlocked air hoses between fifty and fifty-one, freeing the two strings of grain cars.

Monty took his short train back to the very end grain car to get the *flashing rear end device.* He removed his large turnkey, leaving the engines idling while he unfastened this telemetry box from the rear coupler of car seventy-four. The *fred* was critical to their protection, providing the red light warning on their end car, plus measuring air pressure on brakes throughout the train. Then he took the engines forward again, stopping to give *fred* to Fork to attach to the new caboose, old grain car fifty.

Peter saw the quad engine rig with its boxcars in tow headed toward them. He loped up to the switch box where Fork would get off, to tell him the signs were tied on both sides of the first few grain cars, and everyone was clear. He also wanted to mention the police car episode, and the need to hurry to avoid its return. The fourteen minutes it had taken seemed an hour, with a dozen pairs of eyes straining back and forth along the road looking for headlights--and for cars without lights.

The four great engines idled, as Monty tried sounding casual on the radio.

"By the way, dispatch, we're cleared to go over the Range now, right?"

"Say again, 9039. And you sound different."

Monty coughed several times and rephrased. "Coming down with a summer cold is all. We are cleared to Grand Junction, aren't we?"

"What? I show you straight shot south through Subdiv One to Pueblo."

"Nuts! Front Office was to have done all this by fax before they left last night. We just got our new destination late last night en route."

"Well, what's going on? Why the last minute changes?"

"Who knows? Who cares? When you're hauling federal loads, anything goes, right? Will you crank us green lights as far as you can now, dispatch, headed due west over the grades on line 37? We need to keep moving to make up lost time from that stalled junker."

"You're a pain, 9039. Stay put until I get you re-routed on my board," Harran replied from the tower in annoyance. "Five or ten minutes, clear."

Monty turned thumbs up from the radio. Peter nodded.

Harran Winfree had been the dispatcher targeted by Peter for friendship last May. They had shared a Tabasco Sauce one early morning at a counter in Brad's Cafe, as Harran was getting off late shift from the Denver railroad yards. A summer routine developed where Peter waited on Monday afternoons at the 19th Hole bistro by the clubhouse at the City Park golf course. Harran was both an avid golfer and beer drinker, and as he approached sweating and thirsty, Peter would brandish his Shakespeare with a "Hail, fellow, well met!" The boisterous ladies' man would return the salutation with a princely bow and a firm handclasp, shouting, "Hell, fallow, wet mail!" Grain train schedules had been easy to work into conversations. This one from the Dakotas was confirmed last Monday.

Fork was outside studying side compartment gauges on the catwalk, and stopped Peter on the way past. "I'm sorry we had to drop those back twenty-four cars. There's just no way we could get all those grain bins up the Rockies with only four engines. We'll be pushing it to get fifty plus these six empty boxcars over the hump as it is."

"You know, every car we left would have turned into three thousand loaves of bread. To me it's just like twenty-four cars full of dead bodies left right here."

"Pete, try to see folks walking away satisfied from these fifty cars. Even then, it still seems to me like you're swatting at a rogue elephant with a daisy."

Peter climbed down the ladder. "This train will start a movement, Fork. A huge cry will come up from average Americans who still value life to send all our wheat surplus overseas this year, and to grow as much grain as we possibly can next year. Full business for all farmers, full bellies for all kids. We're just the first of a thousand trains!"

Peter walked rapidly from one boxcar to another. Ropes were tied inside across the open doors, a token to safety, since the hijackers all agreed that Americans should see real farmers, maybe even touch weathered hands with like-minded folks along the way. He shook hands with each man, sharing an encouraging word. He closed with the hope that kept them united: "The end of the line is the gateway to the end of starvation, God willing."

"I wish I was going," Ruth shouted to Wilma near the idling engines.

"I wish it was me staying," Wilma shouted back, laughing. Peter and Ruth laughed with her. "But, Ruth, your part is so critical here, as Pete's explained it," Wilma continued. "When you get your three fax messages through, and the packages with your letters and my cpd chip recordings, that will buy us the next few hours. If we can pick up major media coverage by daylight, then we've got a chance."

"Well, from a newcomer, even that limited optimism sounds good," Ruth said. "I'll do my part. You do yours."

"Atta girl, Ruth," Peter said. "Give me a goodbye hug." They embraced as good friends, patting each other on the back, clinging tightly, as if this might be the end somehow. Ruth swiped at a teardrop.

"Be strong for us all," Peter whispered, gently pulling away. "We're going to do this very good thing--and see it through--with you as our Denver anchor. Now head for the truck. Wait to see if we can get this big hummer started, okay? We may need a push." Ruth smiled and turned from the engine. Wilma and Peter climbed up its steps.

With a final wave, Ruth got into the rental truck. This was much more meaningful than the human rights rallies she frequented. Her husband would be proud of her, if he knew, but he was serving two years in Canon City's prison. He had protested a contract logging operation in the pristine national forest wilderness. Even though beetles had killed most of the lodgepole pines, he felt the land should not be ravaged further. So he blew up a few parked logging trucks. Their family had a proud heritage of patriotic protest.

"Ready?" Monty turned from the chief engineer's chair on the right side as the two entered the cab.

Peter shut his door firmly, asking, "Do we have clearance?" Peter had carefully prepared for this critical juncture. When he visited the rail yard tower with Harran last week, he unobtrusively picked up a faxed route change form with the tower fax number on it. Chanto, another group member, was to send the revised fax at precisely 2:15 A.M. this morning, in the midst of the turmoil over a car stuck on the tracks, when it would go unnoticed. Hopefully, Harran would look for it later on cue, take it at a glance, see the handwritten apology for e-mail being down, and not bother to verify the transmitting phone number since it was a standard form, but merely accept the new re-routing orders as his authority. At least, that had been the plan.

"CTC dispatch has given us at least forty-five minutes of green, and is working on more," Monty smiled. "Harran doesn't even know he's in the poker game yet."

"Then let's do it! I told Ruth and the farmers you'd give a short beep on the horn before we move."

Monty shook his head, shooting a look of massive tolerance back at Fork near the rear door. "Pete, you're still talking like this was a car." He pushed the console button, sending a sharp shrill sound briefly through the cab, to the eight farmers in the boxcars, to Ruth in the truck, and for miles out into the Denver night.

Monty eased the great engines into slow motion, which became a lurching action as each car in turn jerked at its coupling, and gripped. Four engines pulled almost reluctantly onto the main track again, followed now by the six boxcars, just far enough to clear the siding switch. Fork had left the cab, to ease himself off onto the cinders as he passed the switch, and now levered it back into its track two position. He radioed, and Monty backed the ten-car string gingerly into the open coupling of the first grain car in the waiting string of fifty.

Clang!…clang!…clang!… Each car bumped into the one behind, starting the ripple of thuds so common to railroad yards. Fork hooked up the air hoses, quickly worked his way along, clearing the chocks and chains anchoring the first three grain cars, and then ran back.

The symbolism was not lost on the fascinated Wilma. Grain was again linked with its producers to help it finally become food. A solemn Peter saw one Grain Train, his dream and nightmare for the next three days.

"We're outa here!" Fork shouted as he burst in. Monty turned the big key into forward position, gave two short air horn blasts, and eased the throttle forward. The new 9039 string was complete and moving.

Monty felt calm and powerful at the same time. Railroading was a joy, a chunk of pleasure that had been wrenched out of him when he was fired. This event was his comeback.

"Here's our westbound track," he announced after several minutes. The long train curved slowly, negotiating a ninety-degree turn away from the southern storage plans of their surplus grain owner--the U.S. Government. The big man's firm hand pushed the throttle lever further.

"Glad we're picking up speed," Peter spoke into the silence. "It made me nervous counting every railroad tie we crossed over."

"Well, bro," Fork said, "we've got our speed limits set for us the whole way. Some places ten miles per hour is as fast as safety allows."

"The limit is forty in the rule books for bulk trains," Monty added. "But we might squeeze out seventy downhill. We'll get there quick as we can."

"And, uh, just where is *there*, me hearties?" Wilma asked in her best pirate tones.

"Play it again, Sam," Fork piped up, and enjoyed her laugh.

"No harm in trying," she sniped. "Can't say I've ever seen Arvada from this perspective. Sleepy little burb right now." Streetlights showed their luminous cones as the group looked out into the blackness. Inside, only the map stand and gauges were lighted, for maximum visibility out, and minimum for any busybodies peering in.

Wilma pointed at a tall white building, floodlit several blocks to their right. "Is the Intermountain Bell control center a bomb target?"

"Natural for a reporter to be questioning," Peter answered, trying to see her dark face. "I hope I'll be able to answer most questions fairly soon. Do you have some writing to do?"

"Thanks for nothing," Wilma snapped. Peter recognized the same tone Janet had used in the barn. He was on thin ice again with a woman who was important to him. But he would worry about repairing the damage later.

"It's 3:15, Monty. More clearance from Harran?"

"He said we're green to Tabernash, maybe two hours or so up the line, past Winter Park. There we pull off and yield to an eastbound."

"Five-ish." Peter calculated a moment. "The engineers will have just been found in the car trunk. Then our deed will be known, and our game will switch to Masters' chess. Let's bluff with this poker hand a bit longer. Monty, radio Harran and ask him nicely to alter either speed or route of that eastbounder, to allow us to pass without stopping."

Peter then touched Monty's arm and pointed silently out the right window. He nodded his head toward the back of the cab.

Monty took the cue. "Wilma, we've doglegged north here on the foothills. It's a fantastic view of the metro Denver lights. Come see."

Petulantly, she sat unmoving. Then she flicked off the penlight and stood.

Peter moved away without a word, and she took his place.

"That's amazing," she said, surveying the thirty-mile view from Broomfield on the north to Littleton on the south, and out past Aurora to the eastern plains. "I had forgotten how sparkly a million lights could be on an August night. Thanks for thinking to show me, Monty."

It was quiet.

"I'll bet you could see to Kansas from here if it was day," Peter offered. It stayed quiet.

"Who'd want to?" Fork opined, not wanting the icy comments of the battling duo to hover long. Everyone laughed, breaking the tension again, but it was going to be a very tedious trip if this kept up.

A few minutes later, Harran radioed back a negative response to Monty's request, saying that 9039 was the newcomer on the line. They'd just have to give way to the 817 and its approved schedule.

Monty, Fork, and Peter conferred and checked maps for a few minutes while Wilma listened. Poker was a mild term to describe what she heard. They were prepared to go to great lengths to avoid being detected too soon as pirates.

"Dispatch," Monty radioed again. "I appreciate your efforts with 817, little buddy. Has she turned north at Dotsero Junction yet? Over."

The radio was silent. "Dispatch, over?" Monty queried.

Another minute elapsed. Peter checked his watch, and announced 3:31. The other two men nodded knowingly.

"9039, this is dispatch. Sorry for the delay. We've just had one hell of an explosion north of our tower. Looks to be on the edge of that oil tank farm. Fire billowing up like you wouldn't believe."

Monty turned off the radio, to insure that the cheering voices in the cab stood no chance of being relayed back to the Denver rail yards. The bomb placed by Jeremy and Manuel had detonated on schedule.

When there was calm again, he turned it back on. "Dispatch, you're cutting out. Maybe interference from that fire you mentioned. Bad one, huh?"

"Biggest probably since Stapleton Airport's tank went up in '90. They say that was an inferno. Anyway, 817 turned north at Dotsero a few minutes before I radioed."

"So," Monty kept his deep voice quite controlled, "they're ninety minutes from Kremmling. Now, here's what you do between watching fire engines go by. Tell 817 to pull off on that Kremmling siding when they get there. We'll pass them ten or fifteen minutes later. They can be back on the track and make up those few minutes of lost time real easy. Over."

"9039, you're losing it. I'm not going to ask them any such thing. Over."

"Dispatch, I didn't say 'ask.' I said 'tell.' They can think of it as a cigarette break." Then Monty shouted, "Now, just do it! Over and out!"

*   *   *

The explosion in the Platte River Valley rocked north Denver, rattling windows six miles away. The ground shock was recorded at 3:30 A.M. by the Boulder Seismic Center as 2.4 on the Richter scale.

Calls about the blast poured into all six Denver district police stations, and the Arvada, Thornton, and Westminster suburbs, plus most radio and TV stations. Trucks rolled from three fire stations nearest the site, and the individuals who stayed to answer phones were giving short, polite replies: "No danger yet. We'll notify you if you need to evacuate. Yes, we'll knock on your door!"

"The red glow is an oil fire, ma'am. No, the smoke isn't poisonous, but try to avoid breathing in too much of it!"

"I'm sorry the sirens woke your baby, lady."

Hazardous Materials Units and ambulances wailed their way from three counties through murky haze toward the oil tank farm.

Major efforts were aimed toward containment. Fortunately, tank number 79 sat somewhat apart from the rest. Investigators soon were circling the inferno at a hot three hundred feet, checking all connection linkages.

The refinery maintenance chief arrived with area maps, to study and explain safety precautions taken to isolate a fire in any tank. His crew was frantically checking seals and valve closures, visually and in the pump computer control room. The people on the refinery grounds were at high risk now. Seams between steel plates on another tank could weaken under heat and pressure, rupturing into a second volcano instantaneously.

Reporters swarmed among authorities, since no firm perimeter line had yet been set up. Questions flew in the hot wind about causes and casualties. The curt answer remained, "We don't know yet!"

The Battalion Fire Chief proudly wore gold leaves on his hat, and became a media target. "Sabotage? Two blasts a split second apart? Well, we're considering all possibilities, but may not know until after it's out."

"How long will that be? With the new chemical retardants, and if we can get a helicopter over it, perhaps six hours."

"Any evacuation orders yet? No direct orders have been issued. We're recommending on radio that elderly people and anybody with lung problems leave, in Globeville and within a three-mile radius. Police will be patrolling to prevent looting."

That was the last direct firefighter interview. The media was herded back to the crowded street, and told to contact the Emergency Operations Center in the Denver City and County Building basement for current information. Denver authorities were shifting uneasily from a peaceful night to a crisis mode, with some discussion of declaring an *Orange Alert* through Homeland Security.

*   *   *

Ruth Fitzwater sighed with relief as she drove south past an empty Colorado Highway Patrol car parked at Sam's Donuts on Frontage Road. She had been precisely obeying every posted traffic sign since leaving Denver more than an hour earlier. She couldn't afford to be stopped, since timing in these morning hours was critical.

Ruth took the next Colorado Springs exit off Interstate 25. The Conoco station had a few cars at the pumps--so much the better to avoid any notice. She parked and went into the rest room as a brunette in a blue dress, carrying a small suitcase. She came out a blonde in a flowered dress, wearing no makeup.

She drove back a few blocks to the big Hampshire Inn, which the Shakespeare Group had decided was the best starting point, and parked in back. No one was near the entrance as she walked up to the only cab parked there.

Ruth gave the sleepy driver ten envelopes with Denver addresses of radio and television stations, and one newspaper. The glue she had used to seal them guaranteed he wouldn't snoop. She hoped the story she made up of phone-back-on-receipt, plus her conspicuously writing down his name and cab number, would be incentive enough for him to meet the 5:00 A.M. delivery deadline.

He pulled away with $250 for his courier service, plus a $50 tip, his look indicating there was something odd about the whole lucrative transaction.

In case he had an accident on the way, she would soon hire a second cab and go through the same routine with identical envelopes. Ruth walked to the restaurant next to the Hampshire. Outside the coffee shop was a pay phone, one of the few left for travelers without cpd's. She waited impatiently for a woman to finish, hurrying her along with some mild foot tapping. She took coins from a plastic bag in her purse. They wouldn't trace this call being made to the one other member of the Shakespeare Group remaining in Denver.

Chanto Kudjakta had first waited at home for Ruth's call that the train was on the way, then drove to a ringside seat for the 3:30 show. He had videotaped it starting at 3:25, then rushed back home for this call. Ruth confirmed that the first cabby was gone, but told Chanto to hold onto his extra set of notices, just in case. She liked the comfort of knowing that if she missed calling from any of her checkpoints to him, he could still get all the information to the media.

They agreed that absolute silence between the train and team was nerve-wracking. To retain group member anonymity as long as possible, Peter insisted on waiting until the venture became viable--hopefully by six o'clock this morning with some media coverage.

She told Chanto a quick goodbye, for she also had facsimile messages to send from the Hampshire service desk, claiming responsibility for the bombing of the oil tank. But what if some fruitcake had already taken the credit? She had to hurry.

*   *   *

Chapter Four

"Can you believe that jerk?" Harran Winfree spoke irritably but to no one, for he was alone in the small rail yard tower office. It was filled with old second generation electronic gear forced by a continuous budget crunch. Yardline maps covered the one wall that wasn't glass.

The last few minutes had been crazy. Joe had radioed him from the tank farm to start re-routing all trains for the next six hours. The fire chief in charge at that mess didn't want to take any chances on the extreme heat rupturing any passing tanker cars.

Harran had also never gotten a message like the one from the loony in 9039 during all his four years as dispatcher. He paced the narrow walkways between three desks, thinking how lucky it was that all transmissions were recorded. That would put that jackass in his place--canned. All engineers think they're God, but that guy had gone off the deep end, Harran knew. This night dispatcher was still in charge here, and he would damn well do as he pleased.

Or, that is, as the rules said to do. He knew he wasn't really in charge. It was just that his tower boss, Mr. Rutledge, was on vacation, and Joe Donaldson, his yard boss, had taken the Dodge yard runner over to the oil tank fire. Great. Guy goes berserk on the run, and no one is around who gets paid the big bucks for handling kooks. What to do?

Joe said he'd be out of the car, away from the radio, and his cell phone device was sitting here on the desk in the cpd recharger. It might be an hour before he got back. Harran knew if he called the eastbound 817 again, they'd tell him to go to hell, and probably report him as incompetent. The big boss Manchester would be furious with another call after Joe already woke him about the fire, and he had roared, "Well, handle it!"

The wall clock read 3:55. All Harran could do was call the maverick back. Maybe he'd just been drinking, as if that wasn't bad enough to get fired over, but maybe he'd sobered up enough to call his bluff.

Harran took a deep breath, thought tough words, and depressed the transceiver switch. "9039, this is dispatch, over."

"Yessir, my track cleared?" The same deep voice didn't sound drunk.

"What's your name again, friend?" Harran put him right on the spot.

"Rintricky, Benjamin Rintricky," Monty read off one of the licenses they had lifted. "What's yours, son?"

"Harran Winfree." *And don't 'son' me, gramps*, he thought. "Now, Benjamin, I don't have the authority to take the 817 off the main line. They've got every rule on their side, and you know it. Plan on exiting Tabernash like I instructed, and they'll be by you in a flash."

There was a pause.

"Sonny, we must still have a bad connection. I told you, I am personally taking that authority which you obviously do not choose to use, and I am setting new rules here. You get that damn 817 out of my way, or there's going to be two hundred cars and their loads splattered all over two miles of track somewhere between Kremmling and Tabernash!!"

Harran hated that stupid shouting. He was apparently dealing with a real psycho. None of the words had been slurred. It was time to call his hand.

"Let me talk to your brakeman."

"Don't have one."

"Put your other engineer on."

"No."

Harran wildly wondered if someone might have been killed. He toughed ahead. "Listen, you bag of hot air, I'm shuttling you off the track at the next siding, and locking the switches behind you--and in front of you. You'll never get within fifty yards of the main line again. You want to cream your train, go ahead."

Silence. Harran's bluff had worked. Benjamin folded, and would pull off.

A full five minutes passed. Harran had returned to his critical re-routing chores.

"Oh, Harr-rran." The radio blared to life with the ominous singsong call. It made his skin crawl. "Do you really think I won't just stop this train right in the middle of the track, out here behind a curve--and see how old 817 can handle a head-on collision?

"Or, I might just as easily put this baby in reverse. Got anybody coming up behind me? I wonder how fast we can take that curve around the houses in Westminster? How does that song go, Harran? Oh, yeah. 'She'll be comin' 'round the mountain when she comes...'" The voice was almost ghostly as it filled the tower room with the familiar tune and insane threat.

Harran was in near panic as he heard Benjamin's voice become very deep, saying, "Now, you young ass, get 817 off of my track, or we all die up here. Over...and...out."

Harran looked out the wrap-around tower windows at the hellacious oil fire blazing a mile northeast of their yards. Had the whole world gone mad, he wondered? Was this the start of Armageddon? He reached for the phone to dial the home number of Sylvester Manchester, the big boss who had delegated the earlier fire call problem to their handling, the boss to whom he had never spoken in person. It was 4:05 Thursday morning, halfway through his most memorable shift, and forty-five minutes before two trains were scheduled to collide.

*   *   *

Small unobtrusive boxes sent invisible laser beams shooting at various heights across the Wayman backyard at night to detect intruders inside the seven-foot-high wood fence. Upstairs in their master bedroom, Frank studied Marion's prone form in the semi-darkness as she slept. It was a night for her to dream, and her restlessness had waked him as she pushed away the sheet. Hers was a tall body, but he was three inches taller--a nice balance when she dressed with spike heels. She worked to keep trim with a tennis group, while he was struggling to get his weight down to two hundred, the target for his second half-century.

They were a good match. They enjoyed bickering about intellectual matters while avoiding work issues, making the limited waking time they could spend together much more stimulating. It also rounded him out by getting a synopsis of every new book she voraciously read.

She was a fine cook, a good mother, and sharp. She parlayed her business degree into a position as office manager for a fast-growing CPA firm. And a big plus, she made great love with him--this blond-haired, blue-eyed doll of his.

Frank congratulated himself on being a good provider for her, as he was rolling over onto his back silently to stare up at the ceiling. His rapid promotions at the Bureau showed what a *brilliant operative* he was, as some said. He smiled, and greeted his dad's memory in the stillness. An early death had left his father's inheritance to finance this abundant home, and the kids' college costs. Some people they no longer called friends had started the rumor that Frank must have *mob connections* to afford it.

Well, somebody high-up should have connections to talk with the gangsters, he began debating inside, again wishing he and Marion could sometimes talk shop. *Because what government officer tries to communicate with all those champions of lost causes who feel nobody understands them, so they turn violent? Yeah, we should learn to discuss our grievances peacefully, to try to strike a balance between radical extremes.* Oh, how could he expect anyone else to honestly give a damn, when he had reached that same point of caring very little for those who were voiceless?

He turned his head to look out at the moon. It was so predictable, unlike his moods. He was being paid to wage combat against that dark side of human nature, so maybe all conflict shouldn't be reconciled away--at least not until after his retirement in twelve years. His mind rambled, wondering if he could even hold the job that long, with his own mid-life crisis shrouding in around him, making him feel cruddy.

The phone rang, startling Frank into half-alertness. He rolled over and fumbled to find the receiver before it rang again and woke the dreamer. His heart started thumping hard.

"--lo," he managed to mumble as he placed the phone to his ear.

"Deputy Wayman, this is Agent Smathers at the downtown office."

"Yes?"

"Sorry to wake you. I see on the schedule you're night-call director this week."

"Right." Frank's fog had lifted. "Get to it."

"Sir, there's been an explosion in the Mountain West Oil Refinery tank farm. One of the tanks is burning now, others may blow. Fresh footprints up from the Platte River may suggest sabotage." The voice was calm.

"Ummm, anyone checking the other tanks for--?" Frank's eyes were still closed, but his ability to size up situations rapidly was coming into focus. He didn't want to say any words that would upset Marion if she were awake enough to be overhearing.

"For bombs? Yes, sir, Agent Matthias is coordinating that now. Fortunately, the agent was returning from a date and nearby, so he was on the scene before anybody. So we beat Homeland Security again by a mile…"

"Stop. Time?" Frank was looking at their illuminated clock radio dial.

"It's, uh, 3:52 A.M., sir."

"Agent." Frank's tone was exasperated. He sighed, and waited.

"Oh, you mean the time it blew? That was about twenty minutes ago, sir."

"Thanks, I'm on my way to the site. No need to call the regional director yet." He carefully replaced the phone receiver and sat up on the edge of the bed.

"Bad?" Marion inquired softly.

He looked back at her, and saw she had one eye barely open in curiosity. "Not to worry. Just a fire at the refinery. They'll have it out soon." He had second thoughts and added, "but I'll probably go on into the office from there. You go back to sleep." He leaned back over and kissed her cheek, and her shoulder. Then he stroked the side of her breast very lightly several times. He was always glad she liked to sleep in the nude.

He got up and took his clothes into their double bathroom to dress. This would be the bargain counter approach because of his hurry: roll a little deodorant, brush teeth, comb hair, dab some after-shave. A rechargeable razor went with him to use in the car. He left.

Backing his silver Lincoln out of the garage, he noticed that Peter's car was still gone. Frank wondered if they should be stricter, then told himself again that it was much too late to change their grown son.

Frank passed a few hundred cars as he sped northward on the Valley Highway. It always surprised him that anyone else was awake when he drove in the wee hours. He turned up the AM station louder than his shaver, studying the ugly glow ten miles ahead.

"This is KDNC, your twenty-four hour radio news station, as the clock hits 4:18. The big news continues to be the inferno roaring out of control at the Mountain West Oil Refinery. A fourth alarm for fire fighters has-- just a moment, a news bulletin is being handed to me--here it is. There are confirmed reports, repeat, confirmed, that an organization has claimed full responsibility for the bombing of oil storage tank 79."

Frank was incredulous. The station wouldn't dare broadcast that without Bureau authorization. He shut his shaver off and rolled up his window, took the cpd from its cradle, pressed *Record*, and held it close to the radio.

"This may be a KDNC exclusive, for I'm reading from an actual fax that arrived at 3:59, just twenty minutes ago, don't know why the delay. Here it is, verbatim--"

Frank switched his Bluetooth phone to #2 in memory. "Smathers, stop this broadcast. It's KDNC. Stop it right now!" Frank's shout expressed his fury, but didn't alleviate it. "And I will hold until it stops!"

"'…and U.S.A.S. stands for *Unite Surplus And Starving*,'" the announcer intoned. "'We have planted other bombs all across the country, and will be issuing our demands in the next fax we send you. America has a right to know, and we have the freedom to speak, thank God, about the surplus grain stored and rotting all over America, while children are starving around the world. The U.S. Government says prices aren't high enough to sell, while poor countries who can't afford to buy watch a hundred desperate children starve to death every hour.'"

There was a pause. Frank was livid when they began again. "This is KDNC in Denver, Colorado, and I am reading the full test of a fax message received just minutes ago. Still quoting: 'The American public has the power to say, *Ship our food to those crying children!* We are sending the SOS to you today, America. Don't let the government stop us. Don't let them stop *you* from reaching out...'"

An abrupt switch to advertisement cut off the announcer.

"Thank you, Smathers," Frank said coldly into the phone. "What are you now doing?"

"The standard FBI broadcast freeze order has been faxed, and wired, to all media, sir." The agent's voice filled with nervousness. "And, uh, we are phoning for confirmation of freeze. Right?"

Frank didn't explode over the taped phone. "Are you asking me what to do, Agent Smathers, or telling me what is actually being done?"

A short delay preceded the report. "Following standard protocol, Deputy Regional Director, we have begun local confirmation calls, as we have staff."

"And?" This was a very real personnel test Frank was conducting.

Another gap of quiet. Frank could hear low murmuring despite the hand covering the office phone. "And, sir, we are using other phones to call in back-up staff, in case of special ongoing needs."

"Do it fast, Agent. Let me know every ten minutes of the number of your successes on both counts. I will call the regional director now." Frank jammed the accelerator hard as he pressed the speed-dial button for his superior.

*   *   *

After fifteen long minutes, Harran Winfree got the call. An unpleasant Mr. Manchester told him what to do, which was exactly what he was going to do on his own in another three minutes if the boss hadn't called. He was to tell the rational engineer in 817, with whom he could reason, to pull off the main line. He'd promise 817 that he'd bring charges against 9039 and keep him from ever engineering again. For now, he'd ask 817 to get as far out of the nut's way as they could. "Run for cover" is the way his boss put it, and Harran used those very words when he gave the unequivocal orders of his superior to the belligerent crew of the 817: "We're side railing you at Tabernash!"

One accident had been avoided. How many more confrontations would there be in the coming hours, Harran wondered? It would probably continue until 9039 needed to stop for fuel and could be commandeered by railway officials and federal marshals. Or the railroad might take the very unusual step of just shutting down the engine computers by override in the middle of nowhere--and dealing with it. He was glad it soon would become Manchester's worry, in the mountains far away from Harran's district jurisdiction.

The unseen and unheard jubilation in the cab of engine 9039 would have seemed incongruous to the frazzled Denver dispatcher, after he grudgingly radioed them the green light through to Dotsero Junction.

*   *   *

"Chanto, this is Ruth. Have you heard anything on the radio announcing our claims for the bombing?"

"Nothing, and I keep scanning the radio and TV. Where are you?"

"In Castle Rock. It's been an hour since I faxed from the Springs. Somebody must have gotten our blasted notice."

They discussed what could have gone wrong. Misdialing? Not that many. No one at the stations? Except they knew of twenty-four hour staffing at most of the places through their early morning test call last Thursday. No one interested? Not a chance--media still thrived on illegality and calamity for urgent attention grabbers. "Could the news blackout get set up so fast?" Chanto asked from his Denver apartment.

"Well, we stick to the plan anyway," Ruth concluded. "I'll change into my green sweater and become a green-eyed redhead, then send the next fax from here. They'll have our name on the warning message before number two blows. I'll send ten of Wilma's first chip recordings by Castle Rock cab. They'll be in downtown Denver forty minutes from now."

"Ruth, do the cab first. Someone will be watching somewhere for that fax to start running. You're just a phone call away from getting caught now. Blessed luck, friend, and may Allah speed your journey."

"Keep scanning, Chanto. Let's have good news next time I call you."

Chanto Kudjakta hung up, then stood to smooth his colorful robe before sitting again. He exhibited solemn pride in being Ethiopian, a tribal chieftain's son. His car license plate authenticated his diplomatic immunity, impressing Auraria College students. However, Chanto was infinitely more concerned that starvation was claiming one of four Ethiopian children under five years old, and one of eight people aged five to ten in the outer districts. He had joyfully told his father that they could eradicate starvation in the homeland by the year 2015, for he had found Peter Wayman and the Shakespeare Group. Chanto rang for tea to be served, contemplating again the danger that his friends might be labeled Mideast Terrorists, because of the color of his skin and that of Ardis.

*   *   *

Miles curved by as the Grain Train climbed higher into the Rockies. Evergreens and aspen alternated with rock faces in the undulating headlight as they followed the canyons up toward the Continental Divide, where waters struggle to decide whether to flow east or west. But powerful diesel locomotives defied Divide laws, instead flowing as the engineer decided-- westward, up the eastern slope for the 9039 string.

Peter radioed his boxcar farmers, who had all left their sets open to channel 136. The Shakespeare Group had decided to use radios instead of cell phones between boxcars and engine, for privacy. "Monty says another slow grade is coming," Peter shouted over the engine noise. "Remember, discourage anyone from jumping in. They might only be hobos, but they could be railroad cops, or Feds, so take no boarders."

Wilma wondered what Peter meant by *discourage*, picturing a shoe stepping on the fingers of someone running alongside a boxcar's open door. Lines of deciding how one lives a non-violent life on this trip became grayer.

She did have a question waiting, though, for when he finished his latest check on everyone's safety. "What are you going to do when you pass the other train, Peter? Wave? Duck down in case they throw rocks?"

"Good question." Peter was ready to deal with details of their first personal confrontation with railroad antagonists. "How long to the 817, Monty?"

"Up to forty minutes, depending on where they exit. But I'm guessing they're mad enough to come as far and fast as they could before sidetracking. So that could put them in Tabernash about now. It's over Rollins Pass, about fifteen minutes."

"How much faster than a safe twenty-five can we run through the town?" Peter asked.

The two engineers collaborated on answering the questions railroaders think about but never ask. "Should hold at forty," Monty replied. "Just hope no local racer expects us to be as slow as normal."

"Anybody able to jump on at forty?" Peter asked.

Fork snorted in disgust at the idea. "Not without losing an arm."

"Unless they'd drive a truck alongside," Monty put in after more consideration. "But I don't remember that much flat space there."

"Then forty it is," Peter decided.

Fork looked sideways at Monty, who just raised his eyebrows before announcing, "Moffat Tunnel in two minutes, Pete."

Peter activated his hand-held radio with several clicks to alert the boxcars. "All right, guys, turn the flashlights on for the next seven minutes. Wet those rags and put them over your mouth and nose to breathe through. Fork tells me there are twenty-nine tunnels we go through in this first stretch. Most have been pretty short…"

The world vanished outside the engine cab. No more pine trees, or moonlit mountainside, only blackness. The headlight bounced eerily off the narrow walls and low ceiling of the bore shaft through solid rock. Anything could happen inside this black hole.

"…but this one we're just entering is a doozy. It's named the Moffat Tunnel. While we're inside, we'll actually cross the Divide at just over 9,200 feet. The old tracks on the mountain above us go around James Peak, some 2,000 feet higher than we are in here. They used to call it Giant's Ladder because of all the wooden trestles over rockslides. It took five hours to go around James, and now we go under it in ten minutes.

"Keep breathing through those wet rags, guys. These trapped diesel fumes are bad," Peter admonished into the radio, waving away the rag offered him. "This six-mile-long monster took five years to build, with President Calvin Coolidge setting off some of the dynamite blasts by telegraph from Washington. The Moffat is the fourth longest in this part of the world, eighth longest in the entire world," he read from a rail guide.

"It cost $15 million back in the 1920's, but Fork said it would cost $15 billion to build today. And we claim to be making progress?" he laughed.

"We've reached the highest point any of the fancy Amtrak passenger trains go in the U.S." He resisted commenting on the humorous hope that they didn't meet the California Zephyr in here. "Southern Pacific Telecom laid fiber-optic cable alongside us. An elected commission runs this hole-in-the-wall with pure politics, some say."

He needed two more minutes of monologue to occupy the minds of his men until they were out of unpleasant inescapable fumes and gripping blackness. So the storyteller next told of Winter Park and its Denver-owned ski resort which waited at the tunnel mouth; the Fraser River, where a president named Ike used to come fishing; and the "Icebox of America" town that sets records for lowest temperatures at less than minus-fifty degrees.

"Flashlights off, guys. There's light at the end of the tunnel!"

Whoosh, they were out. The tunnel had not become their tomb, as Peter had privately worried. It was amazing to him how much quieter the engines pounded, now that they had the universe to absorb their sound. Peter breathed the fresh air of the high Rocky Mountains deeply into his parched lungs. His radio crackled back into action.

"Hey, Pete," Ben Cody barked. "If you said anything in the last ten minutes that we really needed to hear, you'll have to repeat it. We couldn't make out a word on the radio because of the damn engine noise. Say, was that the Moffat Tunnel?"

*   *   *

The security guard at the *Rocky Mountain Herald* newspaper office kept his right hand on the butt of his holstered gun as he dialed interoffice. He didn't take his eyes off of the husky man standing in the dark outside the locked door.

"Mr. Lakey, I'm sorry to bother you. There's a man here with a package. Says he's a cab driver from Colorado Springs. No, sir, he won't give it to me, only to the person in charge...yes, sir."

The guard walked to the door, his right hand still poised on his gun. He spoke into the intercom. "Slip the envelope through the door slot." Then he tensed as the visitor reached in his pocket. The cabby slipped a five-dollar bill through the mail slot, asking the guard to try again.

"Mr. Lakey, the cabby showed me his Springs ID badge...uh, sir, that's right, you told me what to do, but he says some lady is expecting a call right back. He also said to tell you this has a number one on it, and he does have other packages to deliver before 5:30...yes, I know procedure, but he insists on giving it directly to you...yes, sir, I'll tell him you're on the way down."

Upstairs, the newsroom was buzzing. Reporters at desktop keyboards and laptops pecked out last minute details and headlines for the 6:00 A.M. final revision, with the dramatic oil fire dominating the front page. Desk phones and cpd's rang, and other heads were talking to the air, trying to find out about an organization named U.S.A.S., which had faxed a claim of responsibility for the explosion ninety minutes before. The legal desk slaved over wording to avoid the FBI news blackout on the bombing aspect. Three people huddled over pictures of a spectacular hell in north Denver, and the fight being waged against that blaze, to pick the most horrific and heroic.

"This had better be damn important," Lakey said, pushing his chair far out behind his cluttered desk, leaving a reporter standing mid-phrase.

He was still cursing when he returned minutes later from seeing the cabby in the lobby. "Open this damn envelope! Standard procedures, closed room!" Two people jumped to help. Lakey was no man to trifle with when he was running late at press time. Scissors carefully snipped away at the top and bottom of the heavily taped and glued package, then along one edge. They unfolded it quite gently, revealing no white powder. Anthrax scares were not uncommon in the age of terrorism threats.

Lakey brushed it away when they brought it to him, telling them to read it then give it to someone not sweating yet.

"Lakey!" one of the cutters said emphatically. "Scoop--or else hoax." City night editor Lakey loved the sound of that word he called the *s-word.*

"Read it--loud! Loudly!" He continued scanning the mock-up of front-page headlines.

"'U.S.A.S. today stands for *Unite Surplus And Starving.* We have a message of grave importance to America. One hundred people starve to death each hour in our small world. Many are children.'" The reader ran her sentences together. "'The U.S. is blessed with mostly healthy kids, but cursed with productive farmers forced out of work, and wasted food surplus. U.S.A.S. today has taken the first step toward sharing. See for yourself by following main rail line 96 north 3.2 miles from the switchyards. There is a 1972 gray Chevrolet parked near the track on a dirt road, with two messages we left in the trunk--'"

With those words, Lakey stopped studying the page layout and looked up at the woman reader. Implications were frighteningly clear. Lakey nodded for her to continue.

"'...in the trunk for the enterprising media to find quickly. There is a key to the trunk enclosed. The men were all right when we left them tied up...'"

"Thank God," Lakey said, pounding the desk with a fist. A murmur of relief came from the small group that had gathered to listen. Lakey looked around him, but didn't shoo them back to work.

"'...left them tied up. We used minimum force, for we wish to harm no one. But we will not be stopped in our goal to wake up America to her government's stinginess, and her opportunity to save lives.

"'We are serious--watch our oil fire burning. But no one's life is threatened by our property destruction--only the starving will continue to die. Please help us communicate. We need media coverage to carry our message immediately. Every moment of silence now increases our risk-- and costs lives. Your next message will arrive within the hour.'"

"Damn! Damn terrorists!" Lakey fumed. "What more have they done out there? Everybody we can spare is on the fire. Julie, start calling in our day people. Call Wilma Fletcher first, she's always hot to trot. Cookie, radio our helicopter pilot to call me on the quiet band, ASAP. Terry, get downstairs to the guard and find that Springs' cabby who delivered this."

"Shall we hold--" a man in jeans started to ask.

"Oh, damn it all, we can't keep holding the late edition--but we must. This could be the s-word in spades, for the month. Hell, for the year! Yes, hold the presses! Everybody else, get back to work. Now put fire in those stories!"

They all let out a groan at his pun. Intended or not, he got the credit.

"*Gene in the jeans*, find a map and a road that goes along whatever rail line 96 is. Call that yard dispatcher and ask directions, but don't tell him anything. Then get out there. I'll have Barry in our chopper find the car with his spotlight, then I'll radio you. We have got to be first to that car! Now, get outta my sight!"

Lakey wondered how many other packets the cabby delivered, and how many others would take it seriously and be racing to find the old car and its two messages. What if they were dead, or alive with the trunk lid wired to explode? "Legal!" he bellowed.

*   *   *

"Holy shit, what is that?" exclaimed the brakeman from the 817. He stood close to the main Tabernash tracks as the 9039 approached, but not close enough to get spit on or have anything thrown at him by this maverick counterpart. He held his cpd ready to film the offenders as they passed. His own train languished in neutral, sidetracked.

The chief engineer stood beside him, still shaking his fist into the glare of the oncoming train's headlight. "That's the loco rig that ran us off the road, you idiot!"

"No, I mean, look at the signs all over it."

"You look at them," the hoghead shouted as the engines bore down in the cool night air. "I want to see the fool running this circus act."

He shook his fist even more vigorously as he aimed his big flashlight beam at the cab of the engine now opposite them. It caught and held only one young man's face looking squarely at them--hardly a madman.

"You damn punk kid!" the engineer screamed.

"You shithead!" hollered his brakeman in matching epithet. "They must be doing forty-five if they're moving an inch."

"Will you look at those garbage signs and open doors with ropes? 'FEED THE KIDS, FOR HEAVEN'S SAKE.' Now what's that all mean?"

"Beats the shit out of me," the brakeman shouted, relying on his favorite phrase.

"I know it does, but keep filming anyway, so we can show dispatch. There's something damn strange going on that they may not know yet with this jerk." The grain cars continued rumbling past the two who turned their backs in puzzlement and disgust.

The train had reached the town named for brave Chief Tabernash of the White River Band. He was shot in 1879 near here in a rancher feud, Peter had told Wilma. She thanked him for the history lesson, wondering if the whole trip would have running commentary. All four diesel engines were working for the tough climb into the Rockies. The noise level in the lead engine's cab was considerable, but laughter rolled over the diesel whine.

"Oh, if you had seen those two engineers' faces," Peter relived.

"I felt it," Monty put in, "when this engine began melting from their glares."

"I'll swear the air in here turned blue from my lip reading," Fork put in.

"I'm still afraid to take my hands away from my ears," Wilma said, stacking onto the newest pile of one-liners, and all four howled again. The soft glow from the control gauges lit their happy faces.

"It's not all going to be this easy though, is it?" Wilma asked, after the laughing subsided. "It's after five o'clock already, and nobody is afraid of us yet."

"The fireworks at 5:30 may shake things loose," Monty speculated. Wilma nodded, already apprised of the next planned bombing, but still somewhat dismayed at her role in their one-sided crime spree.

"My guess is that they'll try to shuttle us onto a siding soon after daybreak," Peter mused.

Fork agreed. "I figure the first one that makes any sense is Dotsero Junction, little more than an hour out. Easiest to get a posse in, easiest to clean up a wreck if we derail. Lots of tracks going around."

"How long before we can be heard clearly on CB radio?" asked Peter.

Monty scratched his head. "Oh, ten minutes. After Kremmling the road kind of comes and goes again. The train stays right by the river through Gore Canyon."

"Time enough," Peter decided. "Ms. Fletcher, let's write a script that sizzles!"

*   *   *

The ugly fire still roared its rage nearby. The wetted down and wrung out version of Frank Wayman slid into the driver's seat of the government-issued car borrowed from Agent Matthias. If the Bureau thought the deputy regional director would soil the seat covers of his own personal car with this gunk on his clothes, they were dead wrong.

The wind had shifted while Frank was standing on the front lines talking with the firemen handling the foam hoses. Up to that moment of the white spray shower, he had been exhilarated. Now he was just disgusted.

He poked at the second button on his cpd to call his office. "Get Smathers," he ordered, rubbing dried residue off his watch crystal. He guessed at 5:15.

Frank gazed in annoyance at the acrid smoke generated by the huge blaze. The oil refinery tank had become a gigantic exhaust pipe, and was emitting miles of thick black clouds. The billowing mess would darken Denver's dawn today, and maybe tomorrow as well. Gawkers would jam the nearby freeway to see first hand what morning news cams were showing. Even with the windows up, the roar of the inferno was deafening.

Smathers was expressing some concern from getting no earlier response to his page, which Frank had neither heard nor felt. "I was busy. Status?" he asked, backing the formerly cream-colored car out of its place in the misshapen line. He began slowly weaving though a mass of media and emergency vehicles covered with the dirty gray film.

Smathers spoke of no help and constant phones. "Apparently, uh…" he paused…"the terrorist message got leaked in a few other places."

"Like where?" Frank asked tiredly. He took a last look over his shoulder at the enormous roiling tower of black and crimson, anchored to the earth by a flashing array of red, white, blue, and yellow lights.

"Like, Cheyenne and Casper, Wyoming," Agent Smathers was saying. *Could be worse*, Frank thought.

"And Des Moines and Omaha."

It was worse.

"Have a full report on my desk in eighteen minutes," Frank demanded. "And coveralls and boots at my garage parking in twelve."

"Yes, sir," Smathers replied. "My briefing papers are being copied for you now, with another set for the director."

"Make an updated set when he comes later," Frank countermanded.

"He'll be here in six minutes, sir." Frank could almost hear the smirk creeping into airwaves through the phone voice. "I made the decision to call and brief Director Brody twenty minutes ago, when you were out of touch for so long. He seemed grateful, and decided to come in at once."

Damn your ambitious hide, Frank fumed, but said simply, "Patch me through," and took charge again. "Yes, I'm safe, sir. The chief and I were forward when the wind shifted. Covered us in smoke and foam, minimal flame. No serious injuries yet."

"Good news," the Director said. "How long will it take to contain?"

"A day, maybe two. Smaller tank, less fuel than the Stapleton fire, they say. I'll have my initial report on screen for you when you arrive. I'm fifteen minutes behind you, by the time I cover up a filthy suit and wash my face."

"Listen, Frank, we're both here for the duration. Take time to shower and change before you come up. You'll feel better, probably improve your aroma also."

They both shared a laugh, Frank's first since the wake-up call an hour and a half before. Then Winston Brody asked, "Can you tell if this was an accident, despite the bombing claim?"

"The oil company says chances are slim to none, sir."

"I'll begin to organize in that unfortunate direction then. Is Homeland Security in the loop yet?

"No presence on site. I left it up to Smathers to follow protocols."

"Okay, see you upstairs. Oh, is Matthias all right, and still on site?"

Frank confirmed and closed off. *Sharp as a tack*, Frank thought--*a boss who knows and cares about his employees. Concerned about me, too,* he acknowledged, going back over last Monday's conversation with his regional director. It had been a moody start to the week, and Frank had unloaded his list of office frustrations: dictating endless letters, filing reports to make every case look at least minimally successful, and listening to crybabies complain for longer coffee breaks and closer parking spaces--the same softies who filed a grievance against him last year. Managing wasn't the satisfaction it used to be. Then there was the whole rash of changes brought about with the addition of the hovering umbrella of Homeland Security oversight. They called it *I.O.--Intelligence Operations*; he called it *interference and obstacles.*

Director Winston Brody was a friend, trying to forestall Frank's self-made mid-life crisis from spiraling into career burnout. The senior official had reminded the younger that his early retirement would soon leave Brody's big desk vacant. And he iterated that the trust and respect built up between them had put Frank next in line.

To which vote of confidence Frank had stupidly replied that he wasn't certain he was still interested. Instead of berating him, Brody had just chomped harder on his unlit green leaf cigar. He told Frank to put in a two-week vacation slip soon. He wanted him to get his head screwed back on squarely before someone else noticed it was crooked.

*   *   *

Barry's helicopter could have had a loose wire, the way its spotlight flicked off and on. He was merely trying not to attract anyone else as he led the *Herald's* staff car along bumpy ruts in the weed-covered dirt road he had spotted.

Gene welcomed the bright advancing white circle. This was a creepy assignment, sent out to the boonies to check out a nut's story. When the spotlight moved across the railroad tracks, Gene stopped to study the gravel incline up to the eight-inch-square cross ties and high steel rails.

"I don't know but what you'd high-center this sucker, driving across those tracks," Fasma responded to an unasked question.

"That'd give 'em their headlines, when we got hit broadside," Gene snorted. "'*Herald* Car Becomes Caravan.'"

"'Metal and Men Mix in Moonlight Mincemeat,'" Fasma improvised, blocking the words out in front of him with his hands.

"Done deal. We leave the car on this side of the tracks and walk. Barry's got his chopper light on that old car on the other side already."

"Can you get it in your headlights, boss?" Fasma asked. "It's going to be pretty dark when that helicopter takes off on another call, and we've left our security blanket sitting over here thirty yards away."

They parked and walked forward in their headlights, Fasma videotaping the isolated area of scrub oak and yucca and a rocky hill.

"You hear something?" he asked.

"Just rotor blades above us--and your fast breathing," Gene joked.

"No, like pounding…" Fasma insisted, "…like somebody yelling."

Gene now heard the voices over the sound of the chopper. They came from the dirty car twenty feet ahead of them. "A sign of life is a good sign out here," Gene noted. "Ask Barry to climb a few hundred feet so we can talk."

Fasma radioed and the chopper pulled away, but kept the spotlight on them now for safety. Fasma kept filming while he called in the facts they had: gray Chevy, early 1970's model, Colorado license plate, *Po-Fok Rental* sticker.

"Here! In the trunk!" Two muffled voices shouted together. "Get us out of here! Help us!"

Gene stepped closer. "Okay, talk one at a time. Who are you?"

"Train engineers," one answered. "A gang hijacked our train!"

Gene and Fasma exchanged glances and comments. "The James Boys at it again?" "Nah, they're dead."

Gene hollered at the trunk voice. "You've got to be kidding."

"Just get us out of here!"

A chilling thought went through Gene's head as he touched the trunk lid. "Could this car be booby-trapped?" he asked the captives. After receiving no answer, he asked, "Did you hear me?"

"Yeah. We've been talking about that. They had guns, but they left those in here with us. We don't know what else they might have left."

"Damn, where's a cop when you need one?" Gene asked his photographer, only half in jest.

"Your wish is my command." Fasma responded, gesturing toward a second pair of headlights pulling up in the darkness. He then spoke into his radio. "Yes, thanks for the warning. Hit them with your searchlight."

The bright beam cut across the track to pick up the newcomer. It wasn't a police car, and there was no uniform on the tall, gaunt man who got out. He left his headlights on, and walked straight toward them, shielding his eyes. He had a video camera.

"That you, *Gene in the jeans*?" the newcomer called out.

"Donald, you skinny radio rascal! What are you even doing awake at this hour?" Gene whispered to Fasma, "KDNC man. Careful."

The three shook hands, and Fasma waved the helicopter back up. "What is radio doing here?" Gene asked again.

"Same thing as newspaper," Donald answered. "Got a tip."

"Phone? Letter?"

"Nope, taped package by messenger, so other media may have gotten them and will be here soon. You get the story out of the car yet? If not, let's go and share fast."

The men moved closer to the car, filming, recording, planning. "Hello the trunk!" Gene hollered. "Tell us what happened."

"These guys had this car over the tracks, so we stopped the train. Another guy jumped up behind us with a gun, then they marched us over here and stuffed us in. Listen, get us out," the muffled voice pleaded. "We're cramping like crazy."

"We're worried about a bomb, or we would." Gene spoke the truth.

"Hey, if anything happens, my name's Benjamin Rintricky," the trunk voice said. "My partner is Horace Jensen. We're engineers on the 9039 out of North Dakota..." His voice trailed off.

Fasma clicked the belt pack to activate his Bluetooth, relaying the new hard data. He shut it off just when the city desk reporter began, "Legal says don't you dare open--"

"I don't really think they wanted to hurt us," the trunk voice continued. "The one guy took the tape off of our mouths so we wouldn't choke. He said to tell you that they are now unarmed because he put their guns in here. Hey, the guns were unloaded when they held us up. He showed us, no bullets. But how'd we know that then?"

"What else did they say, exactly" Two videos captured every muffled word.

"That they'd call and let people know where we were. And they did, because you're here, right? You ain't them guys, are you? You cops?"

"No, we're not your hijackers, Ben," Donald spoke up. The intrusion surprised Gene, who had been doing all the talking. He realized the radio man also wanted his voice on tape. "Sorry for scaring you by keeping secrets. I'm Donald Trujillo, KDNC radio station." He pointed at Gene.

"And I'm Gene Valore, a staff reporter with the *Rocky Mountain Herald* newspaper," Gene shouted at the trunk lid, then thumbed at Fasma.

"Hi, I'm Fasma, the fantastic photographer," he hammed it up. "I'd sure like to get you guys out of there for a decent group picture. We've got a city waiting to see what you look like." He laughed, and strangely, the men in the trunk did also.

The loud blast of an air horn startled them all. More light poured onto the scene from the headlight of a fast approaching train.

"Gotta go for the action," Fasma said, bolting for the tracks. "We can't hear anyway," he shouted, stepping in front of the oncoming engine.

Photographers are crazy, Gene surmised, aiming a pocket flashlight inside the car's front seat, looking for wires or anything remiss. The short freight train rumbled by, horn blaring at Fasma who had been busily filming from close beside the tracks.

The three men huddled. They had a good story already, with no one seriously hurt. They ought to call the police and not touch anything. The bomb squad should check the car thoroughly before opening the trunk. But police would just force reporters back away from great pictures and interviews.

On the other hand, there could be a time bomb ticking away. Maybe they'd save lives by opening the trunk and freeing Ben and Horace. But, the hijackers showed they had a heart, putting holes in the trunk and providing keys in the mail. You don't do that if you're going to blow it up. Besides, the two in the trunk had pounded the lid and rocked the car already.

Then, again, tampering with evidence at the scene of a crime…yet you have to act hastily in a life-threatening situation…

"Guys," Barry radioed, "I'm low on fuel up here after covering the cow story!"

That prompted their agreement. "Tell him ten minutes at the most," Gene said. They hollered at the trunk. "How bad are your cramps?"

"My muscles are in knots," Ben answered. "Horace? Hey, Horace?"

There was a moan, then a few mumbled words. Ben shouted out, "He's in bad shape. His ulcers are flaring up again. He needs medicine."

"Ben, do we have permission from both of you to try to open the trunk. Sorry to have to ask, but do you waive your rights to sue us if any damage happens?" Gene shook his head at having to say that.

"Yeah, just get us out of here. Those guys weren't killers. Hey, you'll be risking your skins out there, too. We appreciate it."

The three helpers gave thumbs up. Gene was all business. "Donald, make a call to 911 for fire rescue and two ambulances. Give 'em good directions. Both you guys, back up and film me."

Moments later, with Fasma and Donald both shooting, Gene said, "Unlocking you now. Hold your breath."

Gene carefully inserted the key, and slowly turned it. He laid his hand on the trunk lid to keep it from flying upward when unlocked.

Click. Quiet.

He gently raised the trunk lid a half-inch, squeezing shut his eyelids as he did, expecting a blinding flash. When nothing happened, he gratefully opened his eyes and shone the flashlight along the narrow aperture around the lid, looking for a thin wire.

No sign of one. He opened the lid another half inch, and this time looked inside the trunk. All he could see was rumpled clothes. "Hi, Ben," he whispered in relief.

"Hi, guy," the equally relieved voice replied.

Gene raised the lid more, using outside lights to help him see. There were two men, curled up in fetal positions, awkwardly fit together.

"Donald, come help me!" Gene called over his shoulder. "Fasma, you stay away, just in case." Donald reluctantly laid down his camera for the urgency of the moment, and ran to help lift the two men out and carry them away from the car, which might still be rigged with a bomb. They laid them on the ground, and untaped their hands and feet.

Donald raced to retrieve his camera and the interviewing hastily began, along with sobs of relief. "Lie still," Gene cautioned the two, "an ambulance is coming." He fired rapid questions: "Describe your hijackers. Do you know why they took this particular train? Were you hauling anything valuable?" The facts were pouring out.

Two other cars pulled up near the tracks, and a van rigged with a large dish antennae on top with a large number '5' painted on it. Sirens were coming in the distance. The media circus was about to begin in earnest. Barry had landed nearby, keeping the rotors circling.

. "Don, thanks for your help," Gene said, shaking hands and packing.

"Gene, thanks for letting me be a partner. Great story so far. I'm out of here too. Good luck, Ben. Get well soon, Horace." Don ran across the tracks toward his car, before the old rutted road got clogged with traffic.

"Fasma, you mind staying?" Gene asked. "I've got a cover story to write, and the cops will want somebody to quiz at length about all this."

"Nah, man, go for the glory. Here's the film pack, treat her gently. I'll start another one."

"Thanks, buddy. Guard our engineers from the mob. Oh, and shut our car lights off when you get a chance. Sun is coming up, guys, on a new day!" Gene raced toward a ride in the waiting chopper, headed for an anxious editor. The *Herald* had another scoop.

As Barry surged the helicopter upward, Gene looked down at the strange scene--an abandoned car with its trunk open, two men on the ground and one standing, men dashing across railroad tracks from a bushy field which was fast becoming a parking lot, and a parade of flashing lights approaching. Gene was flying away from a story at the point where he usually arrived. And he felt very grateful that he was not staring down at a bomb crater, burning car, and bodies strewn across the landscape.

*   *   *

Chapter Five

Harran Winfree had been backed across the small dispatch office, one step at a time with each new string of cuss-words, until his back was against the tower window frame. Joe Donaldson, his yard boss, was backed into the wall map to the left.

Sylvester Manchester had arrived to take control.

The newcomer wore a lightweight tailored suit, befitting a man who had climbed far up the railroad's corporate ladder, but his language was lifted straight from sweaty yardmen. It didn't take Harran long to conclude that the big boss meant to resolve this maverick train business expeditiously.

"If the two of you made any mistakes tonight, other than having been born, there'll be your blood as two sacrificial lambs all over these office walls!" Manchester stormed. "I won't cover up for you. Where's your dispatcher's log on this mess, Winfree?"

Harran gladly jumped away from the window and toward his radio desk. "Right here, sir," he pointed, "with the transmissions marked in yellow."

Manchester mumbled something as he moved toward Harran. With that first step releasing some tenseness, Joe stepped quickly toward the door, saying, "I'll just go down and see--"

"You most certainly will not! When I'm through with this late night disc jockey, I want to hear again who's paying your salary--us, or that oil company where you spent most of the night." Manchester pointed out the window, then stared for a long moment at the fuming orange inferno. "Make a barbecue fit for all us Texans who moved to Colorado, wouldn't it?" Neither of his employees knew whether to answer seriously or laugh, so they remained silent.

Manchester began thinking out loud, a habit that sometimes got him into trouble. "No use getting the federal marshals up early, just make them grouchy. They can leave at dawn, no sense risking night flying." He concluded, "Never mind your log for now," and turned toward the map of rail lines tracing through the Rocky Mountains. "Where's the next siding where we've got automatic braking long enough for downhill runaways, sixty cars long? I'll just slip him over there, shut him down, shove his ass in jail, and throw away the key."

Harran risked his first smile since he shook hands with his boss and the room started heating up. Harran had anticipated and prepared for this strategy. He walked over and pointed to a spot on the map, in the heart of the Rockies. "Here, fifteen miles before Dotsero Junction, out of our Subdivision but still just within our centralized control. He'll hit there about 7:00 A.M., less than two hours from now."

"Oh, damn it all, I can tell time."

Harran silently cursed himself for his stupid statement. Then he started to again build his courage to share his suspicions. He felt that the crazed Benjamin Rintricky still seemed sharp enough to have anticipated their strategy, and might have an ace ready to play against them.

A voice crackled over the radio. "Dispatch, this is the 321. What the hell's going on up here by the power plant, over?"

Good night for swearing, Harran thought, remembering the earlier infractions from the 9039 engineer. He answered, "The oil tank fire, or something else, over?"

"Well, there's a damn mess of cars on the right, and guys around some old heap of a car on the left, with a damn helicopter spotlighting the whole place. Can't tell if it's police or not. I had to lay on the horn going through them--some ass standing in the middle of the tracks with a camera on his shoulder filming me coming in at him until I almost ran the s.o.b. down."

"Uh, 321, we've got a visitor here--" Harran interrupted.

Manchester grabbed the mike from him. "321, this is Supervisor Manchester. And not just any supervisor, but the one who signs your check. You *will* have a full written explanation to me by noon of just why you believe the federal guidelines prohibiting radio profanity were passed into law. Until noon, and forever after this noon, clean up your act!" Manchester shoved the mike back at Harran, exclaiming, "Damn engineers are going to cost us a fucking fortune in fines for swearing!"

Harran radioed, "321, pull your string onto west 14 line for a breather, and come see me pronto about that old car, copy?"

"Roger, dispatch, see you in twenty. Sorry, Mr. Manchester, won't happen again. Nice to talk with you, clear."

"Oh, that dumb jackass goes from bad to worse with his cutesy personal crap. Never mind about some stolen junk car out by the tracks, Winfree. We've got this maverick to stop, come daylight. That's where the media-- and insurance exposure is."

Ah, ha, thought Harran. *You old codger, dressed up for the cameras in the morning when they get wind of 9039. Have it your way, boss. Maybe there is no connection between the maverick and the clunker, or with the two phone calls from reporters about a train hijacking. Anyway, if there is, and you missed it, then you deserve some of this heat you've been dishing out to us.*

"Yes, sir, no junk cars, by your orders," Harran said, unsmiling again, while unobtrusively logging in the call facts.

"And turn off that damn radio," Manchester continued his demands, "and answer those damn phones, and don't bother me so I can figure this all out."

*   *   *

Ruth Fitzwater felt good, having done her part. Besides arranging cab delivery of media packages, she had sent her own special letter of explanation by cab to her friend Dave Cranmer, regional representative for the National Peace Academy. Now she would carry out her faxed threat.

Ruth slowed her car as she approached the 56th Avenue exit off Airport Boulevard. This divided highway was the major link for high-speed travelers in a hurry from east, south, and west metropolitan Denver into the Denver International Airport, fifth busiest in the nation. Denver planners termed it the Gateway Development Area, as hotels and businesses began to fill the farmland along this asphalt strip.

The two-lane northbound overpass built over the old 56th appeared to the Shakespeare Group to be the perfect target. Destroying it would immediately stop most traffic bound for the terminal, sending a tangible warning to transportation authorities. But it would not be so serious as to warrant Homeland Security issuing a *Red Alert* and closing DIA now. The Group had contingency plans to do that with a parking lot bombing, if necessary later.

She drove slowly through the first short westbound tunnel on 56th, focusing her gaze intently on the last light fixture, upper right side, near the embankment and within easy reach for their placement. Their metal box was still attached there, undiscovered and waiting, containing two blocks of C-4 and detonators. Ruth drove through the second tunnel, supporting

DIA's outbound traffic, and stopped where she could see cars approaching both overpasses. She slipped on a pair of canvas gloves. Her dashboard clock showed 5:30.

She let one final car cross over, then there was a long break. The last to drive that boulevard, she thought, as she started her car and headed slowly westbound on 56th for Denver. Ruth reached onto the seat, picked up the cell phone and placed it on the dashboard. She pressed the speed dial for the number of the cpd enclosed in the metal box, attached to the detonator. Then she dialed the four-digit code number, programmed to insure that no random advertiser would computer call the bomb early.

The thunderous explosion jarred her senses, and somehow even lifted the pavement and her car along with it. Another success for Shakespeare's simple plan: collapse one tunnel and inconvenience highway commuters, thus threatening public air and ground transportation. This gets America's attention, which can then be redirected to the train's message of food surplus and the plight of the children. And Ruth had remained adamant on destroying only property, never purposely threatening life.

In her rearview mirror, Ruth saw the cloud of dirt and debris. She shook when she heard tires skidding, then an unmistakable sound of metal colliding with metal. They had worried about serious ancillary accidents outside their control. It was happening.

Ruth didn't look back anymore, but removed her black wig, and set her mind on getting to Tower Road, south to I-70, west to the exit sign, "I-270 Northbound, Boulder, Longmont." She rolled down her window and flung the cpd into the weeds by the side of the road, its usefulness ended, its incrimination obvious. Then she removed her gloves.

Within five minutes, police, fire, and ambulances had arrived. They set blockades on both sides of the airport access road, and tended to accident injuries. Emergency crews were carefully trying to determine if anyone had been trapped inside the short tunnel when it caved in. The bomb squad was rolling.

Someone was deciding whether and whom to notify in Homeland Security and FBI, since national and international air traffic facilities might be under threat--or not. The nearby airport hotels were mildly concerned, wondering whether it was worth waking up hundreds of guests--to do what? To go where?

Security forces at DIA were debating their proper stage of airport alert, while the night information officer scribbled different approaches to take with the media onslaught certain to find other routes and descend soon on the sleepy airport. The full explosion effects and possibilities of more bombs were uncertain. Were they the target? They decided to hold off notifying regional authorities that airport facilities might be threatened, since it was not their actual property. And it could have been simply a very bad car wreck.

*   *   *

The short recording on the cell phone device SIM chip stopped. Radio station KDNC manager Ron Slider looked at his friend Hargrave, day city editor of the *Rocky Mountain Herald* newspaper.

"We got one, too. Think it's for real?" Slider asked, slowly pulling at his twenty-six-hour stubbled chin and folding into the nearest chair in the office.

"Sounds like Wilma's voice," Hargrave nodded. "We've been phoning for a half-hour, and sent a copyboy to her house. No car, no lights, but milk and paper on the porch." He stood and began to pace behind his chair. "Got a note with it. They want media to create interest." He paused before adding, "Your radio could help involve the public faster."

Slider thought a minute, then queried, "Called the Feds yet?"

"No. I'm not sure what to do. The FBI freeze might tie our hands. Your station could break it with a great scoop--unless it's a hoax, then there'd be egg on all our ties. Railroad isn't talking yet. But their dispatcher could have simply denied any trouble, and he didn't."

The radio man rubbed one bloodshot eye vigorously with a finger, then kept both eyes closed. "Look, friend, I'm bone-tired, and really strung out. We're running a person short, and I got no sleep last night. So if you want logical thoughts or sound advice, forget it. If you're giving us a story, appreciated. If you're asking for help, spell it out." His tone was pure exhaustion.

"Rest a minute, and let me lay out a scenario." Hargrave paused in his thoughts, but not in his pacing. Then he began, "Your reporter and ours were at the car, and talked with those two supposed engineers with no ID from a hypothetical hijacked train. We need to verify that there's a train at least missing, and that Wilma is really gone. You know about the highway bombing near DIA. Maybe the same group will claim that along with the oil fire?" Slider nodded.

Hargrave continued, "When we have hard facts, we can make decisions and call in some favors. We need to bypass the FBI blackout, so you can run that chip recording again, and we can go to press. I'll make a few calls, okay?"

Slider gestured approval, resting his head on cupped hands.

Hargrave phoned his newsroom, then another railroad contact--off the record--and still got no denial. Then he called for a Denver Police Officer, Sgt. Richard Mulvey.

"Well, patch me through! This is an emergency!" he blurted into the phone. "I know he's bomb detail, but they've already exploded, right? So now he's got time to talk about another one that hasn't gone off yet."

Slider shook his head to get his bleary eyes open again. "You got a third bomb?" he asked unbelievingly.

"Nah, just needed to get their attention--" Hargrave broke off abruptly. "Dick, m'boy, this is your drinking buddy from the *Herald*." He winked at Slider, who was slowly coming back to life. "No, there's not another bomb. Listen, have those refinery and *airport* bombs been linked to any extortion yet?" He listened. "I know that's confidential, but I'm in a bind here. I may have a missing reporter, and you've got two engineers from that hijacked train--Dick, you still there? Yeah, I'll hold."

Hargrave nodded, starting again, "Sure, we can meet here, off the record without FBI, right? How's 7:30? Good. KDNC will be here, too." He gave a wink of favored complicity as the call ended, and told Slider, "Dick didn't correct my references to airport bombs or the hijacked train engineers. That's the way he confirms with me. *Facts!*"

Slider next made a call, about being tied up and the station switching to machine number twelve, then the two men headed for the newspaper's staff conference room. Coming awake on his third wind, the adrenaline-powered radio man asked, "Who's the *Herald* ramrod? Quintana on national desk?" He knew of the paper's stormy internal politics.

"No way. Lakey called me in early because of Wilma being mine, and I'm keeping it. But it looks like I'll need TV for maximum coverage fast," the city editor added. "I understand Channel Five got there early. They might come in if you and I are solid--" He waited, testing territory. "I want the story--and Wilma's safety--not necessarily in that order," he added, struggling past the job to express the heart.

"Make your call to Five now," Slider said, counting ratings. At his earlier instruction, the cpd chip recording was now on standby in the radio newsroom control booth, waiting one phone instruction to trigger *News-Flash*. With luck, and Hargrave's help, KDNC would be first nationally to break the full story linking a grain train hijacking, a reporter kidnapping, and bombs bursting in air.

*   *   *

The Grain Train thundered westward through the narrow mountain valley. Darkness remained sovereign for scant moments longer, and headlights of occasional vehicles flashed past on the nearby two-lane Colorado Highway 131 near State Bridge.

From the map, Peter knew they had just seven miles of parallel run beside the highway before they swung southwest into the isolated canyons of Eagle County, where rugged rocks towering a thousand feet above the river bed had inspired the Spanish naming--*Colorado* for *red*.

"It's up to you now, Wilma," Peter shouted in urgent tones. "They must still have us blacked out in Denver. Nobody knows about us, so nobody cares yet. You ready to find those truckers?"

"Ready, willing, and able-bodied," Wilma answered with a shout, trying to lighten the tenseness in the cab of Engine 9039.

Fork had left his fireman's chair to scan their citizens' band radio dial for any active channel. That radio was part of the communication gear they had loaded from the trunk of the old junker car. The automatic scanner stopped at a strong busy channel. Fork waited a few moments for a break, then cut in on top of a slow response.

"Breaker, breaker, let us interrupt with some life or death chatter. Please turn us up louder on your speakers, good buddies." Fork was making urgent gestures for Wilma to take over while he held the switch open.

She maneuvered to take the mike, while Peter held the flashlight focused on the scrawled pad in her other hand bouncing with the train's rapid movement over the rails as she began reading loudly.

"Truckers, believe me, this is no joke. If you have a cell phone recorder, this would be a good time to turn it on. You are about to become an important part of American history." Her first live recitation began.

"This is Wilma Fletcher, reporter for Denver's *Rocky Mountain Herald* newspaper in these frightening early morning hours. I'm in the cab of a hijacked train locomotive, with desperate men.

"There are others on this train--sincere men, dedicated to a cause. They believe it is time to end the curse of starvation on our small planet, for they hear the cries of shriveled children dying every minute. The men are mostly farmers, these men who have commandeered this train. They are not armed. And strung out behind us are fifty train cars full of food--the grain of America.

"This grain was set aside as government surplus, stored already for months. It was on its way to yet another place of storage. But now it is destined for quick use as food, as it was intended when it was grown. These farmers and these engineers are making that possible.

"Our farmers grow more than we eat, and have for years. Our message is urgent: get our surplus to those who are starving right this very minute. American farmers should also be growing more, on land the government pays to keep idle, and selling or trading more crops to those dying for lack of food. America would win, and the world would win.

"That's the story of these railroad Robin Hoods. And their plea to the people of America is to keep listening. Help keep this train moving. Don't let anyone stop this food from reaching the starving.

"This is Wilma Fletcher, riding on America's surplus Grain Train to end starvation."

Peter patted her shoulder. She took a deep breath, continuing.

"Hey, truckers, please relay this word of hope to truckers on other CB channels. And stop when you can safely and call in this message to your own local radio news station back wherever your home is. It may earn you a few *hot tip* dollars, 'cause you may be the first to break this news. But more importantly, it may save kids' lives. What do you say, will you help us? Over."

Wilma stopped, and Fork released the mike key. The three men around her gave her a cheer.

But the CB radio was silent. Was their message heard and ignored?

The radio band finally crackled. "Breaker, breaker, this is the Stone Wall." Fork turned it up. "Wilma, girl, how do we know you're not another faker?"

"Now listen here, Stonewall," Wilma immediately broadcast, combining his names. She had picked up on something in his voice, and gambled. "You sound black to me, and I'm just as black as the night outside this smelly engine cab, too." She lapsed into hard African American dialect, straight from ghetto experience she might rather have left buried. "My mama taught me to never lie, and I sure wouldn't start now with a bunch of streetwise guys and gals like you. You're the ones help keep flashy flax on my back and grits in my stomach. You can take this to the bank, Stonewall, y'hear?"

The engine crew was dumbfounded at hearing her new side, and stayed silent. But Stonewall came back. "Lady Wilma, you done named me right and won my heart, gal. I'll make a call for you. I'm fueling at McCoy in two minutes, over."

"My cell's on the blink, but I'm just five minutes from a booth in Toponas, sister Wilma, and I'm now planning a stop. This is the Ducktail, over."

"Ten miles from here I'll stop for coffee in Wolcott, and make a call to the Los Angeles newspaper. This here's Trapper Ted, over."

Wilma started scribbling the names as they began rolling in, twelve in all. Then she got back on the mike herself. "Boys, I wish you could see the smiles I'm wearing, right along with my engineers and farmers." She was getting wrapped up in the emotional moment. "Thanks, Stonewall, my number one, and Ducktail, and Trapper Ted…" She proceeded to thank each by name off the list under Peter's bouncing light. "You're keeping the ball rolling we started last night in Denver. Bless you, each one. And safe truckin' to all God's children out there. Amen and out."

"Hey, Grain Train lady, add me to that list of *white hats*, pardon the expression. I'm Big Rig Tess, and you folks are riding with my blessing. 'Bout time we started thinking of the wee ones we're keeping hungry, over."

"Power to you and your band of merry men, Lady Wilma," added a new rich voice. "I wondered where Robin Hood had got lost, but it sounds like he, and she, are alive and well. Matter of fact, this here's the Friar Tuck, believe it or not."

Peter, with ego pricked slightly, reached for the mike to clarify which gender was in charge. But he waited until Wilma relinquished it, instead of taking it. His crew was yahooing at the last trucker's name.

"You hear that cheer, Tuck?" Peter broke in. "We welcome your help. They call me Peter. Give us your blessing, friendly friar, over."

"Blessings on you, Peter and Wilma," the trucker said without hesitation, "and on all riders of the Grain Train. May your journey end in full bellies and glad hearts! Over."

The camaraderie was growing stronger. Others joined the list, apparently called onto the CB bank by the first group. The spirit in the cab was jubilant, and Peter radioed the good news of trucker support back to the farmers, wakening them to the dawn of a new day. He praised Wilma and her message.

A trucker named Evangel asked, "Say, is that you I've been tracking alongside since Bond? I'll flash my rigging lights, over." Sure enough, the truck on the highway paralleling the train at this point flashed the yellow lights framing its long side.

"All right!" Peter shouted gleefully, delighted to have visual contact with a friend in the outside world. "How shall we answer?"

Monty punched twice on his air horn button, Fork twirled an old red and green signal lantern from his window, and Wilma radioed back, "That's us, good close buddy. Sure nice to have your company, over."

"I'll try to keep up with you, Grain Train, but you're making better time than I am up these hills. Say, isn't it going to be kind of tough hiding out around here, with those banners you have on your cars? Got enough sunlight to read them now. I like that one: 'If Not Us, Who? If Not Now, When?' CB'ers, I'm looking at four green engines, six boxcars, and umpteen grain cars. What d'ya know, this thing's really for real, over."

Peter spoke into the mike, "To our new trucker family, I'm reminded of what a friend said: 'Have you believed because you have seen? Blessed are those who have not seen, and yet believe.' We're sure not hiding. We want the whole country to know we're here. Thanks for your eyes, Evangel, over."

Peter waved from the window of the engine. The distant truck blinked back a daylight salute of allegiance.

*   *   *

"This is Sylvester Manchester, Denver director of dispatching for Mid-Western Pacific Railroad. Connect me with the U.S. marshal in charge of Colorado railroad illegalities." His two men in the yard tower office watched him. "I know very well it's six in the morning. I've been waiting until it was quite late enough to call. Now I need an awake and alert marshal to hop a helicopter and go make an arrest." He paused again.

"Look, Miss, we have a hijacked train being engineered by a maniac. We are going to divert it in less than an hour onto a siding. The loonies who stole it will disappear into the woods if there isn't some law enforcement waiting to collar their asses!" His neck was growing redder. "What's your name? Wait a minute, you blasted…"

He slammed down the phone. Harran Winfree and Joe Donaldson waited for the tirade, which was sure to follow.

Manchester started. "She hung up on me! The bitch hung right up on me! First she says the marshals are out of town or on the fire, can you believe that? Then she cops a plea and says it sounds like FBI territory anyway. What a pile! Who cares about law and order around here anymore? Well, what are you sitting there for? Get me the FBI phone number, you nincompoops!"

Harran handed him a note pad. "It's written on the top sheet."

"Now just why would you have that number written down already?" Manchester demanded.

"Because they called for you earlier."

"Hell, why in the Sam Hill did they do that?"

"Because the Denver police reported to them that our train had been hijacked."

"And how did they know that?" Manchester screamed.

"The reporters called them after they found the engineers tied up in the car trunk." Harran was trying to keep the gloating smirk from showing. He had all the cards.

"And why didn't you tell me all this until now, young man?" Manchester's tone suddenly grew very controlled, almost icy.

Harran knew that this was the time to play his ace in the hole. "Because, sir," he said simply, "you told me not to mention the junker car anymore, and to leave you alone."

The boss stared through Harran's brain, and in barely a whisper addressed his subordinate. "You took me at my word--to set me up and embarrass me? To jeopardize company property, and expose us to enormous liability by delaying the help we need? Mr. Winfree, that so disappoints me that I am putting you on one week's suspension, for rank insubordination and extremely poor judgment. You will leave just as soon as you finish answering the questions of all law officers on what you know about this hijacking. Is that abundantly clear?"

Harran gulped twice before finding his voice. His cockiness was eradicated. "Yes, Mr. Manchester. Sir, I believe the FBI is already on the way over here to see you."

The tower phone rang again. Joe Donaldson immediately picked it up, glad to become preoccupied.

"And what other surprise information do you have for me, from your evening's myriad of phone calls, Mr. Winfree?" Manchester asked.

"The *Rocky Mountain Herald* called. Their number is on the pad. They said that the engineers were not seriously hurt, sir, I'm sure you'll be happy to hear that, and they may have a reporter on board." He finished the sentence all in one breath, getting quieter at the end.

"I surely am happy." Manchester turned his back to his suspended staffer and walked to the route map. Harran wondered if the full message had registered.

The phone rang again, and Joe softly answered.

Manchester continued, "Mr. Winfree, come over here and brief me on everything you know--everything, about this train numbered nine-zero-three-niner. Any future you may have with this company depends on your absolute cooperation."

Manchester went on, not turning. "Mr. Donaldson, get me the dossiers on the engineer and fireman who were removed from the train, and I want all there is, and I want it now. And turn on the damn radio! I want to hear what the rest of the world already knows."

"Uh, Mr. Manchester, sir." The boss turned his head ever so slowly toward the second man now seeming to give him static. "I do have two calls on hold for you." Manchester glanced at the blinking lights on the phone set, and back at Donaldson. "United Press International wire service wants to confirm that the hijacked train is actually ours, on line one. Line two is a Sergeant Richard Mulvey from the Denver police. He sounds quite upset. I'll go get you that information--" The phone rang. "--as soon as I answer line three."

Manchester threw his arms upward in disgust at the spiraling turn of events.

The small portable radio that had been silenced now caught Harran's attention as the other two were busy on phones. "Good morning. It's 6:00 A.M., and here are your KDNC Radio top news stories.

"Sirens and flashing lights, everywhere in north Denver. At 3:30 this morning, a large oil storage tank exploded at Mountain West Oil Refinery, sending a sixty-foot tower of orange flame into the night sky. A heavy black column of smoke still darkens the sun as this four-alarm fire rages out of control. Denver city officials are not waiting this time, as they did with the Stapleton oil tank fire in 1990, but have called for the Texas oilrig fire experts to come and help.

"One or more of the Airport Boulevard overpasses at 56th Avenue have collapsed, shutting off traffic to and from Denver International Airport, and closing Interstate 70 in both directions. Traffic is being diverted onto E-470 north and south, and onto 104th Avenue for the west side. Bomb squads are checking those highways for safety, so there may be slowing.

"This KDNC radio bulletin: National radio just reported that a terrorist group called 'Unite Surplus And Starving' claims responsibility for the bombing of the DIA access road, as well as the oil refinery. More on this in a special report at 6:25."

*   *   *

Manuel Gomez ate the last bite of pancakes and patty sausage. His flight to Salt Lake City, Utah's capital, had been uneventful.

A restaurant copy of the *Salt Lake Tribune* Early Edition held no mention of the bomb or U.S.A.S., only spectacular wire photos of the refinery fire he had helped set off. The same for *U.S.A. Today*.

He patted his cellular phone, resting on the table by the syrup pitcher, and watched the wall clock as 6:06 became 6:07, his appointed time. At seven minutes after every hour, until the end of the train trip, he would get a call from the cab of Engine 9039, if the plan was going well. If no call was received within thirty minutes of that time, he was to detonate his first bomb. If no call on the next hour, detonate another.

The group had debated using text messaging, but said that someone else who had taken control of Peter's cpd could text a phony message. So they kept voice.

Manuel's belt vibrator alerted him. There was no ringing tone to call attention, for he had planned carefully. He held the phone up and clicked in the connection. A roaring engine filled his ear, and he reflexively moved it away. A shouting voice clearly enunciated one word: "Shakespeare!"

People seated nearby turned to look at the source of the literary message as Manuel switched it off, blushed furiously, and shook his head. He laughed, joining the other smiles and giggles. He would insure that was the last time he took his call, and its changing password, in public.

Now he had to move fast, before someone using a triangulation grid system could find him from the GPS locator in every cell phone. It activated each time a cell tower transmitted a call, and stayed on during the connection.

Manuel walked past historic Hotel Utah for two blocks further east on Temple Street to admire the Lion House grounds. In this mansion, Mormon pioneer Brigham Young had comfortably housed his many wives, for in the 1800's polygamy was a God-given instruction to virtue. The tall statue of the famous bearded husband--and prophet--stood proudly in the front yard.

From Manuel's vantage point, knowing exactly where to look, the new mound of earth in the flowerbed near the porch lightly covered his C-4 package planted four hours earlier. Salt Lakers revered their monuments, and would do anything to preserve them, the Shakespeare plotters reasoned. Temple Square with its world-famous Tabernacle, incredible organ, and vast genealogical library was only three blocks from this spot. The threat would be clear.

Manuel Gomez was proud to be the only Hispanic in Shakespeare, and its youngest member. After this week, he knew his name would be put into the new textbooks on major social change events, like those he had been studying. His family would surely rejoice.

*   *   *

Jeremy Downing, in jeans and plaid shirt, finished filling his enclosed panel van's gas tank. He had rented it on line, to insure he got the type he wanted. It was still cool in early morning Boise, Idaho. He paid for his gas, and a Planter's Peanut Plank, his favorite childhood treat and hard to find in Denver. Then he pulled over to a parking spot to wait.

And to ruminate. Why here? Why the Shakespeare Group? He had come to Auraria on a sports scholarship. His athletic skills came naturally, in tennis and in track. But State funding for college sports dried up, just like job opportunities had for his father in Appalachia. Their family had grown up hungry, and he didn't want to go back to poverty. Somehow, Peter knew, and sought him out. Here he could help the world.

His dashboard clock read 6:08 when the cellular phone sounded. He held it in front of his face, pushed the talk button, and heard loud background noise. He studied the device, wondering if authorities had already static-jammed the line. Then he heard Peter's voice carefully intoning the first code word. Quickly the phone connection went dead.

Jeremy remembered that they had agreed there should be no response, since the group members might be in a compromising or awkward environment. If they needed to talk with Peter, they could open conversation. But that would jeopardize the time chain, as well as allowing someone to more easily pinpoint their remote location. They had deliberately gone to Craig's List on the internet to purchase cell phones made in the early 1990's--before the GPS locators in each phone set were mandated to be activated for tracking at all times, not just when there was a connection.

He drove off to check on the bomb he had placed in last night's darkness. With binoculars he would be able to see the two dirt-colored devices from the shoulder of the highway. They were leaning against two adjacent legs of a giant tower holding up fourteen four-inch-round high-voltage cables, and would cause major electrical disruption in Idaho's capital and largest city if detonated. Then he was off to buy chemical fertilizer and gasoline, and check on parking next to the empty hotel in downtown Boise.

*   *   *

Ardis Borgeba rolled over and shut off the travel alarm on the nightstand. It glowed 5:00, Pacific Daylight Time. In nine minutes, her cellular phone would ring, if their plan was falling into place.

She had gone straight from the Portland airport to the bus station. After watching the sparse 2:00 A.M. crowd to see if anyone looked back at her, she had approached the locker to look for the strand of hair she left caught in the door four days earlier. It was there. She cautiously opened the locker door and studied the suitcase inside. It was still turned at a thirty-degree angle, as she had left it.

She had removed the suitcase with its twelve cakes of C-4, two and one-quarter pounds each of pure heaven in her mind. She then drove her newly rented car across one of the many river bridges dissecting the city, to a nearby power transmission station supplying Portland's northwest section. There, in the dead of night, she had scaled a remote and inadequate security fence to tape C-4 explosives onto a large transformer, the first domino in a line of eight.

Next, Ardis had backtracked to park near the same bridge she crossed earlier, the impressive Hawthorne, spanning the Willamette River. She walked down to the river's edge to search the area with her flashlight for derelicts sleeping underneath the structure, fearless in her mission. Then she climbed back up to the middle of the first steel I-beam as it left the land to span the long space over the river. There her second bomb, this one multiplied to the power of four cakes, had been secured with river mud from a large plastic bag. She could have chosen a bridge over the mighty Columbia River, but this one was very close to the downtown masses. The level of explosion would not completely destroy the structure, merely halt all vehicular traffic on this bridge, threaten traffic on all bridges, and ideally paralyze the nation's second City of Roses.

Finally, she had retreated to the motel, taken off her clothes, and crawled exhausted into the clean bed.

Now only one hour later, the alarm summoned her back for a moment of alertness, then she could sleep again, if there was no threat to their mission. She sat up on the edge of the bed, switched on the lamp, and sleepily eyed her image in the dresser mirror as she tugged a little on one ear. Her dark hair was a mess, but able to be combed, she thought. Her face was smudged with mud and dirty chain link fence residue, as were her hands, but they just needed a deeper scrubbing, she knew. The desk clerk had barely raised an eyebrow. She looked at her skin in the mirror, studying her unchangeable features. Her olive color set her apart as Greek, non-anonymous.

Ardis still jumped when her cell phone rang, and glanced at the clock glowing 5:09. She grabbed the phone, pressing the button before it could ring a second time. She had anticipated the noise of a running locomotive as being the first good news, then she heard Peter's unfamiliar shout confirming "Shakespeare!" And he was gone, a voice in her strange night from a thousand miles away. But he was safe so far, as was she.

They could not triangulate on a five-second call from the hijacked train. Even if *they* traced to Portland, the cell tower had a fifteen-mile radius to search. Even *if they* knew to whom the cell phone belonged. And this early, Ardis knew *they* didn't know anything. Losers. Sacrificial pawns in life's chess game. She was a true believer, and would triumph with her powerful might over the twisted right of the corrupt legal system.

Ardis reset her alarm for six o'clock, shut off the lamp, lay down again, and pulled the covers over her tired bare body. She curled her legs up, then eased both her hands down between her legs for a sandwich of security. She quickly fell asleep again in her womb of secrecy, to dream of a new day of destruction.

*   *   *

In his mind, Tom Buchanan was becoming his alias, Don Thompson. His phony driver's license had given him instant new identity. The record had been easily procured in a large city like Denver with its illegal alien traffic. He mentally pictured his old Denver self being washed away as he worked up rich lather in the hot shower. He rejected the washcloth in favor of using his hands as vigorous scrub brushes.

"Step out a new man," he said aloud. "I am Don Thompson."

He was fully awake after only an hour of sleep. His flight had landed at SeaTac International Airport on time. His drive to the bus station in downtown Seattle was placid. He had walked quickly with his lethal luggage along the docks, and placed the first bomb at an abandoned warehouse, over water. Fire in the famous port would become an immediate crisis.

Then he had driven a few blocks in the other direction, and left one explosive C-4 pack and its detonator in shrubs near the base of one leg of the towering Space Needle, reminder of past World Fair glories. The bright harbor landmark and its circling dome restaurant would not topple, but be merely threatened and closed. His tasks were done within an hour, and he had slept deeply.

Tom stepped from the shower onto the cold tile floor, still dripping wet, feeling very clean. The cell phone waited on the lid of the toilet seat. He reached for a large brown towel, which he began rubbing industriously around one arm then the other.

"I am Don Thompson," he said firmly, putting the towel behind his shoulders, and pulling it hard across his broad back. He toweled the steamy mirror, streaking up and down it. To the man now facing him, he affirmed: "You are Don Thompson, head to toe."

He dried his bottom, his legs, his feet with just as much vigor, then threw the towel into the corner, discarding with it his old self.

Tom brushed his teeth, and began combing his damp hair.

Ringgg. His wristwatch on the marble counter pointed to 5:10. The moment was at hand. Tom picked up the phone set and held it, beginning a grand chapter in world history.

Ringgg. He felt the sound go through him. He put the receiver up to his ear, and pressed the button with his thumb, veteran of thousands of cellular conversations. Noise of the train filled his head, but he kept the phone joined to his ear. Tom turned to face the mirror and watch himself become linked as one of the most critical parts of the chain.

"Shakespeare!" Peter's voice sounded excited, hopeful. The engine rumbled a moment longer, then the noise abruptly stopped, replaced by a dial tone. But Tom's eyes, ears, and brain had recorded those timeless seconds. He switched the tone into oblivion, and remained a statue. Tom, become Don, become unexpendable link-pin.

The human hunk of a man in the mirror had pre-arranged appointments beginning in three hours, seeking support of Seattle's radical activists, illegals asking illegals to go public and risk arrest one more time.

Tom moved his thoughts to later morning, when this same *Homo sapiens*, this leader of humanity would be speaking in generalities with Her Honor, Mayor Taulison, about the typical benefits of using skilled mediators to resolve serious conflict situations. He would extol the virtues of remaining non-violent during confrontation, showing strength by reserving use of force until the absolute last resort. And this talented man in the mirror would seek to rekindle in that powerful woman the warmth of valuing each human life above all else.

His early afternoon appointment was reserved for regional graduates of the National Peace Academy. Undoubtedly, their NPA Crisis Center would already have contacted the train by that time and attempted intervention to stop it. But Tom would offer the broader view of letting it run, and discuss balanced win-win compromises.

This male figure before him was new, the inner man finally coming out. He would be speaking his truth now, sharing his values too long hidden from his peers, leading the way to the new world and brave leadership-- with Peter. Had his leader expected this transformation of his No. 2 man?

With any one of his three appointments today, he was only one person away from betrayal. But this new Don Thompson stood straight and proud, knowing he was up to the challenges. He smiled, for if he felt this confident standing naked, just imagine how strong his presence when fully clothed!

*   *   *

Chapter Six

"Thursday dawns have never been of particular interest to me," Brody observed. He sat facing his eighth-story window, looking at the seven tiers of Rocky Mountain ridges barely discernible through the gray haze. "And this one is particularly ugly."

FBI Regional Director Winston Brody was alert, in dark suit and tie, styled silver-gray hair, emanating a faint aroma of *Outrigger*, while presiding irritably at one end of a large walnut table. Eight rich matching armchairs were occupied around it. His office in the downtown Denver Federal Office Building was leased and furnished years before the restrictive Federal Office Space Guidelines, when there had been ample room and budget for his expansive taste in office furnishings.

FBI Regional Deputy Director Frank Wayman sat opposite with off-centered tie, wavy mane of black wet hair combed flat, strong cologne unable to cover his smoky body odor lingering from the fire scene, tense and out of character.

"I've read your various reports," Brody continued. "Tell me now what I don't know." He spun his chair around abruptly. "Smathers?"

The FBI agent who had been night duty officer relished being called on first, in addition to the honored proximity seating to his superior's left. "We will be up to full staff by seven o'clock, Director. Everyone is coming in early."

"No time for redundancies, Smathers. On with it."

The agent shuffled papers nervously. "Uh, radio KDNC just announced that 'Unite Surplus And Starving' is the terrorist organization claiming the refinery and Airport Boulevard bombings."

"The bombings at both places?" Brody asked, incredulous.

"What happened to the news blackout I ordered more than an hour ago, the one you put in place?" Frank followed up accusingly.

"Umm..." Smathers stammered, off-balance, looking down at his list.

"Next point," Brody instructed. "Let's hear how much mess we're in."

"I returned a call from Denver police ten minutes ago. They were notified by media of a possible...uh...train hijacking."

Brody didn't take his eyes off of Smathers, but began slowly tapping the end of his pen on the tabletop.

Smathers added, "Two men were found locked in a car trunk near the railroad tracks three miles north, claiming to be train engineers. And, uh..."

"More?" The tapping was getting firmer.

"Apparently the *Herald's* reporters found them first, and left in a helicopter after freeing them. It seems there have been several..." He took a long sigh. "...packages delivered by cab, and fax messages sent to all sorts of media, notifying them of the bombings, and the train, and, uh, threatening more bombings if the train is stopped."

In the stunned silence, Smathers felt that instead of serving as the indispensable answer man, he had just put his head under a guillotine blade. "I told the police to fax us everything they had accumulated so far, but they don't have any of the paperwork yet themselves."

"Do I understand," Frank interrupted, "that there has been a media blitz by these terrorists going on for the last hour?" He remembered the early radio news broadcast. "Or even two hours, and we don't have a single scrap from that paper storm?" Frank recalled references to Midwest cities, as Smathers was saying he couldn't be everywhere.

"Director," Frank said, "if those bombers sent extortion packages not only to local media, but national as well..."

"I'm reading your mind, Deputy." Brody pushed back his chair and stood up, striding toward his desk. "It's past 8:00 A.M. in Washington, D.C."

The phone buzzer sounded, as if he had triggered an alarm. His secretary knew never to interrupt staff meetings, except for death or Washington. Brody resolutely pressed intercom, and heard, "III is on your line."

The bombings would be a particular embarrassment to the Denver office. The executive on the phone, number three from the top in D.C. hierarchy, had been in their office only the week before, briefing them on the increasing internal terrorist activity nationwide, insisting on vigilance.

... LAST THURSDAY, AUGUST 4 ...

Visits from III were the stuff of gossip and fear, in advance and after departure. He was impossible to forget. It wasn't merely the immaculate three-piece-suits, but more his very presence. His bearing resonated of European royalty. Frank wondered if he should bow each time they met, as he unconsciously did the first time. Being with III in a meeting was electrifying, but closer to the electric-chair end of the spectrum than the ecstatic.

Frank had done a classified in-depth research on III's background prior to his coming, trying to understand his ruthlessness. And Frank suspected that III knew of this search into closed files. They had shown that in his earlier years, III had a family, a normal life, and an exemplary career in the FBI. He had made numerous arrests of notable terrorists, building his aura of special expertise. Then there was the subway bombing five years ago in New York City. During that subsequent manhunt for the terrorists, he had killed one of the suspects, claiming self-defense Others arrested in the group claimed murder, but were not believed at trial. Four years ago on a Sunday morning, III and his wife and son were standing on the front steps of their church after the service. A car drove by slowly, spraying the worshippers with more than fifty rounds from two AK-47 automatic rifles. III was wounded, but his wife and son were killed. The suspected attackers were later found hanging in parts outside their home. They turned out to be the son and cousin of the terrorist he had shot earlier. III had an irrefutable alibi for the time of their execution. He had not entered a church since. Because of the fervor and success with which he pursued all enemies seeking to destroy the United States, and the constant threats those terrorists posed to our peaceful way of life, a special office had been created for III, with hand-selected staff. The government allowed him to stay within the FBI domain because of his established career network, even though Homeland Security made a strong case that such crimes fall under their jurisdiction.

And that very man, III himself, had stood right here, stridently pointing out that U.S. citizens were continuing to bomb, burn, and murder to further their own beliefs. Innocent-looking moms and pops, next-door neighbor types, even preachers and nuns, were shattering any remaining stereotypes of looks and backgrounds. No crime seemed too horrible to commit, if they could shut down an abortion clinic or a perfume-testing animal lab. Revenging the death of others seemed standard justification for atrocities similar to the Oklahoma City bombing devastation.

The list was long. American environmental activists had gone so far as to burn ski lodges on the mountains extending their runs, blow up timber trucks operating with permits in wilderness areas, torch barns of ranchers who shot wolves for the bounty, and American extremists had expanded to the oceans, setting fire to new oil rigs in the Gulf of Mexico, sinking whaling ships legally killing their allotted quotas, and more. III documented the destruction with pictures.

Terrorists were showing up as rich and poor, with high and low I.Q.'s, failures and big achievers in school and work, all ages and races and gender. The lesson III had brought was much like the McCarthy era spawned--suspect everyone, trust no one.

Frank had been very upset when III ordered re-opening the old files on former groups of frustrated protesters, plus investigating new activist organizations that opposed the Homeland Security Administration's tighter policies. All government workers' records were being newly scanned for questionable memberships or friends. The hunt for potentially traitorous Americans had begun again to prevent any recurrence of a 9-11 ambush. And the Denver office had a role to purge and punish.

III had talked of protest groups being the putrid compost pile from which internal terrorists crawl. He said that when wimpy judges let trespassers and lawbreakers go with only a hand slap, it sent the wrong message, telling them that their misguided ends did justify their illegal means. There was no mention of First Amendment rights from III's mouth, or from their head office.

But the real grabber came after the slides of much earlier protests, which Frank had personally witnessed in Colorado. People he now knew well as older friends who had mellowed were being targeted as examples of malcontents carrying a match, while all of Denver was sitting on a powder keg.

Suddenly, III had switched slides and said, "This is the group holding up the sandpaper for those crazies to strike their matches across." Pictures of Denver newspaper buildings flashed up, then radio and TV station offices. The hard voice of authority had snapped into the semi-darkness: "This irresponsible money-hungry Fourth Estate publicizes each new bombing, headlines criminal activity, provides a forum to these warped terrorist minds. That kind of success on prime-time news throws open the floodgates of destruction. Then when we do make arrests, they stumble all over each other to get more pictures--of their own Frankensteins. "Mark my words," he had whispered, "if there is a master plan to overthrow our democracy, this is the group behind it."

While they flashed more bombings and brutal injuries and bodies, III had shouted, "Who's next? Which protester goes berserk tomorrow, and targets this building? Which cause becomes worth killing for? Can you stop this? Will you ferret them out? Will you stamp out terrorism from a neighborhood--to save *your* city--and *your* family?"

The slides had ended, the lights were turned up. III had stood his tallest, slammed one fist into his other hand, and further inflamed the group. "Internal terrorism must be stopped! And by God, this is the group to stop them! Every person in this room has that assignment as of right now, along with my personal pledge that The Director is behind you one hundred percent!

"And I expect those who have Intelligence Officer Certification from the Home Office to be especially watchful of everything and *everyone*. You are those who have demonstrated in-depth knowledge and true understanding of the insidious national threat environment. You know that only the fullest intell will suffice for our strategic decision-making in these perilous times. And your efforts will not go unrewarded!" And they clapped. Frank's Denver agents clapped.

*

That was the scene one week ago. Frank recalled it all, and was nauseated.

Now there was dead silence in Brody's office. Without hesitation, Brody picked up the receiver and said firmly, "Good morning."

The group around the table listened intently to their director's part of the conversation, but Brody was mostly listening, with an occasional 'Yes-sir,' and even more frequent 'No-sir' in curt response.

So this is what being the Denver regional director has become, Frank thought to himself. *In a crisis, you're not consulted, just ragged on.*

Brody hung up the phone with a short "One hour then," more shaken than Frank ever remembered. He didn't return to the table, but his gray eyes flashed angry messages to each person as he spoke. "To quote several phrases which III left with me, 'Doesn't anyone look at the Internet in your Hick town? Lift your inane local blackout--the whole nation knows!' Staff, I do not recall the last time this office was caught so by surprise.

"Deputy Wayman, send the fax yourself, but assign agents to verify that *all* media receive and respond to the message that our news blackout is ended. Then demand all their information on these incidents for immediate pickup and bagging as evidence. Use gloves when you lay hands on those actual materials, but we need to get copies of the papers and recordings to me here now! Then get the originals into plastic bags and to our CSI lab for fingerprinting. Have my secretary order two more fax lines and two more phone lines installed at once--National Security Priority." Frank was hastily scrawling notes.

"Move Matthias from the refinery to DIA to investigate. Smathers, go camp with the Denver police until you know all they know. Now all of you, go do your jobs like the professional crime fighters you are!"

There was a chorus of affirmatives, and they started moving fast. This would beat III's deadline for a status update in one hour, and provide something new to report.

"Deputy," Brody touched Frank's arm, "get your assignments made within five minutes, then get over to that railroad office. Hijacking of interstate commerce is still our jurisdiction, even if it does fall under that Homeland Security umbrella. They haven't even bothered to call yet..." Brody was glancing at the list of urgent phone numbers his secretary handed him "... or rather, we haven't even bothered to call H.S. back yet. So go take charge in that tower right in our own backyard."

*   *   *

Ruth Fitzwater pulled into a 7-11 gas station parking area in Longmont, thirty miles north of Denver. She adjusted her red-haired wig, deposited a quarter in the outside pay phone and dialed, looking around too nervously not to be guilty of something. A slight breeze fluttered her scarf, and she was glad for her light windbreaker.

Chanto answered, and quickly told her of a breakthrough. "They just broadcast Wilma's first recording on National Public Radio!"

"That's great," Ruth said in an excited whisper, watching customers.

"There's more," he stammered. "A radio club member called, and apologized for waking me, so I yawned to placate him. He picked up some CB truckers talking about a broadcast from a hijacked Grain Train on our make-believe route. Believe it!" Chanto had joined the Model Railroaders, and asked their citizens' band radio enthusiasts to do a project *for fun* last month, linking specific ham operators every forty miles or so, from Denver to the West Coast along a railway.

"Wow!" Ruth burst out, forgetting her openness for a second. Then she said *wow!* again in hushed tones. "That means the word is out."

"Out, yes, but to the right people, we do not yet know. You must immediately get your next fax sent, for decisions are being made right now on what to do. Go quickly, and may the winds be at your back."

"Thanks, friend. They have a fax machine right inside. Next stop, home. Mom will be waking, and needs me."

"I'll be leaving for my radio friend's house," Chanto said. "I'll call you from there, but the message may be garbled if others are near. Go!"

"Gone." She hung up, and walked inside. The sign on the fax machine stated *Out of order*. "Oh, shit," she said, most uncharacteristically, and walked rapidly past the Pepsi display to the short line of customers.

"Excuse me, maybe you could just tell me--" she blurted out impatiently to the one person behind the small counter.

"I'm waiting on someone," the clerk answered coldly. She put a warm cinnamon roll into a yellow plastic bag, in the time it would have taken to answer Ruth's question.

"--where there's another fax machine?" Ruth continued, undaunted, now beside herself with anxiety. The man next in line turned and said, "Roadhouse Motel, about seven blocks west."

"Thanks, sir," Ruth said, adding, "You're a gentleman and a scholar." The cliché was sincere, popping into her head and out her mouth without hesitation.

"Thanks to you, Red," he nodded with a grin.

Another motel, she thought while driving. At least there were no police cars sitting right there, or she would have driven past. She walked to the office, taking her planned list of five phone numbers. In this quieter, more trusting town, the fax machine sat out near a green sofa, next to the Wi-Fi desk--serve yourself. "Bless the small businesses," she murmured, paid the desk clerk, and dialed the first number with no one watching.

The typed message took fifteen seconds to feed through the machine:

TO: Railroad Officials, Law Enforcement Agencies:

You have been given fair warning with the two explosions at Mountain West Oil Refinery and Airport Boulevard. We do NOT want to destroy any more property, or take any more chances on injuring anyone.

You must understand that dozens of bombs have been placed at key transportation and energy installations in many States. Our operatives are everywhere, monitoring the regular transmissions from the expropriated Grain Train.

Do NOT block those signals. If coded messages are not received on time, every time, that will become the automatic signal to detonate.

If YOU block our train, YOU set off more bombs. We have an unending supply already in place, enough to bring this wonderful nation to a shuddering halt.

We want to run the train peacefully, straight through to our destination. Just let us by, and there will be no more destruction or violence--which we abhor.

Our demands are not impossible: 1- Keep our track clear and give us straight green lights, as we announce each succeeding segment of track. 2- Keep our communication channels clear.

Let us go about our life-saving mission in peace, bringing relief to suffering humanity.

'SIGNED: 'Unite Surplus And Starving'

Three minutes and five fax messages later, Ruth pulled back onto the street eastbound, tugging her wig off and shaking her own hair free. As she signaled to turn onto the ramp of southbound I-25, a police car zoomed past her westbound, red and blue lights flashing but no siren. She guessed its destination, took a deep breath of close escape, and headed south to Denver.

Her tasks were over, and she could blend back into the nation of onlookers as events unfolded--unless the authorities ignored her clear warnings, and blocked the train. Her mind tripped and stumbled over the agony she would face in deciding to bomb her own city again, and again.

*   *   *

KDNC's Slider had been editor Hargrave's shovel for twenty minutes, digging out confirmations before making his call to trigger a 6:25 A.M. radio bulletin. He knew no other local station had as much inside scoop on the hijacking. *And even the FBI can't block that which is already public information.*

A media powerhouse was sitting down at the oblong table in the *Herald* conference room as the two men entered. The air had an unusual smell, as of dusty news clipping files somewhere, coffee, popcorn, and fresh paint. The closed door kept out much of the newsroom shouting and phone ringing. Nearest hands were shaken in early morning greetings.

"Strange times, friends," Hargrave said, then added a rare self-deprecation. "I'm a lowly daytime city desk editor, with an aspiring reporter riding a hijacked train that left here hours ago. I've been awake only two hours, but I'm assigned the story--start to finish.

"KDNC radio here started it," he said, motioning with his thumb to Ron Slider at his left, "with his morning news at four-fifteen, and a bit more at six o'clock. He's brought his alert newsman, Don Trujillo," and pointed. "Don, it's your pleasure to sit next to my favorite TV star from KTAD-5, Ms. Donna Harrison. Glad you're back safely from the Montana fire lines, my dear. Good pictures." Hargrave nodded to the middle-aged lady, tastefully attired in a light gray suit and pink blouse. Her dark hair was newly coifed, slightly overdone for Denver viewers, he decided silently.

"Next is Five's station manager, Tiny Tim Timmerman." There was ample reason for the friendly nickname, and Tim returned the smile. "My great chess buddy, we could have quite a Master's tournament strategy going here.

"And Tim, you know my man, Cookie Gilchrist. He'll do our local in-depth for the *Herald*. On my right is our night editor, *Bulldog* Lakey. He lives up to his name, bites right through the gristle." The older man with the square jaw and short sandy hair didn't change expression.

"…missing North Dakota train is now known to have been hijacked from Denver…" The sound system in the conference room suddenly came to life on its own. Hargrave had told Fasma to monitor KDNC, after watching Slider make his call, and to interrupt their meeting with any train news.

"…with its cars full of federal surplus grain being used to dramatize a demand by a terrorist group named 'Unite Surplus And Starving.' On board that train winding west through the Rockies is Wilma Fletcher, a *Rocky Mountain Herald* reporter. Apparently, she is a hostage, being forced to broadcast the terrorists' beliefs. Several farmers are also reportedly on board…" and the news continued with bombing facts and extortion threats.

"In national news…" The sound system went silent. The group of media reps had been glancing at each other during the short broadcast, some taking notes. Hargrave stared hard at Slider, whose tired eyes returned the stare unblinking. The scoop shovel had been busy.

"Unusual, this news and group and hour," Timmerman said dryly. "It's 6:30 A.M., and my TV station KTAD is just barely finding out about your Miss Fletcher. We will undoubtedly be outscooped by your own late headlines, and apparently by tips to our mutual friend here," he gestured at Slider. "Are you now going to try to make amends by tossing us tidbits?"

"No, damn it, I'm trying to figure out how to save a life I care about," Hargrave said as he stood, leaning over as close to Timmerman's face as he could, "and how we can combat a crisis together!"

They measured each other across the table a moment. "Sorry," the huge man capitulated. "Bring us up to date. How do we fit in?"

Lakey moved to the marker board, motioning his animated co-worker to sit and cool off. He taped up a chart, and summarized the hastily drawn chronology of hijacking, freed engineers, bombings, cpd chip recordings, and faxes. "Didn't you get a third fax at six o'clock?" Slider asked. "We did."

Lakey shook his head, along with the Channel Five people. "Maybe they've gotten tired of our silence," he surmised.

"Or got scared off before they finished the list, more probably. Third fax was from Longmont--" Slider stopped, the news wheels turning silently in his head. The room was strangely hushed, everyone wondering about the same possibility simultaneously. Slider whispered to his newsman, who quietly left. Hargrave guessed the reporter would call to see if the Longmont police had picked up the fax sender, and nodded to Cookie to also leave, knowing his reporter was sharp enough to know his assignment without words. Tiny Tim signaled *pass* to Donna. There were no shared exchanges during this *we know that you know that we know what you're doing* exercise, so typical of the Fourth Establishment. Lack of cooperation was ingrained. Scoops sell.

The remaining execs reasoned that local law enforcement had not been included in the communication chain so far, else they would have swarmed the *Herald*. However, they all had heard the freeze from Agent Smathers telling them not to do their jobs. The two reporters came back into the room, looking only toward their respective bosses, each indicating negative responses. Cookie handed Hargrave a note.

Hargrave took over. "Denver police are invited here in an hour. The FBI freeze is lifted, and they are on their way here now, demanding all our material and sources. We need to get our chicks in a box first," he said, adroitly avoiding the cliché.

"Another package?" Donna quizzed Lakey, pointing at his chart.

"Right. Taken to a young local named David Cranmer. He called us and just now brought it in. Wants to work with us--with all the media," he corrected himself. "He's a National Peace Academy grad, recruits for them around here, is on their team of Certified National Conflict Resolution Mediators. Their note to him lays out a very comprehensive rationale for all this. Many wrongs make a right to this terrorist bunch. Government surplus is wrong, starvation is wrong, so are hijacking, kidnapping, and bombing, but feeding the hungry is most right of all--so this whole stunt is morally okay to them."

"We could read a copy on the air," Slider suggested.

Hargrave nodded, and Cookie handed out copies. "Dave faxed to the Peace Academy even before he called us, so they'll be involved up to their non-violent eyebrows also."

"Now listen," Hargrave continued, very seriously, "I want to save this girl, but I can't do it alone. She went along to get a great story, apparently at their request, and with this recording it looks as if they want to go big time public. So to help her, I need to help them do just that.

"I'm asking KDNC and KTAD to hit this fast and hard, to whistle stop right along with the *Herald*. And I mean that literally. Our three groups can leapfrog each other as we find out their route, be in the track cities so Wilma can set up communications--or if she runs into trouble."

Tiny Tim let out a whistle of surprise as the magnitude of the project began to sink in. Several others scooted up closer to the table.

"Our pool will scoop the rest of the media in Denver and around the country. We can guarantee coverage to the hijackers, if publicity is why they're doing this, and hopefully be in the best position to help Wilma get away with her head intact. What do you say?"

There was a thoughtful silence before Slider spoke. "KDNC is in it to the end, but it sure will strain our budget. I think you'd do the same for us though, if it would help save a life."

Donna gave a nod, and Timmerman volunteered her for the circuit, "if guaranteed first copy of Wilma's broadcasts."

"You carry it as lead, and credit Wilma, and you'll share first dibs with radio. You'd be sending Donna anyway, wouldn't you, Tim?" Hargrave looked squarely at his friend, who only shrugged and smiled.

"Appreciated, in any case," Hargrave said, adding, "and we're setting precedent. Every day the train is running, we'll have a special afternoon edition. We're playing it to the hilt, even if the Feds drag us to court."

There were a few soft murmurs around the table. "Big investment," someone said. "But the editions will sell out," added another voice. "Marketing is already making their new ad calls," Lakey volunteered.

"Cookie." Hargrave turned to face his helper. "I know you're itching to travel, but I need you to work on my team here. I'm sending Gene Valore for the story, and Fasma with his camera. You okay on that?"

"Either place is an honor, chief." Cookie answered.

Julie came in unannounced, delivered a folded piece of paper to Hargrave. He wrote on it, and she left. "Can TV-5 find this stupid train, and get us some exclusive pictures? Maybe find Wilma at a window or open door?"

"Well, if KTAD can't," Donna said, "nobody can. Let's pool eyes and ears to spot them, and I'm in the air."

Both stations at the table were lapping up the immense opportunity and story depth. News scoops boost ratings, watchers, and readers--and that sells advertising.

"Headquarter the communications logistics at our place," Slider offered. "Everybody in the country has radio. And we won't hog news, at least not from you guys...and gals," he quickly added. "We're running short-handed," he thought aloud, "but we can call back some crackerjack retired staffers. They'll relish the excitement." He nodded at his good idea, then toward his associate. "Donald, I want you to go on the road with this." From Don's wide grin, it obviously was his wish also.

"Who goes to the Peace Academy for interviews?" Lakey asked from the board, being blessed and cursed with a concern for details.

"A camera person," Timmerman suggested. "The Academy has great background for shooting, and we have contacts at the top there."

"Good. Send back your stuff on a secure com line for us, and we'll time our distribution to coincide as best we can," Hargrave concurred.

"FBI, Homeland Security, and police?" Lakey inquired, writing assignments on the chart.

"Not very photogenic, unless they get violent. Radio will try to pry."

"Good. That leaves the farmers," Lakey added.

"We've got strong farm desk liaison with Greeley and the eastern plains. We'll cover," Hargrave concluded.

"Pool resources and info at my place, twenty minutes after each hour," Slider reminded them, "and the Pulitzer Prize is within reach. Say, how many can share in that?" he smilingly inquired.

"I hope Wilma can, and not posthumously," Hargrave answered. They seemed close to adjourning. "By the way, we have her second recording, relayed over a trucker's CB," he added casually. There were stunned exclamations, as all faces turned toward him.

"Wait a minute," Tiny Tim ventured. "You shrewd old buzzard, is that what was in that note? And you waited to tell us until we were hooked on your line for support?"

"Would I?" Hargrave asked in surprise. "Now, how much am I bid for copies of this mellifluous voice for your special 6:55 news breaks?"

Shouts of "Scoundrel!" and "Charlatan!" could be heard echoing around the conference room, as Julie returned to distribute copies of Wilma's #2 recording, and the revised morning edition just rolling off the presses. The red two-inch banner headline announced: "DENVER UNDER SIEGE!"

*   *   *

Frank Wayman strode upstairs into the rail yard dispatch tower, ready to bail his office and his boss out of this predicament. Holding up his leather ID holder, he looked past the men and through plate glass toward his refinery fire nearby. In daylight, the astonishing flames were eclipsed by billowing oily black smoke.

Miniature columns of dark diesel smoke rose up outside from below him as yard engines went about their duty of switching, breaking, and building trains.

Joe Donaldson and Harran Winfree frantically worked on diversion orders, routing trains away from tracks closely paralleling the fire, while at the same time answering questions from two Denver police detectives. Sylvester Manchester was the only person who responded to Frank's grand entrance with a firm handshake instead of merely perfunctory nods, and even began a thumbnail update.

When Frank learned of Manchester's arrangements to have train 9039 side railed in less than fifteen minutes, with or without marshals being present, he argued hard but unsuccessfully. Then he dialed Brody. His director read from extortion documents just delivered, as they were being faxed on to the tower: "Stop the train, and bombs go off all over the country."

"Not acceptable this early in the crisis," Brody said.

Frank then confronted Manchester. "Read that fax in your hand and prove it's a hoax! We don't even know who's out there!"

"Here, I'm in charge," Manchester retorted. "I think it's a bluff by a few nuts who stole my train. And I want it back!"

Frank grabbed him by the shoulders and spun him around to face the inferno outside. "That's no bluff, mister. That's real. That was a real bomb. If they do that again, it could cost lives and millions of bucks. Your train ain't worth it!"

Frank shouted over the other conversations, "Winfree, how long until 9039 hits the Dotsero side rail?"

"Five to ten minutes, depending on how fast she's been rolling--and that track has already been switched."

"Shut up!" Manchester said, with a look of total dislike. Harran Winfree sensed a second week's suspension--this time for talking too much. Frank also saw the look, then stared straight and hard into Harran's eyes, and made a split-second decision.

"Winfree, put your phone caller on hold, take my cellular, and dial this number: 710--do it, dammit! 710-831-1911. Ask the man to hold on for the FBI. Now, Manchester, that's the personal number for Mr. Harrison Fruehauf, who is president of your whole damn railroad company. I called on the way over, in case I ran into trouble with you. Switch that rail back to mainline right now--or I'll arrest you where you stand, and your Mr. Fruehauf can order Winfree direct. Which is it, you stubborn ass?"

Manchester crimsoned, looked at Harran and Tom, and back at Frank. "Damn you Feds," he said, and ordered Harran to throw the switch.

Frank desperately hoped he had been in time, picturing the train being halfway onto the siding when the switch was thrown, derailing cars and maybe killing farmers or engine crew as they were ordering more bombings.

Harran brought him back to the moment at hand. "Do you want me to tell Mr. Fruehauf good-bye?" He looked directly at Frank, with just a hint of a smile on his lips. The cell phone was pressed close to Harran's ear, the recorded message repeating only to him, "This is not a working number. If you think you have dialed incorrectly…"

The bluff had worked. Frank had gotten only the railroad president's name before climbing the tower stairs, not his phone number. But he had found a valuable accomplice in the abused employee Harran Winfree.

*   *   *

The grain train ground to its first squealing stop. Each car bumped the car in front of it, inching it forward. Each jolt was felt in the engine cab and by the farmers who had been alerted to stay inside the boxcars and hold on. The crew decided too much was at stake to trust the Dotsero side rail switch. They had received no assurances their threats were taken seriously.

This was dangerous. If the train was going to be side railed here, there would be law waiting. Peter had debated long hours with himself on whether to radio for destruction if they were stopped and the plan ended. He was still horribly undecided.

Fork squinted into the dawning sun on his side. Nothing was moving, no vehicles were in sight. The signal was green, but not to be trusted. He jumped down off the engine steps long before it stopped, running ahead to study the switch position.

Straight on the mainline!

He shouted into his radio excitedly. "Green light! Green light!" At once the great engine roared into start-up power and groaned forward, banging like rolling thunder as each car coupled tightly again with its neighbor tagging behind. Fork knew with each stop they risked a failed coupling. That would require backing up to try recoupling. Lost time. They had no tools to repair a damaged link, and would have to abandon cars if that happened. So they needed to minimize stops, for safety as well, the longer they traveled.

On the fourth green engine he grabbed the stair railing and swung up, looking toward the rear of the train, counting moving cars as they rounded a curve--fifty-four, fifty-five, then fifty-six with its red streamers trailing for ID. All coupled. Up in the cab he checked air pressure the length of the train--97 PSI at the last car, and 167 miles from Denver.

He whistled his way back along the catwalks, enjoying the spectacular scene of the Eagle River joining forces with the Colorado River. Right here at Dotsero Junction, a hundred years earlier, surveyors marked their rough maps with a 'dot zero,' and began boating down the uncharted waters. The name stuck, and thinking about all that water helped him decide to take a moment to visit the port-a-john on his way past the cab of engine two.

*   *   *

Winston Brody stopped his diagram work at the white board in his office to take Agent Smathers' call. "Director, you said to contact you as soon as we had anything. The Denver police have names: the engineers forced off the train are Benjamin Rintricky and Horace Jensen. *Herald* reporters who found them are Gene somebody and Face Me, and Donald from a radio station. The reporter left in a helicopter."

"Yes, we have some great pictures taken from that very helicopter in the special edition of the *Herald*, along with bylines and bios of the engineers. But go ahead."

"The police have traced the junker car to Po-Fok Car Rentals…"

This is all in the lead story, Brody sighed to himself, wishing Smathers would get sharper. But he said nothing more to discourage his man.

"--and they are meeting right now with the clerk who was on duty yesterday," Smathers continued. "It took a while for them to find her and get her out of bed."

Brody just shook his head at the level of inane detail he was being given. He much preferred his deputy director's fast-clipped summaries, as Frank had just given from the railroad dispatch office: "The four engines were

Dash models 8-40CW, probably needing to re-fuel before Salt Lake City."

"Hold on a minute," Smathers told his boss. Brody focused on his whiteboard diagram and map. Cabs and faxes from Colorado Springs, north to Castle Rock, north to Longmont, with time enough between cities for one person to drive it--or two or three persons could easily be involved. The bomb at the refinery was too close to the Colorado Springs' time, meaning at least two persons. But the Airport Boulevard bomb was rigged so it could have been set off by the traveling messenger. Unless one or both bombs were timed to go off automatically. He wished his lab would hurry up with the highway bomb fragments. What was Smathers doing?

"Sorry, Director. They just called from Po-Fok. The renter's name was listed as Peter Wayman. That's a coincidence, isn't it? Address: 1122 Antelope Drive, Littleton, Colorado. Might be an alias. Say, isn't that the deputy director's neighborhood?"

But Brody had stopped listening after he heard the name, his mind racing a thousand miles ahead of his subordinate, searching for emergency exits. "What was that you were saying, Agent?" he interrupted.

"I said, they've finished dusting the car for prints, found dozens. They're on NCIC linkup, using my authorization for a quicker search. I'll call you when they're back. I've insisted that our lab boys be brought in on the car analysis work. They said, the more the merrier."

"Yes, good work," Brody answered. He had walked for a moment in Frank's shoes, and they hurt like hell. "I'm a little distracted here with other matters. You plan on staying there and handling the run-down on the fingerprint suspects. I know you're tired from working all night, but we need you there. Catch a catnap while you're waiting on Washington. Good luck." Brody hung up, before his agent put two and two together with whatever math method he had learned.

The director stood and began pacing, stopping occasionally to view the city and the far mountains, as he and his deputy had looked at so often together. He needed a plan to communicate quickly with his second-in-charge, the frustrated sire of the newest *most wanted* fugitive.

*   *   *

Chapter Seven

The two Denver detectives said they were through questioning Harran, as did Frank. Instantly, Manchester jerked his thumb toward the tower stairs. Without a word, Harran Winfree stood, pushed his chair back under his desk with certain finality, picked up his sack of untouched lunch, and walked out--leaving his phone ringing.

"Day shift is due any minute," Manchester explained to a puzzled Frank. The phones kept ringing, faster than Joe Donaldson could keep up.

BOOM!!

Frank saw the huge ball of fire at the refinery a split second before he heard it, and instinctively shielded his eyes with his arm. One huge pane of tower glass shattered inward from the pressure of the blast. In large sharp pieces it fell into the small room, directly on top of one of the detectives. He collapsed screaming.

Frank blinked in disbelief. A cloud of brilliant flame and dense black smoke boiled outward low to the ground, then started raising its hideous undulating shape upward, leaving a wide black and red stem. It formed a mushroom Frank had only seen in documentaries.

The air stank. Frank's other senses registered that a second oil tank had burst, or had been bombed. Manchester and Joe struggled past him toward the door.

"Wait! The danger's over for now. You're needed here!" They looked at Frank as if he was crazy.

"There won't be another explosion soon." He was guessing. "The tower is standing, the windows are safe," he guessed again. "So tell your trains what to do. That might have thrown debris all over the tracks." Surprisingly, the men obeyed the strong directive, and turned back toward the radios and their jobs.

"This fellow needs an ambulance," Frank said firmly, kneeling over the motionless bleeding man covered with glass on the floor. The other detective was frantically trying to pull a bigger shard out of his partner's back. "Leave it! Keeps the vessels closed!" Frank felt the man's neck for a pulse--weak, but regular. No pool of blood indicating an artery or vein severed.

"Detective, stop and call!" The man nodded, and acted on the order.

Frank stood, and looked toward the refinery again, but could barely see the fires. Thick smoke and dust covered much ground area, and the winds created by the inferno were blowing the heated foul air into the tower. He wondered about the firemen earlier standing so near.

"It's them! That train!" Joe shouted into the room's madness.

"Give me that microphone!" Manchester said in a fury, and grabbed it before Frank could make a move. "9039, you sons of bitches! You murdering dogs! Blew up another tank, did ya? Killed a man, and who knows how many more? Why, you bastards? We cleared your track! Ahhh--" Manchester was too mad to say more. But he spoke what was on all of their minds.

The radio also was silent, and then came to life with a voice that was strangely familiar, deep, slightly accented. Where had Frank heard it?

"This is 9039. We exploded no more bombs. You're giving us green lights and clear tracks, and we travel peacefully. Our group did NOT set off another bomb. A tank must have blown itself up from heat."

"What do you want, 9039?" Joe Donaldson took over the mike again, and Manchester let him, kicking at floor glass in sheer frustration.

Frank heard a siren coming closer, but there had been many sirens going by on the highway in the last two minutes.

The train voice answered. "We're sorry for any injuries there, and deeply regret any deaths. But we're running this train to save a hundred lives every hour of every day. So clear this track now to Grand Junction, Colorado."

The dispatchers had guessed this westward leg as the logical path. Frank tapped Manchester on the shoulder, motioning him to follow to the map. The railroad boss shook his head sideways at Joe as he passed.

"Can't do that, 9039. You left our One-A area and moved to Subdiv-Four at Dotsero. That rail is covered by Minturn and Junction towers."

"You don't get it yet, Denver? You're to be our control voice all the way. You understand how serious we are. Unfortunately, you've been touched directly by that same hand of death that is compelling us. So you're best suited now to see that others carry out our demands."

"How can we, 9039? We're not radio linked with Subdiv-Four."

"Get on the horn, you ass, and tell them to green us through!"

"I'm not authorized," Joe said simply, looking back at Manchester, who merely nodded. Frank started worrying again.

"Who is this?" the radio voice asked. "Where's Harr--uh, the man we started dealing with? We want to talk with him."

Frank caught the slip, and cover up. They knew the other man's name. If he had told them in an earlier conversation, why cover up?

"He's left, his shift is over."

"Well, get him back in. He's the only one we want to talk to."

Real odd, Frank thought. Some special connection.

Manchester took over the mike again, and Frank held his breath, waiting for the outburst of anger. It was restrained.

"Look, asshole, you've made your last demand on that suspended kid. He's history," Manchester said calmly. "Deal with me, or you don't deal."

Frank was shocked. He didn't know the job was over for Harran.

"Save your fine family names for friends," the radio started again. Frank was almost bringing back an image of the radio man--those words had triggered a memory. "Now hear this. We will not start over with Subdiv-Four. We are on their tracks already, running under green, just passing Shoshone. First--you had damn well better clear our track to Grand Junction with them. Or else you will not only have two trains making one hell of a collision, but you'll have oil tanks blowing up in every State!"

Frank mentally noted--security checks on all refineries at once.

"Second--get Harran Winfree back on this radio within fifteen minutes, or we will bang a big one. It could be right under your nose."

So they did know Harran's full name, Frank registered, also realizing he might have guessed wrong about the safety of their tower. Note--security check this building, and this whole rail yard. Stop the traffic.

"Thanks for your hospitality, dispatch. 9039, over and out."

Click. With that phrase, a vague image of the speaker locked into Frank's mind. Damn, who was he? But first things first.

Ambulance paramedics bounded upstairs. Frank pointed to the bloody man lying in the glass behind a desk. Uniformed officers clambered up behind them, responding to the radio broadcast of an officer down.

Frank walked up to the detective standing by his friend. "You've done all you can. Medics will take over." He punched the detective's arm to get his attention. "Look at me. We need Harran Winfree brought back here. Did you hear the radio? They'll call back in fourteen minutes. If Harran doesn't answer, they'll explode another bomb. They're serious! Send these officers on Harran's trail. Get the closest car to his house. We'll patch the radio through, if you get him into a patrol car. Then call for a bomb squad to come search this building. *Move!"*

Though still in shock, the detective relayed urgent orders. Joe gave them an address and description of Harran's car, and four officers ran downstairs, radioing his license number and an all-points-bulletin.

All three phone lines in the tower were ringing off the hook, but no one was bothering to answer. Joe was too busy re-routing his trains, and Manchester had apparently run out of answers.

Frank began dialing his cellular while giving orders to Manchester. "At least get your Grand Junction tower dispatcher on the phone." The man looked down at the blinking phones, hesitating. "Just pick up the phone, press all the buttons to clear the lines, and dial out." Manchester ran his finger down a list under the desk glass, punched the line buttons, and dialed.

Frank made his connection, watching the paramedics working. "Director, we've had injuries in the rail yard tower. I'm okay. The ambulance is here. Another oil tank blew, knocked out windows." He talked without pausing. "The train is demanding clearance to Grand Junction. That changes rail yard jurisdictions, and we're trying to get their tower. Will you contact Harrison Fruehauf in Kansas City? He's president of this railroad aberration, and needs to be apprised and involved in implementing decisions immediately. We have serious bombers here, sir, no doubt about it." Brody started to interrupt, but Frank forged ahead. "Two more things. Get our best field radio tech to this tower, pronto. We may need to patch in police and trains. And send an APB to oil refineries in major cities to search for bombs--you may already have done that. The train alluded specifically to oil tank farms. I'm sorry, sir, I must take this other line." Frank couldn't remember ever before hanging up on Winston Brody when his supervisor had something he wanted to say.

Frank punched into Manchester's call, listened, then interrupted to take over. During the conversation, all three men in the Denver tower watched the paramedics carry the detective, strapped face down on a stretcher, but head uncovered. They negotiated him through the debris, over the desks, scrunching across broken glass in their path like clam shells along an island pathway. Down stairs, around one landing bend, gone. Their siren drowned out a few words over the phone, but the conclusion was satisfactory--green to Grand Junction, no stops. But one freight train could get to a siding only if the 9039 could be slowed between Chacra and Newcastle.

With trepidation now, Joe radioed the agreed message to the hijacked train, explaining that Harran was on the way, and their track speed would have to be reduced from seventy to thirty for that four-mile stretch.

"Damn it," Joe answered their accusation, "it's not a trap. Who can jump on a train doing thirty? The problem is your blasted short demand to interrupt everybody's schedule and get them out of your way!" Oddly, Manchester patted his hands downward in the air--to take it easy.

Frank now took time to lean back against a wall, picturing the man with the radio voice, the train's engineer. A big heavy-set man came to mind, hairy arms, smiling, shaking his hand! "Fine family--beautiful home-- thanks for the hospitality." Peter's friend, Monty Montropovich! In his computer files, former train engineer, in his home last night. In the crisis, his memory bank had closed too tightly for too long. Of course Frank knew this man, this terrorist. Monty had left--with Peter. Where was Peter?

*   *   *

Brody hadn't been able to get in a word when Frank called. As he was debating whether to go out to the dispatch tower to personally deliver the news about Peter's involvement, the intercom relayed a D.C. call. Brody pressed the innocent looking button flashing on his busy desk phone set. III's metallic voice was unmistakable.

"We looked over the list of suspect fingerprints from the junker car, before we sent them back to your agent. There are two railroad men, a few still unidentified..." III paused before continuing, "...and Peter Wayman, the son of your own deputy."

Brody remained silent and closed his eyes, waiting for the other shoe he knew would be dropping.

"I'll be on the next flight out. Pick me up at the gate at 10:53, Denver time." There was another pause. Brody didn't know whether he was expected to respond. But III continued. "Keep your hands where I can see them. I hate surprises."

If that standard Secret Service crowd warning was a rare attempt at humor, it failed, for Brody wasn't given time for a laugh, and was in no laughing mood anyway. If the comment was meant as barbed sarcasm, it succeeded in tearing into the flesh of the Denver director.

One more one-way D.C. conversation had terminated.

*   *   *

"Marion, is Peter home?…Well, go look!" Frank had stepped down to the tower's stair landing for urgent privacy in his call home. "Did you check the garage for his car?…So, you're going to be late!…Nothing's the matter!"

The door at the ground floor opened, and a man with a dark blue flak vest moved gingerly into the stairwell, seeming to look everywhere at once.

"Stay calm, I'm FBI," Frank said, holding out his ID card. The man in blue looked up the half-flight, cocking his head. "Just better reception here," Frank said with a forced smile. "Proceed with your bomb search."

Then Frank said quietly, "No, Marion, there's no bomb, just a precaution. Now I need for you to stay home and call every place you can think of until you find Peter." Her reaction wasn't what he expected.

"I know he's grown, and I don't give a rat's…" He stopped his tirade, and began again. "You'll just have to miss your Board meeting…No, it's more important to find Peter! I'll call you on ten-minute marks, don't be on the phone…I can't tell you any more, I'm sorry. Eight o'clock then."

The bomb expert brushed past on his way to the tower office. "Anything you'd like to tell me?" the vested man asked, pausing.

"I'll brief you upstairs," Frank pointed. He stayed propped against the wall, curiously shaking as the man left. This was FBI Agent Wayman who never lost his nerve, even when guns were firing around him--or at him.

Frank thought hard in the smoky stairway. The gang at school, family, Janet. Of course. Peter had that late date in the Springs. They could have stayed down there, the rascals. All this worry--

But Monty still is running the train. Peter likes trains. Stayed out late nights this summer, at the yards, he had said. Which train yards? Night shift, friend's name. Did Peter ever mention his night friend's name?

The downstairs door burst open again, and Harran Winfree lurched inside, helped by policemen whose fellow officer was downed. When he reached the landing, Frank blocked him. "Are you Peter Wayman's friend?"

"Yeah, why? Oh, Frank *Wayman*. He said his dad was FBI. I should have made the connection sooner. Pretty proud of you, usually."

The officer gave him a strong nudge.

"Sorry, I guess I gotta go." Harran climbed up to the tower door landing. He paused there and looked down at Frank. "Hey, Peter was supposed to visit me here last night. He sure is missing a show, huh?" He opened the tower door, and let out a gasp at the sight of the bloody shambles.

Frank was dazed. He looked at his watch--8:00. He entered code seven.

Busy. He cursed, and hit the repeat key several times. "Find him?"

Marion listed four places she had reached, including Janet, who had seemed reticent.

"So they didn't go to Colorado Springs last night," Frank repeated, then said very softly, "Please keep trying. 8:10 then. Call back and interrogate Janet harder."

His FBI radioman came running through the lower door and charged up the stairs. "Good thing they caught me on the way in, boss," he managed to say, breathing hard. "Where do you want the patch?"

"It's on hold," Frank answered in monotone.

"But the office said it was an emergency."

"Damn it, man, I said it's on hold!" Frank shouted, suddenly reaching out and grabbing the man by his shirt.

"Jeez Louise," the radioman exclaimed, taking a step back.

Frank released his grip, and apologized, explaining that the radio operator came back. He asked the tech to set up a downtown office link.

It was time for Monty to be checking in. They had met his deadline. And who else's deadline, Frank wondered, wearily climbing the steps to the crowded hazy little room. What a mess.

*   *   *

It took two centuries, plus three more decades, but the United States had finally created a crackerjack National Peace Academy to rival its War Academies. Night shift chief Kristine Zowadsky hastily turned over its Crisis Center coordination to Jennifer Crussman. Her haste was brought on by an intestinal flu bout Kristine was losing.

Two thin manila folders, color coded from night shift, rested in the Incidents box on Jennifer's desk. These *Threats of Violence--Future* called for review, plus follow-up day calls to check on resolution. One thicker folder also was waiting, color-coded red '3' as an alert.

On its side was a yellow '7' tab--*Hijack with Hostage*, and blue '3' and '5' tabs--*Bombing*, with *Bomb Threat* still immediate. A rectangular image was the bottom State tab, with 'CO' in bold letters. Surprising.

Jennifer glanced quickly around the old remodeled library, in one large wing of a luxurious early-1900's mansion. The burnished woods of the fireplace mantel and its life-sized carved guardian statues, the ornate soffits and floor-to-ceiling built-in bookshelves welcomed her back into times passed, as well as to her urgent tasks. Two associates were also getting a quick grasp on this new day's challenges.

Jennifer stood at her specially constructed study table with the high reading platform. She was a lavish blonde without trying, too tall to be missed in any crowd. She accented herself as a natural exclamation point with bright colors. Today's choice was a lime green skirt and seven varieties of fruit cascading around her long-sleeved yellow blouse. Yellow and white three-inch pumps completed her image, all intended to supplement her rather plain face, presently concentrating hard. The thick folder with the red tab '3' made her immediately uncomfortable. This much paperwork accumulated from an early morning event meant it was serious, or that it involved people with a history of making trouble, or both. She devoured the index page summary:

1.a.-1.f. Six copied documents provided background on illegal Denver events and the possible perpetrator of record, *Unite Surplus and Starving.* Group's claim to moral high ground argued that the beneficial end justified these illegal means, in turn warranting NPA's support in preventing further violence. Hijackers didn't want to hurt anyone, or be hurt, their communiqués said. 2. Situation Analysis, faxed from Dave Cranmer in Denver, with immediate intervention recommended. 3. Historical Precedents, summarized by NPA computers. 4. No communication yet from National Security Branch network.

"Lois, I want to hear the Grain Train recording, please," Jennifer called out to her assistant, the one nearest an e-mail PC terminal with voice transmit.

"Peeling you one," Lois answered. She had been studying the Incident Board on the south wall, and knew a recording had been sent over secure modem lines. Lois looked pure co-ed: dark brown slacks, beige pullover, white blouse and sneakers, cute expression, short brown hair.

Jennifer listened to Wilma Fletcher's tone of voice while looking at the fax picture and *Herald* bio of a pretty black woman. The newspaper had responded quickly to the new Academy's requests, as did most media around the country, for the school had earned strong respect by answering inquiries fast and accurately itself. The instant news processor world had its rules, which Jennifer followed.

Wilma sounded convincing, but her strong phrasing seemed almost rehearsed. No panic, no coercion, which Jennifer could detect. If the woman had been hijacked, she was cool, giving her captors the demanded report, plus much more in depth of feeling. This was not a normal victim's voice.

Wilma's short history revealed ambition, struggle for recognition, steady achievement. Reporters hot for a story were known to play voluntary hostage, as some from the Academy's own Journalism Department had done. It was not unusual to go where you must and do what you have to do for a byline. Being on the train would offer a scoop, even if arrested as *accessory after the fact.* Judges were leaning toward lenient sentencing under a tolerant new federal administration anxious for good publicity.

"How can we reason with this ambitious woman?" Jennifer asked, brainstorming with Lois and her other assistant, Steve. The Academy was becoming noted for creative options during violent confrontations.

"Give her a few more hours of limelight," Steve began, "with her name in newscasts. She'll have maxed then, have nothing new to say, and be looking for a graceful way out before she and the gang get hurt." He was sort of handsome, sort of tall, sort of well dressed, and had an interesting way of putting himself into someone else's shoes.

"Treat her as a professional," Lois said. "Ask our top public relations honcho to talk with her personally. Why, some students think it's an honor to have Dr. Jennings even say their name in class."

"What would he say to her?" Jennifer asked, pushing their ideas.

"Like Steve said, you've gone far enough, people are listening now," Lois ventured.

"You have captured the nation's attention," Steve added. "Stop, tell your story, then walk away as molders of the national conscience."

"But what if she won't listen to Dr. Jennings?"

"Then get her boss at the newspaper to listen, and say it to her," Steve replied.

"And if that isn't convincing, we'll get the president's press secretary to say it," Lois said emphatically, not to be humorous.

"Washington has jumped for us before," Jennifer remembered. "But talk is cheap. The train gang is tired of stale promises, and wants action."

A minute later, their silent thoughts were broken by a two-toned signal, causing all three to turn toward the large screen in the north wall's center, flashing up an image of the *Rocky Mountain Herald's* front page. The headline shouted "DENVER UNDER SIEGE," then the lead article scrolled down with big print readable through the library Center. Jennifer imagined Dave Cranmer in a Denver library, scanning the pages in for an update.

New information typically caused a scene in the Crisis Center similar to an anthill under attack. One associate began entering new names into the master computer's search and print routine. Another began looking through resulting printouts, dividing it into categories, highlighting critical parts. Jennifer sifted through new data, analyzing for rapid recommendations. Any visiting reporters just swarmed.

By 8:20, Jennifer concurred with the ailing Kristine's conclusions, and was confident enough to defend her positions. She would use the speakerphone network with her associates listening. This facilitated training, allowing confirmation of important points and later feedback, without diminishing her authority or the phone line reception.

Jennifer had the authority to initiate calls to key persons during crises. The D.C. intelligence network had not initiated contact on this case, nor had the NSB. So NPA was still flying solo, with plenty to do. "Lois, please connect me with Winston Brody, FBI director in Denver. Steve, got that list of our Colorado contacts who had a train background?"

*   *   *

"Chanto Kudjakta, my new friend, it is good to see you--but so early?"

"Sadrieh, I salute you, and honor your father's wisdom. A thousand times I hesitated calling you."

"It sounded urgent. Come in, come in."

"Ah, merely extremely interesting. I heard on the radio news of a hijacked train traveling--imagine--the exact route we laid out in our hypothetical rail travels from Denver last week. I'm so anxious to see if our network of contact points succeeds equally well in practice as in theory."

"Let us try. We know not how far such a phenomenon might travel in that direction before turning away, but we will toy with it together."

Chanto responded by folding his hands together in front of his face and bowing in appreciation. He followed his host through the tri-level tract home, stopped in the kitchen to have a cup poured brimming with coffee from a familiar blend of Indonesian beans which made the house smell delicious, and walked down the half-flight to the lower level.

One whole bedroom had been dedicated to Sadrieh's hobby as a ham radio operator. Monitoring and broadcasting sets covered with a myriad of knobs and dials and switches, microphones, CB radios with green lights running a search sequence for talkers, maps tacked around the room and in rolls leaning against walls and on the floor. These paraphernalia of a collector, remnants and reminders of trade shows and conferences, crowded shelves and desktops.

Clutter with a purpose, Chanto reasoned, to migrate the man with radio talents through his tall backyard transmitter tower into another world. A cork bulletin board held dozens of pinned cards sent from ham operators on the receiving end of Sadrieh's friendship broadcasts worldwide. He was, as Chanto had surmised, a most gregarious fellow.

Sadrieh unrolled one map marked "Chanto's Track," and thumb tacked it on top of three others. It showed in black marker the right dogleg bends they had plotted from Denver into the Pacific Northwest, with two call numbers written adjacent to the eight junction cities. In the spaces between cities, there were at least five more ham numbers. The longest distance they had gone without finding a checkpoint was the fifty miles from Huntington to Baker, Oregon.

The Shakespeare Group had debated using an Internet setup. But the traffic on World Wide Web had become horrendous, and excluded many truckers without voice capacities. Cell phone reception was too spotty.

"Now let us see if anyone on Chanto's Track is home," Sadrieh said, sipping at his hot coffee noisily. His short frame seemed even smaller to Chanto as he sat tinkering with his dials, saying technical names that Chanto didn't want to know. *If he had as much hair coming in on his head as he did into his mustache, he'd cut a better figure,* Chanto reflected. His rotund little friend, oblivious to the scrutiny, pressed down the microphone key to begin conversation, while pointing out for Chanto the town of Glenwood Springs on the Colorado map with a red laser pointer he had taken from his shirt pocket.

"This is the Sad Sack, calling Hot Springs Hermit, looking for a hot train, over."

The vibrator on Chanto's belt nudged him. He had forgotten the time, watching Sadrieh get set up. Now Peter was making his 8:11 call from the train. The 7:11 call had been received on time.

"Your necessary room?" Chanto asked, in some urgency. Sadrieh looked over his shoulder and smiled, gesturing out and to the right. Chanto quickly headed for privacy.

*   *   *

"Janet's upset, said she'd call me back. Nothing from Peter's sleepy friends." It was obvious Marion was miffed at not being able to leave for work. "Auraria College will be open now. I'll call."

"Try your folks also," Frank said.

"I don't want to worry them unnecessarily."

"Call your parents in Wray! I'll call you again in…twenty minutes." Frank stepped back into the railroad tower office. Another detective had just arrived, and two day dispatchers who were already asking to leave.

A battle of wits began immediately as to who was in charge this round. "That wasn't Fruehauf's number," Manchester spat out, glaring at Harran then at Frank. "I called him. He's never heard your name."

"Well, did he at least recognize my initials? FBI?"

"Oh, he's calling your boss. He'll get some things straightened out."

Damn, Frank thought, you win one, you lose one. What could he do to regain control here while Brody battled with the railroad exec?

"Harran, how can you maintain contact with 9039?" Frank asked the young man, the friend of his son.

Harran looked at Manchester, then looked away and spoke to Frank. "I'm waiting for your suggestions." Harran was definitely buttering up his outside connection, while his inside boss fumed. Career stakes were piling very high.

"We don't feel safe up here, Mr. Manchester. All the smoke and busted windows and blood…" one of the day shift newcomers ventured.

Their boss merely threw them an exasperated look. "Well, sit for a minute where there's no broken glass, will ya? We're working on it. Donaldson, at least keep the trains moving while you're on overtime! Leave the phones on hold."

Frank spoke over the confusion. "Let's play out this first hand. Is there any doubt as to where they'll go next?"

Harran looked again at Manchester, who in turn gave a who-cares look and motioned for Harran to answer, to tighten his noose tighter.

"No question," Harran replied. "Salt Lake City, Utah."

"Then on to the Pacific," Frank added, "to ship to the starving. It's insane. We've got hungry kids right here in Denver."

Manchester couldn't resist keeping his reprieved dispatcher on the hot seat by asking, "What's your best bet from Salt Lake, Mr. Winfree? West to California? Or northwest to Oregon?" His tone iced Harran's nerves.

"The shortest distance between two points is still straight," Harran said, walking over crunching glass to the U.S. map and tracing a line straight from the notch in upper Utah to the nearest bay in northern California--the port of Oakland. The red lines indicating train routes jerked roughly along that way.

"What if…" Frank paced a few steps, "…what if you asked if they want to be cleared further?" Frank studied the Western U.S. "Like Elko, Nevada?

That would dictate California for sure, wouldn't it?"

"Good idea," Harran said quickly.

"The more we know about the bastard's plans, the better," Manchester agreed grudgingly. The Denver detective also nodded.

"Harran," Frank gambled again, "if this railroad company can't get you to Grand Junction to dispatch, the FBI can--and further, if need be."

"The Road can do that, if Mr. Fruehauf decides it's right," Manchester conceded, striving for ground in his own company office.

"Well, good," Frank observed coldly. "Now, Harran, I want you to call 9039, and tell them--why don't you make a list?" he said to the young dispatcher who had taken cues before. Harran was already reaching for a pad and pencil--the infamous pad of phone numbers.

"Number One, confirm that you're back." Frank loved lists, especially when under stress.

"Number Two, confirm their clearance to Grand Junction.

"Number Three…" Frank grimaced at that phrase, while preparing to watch Harran's reaction, "…mention the name *Monty* in passing."

Harran's only response was one of surprise, and he asked the right question back: "Who's Monty?" So he didn't know him. That was a relief.

"I'm just guessing," replied Frank, ignoring the puzzled look on Manchester's face. "I want you to say clearly, 'I'll stay on as your dispatcher, Monty.' Then pause, long enough for him to correct you.

"Number Four, ask if he wants to be cleared to Elko." It took strong willpower for the suspicious father to then finish his directive: "Let's do it."

Frank's hand was on Harran's shoulder, Manchester leaned on the desk, and the detective and newcomers just watched, coughing a little from the putrid air. Harran contacted the hijacked train, and made the first three confirmations in careful order.

No response from the engineer. Inconclusive. Frank circled the number four on Harran's list, and the young man asked about the hypothetical Nevada destination. Again the speaker box was only silent.

With everyone's attention on the radio, no one noticed the reporter from the *Herald* who had quietly walked up the stairs to stand by the open door. He had learned from watching daytime soap operas how incredibly much could be learned by standing outside a room without knocking.

"9039, did you copy, Monty?" Harran queried.

"Son, why are you calling me that name?"

Frank scrawled some words on the tablet. "Because only someone who knew me would demand me as dispatcher," Harran interpreted.

"But I don't know you, Harran," the box squawked in answer.

Frank scribbled words again, his forehead beading with sweat, and Harran read slowly. "But you are friends with Peter, and--Peter--knows--me," as the words flowed onto the paper.

With those last words out, Harran turned and looked sharply at the FBI agent. What was this man saying through him as a radio voice? What was he implying? Harran's eyes spoke all those questions, and more, as he studied the face of his friend's father. But that face was without expression, after years of training. Only glistening skin betrayed the tension.

The radio was still. Frank pictured the man's big hulk seated at controls, while his tall son stood in the engine cab, concocting answers. Saying the two names was very risky, for Frank had watched the taping system link that radio with his downtown office for monitoring.

Harran reached for the mike, but Frank motioned him to wait longer, letting the silence sink in--and deepen--down into their bones. His FBI senses told him this was the moment of truth.

Finally. "Denver dispatch, this is 9039."

There was a pause. Frank didn't breathe.

"We want you, Harran, because you're trusted. You said you'll stay with us, and we'll hold you and your supervisors to that promise. Our mission depends on you believing us--believing that we will do as we threaten. Like the rules in the old Cold War--fear of mutually assured destruction. So it is time to forge that link of total trust."

To Frank's trained ear, it seemed the man was reading. They apparently wanted this to be exactly right. There was no mistaking Monty's voice, now that Frank was listening for it.

"So, no more name games. Yes, I am Monty Montropovich." The roar of the engine in the radio background became deafening to Frank.

"And our guess is that since you had my name, the way you got it is through Frank Wayman. Is that right?...And is he there?"

Now it was their turn in the dispatchers' office to exchange glances of worry and surprise before answering. Frank nodded agreement, and Harran confirmed the guesses aloud.

The next response from the train hit Frank hard, as if the tower roof was crashing in on him.

"Dad?"

Frank felt for the first time as though he was truly dying. His entire system rebelled, refusing to accept the truth. His head shook violently from side to side. He slowly pressed down the button to speak, and could utter just the name…"Peter." Then his throat was so constricted that he choked on his saliva, and he could only cough.

"Dad?" the younger voice said in concern.

The detective turned to get some water for the gasping elder Wayman, and saw a man standing outside the open door to the office. He needed to check ID, but first the water from the cooler. Frank drank from the cup as Harran spoke into the microphone.

"Peter Wayman, is that you in 9039?" Harran demanded to know.

"Damn right, Harran. Is my father all right?"

The whole bizarre hijacking had suddenly turned very personal.

"Of course I'm not all right," Frank managed to get out after grabbing the microphone again, struggling to clear his throat. "What the hell are you doing?" He lapsed into another coughing spree.

"This action is more about heaven than hell," the younger Wayman replied. "And I'm doing what no one in your older generation had guts to do!"

Manchester couldn't grasp it, and just started shouting. "Wayman, if you know who these hijackers are, then get them off our tracks!"

The Denver detective had changed his priority. He was calling in new information instead of quizzing the doorman, when Agent Smathers pushed past the reporter scribbling notes. Giving him a disgusted look, he shouted, "Who's in charge here?" and entered the overcrowded tower.

"Monty, you're the engineer at the controls." Frank was saying as sternly as he could with his raspy voice. Glancing over his shoulder, he guessed Smathers had been sent to take over, or arrest him. So Brody had found out first. "You're the one who can stop the train, Monty," he insistently continued, "and the lawlessness. Let us sidetrack you."

"No!" Peter replied.

"That goes for me, too!" Monty multiplied the feeling.

Smathers took several steps toward Harran's desk. The radio crackled again. "And forget Elko for now, Harran," Monty continued. "Just book us to Salt Lake City. Out."

"The director wants to see you in his office, Mr. Deputy Director," Smathers said loudly to Frank's back. "I am to take command here."

Over my dead body, Manchester thought, ready for an immediate jurisdictional fight. Harran still was shaking his head in disbelief.

"I need to make a call first," Frank said to Smathers as he walked past him in the narrow room without touching, then he stopped. "And Harran," he instructed the young dispatcher, "I am this man's supervisor. Keep that train rolling until you hear from me personally!"

*   *   *

"Peter? Peter, you're positively white," Wilma said as he turned away from the radio mike. "You'd better sit down."

He walked past her, opening the rear door of the cab on Monty's side. The noise of the engine doubled. He stepped out onto the catwalk, closing the door behind him.

"Is he all right?" she asked Monty. "That didn't seem so bad."

"That was the moment he's been dreading the most for this whole trip," Monty explained, swiveling in his chair to face her and be plainly understood. "Peter just divorced his father."

Wilma pieced it together: the career law enforcement officer, the authority figure, the provider of a secure and comfortable home, had just been rejected by his son--probably for all the world to hear. The statement was certain to cause irreparable damage to the future careers of both men, as well as shred their family relationship.

Wilma studied Peter through the door window, the wind roughing his hair. Then she got Monty's nod to place her urgent hostage phone call to the newsroom of the *Rocky Mountain Herald.*

"Roger Hargrave, please, Wilma Fletcher calling!" she shouted, and waited. But not for long.

"Wilma, is that really you? Where are you? You're LATE!"

She thought about asking him what he was doing for a personality this morning, but asked instead if he had received her recorded message.

"Yes. Have you been harmed in any way?"

"No. But the trip has just begun." Nuts, should she have said that?

"What is your destination?"

"Unknown," she answered decisively.

"Did they force you to go?" One of the most crucial questions of her life, and he just dropped it on her, as though it was stuff off the top of his head, with no time taken in planning for this first live conversation.

But Wilma found she was not totally prepared either for spontaneous interview, especially with Peter outside and unavailable for consultation.

"Mr. Hargrave," she responded, "I have a statement I'd like to read, if you'll publish it." She was pushing him to a commitment.

"We'll take everything you can give us, Wilma." He paused. "Can you speak up more?"

Something clicked in Wilma's mind, and she recognized the code phrase they taught her as a rookie in case of a hostage situation. It meant switch to using other code phrases to send hidden meanings. But she had thought the exercise foolish at the time and promptly forgot most of it after passing the test.

"No. I'm too hoarse." She did remember how to say 'not now' for 'life threatening.' Then she read as loudly as she could while still conveying emotion:

"This is Wilma Fletcher, reporter for the *Rocky Mountain Herald*, in the cab of Engine 9039. This train has been speeding away from Denver for more than five hours, stolen to make a heart-rending point.

"These American farmers who have taken over this train are desperate people. They are modern-day Robin Hoods who are carrying one load of our country's surplus grain in a new direction--the shrunken bellies of starving children.

"Since when, they ask, does the most prosperous nation in the world horde its overabundance and shut out the cries of mothers watching their infants starve? Since when, they ask, has our government gotten so stingy as to refuse a man a crust of bread? Since when, they ask, have Americans stopped caring whether families live or die?

"Surplus is still given to us for sharing, these farmers say. And America still has the biggest heart in the world, these men believe. They are acting only in that spirit, and plead for your support, people of America. Keep listening. Demand to hear these reports every hour, and to see pictures of this train still moving westward. Insist on your rights of free press, and full media coverage.

"Talk with your authorities, and your Congresspersons. Tell them that this cause seems just, and right, and these farmers are acting for you. Let this Grain Train go, to help the hundreds who need it to stay alive.

"You can keep us moving, America. Speak out now! For ours is meant to be a government of, by, and for the people.

"This is Wilma Fletcher, riding with America's surplus Grain Train--to end starvation," she concluded, and said no more.

"Got it all!" Hargrave exclaimed after a moment. "When can I contact you again?"

"Can't for awhile, boss." The engine noise increased suddenly as a door opened. "Against the rules. I have to call you."

"Check. Use the X.O.'s phone number. We'll keep it open for you." He gave her the number, and she said she'd call in an hour.

Then she added, "They're serious about more bombs, boss. Pass the word on. Over and out." Peter had come back in when he saw her on the phone, and wrote that message out for her. Then he had given her the *finger across the throat* sign to cut off the conversation.

"I'm sure he had more questions, Peter," Wilma fumed.

"But you sure don't have the answers, Wilma," Peter snapped back. "Not on your own hook."

"You had cleared the statement I wrote, Mr. Wayman," she returned in kind, bristling, "without any changes, I might add. And you did want an investigative reporter to cover this little junket, I believe."

"This is *no little junket,* Ms. Fletcher," he retorted. "We are totally about people dying!"

"Whoa a minute!" Monty suddenly said, turning in his chair and sliding off the seat to face them. He motioned for Fork to take over the controls. "You two young-uns seem to thrive on pushing each other's buttons. And I want it to stop." Monty stood with his hands on his hips.

"We've got too far to go," the big man continued, "in too close quarters to not try harder in getting along. So, Peter, concentrate on keeping us all pulling together on this mission, and give this lady enough information to do the job she has come to do--and some authority to go with the responsibility. That's just good management."

Peter stood in silence during the lecture. It had been only a day since this same friend had given him another dressing down. Dissenters he could counter, but his proponents? He turned the issues over in his troubled mind, team building while his own family was breaking up. Tension increased as the others waited his response.

"Monty," he finally said, "the Peace Academy made you quite a-- formidable friend." Then he smiled tentatively.

With that symbol, Monty was satisfied that the craftsman side of his leader was resurfacing. He returned to his seat.

"Hey, Grain Train voice," Peter turned and addressed Wilma with a sigh, "quiz me on the questions America will be asking."

*   *   *

Chapter Eight

Josephine Williamson flung open the screen door and hurried out into the sunny back yard, her apron in her hand. "Matthew!" she called out.

There was no answer. She called again, almost running toward the big barn. The dented aluminum pan hanging there rang out wildly as she hit the metal spoon around its middle.

It was three hours before lunchtime, so Matthew Williamson knew something was wrong when he heard the sound that was their telegraph. He missed the basket as he tried to put the egg into it. Splat! It fell on the concrete floor, as he ran from the hen house. "Coming, wife, I'm here!" he hollered out in her direction.

She pointed toward the house, urgently heading back there herself. "What in the world is it?" he yelled, breathing hard despite his fitness.

"Marion is on the phone. Peter's missing…no, I mean they found him… but it's bad…oh, just come in to the phone, Matthew!"

They talked with their daughter for fifteen minutes, getting all the facts that Frank had told to Marion.

"She sounded so worried, Matthew," Josephine said, when he got back into the kitchen after hanging up.

"With good reason," he answered. "Peter's got himself in a whole heap of trouble. I can't imagine what got into him."

"Well, I can." The elderly lady reached for the coffee pot, then pulled her hand away. "Oh, I don't want any coffee now," she muttered. "Just sit down, Matthew, we have to talk." They sat down in their customary chairs at the big oaken kitchen table, close enough to hold hands, but she kept hers in her lap.

The farm kitchen was designed to be cheery, papered with a print of various herbs. Morning sun reflected from the row of copper pans on the wall, and the breakfast dishes were almost done. But there was no happiness in Josephine's voice. "Our grandson has been upset for years over two things, husband--the people starving in our world, and our farm surpluses. It seems as plain as a rooster's tail feathers that the boy just up and decided he had to do something about it himself."

"Well, that may be, wife. But seems he already was doing more than most. Why, he speaks at all those meetings, and writes his newspaper letters. And they're still talking down at Jessup's Feed Store about Peter standing up to ol' Commissioner Overstreet out at the Birdwhistle barbecue. Now all that sure seems enough to me."

"Oh, you're slow as a caterpillar sometimes. Remember how peeved you said he was in Sunday School class when Clive opined we had no business worrying about some foreign kids starving and just needed to take care of our own. We should have seen it coming, husband. We might have been able to help." She wrapped her blue apron nervously around her hand. Love for her offspring was a strong trademark, and she hurt when they were hurting.

"I don't know what we could have done, ladybug. We're nobodies in problems that big. All we could do was what we did--listen to him, and love him." He patted her hand.

"I can just see Janet and Peter sitting right over there eating," she said, looking at the empty chairs across from her. They had come visiting again last weekend, sitting close and making lovey dovey eyes at each other at Saturday breakfast, but Janet was sending daggers by lunch. Something had happened, and Josephine hadn't found out what.

Matthew also studied the chairs. "Franklin must be mighty upset with his rambunctious offspring," he mused. "I wish we could do more than pray."

"Well, that's a good start. Let's do it." They promptly bowed their heads in silence a few moments.

"Matthew Williamson! God just turned on a light in this white old head." Josephine sat up straighter, and a sparkle came into her eyes. "We have just become somebodies. Our grandson has made us celebrities!"

"Dear wife," Matthew said tenderly, picking his words with care, "this is a time for sadness, not gladness. Our fame, if we have any, is built on Peter's madness."

"Hist, now, hear me out, old boy. You and I know Peter well enough to know whatever he's doing, he's acting from his faith. Am I right?"

"I would have to think so. It's the way he was raised. Finish your thought, then remind me I have one to tell you about the Lone Ranger."

She looked at him quizzically, but went on. "We may argue with his methods, but we do agree with his goals of reducing our surplus and feeding the starving." Matthew nodded. "And we don't want Franklin and Peter to end up having to fight each other." He again nodded. "Then we must get to Denver where we can help them listen to each other by faith," she concluded.

Matthew stared at the wooden pepper mill on the table, considering her idea. "You may be right," he finally admitted. "This is too threatening to sit here and do nothing. Marion would want us there, but she'd never ask." His thoughts rummaged silently again as he tugged on one of the old-time pork chop sideburns fanning out under his ears. His grandson called them *distinctive*.

"You said 'Lone Ranger' something," she reminded him.

"Ah, yes. Petey told me a peculiar story last weekend, about wearing a mask and taking control. He was watching grain cars loading down at the elevator with me Saturday afternoon, real intent, like we hadn't seen it dozens of times before. Talked about how small the man was as he walked the tops, not even half as high as the car or a tenth as long. Then he guessed you could stand three big cars on end and still not be as high as the elevator stack." Matthew faded in thought back to that scene five mornings before, when Peter asked him a question…

. . . LAST SATURDAY MORNING, AUGUST 6 . . .

"Granddad, how does that old hymn go?" Peter had made up an impromptu refrain: "From storage unto storage, our wheat grain shall be moved--"

"No, hotshot, that's not quite it," Matthew had chided, "but you're close to the truth anyway. Let's see, the words go, uh, 'From victory unto victory, His army He shall lead…'" He had stopped and hummed through it again before blurting out, "'…until every foe is vanquished, and Christ is Lord indeed.'" But the pleasure of quick recall faded as he had stared at the train and sighed, "Somehow we're a far piece from victory here today, aren't we?"

"Maybe closer to it than you think, Granddad," Peter had offered, with a little half smile on his lips. Then he had asked, "Did you ever think maybe we should hijack one of these grain trains, and just ship it off kit-n-caboodle overseas, so hungry people could make some bread?"

"Ho," Matthew remembered exclaiming, turning to eye the young man next to him. Then he had let a big grin spread over his wrinkles and had said again, "Ho! Now there's a radical idea. Maybe we ought to go get our masks and guns right now."

"Oh, the game rules are, 'No Guns.' Got to be non-violent with the people on board, so Jesus will give His okay to our stealing it."

*

Matthew smiled at Josephine. "I can still see the twinkle in his eyes when Petey said that. It made me laugh, and I think I hugged him. I recollect saying something like, 'And this is my wild-eyed college boy, out to change the world. Keep your eyes on the Lone Ranger!' Now it seems he may have been trying to warn me what he was about to do, and I brushed it off with a laugh. He did talk about using no violence, though."

"Well, thank goodness for that. Now if we can just get Franklin to abide by that. Husband, how soon can you get yourself packed?"

"A half hour, after I go back and get the eggs and put them in the frig. How about you?"

"I need to make a phone call, then forty minutes. Let's get busy."

"I'll call our neighbor and ask him to feed and water the chickens while we're gone." He slapped his knee, got up, and hurried away from the table to pack. She went to the phone and dialed.

"Felicia Montropovich, this is Josephine Williamson...my dear, you're crying...I know, Marion mentioned Monty's name. Our Peter is with him...yes, they're on the same train. Now we're packing to go to Denver right away. That's where all the news will be coming in. You know we'll be the last to know anything if we wait for the papers or radio here in Wray. I wondered if you'd want to go with us?

"No, no," she continued, "you would stay with us at the house. Petey's room would be vacant tonight, and hopefully we can turn around and come home tomorrow. There would be room in the car for Monty to come back with us too...good. Now try not to cry any more while you get ready. We'll pick you up around ten o'clock."

Josephine hung up and busied herself washing the few breakfast dishes, and thinking. Then she went into their bedroom to talk. Matthew was putting on his red and green plaid shirt, his reminder to all who passed by of his original *Irish clan*. "Husband, I didn't finish telling you what Marion said at first. Monty is with Peter."

"Montropovich? The retired engineer?"

"Yes. His wife Felicia is coming to Denver with us. She's upset too."

He accepted the extra passenger matter-of-factly. Somebody else was most always invited to everything.

"And Marion mentioned that other farmers were on the train as well," Josephine continued.

"From Wray?"

"I don't know, it could be. What about asking Dan Brown to call around here and see if everybody's accounted for? He should do that, since he's the Serv-U.S. chair."

"Good idea, wife. I'll catch him up on what we know and when we're leaving. Any other families involved can come up later if they want."

"Dan would have to make overnight arrangements for them at some motel or with club members up in Denver. No more room at Marion's."

"I'll tell him. Any other surprises for me?"

"Not right now." She kissed him on the cheek. "Finish your packing and make your calls. I'll bring you some clean jeans to wear into the city. Don't forget the chickens."

*   *   *

"And besides Peter Wayman, there's somebody named Monty Montropowitz who's running the train," the breathless reporter confided into his cell phone.

"Great information," Hargrave said, at once regretting giving a compliment to a cub reporter. "Now get back up to that tower office."

"Cookie!" he hollered out into the busy newsroom, and his assistant appeared at his elbow. "Call Henderson, Greeley Farm Bureau, about a farmer named Montropowitz who knows about trains. Then search our PC morgue files for clippings on Frank Wayman, the family, especially son Peter. Get a feature written; headline 'Under One Roof, Top Cop and Criminal.' Fly on this!" He turned back to laying out page one of the afternoon's Special Edition. "Call TV-5 again for photos!" he bellowed out, and someone reached for a phone.

"They were together Saturday, thick as thieves," Henderson laughed on the phone from Greeley, as Cookie prodded. "I heard Peter tell off the Farm Resources Commish out at the Birdwhistle place. Only the chow bell saved the fellow from getting pantsed by the crowd. Peter's quite a rabble rouser out here."

Cookie thanked him, and with Hargrave's okay, called names to their media partners. During the next hour, Henderson dug in his Greeley files for local items to fax for filler, then phoned that the Williamsons left for Denver--with Felicia Montropo'vich,' not 'witz.' "Now get this," Henderson reported. "The chair of Wray's Serv-U.S. is calling everybody, beating the drums for Peter's bandwagon. A caravan of concerned farmers and townspeople is leaving at eleven for Denver!"

"Holy cow, that's great!" Cookie enthused. "We'll label it a 'Caravan of Concern,' and ask TV-5 for chopper coverage. Listen, find out if national Serv-U.S. authorized the push. Keep in close touch." He slammed down the phone, hollering, "Chief!"

*   *   *

"Manchester here." The district dispatch coordinator had a full time job keeping up with the phones in the railroad tower office wreckage.

"Yes, Mr. Slethering, you heard correctly on the news. We are having a small problem with one of our North Dakota grain shipments…yes, in fact, I think several of your AgriNet Co-Op cars were in the string that was taken." He sighed, and looked at Joe Donaldson for a touch of sympathy. Harran Winfree had left for Grand Junction on a chartered flight. FBI Agent Smathers was busy with his own calls.

"Of course the railroad is covered by insurance, as I'm sure AgriNet is, but…it's awfully…premature for you to be talking about claims," Manchester chided the owner. Finding so many polite words strained his vocabulary.

"Both car damage and loss of product are included, Mr. Slethering, but…" he waited for a break, "but we are working on simply getting a replacement shipment put together within a day or two--no, I doubt if there would be a discount, since it is already so heavily reduced--no, that's between you and the federal government."

Questions of spoilage if the grain cars were recovered after serious delay, and losses in wholesale market prices were discussed and postponed. Then the question of participation in the decision-making process arose: would the Co-Op have a say in how the train would be stopped, since it was certain to be stopped?

Apparently, AgriNet Co-Op had been involved once before in a bizarre incident. A suicide had jumped from one of the grain elevators, complete with pictures in the paper from a farmer with a cpd Polaroid snapshot of the man falling right past their big green and yellow sign. The public had made the immediate connection, and blamed AgriNet for this man's death, and

Mr. Slethering was damn certain he didn't want these new nutty hijackers killed--with AgriNet cars crashing in behind and all over the front pages. "Damn certain, is that clear? Goodbye!"

Sylvester Manchester had decided he was going to his own office with his own secretary to handle his calls, and he told Joe to go home. The Denver police had left a half-hour earlier, and the bomb squad had gone, satisfied there was no danger in this building. The two oil tank fires still burned out of control, blotting the morning sun. The plywood to cover the broken tower window had not yet arrived, so the room was dingy everywhere, in the air and on all surfaces. The regular day shifters, contented with a negotiated hazardous duty pay bonus, were busily diverting all rail traffic to the other side of the river with the untouched Union Pacific dispatch tower and yards.

Manchester told Agent Smathers he could stay and watch if he wanted, but to keep out of the way. The 9039 was far from the Denver tower's radio control range anyway.

*   *   *

The Crisis Center at the National Peace Academy hummed with the Level Two investigation. Computer operators were briskly accessing databases within their restricted network. This facility ranked as the fifth largest electronic repository of personal data on the U.S. information highway, facilitating the Academy's job of "preventing violence nationwide through information, education, and intervention."

Jennifer's crew searched for similar crimes, to analyze their handling and outcome. Files on Academy students, grads, and employees were checked for Denver references and train backgrounds. They sought answers to why the Academy was singled out for the special delivery message? Did that qualify as a formal plea for intervention?

The school utilized specialty software to cull records for successful handling of hijacks and hostage standoffs, when non-violence had defused prior emotional time bombs. It listed today's phone numbers of terrorist negotiators on-call. It biographed the law officers coordinating the chase, predicting their moves. It was unlike any computer the world had ever seen, seeking peaceful solutions like a missile seeks a heat source.

One of the nation's leading computer manufacturers had proudly donated and installed the innovative system. Their chief of software development, Robert Contrary, personally worked with NPA programmers in designing the newest level of 21st century technology.

An *Intervention Team* was on alert. This group of exceptional students and grads was highly skilled in peaceful conflict resolution, at any stage of escalation. They believed violence, even war, could almost always be averted, and fair solutions found when people of good will had proper motivation, informed guidance, and neutral help in deliberating. They were so strongly committed they would put their lives on the line to save others, and they could be on their way to this new Grain Train within fifteen minutes. The news would flash worldwide that National Peace Academy forces were on their way, part of that art of gentle persuasion practiced by their Academy media backup.

The NPA computer network was dwarfed by those hundreds of potential information sources in the United States Government bureaucracy. Four Academy specialists were regularly assigned to monitor and grease the intricate labyrinth of official and informal connections with the awesome barrage of Washington, D.C. authority. Jennifer had asked for three more specialists, as she considered all those agencies that might be involved in this train hijacking incident:

-- The Department of Homeland Security, naturally. They'd be considering whether to raise the threat level from yellow to orange or even red, in the Western States or maybe nationally, based on U.S.A.S. fax claims;

-- The Department of Transportation, along with the rail freight industry, had developed a list of security actions and re-actions to be followed. Their decisions would be critical;

-- The Department of Justice would soon be swarming. The Federal Bureau of Investigation was under D.O.J. jurisdiction, with its own National Security Branch;

-- The National Counterterrorism Center focused on unprecedented information sharing with the Intelligence Community partners. Some operatives still insisted they wanted to know everything you know first, but NPA bypassed them in favor of those most willing to cooperate as equals in interest;

-- The Investigative Data Warehouse developed a similar centralized, web-enabled repository for information, and offered an Alert Capability for automatic notification of uploaded documents that met search criteria. Of course, some of the time the NPA would receive an alert on the very document which they had just uploaded. But it was well worth their time to scour the networks for latest data, and to insure in turn that people in the peacekeeping business had the latest to which NPA had access;

-- The Joint Terrorism Task Force used the Guardian 2.1 system to enter and manage terrorism threats, and share information. Unclassified data was shared with local law enforcement through E-Guardian;

-- Then there was the Law Enforcement National Data Exchange to allow rapid coordination among all strata of law enforcement, which was subdivided into Regional Data Exchange, further subdivided into State and Local Fusion Centers, all sharing information with anyone authorized who knew how to ask;

-- Another very helpful partner was the D.O.J.'s Office of Dispute Resolution. They had many years of experience bringing mediation into government office disputes, and had expanded to offer professional mediation services to disputes involving intergovernmental, private, and public entities. Their O.D.R. mediators served as excellent visiting lecturers and workshop facilitators on the NPA campus, as their calendars permitted;

-- The Central Intelligence Agency seemed to have eyes and ears everywhere, if they would admit to it and share what they knew.

And that was just the tip of the iceberg in official agencies on a huge governmental organizational chart posted on a rolling board in the Crisis Center to say nothing of the challenge in working with sensitive egos and frustrated geniuses in each office. But as a good neighbor, the NPA tried to do its part to add value in its daily contributions to the information highway.

The Crisis Center had its *Technical Teams*, one nicknamed Geek Squad, re-named the Nature Squad. They enjoyed spending lunchtime outdoors with chipmunks and squirrels, along with raucous jays, crows, and magpies. The timid nuthatches and finches kept a respectful distance. Pine nuts and sunflower seeds were the usual menu for critters.

Other techies were in the Marsh Mob, walking further to the wetlands at the edge of the Parking Lot Park. Its meandering creek with cattails and muddy banks was home to frogs, turtles, blue-tail flies, red-winged blackbirds, crawdads, white and blue herons, and an occasional snake or mosquito.

Part of the cost of maintaining the beautiful grounds and intimate touch with nature was borne by the Underwood Family Trust. They wanted to honor the memory of generations of service to the country by their families, in elected and appointed positions in several western States, Congress, and the Interior Department.

Currently, the two top computer whizzes were huddled together at a terminal in a far corner, one typing rather furiously at a keyboard whose screen was rolling rapidly in response, the other making notes as fast as she could write. Their Bluetooth devices were prominent on their ears. They were acutely involved in networking with Robert Contrary, who had logged in with an idea for a program change in the software.

Contrary was authorized linkup with the system whenever he requested, to work through moments of inspiration on a stand-alone beta test site replica of his original and ever-evolving creation. A cracker-jack programmer living in Broomfield, Colorado had been cleared by the National Security Branch to be part of this latest exploration. He had masterminded several Boeing experiments that were successful on a recent NASA mission, and loved theorizing in the virgin territory of computer-assisted peacemaking. It served to offer the same challenges as exploring outer space. One of the FBI computer superstars was also connected with their club work today. Theirs was a living breathing think tank, fingers flying, ideas meshing or trashing, futures changing, as they spoke in fast friendly geek-squawk. The NPA was always seeking out creators as well as practitioners.

There was a commotion nearby in the real world of the Crisis Center. "Jennifer!" Lois said in alarm. "The train engineer is one of ours!"

*   *   *

"No, we tried that!" Gene Valore and Fasma from the *Herald*, and Don Trujillo of KDNC radio had teamed up to cover the story, and now studied the hijacked train below them to the right, arguing with their pilot Barry. Engine 9039 had not responded on any radio frequency. Wind whipped their jackets in the compact Bell Ranger helicopter. They had taken the smaller four-seat model for gas economy, and were crammed in tightly with cameras and luggage.

"Wilma is waving again," Fasma said. "At least she recognized our chopper, and knows we're here." The long train was snaking its way through the fertile Fruita Loma Valley toward Palisade. Rows of peach, pear, and cherry trees in well-tended orchards stretched miles in all directions, making this Western Slope critical to Colorado's economy, with its three million bushels of fruit each year.

"She looks okay for a hostage, don't you think?" Gene shouted. Fasma agreed, zooming his 20x lens until her face filled the viewer. He snapped the shutter again. They spent more time in frustrated animation, using hand signals to find a common radio channel. Wilma just shrugged, then they lost sight of her as they dodged around a grove of treetops loaded with unharvested apricots. Next, Gene tried thrusting a number of fingers toward her, motioning Fasma to do the same.

Finally, Wilma brightened and waved a clenched fist up at the copter, fifty feet away. Then she held up one finger, six, one again, the clenched fist, then five fingers. The men clapped and waved from the copter, and could see the men behind Wilma cheering also.

Moments later, the radio crackled in the helicopter on band 161.5, with Wilma saying, "You guys came all this way to play charades?"

They all laughed, in touch at last, with the train filmed for telecast from the nearby Grand Junction TV studio. She informed them the train was cleared to Salt Lake City, 250 miles west, exactly as far as they had already come. Importantly, the mountains called Rockies were behind them.

*   *   *

"Can you believe a cow on the Interstate?" Frank complained, pacing back and forth in his director's office.

"I'm glad you weren't badly injured," Brody commiserated.

His banged-up deputy had a large bandage on his forehead from being knocked unconscious hitting the steering wheel, and wore a cervical collar bracing his neck after whiplash. Only the passenger's air bag had deployed in the crash. Frank had changed into borrowed clothes and sports coat, but still looked haggard.

"The E.R. nurse told me the Bureau car was totaled. Sorry."

Brody nodded. "So was the cow from the cattle truck spill. Quite a mess."

"We've got more than our share of those."

"I asked a fresh agent to drive your Lincoln in from the fire line. Thought you might need it here," Brody said, and Frank nodded a painful smile.

There was a pause as they approached the subject.

Carefully, Frank sat down in an overstuffed leather chair by the window, resting his aching body. "I got here as quickly as I could." He checked his watch. It was after ten o'clock. "Tell me, is the Grain Train still moving?"

"Yes, crossed into Utah a half-hour ago. Harran Winfree in Grand Junction said you gave some personal orders to keep the train rolling."

Frank's face blushed red against the new white bandage and collar. He sat up straighter, trying to think of how to begin an explanation.

But Brody continued, "Your dispatcher and I talked it out, and your decision still seemed wisest. I asked for clearance through to Salt Lake."

"Thank you," Frank sighed openly in relief, then hastened to add, "but Harran isn't *my* dispatcher in any way."

Brody studied the deputy closely without commenting.

"I don't know what got into Peter," Frank said into the silence that felt awkward. "My son has never...we always..." Words failed him.

"You have a serious family problem, Frank. I think your place is at home with your wife, planning how to handle this. And resting."

"No, sir, my place is right here, helping to get that train stopped."

"We need to separate job and family," Brody said in a firmer tone. "Only you can take care of your family crisis. All of us here will deal with the crime." Immediately, he regretted his choice of words.

"That's just what I don't want," Frank said resolutely. "Peter is no ordinary criminal to be trapped, doing whatever that takes. See, he can be reasoned with, because he's a smart kid. He's only a kid."

"Frank, listen to yourself, talking like a father. That's where your feelings are. That's exactly why you can't be objective on this case."

Buzzwords kept pushing Frank's buttons, triggering frustration with himself and the predicament Peter had created. "This *case*, Winston, is a few nuts acting crazy in trying to feed somebody," Frank persisted.

"And who, in that crazy process," Brody rejoined, "have blown up an oil tank and roadway, caused countless accidents, hijacked a train across a State line, and threatened more bombings." The Director kept up his momentum. "These *are* the internal terrorists we were warned would be coming, Frank. They're here! And they will be stopped, son or no son!"

"Yeah, now I see. Cleared to Salt Lake, my ass. You mean, funneled into that Utah wasteland and total FBI jurisdiction. Set up a road block..." he stuttered, "...a de-rail in the desert, or incinerate the cab as they roar by. That is just not acceptable!" Frank was striving hard to find proper terms and tones, but a throbbing head fought reasoning powers.

"Then provide me with better, Frank! If you insist on staying, work up a foolproof scheme to get them to stop voluntarily. I'm open to a suggestion. But it better be good--and fast--because III gets in at 11:00 o'clock."

"Please, not just me and a pencil and paper. Give me the case."

"So now it's only a *case* for you? No, Frank, your emotions are doing flip-flops. You can't separate things. I'll handle the train deal, and you will not, since there obviously is a strenuous conflict of interest."

Turning his shoulders to face Brody, Frank said bluntly, "We both have bloodstained hands, friend. I won't give my boy solely into yours."

"Don't back me into a corner. You know I go on the offensive fast." Brody moved forward in his chair, and leaned on one elbow toward Frank. "You're fed up with your job, and under tremendous pressure. But don't go overreacting on the home front. You and your son haven't been close for years, always arguing. Now he publicly rejected all you stand for and tried to teach him. Let him go. Just go write up some alternatives if you must-- then go take care of yourself."

A rejoinder was on the way up his throat, but Frank stopped short. He abruptly stood up, fighting off dizziness, fists clenched down at his sides. He saw Brody glance at them, as he also rose.

"I'm calling for a briefing in a half-hour, for all agents," Frank announced tensely. "And going home is out," he finished, striding stiffly toward the door.

"I told you, you are off this case, you stubborn fool. I meant it!" Brody shouted toward his departing deputy's back. The door slammed. Brody moved to his desk and pressed the intercom button of his secretary. "Tell all staffers to disregard any orders from Deputy Director Wayman, until further notice. He is not thinking clearly because of his head injury. When he hears this order and reacts, send him back in here to me. And...please treat the deputy with consideration."

*   *   *

"Milton!"

Peter's 10:11 A.M. call was prompt and curt, conveying only the agreed author's name. Chanto had gone to the shelter of his friend's bathroom again to receive it. He so wanted to tell Peter and the crew that he knew exactly where they were.

A ham operator in the remote village of Cisco, Utah, had radioed five minutes earlier that the train had just passed him. Fully two dozen locals had turned out to wave them on. Everybody in the train waved back, the Ciscoan said, then a helicopter zoomed by. Pretty exciting stuff.

Chanto's first-step plan had worked perfectly. By asking questions during open times on the radio, he stimulated the truckers and people in small towns to look for the train and report it to their newspaper and radio. Now the interest was growing, and people were calling ahead to alert friends and other road warriors that the Grain Train was coming their way.

After Cisco, the map showed the train would soon pass under Interstate

70, linking closely again with Americans on the move. Chanto would know almost immediately over the CB or ham radio frequencies if the train got stopped, even if Peter couldn't call. Then Chanto would act accordingly.

He knew full well that if found out, he would likely be deported for illegal activities as a protected non-citizen. However, he believed himself to be first a world citizen. If one part of his body was aching, Chanto told himself, and another part could bring it relief, should it not do so to become whole again? So, if this train began a long parade of grain shipments, he would have done his part. It was worth the risks.

*   *   *

"Hold on, please. He's just coming in from working on the tractor all morning, but I'll get him." The woman in a nylon slip and hair curlers called her husband's name loudly from the bedroom. She had been busy with housework all morning.

He picked up from their nearby hall phone. "This is Al."

"Mr. Federson, this is Julie Redondo, reporter with the *Rocky Mountain Herald*. May I take a moment to ask some questions?"

"Well, we're getting ready to go out for a fancy lunch, but I can take a few minutes. What's on your mind, Julie?" Al looked at the family grandfather clock as it chimed once: 10:15.

"We couldn't get Harold Swenson at Main Street Drug and Emporium..."

"He's gone to Albuquerque on business."

"You're spokesman, then, as vice-president of Brighton's Serv-U.S. Club? Last Monday night you awarded your Citizen Honor to Peter Wayman of Denver, and we ran a news item in Tuesday's *Herald*, right?"

"Five line news story on page D-7, to be exact," Al pointed out.

"Yes, well...uh, do you have any regrets now?"

"What? Why should we? He's an outstanding young man trying to help the farmers get a fair shake."

"But, Mr. Federson, with what's happened today with the train..."

"What? Hold on a minute...Mabel, will you shut that blame hair dryer off? I can't hear a word this lady is saying...there. Now, Miss, what was your question again?" Al was puzzling over her comment about what happened today with the *rain*, since it was a dry day, and what that had to do with a Denver college kid.

"How do you feel about Peter Wayman now?" she asked.

He answered, "Same as Monday. Couldn't agree with him more."

"So you support his latest actions, Mr. Federson, as a club officer?"

"Well, hell, yes...I mean, sure thing. Use *sure* when you're writing this up. I wouldn't want to upset any city folks with my farm talk. Anyhow, Peter Wayman speaks for us as well when he writes a note to your newspaper or calls on our Congressman."

"When he spoke there Monday, did you know what he planned to do?"

This lady is out of her gourd with these silly questions about what some guest speaker planned to talk about, Al thought, chuckling. But he answered politely, "Yes, ma'am. After all, I was his host for the whole evening. I helped set it up with him in advance, and it went off very smoothly, if I do say so. Just like we planned."

"Uh...umm...Mr. Federson, I'm kind of new at this kind of investigative reporting, so let me ask, may I quote you on that?"

"Well, hel...of course. Wouldn't have said it otherwise. You are kind of green--but we all start learning sometime. You stick with it."

"Yes, sir, I will. May I ask you another favor? I'd like to have my boss call you back and verify what I've written down, if you don't mind."

"Well, missy, my wife and I are stepping out soon, to do some long overdue celebrating. So I need to shower and shave and get dressed. Never know who you might run into. Why don't you have him call in twenty-five minutes, okay?"

"Right you are. About 10:40, right?"

"Yep. Nice talking with you...uh, Julie, you said? Glad the press is finally getting interested in our farm problems, and spotlighting some tough young people who aren't afraid to put their oomph where their heart's at."

"Oomph?"

"Action! He's a smart man with the guts to take some action! The Club is behind Peter one hundred percent. Our award says it all. Now I'm outa here."

Al hung up and headed for the shower, marching past Mabel's scowl. He was proud of thinking fast on his feet, and coming up with good words to praise their Monday night speaker. After all, anybody who can write letters to the editor like Peter did deserved more recognition. Imagine, enough nerve to have gone and talked to a state legislator last March, and a federal farm commissioner just a week ago. That kid's going places, Al thought, and waved to his wife as he closed the door. She was already dressed and waiting to go out for their belated anniversary lunch. "I'm hurrying," he shouted, "so stay hungry!" Then ever the old romantic, he added, "We make a good team, Mabel."

At 10:40 an editor named Hargrave called, and Al confirmed every quote, which Julie had dutifully and accurately written down. Al and Mabel chatted all the way to the Chez Wally restaurant and back home, never turning on the radio, and surprisingly seeing no one they knew well enough to visit with on the day's events. Of course, they went quickly back to outside chores that afternoon to take advantage of the beautiful sunshine, giving no thought whatever to checking on any news broadcasts. For they had news of their own: a thirty-year-long love match.

One front-page headline of Friday morning's *Herald* would read:
"SERV-U.S. CLUB FAVORS HIJACKING 100%!"
And the caption below the smiling picture of Al Federson would say,
"CLUB LEADER ADMITS PLANNING TRAIN HEIST!"

* * *

Talk was lively and loud in the boxcars. These last twelve hours were the most eventful ever lived by many of the eight Wray farmers. They wondered about helicopters over them or alongside, and how long the current one marked *Channel 5* would stay. Peter had radioed back that the *Herald* chopper had stopped at Grand Junction to refuel.

The farmers had been surprised that probably a hundred or so had turned out in Junction to cheer and wave. Of course a few gave them the finger, but they expected that.

They were already tired of being shaken back and forth as the cars lurched along, wishing they had brought even more pillows to prop between their backs and rear ends and the hard splintery wood. Their plentiful food supplies had been barely tapped yet, excitement replacing their hunger. By pairs in each of the four boxcars they debated and argued: How would the railroad react to the hijacking, and what about the State authorities? What was waiting at the end of the line for them as riders: a hero's welcome, or handcuffs? They called families and friends on cell phones, and debated and argued the same things, and tried explaining why they weren't crazy.

The blue-green waters of the Colorado River had departed their company at Whitehorse, flowing southward to the Canyonlands National Park to run into the Lake Powell recreational area behind Glen Canyon Dam. All they saw now was desert. The farmers in boxcars two and four had the doors open facing south. Twenty miles distant, incredible rock formations rose up from their own sand, shaped by wind and rain into the pinnacles and bows of Arches National Monument.

The air had warmed considerably after the cool mountains, gusting hot through the open doors and whirling dust around their rolling living rooms. The interiors were spacious enough--fifteen feet long and nine feet wide. The ceilings at ten feet were higher than in most of their older homes. The picture window taking up fully one-fourth of one long wall, reaching from floor to ceiling, did offer a spectacular view of the landscape. How could anyone fault such a room?

Easy, if that dusty room functioned as their entire home. The kitchen and bathroom and bedroom were all in that same room with no walls between. There was no electricity or running water. There was no glass in the large window, and to leave or enter they had to jump down four feet. Plus, their new home was noisy and moving all the time.

Ben Cody noticed all those faults with his Boxcar Three home, but still he relished the experience. His heart was right here in this railroad car. He and Fulton Skinnard shared the space, learning lessons fast--like never again would they put anything of value in front of the open doors, for one hard lurch rolled it out. So the pathway from the forward sleeping and cooking end to the rear windy toilet end was along the opposite closed side, holding onto the lifeline all the way.

Fulton and Ben sat and discussed the rule from the engine cab about no hobos. They hated to turn anyone away who wanted to ride, so long as the person had more than a two-day growth of beard. That would weed out Feds, they reasoned.

But how would they make sure there was only one extra rider at a time in their boxcar, so farmers would always outnumber the hobos to guarantee control of theft. Who would stand guard? What if two or three tried to board at the same time in one car? And of course, they had no control over the two empty boxcars, so long as the doors were open. All this was also leading to talk about teaming up together in one or two boxcars instead of four, next time they stopped. For *company,* they said; for *security,* they left unsaid. They were now a law unto themselves, since no authorities would be interested in protecting lawbreakers.

Ben smiled, remembering back to the furor Peter had generated at the annual Birdwhistle Ranch Barbecue last Saturday. He challenged old Mr. Overstreet, a commissioner for Colorado's Agricultural Resources Agency, arguing under the twin elms. Gathered quite a crowd...

... LAST SATURDAY, AUGUST 6 ...

Peter had voiced a bunch of facts: Colorado had 22,000 farms with less than $20 thousand in sales last year, so hundreds of Colorado farmers were giving up! With $70 billion in total sales, who did Overstreet think was taking all that home? And with expenses rising sky-high, twenty-one percent of farmland was earning more at thirty dollars an acre leaving it in the Conservation Reserve program and not planting it! And to top it off, only one-fourth were debt-free in the State's second largest industry!

Guests were groaning at the figures, and Overstreet was squirming, saying it's good to talk over problems. That's when Peter had nailed him about needing to take action, and got a cheer.

Overstreet had shot back, "Look, city boy, you're not your grandfather. You're just a weekend visitor..."

"Hey, Pete's speaking what's on all our minds, Commish!" Ben had shouted out, and others raised their voices.

Peter had spoken again: "The suggestions are simple enough, old and sound, and come from these people. Our farmers should earn a fair profit on the open market for growing full harvests. Subsidized regional co-ops should buy up a reasonable reserve for our country. International co-ops should buy the rest of the surplus to sell or trade to foreign countries for their starving millions." Applause broke out, and he kept on: "Subsidizing farmers to help regain lost ground is a lot more important than a little more deficit reduction! Let some of the futures' speculators plow back in some of their profits."

The whole group had cheered, except the tall commissioner. "That's far too simplistic, young man. We'd like to help, of course, but the enormous complications..."

"No! No!" the farmers under the elm had shouted. Peter had glanced over at another cheering crowd, where the lid was ceremoniously being raised from the barbecue pit, and smoke and tantalizing smells were pouring out. He held the leadership reins just long enough to holler out, "Hey, friends, the vittles are ready for us--are we ready to eat?"

Ben had watched the crowd switch priorities in an instant, and move away to the carving table where the first steaming bag of succulent beef was being gingerly opened up. But he had lingered by the twin elm with Peter and slow-minded Larry Shafner. Buck Bancroft and Gregory Smith had strolled their way. Carl Thompson, Drew Manchesky, and his buddy Fulton Skinnard sauntered up. Their talk was of ending hunger much more permanently than any lunch would do. They all had made arrangements

with friends to look after their acreages, if they needed to *leave suddenly.*
These were the Grain Train riders.

Only two had been missing from that group last Saturday at the ranch:
Monty, and the man he had gone to the Cimmaron Trail to round up, Harry
Blake, a sad wreck of a man drinking away his bitter divorce.

*

Ben Cody looked now out of his railroad boxcar at the desert, so different
from the Birdwhistle Ranch. He had wrestled hard and long with this trip
decision. Fulton was beside him, but the other hundreds of friends and
neighbors from the barbecue were far away, safe and comfortable.

*   *   *

"Everybody set? It's almost broadcast time," Wilma announced. This
cab routine had been worked out so that the men in the engine got their
necessary conversations finished, their last joke told, and could be absolutely
quiet while she called in her message. The roaring engine and clacking of
rails had become the signature of her broadcasts.

"Well, I don't know," Fork answered her. "Have you heard the one about
the black lady reporter from the big city who tried pumping the cow's tail
to..."

"Fork, I warned you," she said, wagging a finger in mock threat.

He snickered and turned back to his controls. She treated him good.

"Monty?" He gave her thumbs up.

With Peter she covered the answers they had worked out to the latest list
of questions Hargrave asked. Then she dialed the Rocky Mountain *Herald*
special number.

Hargrave answered, sounding a thousand miles away behind a waterfall.
He said he'd try to clear up the static and she should call back in three
minutes. When she called back, it was no better, and he said the operator
told him the static originated on the caller's end, maybe interference from
the diesels. Wilma and Peter exchanged glances--this was probably not
accidental. In any case, the line would no longer sustain radio broadcast
quality sound.

Wilma dialed the regular phone number for the paper, with the same
problem. So the Feds could claim they were not blocking the line, since
people could still talk, and anybody could have interference troubles and

dead zones.

They switched to 161.5, and asked one of their shadow helicopters how they were being heard.

"Loud and clear," TV-5's Donna Harrison answered.

"Could you record for me, and relay to Hargrave?" Wilma asked.

"Lady, not just to Hargrave but to the nation as well," Donna assured her. "Talk slowly and loudly so we can test you and tech down both of these noisy backgrounds."

Wilma started to object to less engine noise, but decided not to look too closely into the mouth of their new gift horse. She began reading:

"This is Wilma Fletcher, on the hijacked Grain Train.

"We've crossed into Utah, a State of wild variety. It can be lush or desolate, colorful or drab, but ever changing.

"Just now the sagebrush and yucca dominate the softly rolling hills. Their grays and greens are mixed on this palette of grassy plains with dull yellows and faded browns, and lots of plain dry dirt. This is somehow suitable home for a few cattle, roaming near the tracks or seen far away as brown or black spots. We pass an occasional antelope herd, and sometimes they sprint off, but usually just curiously study us with our flapping banners. A coyote lopes through the sage. There are solitary hawks circling, gliding in the gray blue sky of this clear day.

"But this trip is not for sightseeing. These men are on a life-saving mission, carrying surplus U.S. grain to people who desperately need food. This has to do with the farmers who ride with us on this train--men who would rather be riding on a tractor in their field, or sitting in a swing on their farmhouse porch after a hard day with family and friends, or selling their harvest for a fair enough price to last them through winter and buy next year's seed.

"American farmers have serious problems, and a representative few are riding these rails to give voice to their concerns. If our farmers are in desperate trouble today, then so are all Americans.

"The dryness of the land here gives way time and again to the surprisingly verdant valleys where the streams run irreverently, erratically through the countryside. Where the tall oaks, elms, and cottonwoods advertise they have found water for standing strong, signaling hope and life. As does this group of dedicated farmers and ranchers. Take heart, world; America is doing something to help.

"For Peter, Monty, and Fork in the engine cab, and eight other riders in the boxcars, this is Wilma Fletcher, and the Grain Train is still rolling."

After a pause, Wilma asked, "Can you get that out for the noon news, Donna?"

"No problemo," the TV lady responded, "but I need to cut you off to do that. Then I'd like to come back on channel for a live interview with you and Peter, and any of the others who want to participate. We stay with you to Green River, when the *Herald* boys get back. Over and out."

Peter patted Wilma on the shoulder for her latest success, as his public speaker side began thinking of his opening remarks. He could talk about farmers and equipment standing idle, with fertile fields unplanted. Or ripened grain with no place to go.

Or he could describe the devaluing of life by the government, letting hundreds of Africans die every day for a year, finally getting righteous and spending a billion dollars to send troops for a month. Then scurrying home so a weak United Nations' peacekeeping force could replace them, easing the problem off the front page.

But it might be better to be positive, he reasoned. Encourage every individual to speak out now and make a difference. Empower the generous American spirit to follow his radical lead. That was it. He would rouse the sleeping tiger, and see whom it chose to eat.

*   *   *

Chapter Nine

"Peter, help us!"

The radio went silent, as suddenly as it had sparked to life. Peter jerked alert from studying his map. "Where's that from?" he barked.

Monty and Fork were at the controls of the 9039, both looking behind them at the array of phones and radios on the floor by the cab's back wall. "We don't know," Monty answered. "It came so fast."

Late morning sun baked down. They were traveling slowly, since pickers in this last cantaloupe field had left the vines to congregate near the tracks. Five minutes earlier, the town of Green River signaled the same interest with a banner strung along the highway bridge spanning the wide river: "Utah Fruit Growers Support Colorado Farmers."

Fork squinted out the front window at the bright orange media helicopter flying ahead of them. The *Herald* chopper was grounded with rotor trouble, so TV-5 had stayed airborne. "Their copter's steady," he reported. So far there had been no police presence in the air.

Peter grabbed the hand-held radio, which connected him to all the boxcars. "Car One, are you all right back there?" Wilma held her recording mike toward him for action dialogue, but he waved it away.

"Okay here, Peter. Who called for help?" they inquired. So they had heard it on the open boxcar channel.

"Somebody could be playing games on our frequency," Monty offered.

"Car Two, are you all right?"

"Fine here, Peter. Keep going."

"Car Three, are you okay?" No answer.

"Car Three?" Still silent.

"Car Four, can you hear me?" The engines were noisily building speed, leaving green fields behind.

"We hear you with difficulty, Peter. What about Three?"

"Car Three, come in!" Peter radioed insistently. He looked back out of the cab window. No sign of trouble on the right, the side with open boxcar doors on one and three. But they were now on a straight-of-way, and he could see little except the flat edge of the string of cars.

"Nothing over here," Wilma said, looking out the other side.

"Monty, just hold your speed, no faster," Peter ordered, and opened the 161.5 channel to the shadowing helicopter.

"TV-5," he radioed, "can you run a fast check on the right side of the train, third boxcar? We got a strange call for help."

The chopper made an immediate bank to the right, almost standing on its nose in mid-air, even before the reply came, "Roger." In seconds, it was flashing past their engine at eye level. Peter watched it zoom back toward the boxcar, then hover alongside at an even speed with the train.

"Holy Christ!" the pilot's voice blasted out from the radio. "There's a terrible fight in there! Stop that train before somebody gets thrown out and killed!"

Monty looked at Peter, nodding a decisive affirmation.

"Boxcars, brace yourselves!" Peter radioed, thinking through scenarios, then lost his own balance with the fast braking and banged against the window frame, its metal edge flattening his upper arm skin and muscle painfully hard against the bone.

He regained his footing and looked toward Wilma. She seemed okay. He grasped the window frame firmly and issued radio warnings. "This may be a trap. The chopper says there's a fight going on in Three. People may be waiting in these river willows to board us as we stop. Be alert. Shut your doors before we stop if you can, but don't strain your backs." He thought how much easier it would have been for four men to move those huge slabs before the train started than with pairs of men now. The train had an odd forward-backward motion as engines braked and cars banged into cars. Clanking couplings and metal pads shrieking against metal caused an atrocious noise.

"You're going to lose one!" the helicopter voice crackled loudly.

Peter looked closely at about where the third boxcar back from the four engines would be. He saw a shirt flapping loosely from a man who leaned halfway out, desperately holding on. Peter watched helplessly as someone from inside the car hit at the leaning man. And out he went, tumbling like a rag doll down the steep embankment and thudding against a fence post. The television helicopter hovered, probably filming.

"Mark that spot, chopper," Peter shouted into the radio, "so you can go back to help--but stay with us!" He was now giving orders instead of asking. The heavy train was taking a half-mile to stop.

"Was it Ben or Fulton?" Peter radioed the two men he saw peering out from Car One.

"Couldn't tell," Buck Bancroft replied, holding onto the lifeline rope, leaning out further.

"Fork!" Peter directed. "Stay here with Wilma when we stop. Don't let anybody else in here." The train was still braking hard.

"I don't see anybody around," Monty said, studying the terrain. "But that doesn't mean..."

"Monty," Peter spoke to his friend's back, cutting off conjectures, "come with me back to the boxcar. Bring your gun."

"But, Peter..."

"Bring it! It's up to you whether you use it. But I don't want this mission to end because we don't have enough threat power! Fork, same goes for you. Use your gun if you have to. I'll back you..."

"So all this non-violence talk..." Wilma began challenging him.

"Shut up, Wilma. We're doing what we have to do." Peter snapped a shell into the chamber. "We'll try not to use force. But somebody sure the hell is! Monty, let's go!" Peter dashed out the back door. The train was barely moving as he climbed down the cab steps, ran the catwalk, and climbed down the rear steps, jumping off and running back toward Boxcar Three. Four men leaped from it, spotted Peter, and rolled under a grain car to get away.

Buck and Carl Thompson jumped from Car One, Drew Manchesky and Gregory Smith were crawling from the other side under their Car Two. Monty was right behind, but limping with a sudden cramp from sitting still for so long. Peter was in the lead, and could hear the sounds of fighting over the noise of the idling engines and throbbing helicopter rotors. Harry Blake and Larry Shafner stepped out from between Cars Four and Three.

Peter pulled himself easily up into the car. Two men, strangers, were beating and kicking a man on the floor in one corner, and another four were wrestling around at the other end.

POW!

Without waiting for others to get up into the car and break up the fights, Peter had pulled the small gun out of the holster he was carrying and fired it once into the ceiling.

The fighting stopped, as the boxcar filled with farmers. Apparently the helicopter had set down, because a cameraman was in the middle, turning a slow circle to film the occupants as they divided into two camps--neatly dressed farmers barely in the majority, and scruffy hobos with lesser numbers.

"Ben, what happened?" Peter asked the man able to stand. He had a bad gash on his head, blood dripping from his nose, and a mangled finger on the hand he cradled.

"We tried to keep them from getting on, because there were so many. And they got mad. We were going so slow we couldn't keep them all off. Then they just kept coming. It was all we could do to stay inside. How's Fulton?"

Peter looked through the angry crowd around him. Farmers were forcing the remaining six hobos up against the wall, leaning them against the closed door at a sharp angle.

A man was still on the floor. Wilma had come back despite orders, and was kneeling beside the form. Peter went over to the badly beaten man, past the cameraman filming right in the middle of what had been a closed and private group until moments ago. Peter knelt beside Wilma, and took the man's bloody hand in his.

"Fulton?" he said quietly, then more loudly, "Fulton Skinnard! Can you hear me?" There was no movement.

"He has a light erratic pulse, but hasn't moved since I got here. I found no compound fractures, but I'm worried."

Peter acknowledged Wilma's brief diagnosis, and stood up. Donna Harrison came from nowhere to his side with a cpd in her hand. "Mr. Wayman, what happened here?"

He ignored her question, and said simply, "I'm glad your helicopter is here. Can you get him to a hospital back in Green River right away?"

"We anticipated the need for *Flight For Life* capabilities. So we rented this Echostar Lifeguard copter from Centennial for the trip. It can haul two stretchers in emergencies," Donna told him.

"Good planning on your part," Peter acknowledged. "Harry, Buck," Peter pointed, "you know where you put the stretchers. Go get one pronto."

He turned to his other injured man. "Ben, I want you to fly back and get your wounds tended."

"Hey, Pete, I'm not that bad off. Just let me at a first aid kit with some bandages and a stick for a finger splint, and I'll do fine. I'm not ready to go back for jail yet, when the ride ain't half over." Peter nodded, expecting that answer. "Besides, way this is starting, you need my help getting this grain shipment through to the kids."

Peter let a small smile flick across his serious face. "Farmer friends, gang up here around Fulton. Monty, don't let those bastards move!" There was much hollering of "You can't do this" and "We have rights"--but the hobos didn't move anything except their throat muscles in front of the big man with the gun. Donna talked with Wilma.

Peter took charge of getting the injured man onto the stretcher, holding Fulton's neck as stiffly and evenly as he could. After a minute of quick conversation with the farmers, Peter spoke up. "All right, we're agreed: Ben and Larry will join Buck and Carl in Car One. Harry will join Drew and Gregory in Car Two. We'll close and lock the doors on Four and here on Three, after moving only essential supplies forward to One and Two. Let's get out of here in ten minutes. I'm not convinced these are everyday hobos who boarded us. They may have friends on the way.

"Now, we'll all help get the stretcher off the car, then Harry, Buck, Drew, Carl--you four get Fulton strapped into the copter, then help transfer stuff. Ben, get the TV lady to help you with your bandages, and get a cold pack on that head. Cameraman, get a close-up of this gentle man being eased down on the stretcher, whom these hooligans tried to murder." The cameraman looked at Donna, and she signaled okay. The cpd recorder was still running in her pocket.

Peter clicked his hand-held radio. "Fork, we're getting things under control back here. If you haven't already notified the railroad, tell them we are running very slow through here because of debris on the tracks, but not stopped. We don't want anybody joining us, or rear-ending us.

"Now, madam," he said, turning again to the TV lady, "I'm passing this responsibility to you. After your chopper has gotten to the hospital, you may return to the spot you marked, and pick up the other injured hobo to take him to the hospital also, or you may request another emergency airlift to come in for him, or simply call 911."

"Perhaps we could take both men in now..." Donna suggested.

"No! Fulton needs immediate attention, and your bird will hold only one stretcher and two passengers safely. The attacker must wait his turn."

Peter turned abruptly, leaned over and picked up a push broom from the scattered supplies. He walked over next to the wall where the lined-up hobos still leaned under Monty's guard. Holding the end of the long handle, he took a mighty swing with the broom and smashed the bristle end against the boxcar wall, very close to the hands of the nearest recalcitrant.

WHACK! The broom head shattered off the staff.

"I am so damn mad!" Peter yelled. "I could break some knees here!"

He could hear the doors being rolled shut on Car Four. The train was being secured. Fulton's stretcher was being carefully placed on the chopper.

"Cameraman, get a close-up of each of these six guilty faces, for if I find them after we finish this trip, they'll go to jail for attempted murder. All of you, turn around and look into that camera. Now--run out that door straight across that field up that hillside and don't stop. Get out!" Peter raised the sharp spike as if to strike.

The boxcar emptied of frightened hobos with angry mug shots.

Donna Harrison and the cameraman hurriedly climbed down from Boxcar Three, as the farmers busily transferred supplies.

"Thank you for your help here. Safe journey," Peter wished the TV pair, shaking hands for the first time.

"And to you," Donna answered back. "I still have a thousand questions. The main one, your destination?"

"Sorry," Peter said, "I promised Wilma she'd be the first to know." The TV crew turned and walked away fast, ducked under the rotating blades to climb back up into their seats, and the orange helicopter marked TV-5 whirred up and away on its mercy mission.

He watched them go, then turned to help shut and lock the door, and carried the last few supplies on the ground up to the next boxcar with Monty. "I'm worried about Fulton," he puffed, "and the other guy who fell."

"Tough calls, who comes first on triage," Monty answered, also short of breath. "Damn jerks. Just didn't understand. I'm sure from their clothes that they weren't the field workers."

"They won't be the last," Peter warned the farmers getting situated in Car Two. "Got everything you need?"

"How about a gun?"

"No. You're in deeply enough already without that. Let us help you close this door halfway." They pushed together, the farmers inside, and the two from the engine outside. Then they crossed between cars, checked the men in Car One, and helped close that door halfway. The odds were better now.

Monty signaled to Fork, anxiously leaning out the cab window. Fork blew the horn twice, the train engines roared to life, and the two men broke into a jog toward the lead engine. Truck rigs gave long blasts on air horns from a quarter mile distant, where they had been watching the stopped train. Peter and Monty waved toward the reassuring sound, but Peter wondered how many were undercover cops. Rocks and bushes had become bogeymen.

Monty grabbed for the moving ladder, pulled himself up onto the steps, and climbed onto the catwalk. Peter reached up and gripped the ladder handle. But when he pulled himself aboard, a sharp pain in his arm from hitting the window reminded him of what a fragile bond they all held with life. He wished for Janet at that moment, and thought of calling her, but he knew he wouldn't involve her that way. He glanced at his watch. It was 11:30. He had just missed his call series to the Shakespeare Group. The codeword would be *Bunyan*, then adding *is on track*--to signal that the train was still moving, even though late--for a bomb explosion was hanging on every missed call.

*   *   *

Frank Wayman had never thought of his FBI as sinister, until it turned on him so suddenly. Regional Director Brody stood to one side of his own desk, looking down at Frank seated in a folding chair brought in for the occasion. The two high-backed leather chairs and the eight walnut conference chairs went begging.

Seated behind the desk was III, in Brody's chair. The third man from the top in the nation had arrived in Denver forty minutes earlier, and conferenced with Brody during the helicopter ride from DIA to their downtown rooftop. This three-man meeting was the first calculated result.

"I cannot believe," III was saying with zero emotion, "that any career FBI operative, especially one as astute as you have repeatedly proven to be, Mr. Wayman, would not have suspected something."

"I did not, sir," Frank assured the questioner. The cervical collar was too tight, and his bruised forehead was throbbing. His new plans for negotiating with the train rested on his lap. He could smell his own nervous sweat mixed with the dawn's smoke, and hoped they could not.

"Did you ever hold serious talks with your son about law and order issues, Mr. Wayman?" III asked rhetorically, not caring about an answer. Frank winced at an instant memory of their last father-son conversation, about a group stealing a truck for a good cause. He hadn't been firm.

"As I said," Frank iterated, trying to control his emotions, as well as regain some say in the crisis, "Peter never gave any indication that he was capable of such an act, or even of conceiving such action."

"Come now, Mr. Wayman, let's not mince words." III leaned forward, his tweed sport coat, beige shirt, and brown paisley tie boasting irreproachable taste. "This train hijacking is neither merely an *act* nor an *action*, as you suggest. It is a series of federal crimes of gravest magnitude."

Frank blanched as III continued. "It is an indefensible breaking of the legitimate rules of interstate commerce and property ownership. And it is most blatantly a rejection of all this office stands for, as well as a total indictment of the teachings of a weak, ineffective, putrid father."

Frank tasted blood, realized he had bitten into his lip, and said nothing. He looked up at his friend, who stood speechless, undefending.

Impossibly, the buzzer sounded on Brody's phone. III shot an annoyed look at the man whose desk he now commanded.

"Mr. Brody, I'm sorry to interrupt," his secretary's voice began, "but Mrs. Wayman is on the deputy director's line, and says it's absolutely urgent." A flashing light showed which line was holding. Without a word, III pressed the button, putting the caller on speakerphone.

"Frank?" the worried voice of a woman said, "I'm going crazy here!"

Frank stood up, glaring hard into Brody's eyes, accusing him wordlessly of allowing this intrusion into his privacy. His negotiation plan fell to the floor from his lap. When Frank reached for the receiver, III reached it first and put his index finger on top of it.

"Frank? Are you there? Why don't you answer me?"

Frustrated, Frank finally spoke into the icy air of the executive office. "Marion, I'm in conference." He knew she would know from the echo of his voice that she was being heard over a phone's loudspeaker.

"Well, that's just too bad. I need to talk." She surprisingly surged on. "There's a TV-5 truck outside and the camera crew is filming the house. A *Herald* car is parked in front and their man is at the door."

Her rapid-fire list prevented him from stopping her. "There's an unmarked car that two men got out of and came and demanded entrance to search Peter's room. They flashed their goddam FBI cards at me. At *me!* I've never seen them before..."

"Be calm, Marion, I'll call you..." Frank tried to interrupt.

"...and I know everybody in your office."

"Marion!" Frank's tone stopped her. "Hang up now!" he ordered very firmly. "I will call you right back." The phone went dead. "So you're bringing in outside surveillance? To investigate my son? In my own home?" He aimed his fury at Brody, turning his back on III.

"Headquarters felt we needed complete objectivity, Frank," Brody finally broke his silence. "I'm sure you can understand that."

"Without informing me? So I could prepare her?" he asked incredulously.

III spoke from the chair. "She might have destroyed evidence,

Wayman."

"You're a sick person, III," Frank said while spinning around, pushing aside warning bells that normally inhibit a person from name-calling the boss of their boss. "You don't care about a father dying inside, because of his son's stupidity. You sit in a big chair that isn't even yours, with the gall to accuse me of co-conspiracy? Where the hell do you get off?"

Winston Brody had grabbed hold of Frank's arm and now roughly escorted him out of the office, speaking so loudly that neither Frank nor III could easily fling the words of termination that were so close to the surface. Their shoes scuffled roughly across Frank's negotiation plan fallen on the carpet, ripping the copies, crumpling paper.

Astonished employees watched Brody physically force his deputy toward his own office. "Now call your wife! Then go home! We'll talk later!" Brody shouted, slamming Frank's door, and heading back for his own occupied office. No one spoke as he passed.

"Pull that damn Smathers back in here," he hissed to his secretary. "And don't put *any* of my calls through when III is in there--only his!"

*   *   *

"Hurry up with the camera--any angle to start, then move." The two men jumped from the TV-5 van parked hastily at a two-story tan brick house and hustled up the walk toward a college-age beauty standing on the porch. She held the windowed storm door open as if to protect her escape route back inside. A white, short-sleeved blouse and pink shorts and socks showed off a finely tanned figure.

The older lady standing on the top step pointed a small KDNC-Radio microphone, already interviewing on live feed to the station. She had given TV-5 a co-op courtesy call when the name and address surfaced: Janet Binghamton.

"And when did you last see Peter Wayman?" the lady inquired.

"Last night, about 8:30, right here on the porch."

The TV cameraman immediately began backing up while still filming, to give a depth perspective of the rendezvous spot.

"Did he mention his hijacking plans, Miss Binghamton?" the Channel 5 man bluntly asked his first question.

"Just where did you people get my name?" The interview reversed.

The lady was first to answer. "Once Peter's name became public knowledge, we began looking into his background. Several persons at

Auraria mentioned he was dating the junior class president. Here we are."

"KDNC and KTAD and the *Herald* are working together on this, since a reporter was also kidnapped," the TV man added. "Did you know of his hijacking plans?" An affirmative answer would make her an accomplice.

"No, I didn't. If I had, I would have strongly discouraged him."

"Then you don't approve of his actions?"

"Certainly not. He is not the man I thought he was."

"In what way, Miss Binghamton?" the lady asked, playing on any possible innuendoes. Her former radio boss Ron Slider had counted on just this experience when he called her out of retirement two hours before.

"I thought he was a law-abiding student with a promising future."

"Were you two planning a future together?" she pushed.

"We had talked, or tried to," the young girl said, rather wistfully it seemed, "but we're just friends."

"No serious romance yet?" the TV man bluntly phrased his loaded question, and his cameraman zoomed in to capture her emotion.

She smiled before answering, and gave a flip of the raven black hair curling softly over her shoulders. "Not much. He missed a great chance."

"Past or future?" No response.

"What kind of person is he, Miss?"

"Outgoing, churchy, driven by his causes. Good public speaker."

"Was he well-liked at Auraria College?"

"Sure, by his followers." The TV man added that to his scribbled notes. "The men in my dad's Serv-U.S. Club seemed enamored too. And the farmers in Wray couldn't get enough of him."

"Spent lots of time with men, huh? How'd he get along with women?"

"I don't know. I don't think he dated much."

"Do you have any doubts as to his sexual preference?" the man asked. This was one area that, rightly or wrongly, built ratings.

"Oh...," she hesitated, taking a moment to review the memory of his rejection of her offer in the hayloft at the farm. For once both reporters let silence hang in the warm air, hopefully making their subject feel compelled to say more. "I think he really wanted me, but was too much the gentleman... or still a kind boy...I'm saying too much." Longing tinged her tones.

"Has Frank Wayman, or his family, contacted you today?"

"Yes, his mother called early this morning to see if I knew where Peter was. He had told them he was going out with me last night..." A teardrop rolling down her cheek caught the sunlight. "I just hurt for him, and I'm trying to figure all this out myself. Listen, I really don't want to answer more questions. Good luck in your story...or something..."

Both reporters thanked her sincerely, and she stepped back inside and shut the door. The lady waved to her peers, and left at once for her next stop, while the two men began a recap with the comfortable home as background, broadcasting live on *Special Report.*

"And with those words of pain, Janet Binghamton, the one-time companion of train hijacker Peter Wayman closed the door to puzzle out their unusual relationship. The beautiful girl had few good things to say about him, even indicating a question as to his sexual preferences." He glanced down at his notes, deciding to emphasize the risqué he had been listening for, and had heard.

"She characterized him as a boy who lied to his parents. She said other men were *enamored* with him, and that he didn't want *her* when given the chance. This gives us a further glimpse into the peculiarities of this FBI fugitive. Anchorteam, back to you." The two men wrapped it up, and headed for the next name on their list.

*   *   *

"Until this is over, see to it that your deputy doesn't return to the office, or communicate with any of the agents, except those who will be interrogating him."

III was lecturing Brody unnecessarily, for Denver's FBI boss knew his job well. And III was doing it in front of Oliver Laurel, Colorado's Chief of Homeland Security, who had excused himself from a meeting and greeted them at DIA. They walked from the helicopter shuttle pad in the VIP parking lot, a mere hour since III had arrived here. III had seen quite enough of the Denver operation.

"Wayman would not be useful on any assignment while his kid is running loose. We'll make a head office evaluation in a few days on whether he'll be able to return to service, and if so, when, and in what capacity.

"I want that search warrant served immediately, and a thorough sweep made of the suspect's house. You know the drill." III had a way of knocking his subordinates down, then jerking them up and dusting them off. "Wayman and his wife should be brought in for at least two hours of questioning, probably at the nearest police station. Keep him out of our hair, but turn up the heat fast, then call me with answers."

The regional director would have to work quickly to save his friend's career. It would not be an easy task, since III had prejudged him already.

Brody knew that Peter was cut from very different cloth than his father. Frank had been one of his best agents and administrators. Besides, no one was groomed to take Frank's place, and Brody didn't want to spend his final two years training a replacement.

III and Laurel were intently discussing the railroad company's part in their strategic planning. Together they entered the terminal and walked toward the large trees in the hectic atrium area, near the metal detectors, tightened T.S.A. security, and escalators leading downstairs to the conveyor trains. Because of the nearby bombings and U.S.A.S. threats, Laurel and Homeland Security had raised DIA's alert status to *High Orange.* They desperately hoped to avoid the absolute chaos that a *Red Alert* might cause. Frustrated delayed passengers were already openly angry.

"We'll fax into your Situation Room in Salt Lake," Brody confirmed to III, when there was a break in conversation.

"My assistant should have the room ready when I arrive at 2:30."

Brody took the reference to readiness as a poorly veiled insult to Denver's base office, which was lacking in early facts and instant railroad contacts. Of course Salt Lake would be ready, since that office had three more hours to work on it.

"Is the train's cellular messed up?" III asked. Brody affirmed.

"I wish our operatives were in place on the road or train. We should have moved faster. But I still expect us to have this resolved before evening," III predicted. "Don't you concur, Laurel?" And not surprisingly, the Homeland Security Chief nodded very positively, never having faced anything of this magnitude. "Remember," III said, stopping to put his index fingertip near Brody's tie, "Agent Wayman stays all the way out until I give you personal clearance to bring him back. He's high security risk."

Brody thought of protesting, making a counter-argument, but didn't. III was in no mood for reason.

DIA's Chief Security Officer as well as the Denver Police Chief in charge of DIA's police contingent joined the group as they walked briskly. The DIA men offered the comfort of the Security Lounge if they wished. III didn't. Then they offered a quick tour of their new ultra secure communications center. III informed them that he had already been briefed with pictures. And, no, he wasn't hungry.

They continued across the enclosed pedestrian bridge over one broad taxiway, walking past very long lines of travelers waiting to go through the tightened security check, flashing badges at the T.S.A. Officers, then proceeding toward Concourse A.

The last thing III instructed during this grandiose solitary strategy session was to keep his presence in Denver and Salt Lake moderately secret, and to downplay the level of importance the head office placed on this isolated Denver aberration. Then it was nearing time for III's VIP boarding at 12:30, with a scheduled 1:00 P.M. departure.

*   *   *

The Denver TV Special continued: "Thanks to KCOL--Channel 8's help, we're switching from our studio to Boyd Tangent, their 'Sky Spy' in Denver. Let me pause to say publicly how much I admired your bravery in that dramatic rescue two months ago."

The screen showed the helicopter pilot, blue cap and headset, smiling, flying. "Just in the right place at the right time," he said.

"With the right stuff," the anchorman from TV-5 added. "What are you seeing at the present moment, Boyd?"

As the familiar traffic voice began, the underside-camera view flashed on. "We're thirty miles east of Denver, just outside Keenesburg. The first fourteen cars and trucks you see parading west along Interstate 76 are farmers, families, and friends from Wray, Colorado, a small farming community in Yuma County, ten miles this side of the Nebraska-Kansas corner. Those signs on the car doors were obviously hand-lettered: 'FREE TRADE,' 'FREE THE SURPLUS,' 'FREE THE FARMERS,' 'DENVER OR BUST,' 'COME JOIN US.'

"The story behind the picture is that this motorcade sprang up spontaneously in support of Wray farmers who are actually riding on the hijacked Grain Train behind Engine 9039, now in the Wasatch Range four hundred miles west, near Price, Utah. This is very big news in rural Colorado today.

"You can see the strange phenomenon resulting. Not all cars are passing on this divided Interstate. Instead, when they pull up alongside the string, see the signs and the waves and realize who's in those cars, their tendency has been to fall in with them, either in front or behind--and turn their lights on. So the group of fourteen has now become more than forty. Trucks, campers, motorcycles--all cruising at the 65 mile an hour limit down this highway. It looks like a long funeral procession--or a grand VIP celebration."

"It could be a precursor of both, Brad," TV-5 interjected.

"Yes, it could," he continued. "When cars do pass, they're zipping by. There have been a few fists raised by the passers, probably disagreeing with the train lawbreakers--as they themselves break the speed limit.

"So this strange conglomerate is headed your way, anchorteam. I'll be staying right above them anytime you want to take another look."

"For your information, 'Sky Spy,' we are being simulcast by KDNC and others, including USA Radio. So some of those fists you see below may in reality be hands of our listeners waving hello to you."

Arms immediately protruded from windows in the caravan, waving wildly upwards. Brad was pleased, until he saw flashing red and blue lights of two State Patrol cars coming up fast behind the pack.

*

The anchorman said, "Let's switch to *Herald* Farm Bureau Chief Henderson, reporting live from the farming community of Wray. Hello, Mr. Henderson."

"Hello, anchorteam. I'm here with Dan Brown, owner of Wray's local feed store. You don't seem to have many customers today, Dan."

The husky man smiled awkwardly. "No, most of the farmers are already on their way, or getting ready to head for Denver."

"This exodus has to do with hijacking the federal surplus grain train?"

"Right. A few of our locals are on board the train, and the townspeople want them to know we care."

"Does that mean everyone here supports the hijacking?"

"Not at all. Some are sympathetic, some are opposed. But I'll tell you, most are upset over the federal policies of buying grain dirt cheap and hoarding it, while people around the world are starving."

A tractor-trailer rig carrying a front-end loader passed close by in front of the store, forcing the borrowed cameraman from last year's high school journalism class up onto the sidewalk. Henderson had done some quick recruiting for the network special.

"Doesn't that federal subsidy plan keep some small farmers solvent, who might otherwise go belly-up?" the *Herald* man asked.

"Of course. But it's obvious that more equitable and vigorous trade policies would open other world markets, and promote higher grain prices. *NAFTA* butchered us, letting Canadian grain flow in so cheap."

"That's the *North American Free Trade Agreement*. And others say it's working well. Now, Dan, what do the farmers from Wray hope to accomplish by taking these concerns into Denver today?"

A faded orange flatbed truck loaded with bales of hay drove by fast, kicking up the dust on Main Street.

Dan coughed, then said, "Our plan now is to stage a protest. It takes a lot to get us stirred up, Mr. Henderson, and young Peter Wayman's boldness seems to have done just that. But once we're moving, we're hard to stop. It's time to focus national attention on this complicated mess. And we intend to help Peter and Monty and our men on the train to get it."

"What will you do in Denver?"

Several more flatbeds with tractors loaded on them rolled past. A few bystanders moved in to listen to the sidewalk conversation.

"We'll circle, like the pioneers did for safety when they first came here, and like the Indians when they were on the attack. We'll circle around the State Capitol, and the Federal Building, and the offices of our Congresspersons, first with our cars, until the heavy equipment can get there. They're pulling that all together down by the grain elevator now," and he pointed down Main Street toward the railroad tracks.

The young man filming followed his finger obediently, zooming in on the gray octopus arms of the towering elevator. Around its base were dump trucks and stake beds, flatbed trailers and pickups, parked in rough order.

"What's your goal in circling, Dan?" The camera focus returned.

"We're used to the out-of-doors here. We don't want to go into offices and meet people in comfortable chairs behind big desks. We want them to come outside and talk with us, where people like you and me around the country can hear plainly what they say they're going to do."

"How long will you stay?"

"As long as we need to. It's our future we're working out. Our Serv-U.S. Club here in Wray is making motel reservations for everybody, and lining up caretakers for the farms while we're gone."

"So Serv-U.S.'ers support the hijacking?"

"Our Wray Serv-U.S.'ers support our Wray farmers."

"Anything left unsaid, Dan?"

"Why, sure. It's going to take our gang three or four hours to get to Denver. If you are a farmer and live closer, why not take your own rig and equipment in and get the protest going sooner. You know as well as we do what the issues are that these crazy brave guys are raising, the same ones you're struggling with every day. And you know the people who are making the decisions, so feel free to speak out on behalf of us all. Look for Wray cars with posters on the sides. They'll be there by 1:30, if the cops don't get in their way. Come join us in Denver, all you farmers. Let's work together to work this out."

"What do you say about the bombings in Denver?"

"That may have been them, it wasn't us."

Farm Bureau Chief Henderson turned to look into the camera eye. "So that's the story as it's developing in Wray, Colorado, this sunny and serious afternoon. Back to you at the anchordesk."

*

The now familiar face smiled, and took charge briefly. "We go next to our reporter at Denver International Airport. Any change in the backlog out there?"

The television monitor showed throngs of people standing in line, sitting, milling. "No, as you can see from our viewpoint near the bridge to Concourse A, the terminal is still loaded with passengers hoping to get on their delayed flights soon. Three more bomb squads with dogs have been brought in to cover every square inch of this huge building, even checking all the supports of the exotic tent ceiling with binoculars.

"The concourses were searched thoroughly, and declared safe this morning. The Federal Aviation Agency and FBI are taking the train hijackers' threats of more bombings very seriously, and Homeland Security took us up a notch to *High Orange Alert Status.*

"And step to the window with me." The cameraman moved to the window for a long-range shot of the half-mile distant parking lots. "That's where everyone is forced to park. No one is allowed to drive a vehicle up to the terminal building. All luggage is checked out there in the parking area, then put into trailers for x-raying and dog sniffing. Passengers are then being brought in by bus--talk about delays and tempers! We're advising travelers to arrive four--that's *four* hours early, instead of the normal two. All persons working out there volunteered today for double-time hazardous pay. This is all part of an elaborate internal plan for handling terrorist situations. Everyone here seems nervous, since this is the first time they've used it. But bit by bit, it's coming back together."

"What is the mood of the passengers toward the train hijackers?"

The camera picture swung back to the reporter, with the passengers moving around behind him. "FCC regulations prevent most of those comments from being repeated on TV, anchordesk," he said, laughing.

Back in the main studio's control booth, there was a sudden flurry of activity. KTAD station manager Tim Timmerman was monitoring the special broadcast, and spoke up sharply. "Tell that cameraman to zoom in on the five suits walking by, going left, quick!" he said, pointing at the DIA screen. "Switch to camera one for news desk. Summarize or something."

Headset orders were given immediately; the cue person showed the anchordesk two fingers, one, and the red light lit up on camera one.

Tim studied the faces of four of the men now in sharp focus walking twenty feet behind his puzzled newscaster. Even though the fifth man had turned his face away, his demeanor was unmistakable. Damn, that is him, Tim realized--walking with Brody and Laurel and DIA cops, talking so hard right at first that he didn't even see to dodge the camera out in the crowd.

The man Tim recognized was the third man from the top of the Federal Bureau of Investigation. They had met once on assignment in D.C., and Tim never forgot him. His brutal reputation was itself a deterrent to crime. If he was in Denver, then that meant the train hijacking was getting the highest attention already at headquarters.

"Boss?" the show coordinator asked.

"Yeah, back to DIA--finish in thirty seconds." Tim would tell his airport crew to follow and find out which plane III boarded; if eastbound to D.C. connections, he would stay in control by phone; if westbound to Salt Lake City, he would be taking personal control. Poor bastards in the train.

"Boss, Salt Lake City, flight 368," the answer soon came.

Tim buzzed his secretary to place a call to their SLC sister station's manager. A few moments later, he was connected. "Mac, Tim in Denver. Been following our special on the 9039 hijacking? Good. Understand the train is four hours away from you. We're depending on your satellite relay for some great live stuff. Listen, a VIP is headed into Salt Lake International, flight 368, FBI's 'III.' Know him?...Yeah, all true.

"I just thought," Tim continued, "you might want to get your best interviewer out there to meet him, if he steps foot in the terminal. He can take lots of questions fast, if he's inclined to answer. Don't show a camera or lights until the very last minute, or he'll dodge into the nearest room and order your removal. Believe me, I know. My bet is that he's in charge of getting the train stopped as quickly as possible, and he's one guy who doesn't mess around. Get ready, the end of our story may be right in your back yard--and may be ugly."

*

From the studio news desk set, the scene shifted to the Mountain West Oil Refinery fire. A grungy girl spoke into the camera. Billowing pillars of bright orange flame fought with inky black smoke for control of the first hundred feet above the two ruptured tanks.

"One of the problems is the wind," she was saying. "Intense heat from two fires creates strong updrafts, and the ground winds are really erratic. We never know which way the fire and smoke will blow next. That's one thing keeping the Texas oil fire team from going into action. And that's why we all look like this."

She spoke loudly, for the roaring of the inferno behind her and water spraying under high pressure beside her was deafening.

"The other reason for the oil team's inactivity is money. The Texans know that neither Denver nor the State can spend more this year than they made in revenue last year, because of revised Amendment One. Apparently, Colorado doesn't have a million dollar emergency fund to guarantee payment. And Mountain West remains indecisive on their insurance coverage. The governor has asked the president to declare Denver a disaster area, and qualify for federal funds, but we don't have word yet from the White House.

"Meanwhile, we just stand in frustration and muck, trying to stay out of these tongues of fire. Firemen from four counties are working here, cooling down the neighboring tanks with thousands of gallons of water, as you can see..."

The television view expanded to show a dozen great arcs of water being pumped from hoses anchored in place quite close to the dingy unruptured tanks. The containment walls of earth built up years before around each tank now contained deepening ponds. The dirt dams had been compacted to meet Environmental Protection Agency standards, with heavy plastic sheeting layered within them to contain any oil spills, but had never been actually tested until now. They were never designed to hold a lake of boiling water.

"The refinery is trying to empty all of those nearby tanks as fast as the lines will pump the oil out," the woman's voice continued. "Some of the water from the fire hoses vaporizes in this heat, turning into a light drizzle on an otherwise sunny day. This rains the oil smoke and residue gunk back down on all of us, and makes breathing darn hard. Whoever did this should be...caught!" She had rejected several stronger suggestions that came to mind about damaging their masculine body parts.

"Over there," and the camera lady had swung around to film behind them, "are the command trailers for the firefighters, refinery managers, and Texans.

"Specialists from the U.S. Army Corps of Engineers are working with local hydrologists in another of the trailers to design a series of earth and debris levees along the banks of the Platte River, flowing only five hundred feet north of here. Some dump trucks with their fill material are already arriving, waiting for heavy bladers to finish the new road in the valley between the Platte and us. Apparently, the end justifies these means, because the EPA gave clearance to do whatever emergency plowing is necessary to change the riverside landscape and prevent spillage. When these old dams break around the burning tanks, the new levees will hopefully keep the flood of water and any flaming oil from pouring into the Platte River and contaminating it even more.

"The FBI and Denver police also have persons in those trailers, coordinating the search for other bombs. Squads are combing this place, looking like tiny spiders climbing the tall steel and aluminum webs of ladders and catwalks." The camera zoomed in on a man working his way up a distant spiraling tower staircase eighty feet in the air.

"This is an ugly, terrible place to be right now, anchordesk." The camera returned to her blackened face. "We urge motorists to avoid the refinery area if at all possible. State Patrol and Denver police are immediately ticketing any cars stopping along the I-70 freeway to look at the fire, so drive on by quickly. Watch it on TV-5." The camera panned away from her and back up into the sky full of boiling flames.

*

"We'll be back to the fire scene shortly," the woman at the anchordesk said, unsmiling for a change. "But we understand the State Patrol is also busy writing tickets twenty-five miles east of there on I-76. What's going on, Sky Spy?"

The view from the Channel 8 helicopter showed a disorganized parking lot spread all across the westbound side of the highway, and a gawker's block on the eastbound side of the divided freeway.

"Interstate 76 is effectively closed to any through traffic at the moment," Boyd Tangent began, "just one mile east of Hudson. There are upwards of two hundred vehicles already involved in this traffic fiasco, so if you can take an alternate route and avoid it, you're the wiser. Someone apparently gave an order for the State Patrol to pull over one of the lead parade cars with a sign on it. Maybe they thought that would make an example and discourage or break up this strange caravan.

"But what happened is that a few cars passed the one that had been stopped, and then slowed down to pull over on the shoulder, forcing more vehicles to slow down quickly and change lanes. And pretty soon all the cars were jammed in both lanes and both shoulders and into the median, trying to avoid hitting someone or being hit. Far as I can tell, amazingly, no one seems to have collided--yet.

"But the State Patrol better forget about ticketing drivers who aren't breaking any laws, and get some extra officers out here just to clear this massive traffic jam. This is worse than any tie-up I've ever seen after a Bronco football game, or even the Blizzard of '82! I'm sure the officers down there surrounded by angry persons have already radioed for help.

"State Patrol, if you're listening, the easiest approach would be coming up the off-ramp at Hudson, and head east on the westbound side. There sure is less traffic there to interfere with you--except the eastbounders now doubling back over the median strip. Man, we're just begging for road rage out here. And would you believe it? All because of a Grain Train, which is hundreds of miles away!"

*   *   *

Chapter Ten

The media circus was performing in all three rings when Frank screeched his silver Lincoln into the driveway of his home. As reporters and cameras rushed toward him, he was grateful for the automatic garage door opener, which permitted a momentary escape. He honked three times to signal Marion.

She was at the side of his car talking before he could open the door all the way. "There was nothing I could do. They just came in. I'm so mad!" Then she gasped. "Look at you! Bloody bandage, collar brace! My God!"

He got out and took her in his arms. She held onto him tightly. "I haven't cried yet," she admitted, "and I'm not going to now. There's plenty of time for crying later. What's going on with our son? Why are you home instead of staying and getting it all straightened out? You smell like smoke. Mom and Dad are on the way. Does it hurt?"

Her torrent of words kept coming, leaving no time for explanation, as they walked inside the house from the garage. He purposefully buttoned his sport coat.

A young man in a dark suit stood in their hallway.

Frank had planned his first actions, and abruptly stepped in front of his wife. "Show me your identification," he demanded of the stranger. Frank took a moment to carefully study the proffered ID card holder.

"What is your partner's name?" Frank's tone was sharp.

"Agent Gianconi..." The man stopped just short of adding "sir" to his prompt answer.

"Agent Gianconi! Get your snoopy ass out into this hallway. NOW!" Frank Wayman was acting like a boss.

The second agent appeared almost at once, from Frank's office room.

"Let me see that ID, mister," Frank demanded, then scrutinized it and its youthful bearer. "Now, produce your search warrant."

"Sir, we are acting under orders of..." the nearest agent quietly began.

"I've been practicing law enforcement since before you two quit slobbering Pablum." Frank moved forward, pushing back on Marion's arm to signal her to stay still. At his second aggressive step, the two also took a step back. "I *am* Deputy Director Wayman, and I *am* giving you specific orders to get out of *my* house." He kept moving, and they kept retreating without responding.

"And as a private citizen, I'm telling you to stay off *my* property or I will most certainly have you arrested. Now get gone!"

"My briefcase..." Gianconi pointed.

"*My* property," Frank rebuffed him, pointing toward the front door.

"I'm not leaving without..." Gianconi made a move toward the office.

Frank put his hand decisively inside his buttoned sport coat, and looked Gianconi straight in the eyes. He left no doubt of the unspoken threat.

Gianconi turned and went to the front door, followed by the other agent. They left without another word, and without their briefcases.

Marion walked up behind her husband, and wrapped her arms around his stomach, hugging him close. He said simply, "We're bugged now. No more talking."

*   *   *

The Crisis Center had a full house. A Denver TV staffer and several other media newcomers were on their whirlwind orientation to the National Peace Academy campus, while Lois huddled in a briefing room with earlier arrivals.

Jennifer Crussman, the Center's day director, had recommended using an Intervention Team. Within an hour, a trained I.T. investigator had volunteered, and e-mailed a list of specific options to her:

"1. Put team members onto the Grain Train, to delay violence on both sides while reasoning with the hijackers;

2. Get teams working probable destination points:
   a. straight west to Oakland-San Francisco, nearest grain transfer port;
   b. down the southern California coast to San Diego;
   c. up north to Portland;
   d. further up the Washington coast, as far north as Seattle;
   e. either Canada or Mexico, but that seems overly complicated."

Dave Cranmer's call from Denver triggered another quiet alert: blue lights began flashing in the corners of the old library's high ceiling. As

Dave scanned headlines from the *Herald's* Special Noon Edition, Jennifer showed them on the huge wall screen. This was typical of their open file policy, plus all was now public domain anyway:

"Denver's Siege Ends, Nation's Begins"

"Wayman House Divided: Gangster Son, FBI Dad"

"*Herald* Reporter Held Hostage To Broadcast Demands"

"National Service Club Pushing Train:

    Peter Wayman A Hero To Brighton Serv-U.S."

"Denver Media Crisis Co-Op Covers Story:

    Herald, KDNC Radio, TV-5 KTAD Leapfrog For Instant News"

"Hijacking Without Robbery OR Ransom?

    History Has Few Precedents"

Forty copies of scanned articles started spitting into output press trays for eager reporters, while Dave on a private line informed Jennifer that his own regional team would meet at 1:30 this afternoon. She took time to give him inside details, since that often helped spark grassroots alternative ideas for consideration by the Academy's group of information distillation experts.

Jennifer knew this synergism among graduates around the nation was given much credit for the high success ratio. Incredibly, more than half the disputes were settled without litigation, in which Academy grads intervened as neutral third parties. This not only freed up court dockets, but the parties were more satisfied with the negotiated agreements, so deals were lasting longer.

The Academy had developed a long list of solid reasons for trying peacemaking, and shared them with anyone who would listen. In the tours given by credentialed students, this pitch was made for Appropriate Dispute Resolution. They explained that ADR succeeds when people get to know and trust one another, care about feelings of others in conflict, and get experienced mediators involved early to help all sides listen carefully. This was Jennifer's special role.

She told Dave the Intervention Team was planning to call the train around two o'clock. Additional input from his Denver group would have to be received by 1:45. They all were risking violence from the law at any moment, and shouldn't wait longer to offer the hijackers a safe way to exit out to the processes of justice.

*   *   *

Frank pulled a notepad from his pocket, and tore out one piece of paper to put up against the wall for backing.

The phone rang. They let it ring three times, listening then to the message from the caller on their recorder. Well, that reporter could wait forever.

Frank went back to writing the note, and she watched him pick his words:

"Bugs could be anywhere--we'll find most--looks like this:" and he drew several sketches of little boxes and circles. "No more talk, unless in your car. They probably got mine. Help me look for clues about what Peter is doing--before they bring warrant."

He tore off another piece of paper. "When are folks due?" he wrote, then handed her the pen.

She wrote, "Anytime. Mrs. Montropovich is coming too!"

Frank frowned at her, and she just shrugged her shoulders. He pulled out another pen, instead of getting into a pen fight. "Oh, great! Let's open a halfway house for families of hijackers! This will make us look even guiltier! Your job OK?"

She wrote holding her paper against the wall: "I called in sick. What about you?"

"They're trying to decide now--probably vacation. I blew up at III. That'll hurt--along with Peter's train. What a dunce! Let's look for evidence!"

"To save him, or hang him?"

He looked at her quizzically, and they left for Peter's room, newly aware of squeaky floorboards in the strangely silent house. Frank tapped Marion on the shoulder, and tore off another sheet of paper: "Candice?"

"Candice?!?!"

"Call?"

"Can't!"

"Okay. We'll just wait. Now--#1. Don't touch their briefcases. I'll do it with gloves. #2. Never write paper on paper, only wall or counter or tabletop. #3. I love you! #4. Always rip and flush these at once--always."

And true to his new rule, he tore up the three sheets they had used, and flushed them down the bowl in the bathroom off the hallway.

*   *   *

The Book Cliffs in Utah provided a sturdy meandering northern boundary after leaving Colorado. Steep escarpments of fallen rock weathered into sand made up shelves on which layered sandstone and shale 'books' stood, split vertically into a million volumes across the miles.

Fork watched the rocky wall move in closer to the train, almost imperceptibly, since distances were so great in this valley. He thought of the vast land, and the high cliffs themselves, engulfed for centuries by an inland sea. He studied the heritage bequeathed his century: merely desert. A place where death came and went silently.

Clumps of trees broke his reverie. Then more vegetation. The approaching landscape seemed habitable. He monitored his fuel gauges for the four powerhouse engines, and tapped one small glass window. He and Monty talked fueling alternatives, with Peter and Wilma listening. The basic problem: they didn't have enough to make it all the way.

"Where and when's the safest stop?" Fork laid out the dilemma plainly.

"Night will be most dangerous," Peter guessed.

"Mid-day hasn't exactly been duck soup so far," Wilma observed, recalling the hobo attack two hours before.

"Chances are, the longer we wait, the more prepared they'll be to make their move," Monty added to the difficult equation.

"There's another mountain range in a half hour," Fork pointed ahead to the Wasatch. "Hate to add extra weight first. We'll just burn up diesel to carry diesel."

Peter held his chin in thought, scratching his index finger across his stubble beard. "Fork, you've calculated our rate of burn. If we fuel at Helper, could we make the coast?"

"Which coast?" Wilma tried.

"West," the men chimed in.

The engineer in the fireman's seat shifted his eyes back and forth as he went through his mental calculations. It took a minute before he finally said, "Probably. More probably if we slow down a little, and shut off all but one going down hills, and use a few more tricks I know."

Monty answered Peter's eyes. "Shoot, Fork knows this road better than I do. I'll go with his best guess."

"Wilma, any womanly intuition?"

"Thanks for asking. I'm just observing, so you guys decide. Except..." she added, and they all grinned, "I usually try not to put things off."

"Well, in Helper, we've got surprise on our side," Peter began summarizing. "It's daylight, so we can see trouble. Nobody has put any demands back on us, so they're still putting their cards in order." He paced quickly. "We've got our full arsenal left, and apparently they've capitulated to our threat. Fork, how much of the new fuel would we burn off if we load up there before we start the climb?"

"Oh, say, throw away a tenth. And, yup, I figured that in."

"Helper, Utah, you've just won the honor as our fuel stop!" Peter affirmed loudly. "Monty, please radio Harran to set it up for us. Did you say he got into Salt Lake all right?" Monty nodded.

"Wilma, will you contact the helicopter to let them know. That's where they were going to make their relay switch anyway, wasn't it?"

"Yup," she agreed, mimicking Fork for fun. But she was also thinking how to use the mountain gateway stop as a broadcast backdrop.

"Seven minutes to Price, then the same to Helper," Fork said. "Our stop will tick 'em off, holding other trains back even longer."

"Breaks my heart," Peter said, as he picked up his hand-held radio to brief the boxcar farmers and warn them again about unwanted boarders.

As the valley narrowed, cultivated acreages appeared, and farm houses, and trees. The strip of community grew wider, soon filling the little valley with trailers, small homes, streets, stores. They entered the outskirts of Price, largest town so far in eastern Utah.

Nobody seemed to pay much attention as they sped past, Wilma realized. She worried that her public relations efforts through the newscasts might be missing the targeted heartland. But it was Utah, and isolated. Harran said he would arrange their fueling, and halt yard traffic. The helicopter flew on ahead.

Mountainous cliffs on both sides became neighboring walls, only a mile distant. A steady strip of population followed the tracks, and river, and highway. For all three converged and led to Helper--the town named for what it did.

In early railroad days, Fork said off the cuff, extra engines were stationed here to help push and pull trains up over Soldier Summit. Even as he spoke, the rail lines began to multiply, pushing the older pastel-painted clapboard houses and frontage roads further back to accommodate their spreading web. Their Engine 9039 was in the rail yards, slowing to a crawl.

"Is that the fueling rig we'll use?" Monty asked Fork, pointing to a metal tower spanning the track they were on.

"Yup. We'll need to shut all the engines down for safe..."

"Absolutely not," Peter countered. "Only the one being fueled."

"But we can fuel more than one at a time."

"No. We'll take longer but stay ready to move out fast. This train is already a huge risk, so a little more hazard won't hurt."

"You're jeopardizing fuelers here too, Peter," Monty protested.

"We agreed the trip is what counts. Leave three running. Please." He had been forgetting to use that friendship-keeping word recently.

Monty slowed even further, as the four cab residents looked everywhere for signs and sounds of trouble. There were people with hate signs along the far tracks. But their dissident voice was drowned by several dozen supporters with bigger signs. Reserve engines of black and white, and of blue and yellow, stood empty on other tracks, along with variegated rows of boxcars, and a caboose. Peter worried that each could hold a sniper, that every Helper breath could be his last.

"Does fueling take two, Monty, or just one person?" Peter queried.

"One."

"Then why are two on the steel rig we're about to pass under?"

"They want the autographs of some nuts," Fork answered.

"Maybe. Inch along and let me see if I can shake one loose," Peter ordered. He stepped out the cab's front door, onto the narrow platform. The rush of fresh air smelled wonderful as it pushed against his body, and the sound of unconfined space seemed so quiet despite the steady whine of slow diesels. The sun dated first one small cloud then another.

"You there, two persons on the fueling tower," Peter said slowly through the battery-powered bullhorn. "One of you must leave now."

One man obediently headed down, then walked toward the old multi-colored brick depot opposite the fueler. Monty kept the train moving as Peter opened the cab door to ask about the metal shed two tracks away.

"For repairs," Fork informed him. "I'll watch the shadows there."

Peter regained his footing on the engine porch, and turned on the bullhorn again. "All you people at the depot, greetings. To those waiting for a train, we'll be out of your way very quickly. Sorry for the delay. To those here to see the Grain Train, it's for real. Just like the starving kids we want to feed. Are you with us?"

Some of the platform group shouted, "Yes!" and waved their signs. The fifty people were too far away for him to really sense their level of support, or see into their eyes as he usually did at club speeches.

Peter watched the approaching steel tower, which looked much like an old Erector Set model, interlocking metal strips filled with open 'x' braces. Then they were under it, then through it, stopping when the middle of their engine was beneath. Cars clanged together in reverse domino order, but it was relatively quiet since they had been inching slowly.

Peter studied the man attaching the hose coupling to the fuel tanks underneath, just as hard as the man was eyeing Peter. Fork climbed down to supervise filling the bellies of their engines, leaving Monty to insure that gauge needles were actually climbing. Fork checked for more hose couplings or spare tanks nearby, fearing possible watering down, but the line was clean coming right from the standpipe. Surely they wouldn't contaminate a whole diesel pipeline just to foul one train.

"Three or four minutes each," Fork hollered up at him.

"Faster if you can," Peter shouted back. And then he saw some of the onlookers starting across the tracks toward the train.

"No! Stay back!" Peter ordered by bullhorn. "For your own safety!"

One man with a sign lettered 'We want to ride along' shouted out his sign's words, and added, "Let us come closer and talk."

Peter debated the risks, and bullhorned back, "No more than two, come within two tracks and stop there."

As four men kept coming, Peter reached one hand behind him and ran it over the outline of the gun with its fully loaded clip, in its belt holster under his loose shirt. He left it resting there, comfortable with the personal decision that he was expendable to his cause, but would not be gunned down nor allow any of his followers to be harmed, without trying to defend his mission.

*   *   *

The vibration in III's shirt pocket alerted him to a call. Calmly he took out the silver ballpoint and clicked the lever. The digital display showed the phone number and name of the FBI agent flown into Price, Utah. On III's order, the operative was to have begun following the train by renting a helicopter, since the car dispatched in Grand Junction had been unable to keep up on the flatland.

III did not use text messaging. He had learned not to trust that screen words would be either sent or received only by its intended cpd owner. So he left his aisle seat in first class and walked back toward the curtained area, which divided them from coach. His seat companion had unfortunately displayed undue curiosity to the unusual cpd. III eyed each passenger as he casually passed by, looking automatically for any threatening movements. Never was he at ease with strangers.

The *fasten seat belts* symbol was lighted, the plane was still taxiing, as a man in a red blazer walked purposefully toward him.

"Sir, you must return to your seat. We're approaching takeoff." The smiling male flight attendant blocked the aisle, his hands anchored on seat tops on either side.

"Then get out of my way," III said evenly, totally unperturbed by the challenger. "I need to make a private phone call, and I'll buckle into your seat." The plane was making the ninety-degree turn into runway position.

"No, regulations require you to be in your own seat," the attendant persisted. He took an assertive step toward III, who was holding back the disabling punch and subsequent delays it would bring.

Public transportation was such a nuisance, the authoritarian thought as he framed his demands in a degrading tone. "If you'll check your seat manifest, Mister Stewardess, you'll see that regulations don't apply to me. Now, either I go past you, or forward to this plane's captain and abort the takeoff to make my call. What is your career choice?"

The jet engines roared into imminent readiness. By now the attendant had remembered an *FBI* seat notation, and turned back to his own seat, flinging a terse "Be quick about it" over his shoulder.

The plane was rolling past a hundred feet of earth a second as III buckled his new seat belt at an isolated fold-down seat between compartments. He removed his cellular phone from his pocket, just as the pilots removed the plane from the confines of gravity and lifted off. He punched in his billing code, his security code for a closed line, then the Utah agent's number. The phone sounded no telltale ringing tones to be overheard.

"You called?" he said quietly. "Yes, this is he... The train is right there at this instant?...Is the railroad negotiating?...No, they're really not supposed to do anything until I meet with them... And how many engines have been refueled? It would be a shame if their fuel got contaminated, and they experienced some routine diesel failure...Ah, almost finished refueling."

III was thinking intently, putting himself visually in the old Helper railroad depot with his agent, but still acutely aware of whether any passenger leaned too near. "Did you contact the sheriff?...gone to Sun Valley...And the Utah farmers want to board?...Is Wayman letting them?... He's complicating things, so we have to get him moving again...Yes, but what do you think would happen if someone concealed between nearby trains just started shooting?...No, not at you, agent...No, not at them either, just into the ground. Think that would put pressure on Peter to tuck his tail and pull out quickly?...Probably you're right...Yes, that might even happen while we're talking, or when we finish wasting precious time..."

The attendant stopped at III's drop seat first with his inane question regarding beverage service, his eyebrows raised in innocent question. III knew the man was gloating with the prescribed interruption. He just shook an annoyed head, asking if the attendant knew anything about obstruction of justice. When the man moved up the aisle, he continued.

"Agent, do what you can to slow down the media. Question those filming and taking tapes or notes. Get names and station affiliations. Make it plain they are now on our list. Then get back in the chopper and stick with that damn train...Good grief, of course inform the Salt Lake Office when you're airborne--*after* you get the train moving again. Are we clear?" III was very careful never to give a direct order to break any law, merely ask what-if questions, which could be *misconstrued* as suggestions.

"Thank you for notifying me personally. I hope I'll be able to say I picked the right man for the job when I picked you."

III hung up without the innocuous *goodbye*, which was such a frivolous time-waster for him. He pocketed the phone, then saved more time by going into the restroom facility one wall removed, to prepare for his fastidious, though cloaked, arrival in Salt Lake City.

*   *   *

A strange thing was happening in the Helper rail yards. The hijackers were preparing to entertain visitors during engine refueling, enveloped in the security of their multiple bomb threats to ward off arrest.

Wilma had the idea, and after rapid consultations with engineers and farmers, Peter agreed. The Denver newspaper-radio copter had landed, and its three reporters were already in Engine 9039 for their happy reunion with Wilma and scoop interviews with the hard questions. Peter announced over the bullhorn that three more media reps could bring cameras across the tracks and enter the cab and two boxcars for five minutes of interviewing and picture taking. A dozen scampered toward the train. Peter pointed to the three fastest, telling the others to go back to safety. But they just stood one track removed, shouting their questions.

Peter asked the three waiting below him to identify themselves, then he selected one to come up the front ladder. He sent the other two running back toward the boxcars, radioing that they were coming and to help one up in each car. Some people with cameras ran back along the parallel tracks with them, but respected the boundary distance.

Peter answered a few questions for the visiting reporters, then turned them over to Wilma. Through the bullhorn Peter called out to the growing crowd standing on the depot platform a hundred feet away.

"If any of you...who are farmers...," he said, speaking very slowly to be understood over the distance, "...are really serious...about coming with us...

on this Grain Train ride..."

Peter had debated with the Wray farmers and the Shakespeare Group earlier in the summer about adding other farmers along the route. They had guessed the newcomers might be treated by authorities as innocents, merely concerned or confused citizens, not guilty of planning any crime or hijacking. But importantly, they had reasoned, this would show broader support from other States, plus add to the number of persons who would be affected by any FBI counter-attacks. Since the hobo boarding showed an area of weakness, Peter also wanted to shore up his defense shield to insure a peaceful run. Wray's farmers would still outnumber newcomers if only two were added to Boxcar One and three joined Boxcar Two.

Peter was implementing that decision as he continued speaking: "Come one at a time...over to me now...and we'll talk!"

Twenty people ran down the steps or jumped off the platform, and raced toward the train.

"Stop right there!" This was getting out of hand now. They could be mobbed by supporters. His order slowed them to a walk, but they kept coming.

"Please. You are strangers to us. We don't know yet whether you are friend or enemy. You are threatening us by all coming at once."

This time his plea took effect. They stopped, conferred among themselves, and sent one older man forward. The media people standing in the middle of it all were having a feeding frenzy, surrounded suddenly by multiple stories.

When the lone walker arrived beside the engine, he shouted up to Peter, "I'm Brandt Isonberry, a friend of Dan Brown at Wray Feed."

Peter tested that claim, then knelt down on the catwalk, reaching out to shake the farmer's extended hand. "Sorry for all the questions. We had some serious problems with newcomers this morning, so I'm leery. Why do you want to join us, Brandt?"

"Well, near as I can tell, it'd take a miracle to get our government off dead center on the surplus grain issue. You're the closest I've seen to a miracle come through here in the last fifteen years. I'm a widower for four years now, foot loose and fancy free, as they say. Got room for me?"

"Sure, along with enough food, water, and blankets too. But you know we're risking our lives here."

"It's a worthy cause, Pete. I figure this would be a good way to check out."

"Did you bring your gun or knife for protection?"

"Gosh, no, just my prayer book, and credit cards to get back," he smiled.

"That's good, because we're running non-violent. They'll still have to search you, my orders. Sorry there's no time for you to say goodbye's, Brandt. We're about ready to start up again."

"I've said 'em already, Pete, just in case."

"Then go on down to the first boxcar. I'll call and let them know Brandt Isonberry is going to be riding with us."

"That's just great. Say, the fella back there in the green sweater is Doc Nevins. He's been in Helper longer than I have, and I can vouch he's a first class medic. He heard on the news about your getting attacked. He wants to volunteer to go along in case something else happens. He hasn't seen any duty since Vietnam, and kind of misses the danger sometimes, y'know? Would ya talk with him?"

"We can talk."

"Hey, Doc, come meet Peter Wayman!" he shouted over to the crowd waiting thirty feet away in the tracks. Then added, "And he said I could go!" A spontaneous cheer went up from that group, and from the depot platform bunch as well, which finally told Peter what he needed to know about America's early response.

Brandt walked back, well, almost skipped back to Boxcar One in his excitement. Peter interviewed the doctor and accepted him to board.

The clincher was when Doc Nevins said he had called Green River to see how Fulton Skinnard was doing. Peter had done the same, and had let the farmers know there was no serious internal damage, but three ribs and an arm broken, and a dislocated jaw.

Peter also accepted the next two the crowd of farmers sent over for interviews. Drew Manchesky in Boxcar Two knew the first, and Peter made a quick call and talked with the foreman at the Birdwhistle Ranch to verify the second, when Larry Shafner remembered seeing him, but couldn't recollect why.

Fueling had just been completed, and hoses withdrawn. There were now stragglers all over the tracks, despite Peter's protestations. For better or worse, no law enforcement was in evidence.

In fact, though, a deputy sheriff was near the tracks, in touch by radio with the yardmaster, ready to clear people off the tracks at once if any trains were approaching. But since the sheriff himself was in Sun Valley training for search and rescue missions, the man next in charge here was simply keeping the peace, feeling no obligation to arrest someone when no warrants had been issued. No one from the State or FBI had approached him asking for help, so *live and let live* was his day's motto.

BANG! BANG, BANG!

Shots rang out from somewhere in the rail yards. The deputy crouched low, hand on gun, eyes fixed in the direction of the sound, somewhere around the repair shed. People standing around started ducking, and shouting, "Guns!" and running back toward the protection of the depot buildings.

"Go home!" Peter yelled at the farmer he was interviewing. "Monty, get us out of here! Media, get out of the engine!" Then he quickly added, "Thanks for coming. Be careful!"

He radioed the boxcars to ask if anyone was hurt, telling them to stay away from open doors and to brace for rolling, as Monty blew the whistle three short blasts and the train lurched forward, in horribly slow motion if the threat to them was real. Peter had taken cover in the engine, but now scrutinized the few folks who had stopped when the shooting had ceased. They were now waving slow goodbye signals, or holding arms upraised with a clenched fist salute. Some hollered good wishes to departing friends.

Then Peter saw a man in a long-sleeved white shirt, dark tie and slacks, leaving the repair shed two tracks distant, down past the boxcars--an anomaly in these surroundings.

"The shooter," Peter surmised aloud. He got binoculars and watched him walk briskly across three sets of rails to reach the depot. Even though the train was picking up speed, Peter could still see the city man approaching a man filming with a video camera, flash some kind of identification, and motion him inside the depot. Then he went to a second reporter and repeated the actions.

So the shooter was a fed, Peter concluded silently. Didn't hit anybody--so wasn't aiming at anybody. Just to get us moving again--to what purpose? What lay ahead? Peter wondered, but realized immediately that was the question they faced every mile. Looking back along the train cars, all seemed to be intact for the next leg of the trip. The most dangerous stop was completed without serious incident, but the trip no longer held any similarities in Peter's mind to a simple poker game. At this point, he felt his White was still in command of the chessboard, but Black was on the move.

Wilma told Peter that she had followed their plan, and encouraged all those she spoke with to download the pictures and recorded interviews onto the Grain Train blog site on MySpace. Peter had set it up on his last day in Denver--Wednesday--only yesterday. They'd check it and respond as time permitted, to build support with the younger set, hopefully grabbing some parents in the process.

Fork greeted him with a question. "Peter, Helper yardmaster still wants to know how the fuel should be billed." The foursome shared their biggest belly laugh yet.

*   *   *

Shelly Smith-Jones knew she was as effective an executive office administrator as anyone on the East Coast. But this afternoon had caught her totally by surprise, and her head was still spinning. The log of phone calls, e-mails, and faxes provided an invaluable record on an unimaginable day. As it did right now, when Barney O'Brien, national president of the Serv-U.S. Clubs, was phoning her for a status report.

"Have you got the simultaneous fax copy ready for all our club presidents? And what did we decide to put in it?"

"Ten more minutes, Mr. O'Brien..."

"This had better be a *Barney* day, to save time and keep us smiling. Lots of people aren't."

"Don't I know it? Well, we included the *Herald* article that started all this, quoting Al Federson of Brighton saying we endorse the hijacking."

"Did I tell you I finally talked with him personally? Claims he was misquoted. Better put a possible lawsuit on our September agenda."

"Got it. Summary of Dan's interview in Wray. Not much damage."

"*Au contraire*," Barney contradicted. "Ha, every time I say that, I wish an Irishman had come up with a better phrase than the French." He chuckled, and she threw a notepad against the wall. Two other lights on her twelve-line phone set were blinking on hold, and he picked her as an audience for his humor.

She paced behind her desk as he continued on speakerphone. "Dan just told me that he's gotten calls from farm clubs in four States. They're flying into Denver to join the picketing, wanting him to book motels. The farmers are rallying--and they think our national office is backing them!"

"Well, are we?"

"Oh, fudge, S.J., I hope not, but it's not up to me. Set up a teleconferencing call with the national board for a half hour from now."

"But the fax isn't finished." She plopped down in her chair.

"Well, that has to get out also, for them to reference, and to keep my phone from ringing off the hook, probably yours too."

Shelly Smith-Jones' secretary had just put two more callers on hold.

"Be sure to say at the bottom that a Serv-U.S. Board decision is pending."

That will help hugely, she thought, but said, "Okay, Barney," making a note. "We'll include a copy of the board's statement from three years ago, strongly encouraging the government to re-examine its policies on farm subsidies and surplus commodities. They only sent back the *we value your opinion* response."

"Well, we'll follow up now. For your log of my calls..."

My log of his calls? she thought.

"...I just got a call from the Under Secretary of Agriculture, preaching on this Administration's firm commitment, etcetera, to working with farmers to resolve farm problems. Said there would be a news release this afternoon. Then closed by suggesting that non-farmers should stay out of farm issues. How's that for a slap?"

"How do you want to play it?" she asked, hoping he wouldn't say...

"Shucks, reply with a zinger on how many members are farmers..."

She took deep breaths.

"...and why not add to our fax..."

She was shaking her head hard now.

"...that the White House takes note of Serv-U.S. interest in the Grain Train and surplus grain issues, and, uh, will keep us informed of upcoming initiatives, or something like that."

"Fine. You said *the White House*, Barney?"

"Well, the Ag Secretary's boss is the Under-Secretary, whose boss is the Secretary, whose boss is the President, right? And why don't you..."

I can think of a hundred reasons, Shelly's mind answered.

"...get me the number of the president of Mid-Western Pacific Railroad. He may have some input for the Board."

What if he's a 'she?' Shelly thought silently.

"Note on your log that I spoke with Sylvester Manchester in Denver's Mid-Western Pacific at, uh, 11:45, my California time."

I know where you are, Shelly agonized.

"He said the FBI is insisting the railroad do nothing to stop the train, because of the bomb threats. Somebody's going to meet with somebody in Salt Lake to set up plans yet this afternoon. All the more reason to do something soon, if we're going to do anything."

Can I quote you on that, Mr. President? she thought, then asked, "Who else to call?" She knew Barney, and was a glutton for punishment.

"Glad you asked. Call the president of Agri-Net Co-Op. Let's see what position they're taking on their grain hopper cars."

"That's my 2:35 log reference, Eastern time," Shelly said, to be a little ornery. "The wire service recap of their public statement said they have given no authorization to endanger bystanders, the riders, or their rail cars by trying to stop the train short of its destination, and will not be considered a party to any violence."

"Ah, somewhat simpler for them. Okay, scratch that call."

Already done, she thought, drawing a second line through the name.

"What would be on our agenda for the teleconference?" he asked.

Good grief, you're the one calling it, was Shelly's first thought. *You're the president, set it!* was her second. "Well, let's talk through the possibilities," was her actual comment to him, which is why they paid her the big bucks to help the internal organization run smoothly. "Most people believe what they read in the papers," she rationalized, "so the public perception already feels that Serv-U.S. is in favor."

"That's a problem," he acknowledged.

She classified that as very astute, and went on. "If we now retract..." and Shelly used we a lot in her thinking and speech, for she did feel herself to be a key part of the organization, "...we'll look two-faced, indecisive, cowardly, unpatriotic, a traitor to our award recipient..." She began to realize where her strong sentiment lay.

"But how does it look for a national service club to endorse blatant criminal activity?" Barney retorted.

"What about Peter Wayman's claim that the government is criminal in withholding surplus food from starving children?"

"Our radical clubs have called," he confided to her, "always first in a crisis. They insist that we demand publicly for the train to get through, to wherever, and increase public pressure to insure that happens."

"Me, too," she reported back.

"You want that, S.J.?"

"No," she blushed at the truth, "I mean, they've called me, also. Even some middle-of-the-road clubs are tired of waiting, and since the Grain Train has forced the issue for all of us, we should protect the cargo and people, broken laws and all."

"People sure form opinions fast. Well, then, let's add those points to the agenda. Have you thought of any way out of the dilemma?"

As if I've had time to think, Shelly reminded herself. But she answered with a flash of insight from somewhere in her experience. "What if we clarify a *slight misunderstanding* from Al Federson's quoted remarks? Maybe we could endorse the hijacker's concerns, and share their frustration with government bureaucracy's slow response. Uh, then strongly suggest there should be an immediate way to legally link our grain surplus with those needing it. But publicly disclaim and disagree with the means they chose to accomplish those worthy ends."

"Not bad at all. I hope you remember what you just said, because that's exactly the motion I'll ask the Board to consider. Attagirl!"

Me and my big mouth, she chided herself, furiously writing her shorthand memory of what words she had just put together. Then she realized it was pretty good, after all, and her boss had in fact liked it. *Attagirl!*

"Barney, there will be the standard question, even if the board agrees, whether that will obligate individual clubs to that position, or whether they are free to react and comment as they each choose?"dam

"Oh, that haunting ghost. What weight do board statements really carry? Just once in my term, it would be nice to feel the board spoke in consensus with all clubs. Do you suppose...?"

Don't even think it, she sent vibes toward the California caller.

"...no, probably not in this case..."

Good, keep it that way.

"...but even if only a majority felt strongly..."

Oh, turn your back on temptation, Barney!

"...and we could determine that majority view, and it turned out the board shared that same opinion..."

The dam is about to bust!

"S.J., let's poll each club president along with your simultaneous fax. Draw up a short questionnaire for them to fill out and fax back. You know what to ask. Then you can give us the results at our second teleconference in a couple of hours. And keep me updated, S.J., even if you have to stay a little late tonight. Thanks." And he was gone.

Shelly Smith-Jones had just died a thousand deaths. She had no energy left to say there was no way in the world she could get all that done in her lifetime, much less today.

*　　*　　*

Chapter Eleven

"Sure they're going to push us to stop. They must, to stay credible with the Feds." Monty worked to keep Peter open to talking with the Peace Academy whenever they did try to make contact. He was plenty ticked they had not already done so.

"Then I don't have anything to say, if they're with the Establishment."

"Peter, you are..." He started over. "They may be the best friends we're going to have." Monty tried not to push his own temper buttons yet, or those of his friend. This conversation was too important.

The train bumped ceaselessly over linked rails. Wilma listened to the debate, and glanced outside at the TV-5 crew flying alongside in the orange helicopter. They had radioed that Fulton Skinnard was under house arrest in the Green River hospital. The hobo who rolled down against the post was gone when they flew back. Word was out that Mid-Western Pacific wanted no injuries to people or equipment, and that news was welcomed-- even though the railroad wouldn't have the last word on this. And they also reported that another shadow copter had joined them at a respectful distance, so it probably was not media. The KDNC/*Herald* copter team was still in Helper, getting background on the new riders. Wilma turned her attention again to the talkers.

"The Academy people will listen to us. The FBI won't." Monty picked his words with care, and Peter threw them away.

"My dad may listen. We haven't heard from him again."

"We haven't heard from anybody in the Bureau, or Homeland Security," Fork threw in, "and that's got me worried. They're not negotiating."

"Silence may be golden with that crowd," Wilma offered, "so long as we keep getting clearances from the railroad."

Monty saw another lead-in. "The Academy has connections we need. They can probably keep the rail company talking, to buffer out the most violent of the Feds' proposals. And they'll..."

"Broker us into port?" interrupted Peter. "That's what I want."

Monty threw his hands up in futility but didn't stop talking, pressing for reasonableness. "They know more about more than any group I know," Monty said. "If there is any way we can talk our way out of a noose, they'll find it."

"If they're that good," Wilma asked, not waiting for Peter's yea or nay, "why didn't you just go to them first to get help on your project, instead of breaking so many laws? Won't this make everything harder?" She had waited hours for the right time to ask that.

Peter drew in a long breath, then let it out slowly. "That's at the heart of why we're doing this. We've been trying every alternative and contact for several years. All met with very limited and slow progress."

"And as for the Peace Academy," Monty added, "they don't advocate any cause except ADR. That stands for Appropriate Dispute Resolution. They stay neutral, to go into any conflict at the invitation of any side."

"So, see," Fork summarized, "we just had to get into trouble before anyone would help get us out, like breaking a window on a cold night to get thrown into jail." Everyone grinned at his condensed version.

"I see, sort of." She confessed to having more Academy questions. Fork clapped his hands once, gesturing for Monty to take over the show.

"They'll ask our destination. That's not to stop us, but to send in a team to soften up locals, find out who's in charge, where skeletons are buried, what their goals are, get some leverage. So, hey, Pete, we tell them where we're headed?"

"If we did, somebody else would overhear, or take them to court to find it out. Like you say, they play the old game with the old rules."

"But, damn it all, Pete--excuse my French, Wilma--the reason I went to school there is that they're also making up the newest game in town. And our caper fits the profile of who needs their services the most."

Fork was doing a cheerleading routine with imaginary pompoms behind Monty, who had climbed down from his stool. It was for the benefit of his new admirer, a black lady, the first such specimen he ever knew. Plus he was their self-appointed crew clown.

"Fork, I'm going to put you back in the caboose if you don't quit giving me trouble," Monty said ominously over his shoulder.

"But, boss," he said, mimicking Jack Benny's friend Rochester, "we don't have a caboose."

And Peter, Wilma, and Monty all picked up the punch line on cue: "We know, Fork, we know." The tension was broken again.

"Well, a good laugh always makes me have to go," Wilma admitted. "I should have when we stopped, instead of interviewing everybody in sight. Think I'm big enough to walk back by myself, or do I still need an escort?"

"You will always need an escort," Peter answered, "as long as any of us can walk to the next engine with you. A lurching train can throw even the most sure-footed. We can't chance losing our voice."

"I accept the dangerous mission, sire," Fork said, bowing and scraping his orange Denver Bronco cap on the floor. The two left by the back door, down steep steps onto the narrow catwalk with its metal bridge railing. "What shall I hold onto this time?" Fork shouted. They stood in the wind and the sun, right next to the compartments holding the raucous diesel units.

"Me again," she shouted. Unnecessary, but nice. She knew he liked her, so she allowed his arm around her waist or a hand holding hers.

When they got to the other end of the 9039 unit, they stepped down the rear rung ladder. Ties supporting the rail tracks rushed by under the coupling clasps and hoses. She cautiously reached her hand to the giant green machine following obediently. Fork held her trailing hand tightly. Quickly she moved one foot across to the low rung. Fork released her hand in plenty of time to retain her balance, and braced her back.

She felt secure with his watchfulness as she climbed to the second engine's catwalk. They walked close, fighting wind and rocking motion. Fork studied Wilma as she studied the near terrain for hobos, or Feds, or any person. The world was suspicious, even at seventy miles per hour.

Inside the safety of the second engine cab, a unisex portable toilet had been set up. Also a portable dressing room, used in common by any of the four, served as the lady's boudoir to provide her with ample privacy. She liked their thoughtfulness.

"You first, since you called in the reservation," he said. She entered the anchored port-a-john and closed the door. He sat in the engineer's chair on the right side to keep watch, and to think of many things he had not thought of for awhile.

Ahead one engine, Monty and Peter took the opportunity to relieve themselves in the engineer's tiny rest room hidden in the engine's nose. Then they kept up a barrage of why's and why-not's. Monty was becoming adamant on asking for and accepting the Academy's help, and giving them all the information they needed. Peter listened, and really heard his confidante. Yet he still felt that bomb threats, media coverage, and the resulting national public attention would not only get them through to their destination safely, but also assure their prompt acquittal when brought to trial. That left only restitution for property damage--which might take him the rest of his life to repay.

*   *   *

A special 1:30 P.M. KDNC-Denver news broadcast featuring Don Trujillo concluded from the Helper refueling stop. The wall speakers at the National Peace Academy Crisis Center went again silent. Denver and Salt Lake City stations linked into the Media Monitoring Network to provide firsthand information of the ongoing Grain Train saga. Their live specials aired for everyone in the Center.

Outside, away from the hubbub of the Center, the new arrivals from the media circuit were gazing in amazement during their fast-paced orientation tour. The pert young co-ed was explaining: "We'll spend only nine minutes now to take a hawk's eye view of the National Peace Academy from up here in the Carter Carillon Tower." Her small tour group reminded her of owls on a limb, turning their heads all directions to soak up the postcard views.

"In only three years, this campus has developed a mystique for doing the impossible. We're trying again, hoping to stop this Grain Train hijacked in Denver without any violence. That's partly what you've come to witness.

"Leaders here claim that a large part of their success comes from the power of prayer. Down to the east you see the Chapel of Creative Love, built in the shape of a cross. The Presbyterian Peacemaking Program and the American Friends Service Committee were the primary benefactors, but all major denominations contributed. Inside that building, students and staff have signed up to maintain a round-the-clock prayer vigil. We consider this a primary technique of crisis intervention." Even seen from outside, the stained glass windows shimmered like shards of broken rainbows.

"Another strength lies within the students and graduates themselves, freed by the education here to be aware of our own inner resources--who we are, and what we have to offer our world. This *individual* centering is an area too often overlooked or squelched in traditional educational institutions." Her smile radiated enthusiasm.

"Credit for working miracles in diffusing tense situations also is given to the teachers, recruited from all races, ages, and walks of life. They were attracted here by the opportunity to add to a growing reservoir of knowledge, people skills, and hope for making a better world--truly a staff living out a model of what they believe.

"We offer degree programs in business and economics, education and fine arts, political science and history, public administration and law, energy and agriculture, communication and public relations. Each discipline includes special emphasis and creative approaches to Appropriate Dispute Resolution and the potential power of mediation.

"Our curriculum in teachers' education balances non-violent mediation in classroom and playground conflict with self-defense training and its use when there's no other option. Our citizen rights' club trains in handling firearms and learning marksmanship, not for the purpose of killing but for only wounding an armed aggressor, again, if there really is no other choice. It also instructs in how to disassemble or permanently disable any weapon. We certainly don't advocate taking all guns away from the citizenry-- because that leaves only the bad guys with guns. We definitely don't want our country to become defenseless--but rather to provide options for living safe lives in a diverse society.

"All this in the midst of beautifully landscaped grounds, and the familiar historical structures we retained. Plus the spectacular architecture of the new National Peace Academy buildings you saw from the helicopter on your way in. Some of our buildings have quickly become as familiar to American tourists as Colorado's Air Force Academy chapel spires, or the Vietnam War Memorial Wall of the Dead in our nation's capital city."

She pointed toward the high ridge rising behind the north end of the main campus. "On the other side of those hills is our new Museum of Atomic and Nuclear Warnings, which attracts thousands of visitors to its graphic memories, a reminder of what atomic war was like. The top floor of the mushroom cloud concrete structure is an observation deck ninety feet higher than this one. From there you can see the shining glass domes of the World Peace Retreat Center clustered in a mountaintop forest; and in the distance, the horrible scars, charred miles, and building rubble left from the low yield nuclear warhead. You'll remember, it was detonated intentionally during the emergency summit of governmental and religious world leaders, when our Administration sacrificed that pristine valley to show the ugliness of choosing nuclear war when standing so close to its brink. Which in turn prevented an almost certain global conflagration, and allowed us to be gathered here today."

She pointed the other direction, and the group looked that way. "The Clinton Library to your right is another landmark, designed as a gigantic

ocean wave, curling and foaming at its ten-story height. Lights burn
throughout each night in that magic Kennedy cloud level, which houses
scholars, researchers, computers, and extraordinary global pragmatists.
They're racing against time to find workable peacemaking solutions before
violence erupts again in any of the fifteen areas in which we are now
intervening by invitation.

"It's really hard for me not to get excited about life here," she bubbled.
One of the tour members said, "We noticed," at which they all shared a
chuckle in the afternoon sun.

"The whole campus has been built to research and develop, then teach
and practice non-violent equitable alternatives to destructive conflicts. The
nation knows it is an idea whose time has clearly come. We have settled
disputes peacefully in 77 percent of our interventions, which bears out our
claim of knowing what to do, and when and how to do it. America was
right to build and endow us."

She continued with financial explanations. "We are only partially
government-funded. You'll remember the former president who formed
an elite club of public benefactors to help change the image of company
CEO's who took home monstrous benefits on top of outrageous salaries,
at the same time their companies were struggling and stocks failing. To
become a member, one had to contribute $10 million or more to a charitable,
educational, or governmental institution or organization. The president
had met with those wealthy leaders at Camp David for brainstorming
the country's economic bailout, and the idea caught on. Huge gifts and
endowments flowed, tax breaks followed, and it became a win-win situation
for the country's growth. And the many thousands who benefited directly
from the additions to our way of life appreciated the generosity.

"There were new museums, similar to the Smithsonian, Guggenheim,
Getty, and National Gallery bequeaths. Libraries and town halls were built,
following in Carnegie's footsteps. Acreage was again donated for mountain
parks, hearkening back to Denver's Red Rocks Amphitheatre and Genessee
Park Wildlife Refuge. It was a way for the very rich to help the masses, and
it brought some healing between classes. Those in the president's ongoing
America First club say it opens the way for proud legacies.

"Here at the Peace Academy, educational chairs were funded to bring
in those educators recognized as the best of the best, such as the Johnson
Chair of Natural Resources; scholarships were endowed to help bring in the
most promising students, regardless of financial hardship; miles of acreage
were purchased for expanding sustainable energy and agricultural research

projects. Interestingly, all of the recent presidents, in person or through their foundations, made significant financial contributions to this National Peace Academy, and were in turn honored with a specially named place. And all these benefactors have loved visiting *their* new campus.

"The question this Thursday is whether our accumulation of knowledge, people, and prayer will be able to stop the Grain Train, before a violent confrontation? Only time will answer that, but you can be sure we are working at full speed right now to find a way.

"If your time permits, 45-minute bus tours of the grounds leave every hour from the Bush Visitor Center, the crescent-moon building near your helicopter pad. Those buses are equipped to receive broadcasts from the Crisis Center, so you won't miss any special newscasts. I'll take your brief questions now, then we'll take this wild outside elevator down to the van. I know you're going to love your stay here, despite having to work. Your National Peace Academy is an absolutely fantastic place!"

*   *   *

Back in the Crisis Center, Director Jennifer Crussman surveyed the busy scene once more. Operations and information flowed smoothly. Lois and Steve, her assistants, tended to the needs of computer techies and visiting reporters. This freed her time to take the updated printouts to Jerome Blackman, head of the Intervention Team assembled for briefing in the elaborate Ford Briefing Room at the Crisis Center. Beige walls thickly padded, plush red and brown carpet, lowered ceiling spackled with silver glitter, all contributed to soundproofing, once Jennifer closed the carved oaken doors behind her. They showed doves in flight carrying olive branches, on both sides when entering as well as when inside working.

The great round conference table dominated the room, easily seating twelve around its irregular circumference. A windstorm in California's Muir Woods had toppled a giant redwood, and the government held auction for these six-inch slabs of the monumental ancient. One hundred and thirty-three rings of old yearly growth under the clear polyurethane finish reminded those seated of another precious American heritage.

Each place at the magnificent table had a Wi-Fi plug for laptops, electricity for chargers, jacks for headset plugs, and a service buzzer. Only two jacks were in use this day, Jennifer's and that of Jerome Blackman. He was the exact image of his name--very black, and very much a man. His Special Forces experience in Afghanistan and his bearing made him now a commando for peace who could not easily be ignored.

He, Jennifer, and his team of ten listened over the speakerphone to the thoughts of Dave Cranmer, calling from the remodeled Denver Central Library where his regional graduates were in an emergency meeting. Dave said the *Herald*'s Special Noon Edition had electrified their city, starting conversations on street corners, punctuated by a few lumbering pieces of large farm equipment slowing the bustling downtown traffic.

Dave had gone over to the Federal Building, trying to meet with the director of the Department of Agriculture section, but only made it as far as a secretary whose favorite expression was "I really don't know." He hadn't gotten through yet to Senator Frey, but was still trying. He had also phoned his Denver friend Ruth Fitzwater an hour earlier. She had not divulged any personal connection with the hijacking, but strongly suggested that this would be a perfect opportunity for Peace Academy intervention. "The sooner the better," she had said.

"Can you go see her?" Jennifer asked. "She might share more facts face to face. If she is part of the conspir...let's say, one of the activists, she has some keys to helping us resolve this."

Dave Cranmer agreed to try. He relayed their Denver group's serious concerns about the FBI moving against the train, once night came and the tracks distanced themselves from public view.

"We agree completely," Jerome answered. "We plan to put a presence over the train long before nightfall, or on it, with Peter's permission. Any clues on getting inside his head?"

"Peter is for real," Dave assured him. The Denver grads felt he was shooting his personal ambitions in the foot by this sacrificial act. "Treat him as a true believer," they advised. Then they suggested a dialogue strategy: "Try to find out whether it's this actual grain that is critically important to get through, to whomever and wherever. Or, whether it's the message of surplus and starvation that he wants to get through to the nation."

"Right on, my brother," Jerome responded enthusiastically. "If he says, waking up the nation, he may get to that point a lot sooner than to some distant port."

"His answer may save his life," Dave observed. "You know one of our former students is the engineer--Monty Montropovich. When you talk with the train, tell Monty his wife is in Denver at Pete's home, and she sends her love." The nationwide network of grassroots had again provided creative alternatives and an inside track.

The Denver leader spoke again. "Jennifer, a question. Is your position still subject to court-ordered disclosure?"

"Yes, my job is all about information sharing, Dave."

"Jerome," the speakerphone asked, "have you been designated as national mediator in this case?"

"Affirmative, by the chancellor himself. Need a secure phone line?" he anticipated.

"Yes, please. Goodbye, Jennifer. We'll stay in touch, and many thanks. You have my pager number." She hung up, switched off the speakerphone, and left quickly.

The assembled group in the Ford Briefing Room listened only to the one-way conversation, as Jerome Blackman recited the familiar phrases to Dave Cranmer: "By the authority vested in me by this institution, and as a professional in good standing with the National Consortium for Dispute Resolution, I now designate you as co-mediator in the case of the Denver hijacked Grain Train."

Then a phone number, given to Dave Cranmer by Ruth Fitzwater only for direct intervention, was shared between official Peace Academy mediators, whom no court in the land could force to testify regarding any facts in this case. Confidentiality during mediation is protected by law.

*   *   *

The interrogation room of the Littleton police station was blatantly ugly, Frank reflected. He sat at a paint-chipped wooden table, on one of four vintage Samsonite folding chairs, facing the infamous two-way tinted window of too many detective movies. He looked at his watch: 2:00 P.M., two hours since he left his downtown office, with its orderly bookshelves and plaques of commendation. Now Brody was in his face, probably coming direct from DIA after dropping III off. And they had the gall to insist that Marion come here also.

Drab off-white walls matched Frank's mood perfectly. His rainbow of life had dulled in every hue of experience, as Winston Brody ably kept pointing out. "So your son Peter did abandon you," the Regional FBI Director was saying, "and the Bureau furloughed you. That was no reason to over-react by threatening those agents sent to your house."

"Put yourself in my shoes, Winston," Frank said grimly, trying hard to keep his throbbing head straight. He was still adjusting to the neck brace from the earlier collision with the cow.

"No, thanks. You're hurting in too many places." Brody's rare try at humor fell flat. His trusted subordinate was showing his stubborn streak, formerly valued as a strength termed *tenacity* on evaluation forms. "I do think it was a mistake for you to have forced a search warrant to be issued," he continued. "Looks like you have something to hide."

"What do you believe, friend?" Frank asked in tones not friendly.

"Tell me what I should believe, Deputy."

Frank stared at the man questioning him across the decrepit table, then looked beyond that familiar visage to the window behind, suspecting a concealed watcher where there was none.

"I haven't changed, Winston," Frank finally answered. "My son has."

"The Bureau needs more than your assurance. It needs..."

"You mean *III* needs, don't you?" Frank spit out.

"No, I need the facts," Brody continued evenly, making it personal, "to get you off the hook. Give me your educated guess as to where the hijackers are headed--but that guess had better be right on target."

The word *target* hit Frank hard, from many unconfirmed stories of missing persons and strange accidents, and too many stories confirmed.

Moving cautiously, Frank pushed the chair away from the table, and stood up. He rubbed his tight shoulder muscles, wishing Marion could do it for him, wondering what questions she was answering across the hall.

"We don't know," Frank answered, then realized he had included her in his answer. "Marion and I don't know Peter's destination, or any contacts he knows on the West Coast. We looked and didn't find anything before..." He felt antagonism creeping into his voice again, for he bitterly resented the implications of a house search, and by such jackasses. "I would have told you if we found answers."

The moment Frank uttered that obligatory phrase, a definite tinge of doubt darted into his mind. For an instant he questioned what he really would do if he suspected a site. He dared not look into Brody's eyes to see if his boss had picked that up, not even a glance. He turned and paced.

"Would you have told me?" Brody asked the unthinkable.

Frank answered far too curtly, "Of course." Then it was quiet. He was uncomfortable letting the silence just hang there. "I need more time to think about what Peter is doing, to come up with ideas. There was that mediation plan I dropped in your office earlier..."

"Time is another thing Peter has stolen from us, Frank. Your mediation plan will stay dropped. III took one look at your papers after you left, and trashed them."

"I see. And what is this *furlough* I'm on?" Frank bluntly asked.

"Leave without pay, until further notice," Brody answered, just as bluntly. "Sorry. You can petition for reimbursement when this is all over." He sighed. "You should not have..."

"III should not have!" Frank retorted. "III should not have come to Denver at all. III should not have taken over your office and sat in your chair. We could have handled this ourselves!"

"I would not have permitted you on this, in any case."

"I could have helped."

"How in hell, Frank? If you can, you damn well better. That's why we're meeting here now, to give you one more chance to cooperate."

"That's odd. From the agents forcing their way into my home, to the officer serving the search warrant on a distraught family, to your being out here in Littleton now, all seem to stem from suspicion."

"Ah," Brody muttered, extricating a green cigar from inside his jacket pocket. He rolled the smaller end of the stogy between his lips, tasting wet pungent leaves, planning his next words in the quiet his deputy always allowed him during this manhood ceremony. After a moment, "Frank, you must know, and have to tell me, what Peter's ultimate plans are. It's the only way you can survive."

"Why?" Frank burst out, spinning his head around too quickly to face his accuser. A look of agony crossed his own face, but he kept talking hard. "Why do I have to know anything about my son's damn plans? Not every father knows everything about his son, sometimes nothing! So don't give me some phony line about..."

"Frank, stop stonewalling. Tell me something I can use to stop that train, before..." The pause was enough to light up a dozen possibilities, which had been lurking in shadows of Frank's imagination. "...before they end up in a box no one can help them out of."

In his temper, Brody had left an unfortunate metaphor on the splintery table separating the two men. Had they shared sub-conscious thoughts, both were picturing young Peter Wayman prone in a casket.

Then Frank's mind began clicking years backward, to times during Peter's high school days when he welcomed his parents watching his leading role in a school play. When they joined him and his friends in planning his campaign for the Junior Class Treasurer, and cheered for his swim team.

For an instant Frank was back to junior high years and afternoons watching Peter's soccer team, and the canyon picnics when a son and daughter still enjoyed being family. And elementary years with lots of school and church activities and summers in Wray. Wray! Monty and the farmers. Frank's mind jerked back to the drab room and his inquisitor.

"Frank? You all right? You'd better sit down," his boss was saying.

"I'm okay, Winston," Frank said, still standing, shaking his head to clear memory cobwebs, and hurting with each movement. "But you cannot hinge my job on information of which I honestly have no knowledge."

Brody's concern, and Frank's simple statement, seemed to break the tension, even if only for a moment.

"Frank," Brody said slowly, as if gently cradling a head while placing it on a guillotine block, "it unfortunately does hinge on that, so come up with facts, soon." He added plain truth. "It's out of my hands."

"But all the years, and arrests, and convictions..."

"...are on the line," Brody finished, stuffing the cigar in his pocket.

"Damn it, that's not fair!" Frank protested, knowing the response.

"Nobody ever said this career was fair."

"How much time do I have to find this rabbit in a hat?"

"I need something before you leave this room, that I can report in good faith, let's call it. The rest, by the time III gets set up in Salt Lake. Otherwise, it's his move, on his board. The train will be stopped."

"Despite the bomb threats?" Frank asked. And the director only shrugged.

Drained, Frank leaned on the table and looked squarely in the eyes of his boss, his friend, his future. "Winston, I do not know *anything*," he confided.

Winston Brody looked up gravely at his friend and confidante, nodding, "That saddens me. For without your help, I cannot help you."

Silence deepened as Frank thought through options. "Then this is only about selling out my son, since I am presumed guilty as an accomplice?"

Guardedly, Brody answered, "Some eyes are very narrow now."

"Mine are opening," Frank acknowledged.

"So what can you give me to help save your job?"

A passage from scripture oddly entered Frank's mind from Sunday School drills of years past. Then an image formed clearly, the head of John the Baptist being brought in on a platter at Salome's request after dancing for King Herod. "What can I give you?" Frank queried, then answered the question himself in a voice of strong conviction. "Not my son's head. And not my soul. Goodbye, Winston."

The older man stood slowly, the table still separating the two men with their philosophies and priorities now miles apart. "A sad goodbye for me, Frank. Call me, if you find something, or change your mind. And,

Frank..."

To minimize neck pain, Frank turned his whole upper body to face his former mentor, ready for the parting words of a long friendship.

"...don't throw the agents out again, if they are still there when you get home. They are authorized to arrest you the next time, along with all your family. And to use whatever force is necessary."

*   *   *

The Wednesday Quilting Circle was meeting on Thursday in LaGrande, Oregon. Schedules got mixed up a year ago when Marybell Houghton took a library job every other Wednesday. She didn't know how long it would last, so they simply kept their name and changed the meeting day.

This week they were at the widow Barnes' house. Ella was in her early eighties, not sure exactly how far. Her house was painted white, as it had always been. The modest two bedroom home had a large back room added on, the full width of the house. Beds had wrought-iron headboards, her ringer-washer still worked, and shelves were filled with home-canned delectables. Three giant oak trees shaded her back yard, dropping acorns on anyone in the tire swing, and two fan-leaf catalpa trees grew out front where grandkids had climbed.

She and Walter had built up *the place*, as they called it, using the back two-thirds of the lot for a chicken yard and coop, a huge garden, and orchard. Now that Ella was alone, the chickens had been sold and the orchard gone to seed and saplings. She kept up half the garden, and planted the rest in a rainbow of spring-blooming iris by the hundreds.

Ella's garden patch was a vegetarian's delight, and it had provided a large part of this Thursday's lunch an hour earlier. She served a bowl of just-snapped green beans cooked with onions and bacon, tomatoes sliced thick, cornbread with commodity butter, cold sweet milk or rich buttermilk, and for dessert a chocolate meringue pie. This pie was the *all-time-favorite* treat of her granddaughter Ruth, she told them again, and would be placed on the back-porch bedspread along with plates of golden sugar cookies, pieces of dark creamy fudge, and white divinity for the vacation arrival of her daughter's family each summer--before Ruth's mother took ill in Denver.

These weekly quilting parties allowed for sharing memories and concerns, a place to laugh and cry at themselves and their world. It gave friends a chance to create useful beauty in an old American tradition.

The ladies were seated around the living room in the old dark green overstuffed chairs, or on the beige and pink and peach flowered couch, which had been shredded in spots by friendly claws of the tawny cat. Monkey was now sleeping placidly on the back of it by the window. They busily stitched and talked; someone was humming.

"Anyone hear more about that hijacked Grain Train from Denver?" Marybell asked.

Gossip had been quiet, so even news from Colorado made good conversation. "Well," Abigail Stafford began, "some say, if it turns north at Salt Lake, instead of going to California, that means it could be headed for the Oregon coast, which means it could come right through our LaGrande, maybe even by tomorrow morning," She spent a lot of time tending to her grocery store and customers, so she knew about a lot about a lot. "If it really turns north," Abigail continued, "and if it really gets out of Idaho. But I hear they plan to stop it right there at the State line."

"Who does?" Ella sharply asked. "And how can they with the threats about bombing? OW!" She had pricked her finger deeply with the needle, a rare occurrence with a seamstress so seasoned.

Ethel Small said, "Well, dear, go wash that finger with alcohol and get a Band-Aid, or you'll get blood on your pretty quilt. I'll come with you. I know how hard that is to put on yourself." Ethel was a compassionate ex-nurse.

"Thank you, dear," Ella said on her way to the bathroom. "Now the rest of you, talk about something else. I want to hear all about the train when we come back. Talk about my new wallpaper," she grinned.

Her *new wallpaper* was fifteen years old, yellowing fast. They wanted her to pick new, saying they'd help hang. But the old floral pattern reminded her of Walter.

The group was chatting amiably and patiently stitching together various colors of square cloth from their baskets when the two returned.

"Well, it's not so bad but what I can still walk," Ella joked, holding out her finger for display with its tiny white strip, "and I thank God every day I *am* still able," she finished, not wanting to appear irreverent about good health. "Now, who's going to stop those boys on the train?" she asked as she sat down again and got comfortable.

Abigail looked around the group. She had some attention, but spoke in a whisper to attract the rest of them. "Now the way I hear it is that Special Forces from the Federal Bureau of Investigation will stop them."

"Oh, my, the FBI again," Winona Chambers chimed in. "They can be

so tough when it comes to bombs and hijackings and such things. I'm
afraid the jig is up, like they say," she concluded. The group clucked wise
tongues.

"So the bomb threat isn't serious?" Ella pointedly asked.

"Well, I guess not, since Myrtle Sperry said..." and her raised eyebrows
and nod brought similar gestures from others, who knew that Myrtle's
nephew once worked for *The Bureau* as he called it, "...they'd classify this
as interstate shipment of stolen goods, and take the *necessary* steps."

Much shaking of heads followed, then Marybell spoke. "You know, it
distresses me. Those are good boys on that train, just trying to keep people
from starving. Why should they be shot for being neighborly?"

"Good boys don't steal trains, Em," Winona scolded.

"Not usually, I know. But somehow don't you think this is different, what
with that grain getting shuffleboarded place to place? Why, it could have
been God's good harvest sitting down in Old Man Bailey's silos they took,
and that would have been okay with me. Grain is given for full bellies, I
always say. It's not like they're trying to get rich."

"Two wrongs don't make a right, Em," Abigail said. "My mother, rest
her soul, taught me that real young, and I was careful to teach my kids that
too. Somebody starving doesn't make it right for somebody to steal."

"Well, then, missy preacher, neither does somebody stealing make it right
for somebody to shoot," Marybell snapped back, "so the FBI is just as bad,
or worse, by planning to take even more lives."

"Now you two banty roosters take it easy," Ella soothed. "I don't want
anything broken up in here with a fist fight." And everybody tried to laugh.
"Is anyone going to watch the train go through town, if it is headed for
Portland?" she asked. Ethel wondered why Ella hadn't made more of an
effort to move to a calmer subject when she had the perfect chance.

"Not me," Abigail said, though sometimes what she said and what she
did were two or three very different things.

"Me, either," said Winona, following the lead of one of the group's strong
leaders. "I have better things to do with my time."

"Well, I hear everybody at the Hardware is planning to go down to the
tracks when they hear her whistling," Ethel said, as if the destination was
a foregone conclusion, then edged out of the subject. "Ella, who are you
making your quilt for? I see you're using the newspaper for your backing
again." This substitute method dated back to Depression days when muslin
backing was hard to afford.

"Oh, I haven't decided," Ella said, thoughtfully. "I just think it makes it more special, maybe a little lucky, to sew in good news articles, like baby announcements, and weddings, and peace news when I can find it.

"That reminds me," she went on, getting somewhat animated, "I read just a while back about a lady along in years in Denver who started that Peace Ribbon idea. Remember, when people across the country stitched a pattern or painted on cloth what they would most hate to lose on earth in a nuclear war. Then a lot of them went to Washington in '85 and circled the Pentagon with their *love ribbon*. Anyway, she raised fifty thousand dollars to make a movie about the ribbon people and project. How about that from an old geezer just like us?"

"Well," Marybell spoke up, "I'll go along with the *geezer*, but I don't know about that *old* part." And with laughter, their group was at ease again. But the argument over the Grain Train was proving to be not only their newest hot topic, but was also dividing even closest friends in small town America's early Thursday afternoon.

*   *   *

"Nobody was supposed to have the number to our private phone," Peter criticized in general, reaching for his vibrating belt pager. The afternoon sun made him sweat, which was an irritation.

"Except our friends," Monty reminded him.

Peter raised the lid of the trunk at the back of the cab, then raised the lid of a smaller box inside. Now they could hear it ringing. He lifted the cellular phone from its cradle, and answered simply, "Yes?"

"This is Jerome Blackman, mediator with the National Peace Academy. May I speak with Peter Wayman, please?"

Peter could hear the man over the engine noise, so he knew he must be almost yelling at the other end, or using a speaker booster. A pro.

"It's your Academy, Monty," Peter said, turning his head toward his engineer, adjusting his weight to keep his balance as the train took a curve. Then he said into the phone, as he would in any normal shouted business conversation, "This is he. How did you get this number?"

"I am not at liberty to say. May we talk a moment?"

"Of course, for a moment." Peter wiped his forehead with his sleeve. "But the reception is lousy, thanks to the Feds' interference, I'm sure. "But I can still understand you, so let's proceed."

"The Peace Academy has a goal of maintaining peace on our planet, and to find win-win solutions to serious conflicts," Blackman spoke simply, but strongly. "Are you also interested in those goals, Mr. Wayman?"

There was no hesitation. "When I watch a person starve to death, Mr. Blackman, I am not at peace with my world. And I have found no one in authority interested in win-win discussions on giving our surplus food to those dying children." Even though Peter was yelling, a sadness permeated his words.

"You, and your friends, and your farmers are at great risk in this action, Mr. Wayman. I would like to talk with you about just what it might take to satisfy you, what is enough for you to stop the train and get off peacefully."

For a few more minutes they bantered, testing the motives of each man, and the arguable prospects of using mediation. In exasperation, Peter said he would phone back very soon.

For his part, Blackman was pleased with the opener. He discussed the conversation with his team, who, like he, stood at the briefing room marker boards lining the walls. This was their silent dialogue technique, so that each could write thoughts for everyone to see without interrupting the critical phone conversation. Important suggestions were written with green marking pens to help the process flow, warnings written in red, as they all listened in via speakerphone. Jennifer had left the Intervention Team alone to do their task, entering an LED display reading *Do Not Enter* to guard the entrance door to Ford Briefing.

Peter closed the door of the engine cab behind him, to pace the catwalk alone. In his mind, mediation meant compromise, and that meant giving up some demands. He took out his billfold to look at pictures of his foster children in the *Feed My Sheep* program, and greeted Carmelita and Nufala.

He unfolded a worn newspaper article picturing long lines of anguished people. The headline read: 'Refugees Find Little Refuge.' And statistics followed: "Thousands dead, tens of thousands so malnourished they will never fully develop mentally; even if they do live, their children will probably have birth defects." Was it really a hopeless cause that haunted him? The wind suddenly grabbed at the yellowed clipping and flung it away, as if answering *yes*.

His paper people were pulled from his grasp. Peter's mind jumped into tormenting images from his year in Africa. He had been caravanning to Sidamo Province in Ethiopia when he stopped the driver. The small living skeleton beside the road had strength only to squat and brace his body up with one pencil of an arm. His skull hung low in front of his emaciated shoulders, no power left in his neck muscles. The child's bones were long enough for him to be five or six, but he didn't weigh twenty pounds when Peter lifted him off the hot sand.

The boy became absolutely limp, knobby in Peter's arms, his chest hardly moving with breath. His eyes remained closed. Peter put his canteen to the child's lips and poured very slowly. The warm water ran out of his mouth, trickling across thin caked lips, down his cheek onto Peter's arm. For one agonizing moment, the boy managed to open one eye, stared into Peter's face, then slowly let his eye close. He took one deep breath, and no more. Starvation ended quietly.

Now the nameless young armful of bones visited Peter's memory at least daily, triggered by almost anything. Even happy times or delectable meals would bring back that hour cradling an abandoned statistic, reminding Peter of all in life that child would never know. Peter had seen hundreds of emaciated children, standing in endless queues for too little food too late. Or sitting dazed, hopeless, even after the relief truck left.

But today, he was breaking that vicious cycle. No Peace Academy could make him compromise on getting this grain through.

*   *   *

His watch showed 2:10. His flight was a half-hour late in arriving, not bad on this disrupted flying day. At least now he was ahead of the Grain Train. His prey was coming toward him, instead of him chasing after it, as befits the prepared professional hunter.

III turned in his first class aisle seat to watch the exit doorway for the familiar face of Switzer, his handsome aide extraordinaire. But so far there were only the faces of commoners shuffling out of their coach aisle into the telescoping Jetway.

If Switzer had gotten to Salt Lake even an hour in advance, III knew he would have a car waiting down on the tarmac for a VIP exit. But as the passengers thinned to a trickle, his hopes dimmed. Reluctantly, he stood, straightened his shirt and tie, and put on his coat. Then with briefcase in hand, and the small suitcase with laptop recovered from overhead, he began the tedious walk into the obnoxious world of public transportation.

"Thank you for flying..." the steward started to say, trying one more time for a pleasantry.

"No choice," he cut him off, making a sharp right out of the plane.

Around every bend of the accordion Jetway, III expected a person rushing up with a belated greeting. It was not until he actually stepped onto the gray and brown carpet of the concourse that he saw a familiar figure with an innocuous smile, waving. Utah's deputy director--a notch below even Winston Brody. No, two notches.

"Sir, I was afraid you had missed the plane. I was almost ready to come aboard looking for you, but I didn't want to embarrass you."

"Well, thank heaven you didn't have to." When there wasn't the slightest response to the sarcasm, III asked regarding Switzer.

"Just driving in as I was driving out. I told him I had your VIP treatment all arranged. Do you have luggage?"

"Only this ostentatious overnighter," III answered icily.

"Oh, let me help you with that bag. Never a cart around when you need one, eh?"

For once, III was almost glad his underling had neglected any arrangements, so they were being treated as nobodies. The last thing he wanted was recognition, especially by media types.

"These concourses get really long, sir. I usually take the moving walkways. There's one coming up."

"I usually don't. They give me a trapped feeling. But..." III conceded, glancing around at the light flow of travelers, "...I didn't get much sleep last night, or on the two flights today, so I'm tired enough to make an exception."

The Utah deputy led the way. The moment III stepped on the moving steel plates, he wished he had not. A group of reporters, lights suddenly blazing, jumped up from where they had been sitting in one of the side gates, positioning themselves all around the far end of this flat escalator. He would be deposited right into their jaws.

III immediately turned to make a hasty retreat, only to be momentarily blinded by a strobe light turned on directly in his face. They had him surrounded.

"Toby, switch that on dim! Sorry, Mr. Ravenhead," a voice was saying near the glare.

"Shall I get rid of them, sir?" the Utah FBI man stammered, as if he could do something.

"You have the wrong man," III tried.

The reporter's sympathetic tone switched back to business, just as III began to be able to see his questioner. "Mr. Ravenhead, as one of the top men in the FBI, what are your plans for stopping the hijacked Grain Train?"

Being identified as well as trapped, plus mentioned as a power figure, III spoke for the record: "In conformance with Bureau policy, we will use the minimal force necessary to stabilize this situation."

"Why have you let them get this far?"

Their questions were always designed to make a person look bad, no matter how they answered, III decided long ago. He chose to be indirect. "Well, now, they really haven't gotten very far, have they? And we certainly know exactly where they are anytime we want to make our move."

"Sort of like Pancho and the Federales, eh? When will that be?"

"I don't understand the first part of your question, but in any case you will realize that our plans must remain confidential." III glanced over his shoulder. They were halfway to the waiting herd of reporters.

The two blocking his backward retreat persisted. "Can we assume on the basis of increased activity at FBI offices here that you will be taking personal charge of the crisis?"

III looked at his Utah deputy, fully implying a major breach by his scowl. He didn't know the reporter was fishing because of an earlier DIA spotting and phone conversation.

"You are free to assume anything you wish, just don't quote it as fact." Variations of that line would become the standard answer.

Now the shouted questions from the new set of reporters began filling the concourse, stopping curious passers-by to stare.

"Do the bomb threats have your hands tied?"

"What about the hostage?"

"How much property is the government prepared to lose?"

"Will you kill them if necessary, like the Branch Davidian massacre in Waco?"

"Is the attorney general making the decisions? Or the president?"

III just shook his head several times during this line of questioning. "Sir, are you indicating *No* as an answer, or *No comment?*"

"You decide," he answered. Then the barrage of questions started in again, the glare of the lights now making him feel too warm. He stepped off the moving walkway finally, with his local office chief trying to clear their way toward the airline's VIP room just thirty feet away. Customer Service reps had come over, hearing the commotion. Behind their counter, the luxury of privacy and limousines awaited.

But the cluster tightened, and the pace slowed.

Suddenly, III stood very still and straight, speaking louder and more distinctly than any of them, in a tone of unmistakable authority. "Surely I misunderstand. It seems you are blocking the way of a federal officer. But that would be obstruction of justice."

The crowd parted faster than the waves of the Red Sea for Moses. And III strode directly through the airline's waiting open door to the courtesy room, with his embarrassed Utah deputy trying to explain how the media could not have had any way of finding out his arrival plans.

It was no longer a secret that Terrence Ravenhead III had come to take charge of the secret agency in the Beehive State. Salt Lake International began buzzing with the prospect of another confrontation and standoff.

*   *   *

"Do what you want with the Academy, Peter. I'm tired of arguing."

"Fork?" Peter next inquired of his back-up engineer.

"Well, the more leverage for us, the better."

Monty spoke up again. "I told you they're not going to be *for* us..."

Fork rejoined, "Somebody I know once said, 'If they're not *against* us, they're *for* us." Monty silently turned forward again in his chair.

Peter looked at the woman standing at the other end of the trunk. She swayed a little each time the engine rolled over an uneven track, but her train legs were pretty steady. "How about you?" he asked.

"The Academy can get us the extra coverage I can't," she said, matter-of-factly. "Their late night calls would be answered. We need them."

Peter vacillated. "I suppose it wouldn't hurt to talk again."

"No, it wouldn't," Monty muttered under his breath.

"Okay, I will," the young man with a mission decided. One of those stupid cheers went up from his three comrades as he dialed.

The phone rang only once in the Ford Briefing Room before it was answered loudly, "Blackman."

"Let's talk," Peter said.

"Good." Blackman launched in. "All we say is confidential, unless we agree what to tell whom. It's tough to build phone trust quickly with a stranger, but that's what we're all about. Monty tell you how we work?"

"Yeah, he's...Monty is the main reason I'm talking with you at all." Peter rephrased so his friend could hear the credit being given. "Say, there's no more static on the line here. What happened?" Peter asked.

"The Peace Academy has an agreement with the FCC to keep our mediation phone lines clear," Blackman answered. "We are all about opening communication channels rather than closing them."

"Oh," Peter said simply, already impressed with anyone overriding federal law enforcement authorities.

There was a commotion in the cab. Fork punched Monty's arm and pointed out the window, and motioned for Wilma to come see.

The set of parallel tracks alongside the train began to veer toward clustered large structures, some yellow, others tan. Long chutes angling upwards crisscrossed the tracks and each other, concealing the conveyor belts which carried huge black chunks up to be dropped through crushers, only to be lifted on another belt ten stories to drop again through grinders until the large slabs had become small lumps of coal.

Fork was quietly saying there's enough coal in these local mountains to supply U.S. needs for three hundred years, when everyone ducked as they passed under another chute leading up to the tallest mill. But even this huge maze of tubes and towers was dwarfed by mammoth monuments of stone surrounding them. Great white clouds rolled along cliff faces and up over their rugged forest-covered tops, clashing there with startling blue sky.

"Blackman, I'll call back. Sights here are simply taking my breath away."

"Stay on the line, describe what you're seeing."

"Sure. We were wondering why the clouds were so low. Well, they're steam clouds. Billowing steam from a huge power plant we're seeing around this curve. Right behind that is another gigantic mill complex, larger than the one we just rode through. Pennsylvania would be jealous.

"I'm going out on the catwalk to see this better. Wilma's coming too...so is Fork. No, Monty, you character. Somebody's got to run the train!"

Roaring wind combined with diesel engines to shake the speakerphone. Blackman tinkered with dials to suppress background noises.

"Oh, this is just incredible. Great God Almighty, would you look at that?" Only rushing air went in the phone mouthpiece for long moments.

"Blackman? Fork was telling us this is the Castle Gate. There's this giant slab of rock, right by the tracks, slashing upward at least two football fields high. It really seems to be opening up wide for us as we approach... Wow! It's at least another football field wide.

"We're right under its edge, so close and it's so high it hurts my neck to look all the way to its top. We're such insignificant pieces of God's creation. These boulders at its base have been peeling off from it for centuries. Any one of them could squash this engine like a mushroom.

"Now I'm looking back at that unbelievable mountain slice, and it appears to be shutting behind us. God sure did a piece of work here. I just wish the whole country could be enjoying it with us."

"Mr. Wayman, a confession..." Blackman started.

"Call me Peter. What were you saying?"

"The whole country is enjoying this amazing sight with you, Peter, through the helicopter camera. We all went through the Castle Gate with you."

Peter shook his head, a real concern in his voice. "So you were lying about confidentiality? Is the country listening to us right now?"

"No, no, no," Blackman insisted. "We're not transmitting the TV helicopter voice channel, only sending their video on by satellite. You and my team are the only ones on this phone line. Believe me. And your description was fantastic, you're a wizard with words."

"Thanks for explaining our communication links. That had me going for a minute. I'm going to stay outside since you can hear me okay. It may be the last time I get by this way."

One of the team wrote *death wish?* on the board, and Blackman pointed at the thought to show it registered. "I don't blame you, wanting to soak up that scenery. Sounds fine yelling right into the phone. Got headsets?"

"No, forgot those. How are you going to help us?"

"We can become your spokesperson..."

Peter interrupted, "We have a fine spokeswoman in Wilma Fletcher." He was glad she had stayed out next to him to hear that.

"No argument there. Her audience is very broad in the States you're traveling in, and across the whole nation. Your blog site is also attracting thousands. However, our target is limited to those people who have the desire, assignment, and power to stop you. We can help you open up dialogue with that group. Rest certain--if they cannot stop you with reason, they will use other means, and probably soon. You have noticed the second helicopter tracking with you now? FBI."

Peter suspected it. "A threat if we don't use Academy services?"

"A threat either way, Peter."

The leader of the hijackers, the visionary with wind blowing through his hair, considered his options as he watched the two choppers:

--no talk, just wait and hope the bomb threats keep working;

--open negotiations by himself;

--expose his Shakespeare operatives by asking them to negotiate;

--or let the Peace Academy become the go-between.

Peter re-opened. "How would we do long-distance negotiation?"

"We've already begun," Blackman informed him gently of the obvious.

"Now you need to designate our Intervention Team as your mediators if anyone asks. That strengthens our hand here, and affords you some protection there by saying you now are participating in an NPA-sanctioned mediation."

"Agreed," Peter said decisively. All that felt right.

"Second, list your issues to be discussed and resolved, enabling you to stop the train."

"Blackman, it's going to take a whole lot more than discussion to stop this train," Peter said, just as firmly.

"Fine, what specifically is that?"

What would it take to stop him, short of shipping the grain? He pondered that seriously, since it was not in his plans. With many thoughts racing, he asked his new mediator to call back in fifteen minutes.

*   *   *

"I'm so sorry, Mr. Brody, but the director has not yet arrived."

"Look, Switzer, I put him on the plane here in Denver, and I know it has deplaned there in Salt Lake an hour ago. Parachute out, did he?" Brody did not like the man on the other end of the phone, III's special aide. He pictured him as a typical pip-squeak, even though they had never met. He suspected some of the personal relationship rumors had merit.

"I'm certain he did not bail out, and that you did load him, sir. Nonetheless, the director still has not made his way here to the office."

"Have we technology to talk on cell phones this Thursday, Switzer?"

"Of course. In an *emergency*, I can reach the director wherever he is. Shall I log your call in that category, Mr. Brody? I know the director is on the way in, and would rather not be disturbed en route."

Of all the insipid asses, Brody thought angrily. Why did he have to deal with two of them in tandem? This lackey had hitched himself to III's wagon and blocked direct communication whenever possible. This apparently pleased III, since he did nothing about the complaints.

"Well, Switzer, I know I can't trust you to pass all information along, but I'll give it to you anyway. Run it through your litmus test and tell our boss what you think comes out the right color." Brody was furious, being forced to deal with an underling.

"I will certainly convey all relevant information you give me, sir." Switzer's tone was characteristically controlled.

Brody spoke rapidly. "We traced Peter's moves back to his Denver Metro

Credit Union, where he withdrew $3,000 in cash yesterday, and $5,000 from a C.D. on Tuesday. We have compiled a portfolio of mug shots: Peter, Monty, Wilma, and the second engineer nicknamed *Fork* Thompson. Mid-Western Pacific Railroad identified him from the helicopter pictures. That portfolio is being hand-carried now to bus and train stations to see if tickets were purchased here by any of them for the Shakespeare Group. We're checking computer records..."

"What *group* is that, sir?"

Maybe this buffoon buffer was listening, Brody speculated. "*Shakespeare*. We traced one of five cellular calls Peter makes hourly. It was to Ruth Fitzwater, a Denver woman. Peter and Ruth are members of a campus organization titled *The Shakespeare Group*. We haven't found any other connection yet. But we now have all of the Shakespeare pictures and registration information from school files, which we'll have downloaded to Salt Lake by the time the director arrives."

Damn, Brody realized. Switzer has me doing it, giving III the top rank he hadn't earned, and hopefully never would.

"That's nice," Switzer replied.

Brody didn't know whether he was referring to the title or the download idea, but gave that issue no more attention.

"We dispatched agents to all their residences, to determine if they are at home. A team has been sent to the Fitzwater woman's home in the guise of gas meter men to install listening devices.

"Manuel Gomez, one of the group, is not answering his phone or door. But his car is there, so we have the place staked out. We found out nothing from interrogating Frank Wayman and his wife..." This part of the report made Brody want to puke. "...but they are under visual surveillance plus a listening station. Are you getting all this, Switzer?"

"Oh, my, yes. On tape. Your little office has certainly been very busy."

I should have known, Brody thought, trying to recall how he had phrased his reporting. An agent knocked, brought him a document and left, smiling at the thumbs-up sign with which Brody rewarded him. "Switzer, we just found a Shakespeare car at DIA, belonging to Jeremy Downing. That's enough circumstantial evidence to get search warrants for all their homes. We need to know where they've gone..."

"Of course. And the computer records?" Switzer interrupted.

"What?"

"Did you start to say something earlier about checking computer records?"

Testily, Brody answered, "Of course, that goes without saying. We'll get airlines to computer check for name matches, but the Shakespeares don't appear that inept. Oh, one woman, Ardis Borgeba, shows no record of a car registration or driver's license."

"Anything else to report, Mr. Brody?"

Coming from Switzer's mouth, even the most innocuous question seemed slimed with innuendoes of slothfulness. Brody spit out a few closing comments. "We'll begin contacting the campus associates and families of the Shakespeare Group to track them down. With the Fitzwater suspect getting hourly check-in calls, that group has to be part of the bomb network. But there may be others around the country, as they alluded, so the bomb threat could be enormous. It could take a while to get them all in the net, to neutralize Peter.

"I'll call III back in one hour, at 4:15," Brody concluded, reverting to that term of familiarity, and fear. "I expect to speak directly to him."

"And I'm sure he will definitely want to talk at length to you, sir."

A beleaguered regional director slammed down his phone once more.

*   *   *

Chapter Twelve

"Yes, Switzer?" III kept his eyes on the shiny oak veneer conference table when he addressed the man entering. He was studying glass ring marks on the side opposite. Janitors had been fired for not cleaning smudges off every polished surface overnight in the D.C. top floor offices. But this was Salt Lake City, and merely a makeshift office in Utah's FBI Division.

Calvin Switzer's chief job had become that of making III comfortable wherever he traveled on special field assignments, taking orders unquestioningly and implementing them instantly. He had blown it here. First, he had assumed III would arrive unnoticed at Salt Lake International-- a serious miscalculation. Second, he had assumed the Utah deputy meant limousine waiting on the tarmac at the plane when he said he had made arrangements to pick up III at the airport. Despite these blunders, Switzer had not received his termination notice yet, so he continued his job at an accelerated pace.

"Mr. Director, we just learned the identity of one Denver operative," Switzer began, reaching for a handkerchief to wipe off the glass rings.

"Well, you're especially adept at keeping secrets. Think anybody here has a need to know your information, or is it too highly classified?"

Switzer tried never to arouse the biting sarcasm of his superior, especially when working on a case being nationally publicized. This was not his day. He rapidly summarized the information from his printout.

"One terrorist out of six," III shot back. "Notify our questionable Denver FBI office manager to get this Fitzwater's house and car bugged. Think they can at least handle that?"

"I'm sure they'll get right to work on it, Mr. Director. Any more..."

"Just find the other five. I really don't think this circus has any more performers in the wings. We have a few more hours of rope to give them.

You have any specific suggestions from your experience, Switzer?"

This openness from the man with all the answers caught him by surprise, but since he always tried to anticipate, a partial response surfaced.

"Uh, we could bring one of our Montana friends in on the case."

"We have many friends in Montana," III replied, reaching for a pad. "With such vagueness, you should have been a politician." He hastily scrawled a note as he spoke with a smiling voice, but a scowl on his face. Then his tone changed to match the look he had flashed. "If you were referring to outside agencies, forget it. Don't even bring such suggestions into this office!"

He shoved the pad so Switzer saw two ominous words: 'Call!' and 'Gas!'

"Yes, sir, of course. I'm sorry," Switzer said, nodding once at III, to show he understood the note. III nodded curtly back, while pulling three pages off the self-adhesive notes. He folded them carefully in half and placed them in the smoke-eating ashtray. Switzer lit the match.

"Switzer, this asshole is no David Koresh. And this penny-ante Grain Train is no Waco, Texas compound. And stupid farmers are no idiotic Branch Davidian sect like the media is concocting. This is not 1993!"

"Definitely not, Mr. Director."

"We are beyond the point of a 51-day standoff with TV cameras filming our trips to the can. None of that must happen here. This needs the same rapid-fire closure we gave Oklahoma City's bombing in '95."

"Yes, Mr. Director!" his aide affirmed.

"I think they're headed for California. We'll stop them in Nevada. Get me the Governor on the phone. I want to test his resolve for ending this tonight. Now leave." III dismissed him with a go-away hand gesture. The aide left with his instructions: treat a new office in Utah as bugged, and don't talk about activities which could be misconstrued by the public or Congress. Secondly, he had authorization to notify the Militant Officers Neutralizing Team, code-named with the acronym *Montana*. These assassins were relied on for accuracy and discreteness, and the right prices had put many arsenal resources at their disposal.

*   *   *

"Remember paddle-boating on City Park Lake? I was horsing around, and knocked your glasses off into the water?" Dave Cranmer looked into the dark eyes of the pretty girl he dated three years earlier. Before he left for his degree at the Peace Academy. Before she married.

Ruth Fitzwater smiled, barely, at a man she still found good-looking. "You dove in with all your clothes on, trying to grab my glasses, but they sank too fast."

"I never got over that embarrassment."

"We were still young enough, you should have. Just an accident, and a really noble gesture by a wet noodle."

"Thanks." Silence covered the remembering of emotions past. The two friends sat at her kitchen table, sipping a blend of three Ceylonese teas from Sunflower Market, and sampling warm chocolate chip cookies.

"When does your husband get released?" Dave asked obligatorily.

"Two months, if the judge decides standing up for your beliefs isn't totally evil."

This interlude had begun when Dave found Ruth only playing word games about the hijacking. Finally she was moving into activist mode.

"Ruth, I don't understand," Dave puzzled. "Why did you give me the Grain Train's phone number, if you don't want us fully involved?"

"But I do want the Peace Academy to get involved," she insisted.

"Then tell me more," he pressed. "I'm one of the official mediators."

"But it's up to Peter to tell," she iterated.

"Look, Ruth, it's...four o'clock," he said, looking at her wall clock. A variety of chicken-shaped utensils and decorations adorned the yellow wall around it. "...here, and in your barnyard," he gestured, desperately trying to regain her confidence by putting her at ease.

Ruth finally laughed a little. "Mom's been a _fowl_ person for years, remember? You gave her those two chicks...but do you have to leave so soon?"

"No, sorry, I wasn't clear. I mentioned the time only to reassure you that Jerome Blackman would have made contact with Peter more than an hour ago, using the phone number you gave us. I don't know how their dialogue is going, but ours needs to open up." He leaned toward her across the table. "Ruth, you did send me the package about all this?"

A tolerant smile accompanied her silence.

Wheels were grinding in his mind, sentences forming and reforming. "Well, somebody did us a big favor by explaining the U.S.A.S. group. So based on your friendship with Peter, can you guess what's really motivating him? We need to talk his language, to get to his bottom line demands."

"It's so simple, David--feed starving kids," her heart spoke.

"Thanks. I really hear that," he said, thinking how to frame his hundred questions. "It somehow seems a complicated plot, involving a lot of people taking huge risks, for just a token gesture with only fifty grain hopper cars."

"Oh, this is only the first step, to get everybody paying attention. We need to ship lots of surplus grain fast."

Dave had gotten through to Ruth's *we*. Or more likely, he realized, she had given it to a trusted friend. He would handle her feelings carefully as he used them.

"We are going to try to find a way to help get your message through, Ruth, even if the train is stopped."

"It won't be, David. There are all the bombs."

"Would you personally blow up a bomb to get the grain through?"

"Yes, if I need to." She spoke from miles of deliberations and afterthoughts.

Her sudden answer surprised him. "There are more here in Denver?" he pushed.

"A safe assumption, wouldn't you think?" Her voice was chilling.

A cellular phone rang unique tones in another room. Startled, Ruth glanced at the clock--4:12. She excused herself, hurrying to answer. It stopped ringing, as if she picked it up, but Dave heard no talking. She returned almost at once, and sat down without explanation.

During the interruption, Dave had decided to try reasoning with her compassionate side. "You mentioned your mom. How is she today?"

"ALS is a merciless waster, David. It just comes out of nowhere and keeps getting worse. First her speech slurred, then got impossible for anybody but me to understand. You know, you came by to visit her. Now she just writes--scrawls really, and makes grunting noises for emphasis. I have to help her to the bathroom. Those are her only trips."

"I'm so sorry," he said sincerely. "How much longer?" It seemed he was always asking her when things would end in her life.

"Weeks. Or plateau out for years. Nobody in this world knows."

"The '93 breakthrough, isolating the gene causing ALS--hopeful?"

"Not very. More a predictor. There's still nothing to kill it."

"So you're really needed at home." It was truth more than question.

She nodded, fingering the saltshaker chicken on the table. "I'm shopping for a combination salt and pepper chicken," she said absently. "There sure isn't a stupid rooster around here to help." And she flipped her finger against the speckled peppershaker, too hard, knocking it over.

Dave debated picking it up, and cleaning up the spilled pepper, but left it. He looked out the window, through the sheer curtains, toward the street and his parked car. He was thinking that Ruth had little to lose by joining terrorists, and everything to lose, all at the same time.

Dave noticed two men in green uniforms on the porch two doors down to the left, across the street. Casually, he took another cookie and stood, complimenting Ruth on their chewiness, and looked back along the street. A dark green Xcel Energy Company van was parked. He thought quickly about absolutely correct phrases for the pending crisis.

"Ruth, I need to know the train's destination, right now," he said firmly. "The Academy needs to clear violence out of the way, if we can, by prepping that final city for negotiations."

"Why has your tone changed with me, David--your whole demeanor?"

"Because I suspect the FBI is working their way toward your house at this moment. I don't know whether they will arrest you, and me, or just bug your house," he said bluntly. "Probably a planting trip, to find out more."

Ruth stood up quickly, gathering her thoughts, making decisions. She didn't need to ask Dave how he knew. He was a Peace Academy grad, and they taught things like that.

She began talking slowly. "Negotiate for this shipment, David. Peter has his life tied up in getting it load--" She stopped mid-word. Trusting still came hard. Their group's plan was to hold announcements until the very last moments at each junction, keeping authorities off-balance. "I think Peter would die first, before getting trapped, and try to blow up everything in the process."

"How many bombs, Ruth?" Dave needed hard facts.

"Thirteen." The word just slipped out of her mouth.

He was staggered, but prodded her further. "In how many cities?"

"Five." Again quick, decisive, true.

Bing, bong. The front doorbell chimed pleasantly. The two friends turned to stare at the box on the hall wall from where the Armageddon sound had emanated.

Time for one more try. "The destination, Ruth," he asked softly.

She looked into his eyes so deeply his brain felt the penetration. Then she took two steps to stand next to him, cupped her hands on both sides of her mouth, and pressed them tightly against the side of his head. Her word went only into his ear, and into no air for anyone else to hear.

The doorbell rang again, unpleasantly, insistently. "Coming," she called out, backing away from David Cranmer, a hand on his shoulder, then turning her back on him as she disappeared into the hallway.

The greeting from the unseen arrivals came clearly into the kitchen. "Xcel Energy, ma'am. Report called in of possible leaking gas in the neighborhood. No need for alarm. We're here to make a quick inspection of your home, for your own safety. It'll take only a few minutes."

"Certainly, come in," Ruth said without hesitation, and Dave marveled at her calmness. "My mother is ill. Can you skip her room?"

"Of course. Uh, that's her room, with the door closed? Fine. If you'd like to just wait in a spot where you're comfortable..."

And Dave finished the sentence in his own mind: *...my partner and I will take our readings in all the other rooms, then be out of your way.*

The words used by the unseen man at the front door were the same.

"I'll be glad to go with you," Ruth shrewdly offered.

"Oh, not necessary, ma'am. Actually, when we intrude like this, we find it usually embarrasses the homeowner, who ends up apologizing their way through every room, no matter how straight it is. So we can save you that grief by having you just wait." Smooth, Dave thought.

"By the way, may I see your identification, please?"

Good girl, but they'll be ready, Dave knew.

"Our uniforms don't say it all, ma'am?" And the laugh.

"Just can't be too careful these days," she responded, politely but firmly. "Always somebody pretending to be somebody they're not."

"Isn't that the truth," the man's voice rejoined. Words games were all part of the charade.

"Thank you," Dave heard her say after a moment, probably studying the fake ID's. "Please finish quickly. I'll be waiting in the living room."

Dave had been glancing back and forth between the kitchen entrance and the front yard, where Ruth's car was parked in the driveway. The moment the front door closed with the men inside, Dave saw another green-uniformed man approach her car, pretending to be reading his handheld gas-sensitive meter as he waved it around with his left hand. But Dave was watching the right hand as it swiftly inserted a long wire down beside the window on the driver's door. The combo listening device and GPS tracker was now concealed inside the door, without setting off the tampering alarm. The agent was good at his job.

Dave also knew that same agent would have already data-entered the license number of the car parked in front of a suspect's house before entering. His car. And that his presence with the suspect this particular afternoon would not be treated as a simple coincidence. He was now also a suspect.

At a sound, Dave's head turned toward the kitchen doorway as a man stepped through. Dave looked hard into his face. The retelling of those moments when you know someone else knows, and they know you know, always fascinated Dave in class. Up until now he had not had a really good story to tell.

The man in green simply nodded, walking past him toward the door leading to the basement. They were about the same age.

"Want a cookie?" Dave asked on crazy impulse.

The man hesitated, glancing at the plate still half-full. "They do look good," he said.

Dave picked up the plate and held it out. His peer took only one, with a simple "Thank you."

It was enough. The gesture had not been so crazy, after all, or hypocritical, but a throwback to Peace Academy training. One of Professor MacLeod's favorite quotes in his English classes came to mind: "Whoever *they* may be, *they* are not the enemy."

The man's footsteps sounded heavily on the uncarpeted wooden stairs until he reached the bottom. The kitchen was silent as Dave watched the agent in the street finish checking his car for natural gas leaking in the neighborhood. It amazed him how the Bureau agents always seemed to have one more bug in their pockets in case of an added opportunity, as in the case of his car. And how fast they could find needles in the urban haystack, as in Ruth's case.

Dave would stay until the two men left. Then he would help her find one bug, to confirm his suspicions. It would be fruitless to try to find them all and make it feel safe again, for there would never be total assurance. Ruth and her mother were no longer alone in their home. And he and Ruth would be followed wherever they drove.

His urgent task at that point would be to find a secure line to phone Jerome Blackman and his Intervention Team with the new data that was shared between old friends over tea and cookies. He had the whispered name of the destination city.

*   *   *

The great bank of four linked diesel engines pulled steadily westward like a noisy shepherd, with the flock of six boxcars and fifty grain hopper cars following obediently behind in a disciplined line. They executed a sharp curve very slowly as they made yet another switchback during the steep descent from Soldier's Summit. Fork had shared that they were on the highest point in the Wasatch Range, also pointing out graveyards dating back to Johnson's Union Army up here in 1860.

Peter looked back as they snaked downward. The canvas banners on the first few grain cars were still intact on the northern side. On the southern exposure, a Utah antagonist with a long-handled scythe had done quite a lot of damage as the messages sped past: 'OUR SURPLUS' and 'FOR CHILDREN' had long gashes. At another road intersection, those which read 'FOR THE STARVING' and 'PRAY FOR US' had been targets for a powerful paint sprayer mounted on the back of a pickup. But wind from the speeding train had quickly turned the red stream into small pink polka dots on the signs as well as on the painters and some bystanders.

The meaning of the hijacking was still plain for all to read on the remaining banners, however, as the Grain Train rolled through towns and across millions of television screens on late afternoon newscasts, final destination still undeclared.

"I see just one flapping on my side now," Montropovich hollered over to Peter. "How about your side?"

"Mostly tight over here. The copter says seventeen of the original twenty are still readable," Peter yelled back over the whining engines.

"Tell me more about how you got them," Wilma said.

"Well, turns out we had a tentmaker as one of our benefactors. Those tentmakers are always showing up when God puts out the call, like St. Paul. You know what I mean?" All four laughed congenially. "We had several veteran poster painters, who decided they could think bigger, and they blocked out the letters for us. Then everyone pitched in and painted out in the backyard for three days while my folks were on vacation. It was wild!"

"It was a great idea, mastermind," Wilma grabbing the term in a moment of exuberance. "The media must be loving this rainbow picket line rolling by. Was this an Academy textbook idea?"

"We may be an original," Monty answered, sounding unusually proud.

"Then I hope it will be a successful original they'll talk about later, not just a study in frustration," Wilma responded, before switching subjects. "What conditions did you decide to offer the Intervention Team, Peter? Anything short of going all the way?" Peter had not shared details of his recent conversation with Blackman, so she boldly asked.

"I wasn't going to at first. I had always thought of this trip as all or nothing, you know. But our talks have given me more to think about. And we are attracting some attention to our cause, thanks to your talents."

Fork spoke up plainly, as usual. "Is that a yes or no, Pete?"

"Yeah, yeah," Peter chided him, "old get-to-the-point Thompson. As if we had some deadline to finish a conversation out here in the middle of these wiggling mountains." He and Wilma struggled to maintain their balance, standing toward the rear of the cab, as the engine lurched around a particularly sharp horseshoe curve a little fast.

Then Peter reluctantly admitted, "Well, I did lay out some conditions."

"You did?" Monty asked in astonishment.

"Softie," Fork ribbed him again.

"Like what?" Wilma followed up, her reporter instinct itching.

"Oh, nothing big. Like, three-fourths of all surplus grain in storage to be shipped by year-end to starving people, with delivery to the right authorities insured."

"Ah. And what else?" she pressured.

"An international conference convened this autumn under United Nations' auspices, to work out the economics of providing U.S. surplus until countries could become more self-sufficient, and develop items for trade. With one of our group to become lead planner and participate with the U.S. delegation."

"Nothing major, you said?"

"Oh, I'm not finished. There would also have to be amnesty for all on the train, and for everyone who's connected to the hijacking."

"Now you're talking," Fork threw in.

"Plus, the president would have to sign the good faith agreement."

Monty's rolling laugh boomed out. "Well, Pete, I'd say your chances of getting anyone to agree to all that by Saturday morning are..."

Peter rolled his head back, shaking it with a dismayed look.

"Uh, oh, let a little of the cat out of the bag, huh?" Monty stuttered.

"Get that tail back in there, cat! Shoo!" Fork helped out.

Wilma intervened. "Guys, I've given up listening for hints on where we're going. I miss half the things you say anyway, with all this noise. So what do you figure our chances of getting all that negotiated, Monty?"

"About the same as getting this loaded once we get to the dock..."

"Mon-ty!" Peter hollered, and threw up his hands in wild desperation.

And all this brought out the wildness in Fork. Hopping down off his brakeman's chair, he began chasing the mythical cat around the small cab interior, trying in every conceivable way to pull or push or kick it into his also invisible bag, shouting cattle roundup noises all the while he bumped his way into every corner. Wilma cracked up, Peter was going crazy trying to stay serious about a secret determined to be free.

Fork stopped shooing the cat for a moment, to catch his breath. Wilma prodded Peter, "And what is next if you do make it to the coast, Peter?"

Resigned to the arrival of the inevitable moment, he shared their noble scheme. "I guess it is time you should know. They'll get the ship loaded, then take the grain to India. They're hurting horribly, just as in Africa, but it's much closer. They'll split half with farmers for planting where land is still fertile and the weather kind, and half to starving people to grind meal." He explained that this shipment had not been treated yet with pesticides and mold preventives for storage, so it was okay to eat and plant.

"You want others to follow your example? Hijack more grain trains?"

"For crying out loud, Wilma, no. I want our government to change its policy and loosen up the restrictions. I want America to ship its surplus to wherever people are starving, and start producing up to maximum again. That's what will make this trip a success. We need to shock people back to their better senses, their higher selves, and get our food priorities straightened out."

"Then what? You go on a speaking tour, write a book, make a movie?"

"Maybe all of us together, after we get out of jail," he laughed sadly. Then he switched the tables on her with a question. "Why did you finally decide to come with us?"

Wilma got strangely quiet. Fork followed suit, returning to his chair. The men waited. She didn't respond. Peter didn't want to hurt her feelings by going on with the conversation, if an answer was working its way to the surface, but the silence felt awkward. Then he matured a mite more by realizing it was so only for him, and not for any of the three friends in the engine cab with him. So he let the feeling slip through his grasp, to be lost in the noise of the wheels and engines. The train continued its journey, the four travelers absorbed in their own thoughts.

*   *   *

"Damn, I hate being told what to do, and how to do it!" Colorado Senator Stuart Frye's bitter tones matched his frowning face. But only his pretty Denver aide was standing near enough to hear the mutterings, pulling a few lint fragments from the back of the politician's dark suit coat.

"Sir, after all, it was the majority leader who called," the young woman said, reasoning her boss into a better mood before close-up cameras started shooting. "You really had no choice. And what a coup! A plum position as chairman of a new committee. It puts you in a very favorable light."

"Dammit, Jane," the senator fumed, "remember the epithets Britain threw at Neville Chamberlain? *Great Appeaser, weakling, coward.* Just because he gave in to Hitler's first demands for territory. The Prime Minister shoved open the door to his own humiliation, then defeat. And all he tried to do was stop Hitler peacefully, by letting him keep ground he had already violently taken. Sort of like now? Sense any similarities in the ends and means here?"

The senator was getting loud again, unfortunately suggesting story angles the hallway reporters had not yet printed. So his aide brought out the latest statement draft, a result of numerous early afternoon conference calls between the senator and Washington. As Jane pointed to a new underlined phrase, Senator Frye pulled a gold ballpoint from his monogrammed shirt pocket and began changing words. The aide watched, cursing silently at the photogenic man who paid her salary, then ignored her advice.

"Are you certain you've told us everything about Peter Wayman's visit here to your office yesterday morning, Senator?" A tired thin man asked the question as he walked in from talking with Mrs. Johnson, the loyal outer office secretary.

"I'm certain I've told you everything I'm going to tell you, Agent...uh, Matthias, was it? I simply threw out that abrasive bunch of misfits!"

"It still is. Matthias...my name."

The senator didn't ignore the barb, simply returned it. "What brand of cheap cigar have you been smoking, Matthias?"

The FBI man felt a smile starting, and stifled it. "Hottest brand in Denver today, available only at Mountain West Oil Refinery, if you're referring to my pervasive aroma, sir."

"Oh, yes, nasty business out there. I suppose you boys are right in the middle of all that."

Agent Matthias shook his head, and stepped closer to the elected official to speak quietly. "Boys--and girls, Senator. I would think your profession would be more conscious of a new day dawned way back after the Thomas / Hill decision by the Supreme Court. Then Hillary Clinton's broken glass ceiling all around us. But now, back to your three o'clock call to Director Brody. Why did you wait so long, if you read Peter Wayman's name in the *Herald's* Special?"

"Well, I didn't get the paper immediately."

Agent Matthias noted the discrepancy. He had just confirmed with Mrs.

Johnson that she had put the paper on the senator's desk at 12:17. "You said there were five in the group, but you only gave us the one other name, Manuel Gomez. Have you remembered the others?"

The senator shrugged. "I don't know if I ever heard them. We didn't do a round robin of introductions, in the mood they were in. The descriptions I gave should be enough for your very capable branch, however?" The questioning tone destroyed any semblance of a compliment before the agent could grasp it.

"That group had picketed the office earlier," the senator did offer, glancing at his watch. "Sometimes police videotaped before breaking them up, in case there was later damage done. Maybe check their files?"

"Thanks, we are," the agent answered, unaware that mug shots were waiting on his desk from Brody's campus inquiries. "You say they called you a murderer right here, when you refused to do anything?"

"I didn't refuse to help. They refused my offer of reasonable process. Now, it's four o'clock. Come hear my speech, and learn how Washington works." Brusquely, the senator turned, then stopped. His aide looked him up and down, nodding approvingly. As he walked out past his secretary, he picked up a compliment as being the handsomest man in the building today, then he was striding confidently down the busy hallway.

The senator paused at the building's glass entrance doors. Two Denver policemen stood outside. A caravan of slow moving farm trucks and equipment was creating a two-block bumper-to-bumper traffic jam. People marched with signs. They looked so ordinary, compared to the usual bunch of long-hair and filthy-clothes trash, he thought.

The gaggle of anxious reporters now escorted him to the conference room under an onslaught of questions, which he fended off with his best campaign small talk left over from a successful trail two years before.

The half-filled makeshift *briefing room* lit up like a Miss America Pageant walkway as he strode the ragged aisle through the folding chairs toward the podium. He positioned himself behind the sturdy wooden stand, providing him the desired feeling of authority, plus a protective barrier he gripped firmly. He knew the heat from light bars would have him showing sweat in ninety-eight seconds, so he wasted no time.

"Good afternoon, Coloradoans, and ladies and gentlemen of the media. I am pleased to announce that I have finally received agreement from five of my distinguished colleagues in the United States Senate to join me on a new Select Committee on Agricultural Surplus in the Millennium. Our task will be to continue the ongoing interest and concern of this Administration into further improving the strong farming segment of our national economy.

"Our focus will be on resolving many of the complicated and tenacious dilemmas facing America as a respected partner and leader in the world trade community. Several major studies are nearing completion, which we will be analyzing in depth, dealing with commodity globalization, grain surplus foreign market re-stabilization, and hybridization partner with indigenous populations."

After another forty-eight seconds of college-level jargon, the official announcement concluded, and barnyard questioning started. He counted on local media being less rowdy than the Capitol Hill news gang.

"Senator Frye?" a nicely dressed older lady on the front row inquired, raising her hand. "I'm with KDNC Radio. We wonder if this Select Committee is a direct result of the Grain Train hijacking?"

So quickly the specter of British historical comparison appeared, but the senator easily flashed the charming smile. "Mrs. Ivy, I thought you had retired. Nice to see you on the hustings again." A few groaned at the dodge.

"Now, Senator, don't sweet talk your way around my question." Her voice was calm, and very firm, followed by scattered applause.

"That was certainly not my intention. You'll remember that farm reform was one strong plank on which this Administration was elected. It's an on-going initiative, as you are well aware, and this is merely the latest high-level effort at organizing response to fast-changing research efforts. I don't see any relationship to law-breaking hijackers..."

"Are you saying the train..."

"Let me finish, please. The only relationship I see is fortuitous timing. We can now clearly say to this handful of misguided men...and woman...on the stolen train that the needs of *all* farmers, not just a few, will be addressed even more fully by our new Agriculture Committee. Truly patriotic farmers now have old friends in high places, myself included. We're certainly going to listen to what farmers have to say. Why, they make up 27 percent of my own constituency. However, I hasten to emphasize that the proper time and place to do all that listening and talking will be at our hearings, not in street protests!"

"If there's no cause and effect from the Grain Train, why the haste, Senator? I'm Gilchrist, *Rocky Mountain Herald*. Normally, you give us a day's notice of your news briefings. Today it was two hours."

"Well, of course, your federal government is concerned with anyone outrageously taking the law into their own hands, and racing pell-mell across the country with a six thousand ton train, jeopardizing law-abiding citizens by speeding through every crossing, plus blowing up refineries and roads. And..." he shook his finger at Gilchrist, "...*and* threatening to do more damage if we don't agree to their blackmail!

"So a hasty announcement seemed appropriate. If those people have any reasoning left, they will see this committee--which we've been planning for months--as having their best interests at heart, and call off any further useless foolishness. Just yesterday I told Peter Wayman, here in my personal office in this very building, that all his concerns were being addressed. After physically threatening me, and forcing me to call the police, he and his radical group just stormed out. Tragically, he appeared too emotionally and mentally off-balance to hear me. But I put this very answer right into their hands."

Immediately another question: "You used a term earlier, 'grain surplus foreign market re-stabilization,' I believe. What's all that mean?"

The senator beamed and wiped at his forehead several times with his forefinger. "Glad you asked. Our committee will aggressively investigate every possible way to get top dollar for federal grain surpluses in the open world market, as well as in the European Community Exchange. This may be another way to keep paying off the national debt. Next?"

"Uh, my follow-up question." The same reporter stood up. "Why wasn't that already being done? Why did it take a crime to force this?"

The room grew very still, and warm, waiting.

The perspiring senator looked squarely at the standing reporter. "It was. And it didn't. Respectively. You may be seated. Next."

"Honorable Senator Frye, TV Channel 5 here with a question." The big man stood as he spoke. The other reporter had not sat down. A spirit of challenge was subtly growing.

The senator wondered whether he had said enough to satisfy the desires of his Congressional leadership, and whoever in the Administration was steamed up enough to have started all the folderol today. He decided to spin it out through one more. "Nice to see you, Tim."

"Senator, is it fair to interpolate from your comments that you would invite Peter Wayman and his group of farmers and engineers to testify at one of the early meetings of your new Select Committee?"

General laughter filtered around the room. The other reporter took the opportunity to casually sit down as Tim did. With cameras rolling, the freshman senator quickly joined in laughing and easing tension.

"Mr. Timmerman, I'm afraid this FBI agent has other plans for the testimony of the Wayman entourage." As he gestured toward Matthias, many cameras turned to follow his arm. The agent put his hand up to his face, hooking a finger over his nose and covering his mouth as if in deep thought, but effectively preventing a clear picture. He kept steely eyes trained on the speaker anchored behind the podium.

"But I want to make it quite clear," Senator Frye spoke out, drawing the cameras back, "that we will address every concern raised by these hijackers, plus many of greater substance. So if a goal of their misguided mission was to attract attention of this country's leadership to these problems, then I say this to Peter: We were already aware, and we are now even more formally involved as a Congress. My confused boy, lay down the weapon of the train, which you are holding to the head of the country you profess to love, and give yourself up to the authorities. Your day of battle is done."

The speaker was relishing the way the invitation had flowed, when he was interrupted. "Senator?" He looked toward the new voice to cut it off, but too late.

"Isn't it true that there really was no advance plan, and that you never heard of a new Select Committee until you were ordered late this morning to participate?" Whispering started between folding chair neighbors. "And your smoke screen was as hastily conceived as this press conference, as a direct result of pressures from the hijacking?"

The senator mopped his glistening forehead with a handkerchief. Then in utter calmness, he dodged, "Why, I don't think I need to answer, because it really is immaterial. What is of utmost importance is that this Administration is extremely responsive to the needs expressed by all citizens. We are always listening, and people can sleep securely tonight knowing that." He smiled a "Thank you" and moved to leave.

"One more question!" Gilchrist persisted loudly as the senator left the security of the podium. "Senator, why not step outside and send the picketing farmers home with that good news?"

"I'm just sorry I can't. I'm scheduled on a flight to Washington." He shook a couple of hands. "I have some early committee meetings before Congress reconvenes after Labor Day. The farmers know where they can reach me," the senator shouted back, as he smilingly quickened his pace.

"Wonder how long he's had that plane ticket?" somebody snickered.

*　*　*

"Mr. Fruehauf, thank you for coming to Salt Lake City, so we could meet." III was practicing rare diplomacy.

"It's not that far from Kansas City, Mr. Ravenhead. And we seemed to be getting nowhere over the phone."

III studied the man sitting on the sofa across the burled wood coffee table from his own comfortable couch. The husky Harrison Fruehauf had been a miner, a salmon fisherman, and an Alaskan pipeline layer in his twenties. He still had the chest and shoulder muscles to show for it.

His father had made money from a uranium strike in desolate eastern Utah in the late 1950's, and had purchased railroad stock, lots of it, in one company. Fruehauf inherited the large stockholding, and wangled a middle management job. He worked hard learning how to run a railroad, and now, as CEO of that Mid-Western Pacific, he was honcho of the country's eighth largest freight hauler.

That irked III, as his own informal title seemed somehow limiting, now that he was actually third from the top. Up until this career stage, it was merely a college carryover symbolizing his third generation name.

"On the contrary," III eventually contradicted the hulk of a man with whom he was alone in the room. "I think we have gotten somewhere. Taking the measure of one another in a stressful environment is rather like sizing up chess opponents before a match." Then, of all things, he smiled.

The uniqueness of that foreign action was completely lost on the rugged outdoorsman, who was all business. "Maybe so, Mr. Ravenhead, but tell me this. Your FBI offices are on the ninth floor. Why are we meeting on the sixth, in an insurance company executive suite?"

"Simple. I prefer the ambiance that money affords, when meeting with an important well-dressed man such as yourself."

"And?" Fruehauf pushed for the real reason.

III nodded. "And...there is a private elevator in this building. The media camped on floor nine has no idea I am down here on six, even if they recognized you coming in. I prefer they believe your presence in this building is purely a business coincidence."

"Thank you for your candor."

"I would appreciate that being your story as well, if questioned."

"I have no problem with that. However," he shifted forward to the edge of the sofa, "my position hasn't changed. I hope you don't think that my being here means Mid-Western Pacific will allow the train to be stopped by using violence. We will not." The big man of the rail industry looked the immaculate national security powerhouse straight in the eye.

"Your reasoning, again?"

The voice of each showed no hint of concession.

"We have vocal pressure groups represented among stockholders," Fruehauf answered, "who find it easy to stir up bad press. They have made it clear that for various reasons, they want the train to go through. Besides that, we haul a lot of farm products. Some shippers are saying stop, some go. But all agree on *no killing* of American farmers.

"Some grain car owners were hurt in the past," he continued, "by weird incidents, and they don't want a repeat. Bottom line: that damn train is merely an inconvenience which MWP can live with until they're done." He settled back into the soft cushion, distancing himself physically as well as philosophically.

"Ah, you can live with it. And the bombings also?"

"Attention-getters. Baby boomers. They've treated the rails with respect. 'No harm, no foul,' I say."

"We disagree, Mr. Fruehauf." And here III sat up to the edge of his couch. "You have a very provincial point of view, from limited self-interest. I have a nation's security with which I must concern myself."

"Oh, we have the nation well in mind. Maybe you hadn't noticed, but in the direction the 9039 is headed, the rails end at the ocean. The train will stop, without your G-men tearing up a lot of steel and flesh."

"Ah, but what of the lesson, Mr. Fruehauf?"

"What lesson is that?"

"My point exactly. What clear lesson would that be sending the criminally inclined? Come, steal a train, take it as far as you like? Just don't dent it on your joy ride? Not enough firmness there, Mister CEO of MWP."

"Be as firm as you want with them, after they get off!"

"No!" III said between gritted teeth. The moment for real testing of strength was upon them. "No, they will be stopped when and where and how I decide, not they. And not you."

"Just who do you think you are, besides the third person in your family called Terrence Ravenhead, for lack of imagination?"

III's eyes turned hard as any steel rail ever forged.

The CEO went on, when he had already gone too far without realizing it. "And I don't recall the president having nationalized my railroad at this point."

"Ah, *your* railroad. Built it up to be strong, like you?" III studied the man. "The railroad has always stood for everything masculine, hasn't it? Steel, spikes, long straight rails pushing into virgin territory, heavy cross ties supporting the road, giant iron engines...a real man's world."

"What tangential point are you struggling to make, Ravenhead?"

"I really wanted us to have absolute privacy for our chat, Victor."

A sudden switch to informality, a first name, and the new subject made the CEO nervous for the first time.

"Initials of names are very funny things," III switched again, unnervingly. "Kids are cruel, making up words which rhyme and fit our initials--fit us frequently to a 'T.' *V.H.F.*--Victor Harrison Fruehauf. Distinguished. *Very High Frequency* might have been appropriate. Common usage. But what kind of friend would think up a *Very Hairy Fairy* rhyme?"

Harrison had not heard that said aloud since he changed junior high schools. His puberty began too early, when he was eleven. Dark hair grew under his arms and in his crotch one long year before other boys were showing. Unwelcome eyes and hands had toyed with a young oddity in the shower room after gym class, back before it was proper to tell about sexual misconduct. Then he got to liking the feeling of the feelings, and his protests were not so convincing. He even began reaching back.

How had they uncovered a pesky past, Harrison wondered. How was he to answer a dangerous man seated opposite, smiling ignominiously?

"That was a long, long time ago..." he began.

"But Horace Thornberry is fairly recent, isn't he? Some people call him *Ace*, I think because he loves playing cards. You used to tease H.T. about his initials though, because he loved playing with other things too. Wasn't *Horny Thorny* your favorite, Victor?"

This despicable power broker had found out far too much. Harrison rashly decided to fight the fire of accusation by striking another match. "I haven't seen H.T. for years. How is he?"

"Oh, last picture I remember was in another man's bedroom. His new roommate is built a lot like you. H.T. likes his men husky. Matter of fact, I probably have a picture upstairs, if you'd like to see it. A rather good one of you also, with your hairline not quite so receded one year ago."

Harrison's risks, past and present, were compounding his stress at the moment. "Is this blackmail?" he asked with bluntness learned from rugged men during his years of running from his homosexual desires.

"Certainly not, Victor. May I call you Victor? My goal is to keep this just between us. You know, to keep anyone else from finding out. Like those fickle stockholders, so quick to judge and condemn."

Immense satisfaction showed on III's face. This chess partner had been almost too easily checkmated. He much more enjoyed playing against

Peter, and was anxious to get upstairs to that higher-stakes game.

"So what are your plans for stopping the train--Terry?" Harrison Fruehauf's tone was now one of resignation, despite his first name barb, which obviously rankled the FBI strongman.

"Oh, no need to concern yourself with those boring details. You're much too important an executive. By morning you'll have your train back, in one piece. That should really be your goal as CEO, shouldn't it? Never mind the criminals," he added, dismissing them with a wave of his hand, "just leave them to us to handle--hah, so to speak. Oh, and Victor, if anyone on your team should challenge our little compromise, tell them the FBI simply had, um, unmitigated jurisdiction over this affair."

Victor Harrison Fruehauf debated three options as III stood to leave, straightening his tie and coat: one, breaking the coffee table over the back of the FBI's paltry excuse for a man, then finishing the job by strangling him with his own tie. But there were still the pictures. Second, to take a flying leap through the picture window of the insurance office after the bastard left. And third, to perform the second act, but with Terrence Ravenhead the Third tucked securely under his arm.

On reflection, V.H.F. realized all three options could wait to see what happened tonight.

*   *   *

Here the Wasatch Mountains displayed their massive strength in rocky ridges of uneven jutting formations, their pinnacles seeming to scratch the bellies of low flying clouds as Wilma watched. Small fertile valleys nestled between the rough outcroppings, some boasting a crop of golden wheat stalks flowing like lava down the hill toward the train. Farmers were evidently in control, making the most of fertile ground even in mountainous terrain.

"Highway tunnel!" Fork barked out. This had become a ritual to alert the engine crew to the proximity of civilization, thus possible trouble.

This time they crossed under the auto traffic lanes without incident, emerging from the short underpass with the highway merging, paralleling their tracks. For a short time they ran as a team, these two types of road. Then as a hamlet appeared in the distance, the black asphalt veered away to bypass it, shrugging it off with only an exit sign and short ramp. But the cold steel rails headed straight for the small cluster of buildings.

The train whistled its familiar salutation approach to every road crossing:

two long--one short--one long. Peter and Monty could see that there were pickups and cars backed up on the road on each side of the track crossing. People were standing on car hoods to get a better view and to take cpd pictures. Some had made big placards to hold up. Most had words of encouragement; some were vile and negative.

"We're sure getting mixed reviews," Peter shouted as they got close enough to the cards to read. He was smiling and waving at all the folks on his and Monty's side nevertheless, as were Fork and Wilma on theirs.

"Yeah," Fork shouted back, "we're either famous or infamous." He never let up on the throttle as they roared past the small gathering of the curious, well-wishers, and antagonists who were honking and yelling.

"Should I console myself with the thought that they won't even remember us in a week?" Monty asked.

"Oh, I think we'll be remembered for a long time," Peter responded, wistfully. "We're a real piece of national history rolling right through their isolated neighborhood. We'll be in the schoolbooks of their kids, or their grandkids. They got to wave at us, and we waved back and so did the men in the boxcars. We made them part of a big event, and if we all succeed in turning the country's policies around, then they'll be heroes right along with us. Don't you feel that way, Wilma?" he asked his publicist.

"Well, if I stay around you long enough, I'm sure I will. Thanks for the lift, Peter. I'll try to convey it in my next broadcast. Just putting on the final touches, matter of fact."

*   *   *

"Crussman here," the woman answered with businesslike brusqueness. The Crisis Center she directed had accumulated six more reporters since mid-afternoon, and presently had twice as many staff persons since it was the five o'clock swing shift change.

"Jennifer, Dave Cranmer in Denver. Are we off the wall?" Dave certainly did not want his voice being broadcast to all media now resident on the National Peace Academy campus.

"This phone line is secure, Dave...except Cyp is getting on. We're just finishing de-briefing, and he'll be in charge here until midnight." Cypriano Daniello was a treasure chest of talent: computer whiz, a mind which never quit organizing, and a non-violent lifestyle honed while correcting Chicago's inner city injustices. He also had contacts in high places.

"Okay, here goes. I'm at a pay phone. I told Jerome earlier that the

FBI had made me when they bugged Ruth Fitzwater's house and car. I'm surprised they haven't picked me up by now. Maybe giving me enough rope to..."

"If they do," Jennifer interrupted, "you know to make us your number one call. We have an agreement with Washington about our regional reps, but sometimes they forget."

"Right," Dave responded. "Now get this to Aunt Sarah if she's handy..." This was their code phrase for punching in immediate data entry.

Cyp sat down at the swing-out keyboard of the control desk, entered his top rung security name, and selected choices faster than the screen could scroll it: 'Regional Input, Rocky Mountain, Special Code: GT.' The files would begin an automatic sort and scan routine for possible subject linkages.

"Our Denver team still has nightmares about our neighbor, the Rocky Mountain Arsenal. We remember that the Sarin nerve gas was produced right here during World War II and the Cold War era. DIMP is a by-product that contaminated the groundwater, and they're still cleaning up the environment. At least, that's the cover for lots of activity for people in hazmat suits."

Cyp tapped his fingers on the desk, waiting for something tangible to type into the computer. He suspected he knew where this reminiscence was going.

"If the FBI's operatives got hold of a nerve gas, they could lay a cloud of it across the tracks, let the train run through it, and pick up the bodies on the other side. Never know what hit them. No bomb orders go out from someone unconscious in the cab. Then stop the train with a remote signal, and the railroad gets their property back in one piece. That's our scary scenario for this afternoon. We're afraid the government's still got this gas around, and will use it if the wind is blowing the right direction. Getting all this?"

"You bet, and thanks," Cyp acknowledged. "I'll suggest Blackman fly the next three hundred miles of track back and forth before dark. Maybe even later with the night vision radar, to look for a canister of unknown trouble."

"Yeah. Stuff out of those bunkers was designed with killing in mind. Now please patch me through to Jerome. I have the latest weather report from the Seattle area...and that is still confidential, but we can act on it."

*   *   *

Chapter Thirteen

Agent Switzer was taking the damnation from his boss in stride. III got this way under intense pressure on road trips, and would never apologize, just return to normal reliance on his aide's help.

"Hell, if I wanted delays, I would have stayed in D.C.," III cursed.

"Sorry, Mr. Director. Very poor judgment on my part."

III stood studying the fax photos from the Denver office, which Switzer had waited twenty long minutes to deliver until III returned from his visit with Mid-Western Pacific's Fruehauf. Now Ruth, Chanto, Tom, Ardis, Manuel, and Jeremy were spread out on the table before him--guilty of being members of the Shakespeare Group and primary suspects.

He pushed Ruth's picture aside, hissing, "If Brody can find one in Denver, surely we can find one in Salt Lake City, since I am here now and in charge!" His pounding fist emphasized his point.

"Yes, Mr. Director," Switzer quickly agreed. "Probably one or more are here, and we'll find them! Possibly near the most important Latter Day Saints landmarks in or around Temple Square, so a discreet search has begun of grounds and buildings."

"Order surveillance of restaurants and shops within six blocks. Get these remaining five creeps onto one sheet and distributed."

"Right away, Mr. Director." Switzer turned to follow orders.

"Damn it, when I'm through I'll tell you."

The aide wheeled around with one more mistake logged in. "That fruity Fruehauf may be close to going off the deep end under this pressure. He seemed paranoid when I met with him downstairs. Should he appear here, consider him as dangerous. Station an armed agent at our entry door. Don't let him pass, even if he insists on seeing me.

"Next, search this building thoroughly for bombs. I am not exactly low on the list in this game of possible targets."

Switzer wished he already had a search ordered. Too much too fast.

"That accursed train is due here after 6:30 tonight. I'd advise you to be out of this building by 6:00," III went on. "Arrange for my car and driver to be ready at 5:45, with TV reception. Pick a spot on the far side of town, close to the tracks where the train will pass regardless of destination, with no company. Those sickos will see that I could have stopped their borrowed time right there, if I had chosen to do so."

Switzer was making notes of details as fast as he could write.

"Once the maniac has declared his route from here, I must get ahead of him again. His only smart choice among dumb options is California, so get the San Francisco Office primed for my arrival. And this time, Switzer, ignore the president's directive." Disgust crept into his voice. "I don't care if every other U.S. Government employee has to fly commercial, this is a national security mission, and I want a military jet. I will not tolerate another airport mob scene. In fact, someone will lose their job if that occurs again. Clear? Send these five mug shots to the Bay Area, and to Reno and Carson City; I told the Nevada Governor we'd keep him updated. Another long shot: hit Boise and Portland and Seattle also. The fool could turn north. Why are you standing there? You have a great deal to do in less than an hour."

Switzer had become nervous as the list grew, for just that reason. He reached for the doorknob.

"Oh, yes." The door remained shut, and Switzer turned back. "You may mention the possibility of office evacuation to the Salt Lake staff, if you have time after you finish your arrangements. But not the other building tenants. It's probably an unnecessary precaution, and would just worry them. Most of the sluggards will have left by then anyway."

*   *   *

"Sky Spy, your reception is looking good." Denver TV Channel 5 radioed the helicopter in preparation for the 6:30 P.M. Special Report.

"Roger," Boyd Tangent acknowledged, adjusting Channel 8 copter's belly camera for the better long-range angle. Below him, downtown Denver streets were filled with amazing varieties of farm equipment circling the State Capitol Building. Police had barricaded off the parking loop that surrounded the historic granite edifice, for safety of the building occupants and visitors. So the growing contingent of farmers gravitated to blocks around it. Even though the offices were closed, and the bureaucrats gone, the urban parade of rural protesters went on.

Control room technicians in TV-5 studied another monitor. A cameraman was standing at the corner of Colfax and Sherman in front of the State Capitol, filming the line of pickup trucks, campers, and tractor-trailers inching heavy equipment past him. Some carried blatant sign messages tied or taped to their sides: "Farmers Unite!" "Government, Get Patriotic!" "Feed The Babies, And Let The Good Train Roll!" Those signs, and the expressions on the faces of the drivers and passengers, would tell their own graphic story when their segment came.

The sportscaster in a green blazer was wrapping up current baseball standings on the live set monitor, then would comment on Thursday afternoon games. A blooper was cued up to finish sports, then the announcement to be sure and stay tuned immediately following for the special news report and exclusive film coverage of the hijacked Grain Train. Then close with the informal smiles and cheery "Have a good evening, we'll see you again at ten o'clock" would take them to two minutes of advertisements.

Sandwiched in the busy control room was its station manager, Tiny Tim Timmerman. His thirteen-hour workday had tired him, and he had another four hours to withstand, but the adrenaline was flowing for the Special.

His team was ready. Before starting the six o'clock newscast, Tim had told his staff the results of a long conversation he had with network execs. In the minds of his bosses, the Grain Train was not yet of sufficient national interest, despite the play given it by his radio and newspaper partners. The Special would be limited to only the Rocky Mountain and Pacific Regions. But he urged everyone on the crew to do his and her best, since it was designed for national caliber level. He confided that he hoped to sell it to Cable NewsNet, then revved up his team. "Let's go out there and win some awards--and bonus checks!"

Tim Timmerman was very good at many things, including quick decision-making. As he surveyed the many monitors on standby, he made up his mind on another issue. "Lexus," he spoke into the Bluetooth phone in his left ear, connected to the SLC television studios in Utah, "we'll go with your footage of III at Salt Lake International, right after the shot of the Mormon Temple to make the setting." He jotted cryptic notes on the scheduling log. "There's still no way of getting hold of him at the FBI offices there? It's just after 6:28, same as here, and you know they've got to be working on this."

Tim glanced at the wall clock, then at monitor #17 as he listened. The helicopter of Denver's TV-5 team was hovering at an even speed five hundred feet ahead of the Grain Train lead engine, with a zoom lens focused on the number 9039 above its front windows.

One more minute of ads during the break, then the home screens would flash onto that sight, as TV-5's news analyst Vance Walker introduced this Special Report. The lens would draw back to get the whole engine, the copter would slide over and sit in space, twenty feet to the side of the track, and film the train as it roared past them, with gigantic sound. This opening should grab the audience, and the ratings.

"Lexus, what are the chances of the train stopping during our half-hour Special?" Tim asked his Salt Lake counterpart. "It would make dynamite footage...So Harran Winfree says railroad dispatch has no notice yet?... What about the Feds making a move against the train? Any manpower forming along the tracks?...So if it stays running right through Salt Lake, best we can do is the crowd scene. You got the biggest one covered?...OK, I'm with you at the depot on our #14...Say, can you run a clock on there to show ETA of the train at that spot?...Great!"

Tim took one last glance across the bank of eighteen monitor screens, each loaded with tapes on pause from Denver and around the country, or live announcers standing by, or of course another ad if things went haywire. His anchorman Vance Walker had moved to a desk on an hour-old set. Large background pictures Velcroed on those modular walls created a quite incredible composite of wheat field, tall grain elevators, and the long train itself in the distance.

"On Camera 2," Tim heard from the anchor set's speakers into the soundproof control room. In the headset in his right ear, he heard his controller giving the same number countdown to the helicopter pilot shadowing the train in Utah. "You have three, two, one..."

Monitor #17 went live. The block numbers '9 0 3 9' filled the screen, as the controller continued directing the chopper, "Now stand still...fade back..." And Tim saw the huge green engine in its entirety.

Vance Walker announced in mellifluous tones aimed for an Emmy...

"Grain Train 9039:

Mission of Mercy--or Mayhem?"

...as these words flashed on the screen, the first line done in grains of wheat, the second line in block gold lettering. The controller was saying, "The full train! Full sound! Let it pass...yeah, just watch it go by...good!"

The Special Report had begun. Tiny Tim and hopefully three million viewers were glued in.

"Cue Vance, switch to Camera 3 on three, two, one..."

"The trainload of grain, hijacked in Denver early this morning, still plummets along tracks approaching Salt Lake City. In those open boxcars are farmers from Colorado and Utah. In the engine, one retired and one fired engineer, a hostage newspaper reporter who passed up more than one chance to leave, and Peter Wayman, the strategist behind this bizarre plot."

The screen had filled corners with faces of each person in motion as the announcer introduced them, isolated pictures taken by the leap-frogging helicopters. "Bring up monitor #7 full screen," the master tech said, and Peter's image expanded to block out everyone else.

"Thirteen clip on right half," ordered the tech, and Peter squeezed onto the left half of the screen while his bio appeared on the right as the announcer read highlights. The impression was of a mug shot.

"Denver's sky lit up dramatically last night, and fires continue raging," Vance reported authoritatively.

"Take us to #10," the tech said, and the screen filled with boiling flumes of crimson and jet black from two burning oil tanks showing on #10 monitor. The word 'LIVE' appeared at the bottom of the picture.

*   *   *

As the TV announcer credited the *Unite Surplus and Starving* group with that bombing, Ardis Borgeba cheered softly outside, wildly inside. Alone in her latest Portland motel room, the young explosives expert took delight in seeing the destructive results of her students.

The voice was saying the Texan oil fire team hoped for containment by midnight, since federal emergency relief funds had been authorized by the president. The program mentioned the DIA highway tunnel, and the screen showed an earlier helicopter shot of the collapsed concrete structure, with traffic blocked back a mile in each direction.

"Right on!" Ardis exclaimed. "What a team!" She could hardly keep her voice in check as she studied the pictures. She kept her cpd aimed at the screen, recording these small images for replaying again as soon as it finished, and she knew Ruth would be recording it on dvd in the privacy of her Denver home for their enjoyment when everybody got back.

*   *   *

The Airport Security Office at Salt Lake International was a beehive of activity. Every reserve officer and trainee from the SLC police force had been asked to volunteer for a massive ongoing bomb search. Retirees from the Utah State Patrol and federal enforcement agencies living in the Salt Lake area had received a request to report for hazardous duty.

And now the honeycomb of terminal, hangars, roadways, and parking garages crawled with a myriad of uniformed officers, looking at anything and everyone suspiciously. Explosives-sensitized dogs sniffed around parcels, and portable scan booths multiplied outside. More law officers than fearful passengers roamed the Salt Lake airport, but it remained open.

Charts covered Security Office walls, showing the time each segmented area of the airport complex had last been searched. The command post was humming as the Grain Train approached Utah's capital city eight miles to the east. Travelers stopped to watch this television Special as it focused on their area of concern:

"These terrorist bombings, accompanied by threats of more bombs if the train was harassed, forced delays and re-schedulings at Denver International, the fifth busiest terminal in the country. This broken spoke has damaged the wheel of airline travel today, with thousands of delays reported nationwide, as here in Salt Lake City." Long lines waiting at ticket counters flashed on the screen to back up his statement.

"One person whose flight did get through was FBI Assistant Director Terrence Ravenhead," Vance was saying, "shown here as he arrived in Salt Lake City to direct law enforcement efforts."

The clip carried its own sound, and the words 'Filmed Earlier:'

"Sir, what steps will be taken to stop the hijacked train?"

"Whatever steps are necessary, within the framework of the legal system," the FBI man replied.

"Can we assume that includes derailment, sir?"

"You can assume anything you [bleep] well want."

That same man in the same suit studied the television screen from his limousine's back seat. With disdain, III told the driver what garbage this was, as he continued watching.

"The Washington, D.C. headquarters of the FBI and Homeland Security declined comment, as did the White House when we contacted them earlier today," the announcer said.

They damn well better, III thought. He did not want his hands tied in this B-grade Western scenario.

"One-eighth #8 to upper left, ready #12," the master tech ordered in the Denver studio.

The picture of III being interviewed diminished in size up to the top left hand corner, while the announcer returned centered. "Oddly, Peter

Wayman's father, Franklin, is Deputy Regional Director of Denver's FBI office." His image appeared, one-eighth screen upper right, angrily motioning persons away as he drove away in a silver Lincoln Continental.

"No, full screen on #12," and the tech overrode the setting, zooming it up, as the announcer smoothly continued.

"We understand the elder Wayman has been furloughed from his post, at least until this family conflict of interest is settled. It seems obvious the son's criminal activity has strongly impacted the father's career, who was brought in today with his wife Marion to police headquarters for questioning."

In the Motel 7 room near Denver where the Wayman family and Felicia Montropovich had retreated for temporary privacy, Josephine Williamson commented to her son-in-law, "That's a very ugly expression, Franklin." His face went zooming up to the screen corner opposite III again.

"It's an ugly time, Mrs. W. Now, sh-h-h!" he commanded.

"Dad!" Candice chided him.

*

In the control room, the Denver tech quietly instructed, "Fade out to #4, full screen."

"Were you going to have caption on that?" Tim Timmerman asked. The shot showed a shiny gold-domed Colorado State Capitol Building from the air, and blocks of traffic jammed with assorted trucks and large farm equipment. A flicked switch brought up the 'Denver,' and the engaging word 'LIVE.'

"This is Sky Spy," the new voice crackled over the airwaves. Rotor blades chopped the background. "I've watched these vehicles coming from all over to join this parade supporting the Grain Train, and its message. You can see from this height..." and the helicopter was rising, "...the gigantic cloverleaf. These rigs are encircling the Capitol, weaving down around the Federal Building, where the FBI and Agriculture staffs are headquartered. Down a few more blocks around Senator Frye's place, and another loop to surround the block of *Rocky Mountain Herald* offices.

"The sheer numbers of the hundreds of vehicles continually weaving around their four targets have pretty well strangled any other commuter traffic. My advice is, don't drive into downtown Denver tonight, unless you're a farmer with a lot of patience. Listen for traffic reports tomorrow morning to see if they stay, or get tired and go home, or whether the police find a way to break it up--which they haven't yet."

*

"Al," Mrs. Federson called out from their living room, "you should come watch this. They're talking all about the farmers now."

"Mabel, I'm still four families short of finding places for them to lodge tonight," he shouted from the kitchen. "Dang phone," he muttered, as it rang again.

The picture faded back from the elevated shot to Vance Walker at the anchordesk. "And what is this really all about? Well, the farmers driving our streets said they had come to talk. But everybody's left those offices by this hour. Still the farmers drive, and more keep coming. Let's look at some of their sign messages, and later we will talk with them ourselves."

The screen began building a montage of crudely lettered signs through window portions opening and closing. Protesters carried some; others were on the sides of tractors. "And here is what the train itself shows..." he continued, as the banners from the boxcars rolled past.

*

The phone rang out at Serv-U.S. national headquarters, and a weary Shelly Smith-Jones answered, flipping to page five of her day's log.

"S.J., what are you doing still there? It's almost ten, your time." Club President Barney O'Brien was checking in from California.

Oh, really? she felt like answering, Instead, she said, "Waiting to hear from you about the Special. It's blacked out east of the Mississip'."

"They haven't aired any of my interview yet. Think they will?"

"You'd better keep watching to see." *Men are such shameless egotists.*

"I think the Board was very courageous, going public on Peter's behalf, don't you?"

"I think part of the credit goes to your strong leadership, Barney," Shelly said, for the fourth time.

"Thanks. Any more results on *our* questionnaire?"

Our questionnaire was the document *she* drafted, modified, faxed to all 740 clubs, and on which she was tabulating. "Of the one-fourth in so far, 55 percent for the train, 45 percent against, but more than 90 percent favoring a national debate immediately on our farm surplus problem."

"All right!" Barney enthused. "Oh, oh, I'm missing stuff. I'll call ya back. This really ought to start the phones ringing, eh?" Click.

Just what I had hoped to hear this very night, Shelly thought, stretching her aching shoulders and standing up. The national spotlight was about to shine on her boss and her organization, and thus, on her. It had been a long time since she was this exhausted from excitement.

*

"And here is what the hijackers themselves said about their mission."

Wilma Fletcher's increasingly familiar plea to free up the U.S. surplus grain store for feeding the starving was the voice-over for silent scenes of emaciated Africans, South Americans, war-torn Far Easterners, and mid-European refugees.

Anchorman Vance Walker continued: "These excerpts are from the upcoming Special, 'To Have and To Hold, 'Til Death Do Us Part.' This will be shown on most of these stations one hour after we complete this news report. Channel Five learned that Peter and Monty were well aware..."

"Flash #5 and #6 on eighths in uppers," the tech instructed, and the two pictures matching the names appeared in corner windows.

"...of tonight's telecast about serious hunger problems. In fact..."

"Flash #7 and #8 on eighths in lowers," was instructed, bringing up a picture of Frank and one of Marion with her arm around Candice.

"...Peter had actually requested that the Wayman family plan on watching our 'To Have and To Hold' Special. So it may be more than mere coincidence that the hijacking of 9039 was timed for today.

"Certainly America is being gripped by the emotionally charged marriage of *have* and *have-not* nations in our shrinking world, with daily confrontations of the economics of deprivation versus surplus. Two burning questions are raised tonight. First, how much is more than enough in this land of plenty? And second, how will our nation's leaders deal with today's bearers of this question?

"Earlier today, the Wray farmers on board the Grain Train mixed it up with hobos trying to hitch an illegal ride on an illegal run. These remarkable scenes were filmed moments after the hijackers stopped to ward off the attack..."

"Fade out desk, bring up #11," the tech said, following the script. Hard men struggling for physical dominance took over the screen. The fighting was shown from their feet up, making it appear the cameraman was knocked down.

"The TV-5 film crew was outside, standing beside the open boxcar," Vance explained, "having just landed their helicopter nearby. And in this critical moment..." BANG!

Peter's warning shot rang out in four million homes. "...law enforcement officials were put on notice that the hijackers are armed, despite their earlier claims of adopting strict non-violence. The man crumpled in that corner is Wray farmer Fulton Skinnard, now under arrest and in serious condition at the Green River, Utah, hospital.

"The woman kneeling to tend him is *Rocky Mountain Herald* reporter Wilma Fletcher, the hourly voice of the hijackers." Her photo from the newspaper morgue files was moved to one corner. She was originally believed forced to join the train crew, but has passed up numerous opportunities to run for cover with the trailing media, this being the first of those times. Here you see our KTAD Channel 5 primetime newscaster Donna Harrison, in camouflage fatigues for this rigorous assignment, talking with Wilma about escaping to the helicopter..."

Tim had personally insured that clips included close-ups of his team, easily identified by local viewers, putting their station right in the middle of the action.

"Kill #11 on my cue, stand by #13." As he listened to the directions of his crew, Tim answered a control booth phone's flashing blue light.

"Timmerman...I'll take it," he said into a desk phone. "Hello, Mr. Dunnahee. Yessir, glad the FCC is watching...No, sir, this is certainly not... No, we are in no way conspiring to network outside our licensed area. This is our story of origin and we are merely following it...I don't know about any relay transmissions from the train. We've been getting Wilma's broadcasts through CB channel intercept..." Tim sighed, thankful that was the one he chose to broadcast. "No, our being there certainly does not countenance any illegality...Well, I take strong exception to the FBI's insinuation of staging..."

Two segments had been completed while he argued, one with Colorado Senator Frye's news conference expounding on Administration readiness for committee hearings, and the other showing the Crisis Intervention Team gearing up for travel at the National Peace Academy. There was a reference to an astonishing three hundred thousand hits on the Internet blog for Grain Train, exhibiting growing national interest in this story. The Special was drawing to a close. It needed to be dramatic.

Tim watched monitor #14 while listening to Salt Lake's controller in his left ear, and now raised the right hand phone's FCC exec out of hearing range.

"Lexus, the timing is perfect. Have your people tell that crowd they're going live on national TV in thirty seconds. We need more action there with the train coming. GO!"

Down came the right hand phone. "Mr. Dunnahee, I need to cap off this Special. I'll call you first thing in the morning, thanks." Worry about co-conspirator charges would keep.

"Will there be more recruiting of farmers, as Peter did in Helper, Utah, when he stopped to refuel?" Vance questioned, as the screen was reliving that unusual scene. "Will there be more shooting from person's unknown?" And Tim actually ducked along with Peter as shots rang out in the Helper rail yards on re-broadcast.

On monitor #14, the large crowd outside downtown Salt Lake's railroad depot covered the platform on both sides of the scheduled track. As if on cue, which in fact it was, they came to silent life, waving their signs and arms, their mouths busy in the voiceless words of waiting monitors. Tim knew it would be a good sound bite. Then he saw through the camera's eye the approaching Grain Train engine. If it hurried, it would be phenomenally perfect.

"Lexus," he hollered into the phone, "give us a close-up on the engine first, then fade to the crowd. They're rabid dogs--great work!"

Tim motioned to his tech to have Vance move to the remodeled weather map for a wrap-up showing the four possible train routes from Salt Lake, lighted in four colors: west through upper Nevada toward San Francisco; south into Arizona to Mexico and the Gulf; south through lower Nevada toward San Diego; or north through Idaho to the Pacific Northwest. This was just in case Harran Winfree got the destination call in the dispatch office in the next three minutes.

Then Tim picked up a headset from the desk. "TV-5 chopper?" he asked, looking at monitor #15. When the pilot confirmed, Tim gave instructions. "We're almost ready for the big finish. Your elevation shot looks good. Go ahead and zoom back in now on the lead engine. Let it fill your screen... good. Now remember, when you get the signal, start drawing the zoom back evenly. It needs to take five full seconds to get back to the max distance angle where you just were when I called. Got it? Just keep following that engine now, right into the depot crowd." Fortunately for effect, those platforms were not roofed.

The stage was set. Tim surveyed each monitor, like looking at all the candy jars in an old drugstore, but always coming back to his favorite, the one with the cinnamon sticks, the one his audience was looking at. On that one, anchorman Vance Walker was at the map, wrapping up on a serious

244

T.E.J.T.M.

note. "We don't know which route they will choose. That is still their secret. All we can report is that at this moment they are entering Salt Lake City..." and the tip of his finger touched the star in upper Utah, right at the lower end of the long blue lake of salt.

Tim watched as that star became a tiny picture of a train engine coming straight at them, filling more and more of the screen. He regretted his orders to Lexus as the train then seemed to go backward with the zoom lens widening to pick up the crowds near at hand. But it was still a damn good documentary.

"Take #15 out a little, to get the same perspective," Tim ordered the tech, who immediately complied with a cue to the chopper. The top of Engine 9039 expanded to include the tops of all four engines, and that same distance in front and on the sides. "Better," Tim said, then added, "Take us up and away."

On cue, the view switched from platform to helicopter camera, and began slowly ascending with the train growing longer and more of the watching crowds included in the picture. Vance began his conclusion.

"The questions raised by this bizarre train hijacking are many and complex. Who has the answers? What will it take to finally balance the surplus products of the *haves* with the desperate needs of the *have-nots*?"

Tim glanced at the waiting monitor #16, then back to the real screen as the transition was ready to be made from the helicopter camera to a small plane flying 3,000 feet over Salt Lake City. The minimum lens aperture was focused on exactly the full length of the train, just where the maximum chopper picture left off. Without a hitch, the monitor #15 zoom stopped and #16 took over.

"What will become of these persons and this grain?" Vance's tone of concern came over the speakers in the control booth. "If they are modern day Robin Hoods, where is their Sherwood Forest of protection? And how can they put their stolen gains into the hands of the poor they so urgently claim to want to help, with the sheriff ready to pounce?"

The plane's lens continued widening, seeing more and more--with the train always at the center of the picture, but becoming infinitesimally small as downtown Salt Lake appeared. The Temple spires and Tabernacle dome were distinctive, but then within another five seconds also became indefinable as Great Salt Lake made its appearance. First it was shoreline, then a huge mass of blue on the right offsetting green treetops covering most of the half-million buildings on the left.

"How will this saga end? With the destruction of grain? More bombings? With violence and bloodshed? Perhaps even death? It might turn out that in this case, the end may justify the means. But for which side? Pondering these questions, we leave you--with our pledge to keep America informed."

At this magic moment, a third historic camera kicked in smoothly, taking over the continuing ascent into space. The whole lake became a dark irregular ink spot, next to the wrinkled skin of the Wasatch Range and the plainness of salt flats from ancient Bonneville. Within seconds, all of the State of Utah filled the beautiful screen, then the rugged outline of the Rocky Mountains began dividing a continent. The satellite pictures were breathtaking, emphasizing one of Tim's major points of the Special: on this small planet, starvation and surplus seemed incongruous.

"Run the credits," Tim requested of his master technician, giving him a thumbs-up sign. And the list of names began quickly scrolling down, to the right of the cloud-dotted blue-green-brown earth. Tim was very appreciative of his crew.

He looked at the broadcast clock. "Good, twenty seconds. Cue Anchor to ask for votes. Let's put it on top of the Utah helicopter view."

And a moment later, the train was again on the screen, wending its way slowly through the yards toward the control tower. Vance was now reading: "Following our TV-5 custom of polling your opinion, and in the spirit of live-time electronic balloting, we now invite you to register your opinion. To *stop* the train, press #1 on your ballot box, as explained on your screen. To let the train *go through*, press #2. It's a fifty-cent vote. Updated results will be announced hourly and on our ten o'clock news. The totals will also be phoned to all groups directly involved in this event. Make your opinion count: VOTE NOW.

"During the course of our Hunger Special at eight o'clock this evening, we will keep you informed of any further developments in this fast-breaking story of Grain Train 9039 -- mercy and mayhem."

*   *   *

"Pete, this is Harran, over." The radio protocol rulebook had been shelved for this journey, as had the track usage regulations and time schedule priorities. It had come down to one friend talking to another, while breaking all the rules.

"Hi, Harran, where are you now?" Peter's clear voice responded.

"Look to the right of your track, a hundred yards ahead. I'm up here in the tower. Closest we've been since golf last Monday." In trying to distance himself from conspiracy charges, Harran had told his inquisitors all about their Monday meetings at the 19th Hole for a casual beer, and assured them that there was never a hint about any hijacking.

"Can you come to a window?" Peter asked.

Harran looked up at the white-haired, strongly handsome man standing at his elbow. The man in charge, Mid-Western Pacific President Fruehauf, nodded his consent.

The Salt Lake City railroad dispatcher's office was usually informal. Harran and all office regulars wore sport shirts and slacks, but lots of other persons were there in suits tonight. The track board for the city switching yards was lighted with reds, greens, and yellows on the switch locations. On the wall to the left, the district map was similarly lighted, with blue, brown, and orange train colors adding contrasting information. Harran moved across the room and leaned out the window to wave down at the engine passing slowly.

Peter leaned out of the cab window beside Monty and waved up at the smiling face. Then he spontaneously hollered at the top of his lungs, "Hail, fellow, well met!"

Harran opened his mouth to shout his funny re-phrase, then stopped, thinking of the people behind him. He and Peter were the same men still, but the times had changed things between them.

Peter understood the silence, waving a little sadly one last time, then pulled back inside the engine to the business at hand.

"Moment of declaration, Peter," Harran was radioing. "If you wait any longer, you'll have to stop. Which would be the best idea anyway," he quickly added. "You've brought a lot of attention to the surplus..."

"Thanks, Harran, but we're going on."

"Then I'll tell you up front you'll have to go very slowly for five or ten minutes, while I finish clearing tracks in whatever direction you tell me. You've simply waited too long. What's it going to be?"

Visitors in the crowded office had been making all sorts of inquiries about the track switching process, and tracing routes with their fingers west, south, and north on the wall maps. The air had been heavy with second-guessing. Now all talking stopped abruptly, and most of the people clustered around Harran at the radio desk.

"Okay, here's how it will be," Peter's strong voice relayed.

Every word was being recorded, as well as monitored in two other offices in the rail yard building.

"Clear us north, 165 miles, to Pocatello, Idaho. Then leave, and meet us on the radio from up there."

That announcement electrified the room. Every phone and radio on standby went into immediate use. Within moments, the word *North* had been communicated to Regional FBI and Homeland Security offices and the NPA Crisis Center, to Denver's TV-5 and the *Herald* and KDNC radio, to an Interior Department Under-Secretary, III in his limousine a mile away, and all major media in the Western United States.

*   *   *

Wilma touched Peter's arm as he sat on the trunk, running his hourly calls as they left Salt Lake behind them. He looked at her.

"We have a fan waiting up ahead," she said.

Puzzled, he stood quickly, knowing how fast the train travels past points and people. She pointed out the left side.

A black limousine was parked with its front bumper right up to the tracks. One man stood beside it on the passenger side, wearing a dark suit. He stood at full attention, focused on their cab window.

Now the train was close enough for Peter to see the features of the elite man's face. Square jaw, thin lips firmly set, chiseled nose and cheekbones, deep sockets for the eyes.

An eerie feeling crept over Peter, beginning at the nape of his neck and draining downward over his skin. It made Peter drop his gaze to the man's hands, looking for a gun. One fist was empty by his side; the other moved to hold up a billfold. No, a cardholder--like the one his father carried his FBI card in.

The train now brought them within seven feet of one another, and those eyes met his, and locked. Who was hypnotizing the other? A book of thoughts passed between them. Then instantly they were separated by an engine-length as the 9039 roared on down the track.

Wilma watched it all happen, then asked Peter if he knew the man.

"All I know for certain is..." he answered somberly, "...that man wants to kill me."

*   *   *

Chapter Fourteen

A fleeting look on Sadrieh's face gave him away, the reserved tone of voice confirming Chanto Kudjakta's suspicions. The FBI had just linked Chanto through the Shakespeare Group to the Grain Train--only sixteen hours after the hijacking.

Sadrieh had been a very polite host. They had become closer friends during the day's vigil in the ham radio room in Sadrieh's basement, monitoring the train through the high Rockies and the rugged Wasatch down into the valley of the Great Salt Lake.

But the outside phone call to Sadrieh had changed the equation. Chanto had not overheard, but had guessed. By intimidation or lies, someone had persuaded Sadrieh to let a third person join them, a stranger. This would be the FBI plant.

He debated with himself what action to take, trying not to panic. He could leave before the new *model railroad buff* arrived, and go to another club member's house, but at this point he would just be followed. His distinctive African Consulate car license plates had undoubtedly been easy to locate, once they suspected him.

Should he notify Peter during the next scheduled phone call? They could likely have his cellular phone traced for listening in by now.

But how could they arrest him, he wondered seriously, with the bomb threat and Consulate protocol protection? Protection! That's it! He needed his share increased.

Chanto excused himself to another room, and dialed Ruth Fitzwater to talk about the *bugs* this summer.

"I have them everywhere," she quickly assured him, "inside the house and car."

They were both in jeopardy, as was the mission. Who would handle Denver if they both were arrested?

His fast mind decided him on a course of added security. He called his Consul to send one of their Military Attachés to Sadrieh's home, for overnight protection in a rough Denver neighborhood. Because of the intense interest in the Grain Train network they were tracking, Sadrieh had earlier agreed to let Chanto bunk on the radio room's futon. Now Chanto would be moving rapidly toward a major test of his diplomatic immunity and possibly strain international relations between the U.S. and his Ethiopian homeland. But they had known that might happen.

Chanto would break radio silence by saying code words to Peter at 7:11: "The Bills are shaving." "Bills," for himself and for Ruth as members of the William Shakespeare Group; "shaving," for being uncovered; and present tense, for happening without arrest.

Dinner for four would then begin the cat and mouse dialogue at Sadrieh's home, with only his attaché and his host having nothing to hide. He would guard every word.

*   *   *

A diverse fleet of aircraft stood available across the U.S., every hour of every day. With major airlines and metro police departments cooperating, planes and copters were on call for NPA emergency use.

The privilege was invoked again this Thursday evening. An Academy jet arrived with the Intervention Team into Boise, Idaho, at 6:00 P.M., one hour before Peter announced his northwestern route, one hour after Dave Cranmer warned of arsenal gas.

Retrofitting took several hours, with the special parts as ordered. Airport personnel mounted a top unit of eight ultra-bright floodlights pointing all directions by the top rotor shaft. Two fuel tanks were added in the place of a back seat. The Jet Ranger helicopter could now stay airborne ten hours with three people. The teams knew it was more the power of their presence, not their numbers, which induced peace. National Peace Academy identification decals now covered the National Park Service markings of the owner.

They were the only aircraft lifting off at 9:15. Blackman, his pilot, and another team member Ned, all in distinctive white uniforms, sat cramped in beside water, cameras, and flares. The other members would strategize, then sleep, to be ready for Friday morning's relief shift.

The helicopter crew slowly snaked their way southeast along the rails to rendezvous with the Grain Train. They followed the updated rail line maps just printed at the Academy, showing location of legitimate work crews and equipment along the track. Their night mission was to convince Peter to stop, or to at least allow Blackman to board for dialogue. They also were armed with a plethora of night scanning military devices to check the advance miles of track for any derailing efforts. They knew the FBI was now operating from a position of embarrassment, and the Administration was short-fused on criminal activity. Cover of night was a great temptation for law enforcement, even though the Academy had pledged to Washington that it would help resolve this very quickly, and non-violently. Blackman had notified the train of their scouting party presence, not mentioning the unconfirmed possibility of gas, since it might trigger a premature bombing. So first-night jitters inside the helicopter bubble were natural.

*   *   *

In consternation, the Waymans had thrown together a few clothes in carry-on luggage from the motel, swinging by to pick up a frantic girlfriend. Candice had been the go-between, driving over to notify Janet of travel plans, seeing if she wanted to go try to talk sense into Peter, calling back *yes* in code, then returning to the motel to drive her grandparents and Mrs. Montropovich back home.

Frank, Marion, and Janet raced to DIA, stopping for signal lights only when other traffic forced it. Frank had both called and laptopped for reservations, but incredibly, all Portland and surrounding area flights for the next twelve hours were booked solid, apparently with the backups from the morning bombings.

He was certain there would be cancellations, so they left to just go wait in the terminal. They worked through reservation counters when they arrived, checking in person on availability. The story was the same at each. Then in Pacific Northwest's line, Frank heard a man two agents away ask for four tickets to Portland on Flight 268, the one he had just been told was full. But the agent said, "Certainly, sir. First Class?"

Frank turned back to confront the agent who had denied him. "Hey! That man just bought four tickets on 268 to Portland!" He was mad, and loud.

"Maybe somebody cancelled, I don't know, but I won't tolerate rudeness. Mr. Shneidecker?"

The man who had directed them into line in the first place was now at Frank's elbow, with two air terminal security guards.

Frank silently recited a self-control verse, while taking one deep breath and exhaling slowly. He smiled while carefully opening his coat. "I'm sorry. I have identification..."

His hand was stopped as he was reaching. A guard, not smiling, said, "Two fingers only." The other guard watched nervously as Frank pulled out his ID card holder. *FBI* was the only phrase said. The men and Mr. Shneidecker apologized profusely.

"Show me your office computer listings for direct and connecting flights to Portland." Frank took full charge again, exuding authority. He had discarded the cervical collar hinting of infirmity.

"That's on a priority need-to-know basis only, Agent Wayman..."

"Corrections, that's *Deputy Director* Wayman, and I *do* need to know."

"Certainly. Let's go to my office."

"If it's not far. We're in a hurry." The three picked up their luggage to follow the airline host. The security guards left.

There a small screen showed all Portland flights booked. That city had been their best bet for Peter's destination, based on TV news. A check revealed no seats until Saturday for any city within two hundred miles.

"Too late. But thanks." They left the office, Frank mumbling something about stonewalled.

They returned hastily to the terminal atrium, past several FBI watchers. Word was out, surveillance tight. The Waymans would not get to Portland, or near the Grain Train, on any commercial airline. He headed for a phone carousel. The family's cell phones were compromised, and a new disposable cpd would just be traced and monitored, if not jammed. He fished two quarters out of his pocket, and sent them jingling into the coin slot.

"Swansea Aviation? This is Fr--uh, Fred Yarbrough. Do you have a small plane and a pilot available for charter to Portland?...I see." After three more calls to local private carriers, and two more refusals, one secretary said, "Look, Mr. Yarbrough, you're out of luck. We got a high level tip some kook was going to try to hijack a plane tonight, so no one is going to put anything up in the air around here. We're in a High Orange Alert."

Frank methodically considered his options, which had become pathetically few. If he was to play any part in the solution, he had to act decisively, yet he couldn't believe the direction his mind was racing.

"Marion," he whispered as they sat in a crowded waiting area with their luggage, "how much farther out on this limb do you dare go?"

"He's my only son," she answered unflinchingly. "But Candice is depending on us to be around."

"She's in college," he focused their perspective. "She has your folks."

Marion nodded, asking, "What's waiting further out on your limb?"

"I'm not sure, except I'd have to break most of my own rules to get us out of Denver, with a chance to get to Peter."

"Room for me? And Janet?"

"I don't know yet."

"We don't have time to waste. Go find out." Once again her directness helped in speeding the family decision-making.

Frank pushed himself up out of the chair, wincing in pain. But now he was glad to be less conspicuous without the neck brace. He walked hurriedly again to the array of pay phone stalls, certain this would cause someone to be raising earphones in anticipation. Then he lifted the bound white pages, thumbing in the business section to a page titled "Chamberlain--Cinderella." Frank's finger flowed down the names, stopping at Ciliando Ristorante, while he memorized the phone number.

He dropped the book back, told Marion and Janet to wait, and left the area. At a gift shop he bought a large teddy bear and a little spool of dental floss--asking that they put the bear into a box for him. Then he carried the box into the rest room fairly near the Security Office, and left it in one of the stalls, unobtrusively latching the door as he left with a length of the dental floss.

As he walked out, he reported to a janitor that he just saw that man in the yellow shirt, walking away over there, leave a big box in a stall in the men's room. The janitor's big eyes showed he understood the danger, as he reached for his radio. Frank walked away, hoping the distraction would pull attention of most security persons to a locked toilet. For he was now heading toward the only secure phone line he knew of in the huge terminal, to make the most unusual call of his life.

Frank walked at an unhurried pace, knowing eyes were watching. Besides, he needed this time to recall the interior layout of the Airport Security Office. He was planning every step, every word, from the moment he opened the door until he left, seven minutes later.

Now he was ready, counting on the new distraction, general turmoil, and a traditional lack of communication between law enforcement agencies to let him be anonymous. He also depended on a typical hesitation in immediately reacting to bizarre behavior when dealing with management levels like himself.

He abruptly turned, headed straight for the door marked *Airport Security*, and entered. People were talking loudly in rather urgent tones. He bypassed the first officer's desk with barely a glance, going direct to the inner door labeled *Chief*. He knocked, then opened it without waiting for a response.

The man in uniform at the desk was on the radio, and looked up sharply at the intrusion. Frank didn't recognize him, and hiding his relief, presented his FBI card case. "I must use your Info-Cell at once," Frank said firmly.

"Uh, I'm Buckingham, head of Field Security, filling in here. I'll be happy for you to use this office a few minutes. I can wait outside," the chief offered, extending his hand.

Frank did not reciprocate the gesture. Instead he challenged, "What's the matter, Buckingham, don't you know where the key is?"

"Of course, sir. I'll find the forms for you to fill out..."

"Your problem, not mine," Frank retorted angrily. "I need that room for top secret phone communication--instantly. Now open it!"

The ID card, curt demand, and a tough day combined for Buckingham to relent on unfamiliar procedures, and he fumbled for keys on the wire-ring in one of the top drawers. He left the office and walked toward the rear wall of the Security Office and the single door in it, with Frank at his heels. Most of the other DIA officers had left. Frank hoped his being in the Security Office would let his FBI shadowing agents feel safe and hidden by staying outside.

The chief unlocked one keyed panel, entered a number combination from a wallet card, then placed the palm of his hand on the black screen plate. "I think this is the way they showed us. It's brand new."

There was a resounding *clank* as numerous steel bolts slid out of their shafts in the door casing and into the doorjamb. Buckingham pulled the heavy tempered steel door open, permitting vault access for the Denver FBI deputy director, whom the acting chief was certain would be on the approved list. Lights and air conditioning were activated as the stale air assaulted them. A second key opened an inner wall panel, revealing a desk module housing a large screen PC console and printer, built-in hard drive with slots of various sizes for dvd's, flashdrives, cpd chips, and more, plus a phone with visual imaging screen.

"I'll be fast. Shut the door behind me, but do not trigger the locks," Frank ordered, aware of the risk. If anybody got their act together quickly, he could be incarcerated right here for the duration of the hijacking.

"Obviously we would not lock the door," Buckingham snorted, upset that this officious intruder would challenge his intelligence like that.

Frank stepped into the immaculate white room, pulled the door shut as it was being pushed, then locked dead bolts from the inside. These were designed only to slow outside entry, not prevent it. He pulled a chair up to the inset desk and dialed the memorized number. On this phone there were no taps, nor could there be without clearance from one of only four people in the country. It would take time to reach any of those four, even if Frank's *non compos mentis* status was revealed. Frank counted on having at least four minutes of locked absolute solitude.

"Ciliando's Ristorante," the husky voice answered in Frank's ear.

"Mr. Ciliando, please." It was Frank's turn to be courteous.

"Louie, Joe, or Gee?"

"Giuseppe, please."

"I'll check if he's here. Who's calling?"

"This is Frank Wayman, Deputy Director, Denver FBI."

"Yeah, sure. Hold on."

Frank waited, looking at his watch. One minute…then thirty seconds more. It was totally silent in this bomb/terrorism shelter and DIA security control room. Television monitors and communication devices were installed behind alternating sheet metal wall panels, awaiting emergencies-- or VIP tours, as he had gotten during III's last visit. Who would have guessed?

"Mr. Wayman?" An accented voice interrupted his thoughts.

"Yes. Mr. Giuseppe Ciliando?"

"I never thought I would get a call from you. Just occasional visits with your boys to let us know you're still around. Tell me, how was your lovely wife Marion's birthday earlier this month?"

The man was incredible, having information like that to test bureaucrats like him. "It's coming up, August 30th."

"Good. It's your nickel."

"The world is changing, Mr. Ciliando. Do you have a V-I phone screen?"

"Doesn't everybody?"

"You'll need to see me, and where I am, to believe what I'm going to be saying. All this is in strictest confidence. Can you clear your line?"

"Done." There was an almost imperceptible click, as the old man's word became law.

The green light on the base of Frank's monitor lit up, then the craggy face of G. Ciliando, Denver's local Mafia patriarch, filled the visual imaging screen. It startled that side of Frank, which was still every inch FBI to realize that this was actually happening.

But it was only the father in Frank talking now, sharing his story of a heart broken by a runaway son in deep trouble, and the helplessness of being trapped in Denver, unable legally to leave to get to him.

"Ah, I see," the old man said, with a beginning of kindness in his eyes. "And you think I am not bound by the same laws which so constrict you, Mr. Wayman?"

"There has seemed to be a difference of interpretation, Mr. Ciliando. I have developed a respect for your abilities in averting nets."

The man on screen laughed gustily, then asked seriously, "Are you saying, in your case, this particular end justifies using unusual means?"

They were coming to an understanding, but time was running out. Frank set a meet, 1:00 A.M. at Danny's All-Nite Diner. He said he would try to lose their tail. But Ciliando said, not to worry, he would take care of it if they didn't. He asked if Frank would be driving his silver Lincoln.

It was agreed. The Waymans and Janet would leave early tomorrow morning in a small private jet from a short airstrip, which obviously couldn't accept a late flight plan if no one was around. The plane and pilot were pledged to them to use until they found their recalcitrant son. And even afterwards, if they all decided to take a vacation out of the country. Payment was not discussed.

"Now get out of that room before they lock you in and forget the combination starts with a five!" And both fathers laughed together, Frank in relief and then all the more since he himself had only seen the secret combination used moments before, starting with the number five.

Frank unbolted the door and left the Security Office, wasting no words of thanks, undergoing a painful metamorphosis. Then the Waymans and their son's girlfriend, a new comrade in arms, left the airport as they had arrived three hours earlier, in Frank's silver Lincoln.

*   *   *

"Wilma, it's late. Why don't you make a pit stop back in the next engine's facilities, then we'll brake for you to move for the night to Boxcar Two. I'll radio them to get your sleeping bag ready. Want to take some sandwiches or fruit for a midnight snack?"

Wilma said no, still a mite miffed at the plan to separate her from the engine crew. As she reached for the door on Fork's side, Peter suggested she use the other one. *He can't ever let me make a decision*, she thought, changing doors to step into the cool night. As she walked with Fork along the engine catwalk, she admitted that she was looking forward to a good night's sleep after a hard day's work. Then she found herself appreciating

Peter's quiet ways a little more as she surveyed her open view to the west, thanks to changing doors. Wetland ponds of the Bird Sanctuary shimmered silver in the early moonlight as far out as she could see. She held Fork's hand more tightly along the dangerous catwalk. He was nice.

The train soon slowed, then came to a stop outside Brigham City, dangerous in an open area. At Harran Winfree's insistence, they were to pick up a local engineer who held mastery of all rail lines in northern Utah then up throughout Idaho and Oregon. It happened that Monty knew him. So the arrangement had been agreed on before Harran cratered for the night, having gotten them green lights north to Pocatello, Idaho, then 234 miles further west to Boise. The Denver dispatcher said he would reconnect with them in Nampa or sooner, well before the Oregon State line.

The men in the cab watched anxiously in all directions for unwelcome intruders. The helicopter escort hovered nearby. Looking back along the train, they discovered in dismay that cans of paint had been hurled up against the banners during their slow journey through SLC. This had obliterated most of the messages, making them look like some rolling reject from an abstract art museum. Peter wondered if the limousine statue had put them up to that dirty trick.

"Don't worry, guys," Wilma shouted back as she ran to the boxcar bedroom, "you've still got me to deliver the message!" She was getting excited by the prospects of farmer interviews to add new punch to the broadcasts. A man left the solitary auto by the tracks, and ran to climb on board the engine.

As the train was picking up speed again, Monty began introductions in the cab. "Peter, I want you to meet my good friend, Andre Maurantagne. Don't worry about having to pronounce it. We call him A.M. for short. Friend, this is Peter, the young man with a dream." Monty beamed his pleasure as the two shook hands. "Now the man to brief you on the system status is Fork, my right hand. He's very anxious to begin snoring after forty sleepless hours."

"Take my seat, for now," Fork gestured, and the new man climbed into it.

Monty went on talking. "A.M. knows every inch of track between Salt Lake and Boise. Been on this run for six or seven years, right? What kind of shape are they in tonight?"

The dapper engineer opened his notebook of small scale maps and began talking through pages as the train once more roared through the blackness.

In Boxcar Two, Wilma also was shaking hands all around, as five helpful men argued over where her sleeping bag would best be laid out to avoid the wet spots. Five-gallon buckets of urine and feces had been hurled into the open car once darkness fell on Utah.

*   *   *

"I don't know," Monty worried. "I just don't feel right."

"Probably only the weather," Peter offered, standing at his shoulder. "Rain and lightning moving our way. That explain nerves?"

"Might. Might not. Rain's usually no big deal."

Fork was asleep behind them, sitting on the trunk, leaning back against a pillow. He would take his night shift turn at the controls in five hours, at two o'clock Friday morning. For now, A.M. ran the train.

"How about borrowing my earplug for a Fifth of Beethoven?"

"You enjoy. I like listening to my engines, and the rails. They're all the music I need. They'll sing out trouble if any is near." Monty smiled.

"Are you like the old timers who really believe in the *talking steel*?"

"Yeah. Too many stories from engineers not to believe it. Been a lot of wrecks avoided by men who listened, and acted in time."

"Could that be intuition?"

"Oh, partly. But they talk about hearing the steel voice, talking in the rhythm of the wheels. They say, 'Stop right now, stop right now.' Or maybe, 'Go a little faster, go a little faster.' Now mind you, I've never heard the voices, but I still listen for them. Be a fool not to."

"Hmmm..." Peter was thoughtful a moment, watching the tail end of Utah pass by in their headlight. "How'd you like your railroad life?"

"Oh, lots. Being out of doors, not tied to a desk. Fresh air, when I sat in front of the smoke." He chuckled quietly. "Running on schedule, but that was rare. Responsibility for cargo, and lives. Being in charge. When you climb up here and take the throttle, you're Mister-In-Charge. Of course the money wasn't bad, especially toward the end. And there was free time with the Mrs. after a run..." His voice trailed away.

"Only good memories?" Peter inquired, not wanting the two of them to dwell on those feelings of leaving behind a wife, or sweetheart.

"Oh, no, friend. There's bad in any job. Like hours when diesel was so thick you ate it, soaked it up in your pores. Snowy nights when you froze looking outside for drifts." Monty paused. "Constant noise robbed your hearing right through the rubber plugs. Seeing men paid for not working. Deer and cattle that caught us by surprise and got plowed under. Kids in a pickup...bad memories are there, I just choose to down them."

"Hey, Monty, how about you and your Peace Academy?" The train was moving uneventfully through the night, track fairly straight, the countryside sleeping, as was Fork, snoring in competition with the diesels.

"Well, pardner, that's a long story." Monty was feeling more at ease, coming out with his best John Wayne drawl.

Peter returned the familiar intonations. "Well, pardner, I happen to have a few hours I can spare right now." Both men laughed softly. They liked each other's company.

So they talked--of guns in the old Wild West and today, and a National Rifle Association lobbying Congress and losing because of another high school shooting like Columbine in Colorado. The need for weapons to balance power, and pacifism as untapped power. Monty remembered class projects in building bridges of trust. Deeper unilateral disarmament had been a goal to achieve multilateral conversion, along with a United Nations buildup.

"Bring in more students from other countries," Monty was saying. "Oh, and praying more. Academy leaders are great believers in the power of prayer, certain they're on God's side--and vice versa."

"That's a heavy duty organization," Peter granted.

"Just scratches the surface. They're researching peacemakers past and present, rewriting them into textbooks, teaching teachers to resolve conflict in their classes and schools, practicing non-violence. If everybody lived like that campus society, this world would smile."

"So if they're that good, why did you really leave?" Peter asked seriously.

"Because their goals were just so big and it seemed like it would take so long. Every problem had a long-term plan: find water, increase crop yields, control population, and rein in greedy politicians. Oh, the NPA is action-oriented, all right, but they want to mediate and stay friends with influential people. They believe any problem can be negotiated, but that can take time, and some people don't have that luxury left." Monty quit talking again, and the fullness of night filled the cab of Engine 9039.

Peter made his hourly Shakespeare calls. No new reports from Denver after Chanto's warning. Or at least someone was picking up when it rang. Maybe they should have set up a coded response. Too late. But the phone was always on Peter's belt, to place calls out in case of attack.

"Let the wheels keep turnin', let the train keep rollin', while the grain is on the way..." Monty surprisingly began soft but way-off-key singing. He had started composing the ditty in his head after Salt Lake, and was still trying to get the words and melody to come out right. A.M. shook his head in pretended annoyance, and kept his eyes on the track.

"What would the Peace Academy be doing this time of night, besides coming toward us checking track?" Peter put the query into the noisy quiet. He still stood close behind Monty.

"Well, they'll already have researchers studying us, as people and as a phenomenon. They know who we are, our backgrounds, talked with our families and friends, computerized us. They'll try to match our hijacking with earlier ones in what they call their *scientific search for peaceful alternatives*.

"And they've got the guts to get involved, probably giving ideas to the Feds and States we're running in, urging caution, patience. They may try to contact us tonight, if they get any nibbles to your proposal. They'll be sizing up Portland and Seattle, since we turned north."

"Wonder what the FBI's next move is, since their chopper's gone?"

"Hell, I don't know." Monty felt Peter was a close enough church friend to swear with, under cover of darkness. And he was grateful for their friendship.

Time passed. Peter sat in one of the folding chairs at the rear of the cab against the wall, loudly recording some quiet thoughts onto his cpd chip, for handoff to Wilma to put on their blog at the first chance. She had reported that their growing Internet public seemed to be warming up to his words.

*   *   *

'Pocatello, next stop!' would have been announced if they were riding a sleek Amtrak passenger train through Idaho. But they weren't, and they wouldn't be stopping.

The moonlight should have made her feel more romantic and alive, Wilma thought. She was too wired to sleep, though midnight was closing in. The low hills paraded a mile or two distant from the tracks, separated by fields growing hay bales or sagebrush. Nothing seemed big to Wilma, neither the hills nor the upcoming town. She was surprised at how much she missed the downtown Denver skyscrapers of her day job with the *Herald*, and the skyline of 14'er mountain peaks.

She studied the white grain elevators as she sat leaning against the inside boxcar doorframe. Even they were not big tonight.

The railroad tracks were respected here, with the sleeping sunflowers all keeping their distance. Dirt roads began following the line, joined by a thin string of telephone poles and wires as the town lights came nearer. A long bridge atop concrete pillars crossed over the tracks, so cars and trucks did not have to stop for mere trains.

A long yellow crane boom mounted on a flatcar was stationed on a side rail, and the red and white checkerboard of Ralston-Purina marked the upper third of a grain mill a block away. A solitary massive smokestack loomed upwards into the heavens, surely the tallest landmark for miles, but falling short as an inspiring sight tonight. A sturdy platform supported three squat electric transformers between the tracks and the quarter-filled parking lot.

A small crowd had gathered near the old depot. More Lookie-Lou's and flash-picture takers, rather than supporters or detractors, Wilma noticed when she waved out at them. No one who was awake in the boxcar was saying much while passing through small-town America. They may have been worrying that nighttime was most dangerous of all.

A vintage steam engine sat proudly on a flatcar for permanent display, accompanied by its coal-tender car. On nearby working tracks, strings of other boxcars, grain cars, and oil tankers stood silently lined up awaiting orders to hook and roll. It all seemed so normal, as the rhythmic clickety-clack of five hundred wheels rolled across joined rail ends.

Wilma felt totally drained by her second day without sleep. Even talking with the farmers for a while had gone stale. She looked at the Hotel Pocatello sign advertising a large four-story building across the street from the depot, a fine arrangement from days of past glory for train travel. She observed that really nothing was far from the tracks in Pocatello.

They rolled across an overpass while one car drove slowly below them. Large wooden spools of cable rested on their sides in a fenced lot next to the highway. Soon only the lights of farmhouses stabbed the night with artificial light. The town was passed. An exhausted Wilma would sleep now, and worry tomorrow about whether she was crazy.

*   *   *

The Academy helicopter followed the rail line southeast toward Pocatello, flying fast as the Grain Train closed the distance toward them on the same rail line, heading northwest. Their spotlights obediently followed the solid rail lines, as they all looked for breaks. The identification lights required by the FAA blinked their location to unconcerned desert rattlers and prowling coyotes. There was minimal conversation until, "Heat scan screen showing, three miles ahead."

Two team members studied the colorful screen intently. The pilot glanced, and returned his gaze to a dimly moonlit landscape and his rail map. He chuckled, and waited, as they headed straight for the long red line on the scope. Three minutes later they flew low over an Amtrak train, also eastbound with them, scurrying to reach the siding in ten miles where it could safely shut down while a Grain Train took its place on the single set of track.

Miles more they flew, swooping down low enough for the bright belly searchlight to pick up the cluster of pink images showing on the scope: a sleeping group of antelope, which bolted away in startled disarray. Cars were big and red on the little screen, moving mostly parallel with their own east-west paved course. Trucks were darker red on the front end, and longer. They passed over another freight train, but headed west, getting the breaks of forced green lights, plowing the way for the illegal activists coming behind them.

"A good sign," Blackman said. "That train got through okay." Boise dispatch confirmed it left Pocatello an hour ahead of the 9039. "Heads up, crew, somebody else may think it's safe to change the rail bed now. And heaven help us all, we'd probably never see it from this high up moving this fast, unless they were still working on it."

*   *   *

"I say we have some fun with her," Harry Blake whispered.

Drew Manchesky thought both the man and the suggestion were coarse, but he expressed only a negative syllable.

"Why not?" Harry came back quickly. "She's a good looking woman, and we ain't so bad. Besides, odds are we ain't going to make it out of this little jaunt alive anyway. Who'd begrudge us our last shot?"

"Well, Wilma might, for one," Drew whispered. "And my wife would, for two. And Peter might, for three. I think he hopes for quite a different statement about love."

"Yeah, but she's just laying there by herself, wasting all that good stuff on maybe her last night too."

"Hey, Harry, you're single again, and hot to trot. Why don't you go over and proposition her nicely. If she says *yes*, you're on your own. But if she refuses, don't try to force her, 'cause I'll take her side."

With a snort, Harry rose and moved toward her silent figure, stepping carefully around other snoring farmers. There had been a few late night cell phone callers, with odd rings making a disturbance when a cpd had not been put on vibrate. But that all got settled down, and fitful sleep came to most. Wilma lay on her side in the rocking rattling darkness. Harry took his shirt off, spread it out, and lay down quietly facing her. He did have a definite farm hand physique that he was displaying to attract her favors. Several men in the boxcar had still been awake though, and watched this repositioning, male curiosity aroused.

Harry put his hand lightly on Wilma's shoulder, and began rubbing gently, to wake her slowly and in a friendly mood. She didn't move.

He began to stroke her cheek, feeling more hopeful.

"Why did you take your shirt off, Harry?" she said quietly enough for no one else to hear except him. Her eyes were still closed.

Harry was caught by surprise. How long had she been awake, he wondered, and when had she seen him and what he wasn't wearing?

"Uh, I just find it a lot more comfortable to sleep without clothes sometimes. And I thought if you did too, we could just slip under a blanket here so as not to be embarrassed and sort of snuggle up awhile."

She finally opened her eyes and looked into his. Their faces were very close. "That's a nice offer, and you're a fine hunk of a man. But if I made it with you, I'd have to make it with the others, and they'd get excited and things'd get rough. Then I'd be too tired to do my job..."

He chuckled at her humor, reaching for her top button.

She grabbed his hand tightly. "I said, 'No thank you,' Harry. Now respect that answer." Her voice was not shaky scared, but solid.

His big hand moved over her breast, flattened against it, then squeezed for a good feel. She tensed, giving him an unbroken glare.

"Oh, all right," he said, still digging his fingertips into her softness, "but you're missing one hell of a fun time too." He patted her again.

"Enough, Harry. Now good night."

Not good enough, he thought, thanks to these do-gooders around them who would have stopped him before he got in. He gave her a crooked little half-smile as he sat up to put on his shirt.

The silent audience stayed quiet, closing their eyes to look again for hard-to-find sleep. No show tonight.

*   *   *

Peter completed all his 1:00 A.M. hourly calls. Monty was back in his seat at the front console, studying a map.

Andre Maurantagne, the new engineer, pointed a stubby one-jointed finger at the map of section 18-E. "Right along here, in about fifty miles, we'll have to slow down to a crawl. The conveyor chute to the cement plant collapsed on the tracks and there might still be some debris."

"Oh? That huge plant that's been there thirty years?" Monty inquired of his friend, the expert they stopped to pick up four hours before. The rails began a new strange song in Monty's ears. Fork stirred restlessly.

"*Oui*, yesterday, bad," A.M. replied in his lingering French accent.

"Here, between Butley and Eden, a few miles from Twin Falls?" Monty persisted, pointing at the map. The singing rails grew louder, hammering.

"Right here, *mais oui*."

"How far would that be from Boise?"

"Oh, one hundred sixty miles, perhaps."

Monty slid off his seat, passing a drowsy Peter on his way, purposely bumping Fork's outstretched leg to fully waken him. Suddenly, Monty grabbed the back of Andre's shirt, pulling him out of his chair, shoving him hard against that side of the cab. The new engineer cried out in surprise and pain. Peter couldn't believe what he was seeing.

"A.M., you're lying! That old cement plant is on the other side of Boise, not down here. There's nothing this side but ground. Why the lie?"

"Ah, *mon ami*. Ah-h-h...I cannot say."

Fork had instantly come to life, taking over Monty's chair and the responsibilities for running the train over its singing rails.

"I'll throw you out like a sack of coal in two seconds if you don't talk. This is my life you're playing with." Monty pulled Andre struggling toward a door, and opened it. Peter stood dumbfounded.

"No, no, you can't!" Andre screamed over the throbbing engines as he was forced out onto the catwalk.

"Why not!" Monty yelled back, right in the man's face. "You were setting us up!" The small man was no match for the heavyweight, who easily turned him around and thrust his top half over the rail, picking up one leg to tip him all the way over. Andre screamed in mortal terror.

"Talk to me!" Monty yelled over the engine roar. The singing rails were telling him there was trouble.

"*Oui*! Yes!!" the pitiful voice called up. The same strong hands that threatened his death then pulled him back. Peter took a relieved breath.

Pushed back inside the cab, Andre was trembling violently. His teeth chattered as if trying to break each other off.

"Stop that noise and tell us, you devil, or back out you go."

Andre's stare was riveted on his large antagonist's face. Monty slapped him smartly on the cheek to stop the shock reaction. Deep sobs began shaking his body.

"Get hold of yourself." Monty grabbed his arms firmly but no longer brutally. "A.M., tell us now what you have done. What's out ahead?"

The little shriveled man regained enough control to blurt out, "They made me! I had to!" Fear again filled his eyes. Monty grew calmer as the rails grew still.

"I knew you wouldn't want to hurt your friends. Keep talking."

The whole story came out rapidly then: someone threatened to reveal his various female liaisons along the route, which would cost him his marriage and job, unless he slowed the train tonight at that spot.

"Do they plan to shoot us there?" Monty asked bluntly.

"I don't think so. They said I would not be in danger, that the whole thing would be over for everyone in two minutes."

Monty glanced over his shoulder. "What do you think, Peter?"

"I think I wouldn't want to cross you with that temper," he said seriously. "Two minutes. If we believe him, that means something fast...something the engines and boxcars pass by...or through!" They both looked at each other with the same thought, but Fork was the one who beat them in speaking the word out loud: "Gas."

"They planned to slow us down through a blasted gas field," Peter surmised. He saw it all too clearly. "No color, no smell, just collapse without knowing what hit us. That way I don't send any orders to detonate. They seize the train, then appeal to our bomb squad on national radio--shit, they'd have my cell phone. They'd just call all the numbers and tell them that it's needless to destroy any more, since the cause is obviously lost. Then track them down. Take us all to jail...whoever's still alive. That's my ingenious father."

"So what do we do?" Monty asked, looking first at Peter then at Fork, who shrugged his shoulders. A.M. tucked his head down lower.

Peter paced the small cubicle, listing alternatives. "We have gas masks here in the trunk, and in the boxcars for the Wray farmers. But they might not work with whatever gas they've chosen, and the Utah farmers we picked up have no protection.

"We could shield Andre by saying our gas detectors had warned us--if we had some--and if they worked far enough out in front to stop the train in time. But even with that story we'd be forced to stop to protect the farmers. And I

don't know about our TV chopper's equipment and safety..." motioning out
the window toward the blinking lights of the shadowing media.

Monty stated flatly, "The only thing we can do is tell the Feds we know
about the gas trap, blow Andre's cover, and threaten to order detonation of
more bombs hidden along the route. Shall we wake Wilma?"

Peter nodded, a little absently, deep in thought. "Not yet. How long
before we get there, A.M.?" The small figure had given up hope after
Monty's statement about telling all, and hunched against the side of the cab.
He shrugged slightly, and formed his lips into an "I don't know" gesture.

Monty took it as an *I don't care* gesture. "Hey, squirt, answer the man's
question!" Andre started quivering again, but got out a quick reply. "At
this speed, forty-five or fifty minutes."

"Not much time then. I'll radio our media chopper to fall back...Oh, wow,
that Academy chopper! Flying toward us from Boise, right into gas!"

Monty had already picked up the mike from the train's radio, then
slammed it back on its cradle. "Give me one that will contact them, Pete!"
he shouted in frustration.

Peter handed him a cellular already programmed from the last conversation
with Blackman. "Ask them for their first miracle."

Andre didn't hear the comment of hope. He had slumped to the rocking
floor of the cab, trying to blot out all of the world collapsing in on him.
Fork picked up the route book, and began to study it, wondering how many
other tamperings it included.

After a moment's conversation, Monty said in alarm, "Peter, it cut out.
Now there's nothing but static on your cell line." He checked the radios
to the TV chopper, and the boxcars. The phones and radios were all dead.
They were alone in the desert.

*   *   *

In the NPA helicopter, Blackman took the urgent call from Monty: a gas
attack was suspected in their next fifty miles...

Then static started breaking up his transmission, and he was gone.
Suspicious, Blackman contacted the NPA Crisis Center. They agreed that
Kristine Zowadsky would begin working to see who might be jamming
reception in Idaho, and clear it. She would also call the Idaho State
authorities to dispatch emergency equipment in that direction...

At that point, the NPA copter also lost all radio contact. Someone's
jamming equipment was being used very effectively.

"They've muted us all," Blackman said. "Something is going to happen before two o'clock, between us and the train. Let's find it first!"

They watched the night scanner screen for unusual heat, and movement, closing the gap with the hijacked train to under fifty miles.

"Bottom of the screen, check it," the pilot said, pointing. "That big blip appeared after we passed, at a right-angle from the highway, moving toward the tracks. Looks like it may be a truck with a trailer."

"I see it, almost out of range. What about maintaining the same course for one minute more, then doubling back just to within screen distance from it? Maybe they got sleepy, or have a house there, but I didn't see one."

"Roger," the pilot agreed. One minute later he moved the floor stick in front of him to the left and they banked a sharp 180-degree turn, backtracking west.

"How far away can they see our blinkers?" Blackman asked.

"Fifteen, twenty miles on a clear night."

"Can they see us now?" Ned Friedman asked. He was the other Academy peacemaker who had volunteered for this mission.

"If they're looking."

Blackman thought only a second. "Can you turn the lights off?"

"Against the law," the pilot shrugged.

"What they're doing may also be," Blackman responded.

"Let's close in enough to get them on the horizontal scanner, then sit and watch. Maybe keep them from hearing us too."

"Excellent," Blackman nodded.

They went dark, flew just a minute more, then set the struts down on a dirt road paralleling the tracks in a cloud of dust. As they coughed in the hazy air, they watched their target blip move continually closer to the tracks. But no one remembered seeing any heavy cover back there.

"How big a gas cloud would it take…or how powerful…," Blackman ventured in the stillness, "…to stop a train…or to just stop us?"

The blip paused, then turned east toward them, about five miles away. It stopped on the same dirt road that they landed on, which ran right inside the fence line, which in turn ran right beside the track for miles. The copter crew had commented earlier on how long it would take to maintain that many miles of fencing. Now they waited for motion from the unknown blip--with many more miles of track to check, and the train was closing the distance fast. Were they wasting precious minutes sitting here?

*   *   *

Kristine Zowadsky, night director of the Academy Crisis Center, called Engine 9039. Nothing but static. The same with the borrowed helicopter with their negotiator Blackman aboard. She suspected the worst, and also suspected who the most recent activists were. She bypassed those on her call list of next-in-charge, and immediately contacted the FBI First Deputy Director with some critical research facts: loss of all communication; suspected possible gas trap; personal profiles of two farmers on board who had history of heart trouble, plus one other with recent bypass surgery, for whom her campus physicians held out little hope of surviving a strong general anesthetic.

The man in charge of the FBI night watch had responded in testy tones that having such facts brought to his attention in advance, and in the middle of the night, would certainly mitigate the desirability of initiating a gas attack, even if he had authorized it, which he had not, and which he was certain neither had anyone in his organization!

But Kristine knew this was not an idle threat, and could be one master plan to silently end the highly publicized confrontation. One of their computer scenarios allowed the train to pass and be covered by a gas cloud or spray. With a signal bounced from a satellite, the computer signal idling the train engines would be broadcast remotely. The train would then brake to a smooth stop, following directions from someone's laptop. The FBI would move in, gather up the perpetrators before any cell phone call for more bombings, and announce to a waiting nation, and poised group of bombers, that the mission of the Grain Train had failed, and any retribution would be futile and without purpose. Peter's cell phone would be collected from unconscious hands, calls made to his group, telling them in person while triangulating on their location for capture. She didn't know how closely this scenario resembled Peter's fears.

But Kristine did know that even without any further communication, Blackman's peacekeeping force would land at any suspicious site in the targeted slow-down area, and try to assure dismantling of any trap, at the risk of their own lives. That was the nature of their mission, and their commitment. An inspector was en route from the Idaho Department of Health and Environmental Hazards, whose daughter happened to be a student at the Academy and had made an emergency phone call to her father.

With all this in mind, and hoping and praying for lack of injury, when Kristine made contact again with Peter, she would ask for a straightforward trade: *Since they risked their hides to save yours, will you let Blackman come on board?*

*   *   *

"How much time are we going to give them?" the pilot asked.

Blackman looked at his lighted watch dial, then at the stationary blip. "The train's here in less than thirty minutes. We've got lots of miles we haven't checked, and this may be zilch. Let's go look now."

The pilot turned the throttle slowly at the end of the collective floor stick in his left hand, increasing the merry-go-round speed of the rotor blades above them. "What if they shoot?" the pilot asked.

"How fast can you get us out of range?" Blackman retorted.

"Depends on whether they have sniper rifles. Are we going in with lights like sitting ducks?"

"Sure. After all, they may be government workers. Really bright lights will help them see what they're doing."

The pilot pulled up slowly on the floor stick in front of him with his right hand, pushing right pedal to keep balance, lifting the copter. At ten feet, he pulled up on the collective for lift and forward motion, then pushed the stick forward slightly to tip the nose down for more speed. The pilot had checked for wires as they landed, and now broke another rule by taking off straight ahead, instead of first going back out the safe way they had come in to make their landing. Time was ticking away.

The three men formulated the serious plan as they flew dark, fast, and low. When they got within one hundred yards, Blackman would flash the spotlight down on the scene, trying first to see any possible gas containers. Of course, it might just as easily be a derailment, or simply a bomb. Assuming the vehicle didn't move, that would become their primary target. The pilot would be looking around the illuminated area for the closest landing spot. Ned would be watching the people, seeing if they had weapons or watching which way they ran. He would be the one to use the loud speaker in a deep booming voice from the chopper the moment the mega-spotlight bar was turned on, floodlighting their vehicle. And that moment had arrived.

"Get out of the truck, and raise your hands!"

The chopper zoomed straight toward the front of the parked vehicle. It was a tank truck, rigged with a fixed-boom large spray hose coming from the huge metal tank. An auxiliary tank was attached behind. No one was outside the cab, at least not in the broad white circle of the bright spotlight.

"Bingo!" Blackman said. "Nothing the bozos should be spraying out here. And nothing coming out of the hose yet. Let's set down."

The pilot started to land quickly in front of the truck on the dirt road, now a dust cloud, keeping both sides of the cab in full hazy light. But at that moment, the truck lurched forward, right toward the light, and the copter. The pilot pulled up hard on both stick controls, lifting immediately, and the huge boom spray rig just missed colliding with the landing struts of the copter.

"My eyes are burning!' Blackman shouted, quickly reaching for his gas mask. Ned covered his face with the protective gear also, but the pilot was busy turning on a dime to circle back for the chase, making him slower to react. He started leaning forward, pushing the stick down with him slowly, pitching the nose toward upending them. Blackman grabbed the controls and struggled to force them back up.

"Ned, grab his shirt and pull him back! Get him up! And get a mask on him!" Ned obeyed, and Blackman jerked open a window with one hand while he steered with the other. Wind whipped through the cockpit, clean wind, blowing papers everywhere. Some went flying out, but the life-saving oxygen was flowing in. The pilot began to revive, as Blackman maneuvered the copter up higher to get out of the gas cloud.

"That was a close call, I guess," the pilot said. "I've never known anything to act that fast. Thanks for taking over, guys." He now masterfully tilted them back to the right side of the truck and the tracks, away from the deadly spray nozzle. They were all headed fast eastbound, directly toward the oncoming train.

The helicopter spotlight picked up the back of the truck as they gained on it. "Check the mist coming out from the hose, to the side of their tire dust cloud. They're fogging the rail line right now!"

"Is that a man out on the side of that rig?" Ned pointed, just as the copter passed through the outer edge of the dust cloud. The others hadn't seen anything.

"What can we do?" the pilot asked, staying now just in front and to the right of the truck to avoid the cloud of debilitating spray.

Ping! A bullet clanged against their military issue hand-me-down helicopter. Then another.

"That does it! War declared!" the pilot hollered through the mask. He no longer was primarily concerned with the lives of those on the train. Zooming fast ahead of the spray truck as it bounced along the rutted deadly path, he suddenly made a hard 180-degree turn, hovering directly in front of it. He waggled from left to right and back, to make a constantly moving target for the shooter. But he kept his roof and belly spotlights trained directly into the cab, into the eyes of the driver.

"This should slow him down, give him a taste of his own spray!" the pilot shouted. "Be ready with a plan when he stops!"

Blackman spoke harsh tones into the microphone, and his voice boomed out of the loudspeaker: "You have no place to go, no place to hide! Stop now, and surrender!" All men in the copter put on their gas masks again.

Instead of slowing, the truck sped down the dirt road, though blinded. Then it started to veer left off the road, hit the fence line and ran up onto the railroad track embankment, overcorrected to the right, then crashed heavily onto its side--all in an instant.

"Damn!" was the universal comment in the helicopter. They landed on the road, fifty feet ahead of the overturned truck and trailer. The pilot kept the rotor blades turning.

Wheels were still spinning as the two Academy interventionists ran up to the scene. Blackman carried a fire extinguisher, and moved toward the cab. The driver was fumbling with a pistol, and Blackman put out any possible fires along with the gunman. The other man was unconscious.

Ned quickly shut off the pump and closed the valves. The tank on the trailer seemed intact. Miraculously, the overturned spray tank and trailer had sprung no leaks; the meter counts were minimal, so Ned and Blackman took off their gas masks, and motioned the pilot to do the same. The NPA pair checked pulses on both men; they were stable but hurt seriously. After searching them, they left them handcuffed on the ground.

They returned to the waiting helicopter to get chains and locks to secure the valves. Those had been on the *try to think of everything* list of supplies. "What about the guy I saw on the side of the rig?" Ned asked. "If I really saw someone there. I just got a glance."

"I'll take the chopper up and take a quick look-see back along the tracks," the pilot said. "He may have fallen off in that craziness. I want to check on the gas levels back there anyway. As well as the radio. Hopefully we're on the air by now. You guys come up with me for safety."

At the sound of the helicopter lifting off, the man in torn clothing crouched low and turned to look back at the crash scene. He had limped two hundred yards through the sage, back toward the highway. He was dazed, and idly wondered whether anyone would stop for a hitchhiker whose shirt was pressed against his right cheek. The blood was just about congealed along the four-inch canyon gaping open from his sideburn to his chin. He turned and started painfully walking toward the highway, vowing that he would complete the contract to stop this train and its crew.

In the copter, Blackman smiled at a renewed radio. He spoke first with Peter, stating that one gas threat was neutralized, and could hear the cheering in the cab. He said they would confirm with the Academy that the Idaho cleanup team was on the way, and alert them of the chemicals and injured men. And that the copter was already headed toward the train to check the remaining few miles of track separating them. He asked Peter for permission to board the Grain Train as a mediator.

Peter replied that he had already talked with Kristine also, and would be honored to have a miracle worker ride the rails with them. Peter said they would maintain full speed to get through the accursed air near the crash site, and that he would let the boxcars know they would be coming to a stop soon to pick up a passenger, right side, Boxcar One, no need for alarm.

"How nice of them to make room in a boxcar," Blackman sighed when the radio call ended. "But at least we have leverage for negotiating,"

Ned nodded in understanding. "Now Peter knows they aren't afraid to attack him. I wonder if that means they arrested his gang members, or found the bombs?"

"Could be. They may think he's only bluffing now. Or..." Blackman conjectured, "...maybe someone doesn't care what happens to a visionary group, and is willing to bite the bullet on more destruction."

They flew to meet the train, turned, and accompanied it to the designated spot for landing and transfer. The media chopper now picked Blackman up in its spotlight, and guided him back. He waved upwards in a natural reflex toward a friendly source, then waved at Peter in the engine as he jogged by. Moments later a dozen hands were reaching down to help pull him up through the open door of Boxcar One, as the tired crew in the *Herald*/KDNC chopper recorded the physical joining of National Peace Academy forces to the complicated equation of right and wrong. Then that chopper dipped away for some extra footage back at the crash site, with Idaho emergency squads arriving to take charge of the success and failure scene.

*   *   *

Chapter Fifteen

Morning filled the skies with glorious hues of crimson and rose, mauve and lavender.

Inside Boxcar Two, there sat a gracious lady on a crate, surrounded by interested men, and a grumpy Harry. They strained to hear her every word as she radioed the media helicopter flying two hundred feet over their train. This 6:30 taping would run on the 7:00 A.M. broadcasts in the mountain states, 6:00 A.M. on the West Coast. Somehow she looked fresh, though she had slept fitfully in her clothes on a blanket covering the splintery wood floor of her shared lurching bedroom. But this was a new day, and she began with a strong voice:

"This is Wilma Fletcher, and the hijacked Grain Train is rolling.

"Our banners may be covered with paint from vandals during the night. Our clothes may smell like manure, because that's what some other well-wishers threw in on us. But I'll tell you, it gave me a lot more appreciation for what many farmers go through in working their land and cleaning up after their animals, to put food on the tables of America. I'll get used to smelling rotten, if it will help get these surplus crops into the bellies of starving kids.

"One forgets, while living in the city, just how much of our land is used for farming and ranching. We're passing now through good corn country in Idaho. Endless acres stretch away from the tracks on both sides, planted with this valuable food. Plump ears are waiting for roasting or boiling in our corn-on-the-cob feasts, kernels ready to be cut off for canning and creaming, for popping and hominy.

"Corn, to be crushed into meal for making into hot bread or morning grits. Corn, to be transformed into cooking oil for baking and frying the good foods we love.

"Later in the season, when the remaining head-high fields of green leafy stalks and golden silk turn dry-yellow and brown, the harvesting machines will come crashing through, pulling the ears off and slinging them into trucks, mashing and slashing the canes into fodder, wasting nothing, leaving only forage for the pheasants.

"And the trucked corn then will be again sliced, ground at leisure to make the very best cattle feed. Or stored as surplus until prices rise, or the next crop comes in--or it rots.

"But right now, the precise lush rows, thousands next to thousands, are rustling in the light breeze and ripening even as we pass. It brings to mind songs from Broadway on this *Oh, what a beautiful Friday morning*. That's a little *corny*, I guess, but right now everyone on the Grain Train loves this America that the farmers and ranchers cherish and nourish and depend upon. Don't we love this country, fellas?" A resounding cheer of affirmation rose up spontaneously around her from the men.

"Do *you* remember this bountiful America, good listener? Come join us in the spirit of sharing our surplus with the starving. Phone everyone you know.

"Now for Peter, Monty, and forty-two other riders, this is Wilma Fletcher, and the Grain Train is still rolling--thanks to your support."

*   *   *

What was all the commotion last night with the lights in the middle of nowhere? Who was the boarder? And the extra helicopter?
Wilma bundled her questions, and asked Peter all eight in a row after saying good morning to him over the clear connection on the cell phone. His response was that she had wakened him up after a rough night, and he'd talk with her after she came up at the first stop.

He was no help. Time for the 7:30 taping rolled around quickly. Her idea for live interviews with her boxcar family was a sensation. Radio stations around the country, especially in the farm belt, were scrambling for special networking. Don Trujillo radioed her from the media chopper that as the hub, Denver's KDNC was a three-ring technical circus and loving every minute. Wilma held up her hand for quiet, and the rowdy bunch at once honored her signal. She had become hot stuff with them, and even frustrated Harry Blake was congenial.

"This is Wilma Fletcher, on the Grain Train in Idaho, nearing the Oregon State border.

"The patchwork quilt of American farm land is gorgeous: straight green rows of short, early winter wheat; yellow-brown acres of kaffir, a stubby corn cousin; brilliant greens of lush alfalfa, loaded with bees on blossoms; shaved fields of stalks, with the rich brown earth showing through, serving as firebreaks if lightning would strike dried corn stretches.

"I also love the look of our small towns. They usually have two skyscrapers. One is a water tank tower, the other a grain elevator beside the track, probably full of surplus. Those landmarks show up first on the horizon, down the track ahead of us. Then big old trees appear, shading most of the town, a church steeple pokes through, then the houses.

"No ticky-tacky suburban developments out here. Instead, there are all shapes and colors of homes, many with dirt driveways. The places are tidy, and the yards well kept if they're growing grass, with little plots of bright flowers. Americans are a neat people when in small populations.

"There's an inevitable 7-11 Store on Main Street, which usually runs parallel to our tracks. The clusters of business storefronts are becoming familiar. You'd recognize the bank's clock sign, the *Rx* drug store, a barbershop striped pole, a cafe's blinking neon, and the gas station price cards. The biggest low building is either a grocery or feed store. The many *For Sale* signs and boarded-up windows disturb me on the Main Streets of rural America. Our farmers are hurting, and these small towns show it.

"We need *your* personal help as we're rolling into Oregon. Call your state representative and your Congressperson. Call your local talk show, your newspaper office and TV station. Express your own belief that America has enough food, and has enough heart, to share with hungry neighbors overseas. Call people who make decisions. Tell them, *We Want To Share!* Right, guys?" Long cheers almost drowned out her closing words.

"Well, speaking for Peter, Monty, and forty-five riders or more, this is Wilma Fletcher, and the Grain Train is still rolling."

Wilma had seen the head count rising hourly as people were indiscriminately climbing on when the train slowed down to negotiate sharp bends. No one knew everybody, but the bond of doing something important was growing ever stronger. If any newcomers were Feds, they had made no move.

*   *   *

The morning sun still shone with spectacular color display through the stained glass window high in the old library east wall.

"What's this I hear about Oregon? Going to set up a *blockade* to stop the train?" The elderly professor bombarded the color-filled Crisis Center at the National Peace Academy, waving his polished gnarled cane and shakily shouting. In his English classes, he always used a microphone, but everyone in the Center this morning easily heard his entrance.

"Who's in charge around here?" he continued to shout. "Oh, it's you, is it? I might have known," he yelled at Jennifer Crussman as she got up from the control monitor and moved quickly toward him.

He was dressed nattily, as always. Gray tweed sport coat and dark green slacks, light green shirt, brown loafers and the notorious red and orange plaid tam commemorating his Scottish clan heritage.

"Professor MacLeod. Don't excite yourself so." She was rightly concerned, since the old-timer suffered a heart seizure two months ago.

"Don't mollycoddle me, you young pollywog. I asked you a direct question: What is my Oregon doing?!"

"Come over here to the couch, and I'll catch you up. Lois, take over for me, and call the copter pilot on that matter we discussed." Usually Jennifer tried to keep the atmosphere friendly, and one method was by not ordering people to do things. So when Lois paused for a split second, it was enough to remind her of her own rule. She added, "Please."

"Sit down over her, Professor. What have you heard?"

"Just the word *blockade*, and I know the Grain Train has been in my home state for over an hour. I was in a corn field with Wilma Fletcher as I ate breakfast, just as they were leaving Idaho at 7:00 A.M., blessed Oregon Daylight Time."

"All right. Someone from D.C. did some fast lobbying on the West Coast in the wee hours, after the Idaho gas effort was aborted."

"Gas? Good Lord."

"Your Oregon Governor Lee Anderson has now taken a hard line. He promises that the train will never make it through Portland to Astoria, assuming that's their destination since it dared to enter his State. He has communicated that ultimatum to the people running the train."

"And their response is, of course, *nuts to you.*"

She nodded, as Professor MacLeod questioned. "Who else has come out behind Anderson? He doesn't have the nerve to make that statement by himself."

"I agree, sir. Oregon's Senator Sharp has expressed the same hard line. Knowing how that senator has been used to run up test balloons for the Administration, it may have very high support."

The aged teacher coughed to clear his throat. He had a chronic sinus drainage. "Well, what would we have expected from a senator who went to West Point, and a governor who flies with National Guard troops down to Honduras for summer maneuvers? Where's his blockade to happen?"

"A town called Earlham, on the Columbia River."

"Welcome to friendly Oregon--Crash! Not bad strategy. Little town out there, Earlham. What, about thirty-five miles before Portland? Past The Dalles and Cascade Locks. Get those big power plants behind them. One hospital to handle the most serious injuries, maybe keep them from dying, let the others hurt a while to teach them their lesson. But what about the engineer's threat of blowing up oil refineries and power plants if the train is stopped?" The professor had been doing his homework.

"Guv Anderson privately says he thinks it's hot air. Publicly, he calls on them not to destroy America's resources and chance killing innocent people, if they really are doing all this in the name of love and patriotism. His points are valid. I don't know if we're dealing with rational people on the train at this juncture. They've given our mediators impossible demands to negotiate for stopping. I'm afraid they've been caught up by a cause, and can't see any recourse but going all the way."

"When an irresistible force such as you..." he started singing to her, "... meets an old immovable object like me..."

She clasped his hands, and beamed her delight. "Professor, your brain patterns are a breath of fresh air in troubled times."

He smiled back at her, enjoying her spontaneity also. Then he looked deeply into her eyes. "My dear, for some reason this train passage across our land has become very personal for me. It has reminded me of that which I was, and where we all have come from who call ourselves *American*. If that train is stopped, something in me will be stopped too. I don't know how to name it, but it's as real as my joy at making you happy just a moment ago." He paused, and a strange look crossed his face.

"What is it, sir?" she asked, still holding his hands, feeling in tune with this personality from two generations before her own.

"I was just remembering how I hate Dallas, Texas, for something that happened long ago, way back in November of 1963. That *city* killed John Kennedy. In my mind it was never only Oswald or a conspiracy, it was that *place*. I vowed then never to go to Dallas. Don't know if anyone else felt that way, but I never got over my revulsion at the city's name.

"It always brought back the image of the open limousine and my President and his Lady waving and smiling then slumping down never to rise again. Ah, there it happened again, just like it was yesterday."

"I'm sorry." She was genuinely moved by his sorrowful expression.

"I have just decided, my dear," he said, patting her hand, "the death of another American dreamer will not happen in my home State. Not while I draw breath. I was born an Oregonian, and I have loved her, as have many others. I have written of that love over the years as her Poet Laureate. Ah, you had forgotten that honor, my lovely Ms. Crussman?"

Her close attention while he told of his life served to refocus his thoughts, and he began to elaborate. "Yes, I am just here at the Academy on leave, one might say. In absence, I have come to love my State more dearly, despite her miserable representation in high political offices. I have tried to provide some balance by my role here..."

She tried to bring him out of his reverie. "Professor, if the train continues its present speed and course, it will reach the Earlham blockade in less than six hours."

"Not much time for thinking of the past now, eh? Well, I would request a special favor. I'm not exactly sure how such channels work here. I need to get back to Oregon at once."

She smiled, nodding. "We anticipated your request for involvement, but we did not want to approach you because of your health problems. This could be a severe strain on your system. Please reconsider."

"My dear," he began, "my life may have been meant for precisely this time. I vow to you, and this beloved Academy, that freedom will not be stopped within the Oregon borders while her Poet Laureate still has a voice. Get me to Earlham quickly, and get me a microphone, a crowd, and a TV cameraperson for my arrival, and for my departure from here also. It'll jolt them to hear old silver-tongued MacLeod is on his way home!"

"Shall we personally let the governor or senator know you're coming?"

"No, no. They came along after I was appointed. And neither is a native. I wouldn't want them to go to the trouble of baking me a cake anyway, since our tastes are so different. They'll get a clue soon enough."

"Lois ordered our helicopter to be waiting, just after you entered this room. It's ready to take you to a jet, whenever you're packed." She sparkled with the pleasure of an anticipatory crisis management success.

He beamed with shared excitement. "I have also anticipated this worst-case scenario. My bags are already packed."

"Professor MacLeod, you are truly a treasure," she said, hugging him tightly. Then she looked him in the eye, and whispered, "Come back to us." Next, she used her desk microphone to make the first public announcement of his mission. Reporters gathered around the pair, getting great candids, asking important questions. When time was up, he limped slowly out of the room. She sent a prayer on its way for his safety, then returned to the control desk to confirm flight arrangements.

Within twenty minutes the helicopter had whisked the Professor and the three-person crisis team accompanying him to the plane waiting at the Academy's Reagan Field and airstrip. A hasty news conference was held there with the chancellor, who had ridden out in the helicopter with them, offering encouragement and last minute prayers, as was his custom seeing off Intervention Teams. Then the compact Learjet lifted off. They were on their way to the small northern Oregon town of Earlham.

The videotape of that departure was processed at the Academy TV studio, and transmitted on their News-net as an emergency update. The newly expanded mission was also included in the 24-hour student prayer chains, which had been in operation since the train hijacking began one day before. The campus was in full configuration for a major crisis intervention.

*   *   *

On Friday morning in LaGrande, Oregon, Marybell Houghton arrived at eight o'clock as promised. She was to follow Ella Barnes over to the garage on Hobson to drop off her car. Ella unhooked the screen door and welcomed her, heading her toward the dining table with a big plate of fresh English muffins on it.

"Your usual Olde Style herb tea?" Ella asked.

"That would go wonderfully with muffins. But I thought you might be in a hurry to get to the garage."

"Oh, when I called they said to try putting in a can of fuel additive and it should clear up the problem. I don't know why I didn't think of that. So we won't need to go, but I had to talk with you face to face about something very important anyway. Here, sit down and butter a muffin, while I get your tea and some apple jelly." She left, and reappeared with a bowl of her own blue-ribbon shimmering gold. "Now then, do you still feel strongly that the Grain Train should get through?"

"Why, yes, I do. Why do you ask?"

"Em, I'll have to ask you to promise to keep a secret."

"Oh, good. Okay, I promise."

"The helicopter from that train is going to make a refueling stop at our airport, and we can be part of it."

"Ella, you are part of the underground! I can't believe it! Well, yes, I guess I can. You've been awfully active in those Social Justice classes at church, and you've always got some petition or another for *us* to sign at the Wednesday Quilting Circle. But what does the helicopter stop have to do with me? Ummm, these muffins are scrumptious."

"I'm glad you like them. They were Walter's favorites, you know. Almost every morning for his last seven years. But here's where you come in, Em. I'd like your help to finish a quilt and send it in a box with some good home-canned fruit, for the folks in the helicopter. They're probably hungry too, and cold at night, like the people on the train. So I thought we could send along something to show them we're supporting everybody's brave action."

"Oh, I like that idea. I was just going to wave as the train went by, but this is so much more exciting. Sure, I can do some quilting. I was supposed to have my hair done, but I'll call Gerty and switch. And I can put in a quick casserole for Ted tonight. Yes, it will work out fine."

"Good!" Ella struck her small fist lightly on the table in her excitement. "Ethel is coming over to help us work on it too. I figure with the piece I've been working on for the border, we can each take a side and add to it real quick."

"Do you have enough material for a solid color border?"

"Finished hemming that last night. Stayed up until almost midnight."

"You didn't!"

"I most surely did. I used that blue bolt end I've been saving because it felt so good. Remember when they marked it down to ten cents a yard to get rid of it, and I couldn't resist?"

"Well, aren't you glad now you didn't?"

"That will leave enough time for me to pick and wash some fresh garden things to send along too. They're not due in until ten-ish."

"Don't you mean, time for us to pick and wash. I want to help."

"You're a good friend. Sure that's what I mean. This will be so important, for those train folks to know that some of America's heart is with them as they ride. I'm glad we're going to be working together on a gift. You finish your muffin, and I'll start getting the wicker baskets out. I feel just like Betsy Ross, don't you?"

* * *

"Top-o'-the-mornin' to ye. Barney O'Brien here." The President of Serv-U.S. was already on a roll. "What do they say, 'Another day...?'"

"...another hundred calls," a tired Shelly Smith-Jones finished for him. "What's our latest club poll tally? United Media is calling me."

I know, I foolishly gave them your number, she thought. "Hold on." After taking another call, she punched in the California Kid again. "Barney, got your figure."

"Oh, no, you've got a much nicer figure than I'll ever have," Barney rejoined, howling. She howled along with him at his insensitivity.

"We're up to a strong two-thirds favoring support of the Grain Train, Barney. Some locals are even calling back to change their panic votes from yesterday. Uh-oh, another phone. Want me to call you back?"

Of course not, so she took the call, then returned to the California Dreamer. "That was National Farm Collectives Association, boss. They wanted to know what vote process we're using to get results so quickly, so I referred them to you. Better free up your line so they can get in."

"Okay, busy bee," he agreed.

Well, thank goodness, she thought.

"I'll just tell them," he continued, "that it's our phenomenal secretary who's able to keep track of all this for us. They may call you back with a job offer, ha." He laughed jovially as she was thinking, *I'll take it if they do*.

Then she commented, "They also applauded your strong public statement on how disastrous the farm surplus policy has been. They said if their membership gives them any latitude, they'll come out in support of Serv-U.S." In this she was sincerely complimentary.

"Well, that is good news. It was getting pretty lonely with just us and the Grain Co-Ops on the front pages."

"Hey, boss, the National Chamber of Business was right up there on the front page with us."

"Yes, but against the train and surplus sharing!"

"Ah. Then don't forget the railroad. They were the first to say it's just a train and only grain, so let it run wherever with no violence."

"Well, but that was self-serving too, and they've clammed up since, said it was out of their jurisdiction. Weaklings."

I wish you would clam up, she thought, but said, "Gotta go, boss. Listen, I'll call you if there's any change, okay? Operator says if we keep getting calls this fast, we're going to overload the circuits."

"That's a deal. Hey, it's just 8:30 here, but that means almost noontime in your exciting city. You've earned a nice long lunch break. Enjoy."

*   *   *

The backyard was quiet, as was the neighborhood, as was the little Oregon town mellowed by the warm sun.

However, three noisemakers were hard at work trying to disturb the peace: spinster Atkin's big elm tree, chock full of warbling, twittering sparrows, blackbirds, and starlings; Sam Thompson's almost purebred German shepherd barking at the mailman's new bike; and the wind chimes gently blowing together on Mary and Frank Simm's patio.

The next really serious outburst of noise in North Powder, Oregon, should be the 8:47--blaring its way across Maple Street. The Amtrak horn was usually a welcome signal to Mr. Hanson at the Triangle Feed Store, indicating time for a coffee break and only three hours until lunch. But the 8:47 would be unpredictably late today, since all rail traffic had been diverted to clear the tracks for the outlaw Grain Train.

There were strangers in the feed store, which was also unusual.

"Ah heah theah's gwan bee sum doins downda trayn stazhun," said one of the strangers, Chetfield, smiling to be charming. Timothy stood by.

"What's that about a train station?" old man Hanson asked. He was the only one of the three men by the soda pop machine paying any attention.

"Keep still, Chet. Nobody up here can understand you. I'll do the talkin'," Timothy told his friend calmly. "We were just passin' through and heard somethin' 'bout a runaway train," he said more loudly.

"Naw. No runaway." The old man stopped with that much clarification. Getting information here was going to be tough.

"Oh, right. It was a hijacked train, carryin' grain or somethin', as I remember," Timothy said. He hoped the old timer would open up.

"Yep."

"Uh, it been through North Powder here yet?"

"Nope."

"Well, good. We kinda hoped to watch it. Saw it on TV, ya know."

"Yuh duin gud, Tiem," whispered Chetfield, smiling jovially with the jab he gave his friend.

"Say, any idea what time that ol' train might be goin' through here?" Timothy hadn't given up yet.

"Mebbe an hour, mebbe a half."

With that news, Chetfield and Timothy ended their questions, nodded a goodbye to the old man, and started for the front door.

"Yall hava suwell tyem, yaheah," Chet hollered back over his shoulder.

"Eh?" they heard the old man say, as the door closed behind them.

Tim and Chet climbed into their pickup and headed north out of North Powder, on the highway following the tracks, looking for just the right spot, which they hadn't found on the way in. Their pickup was a non-descript gray 1983 Ford, no special markings. They hadn't planned it to be especially ordinary, it just came that way. Their rifles were in leather carrying cases in a large tool bin in the back, instead of up on the gun rack behind their heads, heralding a hunting trip. The men hadn't planned at all before leaving northwestern Nevada. They were just sitting in the porch chairs drinking beer, talking about the hijacking, and cussing the 9-11 attacks, and drinking beer, wondering why the cops didn't just arrest their asses after the Denver bombings, and drinking more beer. Then it was just a spur of the moment *fill it up with gas, kiss the wife goodbye, expect me back when you see me, now let's go get rid of these terrorists for our country* kind of hunting trip for two good old boys.

Tim slowed to let traffic pass them, then turned onto a trail that used to be a road, leading off toward a grove of trees. They didn't kick up much dust because of the weeds and leftover wheat in the ruts. Chet counted only three cars that passed back on the highway before they reached the tree cover, with the tracks close by on the other side. There was no sign of a farm or barn anywhere near enough to be a concern.

Their conversation for the last hundred miles and four beers each had been about past hunting memories. They were getting in their *get 'em with the first shot* mode, which had put a lot of meat on their tables over the years. Until the farmers had posted most of their favorite hunting spots-- just to get back at whatever hunter shot their stupid cows, which shouldn't have been up in those thickets with their plain brown hides anyhow.

"Well, now, where to park?" Tim asked, glancing to both sides.

"Howbout thet guhly yahnder?" Chet pointed to the right.

Tim nodded and pulled forward a little more, then started backing into the little gully. He stopped the truck. "Better get out and take a look at the dirt. Wouldn't want to get stuck when it's time to leave."

"Rahht," Chet said, and hopped out to look things over. He was always glad to have a chance to do something important to help Tim on trips. Tim was the kind of guy who seemed to know how to do everything right, like he had done everything at least once before to know all the tricks.

The ground was firm. Chet motioned the pickup truck back into place, where only the top of the cab was visible from the highway.

"Why don't we wait 'til a little later to pitch camp, Chet," Tim said as he got out of the truck. They both had a good laugh at that.

"Mebbee we shud go luk fuh theah trayuks," Chet drawled.

"Their tracks?" Tim said, then just plain guffawed. "That's a great one, ol' buddy." And they both leaned against the truck in side-splitting laughter. They always had a great time hunting together.

Finally Tim calmed enough to say, "Well, we better go find that game trail." He chuckled again. "It'll be the one that looks like the critters dropped toothpicks and dragged two tails as they went by." And the laughs started again as they pulled their leather rifle cases from the tool bin under the tarp covering the back bed.

They each enjoyed another cold beer from the cooler as they checked and loaded their rifles--a Winchester 308 and a Remington 30.06. They cherished those guns, and would fight to the death to keep them. "If somebody in Washington took away all the guns," they liked to recite in unison, "only the bad guys would have guns!" And over the years at gun shows they had bought personal arsenals to defend themselves and their families from the terrorist hordes.

Chet and Tim then quickly moved the short distance to the edge of the small stand of trees. They had several clear lines of sight to the railroad track, free from obstructions.

"How 'bout you usin' that log for a gun rest, and I'll use this boulder," Tim pointed.

"Nah, ah jist seed anant bigza grazoppah onit. Awl yuse theut rawk."

"Okay. No extra charge for the rattler I saw crawl under it."

"Awl yuse thuh lawg." And both smiled.

They tapped around with sticks to warn away any slithery real creatures before lying down to find comfortable positions.

"Boy, I wish we had time to sight in our rifles. But everythin' can't be perfect, when you're huntin' real terrorists," Tim said, studying the terrain. I make it out to be about goal-post distance down to that clump of bright purple flowers right by the track. See it there? Hundred yards out?"

"Yuh, bout lahk thuh Tweeyun Fowuks spaht."

"Yeah, just about the same. Good memory." His friend Chet smiled broadly at the compliment. "I remember I used the scope there to pick out a scar on the deer hide to shoot into, so as not to spoil any more of it," Tim said, glancing over at Chet to see if he would buy the boast.

Chet looked back at him with eyebrows raised high and chin tucked down. "Ooh yuh?" was the rejoinder. He hadn't bought it.

"Way I figure, if we nail the traitors when they get right in front of us, we might be lucky and each get two shots in before they duck under cover. Shootin' down on 'em like this we could probably pump a couple more rounds into the cab after that. If that steel's American-made, might get some good ricochet damage. The engineers are most important. If the damn farmers are out in the open and we got time, then we pop some of them too. Serve 'em right. Wha' do ya think?"

After a few moments of silence to take the ideas in and consider them, Chet finally said, "Ahh reckunn."

"Want me to shoot that soldier ant off your leg?"

"Owh shuhyeautt!" Chet said as he swiped at the large insect crawling on his jeans. He quickly stood up and dusted himself off vigorously. "Yall kin stay heah fyuh wahnt. Ahm gonna stan siyud uh tree."

Just as well, Tim thought. He'd give away our position jumping around like that. Might as well get up and take a leak. It may be a while.

As he faced away from the light breeze and unzipped his jeans, Tim asked, "Think the sun'll catch our guns?"

"Theay wohn b'luuhkin up eeya no'ow fuh leeky rednecks." Chet brushed a piece of bark off the American Flag patch on his jeans.

"Ha. And they can't order no more bombs to explode, if they can't talk no more neither." Tim finished his handshaking job and his thought. "They're done for this run."

*   *   *

"This is Ron Slider," the KDNC 10:00 A.M. newscast began, "filling in for Donald Trujillo, who's in Oregon right now flying shotgun for a hijacked train. Don, if you're listening, Jimmy Reinholt called to say he and his band will be in Denver *tonight* at eight o'clock for a special Farm-Help Concert. Country western music stations are sponsoring, with four other big names coming to the Denver Coliseum. It should be a great show, but nine thousand is the most that place can hold, so you listeners better get your tickets early. This year, first time, the proceeds will go toward shipping our grain surpluses overseas, to save the starving. Right in line with the Grain Train movement, huh? Nice gesture.

"An estimated five thousand farmers are in Denver for today's impromptu parade and rally on the State Capitol steps. They say tonight's concert might attract even more. DIA looks like a fun set from the old Hee-Haw TV show.

"Other country performers and rock groups on their regular tours are donating their proceeds to the same idea. Now let's hear via relay from the *Herald's* lady reporter, the U.S.A.S. voice."

The familiar voice began. "This is Wilma Fletcher, riding the hijacked Grain Train.

"And this is America, running down the tracks. We're headed for freedom--freedom to share our wealth and the toil of our hands, freedom to share the plentiful harvest God gave us.

"We're loaded with thanksgiving--for coming through more than 230 years of growing as a country, thanks for having the heart to help others who can't help themselves fast enough, and thanks that we're not in the middle of another hurricane or flood or drought ourselves.

"We're loaded with bravery--brave enough to often do what is right when the chips are down, and brave enough to say yes, our God is love. Down deep in our roots, the many faces of God in America are still love.

"We're headed for freedom, along this track of unknown dangers, feeling like Columbus, or Mayflower Pilgrims, setting out for a New World. Or the blessed Indians who welcomed them with food. Or like our pioneers, heading west with new hope. Or like the black race, unshackled to lead free lives. Sure there are problems ahead, but we're stronger for being on the right track again.

"We're headed for freedom. Green lights or red, there's no stopping us now. We're on our way bringing life, bringing grain to starving people! So clear the tracks, and full speed ahead!

"It's 9:00 A.M. Pacific Coast Daylight Time here in Oregon on your Friday morning. This is Wilma Fletcher. I'll be back in an hour, God willing, with more news on this run for freedom."

*

Wilma smiled at the guys as she finished the live broadcast. She was glad to be back in the engine cab with Peter, Monty, and Fork.

The new engineer, Andre, had apparently finished his special part, for he traded places with her when she left Boxcar Two a half-hour before. He looked quite pallid, though, and she inquired if he was ill. He barely spoke, just climbed up into the big freight car. An odd fellow.

She was told there was another new visitor who had joined Boxcar One last night, Jerome Blackman, a mediator from a National Peace Academy Intervention Team. And he had generously provided the satellite hook-up technology to allow the live broadcasting. Her skills would really be challenged today, she thought, savoring the possibilities. Wilma was very glad she came along.

* * *

"Senator Frye, you're getting all sorts of requests from the press for a statement."

"Well, tell them nicely to go play with themselves."

His Washington, D.C. secretary smiled at the typically potent remark. "They are asking whether you will be modifying your position, since there seems to be a grass roots move on for most national service clubs meeting this morning to be voting ad hoc on whether to support..."

"My, my, we're back to our long sentences this morning, aren't we?" He was critical of that trait in her. "I stand for what is right, Mrs. Henderschiedt: the Constitution, and our legal system. The laws passed by Congress, holding together the warp and woof of our democracy. And I was elected to defend those strong principles."

"Oh, if only you would tell the media like that. It's just thrilling."

This reminded him of why he kept her on his staff. So he continued, "That's the curse and the blessing of our modern media. We find out so instantaneously what is going on all around this great land. Some feel they must react just as immediately, but I never have. Haste makes waste, and on Capitol Hill, that's a nasty word.

"Now, will you do me a favor, and bring me everything you can find written against the train. Plus a small sample of favorable views. The Interior Under-Secretary will be interested when we lunch in a half-hour."

* * *

From the outside, the Seattle City Hall Building looked like a newer seven story art museum, finished all in blue-tinted glass and jutting protrusions. Tom Buchanan, calling himself Don Thompson, took time to stroll through the adjoining landscape of terraced gardens and amphitheatre seating in Civic Plaza. The sound of cascading waterfalls and interactive fountains brought him a fleeting moment of peace. He shook off the feeling as untimely and walked into the spacious lobby, past the watchful eyes of cameras and guards. At least they had no reason for metal detector gates and security guards here as in Denver's municipal buildings.

He took one of four elevators to the top floor, and stepped out. The reception area was to the right, balcony to the left. Taking a casual left, he checked exit possibilities more closely, which he had only hurriedly done the day before.

The balcony overlooked busy 4th Avenue. Black glass skyscrapers and parking garages dominated the view. No way out here.

He retraced his steps across the dark-gray carpet squares to the reception area, where four-seater sofas in dark leather faced each other. A kiosk held the mayor's unsmiling picture, stern as a school principal, shoulder-length brown hair curled under and going gray without apology, an American flag to one side. A poster board on an easel boasted the headline, "Best Cities For Business: The Top Ten," from *Fortune Magazine*. Seattle bragged of being first, Denver limped in seventh.

Tom flashed a smile as he walked past the receptionist seated behind the counter and staying busy until he found time to approach her working space. Two ficus trees that never need watering framed the glass door in the windowed west wall, as he stepped out onto the large corner balcony. He surveyed the quiet scene, where Old and New Downtowns sprawled down to the docks with their huge cranes looking like bright-orange Popsicle-stick horses. Then Elliott Bay took over, its polluted waters stretching to Puget Sound. Far islands became horizon. The balcony was high, and went nowhere, so this was no escape route.

He went back inside, almost ready to officially announce his arrival. He quickly studied the interior accoutrements. A short hallway with two doors was to the right of the reception desk. Two modern paintings graced the walls, colors matching some mostly oriental *objets d'art* in the small display case nearby. Official gifts, Tom guessed, which he could use for initial small talk if needed.

He took several deep breaths and approached the receptionist, then announced politely that he was Don Thompson, and the mayor was expecting him.

The lady at the desk smiled, acknowledging him with a polite greeting. "Nine o'clock. You're very prompt," she noted. She escorted him through one of two doors to his left, opening to a large anteroom with a conference table and chairs. The lady ushered him through another door into the long office. Mayor Taulison stood, a stunning executive in tailored navy blue, extending her hand for one firm clasp of his hand.

He smiled, "Mayor, I'm pleased that you called."

"Mr. Thompson, glad you could come." She moved from behind her desk and the seat of power, to a small round table near one of the seven tall glass window panels, motioning for him to join her there--a token of an open administration and an end to back-room politics. But where he would be totally exposed to cameras.

Nervously, he settled into a tan armchair, comfort designed, as she continued. "Frankly, I debated whether to contact you, or call my police chief to arrest you."

That made Tom squirm even more, as she had expected. "I suspected that would be one of your dilemmas this morning," he replied, with a strong amount of understanding in his voice.

This prompted her compassionate tone. "I learned of the gas trap in Idaho a short while ago. Did you say you know the lead hijacker?"

They had bantered around his involvement during his visit the day before, leaving it unresolved. He answered truthfully that he knew one person, offering her limited clarification. She hadn't mentioned the phone call and briefing from the NPA Crisis Center, which had earned him admittance over cancelled appointments. She didn't know if he was in touch with the Academy, or how much anybody knew. They studied one another. Confide? Trust? Fear?

She decided to share a little personal vulnerability. "I made a stupid comment last night to a reporter. One of those you regret at once, yet know will be around to haunt you the rest of your career."

"You mean today's headline? 'Call Me If They Get To Washington.'"

"See? Everyone knows, even the out-of-towners. I can't believe I said that about your train. I pride myself in preparedness, and advance planning. That's a hallmark with me. My staff motto is, *Avoid Surprises!* How those words got into and came out of my mouth, I'll never know."

"Welcome to the crowd of humans, Mayor," Tom said soberly. "But I'm fearful that somebody else's equally fallible judgment is going to cost lives when they make another attempt to stop that Grain Train."

She seized the opening. "But I'm telling you it doesn't have to. If you have any influence with that crew, tell them to call it off now, before anything else happens. There's no way to win from their position." She adamantly stated her conviction.

"You're looking at it from the inside point of view, Mayor. You are Establishment. The upholder of Law. But think back over centuries of social history. Many extraordinary people have died for their beliefs, punished by narrow-minded authorities for causes that eventually triumphed."

The mayor stood, and bluntly asked, "All that aside, does your being in Seattle mean there are bombs here?"

Tom also stood, just as bluntly answering, "That depends in large part on your response." The polite protagonists were eyeball to eyeball.

"Yesterday you asked me to consider what I would do, *if* Seattle was to become the end of the line. Has your wording changed?"

Tom debated telling her, but decided too much was at stake with too many hours left. "Not yet," was his calculated answer, "but you need to be making your plans in case."

"What would you think those should include?" She knew she was dealing with a person concealing facts, making him even more dangerous. But sharing the stage with egotistic activists and active listening under difficult circumstances were two tactics she practiced regularly to maintain popularity and solve thorny problems.

Tom hoped he had read their brief encounters correctly. "You are a take-charge lady," he proffered, "and that leadership will be needed. But for now, let your heart rule your head. You are in a position to release America's love..."

"Ah, so just allow everyone to go free to do whatever they want?"

"Your head is working your mouth too fast again." Tom took himself and the mayor by surprise with his boldness. She moved back to her desk and sat down, leaning back in the big leather chair of officeholder, folding her hands in her lap, silent. But distancing herself in the process.

Was he losing her, Tom wondered. "What will you do with the crowds?" Tom came near the front of her desk and started pacing as he laid out the picture in his mind. "And protesters picketing? And traffic congestion? Won't you want to be there personally, when they stop?" His adverb tense had slipped from *what-if* to a definitive *when*, but he didn't correct it. And he knew she was too astute to miss the implications. "Are you prepared to negotiate the disposition of the grain? And handle all the citizens on board labeled as criminals? With media filming everything?"

The mayor leaned forward. "I understand a negotiator is on board?"

Tom liked the tenor of her question. "Yes, from the Academy. He'll probably keep them safer than otherwise. But just by boarding, he's undoubtedly become tainted and unacceptable as a neutral." Peter had updated Tom very briefly during the night. Then Tom destroyed that cell phone and changed motels. He would not be found until he was ready.

"What about using the Federal Conciliation Service to negotiate?"

"Peter would spot the fox guarding the chicken coop: Federal laws are being broken, federal policies challenged, and federal toes stepped on."

"We've got some good local ADR professionals."

"Mayor, my recommendation is to request another heavy-duty mediator from the Academy. They have some with flawless reputations known nationally, who always seem acceptable to both sides."

"*Both* sides?" she challenged. "I'm just the new kid, wanting to keep my city from getting blown up. Before me, there's the oil refinery, highway department, manhandled engineers, grain car owners, and tons of railroad property. Then there's Homeland Security for internal terrorism, FBI for law, D.C. for policy, farmers on both sides, Peter and his group, Congress... did I leave anyone out?" she finished, managing a brave smile.

"Yes. The National Peace Academy advocating non-violence," Tom added to her list. "And the media, and the grain terminal owner where they might stop, as well as the freighter captain from a foreign country who might be loading there...and the million starving children." He was busy recruiting her help, rather than putting her off any longer.

Shit, she thought, envisioning the terrible complexity which two lines of parallel steel track could be bringing her way. "Double shit," she said aloud as a phone buzzer rang annoyingly, saying "Excuse me" as she answered-- to cover her comment and the interruption.

"I will see him in five minutes, out there, not in here," she informed her secretary, and hung up. "Want to try for a triple cuss?" That made Tom smile. "Seattle FBI is waiting in the anteroom, and they don't do social calls." That brought him a frown, which she noted.

"These damn windows," he gestured, moving away from that wall of glass. He was very glad he had used an alias. A decision point had arrived for them both.

"What's your own long-range goal in all this?" She pushed him for a personal declaration.

He considered dodging her directness, then bought into the concerned look in her eyes. She held so many keys for the future of the train and the Shakespeare Group, as well as their world's tomorrows.

"An international conference," he blurted out. "Convening in October, for debating the ethical and economic dilemmas of farm surplus world-wide." An insight leaped into his mind, from wherever great ideas come. "It would be held here in Seattle, as a more neutral world center than Camp David or the U.N. in New York. Decisions would be made and programs started by January. Next year, we turn things around so the kids get the food and the farmers make a buck for a change." Tom's eyes filled with enthusiasm, and his voice sparkled. It was contagious.

"This is crazy," she said aloud, but speaking more to herself. "Take this rear door. Tell the lady in that office to show you the *4:45 maneuver*. That will get you out without being caught. Come back in the same way in two hours. If they arrest you, tell them to call me. We're going to try to find a path out of this morass."

As Tom was closing the door, he heard her muttering, "Why me, Lord?"

*   *   *

The Grain Train rumbled steadily along the line, minutes after nine on Friday morning. In the cab of the 9039, Peter completed his calls, as Wilma recounted some of the tales she found in the fertile interview field of her overnight boxcar, and told also of the freshly dropped fertilizer that had been heaved in. They decided not to broadcast news of the gas field, giving ideas to others. Then they shifted to the important job of planning their daylight safety.

They had put up with some putrid eggs and old tomatoes being hurled at them into the cab after crossing into Oregon several hours earlier. They had even tolerated a string of firecrackers falling at their feet, though it tensed them up. The incident that really changed their minds was the tear gas grenade. It was lobbed in while passing through Pleasant Valley, three towns back, creating real havoc. Somehow Monty had managed to find his asbestos gloves, bravely picked up the spewing nodule, and threw it out the window--unfortunately back into the sparse crowd, which scattered in all directions. They knew the news headline would be "Engineer Gasses Peaceful Crowd." This could cut down on their draw, and picture them as having more weapons.

But that had decided them on closing the side windows and doors and front vents when going through towns. The problem with this solution, as in so many, is that it created other problems. Public visibility would be lessened; media would be left with earlier videotapes. And they got hot, fast, when closed up in the small cab; the air conditioner was still working only occasionally. They then decided to open the side windows between towns.

The Shakespeare Group had anticipated this, and manufactured two aluminum shields backed with bulletproof glass to cover the windows, but there hadn't been time to attach inside clamps. So Peter and Wilma tried holding the shields in place to keep rocks from shattering glass in on them as they passed through North Powder minutes before. But there were no discernible thumps of objects. Either people were friendlier, or the preventive measures had controlled the antagonism. Though it was too bad, they agreed, not to get to see the people of America face to face.

*

"They're a-comin', Chet. Hear that whistle?"

"Lahk a bueglun ohl ehlk."

"Yeah, I can hardly wait to see their racks...I mean, faces." He smiled. "Say, what are we goin' to do for trophies to take home? We sure can't take the meat or hides."

"Noup," Chet chuckled low. "W'got theyuh nuespaypuh pitchus. H'bout pudn eech won uhnduh zum antluhz?" They both laughed.

"Well, maybe we won't never tell, y'know? They may claim we were poachin' again!" And Tim slapped his leg, that was such a good joke. Then he got serious. "Look sharp now. It'll be a-comin'. See the light blue smoke yonder? Remember, our country's dependin' on us, 'cause if they knew how to stop these suckers, they woulda before now. Them boys think there ain't no vigilantes left in America got another think comin'."

They ducked to hide themselves as one helicopter appeared from nowhere, flying the tracks a mile ahead of the train.

*

Peter just finished checking in with the boxcar farmers when Fork said, "Damn smoke," having opened the window on his side and gotten a face full from an easterly wind gust.

"Yes, but things will cool off in here anyway. What a career you picked," Wilma said, getting a full dose of the summer discomforts of an engineer. "Not much in the way of majestic scenery out there."

"But it's sure pretty," Fork said, "like you."

She smiled and rested her hand on his shoulder, looking out past him. "Just rolling country, pockets of trees tucked away where little hills meet, clumps of flowers here and there bursting into purple, all umbrellaed by bright blue sky..." She was composing aloud for her next segment. "Say, Fork, what's the name of those flowers by the track?"

*

"Now you only got three shells in that aught-six, right? There's only three or four of 'em we really gotta get, and we want to be fair," Tim asked Chet, half joking, half serious.

"Yuhp." Chet held up three fingers, and smiled.

"Besides, those boxcar farmers and whirlybirds may come chargin' up here after us, if we shoot for too long. I'd just as leave drive home casual like, right? Listen on the radio how good our aim was."

He looked down at the approaching train through his scope, the number 9039 clearly showing. "Okay, so when that lead engine gets close to that purple clump...I make out two at the window...you want the gal?"

"Nawh, thuh dood."

"Okay...one...two..." Damn, she's pretty, Tim thought.

*

Fork looked out at the patch of purple they were passing, and smiled at a recollection. "I stopped a whole train once, and picked some just like those to take to my Mom. She called them *Engineer's*..." And his mouth disappeared.

*   *   *

Chapter Sixteen

Wilma didn't have time to scream at the death mask splattering over her. In the next instant a bullet shattered her shoulder, sending her flying against the back wall to collapse in an unconscious heap.

Monty and Peter both dropped to the floor instinctively, staring in horror at their gory friends. The woman's arm convulsed as it hung by shreds of red muscle and tissue from the corner of her body.

Another bullet hit inside the engine cab, ricocheting violently metal against metal. It hit and cracked the front window. Two more bullets banged inside and began their deadly ricochet romance. One thudded deep into Peter's left thigh, and he screamed in sudden pain. Monty pulled himself into a smaller ball.

The shooting stopped. Monty reached up, grabbed the handheld radio, and ducked back down quickly. "We're under attack!" he hollered into the speaker to alert all in the boxcars, if it wasn't too late. "One dead for sure, another maybe. What's happening back there?"

"Okay in One. Who's been hit?"

"Shit! Buck Bancroft just took a hit in the chest here in Two. What in the hell is going on?"

"Everybody stay away from the doors. We're still under full power. Maybe we can outrun them. Fork is blown away. Wilma's minus an arm, losing lots of blood. Peter is hit in the leg."

"Holy Jesus, a massacre. Doc jumped right up to start working on Buck, but he's a target himself now."

"No! They'll pick him off for sure."

And the hunters probably would have reloaded to meet the challenge of a crouching target. But the train was out of sight of the two patriots, back at their pickup congratulating each other on fine trophy shots, and arguing over whether they should have put in five shells each for a herd that size.

Peter struggled to reach his cellular for Shakespeare contact. He pushed two buttons for Boise and put it close to his mouth, pushing his voice to be heard through his pain. "Jeremy, you on?" All secrecy was forgotten.

"Jeremy here. You okay?"

"No...they've hurt us bad...blood everywhere...can't let 'em...do this... and not pay...send message out...blow up your first one...tell them no more attacks on us...or all will blow."

Peter clicked to the third number in memory, telling Ardis the same for Portland, desperate to stop more bloodshed.

"Grain Train, what's happening? Looks like two men down in Boxcar Two." The TV-5 media chopper had apparently seen nothing, and the Academy chopper was much further out on point.

Monty got to the radio while Peter was trying to stop the blood streaming from Wilma's shoulder with his shirt. Both men in the cab had already thrown up from the sickening horror surrounding them, and were beyond that point of shock to be barely functional again. "Fork's been shot dead, Wilma may be, Peter's hit. Where the hell were you?"

"Good God!" the pilot radioed. "We didn't see anything from here." The pilot and Donna began scanning both sides for unusual movement. "Grain Train, which side did the shots come from?" the pilot asked.

There was silence for a moment, then, "They were on the left side, south side. Find the bastards." Radio regulations and procedures were ignored under siege.

The helicopter crew abandoned the blind train under full throttle to retrace the route. They strained their eyes searching the world south of the tracks. Only an occasional car was on the highway nearby, none moving faster than others, and certainly none with rifles sticking out the windows to make the search job easy. There was no motion in the empty fields as they flew back over the ten miles into North Powder.

The media chopper had patched into the Academy lead, and turned them around to search again in front of the train, fast. Their radio was filled with description from Monty about what had happened, and they were preparing to broadcast. "Listen to me, Monty, Peter," the pilot said commandingly. "I've seen a world of injuries. They way you describe Wilma, you're going to have to stop the train for the doctor to get to her. You're losing her. The Academy chopper says you're clear. I'm sure they'll have to airlift, and they're equipped..."

Donna spoke into her headset, interrupting. "Stop the damn train! We'll broadcast your threats to keep everyone away."

The pilot continued. "We're on the way back. No signs out here. We'll stop when you do."

Silence. Then Monty's voice. "No choice but to stop. Be careful."

The TV-5 helicopter made a steep U-turn and headed back, flying low. From a small grove of trees ahead of them, a pickup truck emerged, heading across the field toward the highway.

"Let's take a quick detour," the pilot said. As they came closer, it was apparent that there was hardly a road for the truck to be following. "Middle of nowhere, with a tarp over the back? That's no working farmer. Good view of the rail tracks. Who's inside?" Donna saw two men.

"So not on a picnic." He clicked channels on his radio mike. "Oregon State Patrol, this is National Broadcasting Network Chopper NBN-Twelve. Come in."

"State Patrol, Portland. Over."

"I'm five miles north and west of North Powder on Interstate 84. There's just been a murder of one or more Grain Train occupants. We have possible suspects under surveillance. Light gray Ford pickup, early 80's model, tarp over back, white and silver license plate, spelled 'HUNTFR,' dented right rear fender, two male occupants. now...turning...east on I-84. Repeat, eastbound on Interstate 84, two male suspects of Grain Train murder. Must break away from surveillance for EMT airlift. Request backup, over."

The radio was silent. Then, "NBN-Twelve, this is State Patrol. We have no available vehicles within twenty miles of your location. We will send alert to the nearest unit. Please tell law-breaking train engineers to stop immediately, and we will assist in routing medical assistance, over."

"You son-of-a-bitch," Donna snapped back with all the venom she could muster. "I know you've had a patrol car running parallel to that train all the way across the State. Now turn that car around and pick up those guys for questioning."

"This is Commander Nelson. Your language outburst has been recorded. I can assure you that it will be played back for you at your hearing. Furthermore, OHP certainly does not take orders from you or any media. Our car is following known fugitives on that train, and will not break off to follow some possible suspects in an unconfirmed killing!"

"Hi, everybody. Hate to interrupt such a friendly chitchat. This is an 18-wheeler with my big ears on, handle of *Green Beret*. NBN spy in the sky, I have your Ford pickup driving along right in front of me, so he isn't going to get lost. You go ahead and take care of your emergency. Now, Commander, let me help you get your priorities straight. Those folks on the Grain Train are just trying to get a little of our extra food to hungry people. Nothing wrong with that, in my book. And here I am risking my life by following murder suspects. I want you to do your job by coming and apprehending this pair pronto, or else I'll ask my trucker friends at the next stop up the road to help me with that dangerous job. Anybody up at Frankie's, come on?"

"Green Beret, this is *Stringbean*. We're all here listening at Frankie's, and we're with ya. It's real simple to blockade the bridge down here at the far end, then you close him off from behind once he's on. Only trouble is, could be shooting, other folks on the bridge and all, over."

"Good plan, Stringbean. Oh, you been catching all this, Commander? We've been kind of locking you out from talking much on your frequency. I'll bet ol' Governor Anderson would want you grabbing these suspects right away, don't you agree, over?"

"Now listen, you two truckers and any others, this is not political. You are not to take the law into your own hands. That's just what those train maniacs did. Now there may not have even been a murder, and ever if there was, those men in the pickup may not have had anything to do with it. The Patrol will take the proper action at the proper time after we have all the facts. You just leave those citizens alone, and block no roads. That's an order!"

A familiar voice surprisingly interrupted, overriding the airwaves by calmly saying, "This is Governor Lee Anderson. My aides informed me that an interesting radio transmission was in progress. Hello to all my good trucker friends out there. Hi, Green Beret, and Stringbean. Keep the wheels of commerce rolling, men; our healthy economy depends on you.

"And I'm just sure by now that Commander Nelson has seen on his wire service that indeed there has been a tragic death on the Grain Train in our peaceful State. I'm also sure he has just ordered the three State Patrol cars nearest the vicinity of North Powder to apprehend the suspects identified by the NBN helicopter. Green Beret, will you please give the commander your exact location at present, and verify the license plate number of the pickup if you have it? Then please pull back to a safe distance, so our cars can close in on the suspects without endangering other motorists. Thanks for your good help out there, truckers. This is Governor Anderson, the one who signs your licenses, so no argument, boys. Over and out."

The Academy chopper radioed in next. "Grain Train, Washington has contacted our Crisis Center. The authorities are saying they did not do the shooting, that they don't know who did. They say everybody in America has a gun, and you can't retaliate for a local nut."

Just watch us, Monty thought, as he continued braking the train. Peter kept his blood-soaked shirt pressed tightly against Wilma's ragged side, struggling not to lose consciousness himself.

*   *   *

The three cooperating media enterprises in Denver had been expecting this moment of confrontation every hour of the last twenty-seven. This is what their life was all about--capturing a moment of fever pitch excitement and making it public. But what grotesque twisting of fate for their reporter to become the victim.

"We interrupt this program to bring you a special news bulletin." The TV-5 picture switched to the familiar anchordesk, and KDNC Radio began simulcasting the coverage. The Herald newsroom hushed, with reporters gathered around the TV set on Hargrave's desk. "We switch now live to Donna Harrison, our newsperson accompanying the hijacked Grain Train by helicopter."

The picture and voice changed to Donna's, with much background rotor noise. Her hair was windblown; her eyes were puffy, maybe from crying, and she wore little makeup. This was not a planned appearance. "Via Instacam, you see us in Oregon, but I will not divulge an exact location, for it might increase the danger to everyone here."

The image switched to their bird's eye view of the Grain Train, as her husky voice continued. "You see the train below us slowing to a stop. For there has just been a brutal murder of one of the engineers, whose name we will withhold until the family has been notified.

"Also mutilated in the shooting just moments ago was Wilma Fletcher, ace reporter for the *Rocky Mountain Herald*, on extraordinary assignment in providing live coverage of one of this decade's most unusual stories. We do not know the full extent of her injuries, but they are very serious, and we can only hope and pray that they will not prove fatal.

"Peter Wayman, self-proclaimed leader of this hijacking, has also been shot, but we're told his wounds may not be as critical.

"And there is more. One of the Colorado farmers, riding a boxcar in support of this cause, this effort simply to use our food surplus to feed starving kids, has been seriously wounded in this multiple slaying attempt."

The picture switched back to Donna. "This helicopter's crew was fortunately able to spot two of the suspected riflemen and to lead Oregon

State Patrol to their location, with the indispensable help of several brave 18-wheel truckers, Green Beret and Stringbean, their CB-radio names. We understand Governor Lee Anderson of Oregon finally took a personal hand in overseeing the prompt arrests.

"We are uncertain whether there were more than two shooters, or whether there will be further attempts on the lives of those riding the Grain Train. Or for that matter, aimed at us in the media escort."

The picture changed to the train. "There's a man who jumped from a boxcar, even though the train is still slowing, running up toward the engines, carrying a bag. If we can get a close-up look with the camera...thanks, Ray. Yes, that's Dr. Nevins, a Vietnam Veteran who joined up with the train in Helper, Utah, to be just that--a helper. From the way he's crouching as he runs, he must feel there may still be some danger out here.

"Peter Wayman, in his pain, insisted that we notify all law enforcement agencies that if the train is attacked again, he will order the immediate bombing of power facilities all the way from Denver to the West Coast. Based on what they did to Denver oil fields and roadways Thursday morning, when they began this odyssey, I think he's serious.

"I would be very surprised if this shooting does not lead to some retribution, since that is what he has threatened all along. His statement also clearly implies that somehow this train will be continuing.

"We're going to stay alert at this point...the doctor has climbed on board and is entering the lead engine now...can you get a close-up angle through that door...oh, good Lord, look at him. Oh, no, I'm sorry. I'm sorry, we never should have aired that." Her voice choked up.

"Uh, the National Peace Academy helicopter has medical litter racks for stretchers, and uh, you can see them landing now to assist with the emergency airlift...sometimes this job gets to you. Here, Ray..."

And a male voice finished. "So, that was Donna Harrison from KTAD Channel 5, covering that shooting that just happened out here in Oregon. Right under us--and we didn't do anything to stop it."

The half-minute of cruelty passed into American history.

*   *   *

The special office had been hastily vacated, and re-equipped at Portland's FBI headquarters. III had visited before, but now had come in to take charge. He motioned to Agent Switzer to enter, after the polite knock on the open door.

When informed of the shooting and the results, III said, "Damn their souls to hell!" Which he meant sincerely, for how could they have missed Peter? He pointed a finger at Switzer, and raised his eyebrows in question. The agent shook his head emphatically sideways, indicating it was not an action by the group dubbed *Montana*.

"This will trigger bombings," III reasoned aloud. "They'll think we were the killers." Switzer nodded in agreement, as his boss continued.

"From the Denver bridge evidence, these people are bomb novices. They point and push, so they have to see the target--or just want to. Get Portland officers patrolling on ten-block perimeters around every major bridge near here, and every power plant and refinery within twenty miles of Portland, now! We'll wait for one to blow, then close that net. Nobody gets out of it without ID checks once there's an explosion, and everybody else responds there at once."

He cogitated a minute more. "There's only one of those nuts in each city, I'm sure of it."

Switzer left on the run. The same basic strategy had been suggested by their fax and e-mail in early morning communiques to all cities over 10,000 population west of the Mississippi, which have the same types of infrastructure as potential targets. They might lose power, but they'd catch the prey if they followed those instructions.

*   *   *

Blackman jumped from the boxcar as the train ground to a rough and noisy stop. He zigzagged his way toward the Academy helicopter to draw fire if there was to be any more. Then he signaled to his back-up crew to disembark from the chopper as he neared them.

"Okay, by stretcher pairs," he shouted his orders. "You two, to the second boxcar for a chest wound, male. Doc's got him stabilized and bandaged. Go! You two, with me to the engine. Shorty, move this bird in closer to the train, and keep those rotors hot. There may be more shooting anytime. Keep an eye peeled for visitors. We don't want any! Let's move it!"

The white-uniformed trio ran fast, toward the lead engine through the dust kicked up by the heavy blades. Blackman was already debating what to do with Fork's body, since their borrowed helicopter only carried two stretchers. He wondered if he could now convince Peter to give this all up as a lost cause, and be flown to the fully equipped Pendleton hospital for treatment of his own gunshot wound.

Their EMT training helped prepare the three for the sight that waited behind the closed cab door. Blood and bits of bone and flesh had splattered the walls and run down in bright red lines to add to the pool of life fluids covering the floor. Absorption made the colors indistinguishable on the clothes the corpse wore.

At least Wilma had a face to look at, but it had the look of death on it. The doctor was wrapping her lopsided upper torso with long strips of bandage, while Peter held his sopping wet shirt in place over the hole where her left arm had been. The whole arm now lay in her lap, where the doctor put it after he severed the strips of muscle and veins from which it had been hanging. The stretcher team was ready on the narrow catwalk.

Monty sat at the engine's controls like the train was still moving under his direction, just staring into space.

Within minutes it looked like a war zone, with concerned farmers milling around, some live-streaming cpd pictures, and Academy men in soiled whites carrying the two stretchers with the blanket-covered injured toward the waiting helicopter. The two men in the engine cab had so much blood on their clothes that some farmers who were looking in worried they had also been mortally hit.

The Intervention Team worked swiftly, strapping the unconscious two into the stretcher safety harnesses while the dust flew around them. Oxygen masks had been placed on the two victims, and hooked up to the tank inside.

The lead IT crewmember ran back toward the engine, yelling Blackman's name. The tall African-American stepped out on the catwalk.

"Is Peter coming?" his man asked. Blackman waved him off, saying "Godspeed," and stepped back inside the cab of Engine 9039. He somehow still hoped the stench of blood and vomit would help him in reasoning with the crippled mission's leader.

But Peter steadfastly insisted, "No, we will not stop. We're in a different war now." He was propped against one side of the cab, while the doctor knelt in muck and worked on his left leg. He had cut the pant leg off to get to the gaping bullet wound in Peter's thigh. "How is Buck doing?"

"He may make it. Some farmers are talking about leaving. You going to force them to stay and risk their lives further?" Dr. Nevins asked.

"No--but we can't leave them out here, and there's no room in the helicopters. So, they can leave near the next town. But some will stay. Won't they, Monty?"

The big man in his chair said nothing, maybe not even hearing.

"What shall we do with Fork's body?" Blackman questioned bluntly. No one looked at the horrible mess on the floor that had been a man, and a friend.

"I didn't bring any body bags. I should have," the doctor said matter-of-factly.

"Maybe wrap him in a blanket, and put him in the next engine," Blackman suggested. "When we stop we'll arrange to send him..."

"No!" Monty's first word startled them. "He's going back with me..."

Peter's heart skipped a beat as he sucked in his breath.

"...when the trip is done," Monty slowly finished. Peter bowed his head in relief. "Fork signed on to the end," Monty said. "This is his blood we're wallowing in, so I'll honor his decision."

"As soon as he's moved, wipe up this floor. It's dangerous." The doctor was all business. "How much longer is the trip? The heat might create a problem."

"Through today, if we can get out of this cursed State," Monty answered forthrightly.

"Why can't you just stop past Portland?" Blackman asked. "You'll have ocean freighter access there in Astoria."

"Because that's not part of the plan," Peter said curtly. "Now will somebody help me get up?"

"We'll need to change that dressing this afternoon, maybe sooner if you start bleeding again," the doctor said, taking hold of Peter's extended hand and grasping his arm in support. "The bullet is still in your leg."

"Will you stay with us, in case?" Peter asked, his face showing the pain as he changed position and stood.

"From what you just told this man, my tour isn't up yet."

"Thanks for helping get Wilma off to Pendleton. What do you think of her chances?"

"She'll be a few hours in surgery, to save her. A prosthesis seems doubtful."

"That wasn't her writing arm..." *What am I saying*, he thought. "...but it was one of two perfectly good ones." Then he asked on impulse, "What about her breast?"

"Too early to tell."

Her whole side gone, all because of me, Peter thought. *No, not just me. She believed in this too.* He still felt guilty.

"Are you headed for the boxcars now, Doc?"

"Of course. To wait for the next ambush. You commander-types always have one more mile to take, no matter what the cost. And leave the mess for the rest of us to clean up."

The doctor left the cab, to make his way carefully along the catwalk, now slick with many tracks of blood. Peter stared at the metal door, having heard the words through a fog of pain. He opened the dirty trunk lid to get a change of clothes, at Blackman's suggestion, then said he'd wait.

*   *   *

As the bomb explosion toppled the 75-foot-tall power line tower, flashing light indicators and warning alarms went off simultaneously in the Boise control room of Idaho Power. One-third of its power was interrupted-- no electricity, lights, traffic signals, no nothing. A few emergency power generators kicked in at the hospital, police, and fire stations. The office had been alerted that there might be trouble like this, and immediately dialed the number from the all-points-bulletin on five terrorist suspects, which the FBI had faxed.

Tires squealed, and within minutes the highways were sealed by State and local police within a three-mile radius of the remote power pole that now lay crumpled in twisted steel wreckage. Long blue thousand-volt arcs of loose electricity chased throughout the bombed maze, seeking their lost demanding populations.

Jeremy had reacted instantly when he got Peter's emergency message twenty minutes previously. He had jumped into his car and drove toward this nearest hidden bomb, some four miles away from his motel. There had been little traffic to worry about, and every twenty seconds he had pressed the speed dial and entered the code number on his cell phone, not knowing the range for sure. And there had still been no explosion as he drove.

This was the primary reason they had decided to keep Shakespeare members in each city after placing the bombs. They couldn't be sure they exploded if Peter tried calling the bomb phone numbers from the train. Personal presence guaranteed their threats.

Finally, when he had gotten within a half-mile of the pole, and had the blasted thing in sight, he stopped the truck in absolute frustration. He dialed each number carefully and hard, then the code numbers.

KA-BLAM! The explosion had finally happened, sending a silent pillar of dust into the sky, then the concussion had rocked his rented panel truck.

He hadn't even waited to see if the pole fell, but did a very slow U-turn and headed back for the far side of Boise, awaiting further instructions from his phone beside him on the seat. He wondered how critically his friends were hurt, to force this extreme measure. And whether anybody else had been given the order they had hoped would never come?

Now he saw the taillights glowing red on the car in front of him. *Uh, oh, radar*, he thought. *Better slow down too.* Then he saw the flashing red and blue on top of a black car straddling the two-lane highway. But there was no way this roadblock could be set up so fast for the bombing--unless they happened to be in the vicinity. No, it must be something else, not for him. So he tried to look and think unworried as he drove slowly toward the uniformed men with shotguns. It would do no good to turn around and go the other direction, for all sorts of police and emergency equipment were passing by in the other lane, now headed for the blast site. The road behind him would be blocked as well.

He would be all right, if they didn't insist on checking contents of his panel truck. He had spent several hours already on building up the correct mixture of ammonium nitrate fertilizer and diesel fuel in the six 55-gallon drums. The blasting caps and detonators were still carefully packaged there as well. The Shakespeare Group had been convinced that a bomb of this type, similar to the Oklahoma City Federal Building explosive, would be even more convincing of the seriousness of their threat. But these officers didn't know him from Adam. All he had to do now was to look and act innocent, and show them his Colorado driver's license as they approached his window…

*   *   *

Ardis jumped out of bed, threw on her clothes, picked up her packed bag, and raced out the door of her Portland motel. Unfortunately, Peter's call had been of sadness and utmost urgency. But she was prepared, staying at the closest motel she could find to her first target. A mere mile. She could have jogged within range, as fast as she could get there driving, but she wanted to leave the vicinity immediately afterwards.

Ardis had carefully selected the Northwest section of the city for the blackout--west of the Willamette River, north of Burnside Street. Less population would be affected, but the message was still clear: downtown and Portland International Airport in the Northeast section were spared, but could be the next targets.

She phoned the special detonation number and code. She was genuinely sorry to not stay and watch the transformer station as it began its series of explosions, for she knew it would be spectacular. The little she did see in her rearview mirror assured her of that. But her top priority now was not getting caught, and being in place to instantly detonate the next bomb if Peter called again. She had made reservations at a second motel, only twelve blocks from the bridge, but across town from this isolated corner that would soon be crawling with Feds. When she was midway, she would stop and make one quick threatening call to claim credit for the destruction, and warn of more.

Ardis had many more blocks of C-4 in the trunk, enough to single-handedly insure the success of their scheme. She could have Portland burning out of control by suppertime if called on.

*   *   *

"I'd like to ride here in the cab with you and Monty," Blackman said, "when we get started again."

"Dangerous place to be," Peter said simply.

"My job is still negotiating us out of that danger."

"Good job so far," Peter said in quiet sarcasm.

"Know anything about running a train?" Monty asked, and got a "No."

Peter spoke with Monty, then quickly made his scheduled hourly one-word coded calls, to prevent any more bombings.

"Please get some blankets, to wrap Fork," Peter directed. "I need to talk with the farmers now, then we need to get moving."

Peter hobbled outside the cab. A small brave group was standing near the tracks. They gasped when they saw him. Some newcomers held up their cpd's for better pictures of the leader they were seeing for the first time. He asked them to not record this, since it would be a private conversation. Arms were lowered at once.

After assurances that he and Monty were all right, he spoke of Fork and Wilma and Buck. Then he explained that the train would travel to the next town, LaGrande, and stop to let off anyone who wanted to leave. He asked them to pass the word to the other farmers who stayed hidden in the boxcars. They were to close the big doors for the short ride, to be safe.

A short distance away, there was activity and quiet talking. "This is Donna Harrison, reporting from near the hijacked Grain Train in Oregon. As you can see, the train is stopped, and their leader Peter Wayman has left the cab and is standing on the catwalk of the engine, talking with some of the farmers who have joined him on this dangerous and illegal trip. He signaled that he wanted us to kill the sound and keep our distance during this filming.

"Most of the blood on his clothes and arms is that of one engineer and one reporter, Wilma Fletcher, victims of snipers' bullets. Peter's left leg has been bandaged but is bleeding where he also was wounded. It may be dangerous for him to be so totally out in the open here.

"You see the group breaking up now, most heading back for the boxcars on the run. It's our understanding that the trip will definitely continue, despite this violent setback. Both the railroad and the government are claiming no responsibility for the shooting. They are pleading with Peter to stop the current storm of retribution bombings. There have been new major explosions at power facilities in Boise and Portland, so far, and those cities are reeling from the impact of lost power.

"One man is talking with Peter. I believe that is Andre Maurantagne, the engineer who joined the train when it crossed into Idaho. We don't know why he wasn't in the cab when the shooting occurred, but it was fortunate for him.

"Jerome Blackman, the National Peace Academy mediator who joined them last night in a desert scene worthy of the Iraq War, brought blankets from a boxcar moments ago. He and chief engineer Monty Montropovich now are carrying a wrapped body, undoubtedly the slain engineer. It would be surprising to take time for a burial here...

"No, they are loading the body back up into the cab of the second engine, with the help of Maurantagne and several farmers. So he will stay with the train at least a while longer, a tragic commentary.

"I had hoped for a word with Peter, but the way they are hurrying to the engine, the train is about to get underway after this half-hour emergency stop. The farmers are closing up the boxcar doors now.

"I'll try to get closer. Peter! Any words to the nation watching?"

The handsome young man hesitated by the door, looking extremely haggard. But his voice rang out clearly. "This killing and maiming was so unnecessary. Americans, let us go through. Give us clear passage to help the children. For if this happens again..." and he reached inside the cab and pulled out a blood-soaked blanket from the mop-up, "...truly there will be hell to pay!" He threw it furiously to the ground, close to Donna's feet. The great engines roared their power and the whistle sounded as the train began to move. Cars clanked in coupling. The unsettling interview was definitely over.

The cameraman had quickly positioned himself on the ground, the crumpled blanket large in the foreground of his picture, the departing train pulling away, leaving bloody reminders.

There were calls to make from the train. Monty notified Harran of the shootings, and damage. In tones of stern demand, he told Harran to correct for the delay and keep the track clear--for they were rolling again. A.M. was temporarily back in the cab as back-up engineer.

And there were calls to receive at the train. Ruth called from Denver on a new cell phone to share her horror and concern at the tragic events, and to ask the men to be extra careful. She said she had found out from their *railroad friend* exactly where the train was, then had called her Grandma Ella who lived in LaGrande. It was just minutes away, and she was prepared to give them help.

"Well, we're definitely not stopping again in Oregon. Sorry, it's just too dangerous." Peter knew this conversation was bugged, and he had no way of giving her a clue that they were planning to stop, within ten minutes. "We'll be charging right through there, friend or foe. But thanks. And thanks for risking this call. I hope I won't have to call on you for other services."

"Gotta go, my dear friend Peter. The doorbell. I don't want it to wake Mom. Glad you're not hurt any worse. Bye for now."

Peter had a sinking feeling that she had just put her freedom on the line. And that premonition was confirmed, as three States away, the FBI rudely pulled Ruth Fitzwater outside her house, handcuffed as an accomplice in numerous criminal charges. There would be no more phone calls from that number offering solace or help. For she, like most in the Shakespeare Group, had money neither for attorney nor bail, even in the unlikely event a judge would grant it at this point.

* * *

LaGrande, Oregon. Peter painfully wondered how a town with such a pretty name could be in the neighborhood of such ugliness.

Farmers watched through boxcar doors barely ajar as the valley of the Grande Ron River spread out on the right. Past patchworked acreages on the valley's eastern edge rose the Willawa Range, according to Ben Cody's atlas map in the engine. To the left were the Blue Mountains, sometimes so immediately left that it took a fifteen-foot fence to shield the track from boulders falling off the sheer cliff gouged away.

Why couldn't that shield have come ten miles sooner, Monty scowled, scanning the terrain through a cracked front window. Both side windows were again held covered with protective panels to hide the occupants. Then mountains pushed back to make way for evergreen trees and the highway and the town of LaGrande.

Two trains waited in the rail yard for the 9039 to pass. The Amtrak, parked opposite the station, was several tracks away, with people peering through the windows and from the open doors. A freight train with logs stacked high in lumber post cars was closer. Monty pointed out carved owls roosting atop the depot as totems of good luck. "They were sure asleep on the job today," he added, but pulled the air toward the cab anyway as the train slowed. Peter recognized the Indian way in that.

Many more people thronged the platform than should have been there for a town this size. Some ran toward the train.

"I see no guns," Blackman said.

"We probably wouldn't, until too late," Peter countered. "A few bad posters. Keep the train moving very slowly," he instructed Monty, "to keep them off the tracks."

Camera slung around his neck, Fasma ran and grabbed the ladder of the fourth engine as it passed, to get action pictures for the *Herald*. Peter would probably have suspected sabotage, if he had seen the stranger. The two media crews were continuing to leapfrog by helicopter. Fasma, Gene, Don, and Barry had landed an hour earlier to get ready for the next leg. The copter from TV-5 was now setting down.

A group crowded closer to the tracks. Peter relented, moving a shield open slightly on Monty's window. Loud voices were respectful. "Sorry about Wilma." "We're sure sorry it happened." "We're with all you guys." "Hang in there, Pete." Homey sincerity reached out, and the train had to slow even more.

Maybe Ruth's idea was a good one. Peter called out to the crowd, "Does anybody know Ella Barnes?" Many walking alongside said they did. Some ran toward the depot, yelling to Ella that Peter was asking for her. And a grandmotherly lady standing on the platform wearing a rose-flowered lavender dress began waving. There was no sign of uniformed officers.

"You have a friendly reception committee," Blackman observed.

"But all it takes is one bad apple," Monty reminded him. "And keep sounding that horn, A.M. There's no way I want to get blocked in here."

"Let's risk stopping," Peter decided, "just to let those few get off, if they haven't already. Stay glued to the controls." He had spoken with the farmers on the way in, about life and death, about leaving or staying. Eight would get off.

The moment they stopped, the sprightly nymph named Ella started climbing up the ladder to the engine, assisted by friends. "Oh, what does she think she's doing?" groaned Peter as he limped back to intercept her.

"My, you're a mess, young man," the elderly dynamo greeted him, "but you're every bit as handsome as Ruthie said. Now back into the cab with you, we have to talk."

"Ms. Barnes..." he began his urgent protest.

"It's grandma to you, Peter. Back on up now, and mind your leg."

As he did, he asked her if the entire crowd was friendly. She stopped in her tracks, turning to face the depot crowd. "Peter wants to know if we're friendly, LaGrande!" she shouted at the top of her old lungs.

They responded with the loudest cheer he had heard since his Brighton Serv-U.S. awards dinner. "Now into the cab, young whippersnapper," she ordered, pushing gently on his back. "Hi, fellas, I'm Ruth's grandma."

Once inside, she reacted with amazing calmness at the terrible mess, while tying on a yellow apron. "Looks like some calvings that went real bad," she observed simply, and began to lay out what would be done in the next fifteen minutes. Her quilting circle had talked with the *Herald* chopper folks, then watched the depot TV. They saw they'd need buckets of hot water, cleanser, and sponges. Now she insisted that the cab crew was to take ten minutes to shower and shave and change into fresh clothes inside the depot. They objected that they didn't have time for that, and she just said fiddlesticks, the cab would be ready before then anyway. And that shaving kits and soap and towels were waiting inside. And not to worry, her nephew was manager and a good boy.

Peter debated his options. None were red-hot. If he and Monty left the engine and the radios, it could be all over. If they didn't, the sights and smell of the cab could drive him crazy with sickening regrets.

Ella was still filling them in. The LaGrande undertaker was bringing the right stuff to take care of their friend's body. They could leave Fork here safely hidden, or they could take their friend on with them, in a nice pine casket, with the respect he deserved.

"What about the law, Grandma? They want us real bad," Peter said.

"Well, I talked with Em, and she talked with her Theodore whose brother is sheriff, and he said the governor already called every town on the line to arrest you if you stopped, but said the governor doesn't sign his checks, that this town elects and pays him, and since most of us coming down here to the station want you to keep going, he's listening to us instead. Now that were a mouthful, weren't it? Bless my britches."

The men smiled a little, the first time during the grizzly hour. This was probably as close to home as they would get on this trip. Peter wondered what his family would be thinking. What would Janet be doing? He quickly gathered his sad thoughts, and accepted Ella's plan gratefully. Monty locked the engines in idle, took the key, and the three men moved down the ladder and back up the steps onto the platform.

Townsmen reached out and proudly shook their grimy hands. Some women cried at the clothes stained with blood in their own backyard. Fasma captured scenes for the *Herald's* second Special Edition, and TV-5 gave the moment to America--which of course alerted the State authorities.

Andre and Harry Blake went back to help scrub boxcar floors, each with their own thoughts. Townspeople pitched in, visiting with farmers, sharing fruit and desserts, cigarettes and chaws. Three times as many joined up as left. Despite tearful goodbyes, it was what some LaGrande men felt they must do, and four wives did too. Wilma had touched them.

Laptops were plugged in at Wi-Fi stations in the depot, and lines formed for picture-takers to download their photos to any and everybody nationwide. The airwaves were filled with Peter's struggle to save starving children, even at the risk of many other lives.

And lines of men were also waiting to use both restrooms when Peter's group entered. The farmers insisted that Peter, Monty, and Blackman go to the front of the line for the men's room. Doc Nevins had asked to come along to take a look at Peter's gunshot wound, and to clean up himself. As they entered the locker room door, the line just moved over to form two for the women's room, giving the four men privacy.

The main depot floor was worn linoleum, but the bathroom was the familiar white octagonal tile about an inch big, outlined in black grout. There were two sinks with a mirror over them, and two shaving kits waiting, one toilet stall, two urinals, a wooden bench and four lockers. Very nice provisions for weary travelers, and a very welcome sight for these men.

A few gifted clothes from the townspeople had been quickly gathered, and were spread out on the bench and hanging in the lockers. The station manager helped them select from assorted sizes, saying he probably would get a week without pay, but wouldn't be fired, because small town replacements were hard to find. The men took off the horrible reminders of the past just lived, piling them in a corner. The two small shower stalls were soon put into use by Monty and Blackman, with a metal bar and hooked plastic shower curtains over each entrance. Doc took the outer dirty bandage off of Peter's leg. The wound had bled a lot and dried, adhering the gauze tightly. He told Peter to go shower and loosen it, then he'd work on it again.

Those first to shower finished quickly, got towels wrapped around them, and moved to the sinks to shave. Then Doc started his fast shower also, for he was as battle-bloodied as any of them. Peter had washed hurriedly to start. Then pain in his leg forced him to lean against the shower wall to steady himself. The water was hot and felt good and hurt. His senses reeled--he heard the shot, saw Fork ending existence, a shot, Wilma flung backwards, shots, everywhere around his world. His eyes snapped open, water running in them, over him, shower stall, safety.

He lathered and washed, and did again, and still he could feel the bloodstains all over him. Slowly he pulled the bandage loose a little more. Stubborn stuff, but he didn't want to rip it off and do more damage.

Peter turned in the confined space to let the hot water hit his back and shoulders, and hit him…his head sagged forward…hit him…Wilma's voice drifted into his ears…"Yes, you can." The old campaign chant--she came to encourage him. "Yes, you can." Janet's voice joined in, then his mom's, and his dad's. They were all here! Peter suddenly cried hard tears for his loss, for his cross and pain, for his loneliness.

The sound of two electric shavers working started bringing his senses back. The surreal blessed moment yielded to a simple shower running over him in a train depot locker room. "Yes, you can!" the chant now came loudly through the open window from the crowd outside. "Yes, you can!"

He finished pulling off the soggy dark bandage, and looked at the ugly hole it had covered. Doc had laced in some stitches to help control bleeding, and Peter hadn't even been aware of it. The other three men were dressed as Peter finished drying. He sat on the bench with his leg up on it, shaving with a cordless razor as Doc rebandaged the puffy wound. Grandma even provided new toothbrushes and toothpaste for all of them, and deodorant. "Grandmas are a special gift from God," Peter shared with Donna Harrison, and the men agreed with a smile. Donna had been interviewing them from outside the screen window through the closed Venetian blind.

Peter, Monty, Blackman, and Doc emerged from the train depot office, looking refreshed and stronger. Doc headed for a boxcar. Blackman, now in a red and white checkered shirt, got a call on his Academy-band radio from the one friendly chopper that was still airborne, saying the State Patrol was only five miles away, coming in force. When the three walked a clean catwalk into a shiny cab, they could only hug grandma and the flock of ladies standing there waiting for just that.

Andre had been busy in the meantime. He had heard two local reporters say they would stay aboard. If there were opponents, they were someplace else now. In small towns, Andre knew, issues like the train's morality would last a year or two, but neighbors lasted a lifetime. He counted twenty-nine in Boxcar One, and thirty-five in Two. When someone asked about opening other cars, Wray farmers all said sure, glad to have good company. It had been agreed that Fork's casket would be secured in Three.

An undertaker scurried forward, reverently saying he had left their blankets, and a bag of personal belongings back in the engine cab, but that a casket wouldn't fit on the catwalk and would be exposed to abuse and elements, so he anchored it in Boxcar Three, and hoped that was all right. Blackman tapped his watch at Peter. It was 10:40, a much longer stop than anticipated, but necessary.

But the man in the black suit continued explaining that Fork was much nicer now in clothes personally donated. He warned that even Fork's family should not open the casket the townspeople had bought. Only an undertaker or coroner in the final resting place should, so it was locked. He tossed the key up. Peter thanked him for his professional work and generosity.

"Let's move!" Monty said, in his fresh green shirt and khakis.

Peter hugged Ella, said how much he liked his blue shirt of Walter's and it fit fine, and helped her step down to waiting arms. A.M. sounded a horn warning farmers to steady themselves, and others to clear the tracks. Side railed train crews even gave thumbs-up signals. Fasma stood in front of the train, fast becoming his favorite position.

Peter didn't know how to thank a whole town as the train started away. So he waved, then painfully lowered himself to one knee, bowing his head in thanks for this love outpouring. Impulsively he reached out and brushed the good luck air of this town and people around him and his train. Monty nodded as he watched. Townspeople and the carved owls on the depot roof were soon lost in forest.

The Oregon State Patrol frantically arrived, lights flashing and sirens wailing, having been detained at the narrow Wolf Creek bridge for twenty minutes while a fellow called Stringbean was trying hard to get his big rig started and moved out of the way. When they pulled screeching to a stop blocks from the depot, there was neither a parking space nor a Grain Train to be found. But lots of people were smiling.

*   *   *

"Oregon must consume a lot of tripe," III said over the phone to Lee Anderson, the State's Governor.

"How so?" Anderson asked, hesitantly.

"To have so many people so full of shit," III replied, just warming up. "I thought you said you could put an end to this hijacking."

"I did say that, and we can!"

"Instead," III slathered on, "you give them a damn martyr, then top it off with a heroes' welcome!"

"I'm just as furious with La Grande as you are, Mr. Ravenhead," Anderson assured him, perhaps emphasizing the lesser title of *Mister.* "They should..."

"If you'll give me the name of the person who's really running your State," III interrupted, "I should be dealing with him--or her."

"Now you're going too far..."

"No, Governor," and the title spit out sarcastically, "the problem is you're not going near far enough. I gave you the chance to be the tough guy, because you asked. But I'm seriously disappointed in your performance. You've cost us precious board position. Must we take over your office to gain control of this deadly chess match?"

The game reference was somewhat unnerving. But Anderson responded in kind. "You do what you like with your *pieces.* You have the authority. But what I'm telling you is that I'm going to stop them at Earlham, if they're still running three hours from now. Make no mistake about that. I have a sheriff there who thinks more of the law than of his relatives' opinions."

III let the chief executive ruminate, anxious to know his plan, if he had one. He was saying his State Patrol would be there in advance this time, and that he would be in constant radio communication from his office in Salem. Brave fellow, seventy-five miles from the confrontation site, III thought. Then he backed off his silent criticism when it got a little close. Anderson was saying there should also be federal agents there, when Peter gets to the end of his line.

"Rest assured there will be."

"What about the bombings?" the governor asked, trying to make it sound like strong annoyance more than fear.

"We have two of his gang behind bars, and a third under constant surveillance in Denver. You obviously have one still loose in Portland."

The governor quickly took the offensive. "No, I think it's your agency which still has one at large there in Portland where *you* are. I damn well want an arrest made before we pull out the stops at Earlham. I want no further threat to our citizens."

"You keep wanting then, Governor, and we'll keep working. But finding that terrorist has no bearing on whether the train will be stopped--dead--in Oregon. Are we quite clear on that? I have no more pieces I care to lose in this over-extended match."

III wondered for a moment how many lives would be lost in another massive downtown bombing, this time in America's *greenest city*. U.S.A.S. had the materials and know-how to pull it off--Boise's van proved that. Who would get the blame?

"You talk of losses?" the governor retorted. "Do you realize the damage that would be done if they've planted explosives in one of those huge dams on the Columbia? Even a two-foot rise in water level would wipe out highway and rail traffic for a hundred miles, and take out every dam downstream. Northern Oregon would be devastated, to say nothing of southern Washington."

Could they drive a truck of fertilizer across a dam? III posed the question in his mind.

The governor let that magnitude sink in, then swam into murkier territory. "What of that Academy mediator?"

"Go for the jugular when you're talking with Blackman. Get him on our side, or get him off the train and out of the way if he doesn't want to be hurt. But make him understand your State is taking back control."

III hung up the phone abruptly, with no rejoinder, no goodbye. He looked up at his seemingly ever-present aide. "By the way, Switzer, any idea why the train came all the way up here to Portland and Astoria? Who do they know here?"

When the shake of the attentive head was negative, III fumed, "Well, call that Brody fellow and find out! It's noon in Denver, get him out of lunch! I want that ship connection found, unlinked, and permanently disabled! The Salem simpleton says they're not going to get this far. But if they do, it's the end of the line--and of them."

The agent turned to leave, and was instantly stopped by another outburst. "And Brody had damn well better...have found..." His anger was tripping up his English. "...that damn flaky deputy of his by now! If Wayman and his family got out of Denver, it's Brody's head!"

*   *   *

Chapter Seventeen

Leaving LaGrande, following the river, the train began its ascent to 4,100 feet. The companion interstate highway shadowed them a short way, with mighty concrete bridges spanning the river channel in graceful curves. Traffic flowed by, same numbers of cars going both ways, as if no one was ever satisfied.

"Are you in any shape to be making decisions, Peter?" Monty was obviously worried, and still traumatized from the shooting.

"If you'll double-check my reasoning," he answered quietly, standing close. "First, can we keep going? Second, should we?" Andre seemed occupied in his thoughts, and Blackman was glued to the cellular.

"Good start," Monty responded. "We've got ten hours to the port, if we push all out. That puts us in late at night, which doesn't work, because we need a big turnout now more than ever.

"And even ten hours are too much for me to do alone. So if we could safely stretch it out another ten on top of that…I'd need lots of relief." Monty looked out, trying to decide about trusting his erstwhile engineer friend. He absently studied the old road, now used only by local traffic going to cabins built among the pines. Simpler lives. He wondered if he should have wandered this far from Wray, from his dear Felicia. "I think we can count on Andre," he declared. "His life is tied to ours now, wherever it was before. Better him than chancing a new pair of eyes for lookout."

"You've got mine also. Let's just push hard to get out of this infernal territory, then we'll discuss slowing down tonight."

Then Peter spoke more loudly for the other two to hear. "What's the vote on lowering shields through this wilderness?" Brackets had been hastily welded in LaGrande to hold them. All agreed, and Peter radioed for farmers to vote in each of the four boxcars about opening the doors for air and incredible natural beauty, but not to stand in the open as Buck had.

Oregon forest engulfed them. The farmers had felt some power over the autos they passed, because of their rail car size and speed. Now great pines three and four times higher than boxcars dwarfed the riders. The train rolled slowly past these dark green giants, the turning wheels muffled, seeming like intruders in a land abandoned by time.

For mile after mile, the train wove the curving path beside Clearwater River, among the trees. The water patiently followed the law of nature, running westward out of Idaho, away from the Great Divide of the nation's mountain rib, pulled toward the Pacific Ocean as its destination, just as surely as the 9039 was being drawn. The travelers observed the grandeur of the world in silence, some in prayer. Here their mission seemed very near to heaven itself. Peter prayed for those missing, and those working to preserve these forests, urging God to make compromise a more attractive lure to lumber and paper and environmentalist negotiators.

Reluctantly, he rekindled the urgent conversation. "Now, how do we keep the enemy from shooting and stopping us again?"

"Uh, you know, they can stop us anytime they want with a derailing," Andre offered, showing his worry.

"The only thing keeping us going is our bombing threat," Monty reminded him. "That plan is working, with the authorities anyway--if we can believe them."

"Peter, we should get on with the business of mediating, as soon as you're up to it," Blackman suggested.

"Meacham," Andre interrupted, pointing, "an old stage stop." Somehow, sitting in that second engineer's chair seemed to draw a person into reading maps and sharing. After all, they wouldn't pass this way again. Those cabins could have been from the original settlement; others were probably only fifty or sixty years old. Why would a handful of people hang on here, Peter wondered. Why, indeed, would a handful of people ever try to do anything to alter this world populated by billions?

Misty clouds wrapped themselves around the nearest peaks. Rain dotted the windshield, then little rivulets began streaking along the cracks. It smelled incredibly fresh, and nobody moved to put the shields back up. A beaver pond danced in the light drizzle as they passed Bonifer, where two redheaded ducks lifted off in frantic flight.

"Wilma would have had a ball describing this," Peter said wistfully.

"And Fork would have loved just seeing it with her," Monty added.

Andre continued studying the maps and notes of this road less familiar. Blackman broke the reverie. "The Academy is passing on media replacement offers. The newcomers may see it as sure-fire headlines, even film rights onto easy street."

Andre mentioned that two new reporters got on at LaGrande.

Peter nodded. "Monty, what about designating any royalties all this might generate for medical and funeral bills?"

"Sounds fair to me." Nobody else was consulted.

"How about getting a reporter into the cab?" Blackman followed up.

Peter looked around and drew his arms and shoulders together. "It's already pinched," he noted, "but we really need someone to keep the story alive from inside." He sighed with his own words. "Let's see how Donna and Gene and Don want to handle it now, since they've come this far with us in the helicopters. Tell the Academy we'll let them know, okay? And ask them if any government counter offers have come in."

"Continuing the trip is a go, then?"

"I don't see how stopping would help. Jail is waiting for us already, same as at the end of the run." This was the first time Monty heard Peter describe jail as so predestined, his new reality instead of merely a strong possibility.

"Besides," Peter continued, "a bullet shouldn't be able to stop a righteous cause." Monty recognized the talk of a full-blooded religious martyr. Things were apparently solidifying in the young man's mind, with remaining gray areas breaking down from pain and loss, becoming plainer.

"Don't you vote for keeping on?" Peter interrupted Monty's thoughts.

"Some democracy! Now? Now you're asking for a vote? I'm in it with you to the end, buddy. Have been from the start."

"Thanks, Monty--sincerely. Man, I'm tired," Peter sighed long and deep, looking out the window. Green moss rock protruded from the hillside grasses, allowing small waterfalls to wash its face. Pristine, unspoiled by humans. "Awesome," Monty quoted his grandson's favorite word.

Surprisingly, A.M. sounded the whistle. Two long...one short...one long--the four tones required for civilization. A paved road came into view with yellow painted middle lines and white striped shoulders. They were back into the modern world already, and oddly voted to leave the shields down. Some lower hillsides were cultivated for crops, and horses grazed in distant front yards. Birch, ash, and elm replaced fir and spruce. Vines prowled in underbrush, and cattailed marshes were thriving. For a while they had run without a river, but the Umatilla now became a broad flow beside them, born in heights above, just as it showed on their map.

"How far to Pendleton?" Peter asked. "And how soon can we find out how Wilma and Buck are doing in the hospital there?"

"We could stop," Blackman said, "and spend some time talking."

"You bet," Peter threw back at him, "and every stop could be our last with those bastards waiting and watching out there."

"Yeah, they could have just let us go through with the grain."

"You know better than that, Monty."

"Yeah, right again. Get the *Herald* chopper to ask the hospital."

A.M. answered an earlier question. "I judge we're ten minutes to Pendleton. Want me to notify the boxcars?" Peter was glad to see him taking on added spark in trying to make amends, and nodded his okay.

With the river soon came its broad valley, green and gold and brown from active farming, reaching for miles before pushing back up into the Blues. A.M. pointed his arm so quickly it made people duck, but then they followed his directing. A Umatilla Indian burial ground lay fenced off, he read from the guidebook, by special treaty untouched, brown with natural field grasses in the middle of plowed green acreage.

As the train crossed between the steel arches of a bridge, a Great Blue Heron took flight from the river below. Then it was Monty's turn to point, toward a pasture by the banks where a young steer was mounting up on the back of a mature bull, which looked around slowly in annoyance. The place was almost idyllic; the position of the train crew was not.

Peter and Monty discussed staying in touch with Ardis all the way through Pendleton, just in case of a trap.

"Would you really tell her to blow the bridge?" Blackman asked

Peter studied his bandaged leg. "At this moment, yes!" he said.

"What would you gain except revenge?" Monty asked after a bit.

"Oh, Monty, you're so...moral!" Peter replied, sitting on the trunk and leaning back. Blackman stayed quietly alert for insights.

"Nah. Moral folks love the Peace Academy and stay to graduate." He was quiet for a short while. "I just want you to analyze your motives, friend. Be sure you can justify your decisions to the press, or to history--or to God, whichever happens first."

He looked over his shoulder. Peter seemed to have dozed off, but more likely was deeply in prayer. He had done a lot of that on this trip.

Monty radioed dispatch and listened carefully to Harran talk about rail traffic ahead of them, as he slowed to let a short freight pass on the outskirts of Pendleton. A young tan llama raced away from the commotion toward the safety of its mother and the ranch herd. The sign announced that the cluster of low buildings on the right a mile down a spur was the original

Pendleton clothes manufacturing plant--a reminder from simpler times growing up.

They picked up a little speed. Old mansions dotted the nearby hillside to the left, one blue, one a barn red. The valley was not wide here, but filled with the original downtown brick buildings and clustered shops in this Oregon town of 7,260, according to the old sign. The hills on either side were given over to green and gray roofed homes with brick fireplace chimneys and occasional churches.

Peter had decided he still would not be intimidated into shielding the windows, but he put it once more to a vote in the cab. The consent had been strongly unanimous, and they looked now into the faces of the people who had come to watch them pass. Many waved.

"Peter, problems," the *Herald* chopper radio announced. "The hospital here won't work on Wilma beyond having stopped the bleeding. Insurance hang-up with FBI criminal accomplice charges. Hargrave is collecting a fund in Denver, but doesn't have much yet in this short time. Any ideas?"

"Those stupid..." Peter's answer was immediate. "Sure. I've got $1,800 cash left from the credit union. Any my credit card that has $10,000 on it--whatever that's worth now. Hold on...okay. I have credit cards from everybody in the cab. Thanks, guys. So it's all theirs, if they can get down here to the train to get it. How's Buck?"

"Roger, that's a great start. I'll get them on the way. Buck is stable--he's tough. Slow it down if you can."

Monty reduced speed and notified Harran. They looked out on small but nice homes on streets ending at the tracks, instead of the shanties in some towns. Wood siding and pastel colors, some chipped paint, some broken shingles, low picket fences enclosing meager grass yards. Old locust trees and bright flowers were common. Logging trucks drove through town, past men standing on the streets talking in front of a closed theater and shops for rent. No white paint wasted on striping the side streets here.

A new shopping center had been built nearby, and was doing pretty good business on the basis of the cars parked there fifteen minutes after noon. A.M. wondered casually how many small shops had closed up because of the bargain chains, and the hard times around 2008. A huge correctional facility, old, sturdy as Gibraltar, fenced and barb-wired in double rows, exuded such an ominous presence that no one spoke as they passed it. The Blue Mountain College campus was right next door.

"We have a meet set," the radio interrupted their thoughts. "He said just past the big PGG chemical fertilizer plant and storage elevators there's a

Fleetwood Camper manufacturer. Board member there will be out by the tracks waiting for your envelope. Thanks, Peter, we appreciate that a lot up here in the copter." Peter looked up and waved at their shadowing friends. He felt good--and horribly guilty--and mad, in all his being.

Some people with signs asking "Can We Come?" grabbed his attention. They were an odd assortment: a few white-haired retirees, some drifters, college men and women. Peter didn't give them any sign of an answer, they took him so by surprise. He watched as the train engines rolled past them, then he was dumbfounded to see hands and arms reaching out from the boxcars to help first one, then another on board. People were running alongside the train, and Peter realized that five boxcars had now been opened and occupied. In amazement, he radioed back along the string for a headcount. They were carrying eighty-three.

"Say," A.M. commented, "some Amtrak runs would be happy to have this many folks." Responsibilities were increasing well beyond their original plan. A.M. also let them know that port-a-johns and cartons of TP had been loaded at LaGrande, along with more food and water which Ella and her quilters had quickly arranged.

A viaduct lifted the vehicular traffic over the tracks, up toward the freeway. They passed a park with swings and a jungle gym, a small pool and a statue of a man on horseback, picnic tables and a slide and bouncy horses on springs, and a well-worn path where a sidewalk wasn't but should have been. Kids waved from windows of their school, and Monty sent them three horn blasts.

Blackman went out and down the steps to make the cash and card hand-off to a man in a tie, who smiled and waved as the train continued on its way up the narrowing valley. They followed the highway and the peaceful tree-lined river between the sloping hills with occasional farms and grazing herds of cattle. This had been the stuff of hundreds of quiet miles up until three hours ago.

*   *   *

The sparring partners were sitting through their next round in the small private office of Seattle's Chief Executive, away from the wall of windows.

"You know the risks you're taking coming here now, Mr. Thompson?"

"That's why I was late," Tom Buchanan responded to his alias, glancing at the clock which read almost twelve-thirty. "They're not exactly sure which one of us to look for in which city, or even if we're in Seattle. As far as I know, no one except the Group is sure of the train's exact destination."

"Am I?" the inquisitive Mayor Taulison asked.

"I am here."

"And that says it all?"

"That says a lot."

"Boise and Portland were bombed since we talked three hours ago..." the lady began, accusingly.

"...and one man was killed, and two persons seriously wounded on the train," he finished angrily.

"Not the government's doing," she explained. "I called and asked."

"Peter believes it probably was not. Still, terrible harm was done on both sides."

"You have the power to prevent more--Tom Buchanan. We can cut to the chase."

He paused. "You've been busy. I came in here as Don Thompson. So, are you prepared to help us get out of Oregon in one piece?"

"Are they still in Pendleton, with no insurance for the hospital?"

"I don't know." Tom was impressed with her currency of status, and perhaps should not have shared his sparsity.

The mayor added more information. "I spoke with the Academy. They're looking for new mediators."

"Get them here, fast."

"Here, in Seattle?" Confirmation, finally.

"Yes--if you can get us out of Oregon."

"I can call Governor Anderson when we're through. But why should I not want him to halt your group down there?" The language was very personal.

"I guess that depends on whether you believe at all in our cause, Mayor. Do you think America should find a feasible way to ship our surplus to people starving all around our globe?"

She hesitated, re-training herself not to speak in haste. Then answered, "When you put it so simply, of course..."

The lawyer in Tom cut her off before she could qualify her affirmative statement. "Let us come to Seattle, then give us sanctuary. With the world watching, the president and the U.N. Secretary General will work with you in convening the *Taulison Conference* we talked about. Your place in history is guaranteed."

She had to admit he pushed the right buttons. Her pride and ego stepped up to the plate, ready to take a swing at conventional wisdom and its confining legal precedent. One woman against a whole system. Like Eleanor Roosevelt...and Wilma Fletcher. Yes, look at that maimed lesson!

"There is still much to think about, Tom. I will also call our governor. And I have a neighbor who is a federal judge..."

"Judge Hannerfing," Tom interrupted, wanting her to know he had done some homework also.

"Yes," she smiled. "I'll ask him some *what-if* questions about jurisdiction if the U.S. Attorney General injunctions our grain elevator against unloading, or allowing the foreign freighter to leave with stolen goods. Which dock elevator did you say would be used?" He stayed silent, so she applied logic and guessed. "Has this been arranged with the Mannheim people? Or should you now warn them, to avoid surprises?"

"We'll take it as it comes. Bomb threats work wonders against a city's conscientious business execs."

Great, another hurdle, she thought. But it would be the Mannheim Elevators on Pier 86, and that particular exec always acted like he owned the whole North Bay. This would not be easy. She switched subjects.

"If you get the train out of Oregon, would you guess a regular four-hour run to get up here tonight?"

"No. After daylight tomorrow, maybe mid-morning."

Eighteen hours to do the impossible, she calculated. That was more time than constituents usually gave her.

"It's time for you to match my good faith efforts, Tom. Tell me one of your bomb locations now, so we can disarm it."

The thunderbolt stood him upright, as if under attack. And he virtually was, now thinking defensively. An implied threat of immediate arrest was very real if he didn't cooperate. But if he gave up one bomb, he had only one other. His bargaining position clout would be cut in half. But she didn't know that.

She was bartering power only in the physical realm. How had she responded to the real message? This meeting had escalated to a world-class competition, with life and death as white and black teams, involving many players moving on both sides of the global chessboard. The moment was prime time live; his was the next move in forging an alliance between the queen and the king's white knight.

He paced in front of her simple desk. She stood. He paced still.

"Let me rephrase that," she offered. "What is more important to you, Tom? The threat of blowing up Seattle, or getting the grain through?"

He stopped and leaned on her desk to study her face. "And you promise..." he finally began.

"No promises, Tom. I have said what I'll try to do. As you can guess, the pressures on this office will be astronomical."

Which is just what..., he thought, and decided to say aloud. "Which is just what makes your world go 'round, I believe. This is partly why you ran for office, to see what you could do, what you would do, if you were given the chance to change your corner of the world. I've brought the game to you, Mayor, and you and I are writing the rules."

With a raised hand, he stopped her from responding. "I think it's still my turn. I compliment you on your last maneuver. Insightful, even daring. Go after your self-interests, one piece at a time." She kept a smile on her face, and it was slowly becoming stunning.

"Now," he said, "know that my very soul is wrapped into this venture, so I make decisions from strongest strengths, not weakness. Yes, I will tell you of one solitary bomb location, for I have more. Disarm it carefully, so no one else is injured this day."

"You talk a good game, Tom. Will you disarm it for us?"

She pushed, and it was his turn to smile. He felt he had given more than he had gotten this move, but he would walk away without arrest, and maybe next time she would owe him. "I don't know how to disarm, only to set and explode it," he responded. "So I'll call you with a location, one for which I carry the remote triggering device. I must remain certain I now leave the building and become just another tourist again. Our next meeting, Mayor?"

"We'd best talk only by phone. This card has my private line and home phone." She wrote more on her card. "This is my bug-free hotline. Whatever happens, anywhere, don't act rashly without calling me first. Agreed?"

He took her offered hand, matching the firm single shake. Peter had sent the right man for the job, for Tom was recruiting a most critical ally.

*   *   *

"Well, we're here, and helpless." Marion spoke their common frustration. Janet stood pensively at the lounge window of the small airport tower building, squinting in the sunshine. Nearby, the Columbia River's mouth opened into a shimmering bay about to become an ocean.

Frank was seated near a large transmitter-receiver, scanning the dial for

news. He reset his watch back one hour to 12:45 P.M., Pacific Daylight
Time. The room was nicer than would be expected at a short-strip field
like this, where their loaned jet had landed. They were somewhere near
Warrenton, on the Oregon side of the river. A railroad spur leading directly
past Portland to Astoria docks on the nation's West Coast ran within
eyesight. This destination was their guess as Peter closed the 250-mile gap
now separating them.

"Hey!" Frank announced. "Public Radio has KDNC from Denver. Come
listen!" Marion and Janet pulled padded folding chairs to the table as Frank
turned up the volume. Their armed pilot waited outside on standby.

"This Special Newscast highlights one of the strangest phenomena in
recent history," the announcer was saying. "Country western stations are
playing train songs and gunfighter ballads, with a lot of crossover on pop
and rock stations. Patriotic songs are cropping up, as if it's a holiday.

"Classes of school kids are showing up along the Grain Train's path to
watch it pass. Many kids carry American flags or hand-lettered messages of
greeting and support. Even a few flags are flying at half-mast to memorialize
the engineer who was killed.

"A network has pre-empted its programming to show the old Errol Flynn
version of *Robin Hood*, bearing remarkable similarities to what's happening
in real life today. *Grain Train* T-shirts are already hot items.

"Denver is where it all started, with our own KDNC being first to break
the story." Frank thought back through the thirty-four-hour eternity since he
heard that early radio announcement on his way to the fire, and he reached
over to hold Marion's hand. He would never take anything for granted
anymore.

"An outpouring of support from Rocky Mountain farming communities
is boggling transportation systems here in Denver. For those who did
somehow make it downtown this morning, they will be hard pressed to
leave. City buses are running an hour late, if at all. If they get out, they don't
get back in. The congestion looks like Manhattan's madness. The farmers
are out in force, leaving no doubt of their concern with food surpluses co-
existing with starving people.

"Denver's reputation as the Queen City of the Plains will be strengthened
again tonight as four of the biggest superstars in country music fly in for
a concert and fireworks spectacular at Invesco's Mile High Stadium. The
venue has changed from the old Coliseum, since with tickets on sale only
two hours, there were twenty thousand already gone. At this rate, the
seventy-five thousand seats will be sold out, generating a cool $1.5 million

to benefit the U.S.A.S. fund, 'Unite Surplus and Starving.' We hear several Hollywood luminaries vacationing in Aspen may just drop in for what's being billed as an all-night gig.

"We understand the Grain Train blog on *MySpace* is nearing a million hits. Folks are starting to make up their minds on these issues, and letting their opinions be known around the country.

"For our part, not to be left out, we will break these four broadcast segments with a piece that just about says it all for us here at KDNC. A choir sings the words of Katharine Lee Bates and the familiar music of Samuel Ward:"

"O, beautiful for spacious skies, for amber waves of grain,
For purple mountain majesties above the fruited plain!
America! America! God shed His grace on thee,
And crown thy good with brotherhood from sea to shining sea!"

The KDNC announcer's smooth voice continued the Special's second segment. "The U.S. Attorney General's Office has issued a statement deploring these two days of criminal activity, including the train hijacking, the bombings, and the murder and maiming of members of the terrorist group two hours ago. The Office plainly states that no agents of the U.S. Government were involved in the shooting, and calls on the terrorists to cease any more bombings in retaliation for the actions of two suspects in custody, who apparently acted independently. The Office is seeking to re-open negotiations.

"Oregon Governor Anderson also says State law enforcement agencies were innocent. Therefore, bombing a Portland power-generating facility was totally uncalled for, a reprehensible act of lowest terrorism, in his words. He vows retribution for Oregon, plus Idaho and Colorado which also were bombed, pledging that the stolen train and grain will not leave Oregon.

"We cut away now to pick up on an interview from Washington, D.C., with Colorado Senator Frye and Oregon Senator Sharp:"

"...so neither of you plan to express sorrow about the shootings?"

"I'll respond," the mellifluous Coloradoan intoned. "It will be a sad day of screwed-up priorities when a U.S. Government representative says he's sorry a criminal was hurt or killed while in the very act of committing a crime. A new day of toughness is dawning. Petty terrorists, gangs, and all the rest of the criminal community had better beware."

"At the same time," the rapid-fire speaker from Oregon cut in, "we will also expect to see the other suspected perpetrators, that pair of hunters, prosecuted to the full extent of the law. Justice will not be mocked in America. I'm sure we can process these several dozen people on the train expeditiously in the courts..."

"Our count is now up to eighty-six, Senator," a reporter interrupted. "For some reason, Americans are climbing on board."

"Well, they are a misguided lot, if that is the case," Senator Frye responded. "Our new *Ag Committee for Farm Opportunities* is the place they should be directing their energies."

"If they are real, real smart," Senator Sharp added quickly, "Those eighty-some criminals will jump off that rolling jail house before it is stopped-- which it will soon be--and they are all arrested for theft and extortion."

"Senators, the national Board of Serv-U.S. has begun a campaign to get their members to phone congresspersons, asking for an international conference on surplus food disposition, and to phone the president asking for clemency for the hijackers. What is your opinion on this move, and do you feel other service clubs will pick up on this call to action?"

The Oregon Senator was the first to answer into the microphone to the nation. "I cannot imagine that there would be very many true-blooded Americans who would turn their back on law and order in this great land, and who would spit on all our flag stands for."

The Colorado Senator leaned forward to take up the cause. "And there will be very few traitors who would trample on the graven memories of those who died to procure our sturdy Constitution, so well defended by the brave and wise Justices who dispense the law daily at our Supreme Court..." The voice was faded out, the music modulated in:

"O, beautiful for pilgrim feet, whose stern, impassioned stress
A thoroughfare for freedom beat across the wilderness!
America! America! God mend thine very flaw,
Confirm thy soul in self-control, thy liberty in law!"

The KDNC radio announcer continued:

"From the firmness of Washington, D.C. rhetoric, we travel now to the mid-day darkness during Boise, Idaho's emergency. Come in, Boise:"

"Yes, it's been three hours since the explosion at the power plant here. As we reported earlier, the Grain Train terrorists' group has claimed responsibility for the blast, saying it was an eye for an eye in exchange for the attack on the train. Of course, it had already left our State.

"They do emphasize that they will not take lives, even though one of their group has been killed--that they will only attack property.

"But that is small consolation to our surgeons operating under temporary lights from emergency generators, or our people hospitalized from accidents at intersections without traffic lights.

"We are on emergency alert here in Boise. Security services have brought in all their employees to guard banks, jewelry stores, big money places which are without lights and security systems. There just are not enough police to respond to any but the most serious situations.

"One male suspect has been apprehended here in the bombing. We have it on good authority that if there are any deaths that can be directly related to the power outage caused by the bomb, *manslaughter* could be added to the internal terrorism charge he faces.

"If power is not back soon, National Guard may be..." Voice fades...

"O, beautiful for heroes proved in liberating strife,
Who more than self their country loved, and mercy more than life!
America! America! May God thy gold refine
Till all success be nobleness and every gain divine!"

Then the announcer began the final segment:

"And from a plane to talk about a train, here is scholar James MacLeod, Visiting English Professor at the National Peace Academy and Oregon's State Poet, enroute at this moment by jet to rendezvous with the train in his home State at Earlham, perhaps the final point of confrontation. Professor, your comments?"

Jet noise made up the background, while the old man cleared his throat loudly, then spoke in a deep resonating voice. "I have watched this violent drama unfolding, with ample good and evil on both sides of the issue so quickly dividing us now as a nation." He was broadening scope, in the process of defining it.

"It reminds me of our shared past, and I have written this morning of those ruminations." There was a distinct rustling of pages being shuffled into some order. Then his timeless voice began the recitation via satellite over national radio airwaves:

"In the lush green valleys
        of Lexington and Concord,
                our patriots revolted against tyranny.

"In the mountains and plains
    after our second Civil War,
        Native Americans resisted waves of powerful immigrants.
"In the muddy shallow trenches
    of scarred French fields,
        our doughboys bravely resisted the dictator.
"Madame Curie and Jonas Salk
    isolated in sterile tubes
        the cause and the cure of diseases.
"The Wright Brothers and astronauts
    at Kitty Hawk and Canaveral
        loosed the tugging claws of gravity.
"On the steamy island of Corrigedor
    to the very walls of Berlin,
        we bloody-well beat back the aggressors.
"And we tried to do it again
    in the sweaty jungles of Vietnam,
        but times and the world had changed.
"We sent Guard doctors and businessmen,
    military and environmental might,
        to resist an Iraqi invader.
"Al Quida has felled
    our twin towers of the world,
        and we'll hunt them to turn them into dust.
"And as AIDS and abortion
    rear their hideous masks,
        our blood boils and we rise in resistance.
"For we are a warrior-nation,
    and we fight that which is wrong,
        by our nature, and our history, and our love.
"And the newest American heroes
    are now carrying on our rails
        our surplus grain to the bellies where it's needed."
Then the poet's voice is silent, the jet noise fades…

"O, beautiful for patriot dream that sees beyond the years,
Thine alabaster cities gleam, undimmed by human tears!
America! America! God shed His grace on thee,
And crown thy good with brotherhood from sea to shining sea!"

*   *   *

The train crew picked up the mile-wide Columbia at Boardman, and stared speechless across the river milestone and barrier to the low hills of Washington State. How they had planned on paper to celebrate this moment, and how differently it had worked out in today's life. The voice on Peter's phone brought him back to the conversation with the Oregon Governor from his Salem office at 1:30 on this Friday afternoon.

"I asked, who made you God, Wayman?" Lee Anderson was in a vile mood.

"Nobody did. God is still on the throne, in control. Why would *you* ask that?" Peter pressed his tough questioner. "You who already decided who should live and who should die on our planet. I thought that was one of God's duties."

"It is. And a man with blood on his hands shouldn't be lecturing me or anyone else on religion!" Anderson shouted.

"Gentlemen..." Blackman tried to interrupt as mediator.

"Everybody I've killed was during service to my country, upstart."

"And everybody I'm saving from starving will have no doubt that I am truly serving this country, you old..." Peter blasted back.

"Gentlemen!" Blackman interrupted the conference call from his own cellular in the engine cab. "I remind you that we agreed there would be no name calling or character slurs, during this mediation session."

"Right," Anderson admitted. "Say, what's in this for you, Blackman."

The peacemaker sighed, and looked at Peter, smiling slightly. The engine was bouncing them as they rounded a curve. "The same for me as for the Peace Academy, Governor, and that is harmony. We seek to maintain harmony, and restore it non-violently when it's disrupted."

"Then just why have you not convinced Mr. Wayman that he could restore harmony by stopping that damn train?"

"Governor, no swearing, please. Mr. Wayman can testify that I have been trying to accomplish that very feat since I arrived."

Peter remained silent during the pause. Thanks once more for nothing, Blackman thought, then asked, "Governor, what will you gain by trying to stop the train in Oregon?"

"We won't just try..."

"Please answer my question, sir, don't just nit-pick my choice of verbs." He was running short on patience, a bad sign for a mediator. But this conversation had already lasted ten minutes with little to show.

"I'll re-establish law and order in Oregon as an operating principle. I'll show those who might consider following the same lawless path that we won't tolerate it. There won't be a next time in my State!"

"If you don't clear these tracks all the way through Portland into Washington..." Damn! Damn!! Peter had let too much slip that time. But he had to follow through quickly now to make it stick. "...I'll blow that city sky-high!"

Blackman realized a piece had just been moved on the chessboard of this high stakes game. He wondered how to react, and whether the governor had picked up on it.

He had. "So you and your little train are just passing through?"

"This information changes things, Governor," Blackman interjected, glancing at Peter as he spoke, trying to keep his confidence intact. "Oregon doesn't have to become the place American law and order take a final stand. The train can leave your jurisdiction peacefully." In some disputes, he didn't offer suggestions. But in this Mulligan stew, he said whatever came to mind that might help one or the other save face.

"Ah, but it's too late to leave peacefully, isn't it?" Anderson pointed out. "This trigger-happy clown already ordered a power plant blown up in Portland!"

"Gentlemen, please--the rules. Mr. Wayman, no threats during this dialogue. Governor, avoid the demeaning terms. Now then, Mr. Wayman, what exactly would it take to get you to stop?"

Peter answered somberly, "Bring back Fork. Restore Wilma's arm."

"There's no way, kid," the governor tossed it off, "and you stand to lose a lot more limbs and lives if you try to run my blockade. But that's your choice to make, not mine."

"It can be your choice to remove it."

"No way. Think it through. If you want to wreck the train, and mangle the people on board, and ruin the grain so nobody can eat it, then you won't really have stood for anything worthwhile, now, will you? But if you change your message to a plea for people to call and write Congress, to go to D.C. and testify and picket? Say, what about a march, like the million gays in '93? Even the president paid attention to that."

"And what changes got made, Governor? It sold more newspapers."

Stalemate. Blackman calculated quickly to keep the lines from being closed. "Governor," he asked, "you said earlier that Mr. Wayman's father had called you to intervene. Did he leave a phone number with you?"

"Yes, he gave his cellular, said not to try tracing it. As if I give a fig where he's hiding, unless he's part of this bomb conspiracy."

"Oh, don't be an ass, Anderson!" Peter said sharply.

Blackman shot him a disapproving look. "Governor, would you give me that number, and can we break for special caucus?"

"Sure, you can play the game any way you like. It's going on two o'clock, and I definitely have other matters which need attending. So call me back again if you have something to offer. I'll try to break away. The way the train is putzing along, you've got two or three hours left before Earlham. Enjoy the scenery while you can."

Blackman's plan was to reconnect the Wayman family with the estranged family member leading this expedition. He hoped this would change some chemistry in the decision-making process, perhaps soften some stands and lead Peter to reconsider more traditional approaches.

For whatever reasons, Peter agreed to talk if Blackman got through. The young man looked out at the broad Columbia, flowing so smoothly westward beside them that the only motion seemed to be the small waves coming up to slap the shore. There was just enough room for the tracks and highway to share the slope between the river and steep hills. *A flood would be disastrous*, he thought.

"It's ringing," Blackman announced, then asked the operator to let it ring a minute longer. He turned to Peter. "They probably don't recognize this number. Do you have a calling signal in your family?"

"Sure. Let it ring once, hang up, call back again."

Blackman asked the operator to do that. Peter clicked in on his set.

"Hello?" Marion answered, and Blackman hung up.

"Hi, Mom."

After the briefest pause, "Peter Wayman, you should be...spanked."

Peter laughed heartily. "I probably should be. But don't leave out our president. He should be too."

"How badly were you shot?"

"Upper thigh. Missed the bone, thank God. It'll be okay, just hurts like hell with the bullet still in it."

"Peter, we could have helped you find other ways to do this."

"Damn it, I tried talking," Peter said, letting his anger say the words he normally would have stifled. "Everything was taking too long, Mom."

"I've never known you to swear so much."

"Bad times bring out the worst."

"I can vouch for that," Marion affirmed. "But let them bring out the best in you as well. No more swearing. We raised you better than that. Uh, your father is saying something about remembering triangulation."

"Yeah, they'll be honing in on your location. Better put Dad on, if he'll talk to me. Oh, Mom, thanks again for staying home to make that great spaghetti. I love you lots."

"We'll do it again soon. I love you too, my boy." She was crying. Peter drew in a deep breath.

"Hello, son." His father sounded just the same as ever.

"Hi, Pop. You're on the run too?"

"Yes. I don't seem to fit their image anymore."

At once, Peter spoke loudly. "If any of you FBI jerks are listening on this line, my dad had nothing to do with all this! Might as well blame the starving kids!" Peter paused, then apologized for messing him up.

"That's water under the bridge. We're worried about you now. Let's work out a place to stop. I'll join you. We'll get you out in one piece."

"I can't stop now...but thanks." They were silent a moment. "Dad, I tried to write my ideas of a better world. If anybody'd like to read the green binder on my desk...I guess it's a lot about who I am."

"We brought it with us, champ, and we have been reading it."

Peter hadn't been called that nickname in a long time. He was glad to hear it, and happy they cared.

"I guess you're doing what you believe is right, and that's the way we raised you," Frank admitted, "only..."

"Is Candice with you?" Peter interrupted before a negative phrase started a no-win argument.

"No," Frank sighed, "but we brought a friend. Tell her where you're headed. We'll meet you. Love you." He was gone before Peter could say more.

"Janet, is that really you?" Peter asked the next voice.

"Really me, you skunk. Why didn't you clue me in?"

His heart was pounding hard. "What then, babe? You would have just tried to change my mind, and we'd have had another fight."

"Probably. I'm sorry you're in trouble."

"Our world is in trouble. Maybe this will help move us in the right direction. Can you understand at all?"

"I can! I like reading your words, and I agree with so much of what you believe. It makes me feel almost like you're here. I wish you were... because I love you."

"That's all I needed to hear. I love you too." He held her in the silence.

"Say, if I make it through, we'll go enjoy that salmon dinner we talked about. Remember?"

"That's a deal, doll. But say *when*, not *if*, because you've got to make it. There's a bright future we need to work on together." Her voice was as choked as his own as he said goodbye.

Blackman allowed Peter the space he needed. Time for rethinking who he really was, and how much a safe return home might mean to him.

And the Waymans literally ran from the lounge to join their pilot warming up engines of the private jet. Undoubtedly there was a plane with arresting officers headed straight toward this pinpointed airstrip.

But the family knew Peter's destination now, and thus theirs. The salmon dinner date was one Peter had dreamily told Janet about one night: slow-baked fresh King Salmon smoked in sapling frames by the Tillicum Indians. They welcomed you along a path of broken shells with a cup of hot steamed clams, then shared their tribal dances on an island reached by ferry--from Seattle!

*   *   *

Chapter Eighteen

FRIDAY, AUGUST 12, 3:00 P.M.

Dozens of reporters together in any one room make for a lot of noise. The library of the old mansion converted into the Crisis Center was no exception.

The National Peace Academy attracted so many media reps because it was the next best thing to being in the middle of the action. Radio linked Engine 9039 through Blackman. TV coverage was a moment away with helicopters--that which the Academy modified and those of the Denver media crews. Another network had sent a fourth, and the FBI a fifth. But there were rumblings that Oregon or the Attorney General might soon claim air rights over the train, and send the media packing--or treat them as co-conspirators and force them down.

The Center was also helpful about making periodic calls to hospitals and police in Denver, Green River, Boise, Pendleton, and Portland, status-checking on the many direct and indirect victims of the train's journey. They stayed in close communication with Governor Anderson's office, even after their strong disappointment when the governor issued his public radio ultimatum" If you do not stop at Earlham, you will be treated as a hostile invading force." And they kept one line open with their Academy representative now on the scene in Earlham--Dave Cranmer from Denver.

Most information got through the filtering system to the waiting reporters eager for the latest changes. This was a good hot spot for news, since here they treated truth as a friend, communication an ally.

But there was a problem, as Jennifer Crussman huddled with her assistants at the director's desk. "We're getting stonewalled on this," she apprised them, "at the highest levels. My D.C. contacts say there's no room for discussion on the Earlham blockade--period. That means the A.G. herself must have put out the word. Which puts all the riders on board at their own risk."

"Well, that sucks."

"Steve!" Jennifer reacted to the unusually strong expression from her subordinate, and glanced around. No one nearby was paying attention.

"Well, it does," he continued. "It's a wasted day when your government leaders won't keep looking for non-violent alternatives to ending a conflict."

"It really hasn't been that long on the hijacking that they should be so desperate to end it," Lois added.

"Think it's time for our Chancellor to use the chit from our help with Louisiana's tidal basin tiff?" Jennifer asked.

"I don't see we have any choice, with only an hour and a half left," Steve said.

"What's our proposal? We can't just have him ask her to back off."

"Why not?" Lois questioned. "Back off now, let the train go through. We know from Dave and Ruth they just want to get through Oregon and turn north. We need those extra night hours to mediate a peaceful resolution."

"So the chancellor just needs to know they're headed for Washington State. Anything more definite and the A.G. would pry it out of him for national security," Steve spun out the details.

"Good job, crew. I'll call him and lay out the need, and the plan. Then tell him we need his clout on the hotline one more time. And suggest that he ask her where the buck will stop this time when more bombs start exploding around the country."

*   *   *

About one mile after the tracks pass through the town of Earlham, where a dirt farm road crossed, a jumbled stack of railroad ties was scattered on the tracks, near a front-end loader. Safely away were two Oregon State Patrol cars, an old ambulance and two of the town's five doctors, some nurses, a fire truck, the sheriff and most of his deputies.

This was Oregon State's blockade, with federal acquiescence, and this is where the helicopter from Portland International landed. Dave Cranmer and all sorts of people were already there to greet Professor MacLeod, thanks to the networking of the Crisis Center with the five States involved. A quick news conference was held with the professor who looked like someone newsworthy, the elder-statesman type, flanked by the three Academy interventionists dressed in their easily identifiable all-white uniforms.

The crowd included all ages and descriptions of people, who came in curiosity, support, disagreement, or just for excitement in a small town.

They had cell phone devices with live stream videos, digital cameras with movie and sound capacity, TV cameras and radio mikes--they were ready for the action. The mood seemed to be, *Let the games begin!*

The sheriff was trying to be in charge of the hodgepodge scene, standing on his car bumper, fitting the description given of him by the Crisis Center: "Thomas (Shorty) Brighton, 5'8", 140 pounds, forty years old, sheriff for eight years, no military experience, divorced six years, no children, rumpled appearance, casual approach to law enforcement, no record of continuing education classes after graduating with C's in *Social Sciences* fifteen years ago from Oregon State University, defender of status quo, tough on Main Street speeding tourists, $150 contribution to governor's campaign; warning--likely candidate to be the scapegoat if the blockade gets out of hand, so could feel very threatened."

In response to questions, Sheriff Brighton said the rest of the medical and legal personnel were in town to protect the law-abiding citizens and to receive those injured and arrested when the train stopped. Or when it didn't, and crashed. Three FBI agents were also present, as promised by III.

The public address system had been set up by the NPA contingent near the obstructed tracks, as the professor had requested, much to the consternation of the local authorities. But it was on the farm road, a county-maintained road, and the county supervisor's wife's niece in Omaha happened to be married to an NPA graduate. Their alma mater's computerized network had connected again. The microphone was clicked on, and the man of letters began his exercise in freedom of speech. The rest of the Academy representatives, who had each buttonholed themselves with anyone of influence they could find out at the site, grew silent. They fervently hoped that the poet-professor could convince someone there to countermand the order and remove the ties.

If he failed, the agreed-upon backup plan of the crisis team was to begin quickly removing the creosoted timbers, ten minutes before the train was due. This action would be peaceful and hopeful in orientation: to eliminate the risk of a crash and serious injuries, for they fully believed the train would not stop.

The likely outcome of that action would certainly be their arrest, and the throwing back onto the tracks of any logs removed. Sheriff Brighton stated flatly, as if rehearsed, that he believed the train would stop, rather than risking the lives of any on board, unless the engineer was just plain crazy.

Communication with the train was still open, through Blackman, but there was no change in the intransigent position of the wounded Peter and his engineers and the farmers in the boxcars who had been polled when news of the actual blockade was radioed. They were all convinced that the authorities must have a contingency plan, like the waiting loader for pushing heavy ties out of the way when it became obvious that the train was not slowing down as it approached the blockade point.

Dave Cranmer listened carefully at first to the professor's flowing wisdom and emotion, but then his training in Confrontation Psychology took over. His mind became sharply analytical, searching for ways out of this web of no-win positions. As coordinator of all the NPA teams present, he was under enormous pressure to prevent bloodshed. His whole purpose in life was focused now on this precise moment in time. There must be a way. God, show a way, he prayed, fighting off both panic and inevitability.

He wore the white shirt and pants common to Academy volunteers on the line in crisis, with a blue and green bandana and similar colored beret. They stood out in any crowd, as was the intention, to be identified as trained cool-headed peacemakers.

Dave felt a peculiar gnawing thought--felt it but couldn't grasp it. His few years of experience in these situations gave him an intuition that he respected. He tried to tune it in.

Comfortable. That's part of it, he thought to himself. All the neighbors were here to watch the show, and all the Academy people were tense and anxious, but those on the other side of the issue were not. They were almost at ease, even in front of TV cameras. Some joking, some listening to MacLeod, others casually picking at cottonwood fibers on their shirts, but none really ill at ease. This almost seemed an exercise. Not one of them had seriously debated the issue with him since noon today. It was a closed topic. As if...somebody someplace else had made a big final decision. What could have happened...? Somewhere...where! That's it! It's not going to happen here at all. They are play-acting for the cameras here. Oh, God, is there time left to find the real spot?

*   *   *

Friday afternoon harbor traffic bustled in Elliott Bay, but Captain Pradesh had never seen it otherwise in his seven visits to Seattle. Ferries carried commuter cars and tourists, a U.S. Navy Destroyer awaited retrofitting, and two oil tankers headed for the inland channel.

Little did Midshipman Sam Elliott of the 1846 Wilkes Expedition realize what a sleeping giant he was surveying in this bay, its belly reaching down a hundred fathoms to accommodate the biggest ships in a new world.

The grain freighter *Godavari Sunrise* was at the mercy of a small strong tugboat now. The two-mile limit for maneuvering under one's own power was strictly enforced. They may have made it across a thousand miles of ocean but were not trusted near land, and maritime unions of the U.S.A. were not to be toyed with, Pradesh had learned.

Slowly they headed straight for fueling dock #22, next in line. Their timing was perfect, despite the delay on the Columbia River sandbar in Wednesday's storm. The original schedule had called for Friday afternoon loading, but mysterious engine problems that Second Officer Sheefah could never quite explain had forced grain buyer Ben Kenpur to radio for rescheduling first thing Saturday morning with Mannheim Grain Elevators.

They would take on a few more sailors of international origin, but none of U.S. citizenship, differing from other trips. At the captain's orders, they would remain a totally foreign vessel.

After refueling, they would anchor three miles out, since the weather reports were now favorable. At sunrise, they would return for a tug into the long grain loading dock at Pier 86. Mannheim was a half-mile north of Seattle's Pier 47, where the tourist traffic began or ended their shopping sprees with the smell of salt-water. And Mannheim was a half-mile south of the large public marinas, leaving it an isolated world-class wart on a congested coastline.

*   *   *

Dave Cranmer squinted in the sun at his watch--3:30. The train was only ninety minutes from the blockade at Earlham in northern Oregon.

Earlier in the engine cab, Blackman had convinced Peter to slow down yet one more time, to allow the process of mediation to weave its magic. But they were still moving inexorably in this direction.

Dave, the visitor from Denver, backed away from the crowd near the tracks, and the waiting pile of railroad ties, catching the attention of a few of the NPA volunteers as he moved. He motioned for them to follow him. When they reached a secluded spot among the randomly parked cars, away from the police cars and fire truck, he began his radio contact.

First to the Academy helicopter, which had been flying lead for the train since the wee hours of the morning in Idaho: "PA920, this is DC in Earlham. Are you able to carry out a 180 RCO at 60 to EO and report pronto. Acknowledge."

The helicopter repeated the code, instructions to proceed due west down the tracks ahead of the train, make a rail check for obstacles all the way up to the Earlham blockage, flying at sixty feet or lower. They tried with the use of codes not to make it too easy to be second-guessed by law enforcement listeners. PA920 confirmed.

Dave then radioed the helicopter from Portland standing by in the small town square of Earlham: "PA641, how many emergency vehicles still in town?"

"One fire truck. One ambulance. Two sheriff's cars. Two school buses pulled up to the Municipal Building, then the drivers went into the Sheriff's Office. Three OSP at the Bluebird Café, along with one clean black panel truck. Over."

Dave gave that pilot the same order, but to fly eastbound over the tracks back in the other direction toward the approaching train. Then he shared his suspicions with his few team members: to avoid raising suspicion, those other emergency vehicles would remain in town until the last minute, then head east to a surprise crash site. A surprise would catch the train's occupants off guard a few minutes early, and maybe prevent them from giving any orders to blow up refineries or power plants, if there were any bombs or bombers left. If word then got out that the train was stopped permanently, there would be no moral rationale for retaliation anyway. And these hijackers were still being given some benefit of the doubt morally. It all seemed a very plausible offensive strategy to Denver's Academy rep, who was trained to put himself in everyone's shoes during a conflict. Those insights were one reason the Crisis Center left him in charge of advance intervention teams in this present case.

Dave's group quickly decided if that was the governor's plan, it might work to get him off the hook of dirty tactics accusations, especially after he warned the train with his 3:00 o'clock radio broadcast: "Go no further, on penalty of derailment, possible injury or death, and imprisonment." Anything becomes fair in a declared war zone.

One national network and numerous local stations were hooked in as the elderly Professor MacLeod from the NPA was still speaking. Oregon's Poet Laureate was getting hoarse and looking very feeble, but winning over some of the crowd of townspeople with his sharp debating skills in answering the reporters' shouted questions. He eloquently spilled out his heart in urging his beloved Oregonians and the law officers to avoid violence by removing the railroad ties. The law had left the crowd alone to behave itself so far.

Dave's radio crackled to life: "PA641 to team leader. Spotted a couple of pickup trucks beside the tracks, about seven miles east of town. A bunch of men started running into cover, carrying tools or rifles, when they heard us coming. Can't tell about the tracks there without getting into target practice range. Several men still in truck cabs. Over."

Dave knew this transmission would be monitored in town. He thought quickly and spoke accordingly, to use their nosiness to his advantage. He didn't want more of the authorities heading out to that eastern site leading into town.

"PA641, begin your zoom-lensing of that site to identify any men who tamper with the track or if they start another blockade. That's still a federal offense. Keep well out of weapons range however. Over."

"This is PA641. Negatory, leader..." There was a pause. "Affirmative, leader. Message understood. Will hold distant position for filming of illegal actions. Over."

Dave let out the breath he had held since the word *negatory* was broadcast. He knew that particular ferrying helicopter was not carrying the zoom lens mounted camera, only handheld short-range videos. But he gambled on scaring the townsmen into stopping work, assuming the pickup trucks were in touch with the base radio in the Sheriff's Office. And the pilot had caught on, going along with the bluff.

Very shortly after that, the pickup trucks bounced across the tracks and disappeared into the trees where the rest of the pack had run.

Earlham's Sheriff Brighton and his deputies soon began moving the crowd back from the road, into the willows and mosquitoes at the western blockade leading away from town, saying, "Five hundred feet for safety, folks," and tying up their yellow "Police Line, Do Not Cross" plastic ribbon from branch to branch chest high.

The train was forty-five minutes from the place where Dave stood thinking and the poet pleading with everyone to find a peaceful way.

*   *   *

The anxious men in the cab of Grain Train Engine 9039 monitored the radio transmission of Dave Cranmer to the NPA helicopters.

"Anderson isn't going to budge, is he?" Peter asked Jerome Blackman.

"The Crisis Center hasn't yet been able to dissuade the governor, or get to the person pulling his strings," the Academy mediator answered somberly. "The Center also has word that he's moving wreckage cranes east out of the Portland rail yards along this line."

He continued, putting a hand on Peter's shoulder and looking him straight in the eye. "Isn't there some way that you could be the one to budge? Even a gesture might get the ball rolling. That's the way mediation works sometimes." He waited for the answer.

It was a pensive one. "Jerome, I've thought a lot about your suggestions, and your Academy lifestyle. I've talked with Monty, as you know. And prayed about it. Your ideas would depend on leaders carrying out their promises, and those would be coming from their public image shells, not their hearts." After a pause, he ended, "I'm afraid today's expediency doesn't lead to tomorrow's commitment."

Monty turned in his engineer's chair. "I have to second that. Finding solutions to the surplus and starvation problems hasn't been on their agenda. I don't think this trip has put it there yet."

"But you have created a voice now," Blackman emphasized. "You have become a focal point for the nation to rally..."

"Thanks, Jerome, but that wouldn't be so true from a jail cell," Peter said. "I'm no nationally known priest like a Daniel Berrigan."

"And I'm no Pulitzer Prize Nelson Mandella," Monty added with a little laugh.

Andre Maurantagne stayed silent, the man they called A.M., knowing he had not earned a voice in this part of the conversation. The FBI's saboteur replacement engineer may have changed allegiances, but would never be consulted in major decisions.

"What will be your next moves then?" Blackman asked.

"I told Governor Anderson point-blank that there would be a bomb every ten minutes until he cleared the track. My threat hasn't worked, so I have no choice. I have to call for bombing to begin again in Portland--to try to pressure them into changing their minds," Peter said firmly.

"You know that will also leave me with no choice but to exit the train. I cannot become a party to violence," Blackman said just as steadfastly.

"So you're leaving when we need you the most?" Peter prodded.

"You don't need me, if you're not going to use any of my ideas."

"Do you just want to go back to a boxcar?" Monty inquired, knowing the answer before he asked, and planning the wording to his next question.

"No, I'll have to get off."

"Others may want...uh...an opportunity to leave, Peter, before we run the blockade," Monty suggested tentatively.

"We reach a small town, Hood River, in ten minutes," A.M. informed them.

"Good idea," Peter sighed, turning the facts into suggestions then decisions. "Monty, talk with the farmers a little about what's going on, while I call the Group, or what's left of them. Then I'll get on the radio with the boxcars. A.M., keep us on track."

"Don't order bombings, Peter. Please!" Blackman asked one last time, receiving no response, then opened the door and left the cab to go stand on the catwalk and look out over the Columbia, realizing he had no more control over Peter than he did that wide river. Only dams slowed the Columbia, as a dam of railroad ties would slow or stop a train. He could try to overpower Peter, maybe take one of their guns, and force a stop. But using violence as the means to thwart violence would invalidate the end he sought: a world ordered by non-violence.

Peter dialed down his hourly check-in list, first to Ruth in Denver, who had not answered since she called him as they were entering LaGrande this morning. Still no answer.

He next dialed Jeremy in Boise, also to no avail. News reports had mentioned that suspected terrorists had been arrested in those two cities, but no names were mentioned. He now feared for them.

He thought of Chanto, with his diplomatic immunity. Peter decided to save him to use as a last resort, little realizing that an FBI agent was in the next room with the ham radio gear in Denver, and acting now as Chanto's second shadow.

Another moment of decision. The rest of his group still held bombing threats. How he hated being put in this position.

Peter shifted to pull out the remaining newspaper clippings from his bloodied wallet, grimacing at the painful bullet lodged in his leg. He studied the gaunt faces and spindly little bodies in the stained pictures. He remembered the picture lost to the wind of the long lines waiting for a handful of food--and all those people would be lost to the wind by now also. He finished dialing Ardis. "Go ahead with the second one--quickly!"

*   *   *

"We have been in touch with one another most of the time since the power station bombing in northwest Portland at 9:30 this morning. Thank you for joining me now in my office this afternoon," Jonathan Davies welcomed his guests. He was in his second term as mayor, enjoying his quietly bubbling pot of independent liberals and microbreweries.

He turned the meeting over to Oregon's Governor Lee Anderson, speaking from the large plasma screen on the side wall.

"I have spoken with the FBI at one o'clock this afternoon, which was a waste of breath," the governor said, remembering his heated exchange with III. "They are doing nothing, less than nothing, to stop this illegal Grain Train. Or to catch the bombers here and eliminate the threat. They are leaving that to us.

"I've spoken personally with Peter Wayman in the train engine, the primary schemer of these crimes, to no avail. Minutes ago, at 3:00 o'clock, I ordered him to stop the train himself, or we would stop him forcibly. So far he has refused. I believe that he will stop at nothing to keep his train rolling to his destination, and I still firmly believe that to be the Port of Portland. He tried a smokescreen about going on into Washington State to throw me off, but his cargo is wheat. Portland is the largest shipper of wheat in the U.S., the second largest in the world. Why risk going further?"

The authorities gathered in the mayor's office were paying close attention to the man on the screen who had so much firsthand information. "I know your port is eighty miles northwest in Astoria," the governor continued, "but his train must go through your beautiful City of Roses. This places your city of a half-million plus a hundred thousand more workers in imminent danger. I'm very close to declaring a *Red Alert* to keep any more Oregonians from dying. Mr. Hofstetter, your thoughts?"

The Oregon Chief of Homeland Security leaned up toward the speakerphone in the middle of the table. They were not yet used to simply talking to the new wall screen. With strong tones, Hofstetter replied, "Given the enormous demands and stresses of a Red Alert on the citizenry, and with only a power installation lost and no loss of life in this vicinity, I hesitate. Perhaps a broadening of the Orange Alert to *High* at Portland International…"

"Who else has an opinion?" the governor interrupted in an annoyed tone.

The police chief changed position, leaning forward slowly to look around the table as if hoping someone else would be next. All deferred. "It's almost 3:30. Why don't we take a chance and let the downtown buildings empty normally over the next two hours? Then our number of potential victims will go down dramatically, without creating a massive traffic jam of commuters in panic."

The head of the Metro Area Xpress nodded, and spoke up. "This is Gustafson, MAX Director. I agree. Our light rail system will clear the city by 5:45 operating normally. An overload all at once would jam our line, create fights, and maybe get people run over trying to stop a car to get on. It would have to be a real emergency…"

*   *   *

Ardis Borgeba drove the rented car toward the Hayden Island Bridge, twelve blocks away, and parked just off North Marina Drive. This was a moment she relished with all her being. Her explosive device was in place under the bridge. And Peter had just given her a green light to trigger it quickly.

She tried studying the bridge in its wholeness, but passing traffic interfered with her view. So she left the safe anonymity of the car and walked across the frontage parkway, to the embankment above the Columbia River, carrying the remote trigger cell phone. Here the view was unobstructed.

Traffic flowed almost endlessly across the long bridge at 3:45 in the afternoon. They would never know what hit them. She knew she had sort of promised the Group there would be no injuries. But she had her orders now from Peter, and every second was precious. She would just wait to press the button for the next break of four car lengths on both sides of the pillar holding the bomb. That would probably give them time to stop fast. Not yet…no…there!

KA-BOOM!!

It worked perfectly. Awestruck, she watched the huge slabs of concrete heave upward. One settled back in place, held by strong rebar, with only a gaping hole. But on the other side…perfection. How beautifully it kept plunging down into the Columbia, followed by one, two, three…maybe… yes, four cars sending up giant sprays as they hit the water's turbulent surface. A sight to last a lifetime. How she regretted not having a videocam for this career highlight.

"That will teach them not to mess with us," she bragged aloud.

Then the bridge was just a bridge again. Smoke and dust were clearing already, traffic at a dead standstill with multiple chain reaction collisions. No more to see. She turned for her car, but instinct gave her second thoughts. Just in case they might try roadblocks, she rationalized.

The sirens started then, and to her it seemed from every direction. The Fire Department was on the ball. And the police, moving in for traffic control. Ambulances, automatically. This would stir up a hornet's nest in their Office of Emergency Preparedness, or whatever they called it in Portland.

But the next bomb beckoned. She needed to get to the other planted explosives in case Peter called again. And soon.

That meant she had to drive. But the car seemed even more threatening now. Ardis decided to walk along the river two blocks, then up toward the motel to arrange for another rental there. She might jeopardize the Group's plan by taking that much time, but staying free was now all-important.

She turned her back on the bridge scene with one last look at her messy handiwork, and began walking up the grassy slope on top of the high-walled embankment. The sirens grew louder, probably coming down the frontage road she had parked on.

Vaguely she became aware as she walked of some object on the river itself. She glanced that direction, then looked forward, tensing. Harbor Patrol cruiser, moving her direction fast.

She steeled her muscles against running, but changed her path to move up toward the street. She took one more quick glance. The man in the bow had binoculars trained straight her way.

Now the sirens seemed almost on top of her. Then Ardis heard the scariest sound of all. Brakes were screeching cars to a halt.

She looked over her shoulder toward the Columbia. The white Harbor Patrol Cruiser with bright markings was only a hundred feet off shore, and three men armed with M-80's stood at the ready on its deck, facing her. She turned back to see the caps and heads of a number of officers prone on the grass directly above her, pistols drawn and aimed.

The inevitable bullhorn began its invitation. "Police! You are under arrest! Lie face down on the ground, and put your hands on your head. Make no sudden movements or we will shoot you without further warning."

She looked around as if it could possibly be someone else they had in mind. But she was also thinking how great it had been. It was a sensational bomb. And her being here was all so circumstantial, she was just another tourist...except for the cell phone device stuck in her back pocket.

* * *

"Well, Pete, the vote's in," Ben Cody said from Boxcar One.

Peter and the cab crew tallied each boxcar as it radioed its count of those who wanted to leave before the blockade. Peter made it clear he didn't want to risk the life of anyone who wasn't prepared to give it, and he knew they had many important life commitments.

Monty was first to speak afterwards. "In positive-thinking school, we'd say we're going to be half-full." All the Wray farmers were staying, and thirty-nine more. Fully half of the Utah and Oregon newcomers were not.

"Ben, Mr. Blackman will be leaving the cab, so we'll have room. A couple of Wray people want to come up with us?" Peter had his reasons for radioing extra hands. Ben and Drew Manchesky jumped at the chance.

The train sped through the town of Hood River, hectic with the work of river and dams, electric power and tourists. The majestic Mount Hood rose to 11,000 feet in blue and purple hues twenty-five miles off to the left, and 12,000-foot Mount Adams could be seen clearly across the Columbia, up the canyons, past the hills, forty miles away. Peter waved mechanically to spotty crowds of curious well-wishers as the train whistled through town.

Then Monty began slowing dramatically. "Good underbrush coming up," he pointed out. "What say we tell the odd-numbered cars to jump first, where the doors are open on the right? Maybe it will take the Patrol a few minutes to figure what's going on." He jerked a thumb over left toward the highway, and the two black and white OSP cars pacing them. No flashing lights, just constant presence.

Peter nodded, reaching for his radio. "Listen up, all boxcars. We're going to be rolling very slowly but not stopping. It's just too likely we'd be boarded. The first ones to be jumping off will be those in cars with doors open on the river side. Work your way back to that town we just passed, rent cars and vans and pool together to get back home. Please hold your phone calls until you get close to town. We don't want to give away our plans too early. God bless you for coming this far with us. Keep us in your prayers as we part company. Be very careful in getting off. We sure don't want anyone injured." Monty gave him the signal. "God go with you. Leave quickly on the river side, now!"

"Shall we tell the media choppers?" A.M. asked.

"They'll know soon enough," Peter answered, looking back at the exodus beginning. "Can we go any slower? Some are falling as they land." Monty nodded, and A.M. throttled down from four to about two.

Blackman stepped gingerly off the bottom rung of the engine ladder, and started jogging toward an open beach area a hundred yards away. The Academy chopper hovered there, as arranged. He didn't look back.

Now the Denver media chopper saw what was happening, and peeled over to the right side for camera coverage. The local news chopper followed them, drawing the OSP chopper over to that side also. Those airborne additions had joined them when they met the Columbia.

"They're onto us," Peter said.

"Great trees coming up on the left," A.M. notified him.

One of the Oregon State Patrol cars stopped, its lights now flashing their warning. Peter watched the man in uniform step out, and take the bullhorn with him. He was probably announcing something to the people about stopping as the fifty grain cars rolled slowly by, but there was no way to hear.

At least we've got them outnumbered here, Peter thought. Most would have a chance to escape. "Ready the boxcars, open on the left," Peter said into his radio. "Go now with God. Please be careful." And the people started spilling out on the highway side. The overflow of forest would offer some cover.

In a minute, the second OSP car stopped, lights flashing, and two uniformed men got out, this time carrying shotguns.

Peter thought at once about using the bomb threat to get OSP to leave the people alone. But he realized his threats weren't even working to clear their own tracks yet. He verified on the Academy channel that there had been no change in the status quo at the Earlham blockade scene, or with the train's status even though Blackman had left. Then he pressed the phone's memory block code for Manuel.

*   *   *

In a Salt Lake City police car the cellular phone rang. Everyone in the car looked at it on the back seat, but no one reached for it. Manuel couldn't in handcuffs. He had been picked up a half-block from his motel, on his way to the Lion House landmark in answer to Peter's command for an explosion.

"Shall we answer it?" one officer asked the other. "Keep the train from knowing we got him?"

"What would we say?" the other answered. "They probably have some kind of code. Or maybe just listen for orders?"

"What do you usually do?" the first officer asked Manuel.

But the cuffed prisoner's mind was hundreds of miles away by Peter's side, feeling his frustration and disappointment.

Peter tried Manuel's number again. Then he dialed it in himself. Still no answer. He couldn't wait, and didn't allow himself the time to either worry, or be upset with lack of dependability. Ardis wouldn't be in place yet for the next one, so he didn't bother dialing her, but went direct to Tom.

*   *   *

The dispatcher for OSP patched in the state commander to answer a request from the mass exodus scene on Interstate 84. "No, you can't have backup. Those are small fry. Make as many arrests as you can, for *aiding and abetting*. Take them to Hood River for jailing. Say, if some have their ID, just get the information and release them on their own recognizance. Red-tag them like abandoned vehicles.

"OSP Chopper 21, you listening? Help keep track of the herd. I'll call Hood River to send cops up the tracks to greet stragglers. Did someone once make a movie about rats deserting a sinking ship? Over and out."

*   *   *

People at the mayor's conference table began to reach for their vibrating cell phone. The mayor's crisis phone was ringing. Even the governor could be seen excitedly talking with someone in the background on the wall screen.

"Is it confirmed?" the governor interrupted. "Has a bridge been bombed in Portland?"

There were nods of assent from half of those around the table. Worried looks were exchanged, some pushing their chairs back as if to leave.

Mayor Davies took charge, and spoke loudly. "Hold your places, people. Yes, Governor, we have just received the messages. Hayden Island Bridge over the Columbia River has been bombed, one mile from this office. Several cars into the water, no word on casualties--we've ordered the bridge closed to check full extent of the damage."

There was shock and disbelief on the faces of the assembled leaders. This was their quiet, great city--under attack.

Questions began flying: "Shall we close the other bridges until we can check them?" "Shall we *evacuate* the tower buildings?" "Is downtown the next target" "Did they catch the bomber?" "How many terrorists are here?" "Was there gas?"

The governor interjected. "The FBI tells us they have one suspect, who may be the only bomber in Portland. But they also say that the bombs are triggered by cell phone. There could be more bombs hidden, which could be triggered from the train."

The mayor stood. The voices silenced. "Is there further discussion on declaring a Red Alert? Or are we of one mind?" One after the other raised their hands, solemnly, nodded, and voiced, "Red."

"Mr. Governor, we are agreed. A Red Alert should be immediately declared in the greater Portland area, and the Emergency Plan put into operation."

"I do so order," the governor spoke definitively. "Keep me posted hourly on your progress, Mr. Mayor and Mr. Hofstetter. Let's get to it."

The group stayed just long enough to clarify their next movements with each other. They departed with cell phones to their ears, or talking to themselves on their Bluetooth, or text messaging madly as they took the stairs rather than waiting for a now risky elevator ride.

The mayor walked to his outer office. "Mrs. Jennings, please trigger the building's outside emergency siren. Not the fire alarm, the air raid siren on the roof. All of you, gather your most important personal belongings, and prepare to leave. Put only the most essential files and documents in the fire safes by the doors for pick up, as we did in the drills. Hopefully, this is only a drill. But for your safety, get home as quickly as possible. Now hurry, get a head start on the mob."

Mayor Davies returned to his office, having decided long ago that he would stay at the helm of his own particular ship of state, here to answer his calls and make the hard decisions. Hofstetter stayed, so he and the mayor could then make the astonishing calls and confirmations together. They activated the reverse 911 system to simultaneously contact all media broadcast stations in the designated market area of more than one million homes, with the same message: "Activate Emergency Broadcast System."

The mayor placed a call to his war room, the Portland Crisis Operations Center, to see who had reported in for assigned emergency duty, thus also placing their own lives on the line today, and to check on progress. Hofstetter instructed the Homeland Security operator in the Center to start the pre-recorded broadcast: "This is not a drill. Repeat: this is not a drill. Proceed calmly to evacuate downtown Portland. Use every street available to leave the downtown area. Do not panic, but evacuate downtown Portland at once."

*

This was the first time anyone had heard anything but the old familiar, "If this had been an actual emergency…" instruction. And for those who were listening to radio or TV, it was a shocker. Families started calling out and in, to give warning and make plans. Within minutes the circuits were jammed.

Office workers heard evacuate, but in the tower buildings they had only practiced fire drills, emptying offices at the sound of fire alarms, and heading for nearby street corners to huddle in casual groups to be head-counted and visit and gossip about whomever wasn't there. But there were no fire alarms, only wailing sirens from City Hall and downtown fire stations. The workers milled around at first, until the safety officers on each floor began to order them to leave, and take all the personal belongings they could bag up. A feeling of panic began to spread.

In one building, a worker got impatient with a stairwell clogged and not moving, so he went back out onto a floor and punched the fire alarm. That got them flowing--and brought the big fire rigs racing toward the entrance, further impeding traffic, and then in turn trapping those rescue units at that location, stuck in gridlock.

A few minutes later, a hungry homeless man watched the mass of people running from the building, with nary a dime thrown his way. He looked inside at vacant security checkpoints, no guards with wands and badges. He wondered how many desk drawers might have quarters for the coffee machine, and how many refrigerators might have leftovers from lunch. No one was using the elevators for some reason, and he entered, uncontested and happy.

A woman made it out of the parking garage, but then waited anxiously for the traffic light to turn. She had waited through two already, thanks to the inconsiderate men who went through the yellow when there wasn't any room, and blocked the intersection. She was determined to make it through the next time, and kept close to the bumper in front of her. Yellow, he had still been moving, red, he was still moving slowly, but she then became the one in the middle of the intersection with nowhere to go, and stopped. Horns were blaring. She could see the angry fists waving at her, and just looked straight ahead. One car had his fender almost on her door. She locked it quickly, and hoped for her lane to move soon.

It only served to stir the pot, where panic was already reaching a boiling point, to have Air Force jets suddenly appear low overhead. The airspace had been sealed off, and only planes short on fuel were still being allowed to land at Portland International. The Air Force jets took turns following each airliner in to insure they remained in the flight pattern. So people on the streets, and still in the buildings, who had a view of the nearby airport, watched intently as each plane came in for a landing--wondering if any would turn toward downtown at the last minute. And what if they did? If a jet had orders to shoot them down, they'd crash somewhere in downtown anyway, with the airport just five miles away on the banks of the Columbia. It was a no-win scenario, and most people figured it out.

The mayor confirmed the Red Alert on a call from the *Oregonian*, apologizing to the newspaper editor for slow notification, and put him off on his offer to help. And he called the CEO at Intel, Portland's largest employer, to give him a head's up. They agreed that their location to the west in Hillsboro should be safe--except for the large numbers of people congregated in one place as a target. The other twelve hundred technology companies in the metro area would not get a personal call, and were on their own.

*   *   *

"Go ahead, Robert," Mayor Taulison spoke into the red phone bearing her hot line number. This was her personal bodyguard calling.

"I've been following Tom Buchanan as you ordered. I'm certain he hasn't seen me. He's sitting on the grass by the Space Needle's lower Gift Shop right now. First he looks west toward the Sound, then out over the city, then cranes his neck up to stare at the Needle. Then he does it all over again, like he's maybe struggling with a decision."

Tom had not yet called the mayor with a bomb location, as he had promised during their noontime meeting. He had not given her a phone number to call him, so she just watched the drama building in the television reporting of the Earlham blockade one State away. Time was very short before that confrontation, and Tom's Seattle bomb could be a key factor in intimidating Oregon's Governor.

"Shall I pick him up?" The detective's question pushed her to a decision, which if wrong, could cost her job. For if her suspicions were correct, Tom was considering destroying the world-famous tower, plus endangering many lives.

"No," she said, with a great lack of finality. "I still think he'll call me. Stay with him, and contact me the second he moves from that spot!"

She hung up, then called Police Chief Simonet on a regular line. She told him she was still delaying arrest, but asked him to move a bomb squad into standby position at the fire station three blocks from the skyline-piercing Needle. And to put all downtown fire stations on full emergency standby ready to roll. The mayor did not ask for his opinion of her decision, nor did the chief offer it.

She completed the list of names she planned to call for the Seaticon mediation night session, as soon as Tom kept his bargain. What if she was wrong about him? She waited and watched Earlham developments intently-- along with sketchy early reports of a bombing and Red Alert in Portland.

*   *   *

"What do you mean you can't?" Peter asked unbelievingly from 9039.

"We're so close to an understanding here," Tom replied, knowing he would have a tough time explaining his position, especially sitting in an outside public area talking on his cellular. "The mayor is willing to listen to us, once you get here..."

"That's the problem! We won't get past Earlham if you don't detonate your first bomb right now!" Peter shouted into his phone from the noisy engine.

"But if I do that, we lose this mayor's support. She's made it clear she'll side rail and arrest you and everyone on the train the minute you get into her jurisdiction if there's a detonation here in Seattle. We'll lose everything we've..."

In the stony silence he realized he had given away the destination, if there was still any doubt by now for those tapping their line.

"Thanks for nothing, Tom. You have too big a mouth, too many dreams, and not near enough guts. I'll see ya around sometime." And the phone connection became dial tone.

Tom wrestled with his decision, and his commitment. He fingered the remote detonator in his pocket, and looked at the bushes at the base of the gigantic hourglass soaring above him. How could he not follow through with what he had been sent to do?

But wasn't their main hope always to get the grain loaded and shipped, and maybe clemency for them? Didn't this mayor hold those keys? He was just as much her captive as she was his.

He had a promise to keep--to the larger mission. "God, wake up in your heavens, and hear the cries of your children," he prayed suddenly aloud in an unusual act of desperation.

Then he dialed the mayor's special number. She answered quickly. She seemed relieved and surprised when he gave her the location of a bomb-- the one at the dock back of the warehouse on Pier #29. He got up and left the forbidden comforts of a soft lawn and beautiful view, to walk and think. His hotel was four blocks away, where he could watch TV showing the close encounter of friends with a blockade in full blazing color.

When the detective notified the mayor that Tom was on the move, she ordered him followed. She also put into effect an immediate staging of pre-planned incidents: a fight in the garden level Gift Shop to break out a window, and a reported gas leak in the rotating Dome Restaurant.

Both public areas were quietly evacuated, and the surrounding blocks sealed off, without using sirens. Plainclothes officers began searching inside and out for the bomb she knew was there. Soon the package was found in the bushes, scanned for contents, and gingerly lifted by robot into the waiting compact three-wheeled trailer with its eighteen-inch steel-plated and padded blow box.

*   *   *

Dave Cranmer had ordered his selected Peace Academy team waiting in Earlham to quickly load up some strong sympathetic townspeople they had found, taking pickaxes, cables, ropes, rail spikes and sledgehammers, then head east for seven miles, watching for the small Academy helicopter. It guided them, and they soon arrived at the site. The pilot had seen no sign of the two trucks leaving the woods, which was just as well, he thought, to keep them from going someplace else and tearing up track.

The new expanded team from town walked the tracks and found that one section of rail had been completely loosened and moved over just an inch so it wouldn't show from the air. Only a few spikes on the rail opposite had been removed so far, but it was still in place.

The train was twenty minutes from the detached rail at their feet.

*   *   *

Peter's call to Ardis rang unanswered. She was still out of pocket on her way to the next site, or...? *Where was everybody?* he wondered desperately. Should he try to detonate with a long distance call to Portland? Would he then phone and claim credit for a bomb that may not have exploded--and lose all credibility? What if Ardis was working at that bomb right now?

"Well, we're going to hit the blockade, hard enough to go through!" Peter announced solidly, his final decision made alone. "We've got only ourselves to count on now."

A.M. had stayed, and now cranked the 9039 up to full power, while Monty, Drew, Ben, and Peter moved the lead shields and other protective materials into place over the side and rear windows to deflect bullets. Only one small square of the cracked front window remained uncovered.

Strangely, it brought to Peter's mind the armored bus that Clint Eastwood drove in *The Gauntlet* movie. Peter never imagined he would be running one for real.

Blue diesel smoke poured skyward as the three reserve engines roared into power. In the shadowing *Herald* helicopter, Don Trujillo yelled to the listening nation, *"They're going to run the blockade!"*

*   *   *

Chapter Nineteen

While the crew on the east side of Earlham worked feverishly, driving the spikes back into tie holes, and struggling to lever the other heavy rail back to proper distance, Dave moved his group into place at the yellow barrier ribbon west of town. Sixteen of them had gathered from six States, proudly wearing the white working trademark of the National Peace Academy Intervention Teams. They had just informed the authorities that it was their intent to save lives by moving those railroad ties blockading the track.

Sheriff Brighton warned them loudly as they formed into lines, leaving no question that they would be arrested and forcibly detained the minute they touched the ruinous pile of four-foot-long 4x4's. He went to his car when a deputy motioned, and switched his police radio to broadcast through the loudspeaker on top of his car. The crowd clearly heard Governor Anderson issue the final ultimatum from Salem by radio to the train crew: "Stop--or be stopped!"

The sheriff left his speaker switched open to that radio frequency, effectively competing with Professor MacLeod's makeshift speaker capabilities. The police dispatcher again blared out: "They've shielded the cab windows, and closed the boxcar doors. They're on full throttle, doing at least sixty. ETA at Earlham: eighteen minutes--if they don't jump the rails at that speed."

Dave knew that meant only ten minutes until it hit the split rail east of town. He prayed his other crew had found enough strong helpers and materials to get the rail back and nailed into place. He prayed that no other sections had been torn up in other places. He also prayed for courage to do the job left to him by default. All other non-violent recourses had apparently failed.

Dave wiped sweat from his forehead with the end of his turquoise bandana. He smiled individually at each of his team, shook a hand or patted a shoulder, then made a sweeping motion forward with his arm, shouting slowly: "Four by four, no blood--shed; four by four, no block--ade," and he kept repeating the refrain as they marched quickly up toward the stack of ties thrown across the tracks. Photographers and anyone with a cpd walked along with them, stride for stride, filming now to live audiences watching spellbound somewhere far away in safe comfort.

A line of deputies and state patrolmen stood between them and their goal. Those armed men also sweated, and held truncheon clubs and mace cans at the ready, and shouted: "Stay away! Outsiders! Go back where you came from! Law breakers!"

The volunteer peacemakers in white kept walking, arms linked, four abreast now, four lines deep. Dave started them singing the familiar refrain of freedom, "We shall overcome, we shall overcome..." The old Poet Laureate moved from the stage microphone to join them by the timber pile, his hoarse voice useless but not his body and soul, hobbling with his polished cane.

*   *   *

The train was now nine minutes from that blockade through town on the west, but only one minute from the derailed track on the east side, with no sign of slowing. The outside metal spikes were all back in. The inside spikes had yet to be driven, yet only one sledgehammer was working. The handles on two others had been broken off trying to wedge the five hundred pound rail back in place. One more spike slammed in; only two missing. The train was a block away, bearing down fast. It whistled, long and loud and shrill. The man with the hammer took one more swing, looked over his shoulder and threw himself backward. The engine roared past, a foot away.

Then boxcars, then grain cars rumbled over the replaced rail. It bounced with every wheel rolling across. The men alongside the track agonized, helpless as the spikes on the front end worked their way loose in the used holes, inched up, then popped out.

The rail end was falling and rising two inches with each passing set of wheels. As the wheels hit that lifting rail tip, bright sparks flew. Every heavy jolt to the ground rippled through the men standing as statues, watching, praying. The only hope was that the far wheels would stay rimmed on their rail, and the train wouldn't start to sway. They were all much too close to escape injury if the train did derail, but they stood hypnotized. Nine cars were still left to pummel that fragile steel bar.

*   *   *

The distant train whistle startled everyone at the western blockade site. They all turned to look east, down empty tracks. The sound continued, three blasts at a time, two short and one long, as if saying, "I am coming!" Dave guessed the train was passing the crew at the split rail. Thank God they had done their job. Now he must quickly do his.

At that precise moment, Sheriff Brighton knew the derailment plan on the other side of town was failing, and the train must now be stopped here at his blockade. He looked at the approaching white shirts, then smiled as he grabbed the red five-gallon can of gasoline from his car.

Dave saw the sheriff run toward the stack of creosote-soaked timbers on the track, carrying the gas can. Professor MacLeod had moved close to the timbers by now, untouched by anxious deputies since his frailty was seen as harmless. At the sound of Dave's warning scream, the professor turned just in time to see the sheriff on a dead run, coming straight for him and the wood. He stepped to one side, barely avoiding the extended straight arm, but left his cane in place. The sheriff tripped and went sprawling, landing hard with the can under his chest. The cap popped open, gas gurgling out.

The Academy team was now lunging through the police line to get at the timbers and move them before the wood could be torched, before the whistle reached them. But there were so many opponents and logs, and so few of them. Truncheons thudded against the white uniforms, hitting into the flesh and muscle beneath, mace sprayed straight into eyes, no quarter given.

The professor had lost his balance and fallen. Now both he and the lawman struggled to get back up onto their feet. The sheriff, pain-crazed with three broken ribs, picked up the half-empty can and swung it furiously at his antagonist who was steadying himself against the timbers. The crunch of old bone was more strange than loud. Then horrible, as the once-poet-for-Oregon crumpled onto the logs--those damnable logs--with his skull caved in.

Most of the crowd from town, the silent or mocking spectators of this afternoon circus, now were galvanized into one body by that ghastly sight. As the sheriff agonizingly sloshed the remaining gasoline onto the blockade with its crumpled corpse, he saw the smoke of the train coming through town one minute away. The long whistle drowned out the sobs around him, and he didn't see the townspeople raging forward. The mob grabbed the sheriff and each of his enforcers, wrestling them roughly to the ground, almost oblivious to the flying truncheons and even several hasty shots by deputies.

Academy team members who were still on their feet saw their rescuers coming, and raced to remove the logs. Townspeople rushed to help, and a hundred were all at once on the track with the train now in sight. Cameramen for the people of America were in the middle of the action, watching in tears and disbelief as their instacams filmed the scene live and in bloody color.

The tracks were almost cleared. Only two railroad ties were left when the steel nose of the 9039 slammed its way through. The solid 4x4 logs splintered apart in a dozen directions. One jagged splinter at least two feet long imbedded its tip deep into the chest cavity of an astonished deputy. The man clutched at it desperately as he sank to his knees. An Academy woman lunged over to keep him from falling forward, but missed him by an inch. The earth on which the deputy fell pushed the red spear point on through the back of his shirt as he collapsed. His final breath was spent on a curse. The train that wouldn't be stopped went charging blindly through the carnage.

Oregon's Poet Laureate was dead. So was one deputy. Seven from the crowd were seriously injured along with the sheriff and four of the Academy team. A strong recall effort would be started within hours, targeting the stop or be stopped governor of that quiet peaceful State.

*   *   *

Mayor Davies paced back and forth in his large office, ignoring the soft plush carpet beneath his shoes. The weight of his elected office was heavy this day, for his was the responsibility for having cancelled all major events to be held in large public venues for the next week. His to have closed all schools and colleges, and put the Oregon Health and Science University staff and students on emergency medical standby. His to have ordered the closing of the airport, scrambling air traffic around the country and the world. His to have closed the third largest port on the West Coast, and to have cleared track on the Coast Starlight and Empire Builder intercontinental rail lines. His to have cancelled the Portland Trailblazer games at The Rose Garden.

His was also the responsibility for the order to have closed inbound lanes and turn all lanes to outbound on Interstates 5 and 205 bridges over the Columbia, and Interstate 405 and Bypass 30 and Highway 2 over the Willamette, and to do the same with virtually every major thoroughfare leading into Portland. But that plan had disintegrated as the one inbound lane on each highway designated for cabs and buses to return to make round trips was soon blocked with crashed cars, which had tried to break through and get away.

Thousands of motorists, angry at being refused entry to pick up spouses and children, or to return to their home in downtown, vented their rage on other motorists, who in panic to get away from an unknown terror, wouldn't give an inch to let another driver in. Courtesy was dead, dogs eating dogs ruled, to the most aggressive goes the prize.

With traffic clogged in all directions, no emergency vehicles could move. Accident calls and desperate medical calls for help went unanswered. The mayor heard them all on his scanner in his darkening office.

Close advisors had chosen to be near him, rather than going to their families in the mass evacuation of downtown Portland. He and they could see a dozen different intersections through his office windows in the late afternoon sun, all in gridlock, with no citizens escaping by car from here to safety. He could see past the buildings to a forest canopy of trees over residences, for Portland had been called the greenest city in the United States. *Soon in flames*? he conjectured.

"That incessant siren…" he muttered, but quickly added, "…leave it be" when someone moved to have it turned off.

Word had come that the Grain Train had run the Earlham blockade, and two people had died--one law enforcement, one civilian. The governor would be irate; the FBI would call it murder. And that unstoppable train would now be in the Portland yards in minutes. The mayor debated options with his staff: He could order cars parked across the tracks, wreck it, kill the dozens of innocents and not-so-innocent on board, stop it here, be a hero-- or a killer of patriots in his very individualistic, free-thinking, independent-minded township.

His city was a safe haven for punk, hardcore, crust punk, anarchist movements, layers of subcultures, and even a lot of people who didn't like wearing any clothes. And now this piece of domestic terrorist trash from Colorado had brought his tranquil city to its knees in a day?

An assistant called the mayor's attention to a fire they could see flashing and growing in an upper floor window of an office building several blocks away. They watched it spread to another window, and another--then it went out rather quickly. It later turned out that an irate office worker, furious at his boss over something, stayed when everyone else evacuated, emptied all the files, and lit the blaze. The sprinkler system contained the damage to four offices, except for the water and smoke.

Looking down, the mayor saw a gang of people running into a smaller building, past a few workers still running out. With binoculars he followed their progress through second story office windows, watching them select computers and laptops, paintings and artwork for pawning, dumping bookcases and trashing files for the fun of it. *Scavengers and rats from the gutter were only inches away from us at any moment*, he noted.

The window at the elite jewelry store on the corner across the street was soon broken, and scores of people, some in nice clothes, even suits, went in and came out with pockets and hands full. There would be stories of other shops, where owners stayed, with their guns. And the thin blue line of police and security officers had been stretched so tight so quickly that it broke-- right in front of his eyes.

Drivers, blocked and frustrated, tried to keep going by driving on the sidewalks, knocking pedestrians aside, some gently and some not-so, then when there was no place to go on, some of those drivers were pulled from their penetrable steel weapons, and beaten, and the contents of their car and clothing taken. Guns with concealed carry permits didn't stay long in glove boxes. Shots were plainly heard from the streets below.

People roamed freely over the hoods and roofs and trunks of the sea of abandoned cars, trying to get away from they knew not what, only obeying the wailing sirens all around them, screeching at them to flee.

In his time in office, the mayor recounted to his staff, he had seen stress bring on many symptoms--rage, frustration, tears, depression, and heart attacks. The 911 channel was clogged now with all those symptoms, plus sadness, fear, and death. And it had now all happened in one hour of mass hysteria, he acknowledged rather sadly, brought on as a result of the destructive actions of one individual, followed by a decision then a declaration by the officials whom the people had chosen to protect them from such things.

The police chief called to airlift the mayor and his cadre out of the threat of attack. But the mayor realized with a hint of a smile that during this last hour's master plan response in preparation for the battle of Armageddon, there had been no more news of bombing. No more destruction of power plants, or bridges, or buildings downtown, or threat of weapons of mass destruction. There was only silence from the explosive enemy, while the huge bureaucracy of everyday life ground to a halt as the collateral damage of his two simple words: *Red Alert.*

*   *   *

The Grain Train blistered the tracks toward Portland. Monty was talking on the cab radio with Harran at the Portland dispatch tower, assuring clearances. Peter kept his earphones pressed tightly in one ear, listening to the news on the radio, while also hearing one media helicopter reporting on the incidents at Earlham. He was struck with remorse to learn that more lives had been lost in reaching his dream. But his grieving would have to wait.

He tried all of his Shakespeare phone numbers again, except Tom in Seattle, wondering if he had any bomb threat leverage remaining.

*   *   *

III mulled over his options as the FBI helicopter lifted off from the rooftop of downtown Portland's federal office building, using an emergency variance through the secured air space. He looked down at mile after mile of crammed parking lots--that an hour ago were flowing streets. "Switzer, I'm even more certain that the train is headed straight for the ocean," he said to the trusted aide sitting very close to him in the copter. "Get every federal law officer that is still mobile to convene at the entrance to the Port of Portland to meet me."

III considered the criminal's options. "With that maniac and his train almost within sight of those grain elevators and waiting freighters, why would he ever veer northward? Makes no sense at all. He's out of bombs and bombers. We will nail his hide within an hour, mark my words. Pilot, get us out to those docks fast!"

*   *   *

Mayor Taulison couldn't tear herself away from the television screen in her Seattle office. The scenes of utter chaos and bestial behavior horrified her in her proud neighbor city. "How could a place so beautiful and clean become so ugly and dirty so fast?" she asked. An aide answered the obvious: *Red Alert.*

"That will never happen here, not on my watch. Never! Never!" She thought for another moment, studied the Portland hell, and concluded, "We must find a way to deal with them--honorably, or else stop them cold and hard, before they get here. Get me our governor on the phone. We will not see Seattle crippled by any order from our national security department!"

*

"Well, tell Mayor Taulison this is another emergency she'll have to squeeze in!"

Jennifer Crussman paced the floor around her desk mounded with excess paperwork, speaking into her headset. Their large TV screen on the multi-media wall of the NPA Crisis Center was replaying the dual death scenes from Earlham. The gathered reporters watched again in astonishment.

"Mayor, did you watch the running of the Earlham blockade?...Yes, MacLeod *was* one of our professors, and *was* a friend of mine. Plus, the accidental death of that law officer will give the FBI a free rein on doing anything they want to stop the train, even blowing it up themselves...Oh, yes, they would! That's the main reason I'm calling you. We need your help in getting this violence stopped..."

Jennifer listened impatiently a few moments, then interrupted. She had a remarkable way of being treated as a respected equal in long distance calls. "We have solid information that Peter will tell the train dispatcher to clear the tracks northward to Olympia. He's headed your way--where he'll stop on his own! There's been enough bloodshed...Good, you knew already, so we're close to an understanding. Now you must call the Attorney General... yes, the U.S....No, she's not taking any more of our calls, but she will take yours. After all, you both graduated Vassar, right?"

The director cocked her head a little, adjusting the earpiece as she was being asked for advice. "Well, you can tell the A.G. that you need the extra hours tonight to prepare for negotiations. Listen, some good news! We've got the very best coming in to work as your mediator at Seaticon. Her name is Cowdrey, and she's flat wonderful. But she prefers dealing with live people! That's why you need to call the A.G. right now. Get her to order Homeland Security and the FBI to back off...Bottom line reason?" Jennifer sighed. "Haven't both sides battered each other enough for one day? Also, how would she explain a death sentence for forty citizens versus trying overnight mediation? No, too much is at stake."

She listened even more carefully now as she scribbled a note for Steve who was standing nearby. He hurried to another desk and picked up a phone. Jennifer asked, "What about your own governor's position?...That's good, wait until they're really needed. Preventive actions with a nervous National Guard too often escalate...You bet. Oh, we're going to try to get

Jerome Blackman back into the 9039 cab, to do some hard reasoning with Peter tonight while you folks are positioning in Seattle. He needs to be in there in the morning..." and her sentence was left hanging.

Then she continued. "Mayor, I've just watched two men die for the third time on TV. I need time alone. We've got the A.G.'s office standing by to patch you through. Let's get this thing to wind down into bad memories." Jennifer nodded to Steve to punch in the connection as she hung up, then walked rapidly in the direction of the nearest rest room, not knowing whether her stomach, or screams, or tears were coming up.

*   *   *

Portland during this evening madhouse was a tangle of hot cars and blistering tempers at the railroad crossings. Harran repeatedly warned the 9039 to slow down even more for irate drivers running past the striped flashboards, because of the closed bridge and resulting traffic jams.

Peter looked up-river at the legacy left by Ardis: two clusters of flashing lights on either side of the gaping concrete, boats swarming the pillars at the base of the bridge. Then he looked back at the mist-shrouded skyline of the city. A strong feeling surged up in him that somewhere near those dimly lit office buildings was the man who wanted him dead, and who would now leave town to get ahead of him one last time.

*   *   *

"Mayor Davies, the TV!" Portland's mayor pivoted quickly to see an aerial view of the Grain Train, moving rapidly. And a voice saying, "Unbelievably, the train has turned north! She's headed out of Oregon, to everyone's surprise! And she's now crossing that Washington state line!"

The mayor sank exhausted, almost in a stupor, his head splitting, and his chest in gripping pain. The red phone was ringing somewhere in the fog.

"Mayor, it's the governor, for you."

The mayor slowly picked up the phone.

"Mayor, you didn't call me as promised. Looks like you've got a mess on your hands to clean up. The train is still moving, so they can yet be a threat to Portland, but it looks like Seattle may be their target after all. Good riddance. I'll leave it up to you and Hofstetter to decide what to do on the alert. Good luck."

And he was gone. Along with the peace of Portland. The mayor buried his head in his hands, his future in the shambles he had feared for his city. He guessed that the many microbreweries for which the city was famous would be doing a booming business, filled with people with no place to go and no way to get there. He wished he was sitting on a barstool right now himself.

*   *   *

A half-hour had passed since the woman with the most political clout in Washington State had spoken with the woman who held the highest legal position in Washington, D.C. Power continued being exercised this evening.

"No, Mr. Director, we will not do another Waco assault. I removed all pictures of that decades-old inferno when I took over this office, and I don't want them replaced!" She felt like hammering the phone on her desk.

"But, Ms. Attorney General." The director of the FBI had never felt at ease with the forced title or the woman in charge one block away. "I am assured that no one will be injured except those in the engine cab, who are directly responsible for these criminal acts."

"Ah, just the people at the controls. Then how would this runaway train be stopped?"

"There are many side rail yards in southern Washington, where the train could be switched, slowed, and stopped electronically."

The lady executive paused to consider, then asked, "Just what does the FBI have against letting the engineers stop when and where they are ready, Mr. Director?"

"Madam, it is decidedly a signal of weakness, the wrong message to send to those watching us at home and abroad for such signs of passivity and helplessness."

"I see. Did I understand you to say their bomb threats are now useless, because *all* of their gang members have been arrested or are under surveillance?"

"We believe that is correct. We can make our move at any time..."

"And you plan to arrest all on board when the train stops?"

"We have contingency plans for an airlifted SWAT team, Madam."

"Then tell me, what immediate risk does this train pose to the United States?"

He quickly extricated himself from the logical box. "Disruption of regular rail service, engineers unfamiliar with the track, curious citizens wandering into its path, people killed and injured...I could go on."

"Precisely, Mr. Director. We have three deaths, thirteen hospitalized, and many more injured already during two attempts at stoppage..."

"We had nothing to do with several..."

"As I was saying, two of the dead were innocent of conspiracy. So who's left? A train full of discontented farmers and citizens, a recalcitrant student, and retired elderly voters who in their own minds are trying to save lives of children. Doesn't your perception reach past tonight? Continued wrong handling of this, or pictures of more mangled bodies could bring on a crisis of confidence with this Administration! No, I feel mediation is our best chance for finding the *help-help* solutions and saving face."

The director's own face grimaced at the innocuous term of help-help. That was the newest phrase for the old *win-win* school of thought, peopled by those who spent a lot of time arguing about semantics, and talking courts out of prosecuting law-breakers.

"Then there will be a *next-time*, Ms. Attorney General."

"It's your job to avoid a next time," she concluded. "Have I made myself totally clear, sir? *Don't stop that train.* Goodnight."

The FBI Director hung up the hotline receiver in his spacious office. He muttered under his breath as he dialed across the continent to a cpd in Portland. "Spineless, cowardly, female political hack..." and he would have added more except for III answering at that moment. "Sir?"

"Don't...stop...the...train," he said, belligerently laboring the words into the phone.

"What?" III asked in disbelief.

"The exact quote of our astute Attorney General, to avoid more bad press, thanks to your expert handling of this matter out there."

III blushed furiously at the insult, and turned toward Switzer, who was standing very near. "But now they've done themselves in. Did you remind her that an officer is dead? That justifies use of maximum force!" III insisted.

"I told her everything, my inept friend. Now we will take her history-making orders to not stop the criminals, and see just where that leads our country. And disassociate us from Governor Anderson's actions. He's too far out on the limb already."

"I see. If that is all, sir, then good night." He broke his own rule of avoiding that closing phrase, and at once regretted becoming commonplace.

"No, it is a terrible night for America. I wish there was something we could do." Then the conversation abruptly ended with a click.

His aide stood at III's elbow as he clicked off the phone. He had just received a red light, personal insults, but also what in his mind he perceived as a clear green light in the Director's parting phrase.

"You know, Switzer, I may take that vacation this year."

"Sir?" His trip arranger looked very puzzled, since there had been no mention of any time off. They stood at the Astoria port rendezvous point, with an array of law officers waiting nearby.

"You remember, the hunting trip I've been promising myself in Montana."

Switzer's ears perked up on the cue word. "Oh, yes, Montana."

"There's a big buck I'd like to get my scope on. Been after him a long time."

"When would you plan on going, Mr. Director, so I can make arrangements."

"After this game is ended, and that damnable train finally stops, so we can put this behind us."

Switzer leaned over and whispered something in his director's ear, which made him smile. The aide then left to make the contract call to the killing corps. They were still smarting from Academy intervention at their late night gas trap in Idaho, and the capture and wounding of their elite operatives.

*   *   *

Peter finished apologizing to Harran for having kept his dispatcher in the dark about their direction change until the very last second. Fortunately, all other rail traffic was stopped anyway because of the Red Alert, and the tracks could be switched rapidly. Then Peter radioed a response to the Academy helicopter again flying their point as they left Portland behind them. "Jerome, you are one of the few hopes I'm holding onto in getting us through. And I trust you enough to honor your request to re-board. We'd have to be out of Oregon and in a safe place away from the highway. You come down low over the tracks when you want us to stop in about a mile, but don't say anything more over the radio about it."

Monty pointed out to the side, and Peter moved the shield enough to see the OSP chopper peeling angrily away and heading back. The 9039 must have just crossed the State border out of Oregon. *Into the setting sun, they ventured boldly*, Peter's memory triggered somebody's quote. Into Clark County, Washington, leaving behind them one governor's ultimatums, and wondering about the next.

Peter spoke decisively into the radio transmitter: "When we stop, Jerome, we will stay no longer than ten minutes. And if any chopper lands other than yours and TV-5, we'll leave immediately."

"A suggestion, Peter," Monty rejoined gently. "Television is becoming a strong ally in generating public support. If the media want to land to create more human interest story settings, that might give you greater voice in negotiating. Think on it." Then he added quietly, "What would Wilma have wanted, I wonder?"

That clinched it. Peter knew from their brief time that Wilma counted major station cameras in each city they passed. It was a sign of their box office draw, she said. He could almost hear her words...

He shook off the reverie, and pulled the left shield open slightly. A beautiful body of water reflected the reddening sun.

"Vancouver Lake, here on the map," A.M. pointed out. The map also showed the highway off to their immediate right, paralleling their run.

"Keep the speed up through here," Peter instructed, imagining the highway crowded with the new State's Patrol cruisers. Had he looked, there was only one, a traffic controller if too many gawkers stopped.

He asked Drew to take down the left window shield, letting the low sun and fresh air stream into the cab, feeling safe for the moment.

"Terrific sight," Ben said. "Want to tell the boxcars to open up too?"

"Thanks for the idea, but it might be dangerous to have them shoving on those doors while we're moving this fast. I'm guessing we'll get the sign to stop from the chopper in just a few minutes, and they can get some air then. We'll be here at the throat of the lake," he pointed, "after we pull away from the highway into the wetlands and slow down. Make sense?" The two farmers agreed.

Now the choppers around them numbered five. Peter studied each with binoculars. One held Blackman's flight crew from earlier. They decided at the Earlham blockade site to carry the most seriously injured Intervention Team members into the nearest Portland hospital. The second NPA helicopter continued to ferry the injured under Dave Cranmer's direction from Earlham.

The orange TV-5 copter flew with rear doors open, and Peter could see one end of a light pine casket. The TV crew had collaborated with Blackman to arrange for a Portland undertaker, an NPA contributor, to pick up two bolts of black crepe cloth plus red, white, and blue bunting in the shape of shields. The undertaker had brought that to a small hub airport outside Portland along with the casket.

No one at Earlham had interfered with the removal of the feisty professor's body when it was picked up on a stretcher and carried by NPA volunteers who were still able to walk. The stretcher was loaded in the same spot where Fulton Skinnard had earlier rested on the way to the Green River, Utah hospital--the same spot where the strapped casket now carried the silenced peacemaker.

Peter saw that the *Herald*/KDNC Radio copter had finally caught up with them, after covering the blockade aftermath and interviews. FBI occupied the mosquito-size copter, so far just an annoying observer accurately reporting one side of the story to whoever was listening and wearing a gun. The fifth carried the pool camera/news crews for the Pacific Northwest stations, by agreement with Denver media and the FCC. They all generally kept to their assigned airspace segments surrounding the train, for safety, and under threat of arrest and loss of license if flagrantly violated.

Up ahead, Blackman's chopper dipped twice, each time lower to the tracks, to alert the train. Then the third time almost touching, and landing near the rails. The TV-5 copter quickly followed suit. The *Herald* chopper set down one hundred yards further north up the tracks at the next clearing. The other two choppers hovered overhead, frustrated by the lack of further landing space available.

The train had been slowing steadily for the last mile, but Peter warned all riders to brace for a quick stop. Moments later Monty applied the air to the brake pads. The engine passed the first helicopter's landing spot, but was expertly stopped by the time the agreed Boxcar Four was directly opposite the TV-5 crew and their precious burden of Professor MacLeod's body. Blackman ran to meet Peter, Monty, and Drew as they walked from the engine toward the casket. Ben stayed with A.M. in the cab. Doors of all boxcars had been pushed open enough for occupants to be climbing out on the lake side. Most of the train riders were also making their way toward the TV-5 helicopter, as media cameramen were busy filming, along with anyone whose cpd battery was still charged.

"Monty, can you get me higher?" Peter asked his friend. Monty motioned to the husky farmer at his side, and together they lifted Peter up to sit on their combined shoulders. He stifled the cry of pain that rose into his mouth as the pressure increased terribly against his bullet wound.

"My name is Peter Wayman!" he shouted to the throng gathering around him. "This is Monty, the train's engineer and my friend, and another farm friend Drew," he gestured at the two supporting him.

"And you are the people who are helping us," Peter said, waving across them. "Farmers from Wray, raise your hands in bravery. You have been with us all the way.

"And now we mourn the passing of one I never knew in life, and greet now in death. I understand from news reports that he spoke for non-violence as a poet and teacher, and at Earlham until the last. He then joined the Intervention Team from the Peace Academy to try to take apart the blockade of railroad ties." Men were moving the casket toward the boxcar.

"He--and they--succeeded, with the help of local townspeople just like yourselves. But at the blockade, Professor MacLeod gave up his life for his friends, for all of us, for all the starving children crying out to America. The professor heard them, and understood.

"Another died with him at Earlham, a deputy sheriff doing his sworn duty. We offer condolences to the families and friends of both men." Eight men lifted the heavy casket and began slowly pushing it inside Boxcar Four, into the waiting hands up there.

"And we will honor Professor MacLeod with one final action, adding his body and coffin to our Grain Train. We already carry in respect and sorrow the body of our slain engineer, Fork Thompson."

Peter saw that some had been stringing black crepe outside Boxcars Three and Four. The doors had been opened on both sides, and the bunting shields were attached just to the left of the openings. The paint-splattered, wind-whipped banners that had served them so well had now been removed from those two special cars.

"It will be an honor to ride with them, and with you. The train will stop in twelve hours, after sunrise. Any who want to leave then can safely do so. We welcome your presence. Be cautious through the night. Pray for our mission if you speak with God. Hold positive thoughts for our success. Now shake hands with a new friend, embrace your neighbors, then let's hurry back on board. Five minutes." Peter was carefully lowered, and limped back with Monty's help. His wound was bleeding again through his pant leg.

There was no applause, only silence, as the group mingled and pressed the flesh. Then they moved back toward their Grain Train home, uniting in uncommon bond as people now numbering millions watched live on their evening news. It may have been Blackman who started them singing. "We shall overcome...we shall overcome..."

Evening fell as quietly as the brown fluff blowing off cattail stalks by the tracks. Monty had started the train very slowly from their stop at Vancouver

Lake. Peter radioed Drew Manchesky, now in charge back in Boxcar Four, to confirm that the new casket was anchored solidly. It was fine, so they could speed up past the twenty mph they were going.

But Monty held back. Somehow it seemed the proper speed now. Plus it was night on unfamiliar track, and they did have until morning. He turned in his chair and raised his eyebrows in question to Peter, who pursed his lips and nodded slowly in unspoken agreement. Ben Cody had been asked to take charge in Boxcar Three with Fork's bier to insure that no disrespect was shown. Blackman had taken his former place in the cab of Engine 9039, talking at length with Peter to open areas for negotiation as miles slowly crept by.

"Fellas, what do you make of this scene ahead on the left?" A.M. asked. Alarmed, everyone in the cab looked down the track.

Shapes of people were outlined in a strange kind of glow, with a few flickering lights in front of their small group. No signs of protest. "They're standing still enough to be friendly," Monty ventured, as the train drew closer.

"But they're very close to the tracks," A.M. cautioned. "Shall I slow down? Speed up?"

"Shall we warn the people to stand away from the boxcar doors?" Blackman asked, leery of more violence.

"I am at peace inside," Peter answered their worried questions. "I think this group means us no harm. Let's just pass as we are." And he opened the rear door of the engine cab and limped out onto the catwalk.

"Where are you going?" Blackman asked in surprise.

Peter did not respond, but leaned out to peer around the engine wall at the group not thirty feet away. They were holding candles. That was the peculiar light. Several of them held small crucifixes up in front of them, and most made the sign of the cross as the engine rolled past.

This was not a ritual of his own church denomination, but Peter had sometimes wished it was. He crossed himself in response to their prayers-- touching forehead, chest, left shoulder, right shoulder, then lips. Softly he prayed, "In the name of the Father, and the Son, and the Holy Ghost. Amen." He smiled in the deep joy of returning to the palm of God's hand, and pictured the Grain Train running down a long crease in the palm of that huge cupped hand of love and acceptance.

Peter watched back along the track as the boxcars reached the group. He was surprised to see several persons step closer to the big passing cars and stretch out their hands with the lighted candles. Of course the wind blew out the flames, but people on board reached out trying to take the proffered wax batons. Some missed and dropped them, but some were passed.

Pleased by the gestures, Peter carried the story of the event back inside to the crew. "If we see candles coming again," Peter said to Monty, "let's risk slowing down enough to let the people touch each other."

"What about the shields? Monty asked. "Are you ready to take them down?"

Peter liked the tone of the question, and reframed it. "Are we ready, men?"

"It's night," A.M. said simply.

"And it's Washington," Peter said as simply.

"Ready," Blackman answered, "if I have a vote."

"Ready," Monty seconded.

"Ready or not, here I come," A.M. affirmed, accepted. He switched off the overhead lights, then the shields were lowered. They were again at the mercy of any individual.

"All it takes is one with an Uzi," A.M. said on second thought.

"All it takes is one with a dream," Peter countered.

And Monty said the amen.

Nearing the outskirts of Woodland, more candles began twinkling their greeting. With a feathered touch Monty slowed the train. No one would have lost their balance in that gentle decline of speed, for he had been a very good engineer.

Blackman and Peter both studied the upcoming group through night scopes. No expressions of anger on the faces, only sadness. Not any sign of weapons. This time the people were dispersed on both sides of the track.

"May I take the right side, Peter?" Monty asked, as Peter reached for the left door again. "Just to feel what's going on with the people?"

"I thought you'd never ask," Peter replied as he exited, then added, "but watch out for a trap."

Here the small town residents had begun to gather. An older couple had set up a card table covered with white linen, with figurines around which small candles burned in green, yellow, and red votives.

A father and mother and four young children stood apart from others with their family altar statue of Mary, whose arms were raised in blessing. The Catholics had been touched.

On his side, Monty shared the same feeling that people had come down to the tracks to see a funeral cortege. Here a small choir stood together in their church robes. He could see their lips moving, but couldn't hear the

"Ave Maria" they were singing. He could tell that purple was the color of their robes, from the extra lightcamera spotlight.

Even if he could have seen the enterprising photographer, he wouldn't have recognized him as Fasma from the *Herald*. From their lead helicopter they had seen the advance preparations being made in Woodland, and had quickly landed in a nearby parking lot to capture the scene for a State and a country becoming enchanted with the beleaguered Robin Hoods.

A.M. slowed even more, almost from necessity, as Peter came in to say the citizens were walking right up to the train. The offering of candles and rosaries, then virtually any item, was just a spontaneous gesture. Scarves and hats, Bibles and wildflowers were handed up by the crowd to the passing boxcars filled with people just like themselves.

That feeling of oneness is probably what compelled watchers to reach up and offer themselves. Peter was astonished to see the first person lifted from the ground up through an open boxcar door.

"Ben, what are you doing back there!" Peter urgently radioed Boxcar Three.

"Peter, it's unbelievable," he answered at once. "I was just going to radio you. It's like some spirit is moving them. They're yelling up at us that they care about the starving too! One ran along saying he's been waiting a lifetime to make his life count for something--and we're it!"

"A.M.! Stop now!" Monty yelled into the cab, then he turned and looked back along the track. Two people on his side of the train were frantically pushing a wheelchair-bound person alongside the rough gravel shoulder of the rails, and he was reaching up toward the boxcar. Incredibly, arms were reaching down to grab him--a tragedy waiting to happen.

Two rails later the cars were clanging together in their domino drumming. Peter rushed into the cab to see why they had stopped without an order, and Monty gestured over to his side, explaining angrily. Blackman had been watching, and said, "Well, he's inside, with his wheelchair, along with a dozen others on this side, including a couple of kids. Want to make a federal case of clearing them off? Or get started again?"

This moving of a people's spirit was more than Peter could explain, or undo. He decided on the lesser impossible of his alternatives. "Monty, start inching us ahead again, as you did before. Let them know with your horn."

A long half-pressure tone emitted, turning into a full-power blast. Then it sounded again as the rails began moving backward under the wheels. Blackman and Peter went back out to watch as people reluctantly let go of firm handclasps. A few more were pulled up.

Peter shook his head, wondering what kind of ground work Tom might have been able to lay for a peaceful entry, or what kind of nightmare he might be taking these people into in Seattle tomorrow morning.

*   *   *

"America is getting on board, figuratively and literally," Donna Harrison reported from the hovering helicopter transporting the Channel 5 newscaster, "by ones and couples and families, young, elderly, handicapped, and the colors of all races.

"Respecting the solemnity of this evening's journey, we are flying five hundred feet over the Grain Train to avoid disturbing those who have come to pay their last respects. Below us the people wait, some reading scripture or being led in worship by clergy, some explaining the unexplainable to their children, some simply silent. They are wanting to share this moment in some way, to touch, to pass along their caring.

"Where crowds are gathered, the train is now stopping to allow lines of mourners to file past the two black-draped funeral cars. This, despite the repeated attacks and threats. The poet and the engineer surely have a stronger voice in death than they were able to have espousing this cause while alive.

"Hopefully you can see with us the remarkable sight stretching miles northward, as the dark earth is tied with a dotted ribbon of candlelight vigils. Homes in the little towns along the track are putting lighted Christmas decorations in their windows, and last December's strings of lights are plugged in again, outlining their houses and trees. It's almost as if the people of Washington have set up lighthouses to guide loved ones safely home. If this isn't the heart of America we see beating, I don't know what is.

"We'll be following the train all the way to the end, and we hope you'll stay with us. Peter Wayman did request a favor of this reporter, that we let Americans know that an official cease-fire has been declared through the night. A twelve-hour non-violence agreement was reached between the Grain Train, Washington State, and the U.S. Government. I just hope all the dissident warriors listening out there will honor that pledge of peace."

*   *   *

Lights burned late into the Seattle evening hours Friday, as Mannheim Grain Elevator company officials delayed starting their weekend, indefinitely. They were angry as they gathered in the small conference room. The manager Antonio d'Almeda was there, and also annoyed, but would be leaving soon for the Seaticon Hotel for a larger meeting. His story to his officials was sketchy, simply that the hijacked Grain Train would be arriving in town in the morning, and their company was apparently the targeted destination. Beyond that, the details that they were staying now to work out, he neither wanted to know, nor approve.

For reasons d'Almeda left obscure, their East Coast management group was interested in having some of that grain transferred to a freighter. He didn't mention the phone call from his father's friend in Denver, Giuseppe Ciliando. Those were the infrequent calls that were always put through immediately, and never treated merely as requests.

*   *   *

The benefit concert at Invesco's Mile High Stadium was rocking the nearby Denver neighborhoods with high decibel sound waves. Country western music was the *gold in them-thar hills* tonight, from the million-album recording stars performing to the eighty thousand fans jamming the ballpark with a standing-room sellout.

Al Federson had been introduced to the enthusiastic crowd as the first person in the country to stand up and be counted in favor of the mission of Engine 9039. He had Mabel stand beside him to soak up the cheers, along with Harold Swenson, president of Brighton's Club.

Then Barney O'Brien, national president of Serv-U.S. who flew in from California, was handed a check to hold in trust for the U.S.A.S. cause-- totaling the full $1,610,820 in gate proceeds. The huge crowd of visiting farmers and locals stamped their feet in a bleacher hurrah for two minutes. That scene would make the ten o'clock news for sure.

*   *   *

Two tired concerned grandparents, Matthew and Josephine Williamson, along with Candice and Mrs. Montropovich, were glued to their Denver TV set for any and all newscasts about the train odyssey now consuming their lives. Candice had begun answering all phone calls, for one might be her parents, and one might be Peter and Monty.

*   *   *

Portland's Red Alert had been lifted two hours before, and flights resumed. Evening flight 1213 continued its approach to SeaTac, the international airport serving the Seattle-Tacoma area. One VIP passenger had changed to a fresh suit en-route from Portland, aggravated to be flying commercial again, but refusing to look rumpled when he left the plane.

"Portland is what's rumpled," III mumbled to himself. "That phony Governor Anderson, and all of Oregon, could drop off into the Pacific, and the U.S. would be better for it. Damn train should never have gotten this far. Never!" III was arriving to assert his fullest authority in the final plays of the game. He felt the championship would soon be in his grasp, if only his forced partners would keep their hands off the pieces once they reached the Seaticon conference room.

The landing pattern brought them in two thousand feet above the suburb of Tukwila, its lights twinkling dimly up at him through the evening mists.

*   *   *

The trio of tired travelers was not aware of the stream of planes coming in low over the well-insulated house. Their host was busy helping them feel at home for the few hours they would be there. They were on the fifth course of their dinner: truffles, brandy, and blackberry tarts made from the fruit of bramble undergrowth around trees south of the house. Oddly, but politely, this was one living room conversation in America in which the hijacked train would not be a topic of discussion this night, though that gorilla in the room was really on everyone's mind.

Frank, Marion, and Janet had been safely landed at a small strip near Isaqua, after their close escape from the Oregon coast. They were then picked up by limousine and whisked away nine miles to this luxurious Tukwila estate. Washington State wetland preserves, lush and wild, bordered the neighborhood street as the chauffeur had turned onto a gravel drive leading off to the right. The large home was set toward the back of rolling terraced lawns, which led down to a sand volleyball field and barbecue pits. A little drainage stream from the wetlands meandered the lower property, creating cattail havens and duck ponds graced by water lilies.

Frogs still croaked nighttime welcomes through the big room's one open window. Would that government workers had it so good, Frank thought, wincing slightly from a stiff neck as he nodded amiably at his Mafia-connected host.

*   *   *

Chapter Twenty

The mediator picked by the National Peace Academy was a tough old pro named Cowdrey--Cassie Cowdrey. Her folks had chosen *Cassandra*, but she grew up to be a *Cassie*.

She was known in professional mediation circles as a neutral's neutral, treating every side with equal disdain for being unable to already reach agreement. Her style came not so much from textbooks as from growing up the oldest of ten, six brothers and three sisters, in rural Tennessee.

There was never enough food on their table, but always plenty of hand-me-down clothes for the younger kids. Her mom died when Cassie was eighteen, and the eldest stayed home to keep the family going until her next older sister finished high school. Then Cassie entered Tennessee State University part time, worked full time, and sent as much money home as she could.

"Nothing was ever given to me," Cassie used to say, "except my talent as a peacemaker." She helped people stop fussing with each other everywhere she went--at work, in church, around the neighborhood. She got so good that the National Peace Academy recruited her to teach mediation skills to their students.

Occasionally Cassie was asked to personally mediate a serious dispute, and that's why she was flying to Seattle at the shared expense of Academy and government. She was briefed in triplicate. The Academy faxed dossiers on all the known participants in the Grain Train dispute, plus a full legal brief prepared by their Law School faculty and interns was sent to her laptop computer. This was the product of one Academy specialty: researching a dispute in progress, finding the salient precedents in State, District, and Federal case law, defining untested issues, and boiling it all down into layman's terms accessible to negotiators as well as all sides. "To facilitate a just and peaceful settlement of any dispute" was their motto, and they ambitiously pursued it at the NPA School of Law.

The mayor of Seattle had arranged with the FBI for the Academy mediator to be brought straight to City Hall from the SeaTac Airport. They had agreed an FBI helicopter was appropriate in this case involving national security.

From her commercial 747 flight, Cassie Cowdrey phoned Mayor Taulison a half-hour before landing. "Your Honor, thank you for accepting my call this late."

"Crises come at all hours, Ms. Cowdrey," the mayor replied matter-of-factly.

"I wanted to let you know that I will be shuttled by the NPA's helicopter from SeaTac to the rooftop landing pad at Seaticon Blue at approximately 10:50 P.M.," Cassie said. "The Academy has made arrangements with your Manager of Safety Gillespie to have that area secured for landing, then escort me to the Executive Suite. The media has been notified of our mediation plans, but will never be present during the negotiations. My first meeting with you must be private, since I see you in a pivotal position as CEO of your city. I should be able to be in the suite by 11:14. We can have until 11:30 together, then we must join with the others who will be waiting. Are there questions?"

"I have already made other arrangements for your transportation, Ms. Cowdrey," the mayor said stiffly.

"Thank you. However, they must be done my way, to assure that I am perceived by all sides, and the public, as absolutely impartial, beholden to none, for any past, present, or future favor. I'm sure you understand. Have you and I ever met?"

There was a short pause. "No, we have not, but I have researched you, and know you do things for valid reasons. So I will honor your arrangements for impartiality, but also keep mine as backup reserve, in case of any problem. I will ask the Bureau's pilot to follow you in. And I'll chat with my Manager of Safety about communicating."

"Of course. A pleasure doing business with you, Mayor Taulison. I'm sorry my staff did not reach you earlier to prevent this duplication. See you soon." The long distance test of power ended cordially enough, in Cassie's book.

The phone call to Tom Buchanan was a different matter. She had gotten his secret Seattle number from Blackman, who got it from Peter, who told Tom an hour before that the call was coming. Peter and Tom had worked at reconciling hard feelings and re-establishing loyalties.

"This is Cassandra Cowdrey. With whom am I speaking?"

"Call me Tom. May I call you Cassandra?"

"No, Ms. Cowdrey will be fine for now. The full group will have to agree on that level of familiarity. And what is your last name, Tom?"

"I don't care to divulge that." He didn't care for her rebuff either. "It is of no consequence to our discussions."

"On the contrary, it is of the utmost importance to you as an individual, and I only deal with persons who are trying to be honest with themselves first, and with their disputants second."

"Valid opinion, Ms. Cowdrey, but not applicable here. I'm not the FBI. They're the ones who need your honesty speech. And I'm not Peter Wayman. He's the original Honest Abe. But he's in the train, unable to come to the phone because he's trying to sleep with a bullet hole in him. I'm only a stand-in to talk about talking. And *Tom* will do fine for this interim job."

"Young man, we've got a long way to go and not much time to get there. People around the Seaticon table tonight are going to be sleepy and grouchy. They'll blame your group for making them that way. So they'll be mad at you. Will you be in the room?"

"No, on telecom screen, to keep from being arrested."

"It will take more than that to keep you free."

"The mayor named me a co-mediator in this case. That gives me the same protection against prosecution as Blackman has."

"Don't kid yourself. Mr. Blackman doesn't have an APB out on him. Any law officer will nail you on sight as a suspected terrorist, Mr. Tom Buchanan."

Silence stole into the phone connection. His cover was blown again.

"And if I know your name, and am looking right now at your picture stapled to a thick dossier, you'd better believe the FBI is just as fully apprised. So rethink your secrets and your stands before we bring you up on the screen at 11:35, or else I'll agree we deal only with Peter Wayman when some others there start demanding that."

"I'll think on these things," Tom said, some of the strength gone in his voice.

Cassie picked up on the changed tone. "And don't you dare let me cower you either. I'm here to *empower* you into *equal* status with everyone at the table. No more, no less. That's where the win-win solutions are waiting, between equals." She paused just a moment. "But the stewardess is telling me I am not her equal since we are landing, so goodbye for now, Mr. Buchanan. And be sure to have Peter Wayman talk with Mr. Blackman about the Academy's conference blanket. Got that? The conference blanket."

The night was just beginning in Seattle.

* * *

"You ask about our conference blanket? Well, we will not help hide any individuals in the Grain Train team in their various cities. They communicate with you using their own devices," the night shift chief at the NPA Crisis Center told Peter.

"But we will help facilitate the Seaticon conference with a blanket," Kristine Zowadsky continued. "Tom needs a safe place from which to mediate a peaceful solution out of this morass. The NPA has been authorized by the president to use a super scrambler technology. We can hide the location of any communication device, be it cell phone or laptop, wireless or cable, for up to twelve hours.

"It's the same system used by the FBI's counterintelligence unit, and the Department of Defense and CIA. But the fun is that we all know that we all have it. And we all know that we can tell when a hacker is trying to break into it, and how far they've gotten. If they get within twenty miles, then we shut down, and start the system up all over again, using a whole new random network of clones around the globe. It takes hours for them to get close again, and they never fully succeed, so they rarely even try. We can insure that his hiding place remains secure, so long as he is negotiating in good faith with our mediator."

* * *

Seaticon. The very name conjured up images of elegant dining, luxury hotel accommodations, and a conference center *par excellence*. This was to be the gathering place of executives yet one more evening for the deciding of fates.

Mayor Taulison, with her police chief George Simonet, along with Mannheim's exec, Antonio d'Almeda, were just finishing coffee in the fifth floor French Bistro. A latte spiced with almond, butternut, and a sprinkling of nutmeg on the rich whipped cream offered a decadent attraction to the mayor each time she came. Each of the seven floors in the food court tower was finished in exquisite replication of varied world cultures, featuring their chefs and secret recipes and aromas. This circular tower of international cuisine, lighted with exotic pastel shapes and shades that showed through the outer glass walls, was centered in a manicured floral inner courtyard.

An enclosed arboretum offered a beautifully maintained color feast of flora, fauna, and fountains separating the triangle of walkways leading to the three pods of the conference center. Washington's Lieutenant Governor Dunlap, as designated negotiator for Governor Archway, was at that moment approaching one of the connecting walkways on a parking garage monorail. He knew his way around the huge complex, with its green, yellow, and blue triad of concourses, and had agreed it was the best location for a midnight mediation.

When he reached the Blue Point arm, he stepped out and onto the moving walkway curving to the left, passed the McDonald's and Panda Express bubbles then saw the large round blue-carpeted lounge area. It was designed for casual conversations, with chair clusters as well as tall round tables elbow high with foot rests and stools. Vending machines flanked either side of seven automatic sliding doors around the perimeter leading into the hallways of meeting room pods with movable walls to accommodate two or a hundred persons easily. Windowed walls separated each pod hallway, showing grounds outside planted with hundreds of trees and shrubs now twinkling in a wonderland of multicolored lights.

Above this blue room with its high ceiling was the much larger second floor, equipped as a giant auditorium with movable stages and flexible state-of-the-art audiovisual equipment. Floating circular walls and platform seating could let two hundred or one thousand fill that room for presentations.

The yellow and green pods on the points of the equilateral triangle leading away from this sixty-degree corner were identical size, providing the most modern facilities for five thousand conference delegates.

The spiraling twenty-floor adjoining hotel could host all of that number and more, and was the immediate destination for the man exiting the helicopter on the pad not far from the main entrance. It was the grandest way to have made an entrance that III could have chosen.

The night concierge, the Seattle Bureau Chief, and Agent Switzer were on hand to greet him. A flock of bellpersons stood by to handle his one suitcase. This small FBI contingent was whisked through the orchid-laden granite lobby to a fifteenth floor suite, offering more than the comforts of home. There was a full hour before the hijacked train conference began in the Chess Room of the Game Pod in the Blue Point. He had not been given the choice, but that would have been his room selection when choosing from animals, plants, fish, or five other categories from which rooms were named and decor carried out.

As soon as one woman named Cowdrey arrived, III knew the final irrevocable solution would begin falling into place at Seaticon.

*   *   *

Helicopter arrivals, lattes, and private caucuses were concluded. Formal introductions had been cool in the Blue Pod, done either in person or on remote screen via satellite. Cassie was standing and writing at the whiteboard wall, clearly establishing control. Her plain white blouse, red blazer, and navy blue skirt helped keep attention drawn to her.

"Thank you for correcting me, Lt. Governor Dunlap. Each of you speak up, as did the Lt. Governor, to insure my notes say what you say. So to paraphrase you, sir, arresting everyone would be like trying to catch all the ants on an anthill for a bottle farm: you couldn't get them all, would get stung trying, and seem mighty cruel in the process. Plus the ants get madder every minute you keep them locked up, and might stay fighting mad for months even after you turn them loose." Some smiled.

"That contrasts with U.S. Deputy FBI Director Ravenhead, who speaks also for the Department of Homeland Security." She strung out the full title, for she had not gotten them to agree on using either 'Mr.' and 'Ms.,' or first names. "You want all arrested, all fully prosecuted, correct?" III nodded assent, arms folded across his chest, leaning back in his chair as if now merely an observer since he had drawn the #1 token and spoken first. All chairs were equal in comfort, and in the number of squares in the checkered light and dark gray upholstery, which happened to match his impeccable gray pinstripe.

"And that also differs from Mayor Taulison, who feels that citizens of Washington State could not have premeditated their actions, and should be excused for being caught up in the spirit of the moment. Her target for arrest would be only the crew and farmers from Wray. Right?"

The lady executive nodded, glad she had worn her blue suit instead of the gray pinstripe. Not only for contrast, but to give her an extra bit of confidence. For tonight, every power avenue would be traveled. She stayed more involved, leaning forward on the huge round ebony table. At its center was a pattern of three squares joined to form a triangle, each large square comprised of fifty white and black alternating squares. In essence, three chessboards resting at the heart of Seaticon's Chess Room.

Cassie would not mention privileged information from an earlier caucus that the mayor was also concerned for the safety of that entire Colorado group, seeking to hasten the quick departure for security purposes. That was up to the mayor to disclose or not, in her own way and time.

"National Guard Commander Guinn, your position statement mentioned possible unruliness when residents saw women and children being arrested. Which reminded me of a story about a herd stampeding...if we had more time. You assured us your wranglers could handle any crowd problem if given authorization to use whatever force you deem necessary." The officer bedecked in camouflage fatigues nodded yes, ready to leave for instant duty if called.

"Mr. Buchanan, you drew a random #5 at the start, and it is now your turn to briefly outline your position on arrests. Can you still hear me through the remote hookup, and see us clearly on screen?"

Tom's viewing screen was a four-foot square plasma screen displaying the entire room at Seaticon, plus inset pictures of each participant around the border. These insets were live pictures being taken by the small angled camera screen in front of each table position.

In turn, a picture limited only to Tom's upper body image was in each of the six large plasma screens around the perimeter walls of the conference room. A sheet had been draped behind him to block any background images.

"You're very clear, like being there." Tom seemed assured, even casual in his Pendleton shirt checkered with shades of green. "My position is that no one should be arrested. It would be a waste of time. In defending their actions in court, the Group would claim *the lesser of the evils* defense, well established over the years in legal precedent in various Circuit Courts. Breaking the chain of the greater evil of starvation was a compelling act, a greater necessary good for the whole of humanity over the lesser evil of breaking any number of civil laws. The case would quickly be dismissed."

"Rubbish!" III exclaimed.

"Excuse me, Mr. Buchanan," Cassie said abruptly before Tom could react, and turned to III. "Deputy Director Ravenhead, you personally agreed, as did we all, not to interrupt anyone when they were speaking."

"But, really..." he started, intolerantly.

"Did you not?" she queried. He nodded assent. She finished, "Then don't. I hold everyone to our agreements. It's part of my job. Now, Mr. d'Almeda, what say you as manager of Mannheim Grain?"

"No opinion on the present subject. They have done nothing to threaten or damage our company persons or property." The heavyset man had not yet taken off his tan sport coat, but was sweating in anticipation of doing so.

"Colorado Senator Frye, you drew #7. For your State, and your Senate Agriculture Subcommittee, where do you stand on arrests?"

The wall screens around the room now split in half, showing both Tom and the congressman. Senator Frye looked ready to launch into a State of the Union Address, with dark blue suit and tie, seated at a grand desk in front of a wall lined with books, hands folded in front of him. "I agree in part with many of you sitting across the continent from me in these early morning hours. But there is a pressing need to demonstrate firmness now. Give all *non*-Coloradoans one last chance to leave peacefully, at a stop before entering Seattle, then arrest all those who choose to stay. All lawbreakers from Colorado should be arrested as soon as they stop, and brought to swift justice, as an example to discourage others. The same way we would do things at home."

As mediator, Cassie made no judgment and expressed no opinion, but simply documented her written notes on the wall, and continued. "Mr. Fruehauf, CEO of Mid-Western Pacific Railroad, whose train is in the middle of this furor, has declined to participate this evening. He said, quote, 'What the hell, it's just one train.'

"Seattle Police Chief Simonet is here as an observer at the mayor's request." He sat back away from the table, the full authority of his uniform, badge, and gun bespeaking power even when silent. "As are FBI Special Agent Switzer and Seattle's Bureau Chief, at the Deputy Director's behest, seated behind him.

"And though there are a number of other interested parties, such as the Serv-U.S. Clubs, and the United Nations' World Health Organization, we have decided in this initial meeting to exclude them as secondary in interests. Everybody still comfortable with that decision, after this first round of statements?" By framing the question in positive terms, she allowed the group to achieve common ground again by agreeing on yet another issue, as they did in agreeing to start with the question of arrests.

The room and radio speakers were silent.

"Fine. I've gotten all those positions written as our starting points. Will each of you please print that list from the wallboard for easy reference. Just scroll up the screen window using the mouse to Board #1, click on 'Print,' and you'll have it coming off your printer any moment. Then I'll move it over to a Save-Board #2 here on the other side. Everybody with me?" The quiet hum of laser printers at their workstations answered her.

"We'll continue focus on our various opinions first, to see where we're already close to agreement. Then we can come back to where we seem to need more discussion.

"So on to our second major question agreed upon. Senator Frye, let's begin back through the group with you. Who should pay for these several kinds of damages, not necessarily in order of importance: to the train and the tracks, to grain cargo, to the bombed cities, to the people injured and killed?"

He didn't hesitate. "Simple. We may be approaching $100 million in property damage, and possibly five billion or more in liability lawsuits. There's no question," the suave lawmaker dictated. "Insurance will kick in first. But then the insurance companies and the self-insured have recourse to the criminals. This is the sole responsibility of the planners and perpetrators of the crimes. Take it out of the hides of everyone arrested. Sell everything they and their families have. They won't need anything, sitting in jail for the rest of their lives."

Mr. d'Almeda said that he again declined comment.

"Standing on the Fifth Amendment?" Cassie asked with some jocularity, but received surprisingly few smiles for her effort. She chalked it up to the late hour.

Tom Buchanan naturally took exception to the senator's stand. "The U.S. Government forced this action onto us by their errant policies. Therefore, they should pay for the rebuilding of the damaged facilities. These could be public works projects for unemployed skilled laborers."

And when the time came for III to respond, he added another demand besides billing the train crew. "Tell us where the other bombs are. Or admit that you bring no *good faith* to these negotiations, so we can all go home and just wait to see what happens tomorrow morning." III had the nagging concern of a lawman that there might be another terrorist with a detonator besides Tom who slipped through the tightening of their net.

"With that comment," Cassie noted, "Question Two ends. Go ahead and print my atrocious handwritten summary on Board #2. Since it's very late, let's not take time for any of you to repeat what you've already said. We heard it, I wrote it, and it's in the group memory. So let's move on to some significant ideas on how we can find a bridge between our differences, and put those forward. If there is a point to clarify, ask that. Deputy Director Ravenhead?" Cassie responded to his quickly sitting up to the table.

"I still want to know where the bombs are!" III adamantly stated. "If their group insists on holding onto all of them, I'm walking right now."

"Did you say *all*?" Cassie asked, passing by an ultimatum but picking up on a possible negotiation piece to keep all the players at the table.

"You heard what I said," he answered caustically.

"I'll tell you where one is right now, if you'll promise to go pick it up personally," Tom shot back from the video screen.

The night was stretching not only long, but taut.

Friday became Saturday at Seaticon, and the minutes dragged on. Cassandra Cowdrey felt the mediation wringer starting to squeeze. However, all participants had agreed on the foolishness of full titles and switched to the Mr. and Ms. prefaces, an agonizingly small step toward more common ground. Yawning was both stifled and open by 1:00 A.M., fingers slowly rubbing across bloodshot eyes.

"Well, it's time for a break--and I need a break," Cassie admitted. "But first, we need to see some position switching by somebody on something. Surely there is a demand of lower priority that could be modified at this moment, just to see what that might...allow someone else to yield." She almost said *trigger*, but sought to avoid words of violence and conflict. "Who'll break our current stalemate, so we can all take a half-hour break?"

Sometimes a little extra incentive in good humor actually helped a mediation. Waiting in silence was another technique, letting participants feel an awkwardness, that someone in the group should do something.

This usually worked its pressure on persons in the same room, but it was Tom, distant and youngest, who broke the prolonged silence. He had earlier surrendered one of Jerry's bomb planted in Boise to keep III at the table. Strangely, this seemed to increase his intimidation leverage, rather than diminish it.

"This is not a primary goal for us, but a serious concern. We would like for all the Wray farmers to be released to go home to their families and farms. Agreement on that would be worth another bomb location."

III responded without waiting for recognition as Cassie was saying her thank-you to Tom. "You might as well give up all the bombs, Mr. Buchanan. They're useless, with no one left to detonate them."

Cassie turned to chide III for speaking out of turn, when Tom jumped back in. "That's your assumption, Mr. Ravenhead, not our admission. And do I personally look ghostly to you, too ethereal to push cell phone buttons myself?"

Mayor Taulison was getting nervous at this turn of conversation. She motioned Chief Simonet up to her chair to exchange quick whispers. Then poised a hand halfway in being raised for recognition, delaying Cassie's question about her disturbance. Cassie needed to regain control, but felt something was cooking.

"If Mr. Buchanan would consider..." the mayor began, thinking her words carefully as she studied Tom's face on the large screen, "...uh, relinquishing two bombs, one of which could be in the Seattle area, I would then propose that...we charge the Wray farmers with reckless endangerment and accessory to grand theft, then plea bargain a sentence of thirty days in jail and one year's probation."

"It's not your jurisdiction, lady!" III shouted out.

"That's just not acceptable!" Tom also shouted to be heard.

"It most certainly is my jurisdiction! And why isn't it acceptable?" the mayor hurled back at both men.

Cassie breathed a quiet sigh of relief. They were talking serious possibilities again. She would work them through this series of intolerances and concessions, then allow them a break on a positive note. Hopefully, the informality of the large Blue Room's social atmosphere would permit the bridges of compromise to continue building.

*   *   *

Third Mate Kasir hung up the cellular phone on its cradle near the wheel, and turned to the night watch.

"You were wise to wake me. That was a strange call from the grain elevator person. Mr. d'Almeda himself. He said we should move to their dock at once if we wished to assure loading in the morning. And he gave me a night number to get a tug ship. What a strange way to do business. Now I must wake the captain." Both men tightened their ties anticipating his presence.

One hour later, lights from a small slow tugboat approached the *Godavari Sunrise*. Captain Pradesh noted 2:34 A.M., as he watched from the freighter's tall steering bridge at the stern, standing outside the cabin in the cool moist night. He drew in the fresh sea air, cleansed of the busy port's diesel fumes from the day. The distant shoreline blinked to him, a thousand semaphores of civilization. Soon he would order the raising of the huge anchor holding them to the floor of Elliott Bay. And the tug would guide them slowly toward that Seattle skyline, toward the berths for ferries and pleasure cruisers and lesser craft. Then veer north past a quarter-mile of bare shoreline to the long dock and tall towers filled with grain.

Around eight o'clock the transfer of grown gold would begin from land to sea. The captain often told the crew what an essential link they were in the supply chain, and that was why he expected such high performance from them. Their obedience would be tested this day, he was certain.

Then it began with a shout, as the lead to the bow rope was tossed down to the tug, dwarfed by the steel hull towering eighty feet above it.

* * *

"It's going on 4:00 A.M., gentlemen and lady," Cassie informed them. "In ten minutes, the Seaticon monitors will begin broadcasting three television networks on the dark unused wall screens here in the Chess Room. They will scan and videotape all of them, elevating sound on whichever has news on their 7:00 A.M. East Coast broadcasts relating to the Grain Train.

"Before they begin, I would like to direct our mutual attention back to Board #6, on which I've listed our agreements so far. I remind you that mediation is a voluntary effort, with all agreements made in good faith, and to be similarly honored.

"There should therefore be no reneging, since none of you were under coercion. They are in the best interests of all groups represented, and because of the nature of this conflict, the best interests of the United States. This cooperative spirit is one reason mediated agreements last longer, and I commend you on your use of the process thus far."

The perky woman read down the list of seven items, including Senator Frye's commitment to personally attend an international farm surplus and world starvation conference to be hosted in Seattle. Part of his initial reluctance had been finding federal funding, but the governments of Washington State and Seattle along with the federal group, plus Mannheim and its affiliates guaranteed joint efforts. The Seattle Chamber of Commerce was also listed as a generous donor, after a special wake-up call by the mayor to its director. The Seaticon facilities had been offered *gratis*.

Senator Frye had also been concerned that his staunch compatriots, those honorable senators from Washington State and his own counterpart from Colorado, not feel insulted by not being invited at the same time as he. So they also were awakened, invited, accepted, and wondered why they weren't also linked into the current Seaticon mediation.

The same kind of funding appeal, this time a conference call with Lt. Governor Dunlap and Senator Frye on the line to Barney O'Brien, president of Serv-U.S. Clubs, still in Denver after the concert. He pledged his sleepy but full support. "Don't be so surprised," Cassie had said. "Win-win happens time and again with mediation." There was no doubt she was a true believer, and an expert at helping people to stop tearing down and start building where they could agree, despite deep differences.

The newscasts began, drawing the full attention of the tired group:

"Overnight the train of death has become the train of life. At every hamlet and town on its route through western Washington State it has stopped. Just plain people of every description have boarded, their only common denominator being Americans. It's impossible to count how many climbed on, for it was done by moon glow and candlelight, but estimates range up to one hundred new riders. If this train was to be wrecked now, it could become the worst disaster in our railroad history..."

The second channel's commentator was turned up:

"It's still dark outside Nisqually, Washington, but you can see and hear the hundreds of mourners and supporters, singers, and a few hecklers who have come to see the train of grain and the people urging changes. The strident voices of the dissenters seemed unimportant to the reverent crowds. Not surprisingly, most protesters stopped of their own accord when they were just ignored, or were perhaps awed by the spirit of togetherness so prevalent in the night.

"This is the Fourth of July come around a second time this year. Ordinary citizens standing up against a strong central government, which they believe to be wrong on this issue. When revolution happened in Central America and Africa, some dismissed it as irrelevant. But now it's in our back yard, folks fighting against the combined might of all branches of the law, with only the three weapons of Faith, Hope that right makes might, and Charity motivating their boldness..."

The third channel was replaying a montage of footage from the past two days, reliving the journey for people on the East Coast who had not been part of the drama:

"...and the nation is dividing bitterly again," the announcer was saying to the backdrop of images, "as it did over Vietnam, and abortion, and Iraq, as to the morality of the issues, this time surplus versus starvation. And dividing over what to do with the lawbreakers, just as we disagreed over the ATF siege and storming of the Branch Davidian compound, creating the Waco massacre. Americans fast become experts with a few broadcasts of the facts, and everyone likes to form strong opinions of what's right and what's wrong. The eyes of the nation will be looking to the west, for this may be Judgment Day in the State of Washington for the so-called *misguided mission of mercy.*

"We understand the decision-makers have been mediating through the night on the best ways of resolving this conflict. Our reporter is standing by at their Seaticon headquarters, but so far there has been no news released by the National Peace Academy negotiator Cussie Cowdrey. Stay tuned..." The last screen darkened.

"So the news hounds are waiting for us," Cassie said. She smiled at the wildness of her new name, but said nothing about the mispronunciation. "I want to keep it *no comment*, as I've been telling them by phone on breaks. Our blue conference pod is sealed off here to outside visitors until seven-thirty. We have way too much more to accomplish together, and I don't want us interrupted by premature news conferences. I trust we are in consensus on media blackout for three more hours?"

And she added that to the list of agreements on Board #6 before they left on their break. She reminded them that their task was to re-energize, and together search for solutions to make all of them winners.

*   *   *

Truly metropolitan cities never sleep. At 4:00 A.M., Seattle was merely resting as the limousine drove through. The car had left the Tukwila estate with its driver and Frank Wayman, who was trying to rouse himself to full alertness after only two hours sleep. Frank had busied himself in the den studying the full wall topographical map of Seattle. He had analyzed the home-theater aerial pictures his host had provided, after saying that he found the Mannheim Grain Elevator more fascinating than any other tourist spot in Seattle for anyone interested in grain trains. Frank had taken the hint of train destination at full face value, considering the source, and scanned all the area within rifle view. He had known what to look for, still feeling that an assassination effort was a dead-certain possibility.

Then he had worked in his host's basement firing range with the FBI-issued Beretta nine-millimeter caliber pistol. The polished semi-automatic held thirteen rounds of firepower in the magazine, plus one in the chamber. After a half-hour it was again Frank's accurate friend.

Now he was dressed as a middle-class transient, neither bad enough to be arrested nor good enough to be mugged, just right to be accepted at a glance, and ignored. They drove circuitously to lose initial tails, then on to the Interstate and north toward downtown. Passing the exit titled *Seaticon*, Frank studied the interesting architectural spectacle of glass and twinkling lights and circling tower. He had seen the facility described as world-class, attracting elite clientele. The large blue room was lighted. Too nice for III to be enjoying, both men agreed. Frank silently prayed for the mediation there to be successful.

They took the next exit, drove several blocks into a warehouse district, then turned slowly into an open garage. The overhead door closed behind them. They moved quickly to a very ordinary blue Honda, and left again through the rear garage door for downtown. Now Frank and the chauffeur had a few relaxed minutes for talking, about family problems and disappointments.

Through the business district, down the steep hill past Pike's Market with fresh fish already being iced, across the railroad tracks then north on Alaskan Way fronting the docks. Because of the peculiar narrowness of the waterfront near Mannheim, it was the only street following the coastline providing business frontages. The steep hillside rose inland from its shoulder up into the Queen Anne area. They doglegged, and with the coming excitement of the train stopping at Mannheim, Frank was certain this Elliott Avenue they now drove would soon be closed or badly clogged. Not a good escape route, so not the choice of a paid assassin who specializes in living to kill another day.

Logically, the houses and woods on Admiral Hill became most suspect as providing both sight line and uncluttered escape. In the light of morning, he planned to check house to house, so he would change to the tie and business suit he had packed in his small suitcase. But in the remaining darkness he would get a feel for the dirty and stubble-faced park sleepers. That way, newcomers in the daylight would be obvious. Unfortunately, his targeted hill was high and his time short.

They continued scouring the district by car to give Frank total familiarity with his new surroundings. The images from the pictures he had studied took on dimension. He discarded some sites he had held as possible shooter bases, and added others. They drove every street back up the hillside overlooking the huge Mannheim grain storage and loading facility.

In the darkness, the job of finding one hidden person seemed overwhelming, much less two or three if they had brought an assassination team. Frank sent up a silent prayer for some sort of a sign.

They parked the Honda a block above the forested Queen Anne Park. The two men watched nothing happen for a few minutes. Frank turned down his driver's offer to stay and cover him, never for a moment doubting the man's claim of being an excellent shot.

When Frank gave a parting handshake and started to get out, the driver surprised him again by saying he would be leaving, not Frank. The Honda would remain at Frank's disposal. At the given signal, another car pulled alongside where they were parked, and the chauffeur left. His Seattle host had done all he could to insure success. It was no wonder their organization had lasted as long as it had. Nor was there any question that they would someday ask him to repay the favors.

*   *   *

"Damn it, Cowdrey, there's no more time for your moral suasion," III spoke angrily. "You see the sun rising out there?"

Cassie had eased the ban on swearing, and also tolerated the use of surnames only. It was too late and too urgent to be arguing over lesser things.

"And I'm not going to give in on the grain issue!" he concluded. "Not a kernel of stolen wheat is going to be loaded. I'll disable the damn machinery first!"

"Over my dead body you will," d'Almeda said, his red aching eyes flashing in anger. And no one doubted him.

"Buchanan, have you backed away from your tight-assed ultimatum?" Cassie was hoping for shock treatment in lowering her standards of communication. But she also was frustrated on the final deadlocks over grain disposition, damage claims, and crew arrest.

"All the kernels go--or energy plants start disappearing again," Tom said unflinchingly. He had not given up all his pieces during the negotiations, and he could still bluff.

"Damn your stubborn hides, emphasizing the plural." Cassie indulged herself in a small outburst. "I can't believe *all* the grain is that important to either one of you!"

Mayor Taulison intervened with a hand raised and a calm voice. "Tom, when we spoke earlier, I thought you said this trip was more about helping the starving and sharing surplus, rather than this train, or these fifty cars of grain. Didn't you say that?"

He was quiet for a moment, then answered thoughtfully. "I may have said that. But if none is shipped, the mission has failed."

"Then what about ten cars, Tom, or one car? One carload of grain to be your symbol? Fifty cars aren't going to save that many lives anyway. You need thousands of thousands to even make a dent."

III spoke then, no less strong, but quieting in tone, perhaps unconsciously following her lead. "Mayor, if even one car is unloaded, then the criminals in our country will take law enforcement as powerless to stop hijackings or bombings. Can't you get that through your head?"

But Cassie had spotted her chance. "Tom, what is your bottom line?" she followed up.

Tom saw it too. There was no sense fighting for ground they didn't need for winning. This mediation had drilled that into him. Compromise was logical, and it worked. "Our bottom line is to wake America up. We can do that by shipping one carload of surplus to the starving."

"Mr. Ravenhead?" Cassie queried of the new offer.

"Not acceptable. The stupid asses can't bargain with stolen goods!"

The minute he said it, he regretted it. It cut him, deep down inside. For he knew he had just opened a screwy logical door to these do-gooding, bleeding-heart liberals.

The room was silent, very unusual since the wee hours of the morning. Had everyone picked up on it, III wondered? He could almost hear the brain waves undulating between them, and didn't even want to hear what dumb thing the first one would utter. "Shall we take a quick break?" he postured. "I'm in need of..."

"No, I think we'll stay together a few more minutes. I feel somebody has a new suggestion to offer." Three hands went up. Cassie thought it might be better coming from someone other than Tom. "Mr. Dunlap?"

The Governor's Lieutenant laid out a scheme for the people on the train to be given the opportunity of buying the grain in one car from its co-op owner.

"But it's illegal to buy transported stolen property..." III protested.

"Even if you buy it from the owner?" Mayor Taulison asked.

"Who would like to call Mr. Fruehauf of the Mid-Western Pacific Railroad?" Cassie asked.

Surprisingly, Tom spoke up. "I will," he said quickly. "We may have enough left in our reserve to do it all, or most of it." Suddenly he remembered that Peter had given it up for Wilma's operation. But conference room activity prevented his speaking out.

"I have a call I need to make also," III said, pushing his chair vigorously away from the ebony table, "recess or not." His director would soon hear about this move. So would the Attorney General of the United States. People paid dearly for antagonizing his team with trivial legal technicalities.

* * *

It would have seemed somewhat odd, a man not shabbily dressed wandering rapidly among sleeping hobos in the Queen Anne Park just before dawn. Odd to anyone paying attention, that this man carrying an old suitcase would walk from one side of the park to the other, each time fifty yards further down the hillside. But no one paid the wanderer any mind. And day broke grayly, with only the birds seeming joyful.

Frank's strategy was to work his way closer to the Mannheim rail yards, thinking the nearer the target, the surer the shot in an assassin's planning. When he got down to First Avenue, he would begin his way back up Admiral's Hill of homes and bushes and trees one mile wide. For now he was making mental notes of those unoccupied park spots that would make perfect shooter nests: hidden from passers-by, a clear view of two hundred yards of track, easy escape. But there were so many.

Frank studied each sleeping person he passed. Stubbly beard? Filthy smelly clothes, not just dirty? Shoes with holes? The park was empty of other walkers down this far. But in the distance he could see the dedicated runners beginning their endurance play along the path.

Marion had asked a sour question last night. Now he realized how wise she was to ask. Should he notify the FBI here of his suspicions? He had dismissed it out of hand then, but it was clarifying his shifting position this morning. He knew III would have contracted for outside help. And if this were the target area, no way FBI would be assigned anywhere near. No, if he were right, there would be no feds around, with or without his call. The local police would be busy along the known rail route in crowd control, so none would be here either to help or hinder.

It was nearly six o'clock. The train could arrive any minute, or it might be another four hours, that is, if their clues had been correctly surmised, and Mannheim in Seattle was Peter's destination.

Frank walked in the stillness toward one of *those spots*. If there wasn't somebody now stationed by the huge moss-laden tree near the blackberry thicket, there could be later, so he'd have to revisit.

But already there was a person. Frank just spotted the blue shirt through the bushes, as the thought flashed by, *there ain't no blue in blackberries*. He allowed a small smile, even as his spine was tightening. He could see the person lying curled on his side, back against the thicket, facing downhill toward the Bay. Frank kept up his quiet walking until he got to the large tree, then stepped behind it and set the suitcase down. He looked all around, spotting no one else moving.

Thinking through his next six movements, he pulled the Beretta from the belt holster under his sweater, and cursed not having a silencer. Frank clicked off the safety, and grasped the gun in both hands. He looked around, took several deep breaths, and boldly stepped from behind the tree, aiming the blued steel weapon straight at a prone man.

He thought he saw the man flinch, but nothing definite. Frank studied hand positions immediately. The left was tucked up under a jacket the man's head rested on, the right down between his legs. Either could conceal a weapon, or a radio to alert another.

Frank walked steadily closer, directly up a thirty-degree angle emanating from the man's middle. Physiological defense classes showed there was no way either of the man's wrists could presently be flexed to have a gun aimed at him inside that narrow angle. The forearm would have to move to take aim, and he would kill the bastard before that could happen.

*   *   *

Chapter Twenty-One

Not a second was wasted as Frank studied the hobo on the ground. Smudged blue shirt but no worn spots. Dirty jeans with kneeholes, could have been from an expensive fad store. Brown shoes scuffed, convincing. But socks were another story. They matched each other, remarkably like the pair Frank had on. The elasticity was still tight. And they were not dirty.

Frank now stood seven feet away from the figure lying there, just out of lunging reach. He had noticed when he looked at the man's face that one eyelid moved, as if squeezing shut from being open a slit. He was awake. It was time to get acquainted.

"If you twitch a muscle, I'll blow two new holes in your face," Frank said, matter-of-factly, pointing his Beretta directly between the man's eyes as they slowly opened wide.

"I'm assuming you have a gun out of sight in each hand. I could kill you, then find out I'm right. Or you can prove me wrong. Very slowly pull your left hand out from under the jacket beneath your head, one finger at a time, while I spell a word. Ready?" The man had not moved.

"D." The little finger of the left hand began to protrude from under the jacket pillow. "E," Frank said, and the ring finger appeared on cue.

"A...T...H." As Frank uttered each letter, another finger showed, until the whole empty hand was exposed. His peripheral vision had never left the hidden right hand. "Now stretch that left hand along the ground straight above your head." Frank studied the man's fingernails in the day's new light. "Dirty, but no prize. No hangnails or split cuticles. Evenly cut. Now that shows someone who cares, don't you think?"

Then Frank instructed the man to repeat the same maneuver with his right hand, as he spelled out *P-E-T-E-R*. "That's the name of the man you came to kill today. Did you even know his name? He's also my son. Are you surprised?" The man didn't change expressions, from what Frank could see of his face with both his arms now raised above his head.

"Next, roll over once toward me, away from your jacket and whatever was in your hands. Do it now!" Frank commanded, emphasizing his words with his automatic.

As the man began to roll, Frank sprang to his left, dodging down past the man's feet in case he tried to kick. But he was docile.

Frank glanced at the vacated ground. Nothing left behind where the man's butt had been. Maybe he was a nobody, keeping his hands warm.

When the man couldn't see Frank, he made a move to get up. "No, no," Frank said sharply, "you're fine stretched out just like that. Matter of fact, why don't you roll over onto your stomach and do a spread eagle so I can search you." The man hesitated. "Or, I can shoot you in the back first..." The man rolled and spread his arms and legs.

Frank took several steps and lifted the jacket, uncovering a shiny brown-handled Colt .45-caliber pistol. He simply shot it with his own weapon, sending pieces bouncing in different directions. The man on the ground turned his head to look back toward the noise, and Frank said, "Grown men shouldn't play with guns. Turn your face away!"

Frank looked around. No one near. Then stepping backward, Frank began walking the perimeter of blackberry brambles, looking back and forth between the man and the bushes. "Where's the damn case?" he muttered softly. "Can't make a case without a case...probably wrapped up in something...there it is." An old Army blanket was folded, and hidden about four feet back into the prickly vines, if he could reach a little further...

Out of the corner of his eye, Frank saw the man's lightning movements rolling over, reaching down, sitting up. That was his mistake. Frank pumped three loud 9mm slugs into the man's chest as the hidden weapon was being drawn. He felt strangely distant watching an unknown cipher topple over backward onto the lawn, in a blue shirt becoming dark red.

Frank glanced around, knelt, and reached again into the bushes to pull out the drab green parcel. He unwrapped it quickly, opened the attaché case that was inside, and looked at the nine pieces of precision metal in their fitted pockets covered with soft gray felt. He looked around again for any intruders, assembled the rifle quickly, snapped on the scope with its deadly cross hairs, closed the case, and carried all his parcels to deposit back at the tree.

He walked down to the body, felt for a pulse on the non-entity he had just created, then pulled him by the arms over to where he had been feigning sleep near the thicket. He was careful to get no blood on his own nicer clothes.

Frank picked up the rifle, held it by the barrel, and swung it heftily against the tree trunk. It shattered loudly into many more than its nine component parts. He saw the scope lying nearby, and walked over to deliberately smash it under his heel.

Then he turned the body on its side and covered it with the Army blanket, leaving the relatively undamaged head uncovered as if still sleeping. The barrel of the rifle was among twigs a few feet away. Frank picked up the black tube of death and flung it as far as he could into the blackberry thatch.

One down, how many more to go? he wondered. At least there had been no radio warning to others. Frank's stride was purposeful as he picked up his bag and resumed the search. But his mind was tortured. "Damn you, Peter, for starting all this," he complained. "And damn you all to hell, my federal security brethren."

*   *   *

"Be sure to have the foreman show you the under-rail beltway and its master switch. That's our speed dump," Mr. d'Almeda said. He had stopped by the Tukwila estate to pick up Marion Wayman and Janet Binghamton on his way to work after leaving the marathon Seaticon mediation early. "If all machinery works smoothly, five cars are unloaded in less than a minute. If not, I fire someone." He really laughed for the first time in hours.

The two women smiled at his joke. They looked like office workers: Marion in a tan suit and heels; Janet in a brightly flowered gingham dress and flats, with her hair pulled to one side in a ponytail. Marion wore prominent unnecessary glasses; Janet sported loose braces on her teeth. At a glance, they did look different from newspaper pictures.

Marion still didn't know logically why they had come. But from the early telecast, she felt they stood a better chance at Mannheim of seeing him. Most train riders would probably be forced off this morning. But if the train got through, Peter would be on it, and they would be there for him. *For him?* she challenged her thoughts, *or with him? What would she do with a criminal she had raised to be a Christian? And where was Frank?* He had slipped away again with only a quiet kiss in the night.

"All non-essential personnel have the day off," d'Almeda went on. "Two desks will be vacant as you enter. Large stacks of filing have been left there, and empty folders have been marked *Miscellaneous* in every file drawer for you to put those documents into."

They drove north past Myrtle Edwards Park, a beautifully kept strip of lawn and flowers and paved path, situated between the railroad tracks paralleling Elliott Drive and waves lapping at a boulder strewn shore.

Janet dreamed of walking there with him. She missed Peter, longed for him. She wanted their rough romance and tumbling emotions to have a chance of soaring. How was that to happen, when she might not even get to hold him before his arrest? How could he act so uncaringly...?

"File deliberately," d'Almeda was explaining, "and it will keep you busy under very watchful eyes. My secretary will answer phones."

The enormous collection of grain elevators loomed skyward as the park ended at the Bay's edge. Two connected rows of eighteen round white storage bins towered two hundred feet. "Up to four million bushels," d'Almeda bragged. Tubes connected their tops to a long enclosed storage gallery and distributor belt feeding into the tallest building of all, the *headhouse* their host called it. From its transfer gallery base another conveyor shaft shot up to the top of the first of five huge steel scaffolds supporting the shipping gallery conveyor out along the dock. The dock platform was broad, surrounded on all four sides by water, connected to the mainland by a wide wooden walkway. Each steel tower's top had one long white snout reaching from the grain conveyor belt back down, almost to Bay level. Here, gravity was king.

The grandiosity of the whole operation made the ladies feel somehow momentarily insignificant. D'Almeda knew those sounds of silence from visitors, and brought their thoughts back to other realities.

"Your new names are on your ID badges. Please answer to those names when called." As they drove into the security check, they noticed that somehow their pictures were also on the cards. This morning there were two guards on each side of the entrance with automatic weapons pointed at them, plus the usual solitary old man who shouted, "Good morning, boss!" and waved them through.

A huge dark freighter was moored to the far side of the dock. Janet read the unusual name on its bow: *Godavari Sunrise*.

*   *   *

Peter snapped awake. He stared a moment into Blackman's face, then turned to look at the man's hand resting on his shoulder. He took several deep breaths, and straightened up with a groan from slouching against the back of the engine cab. "You woke me?"

Blackman smiled. "Governor Archway of the great State of Washington would like to speak with you again." He indicated the phone in his hand.

"How long have I been asleep?"

"It's 6:40 Saturday morning."

"Mmmm," he moaned softly as he moved his stiff bandaged leg carrying the bullet, and reached up an open hand. Blackman handed the cellular phone down to the leader of the pack.

The two men talked briefly, almost casually, then Peter handed back the phone and yawned. "Sounded more like Pilate to me, washing his hands for all to hear. 'No responsibility for what happens,' indeed. What a gutless wonder." Peter's bitterness toward politicians was obvious in his sleepy tones. "Governor Archway is begging us to stop before getting to Seattle," he explained as the men quizzed him further.

"Wonder if that means he knows something we don't about what's waiting there?" Monty questioned. "Course, nobody should know which city for sure yet, unless it came out in the mediation last night."

"So who is in charge of murder around here when it happens?" A.M. asked, sounding worried.

"Somebody like my dad," Peter answered, more serious than snide.

Neither of the engineers commented, nor did the tall NPA mediator near him. Peter stood up to reactivate his muscles. Sharp pain shot from his leg through all parts of his body, and he would have collapsed except for Blackman's fast grab. Now he was acutely aware that much of the medication's numbing effect had worn off. He wondered how clearly he was thinking.

"When are you going to let a doctor take that bullet out?" Blackman asked his hurting new friend.

"From what I've seen of ships' doctors on TV, they're better at making love." That caught them off guard, and they all laughed. "So probably a prison doctor will get the honor."

"From what I've seen of prison doctors on TV, they're better at smuggling prisoners out," Monty threw in, and got another laugh.

"That's not such a bad idea," A.M. added, to general agreement.

"Tom called, just before the governor," Monty spoke up from his chair, "and by the way, it's good to hear you laugh."

"Good morning, everybody. Good morning, world!" Peter shared a greeting, trying to lift his own fog that matched the gray mist outside.

The slow clicking of rails beneath them, and the lack of jostling let him know without asking that they were traveling only about five miles an hour. "Well, how did Tom think the mediation was going?"

"He said there had been a possible breakthrough," Blackman answered enthusiastically. "He's working on buying one carload of grain to legalize it..."

"...but he also wants us to stop the train now, to give him more talking time," Monty finished. "Otherwise, the mediation team will be making their final decisions, and adjourn. They each have to go get ready to do their own thing with us."

"What do you think about stopping to talk, Monty?" Peter asked, double-checking his own decision.

"Times like this I used to say, 'Katy, bar the door!'" He grinned at some memory.

Peter knew they were in synch. "We'll go straight on through then. I'll call Tom..."

"If you ask me..." Blackman interrupted.

"But I didn't," Peter clarified, unusually blunt. "A.M., where are we?"

"We're just now leaving Tacoma. Next town is Puyallup, in about fifteen minutes," A.M. answered, anticipating Peter's thoughts.

"Monty, whistle short five or six times to get the boxcars' attention. I'll get our farmers on the radio, and have them start quizzing their riders on who doesn't want to be arrested. I figure we'll keep last night's plan and drop off everybody with wet feet on the other side of Puyallup in a three-minute stop. No more meeting and greeting them, though. Too many strangers." He looked at his watch, and thought of his grandfather. "You got seven o'clock, Jerome?" wanting to start them conversing again without having to apologize.

"Yep. You going to call Tom first?" He was still pushy.

"I probably should run my numbers first, discouraging or not. Thanks for reminding me," Peter smiled, nudging Blackman's arm as he needled him. He tried every coded phone number for the Shakespeare Group, except one. Only Chanto picked up, to say in code that he was trapped. *Mr. Diplomatic Immunity* couldn't move.

Then Peter called Tom, who immediately excused himself from camera view in order to hold caucus. "I have left our fate in the hands of you and the Lord Almighty," Peter began. "How's your half of the team doing?"

While he spoke with Tom, Peter had asked Blackman to discuss their plans with the farmers, and make his personal *exit for peace* appeal.

Minutes later, Peter changed his mind. They stopped the train at the clean little depot right in Puyallup, as they had been stopping through the night and his exhausted slumber. Only seventeen left the train for assorted reasons, and nineteen more climbed aboard. Their accumulated numbers totaled 193, plus two comrades in coffins. The motley group had become a sizable force to be reckoned with fairly, Peter kept hoping.

*   *   *

The Seaticon prolonged session came to an end, as do most complex mediations, with some consensus agreements and some stubborn unresolved issues. The enormous property damages did not go away, and major surplus policy shifts did not occur.

The exhausted participants departed well past dawn with no sleep, each to their own strenuous area of continuing crisis. The remaining details would have to work themselves out with many more players publicly involved, for the next mediation was scheduled for whenever the train arrived at Mannheim Grain Elevators in Seattle.

*   *   *

It was going to be one of those no-holds-barred news days, for the nation was tuned into Seattle. One editor said that if the White House could have had one wish that Saturday morning, it would be having Elvis back for a verified sighting and singing news conference--in Florida.

The two helicopters carrying the wrung-out Denver crews from KDNC and TV-Channel 5 were bucking all outside attempts to control their pre-emptive flight patterns, just as they had fought their way through the four previous States. They said they would have to be shot down before they would relinquish their *track air rights*, a new term in media jurisprudence.

The small planes used for Seattle and Tacoma weekday traffic reporting were airborne on a weekend, rare except for game days, but now flying thirty miles south or north of any mild 7:10 A.M. vehicular congestion in their respective cities, covering the 9039 story.

Reporters of every ilk clambered aboard the creeping train to get rider stories for their tabloids and national news syndicates. The affixed warning signs on the engine catwalks did little to deter enterprising journalists from trying to get into the cab. So Monty and Blackman had become door guards to control the number of interviewers to two at a time getting inside to see

Peter, then bouncing those so the next two would have room to get in. Peter wished he knew how Wilma would have handled it. At least the Wray farmers were loving it, and the story was getting out to more people.

*   *   *

Scaffolding for a three-platform stage was hastily being constructed at the paved northern part of the Mannheim yards. The media plan was that the train side rail would head straight for the platform next to the tracks, with the Seattle skyline behind on their left, and the dock with its freighter loading from the steel statuary on their right. That way the cameras would catch all the action, and Mannheim had surprisingly agreed at 2:00 A.M. to help, after the anonymous tip to all major networks. Nothing would be missed of the final chapter in the Grain Train's infamous August run.

With the help of Seaticon technicians and National Peace Academy influence with the networks, a remote studio van was on the way across town to Mannheim. Video screen and satellites would again link all players in the final moves.

There were some substitutions. III was out of the mediation phone dialogue loop, along with his director; the U.S. Attorney General was in. Colorado Senator Frye was out, period. The Administration would have the Secretary of the Interior standing by to speak to the unresolved issues of changing farm surplus policies.

Tom deferred to Peter as spokesperson for the Group. Washington's Lt. Governor Dunlap had been asked to stay as an observer, but Governor Archway himself would be on the line. Mayor Taulison would represent Seattle interests and ordinances. Mannheim stayed with d'Almeda; Mid-Western Pacific remained in Fruehauf's unsoiled hands.

*   *   *

An industrious bank in suburban Renton saw the golden goose flapping by, and captured it through advertising. The bank president bought ad-liners to run at the bottom of TV screens every half-hour on network channels, and fifteen-second spots were read on major radio stations:

"Want to help rescue a child from starvation? Want to play a part in keeping an American farmer out of jail? You can do both with your contribution to U.S.A.S. today. Bail the Grain Train out of trouble. E-mail us your deposit or call in your credit card amount. Operators are standing by. Hurry!"

Special tellers were already averaging $300 a minute. And cars were lined up two blocks for the drive-in deposit windows.

Some fire stations had responded spontaneously as with the Labor Day campaign for Jerry's Kids. Trucks with flashing lights were parked at intersections, and the firemen in yellow flame-retardant suits were holding the big rubber boots for cash donations from passing motorists.

Another newscaster opined, "At this rate, they'll soon have enough money to buy *all* the grain, and the *train!* Now there's an idea."

*   *   *

The Washington State Patrol was battling near gridlock in smaller communities as people just stopped their cars at railroad crossings to wait for the train, sometimes up to a half-hour. Traffic on State Highway 167 was dangerously snarled, with people parking on shoulders and walking to railroad overpasses for a glimpse, and traffic then slowing to a crawl for safety, and a look for themselves. In another hour, Interstates 5 and 405 would be similarly wiped out.

With the Governor's approval, the Patrol sent in a request to Commander Guinn as he was leaving Seaticon to call out immediate National Guard help along a 25-mile stretch of six different highways bordering the likely tracks. They wanted people in military uniform within one hour stationed along 99, 900, 599, and 519, plus along the major vehicle carriers of Interurban, Marginal, and Airport Way. Besides, of course, the final leg: Alaskan Way and Elliott Avenue.

One other talk-show disc jockey said to a mystified caller, "Buddy, if you don't know about the Grain Train, you either don't have electricity, or you're an alien!"

*   *   *

Agent Switzer drove the white G-12 licensed car past the guards with a flourish of three fingers of his left hand. Disregarding the Mannheim parking lot, he pulled up to the front door of the office building and double-parked. The chief of the Seattle FBI office exited from the front seat passenger side, III stepped aristocratically from the back. Finally he was away from the Seaticon mediation turf of forced equality. Here on the real battleground, he intended to regain command.

An identical G-12 auto parked nearby, and four more agents climbed out, heading for various parts of the complex. Uniformed Seattle police were already a prominent force, many with motorcycles to help cover the fenced ten-acre site. Three prison buses parked near the tracks; more school buses were being commandeered.

Inside the offices, III walked briskly past the two women at the outer desks with barely a glance. He was intent on reaching the obvious *Executive Secretary*, asserting his authority, and getting one-on-one with Mr. d'Almeda in the closed office. Marion recognized him from upper echelon pictures Frank had shown her. But she didn't say anything to Janet, since the man's driver was coming toward her with card in hand.

Mr. d'Almeda's office was comfortable, but obviously intended for work and cost cutting, as the two men met again.

"Here's how it sorts out, d'Almeda." III then demanded that the *Godavari Sunrise* immediately stop loading and leave, and that no other ships dock until the train matter was settled. Under no circumstance was hijacked cargo to be unloaded, much less shipped. III would give the order to the ship's captain, to insure prompt departure.

"On my company's private property, guests are free to talk with whomever they wish, who want to talk with them," d'Almeda snorted gruffly. "This differs from some jurisdictions." The pointed barb did not go unnoticed. "So you may request permission of Captain Pradesh to go aboard his *Sunrise* and talk, since there you'll be on foreign soil. However, I will notify him as soon as you leave my office that he is free to stay until he finishes loading, no matter what threats you may make."

He held up a hand to stop III's rejoinder. "I haven't finished my statement, Ravenhead. And I didn't interrupt yours."

III fumed at the leftover rule from mediation, but forced himself to remain silent, hoping the forceful supervisor would hang himself.

"We run a successful international exporting business. The president himself always finds time to call when he's in town. So don't try to bully my buyer. He'll leave when he's loaded, and that's after the machinery is repaired, and we can finish the order."

"Convenient, like a truck breaking down in front of a bank just before the holdup."

"Are you charging me with a crime?" d'Almeda bluntly asked.

"Not yet."

"Then shut the fuck up!"

III vowed to himself to make this man and this operation his next target.

He left abruptly, signaling Switzer with one angry glance to break away from visiting at the desk of the pretty girl with the ponytail.

As Switzer pulled the car away and sped toward the docked ship, he told III, "I don't think that young lady is who she says she is."

"Later," was all III replied.

"Yes, sir," Switzer obeyed, taking in a deep breath of the sea breeze instead of sharing his suspicions. He was nothing if not instantly obedient, when his irritated boss issued an order.

*   *   *

"Mr. Wayman," the voice filled with gravel said over the phone in the rolling engine, "my name is Cassandra Cowdrey. Call me Cassie. I'm the mediator designated by the National Peace Academy because I'm damn good. Tom Buchanan has communicated very clearly on behalf of your group, and negotiated strongly all night. He speaks highly of your leadership, and asks to pass the torch now that you're in the neighborhood. May I count on you to listen carefully, speak thoughtfully and considerately, and accept the premise that win-win solutions are our mutual goals?" She finally took a breath.

"Sounds like you have a Bible waiting there for me to swear on, Cassie," Peter answered the husky cellular voice. He didn't laugh, but she did. Tom was listening intently to insure she got the facts right.

"I appreciate occasional humor, Peter. We also need to say on track, pardon the pun."

Peter beat her to the laugh this time. "That's exactly what we're trying to do in our fifth State, Cassie. Glad to have your help." He casually tried sucking her in.

"I remain neutral, Mr. Wayman. My job, you know. Are you traveling with your metal shields up right now?"

That caught him by surprise. "No, ma'am, they're down, and we're waving at the crowds. They seem mighty friendly."

"Well, that's dandy, if your mission is grandstanding. However, if it is to reach the Mannheim Grain Elevators alive, I would strongly suggest that you put them back up at once."

It was the first time Peter had heard their destination stated so specifically and publicly by an outsider. It sent him into awkward silence. "Tom?" he asked of the only other known person on the line.

"I told them last night." Short, pointed, not bothering with the detail that they had known early enough to invite the manager to the meeting.

"No more time for games, or playing the talk-show guest, Mr. Wayman," Cassie cut into the unspoken recriminations. "You now have the *creme de la creme* in your special interest area, waiting to be clicked into this conversation. You also have the keys to preventing violence here today, Mr. Wayman. Are you ready to give your undivided attention to discuss using those keys?"

"Discuss, yes. But this has never been a game for us, Cassie."

"My bad choice of phrase, sorry. Here we go then." And the caucus immediately double-clicked into a conference call replete with decision-making power. The still youthful college student in Peter was amazed during the introductions, repeating the names aloud for the men in the cab, and watching their eyes bug out in disbelief also.

Peter left the shields down. It was the people of America they were trying to reach, and those people were right outside. Reporters continued to be escorted into the engine cab's interior, but as observers only, hearing but one occasional side of the eight-way conversation. The man Peter had become on the journey was back, so critical subjects were dealt with quickly and decided, or tabled for later, of which there remained precious little time.

One intractable item bit the dust: property damage would be left up to the courts to decide the fitting restitution.

Another mile passed under the train, then two, as they debated multiple criminal charges against Monty and Peter. Those two men held a short muffled conference in the cab while Peter listened in the other ear to what the Attorney General was iterating about her Constitution. Then Peter nodded at his engineer, like a pitcher agrees with his catcher's signals, and waited for a break. He spoke with utter finality into the phone.

"We will agree to arrest without resistance or retaliation, under condition that the spirit and intent of our nation's laws will be debated in court, probably numerous times with appeals, with the people watching on television, and with full opportunity to explain what forced us to take such desperate steps. Then juries of our peers will determine our innocence or guilt. Let God and fate take their courses."

Cassie breathed her sigh of relief in the telecommunications van parked next to the tracks in the Mannheim yards. She checked that item off the list by writing 'NFD'--no further discussion. The other decisions on arrests stood firm: locals get off the train with no charges when it stops; Wray farmers arrested and charged, then allowed to leave on recognizance, with light sentencing already agreed; A.M. and Blackman respectively getting

FBI and NPA observer status.

The train had reached Tukwila, the edge of the Seattle metropolitan area, the beginning of even worse traffic nightmares.

As mediation continued, reporters coming into the cab were bringing news of not just streets but major highways completely immobilized by the gawking public. At least that part of the public that wasn't jumping onto the train for the ride of the century. They kept coming, up into the already crammed boxcars, or onto the ladders at the ends of each grain car, and even up onto the tops of the cars. Now the crew could not speed up for any reason, or stop suddenly, without risking critical injuries.

Peter asked Monty to call Harran, and request the final side rail switch--into the Mannheim complex, at the very edge of the deep channel to the Pacific Ocean. They were so close. Peter asked for a ten-minute recess in the mediation, needing time to put things together. He knew the leaders of this State and nation would expect him to give up more ground, but he would hold onto his beliefs in the rightness of this cause.

*   *   *

The distant scene was incredibly tranquil. Huge orange mechanical cranes seemed to be stalking the waterfront, as if searching the shallows for more bright containers to lift in their beaks. They formed a sharp-angled skyline all their own from the level of the engine cab window. Graceful bridges arched in the distance, connecting Seattle with Bremerton. The Olympic Mountains were in plain view off to the west across the Bay, some higher peaks still snowy.

Behind the train, as it wound now to the left, Peter saw Mount Rainier rising majestically in isolation, a huge cone mostly snow covered, offering towering strength. He confirmed to himself that the motives and image of this Grain Train were every bit that strong.

Peter gave up a moment of the present to think about the past, of what he would have done differently in his planning. He would not have assumed that the five-second hourly calls to Ruth and Chanto would go untraced over time, nor would he have assumed that four nobodies could make flight reservations under their own names and not be traced to their destination cities. He would not have brought the group together in an identified campus club for convenience, only to be easily linked with pictures and ID early in the trip, nor would he have taken the lead shields down from the cab windows until now. But he would still have made the run.

Their designated track threaded through the maze past the King County Airport, so reasonably named Boeing Field. That giant corporation lined the perimeter of the airstrip with dozens of office and research buildings and hangars, and many more of their large plants dotted the region. *Boeingland* was still home to thousands of employees continuing work on Defense Department contracts, despite the improved East-West relations and winding down of several wars, and in spite of GAO lawsuits over sub-standard parts and the massive engineering layoffs after the turn of the century and the recession. This politically-sensitive management, and those they influenced, would certainly not welcome a trainload of anti-government lawbreakers.

The spiny silver clamshell topping the Kingdome came into view. They would pass within a stone's throw of that great sports center. Peter's mouth was dry. He wished this trip was only for a Kingdome game, then he took back his wish. They slowed even more as the myriad of tracks approached the waterfront of Elliott Bay and its business district. It would take another hour to go the last four miles.

Mediation had resumed, but Peter's attention to the bickering on the phone was interrupted again by the throngs of people lining the tracks while youngsters played chase through their legs. How far would they ride when they hitched? What would they do at the end of the line? Peter knew he was also excited by their arrival, and by the sights in the Pacific Northwest's colossus. His attention wandered, his head hurt, his leg throbbed. *Just let me unload the grain*, he thought*, and hug Janet. This is such a pretty place....*

The skyscrapers of Seattle clustered tightly, beginning their growth scant blocks from water's edge and rising precipitously from the steep hillsides. Several high-rises were under construction, a sight typical during recent years. The Space Needle hourglass of aluminum stood tall and naked shiny to their right, isolated from the other structures, a 1962 World's Fair monument. It was so close they saw people in the little elevators crawling up the side of the massive shaft to the flying saucer top. Peter was very glad that Tom had argued him out of its ordered bombing.

From elevated Highway 99, which races between the glassy steel towers and the aging wooden docks, the smell of fish and ocean was the strongest. This roadway parallels the tracks, and that was the reason this particular Saturday morning for the remarkable traffic jam. Car drivers were gawking out their windows at the newest attraction in town, just arrived: a first-ever hijacked Grain Train. They were slowing to almost crawl speed on the

65 mph freeway, as they always did down on Marginal Way when a huge aircraft carrier tied up for shore leave. Peter's nerve endings shot up to keen edges with the sight of hundreds of National Guard troops working the highway problems on both sides of the train--all within rifle shot, and all trained in the use of government-issued firearms.

*   *   *

Chapter Twenty-Two

Frank wished he had hours more, or a photographic memory. He needed to go down to the train tracks at the grain elevator and look back up at this Admiral Hill. Which houses had upper stories clearing the tree line enough to offer a shot? He couldn't remember which ones out of the hundreds.

But by now the Mannheim yards were swarming with detectives of all flavors. Traffic had already started to bottleneck, even under police direction at intersections. So he was stuck up on the killing hill, limited to his sight and second-guessing.

Frank had swept the large Queen Anne Park once, bagging one. Then he changed in the Honda to white shirt, tie, and cardigan to canvas the homes he had picked from pictures and his chauffeured nighttime tour. He had brazenly shown his ID card, covering the name with one finger and using an alias, and hurriedly paraded into every room with a western exposure. The panoramic views would have been breathtaking, and some of the bedroom scenes memorable, given time and inclination.

When he left each inspected home, finding nothing suspicious, he asked one question: "Who else in the neighborhood has a view this spectacular of the Mannheim Dock?" Then he closed with a warning that the bureau would closely investigate anyone who tattled about his visit, plus instructing the I.R.S. to run an audit of their tax returns!

One hour and eight homes later, he had turned up absolutely nothing, and had a list of dozens of other addresses with great views. The transistor radio he had brought announced that the Grain Train was leaving Tukwila, but running north only at crawl speed. He made their E.T.A. at the dock as 9:30. Thirty minutes away. Thirty ridiculous minutes to find a needle with a rifle in the haystack.

He sat down on a bus bench to decide where to search next. The sun poured down on him as he looked out at the blue body of water fed from

Puget Sound. Somehow it reminded him of a commercialized Lake Tahoe, where he loved to go fishing. Bitten with that memory, his decision was made instantly. Back to the park! Back to the fishing hole where he had been lucky before, like any good fisherman would do.

Four minutes spent in jogging to the blue Honda, sweater and tie in hand to not be totally conspicuous. Change clothes back to leisure-hobo, then implement his new strategy: check out the three spots that felt prime when he found them earlier. Following his instincts, he began jogging toward the southern end, the closest, with a tote bag of his weapons, ID, and binoculars.

*   *   *

At the northern end of the park named after Queen Anne, a man walked alone, casually dressed and wearing a light windbreaker, stiff-legged on the left side, using a cane. His long gym bag was stuffed and bulging. He seemed to have no particular destination, ambling generally in the direction of a small heavily wooded rise just a half-block from the street, but well away from the beaten pathways.

He was a very ordinary looking man, except for the long gash closed with new stitches pulling the right side of his face down toward his chin, which he made no effort to hide. He touched this souvenir of a very recent accident in Idaho, recalling the spray truck on which he had been riding to a job left undone.

*   *   *

"Mr. Ravenhead," Captain Pradesh said in heavily accented English. "I respect you as an American citizen, an officer of law, and a fellow human being. May I ask, are you also fully cognizant of maritime law?"

"Fairly, I'd say." III knew he was a bush leaguer, but at least he had gotten up there to the second level of this stacked building on the freighter's stern. He had been escorted ceremoniously by a number of the crew to the seaward side walkway. There the Captain, rigged up in his starched white medal-bedecked uniform, had been standing at the rail, studying the Bay's ship traffic with binoculars.

"Interestingly," the captain continued, "a ship--any ship--even this ship has been characterized as an island nation. And I, the captain--am of all things, the president, the reigning monarch, the absolute dictator, Il Duce, the tribal chieftain. My word is law, on board this ship."

"You are in American waters, a guest..." III challenged.

"We are, nonetheless, a most sovereign extension of our foreign nation," the captain reaffirmed. A gull circled squawking near them in the light breeze. And the foghorn of the large Spirit of Puget Sound ferry blew its noisy entrance to the docks a half-mile south of them.

"A criminal is on his way here, and will possibly attempt to make you an accomplice in this train hijacking," III chose his firm words with care, as if dealing with a dark-skinned peer. "To avoid breaking any of our laws while tied up to an American dock, and to prevent an international incident which might jeopardize your ability to ever return, as well as future trade with our country, I suggest you cast off immediately."

"And should I give that order now, would you therefore journey with us as a guest on our voyage?"

"No, of course not. I meant after I get off."

"Then you should more precisely say what you mean, Mr. Ravenhead. Misunderstanding is a veritable bane to our civilization."

"Then you will leave without further adieu?" III ignored the slight.

"Please, what is this uh-dew?" the captain quizzically asked.

"Uh, let's just say, before the train arrives?"

"Certainly."

III nodded his satisfaction at the favorable gentlemen's agreement just struck.

"We will begin our preparations--just as soon as our holds are filled with the cargo for which we came."

Frustrated again, III inquired, "And just how soon is that?"

"You would have to speak with Mr. d'Almeda on that subject."

The only thing missing was the whistling calliope music to make the merry-go-round feeling complete for III. He looked out to sea, then back at the imperturbable ship's officer.

"I could arrest you, Captain Pradesh, and all your crew, for conspiracy to commit a crime." III was forced into his brashest corner.

"Oh, possibly. But not from your position on the hidden side of our aft deck. Here you are alone with the sea, and all those you just threatened. None of your friends--agents, I believe--can see you here."

In a moment of insanity, III reached inside his suit coat. The very audible clicking of numerous weapons into firing readiness bounced off the steel walls of the cabin housing and floated out over the water toward the islands. III stood utterly immobile.

"Did I mention, Mr. Ravenhead of the FBI, that our radio operator is practicing this very moment to keep his satellite relay skills current? He is listening on this device..." and the captain touched the small bar on his left collar, "...and beaming this conversation to our embassy in your own Washington, D.C., to avoid any unfortunate misunderstandings."

III studied his environment a moment, then nodded at his hand still inside his coat and asked, "May I?"

"Certainly," the captain responded. "You have not risen to your level of importance by building on stupidity."

III slowly slid his open hand out into view.

"If you know what's good for you," III said slowly, enjoying the words, "you will leave, and never come back."

"Oh, ditto, I believe you say," the captain quickly retaliated. "Your visa has just expired here, making you *persona non grata*, whatever that means. In any case, please go away."

III turned to leave, feeling it prudent with this audience to make no more speeches. Not so the captain. "Oh, Mr. Ravenhead. Know this fact doubly well. If any unauthorized hand lays hold of our mooring hawsers, or attempts to board this vessel again, we will consider it an act of aggression, and take appropriate steps to defend our property and persons, and our nation. Am I clear as a bell, sir?"

III was just about to turn the corner, under guard, when he answered, "A cracked one."

The captain inquired of his comment.

"I said, our Liberty Bell is a cracked one." III took one last fling at blending insult with patriotism, before being escorted clearly at gunpoint to the long gangplank. He motioned his anxious agents to hold their fire.

Minutes later, Ravenhead stepped in to interrupt the mediation dialogue being coordinated in the media van. Cassie listened in astonishment as he described his version of the *Godavari Sunrise* ultimatum to the U.S. Attorney General. In short order, III had undone much of the goodwill and several tenuous settlements earlier won by losing sleep in the Chess Room at Seaticon.

*   *   *

Failing to find anyone occupying the first perfect site, Frank started jogging toward the middle of the park. He intently studied every person within eyesight as he moved, looking for anything out of order in the image they were supposed to be. Even one couple necking under a tree had halted him to jog in place to watch the kiss. They were not role-playing.

When within a hundred yards of the second site, Frank allowed himself idling time as he approached the place of suspicion. He didn't want to make a beeline right down the muzzle of a gun. Trees and bushes provided some cover, but it was the small 8' x 8' shed that held his attention. He knew from his earlier pass that there was a little barred window overlooking the bay.

His hackles rose again as he walked slowly toward the door in the back with the ancient "Keep Out" sign. Then he stopped abruptly, and knelt to tie a shoe that wasn't undone. A young man in sweats puffed past, waving at the kneeling stranger, much like Peter would do.

They won't get my son--not without a helluva fight, Frank silently vowed. That strange acronym came to mind: T.E.J.T.M. The words and philosophy his son hated because his father lived by them. But now Peter had come 1,500 destructive miles using them. And now Frank was justifying murder by them: The End Justifies The Means!

The jogger was far past. Frank looked around one final time, drew the Beretta pistol from the bag, and stood up. Taking two deep breaths in and out, he strode four quick paces to the side of the door. The twig he had placed on the lock was gone. Wind, or...? He shot the lock into smithereens, kicking open the door and dodging to the side. The expected volley of shots didn't happen.

Frank whipped his head around the frame and instantly back out. No sign of anything but tools, and a cleared area in front of the door.

Into that spot Frank jumped, turning in mid-air to face the rear of the shack and behind the door. No one there. The breath he expelled was very audible. He went back out, replaced his weapon in the bag, then pulled a twenty-dollar bill out of his wallet to leave as payment for the lock.

His second thought was better. A shooter could still come here after he left. He spotted the kerosene can, and within seconds had splattered the fluid around the old shed. He stepped out, lit a match and touched off the flames. Maybe the FBI had declared the park off-limits, but not the Seattle Fire Department. He needed some extra people disturbing the peace up here, he decided, jogging urgently away toward the north end, looking everywhere as he ran.

*   *   *

The man with the stitched sagging cheek turned and saw black smoke rising a quarter-mile away to the south, in the center of the park. He idly wondered regarding its origin, and whether green trees in coastal cities burn. Then he returned to his task of pulling the camouflage blanket over himself. In the dense undergrowth of the hillside he would become another bush, his rifle and tripod just more branches. The Mannheim Grain Elevators lay unimpeded directly down the slope in front of him.

He turned the dial on the powerful sighting scope. The brown and white pigeon filled the eyepiece, feeding on the mixed kernels of yellow corn and brown wheat spilled between the two tracks of rail. One downy feather was loose in his right wing, and would surely drop off when the bird flew away after its breakfast. Or sooner, if interrupted before that by a train coming in on those Mannheim side rail tracks.

*   *   *

Wind put whitecaps on Elliott Bay. The large body of water rolled with even waves as Peter gazed out the left window of the engine, Fork's window.

The sky incredibly was cloudless, a coastal rarity. Jagged white teeth of the Olympics Range rose high above Bainbridge Island with its base of blue waters. Peter studied the seascape, consciously absorbing the beauty of it as if through the eyes of his absent friends.

"We're almost there, Wilma," he mumbled low under the engines' whine. "I can see the gulls circling for food. A few cormorants are floating around. Hey, there's a pelican standing on shore rocks.

"Fork," he smiled, "there's a big freighter sitting out there. She's so high out of the water that half of her pink rudder shows. You would have made some kind of joke out of that, I'm sure."

They passed the square red brick Old Spaghetti Factory on the right, and next to it a Shakey's Pizza. Monty kept one eye on the tracks, but glanced at the big city sights also. He had not heard Peter's words, but was thinking along the same lines. Monty remembered their last meal, when all four of them were together in the cab, scheming the vision.

Peter saw the old Port of Seattle building on Pier 67 newly remodeled, the sign said, for use as a luxury hotel. The new Port Authority Headquarters was Pier 69, gray-sided, turquoise-glassed, pilings painted.

A small cruise ship loading a line of travelers occupied northernmost Pier 70. "Always pleasure first," Peter said, pointing it out to A.M., who in turn pointed out the Waterfront Trolley garage, signaling the end of the line for that primary tourist attraction. "Or the beginning," an optimistic Peter rephrased.

Then came their first clear view of the Mannheim white towers seeming to soar up ten stories high out of the water. The long top shed connecting them was anchored back to the mainland by a hundred sloping feet of enclosed chute. These coastal elevators were not part of the surplus problem, receiving only grain that had already been sold for shipment.

Suddenly a white and gray gull flew close beside the engine window, carrying in its beak a small crab with claws still thrashing. "It's a hard life for all God's creatures," Peter breathed. Monty only nodded.

Some people kept jogging along the waterfront path down the line of land separating the train and the slapping waves, which the sign proclaimed "Myrtle Edwards Park." But most stopped to join the crowd of waiting watchers. This train's arrival had turned into a picnic event on a beautiful day. The long strip of green grass had become the ringside seat of the rumored finale of the cross-country excursion. For at the end of this park was the fence surrounding the Mannheim grounds.

Some in the crowd were asking, why this distribution point, instead of Portland, or Tacoma, or Vancouver? But no one had the answer. All they saw was a train approaching, covered with people like a New Mexico storyteller clay sculpture, and the nearby array of waiting law officers.

In the cab, Monty looked again at his wounded friend, who smiled and nodded a weary agreement. Monty radioed dispatch, "This is 9039, requesting immediate switch of rail into the Mannheim Grain Elevator station. We'll be a while here...no, in fact, we're stopping. Resume regular scheduling when we're inside."

After a moment, Harran radioed back, "Roger, 9039. It's been real. See you at the 19th Hole, Peter. Just holler out, 'Hail, fellow...'" His voice cracked.

Peter took the mike and finished for him, "'...well met.' Listen up one last time, railroad, and Feds: Harran Winfree is guilty only of being my friend, and a skilled dispatcher in an emergency. He is very innocent of any complicity with my actions. Over and out."

"Can you believe the trip is over?" Monty asked as Peter was putting his ear back to the ongoing phone mediation.

Peter only nodded a slow yes several times as he limped to the rear door. He looked behind them at the towering Mt. Rainier, still pushing distant clouds aside on its way to the high sky. "This is one spectacular shot for the media, Wilma," he said to her memory. Then he turned and looked ahead on the tracks to the gauntlet of photographers lining the tracks. "Your hour has come, for you helped get us here."

Monty continued to slow the train, and touched Peter's arm, pointing up to the right. They were passing the *Post Intelligencer* newspaper building with a large green and blue earth spinning on top, with script lettering reading "It's in the P.I." around it. "That's our one small world, my friend."

"Let's hope the people got the message, compadre." Then he added, "I still can't help looking for people on the rooftops."

Both men looked up at empty roof ledges. Peter's eyes were drawn back to the globe, then beyond it to a steep hillside. Some homes lodged there, but it was mostly trees. A park--or a hiding place for another sniper. He shook his head to clear away the morose thought.

"Yes, Cassie," he spoke into the phone. "I'll radio that procedure to the boxcar farmers. But understand they may not be able to make themselves heard. It's getting pretty noisy down here. Besides, they can't speak to all those outside on the cars. You'll have to find another way."

An unusually big wave broke on the shore fifty feet away, sending white spray high over the rocks. The back row of watchers let out squeals of surprise. Two seagulls sailing overhead shrieked at each other. The train slowed even further, then meekly followed the switched rails leading away from the main line it had followed for a thousand and another half-thousand miles.

Forward went the 9039, with its three strong helper engines now silent, then the six spray-painted and tomato-smacked, crepe-draped and bunting-bedecked, banner-flapping and rider-cheering boxcars, on through the opened gate into Mannheim. The fifty cars of wheat grain followed, one by one pulling the next inside the tall chain link security fence, which normally kept the curious public out. Except for those persons who now filled every square foot inside the boxcars, and climbed onto every rail car ladder during the last few Seattle miles. Five hundred free loaders created the logistic problem now being discussed, even as gates swung quickly shut behind the red freddie on the tail end of the last grain car.

"Stay on the train until it stops. Then move in orderly fashion to the nearest school bus waiting on either side of the train. Only those who boarded the train in Denver should stay on the train. I repeat..."

The amplified message rolled across the yards, through the boxcars and over them. The familiar yellow school buses waited along the side rail, idling away more diesel fumes than the one working engine passing them. They had arrived in the last hour with the help of motorcycle escort, negotiated through mediation. Officers stood at ease, waiting for the train to stop as agreed.

Then the brakes screeched on almost a thousand steel pads as they gently met their neighboring wheels in one last moment of friction. The clanging of car couplings filled the air. Mr. d'Almeda had said there would be a red line sprayed across the rails at their stopping point. The nose of the 9039 now rested on it. In the cab, Monty reached over and shook A.M.'s hand as a fellow engineer who had proven himself again worthy.

"You may now disembark carefully," the loudspeaker voice instructed repeatedly. Soon it changed to, "It is safe to get off now." Neither message worked. Only a few riders jumped off. And when they saw that almost everyone was staying, they climbed back on board themselves.

Mayor Taulison shot a worried look at Police Chief Simonet, standing near his command car, as she continued to hold the negotiation phone to her ear. Where was the mass exodus they expected? And how do you get women, children, and men out of boxcars and off grain car tops, if they don't want to leave? Tear gas would be a catastrophe on live television. And the thirty or so media reps flowing off the platform near the lead engine assured that red active lights were flashing on those cameras.

The mayor took a few steps and leaned into the communication van to ask Cassie for a five-minute caucus break. Cassie debated the benefits of interrupting for consultation versus breaking momentum, and decided it wouldn't hurt. Anyway, she wanted to meet Peter. So she asked the phone team to reconvene at 10:00 A.M., Pacific Daylight Time.

Then she stepped from the van, stretched, looked into the sun and around the blue sky, and walked smartly the fourteen steps to the left cab window of Engine 9039. "Mr. Wayman?" she called up.

Peter came to the window and looked down. "That's a familiar voice," he exclaimed. "You must be the better half of the National Peace Academy team." Blackman joined him at the window, and greeted her with a warm, "Good morning, Cass!"

She let out a good laugh. "Well, sir, at least we are a wee small part of that team, still trying to be of service in this predicament. May I bring myself and my phone up to your borrowed domain?"

Peter liked her style. "Come ahead, there's just enough room." And he gladly stepped back into the interior, having felt nervous being at that window.

III watched in disgust from his own car a short distance away. He dialed a familiar number, discussed a suggestion with his boss, then listened as the connection was linked to the Attorney General's Office.

Those three persons hastily agreed to order d'Almeda quietly to divert his ground conveyor lines, so that no actual grain from the train would reach the active elevators. The freighter would finish loading as fast as possible from existing supplies, then leave. A win-win solution, as D.C. saw it: the ship gets a full load delivered by the elevator, per agreement; even if one grain car is unloaded, no stolen grain leaves the continent. They also agreed not to mention this new arrangement to Peter or Cassie.

Those two parties were just shaking hands on their rapid understanding of his newly mediated agreement: unload one grain car as a token, and give time for it to reach the ship, then allow the ship to not only leave but insure that it reach its destination without interference at sea. All Coloradoans would turn themselves over to the custody of the federal marshals, to be arraigned for a trial early scheduled. And when Peter left, the train could be speedily evacuated without violent incident, for the show would be over.

Cassie reconnected all mediation participant channels from the cab, and began by saying that Mr. Wayman had a revised proposition. But after he presented it, she was totally unprepared for the immediate acquiescence by everyone. Something had gone on that changed too much chemistry of the previous recalcitrant interaction. From the questioning look that Blackman gave her, she knew he was suspicious also.

However, a cardinal rule of most mediators is to accept the agreement reached by the parties, if it did not do great injustice to the rights of the weaker. So she made no mention of her bewilderment, or premonition of insincerity. Her immediate job was to rephrase the full final agreement to the satisfaction of all principal parties.

She did precisely that, and there was consensus. And it was 10:24 A.M. on Saturday, August 13, in and around the Grain Train.

*   *   *

The Grain Train had whistled its entrance into the Mannheim compound fifteen minutes ago, and Frank was trying hard not to panic. There was so much more ground to cover. He knew if he stopped and stared with binoculars at the motionless train down at the bottom of the hill, he might catch a glimpse of his son. But that would waste precious moments, life-saving moments. He did glance at the Bay sparkling like a blue diamond, blemished by ship dots, as he hastily neared the third natural ambush site.

Frank went over options as he loped along in his desperate search, breathing in the smoke-tinged air of his making. If he had only one shot, and had a choice of killing or wounding an assassin, what would he do? Aim for the sniper or his rifle? If he didn't kill the man, the rifle could still kill Peter. If the rifle was disabled, the man would have to get much closer, like Jack Ruby awaiting Lee Harvey Oswald. Was one in the crowd already? Many more questions than decisions flooded his mind.

Frank saw him! Rather, sensed movement in bushes that shouldn't be moving. His heart stopped, and his feet wanted to also. But he forced himself to slow only to a cooling-down stroll. His eyes bore holes into the underbrush ahead, seeking out the source of the movement. Only a squirrel? He listened for its fits and starts in the leaves sixty feet away.

Then Frank's eyes sent the faint message to his brain...colors. Some colors don't match. There are yellows there not anyplace else, and darker greens, amid the roots. Camouflage! Over a form on the ground.

His first instinct raised the question of how to reach for his nearest gun. In the damn tote bag for daytime concealment.

His second compelling thought was to let his eyes crawl up the blanket to an exposed head, to see if he had been seen. He instantly said no to his eyes. Eye contact was the last thing he wanted, for it would force immediate action by a discovered camouflager, now only suspicious.

No place to roll and duck for cover. No time to come from behind. Frank was in the wide-open lawn. He knew he had made three mistakes: No gun, being too close and too exposed. But he had not yet struck out.

The old rock in the shoe scam, from the chapter on buying innocent time. But make it look real, he remembered. That would take one or two sudden broken strides, calling attention if it wasn't already focused on him. Do it!

Frank tripped once, avoiding putting his other foot down firmly, just balancing to plop down, a smaller target, going through his next motions.

He took off a problem shoe and tapped it upside down, knowing any movement could be his last. He put it casually on the grass and reached over inside his bag on his far side, hidden from the bushes.

His fingers tightened around the gun handle as he flicked off the safety. No deep breaths to give away his next move.

Suddenly twisting, he brought his upper body and outstretched gun hand into direct line with the front end of the camouflaged form. And the black line of the rifle was there, like a thick branch pointed downhill. And the head was there, and also the eyes of the hunter, looking straight at Frank.

The hunter's hand was swinging up. Frank's terrible split-second choice for his first shot--kill the rifle or the rifleman. Save Peter or himself?

Frank shot into the center of the rifle's guts, commanding his reflexes to instantly swerve right and squeeze the trigger again.

And Frank's reflexes did just that, for his brain was sending no message as a third of it flew across his back.

The assassin's quick shot had found its mark. But so had Frank's second shot. The ruined man lay under camouflage, his ruined weapon in front of him. Frank Wayman had again given the gift of life to his firstborn.

*   *   *

Chapter Twenty-Three

CEO d'Almeda would have told anyone who asked that the Mannheim Company had pioneered a technical revolution in the unloading of huge railroad grain hopper bottom-dump cars. Steel caissons anchored in cement footings on bedrock supported a steel-girded superstructure of cross rails and tracks, with the gaps left open in this ultra-strong latticework. The grain gravity-flowed out of the grain cars through the three openings in the bottom of each hopper car, dropped into conveyor belt bins directly under and between the rails, then lifted to the top of storage silos, or directly to a chute with ship-feeding snouts.

On the older cars, some could be tipped and dumped. Others required each of the three metal bottom covers on the stubby funnels to be manually opened and closed, but the newer cars were spring-hinged, and magnetically locked. At this Mannheim hopper dump, a long set of vertical parallel bars on each side of three rail track sections in a row could be activated to reverse polarities, demagnetizing bottom cover mechanisms in five cars at once, allowing them to drop open and stay open. The gravity pressure of the grain in the cars would begin emptying cargo through the open spring hinges, so five cars unloaded themselves in one minute. As cars passed beyond the two parallel bars, magnetism was reactivated then lack of pressure plus spring hinge pulled the bottom covers shut again, held firmly by the magnetic field manufactured into each car.

From an office window, d'Almeda saw that most of the hijacked grain cars were the new magnetic type. He picked up his interoffice phone, and gave the instructions to both his track foreman and elevator supervisor: demagnetize only grain car number one, and send that car's grain to *fat*--first available tower--not the ship. He had kept his new forced bargain with the government. The other cars were not his problem.

From her vantage point in the stationary engine cab, Cassie saw wheat dust flying from under the grain car just past the last boxcar. The shed's dust suppression doors had not been closed because of the milling crowd. She was quietly grateful the cloud was neither gas nor smoke. A monumental cheer went up from the watching crowds, inside and outside the fence. Riders scrambled away from the cars nearest the dust cloud.

Marion and Janet with their Mannheim ID tags had meandered near the stopped train. Janet was following her heart toward the idling engine and Peter. But strangely, Marion's instincts pulled her toward the grain shed, the conveyor belt area--into the dust and away from her son. She recognized no faces in the dozens from the boxcars, who were in turn looking at the lady in a tan suit and high heels, tiptoeing in the gravel work yard.

Cassie pointed out the dust to the men in the cab. "Peter, you've got your national attention to the problem, and the grain going to feed the hungry. Now it's time to pay the piper. Five minutes for the grain to be lifted up the conveyor chute and to drop into the ship's hold, ten or fifteen minutes for the ship to get underway, I understand. Then time for your grand exit. I'll be out in the media van if you need me."

Peter thanked her sincerely. Then Blackman said he would leave with her, that his job was also done. Peter grasped the man's large hand, shaking his head for loss of words, then both of them added their other hand to that grip. Four strong hands that had pulled together in the same direction for different reasons. Peter thanked them again, then turned his back to the door. He began answering the earlier question of a reporter, when Monty cleared his throat loudly. Then he did it again, even more loudly, almost gagging. Peter looked at him in mild annoyance, and Monty nodded toward the back door where the mediators had just left. Peter followed his gaze.

There she stood, the most beautiful girl in the world. His girl. She had tears in her eyes as she stood immobilized in seeing him finally, taking in his bloodstained pant leg, his dirty face and haggard look, his windblown unkempt hair. How he had aged in three days, since last they kissed. She flung her arms open to accept him as he limped the few quick steps to reach her and enfold her joyfully.

They exchanged no words in the ecstasy of touching again, of being held so tightly that breath comes hard, or is it that the heart stops beating? Then she turned her face up and kissed him so urgently that the other men one by one looked away from the private moment.

III watched the reunion through his binoculars, furious that his agents had allowed her to board. Where had she come from? Then in a flash of terrible awareness, he knew that meant the Denver deputy director must also be here, somewhere. He played his field glasses carefully over the crowd near the engine, then started making bigger rippling circles away from that center. Frank would be trying to get to his son to protect him. III looked frantically to his own left and right and behind him, then started through the crowd again, wondering also about the right side of the train hidden from him, the hill side. If only the Seattle agents knew what Frank looked like, to neutralize him.

Marion had seen III see Janet, and knew their time was short. She moved out of his sight lines, around the corner of the grain shed. She could still see the engine through the lingering filter of grain dust, but she could not see her son yet. And where was Frank?

The masses on the train were stubbornly refusing to get off, despite the repeated urgings over the bullhorn of officers very near. She could hear bits and pieces the farmers were shouting that Peter had said, about one car getting shipped, so they had won, and thanking everybody for buying that one car of grain, and him being arrested but not to worry because his trial would be fair. She stood transfixed by the strangeness of the scene, not knowing why every nerve was tingling alarm inside her.

*   *   *

Impassable was the only way to describe the Elliott Avenue thoroughfare. Not even pedestrian traffic was allowed past the yellow-taped police line now. Black-and-whites blocked the street at both ends of the long Mannheim yards, creating an island of divided humanity.

Many of the people who were turned away had decided to go see this new island of activity from a different perspective--from Elliott Bay. Many headed for the two marinas just to the north. Hundreds of craft were moored there, either their own or available to spontaneously hire out for the morning show.

Others were parking up on Thomas and John Streets and Denny Way, and under Alaskan Way Viaduct by the trolley lines to hike up the hill to Queen Anne Park where they could look down on the event, as well as seeing how much damage the morning fire had done up there.

In a posh empty house on the side of nearby Admiral Hill, the 'Immediate Occupancy' portion of the 'For Sale' sign in front had been taken literally. The lockbox on the door had been picked, the key removed and used, and the dead bolt then locked from the inside. One man sat at the window in the master bedroom, with a commanding view of Elliott Bay, and the

Mannheim Grain Elevators, and the tracks with their solitary train this sunny morning. Three blocks away, as the gull flies. Four hundred yards, for scope sighting purposes.

No portion of the twenty-four-inch stainless steel barrel protruded through the open window though there were no neighbors behind the house to wonder about that, only low treetops on the steep hillside. The polycarbonate stock of the Remington A-4 Varmint rifle fitted comfortably, almost naturally, into the pocket of the little man's shoulder. The Harris bipod support rested securely on the rigid plastic chair mat borrowed from the office to cover the carpet below the dirty windowsill. It was a nice day to be waiting for a target.

So far he had seen only the burly older man at the right window of the cab of Engine 9039. Apparently he had a chair there. The person instructing the sniper group had been very plain: "Forget the old man, he'll be dismissed as an angry drunk. Get the boy, he's the hero." And there had been no conditions, like only when this happens, or just if that doesn't happen. It was a plain and simple kill commission--the kind he relished.

The man in the bedroom knew he would have to shoot very quickly when the target presented, for the other two on his team would probably be shooting at the same time. And they might knock the target out of alignment for a clean shot. He liked shooting for the heart. That way, if the wind lifted or dropped the shell trajectory, he would still hit a major vein or artery to pump blood out quickly. If wind pushed to his left, the lungs and spine punctured. To his right, too bad. His hope then was that the target would be pushed back and thrown right by the impact, so a second or third shot could decapitate.

Of course, with no wind, and his true aim, he had never known a heart shot with an eighty-grain .223-calibre flattened shell to leave a survivor. But for his own peace of mind, he asked a military munitions retiree to modify the Remington weapon to new specs, setting it for a three-shell burst. Today, he simply factored in the updraft off the white-capped Bay.

"We understand Peter Wayman is coming out now." The sound from one bullhorn reached faintly up Admiral Hill, weaving in pitch through the trees, over the populace. "Please get ready to leave the train peaceably, people."

The bedroom interloper watched activity increasing near the engine. He knew a moving target walking away from the other side of the engine would be more of a challenge, and he was up to that. But he would prefer the certainty of a portrait in the right-hand cab window. Through the Leupold

Mark 4 scope he watched the heavy-set man move stiffly out of the seat, vacating the window. Then into that place stepped the young man, the face from the TV specials he had been watching. Peter gave a quick victory wave to all the people cheering outside the fence on the right side of the train whom he had not acknowledged since they stopped.

The heart was in the cross hairs. The small man in the borrowed home slowly squeezed the two-stage match trigger, and kept his finger pulled against it for one-half second. The three-shell burst was delivered. His eye remained fixed to the gun sight to see the body jerk, falling back. He triggered another automatic three rounds through the cab window. That left fourteen in the AR detachable magazine clip.

Without looking back, he moved to the side of the window, propped the rifle against the wall, unclipped the bipod and folded it into his large fanny pack, then removed the magazine and placed it in the pack. He retrieved six shell casings on the floor, then took his dark rain jacket from off the back of the chair and put it on. It was heavy from the grenade in one pocket, the small revolver in the other. He picked up the rifle, covering its forty-two inch length with a sweater to hold draped down at his side, his rented car keys in his other hand. Then he left the bedroom, and the house, door ajar, for others to soon swarm in 'Immediate Occupancy.'

*　　*　　*

The bullet splashed through the right edge of Peter's neck, clipping the tendon, then pinging around the cab. He yelled out in pain, tumbling backwards as the second bullet thumped into the right side of his upper chest, just below the collar bone but shattering the shoulder blade as it forced its way through the body. The third shell smashed a high rib and took a destructive path down through tender organs into the intestines.

Janet and A.M. had just left the cab, and Monty was outside the doorway when Peter screamed and the first bullet began ricocheting. Monty's reaction was immediate, for he had berated himself brutally for cowering in the earlier shooting. He threw himself back into the cab on top of Peter as he was collapsing onto the floor. Almost at once the second volley of three shots began. Bullets violently ricocheted off the walls, hissing to the floor and ceiling and back again. One pounded into Monty's right arm like a sledge, another imbedded in his strong back, but he didn't feel it go as deep. He waited on top of Peter to die, helpless to stop the next burst. But it didn't come.

Monty heard the screams outside, heard A.M. yelling at him to get out of there. Someone pulled on his bloodied right arm, which brought a loud protest, but cleared the fog and got him moving.

"Oh, my God!" Monty exclaimed, rolling off of Peter. His friend lay limp in his own blood. But his lips were moving.

"Shut up!" Monty yelled at those behind him who were urging him out. Then he leaned over to try to hear what the wounded man was saying.

"...ship..." came out clearly, then one other word, "...friend..." Monty didn't know whether Peter was referring to him or the ship, but it gave him a desperate idea. They needed sanctuary, someplace they wouldn't be killed. The only safe place would be the ship, if they could get on board.

"Come on, Peter, let's get out of here," Monty groaned as he started trying to lift the limp form. He no longer had the strength.

A.M. knelt and tenderly grabbed under Peter's arm and around the soaking wet waist. "God Almighty," he muttered.

"God didn't have much to do with this," Monty said simply, slowly shuffling toward the door with Peter dangling between them.

"Listen, A.M.," Monty spoke in low tones, "once we're off, start the train up again real slow, then you leave. Make it so they can't stop it easy."

"Why, mon ami?" A.M. asked, grunting with the awkward load.

"I dunno. We need a distraction."

"But the people on the tracks..."

"Damn the people."

Both men were surprised to hear fairly loud words from Peter's lowered head. "No! Praise...people." And he coughed up blood.

"We've got to hurry," Monty said as he stepped out of the cab and into pandemonium. Most people were running and shoving and screaming to get away from the train and find protection. Some had taken refuge against the engine's bulk and on the catwalk, and now jammed it to see or help.

Tears flowed freely down Janet's cheeks, but she had not broken down in sobs. And she had held onto first position by the door. Now she turned to face the nearby crowd standing in the way.

"Make room for us," she said in a cracking voice. Then squaring her shoulders, she said again more firmly, "Make a path for this man!"

Once the gawking persons had direction, they turned and began climbing back down the ladder or over the rail onto the wheels. Janet focused all her thoughts away from her horror and onto the bullet-riddled man she loved. She didn't know the plan, but saw a hurdle to be overcome.

"You down there, yes, you," she gestured to the few who looked up. "Go back to the boxcars and get blankets! Go on, now!" And four people raced down the track, putting aside their fear to do a helpful thing.

The mayor had been whisked away to the isolated northern end of the docks and into the equipment garage with Lt. Governor Dunlap. The media van was shut tight but unmoving, with Cassie and Blackman inside. Reporters and camerapersons on the platforms had held their positions, really very bravely, just ducking down and filming everywhere. Their conscious job was not only to capture the action, but for later study, possibly capturing the shooters on film.

As a few were panning up Admiral Hill where some people were pointing and looking, the police chief was ordering all available mobile units to close in on the crowd on the right side of the engine, outside the fence, drawing a net around the most likely area for the shots to have originated. People were still madly climbing down off the rail car tops they had so defiantly occupied moments before, as the word *shooting* traveled the length of the train.

Blankets came, with helpers. Janet directed them to stack three fully open, and others to be folded in half and laid criss-cross fashion. And to hurry and hand two up to her.

She spread the first one, an Army blanket, on the catwalk, and laid the second one on top, a handmade quilt with a blue border and the name Ella stitched in. Monty and A.M. just turned around, leaving Peter's feet at the edge of the quilt, then they backed up and let his broken body lie down softly. For the second time on the catwalk, Janet looked at him fully. No part of the once eloquent speaker was without splotches of blood, either his or Monty's own life store. The tanned skin from her hayloft memories was now pallid in the bright sun. And the poor legs she had admired running the school track...

"Hurry!" she ordered. "Two more strong men up here!" She knelt beside the terrible sight, and reached with two tender fingers to wipe away the frothy blood from her lover's lips. Then she bent down and kissed him twice with just a brush of her lips, careful not to block his air. He opened his eyes barely a moment and closed them again. Along with a twitch of his lips into a smile, she was sure she saw him say the word that said it all for her.

"I said, hurry!" she blurted out from her kneeling position near the blanket. "Get him down off here! But be careful!" She stood and looked at Monty, lifting and grimacing in his own pain.

"Monty, where do we go?" she shouted, fearing more shooting.

He merely pointed with his bad right arm. Toward the freighter.

Tenderly, Peter was lowered from the catwalk, through the gap in the guardrail at the steps. Dozens of hands supported the bottom of the blankets as he came over, even though blood was already seeping through. They carried him quickly to the layered blanket stretcher and laid him in the center.

"Five or six on each side to lift. We're headed for the dock." People looked at one another, puzzled. Why move him at all, since they could hear the ambulance coming toward them through the crowd. The few FBI agents standing near began to get nervous, but they had no direct orders for handling this type of situation, since there was no clear and present danger.

"Do it, or stand aside!" Janet commanded again. "Now take hold, on three, lift. One, two, three!" The blanket rose as evenly as a tabletop. She was surprised at how much she was remembering from her first-aid training. "Now start off with your left foot as I begin, and keep up. Ready, left, right, left right..." and she counted in rapid cadence. "If you get tired, ask for help. All of you around here, come with us, but stay out of the way until you are picked. Left, right..."

The agents stepped away from the crowd. There was no place the group could go, trapped on one side by water, fenced in on all the others.

Monty walked with Janet at one side to keep a close eye on Peter. But he glanced back over his shoulder to watch A.M. re-entering the engine cab. Seconds later, the sounds of rail cars slowly coupling began to domino softly across the yards. It was so subtle most would have missed it in the general confusion.

The safety concern got the better of A.M., Monty knew, as the engineer started blowing the air horn of the 9039. Three short, three long, three short, and he repeated the signal. It not only startled the crowd but also warned them of the moving engine. More importantly, it started them in a chant of growing magnitude: "Share Our Surplus...Save Our Starving... Share Our Surplus..." and so it continued.

Monty looked back again. A.M. was exiting, locking the cab door behind him. Good man, Monty thought, turning to look at Peter. "Hold on, friend, we're almost there." The bloody man in the blanket only moaned. And Monty joined him in that sad sound.

*

Marion heard the first series of shots very plainly, as if the only sound on earth. The second ricocheting group thundered twice as loudly in her ears. Enormous fear rose up into her throat, physically choking her and constricting her chest in sharp pains. She kept looking at the cab door of the engine where Janet and the other engineer and Monty had just emerged laughing. She had known her son would be the next person coming through the door.

But then Monty had leaped back in, and the engineer. People began running everywhere, like on an ant hill with fire put to it, except Marion stood still, watching, waiting.

Then two people had come out, carrying a third between them, who was covered with so much blood that he was unrecognizable. About Peter's height, except his head was bowed down. And Peter's build. But not his clothes, from what she could tell. Not anything she had ever ironed and hung up in his closet, and her hopes lifted.

Marion thought she saw that man worst hurt move one leg, and her heart jumped, just before they laid him on the blanket. But standing ten long cars away, it really was impossible to tell for sure.

Frozen, she watched Janet and Monty and the crowd carry him rapidly away, knowing not where they were taking the man. And she saw the other engineer re-enter the cab, and the empty grain car in front of her began to move forward inches at a time. Then the whistle blew loudly, startling her, and some people began chanting something. And the engineer came out, and locked the door, and left. She saw it all.

Why would he do that with Peter still inside, she wondered? Maybe he climbed down on the other side to escape. That's it, she reasoned furiously, or he's in the cab and taking the train to another dock and leaving Janet and Monty here...

But her logic left her, as tears began welling up in a mother's eyes.

"Oh, Frank, why couldn't you stop it?" she questioned to herself. "And why did Peter have to come here anyway?" The second grain car was passing in front of her, moving so slowly, but not dumping its cargo.

"He came to bring this grain," she was now speaking openly to herself. "And somebody's trying to keep it for themselves. The selfish pigs, the stupid killers..." Into her mind clicked the early morning comment from the elevator owner who had driven them here: "Be sure to have the grain shed foreman show you..."

She turned and entered the small office, and shut the door on the dust and screams and blood. The man sitting at the desk asked, "Yes?"

"Mr. d'Almeda said to show me how to unload five cars all at once."

The man stayed seated, but picked up the phone. "Come behind the counter," he instructed her, and he said quietly into the phone, "She's here." Then he nodded and hung up.

"It might be those three green buttons in that top row of the console, but I'm the only person authorized to press them..."

With the fingers of both hands Marion pressed all three at one time. And she kept them depressed, even as the great whooshing sound started outside the office, and the air there was filled again with dust of wheat kernels dropping onto conveyors now rolling under the tracks. She didn't know to also turn on the air filtration system.

Marion didn't look at the foreman, who had not raised a finger to stop her, but she looked instead for the back door and was gone, running painfully across gravel toward the group carrying her son away from her.

*

The media persons covering Mannheim were having a black field day. With no one left to worry about containing them, there were news stories breaking all at once for them to choose between: the assassination attempt on Peter Wayman and his chanting parade, the runaway train and its danger, the rapidly unloading grain and its cheering crowd outside the fence, oblivious to many of the problems Bay-side or the reason for the wailing siren.

An ambulance was struggling to get through the tightly packed crowd rapidly nearing the edge of the dock. There was danger of someone being pushed into the deep brackish water between the pier and the ship, so some of the police were trying to set up a barrier line to keep people back, as well as cooperating with the FBI to keep anyone from boarding the freighter.

On board the *Godavari Sunrise*, Captain Pradesh had watched the growing melee in the yards below. Through binoculars, he saw Peter being carried off the engine, and his own heart broke at the sight of such inhumanity in this most caring of all nations. Had not Peter himself arranged with the captain to transport this stolen grain as an international gesture of goodwill?

Therefore, when the additional grain cars began to be unloaded, the captain requested the long snouts to be lowered again, in case Mannheim decided on direct conveyor access. But he had also been ready to leave after only one car, to keep the mediation agreement.

The snouts indeed did begin disgorging their precious food supply, and

Captain Pradesh ordered them raised ten feet up out of the hold, so the people on shore could see them and have no question their grain was coming on for transport. Anti-air pollution mandates were thrown to the winds.

The captain had also seen the high-heeled lady disappear into the grain shed, and figured she had something to do with starting the machinery. Then he had watched as she came out the back, just as his earlier unwelcome FBI guest was disappearing into the dust cloud in front. The lady headed straight for the crowd approaching his ship.

"Lower the gangplank," he ordered.

"Sir?" Some of the crew still wondered about the strange behavior of their captain on this trip, and his motivations.

"Obey the order, Second Mate."

The telescoping aluminum planking began winching outward on its double cabling, down toward the dock.

Marion caught up with Janet, and grabbed onto the young girl's hand hard as she looked down into the sagging center of the blankets. The corpse-like form was her son.

"Oh, no, no," she gasped in agony, "oh, my God, no!" She scraped tears from her eyes to be able to see where, and who...

"Monty, where are you going with him?" she blurted out to the man she had just fed supper on their last night at home. Then something in her added, "And how badly are you hurt?" as she struggled to keep up.

"I don't know, ma'am, I took a couple for Pete. And we're going onto the ship, 'cause that's what he wanted at the end." Monty saw a wave of grief wash over the faces of the two women. "Hey, I don't mean he's dead. Lord, no. That's just the last thing he said to me."

Janet thought of Peter's last word to her, and their last kiss, and she cried again. The crowd kept advancing.

"Mrs. Wayman, how's my Felicia?" Monty asked the pale woman, grabbing her arm to help steady her as she stumbled. She flinched away from his bloodstained clothes, not wanting him touching her.

"For God's sake, she's safe in Denver!" Marion spat out, shuddering, ashamed. Janet squeezed her hand more tightly as they lurched along. Marion blinked away tears to look into his gentle face with its pain contortions, and finally was able to rasp, "What can I tell her for you, Monty?"

"Aw, tell her I love her..." and he was crying hard tears too, "...and the other stuff she'd like to hear. I'm not very good at that. I just hug her. And tell my grandkids I was thinking of them."

Marion was trying to pull herself together. "I'll hug them all for you,

Monty. Or maybe you can come home and do it yourself." She at once hurt along with the hurt her words had caused. Nothing was right.

"I think it will be a long time, Mrs. Wayman," was all he said.

"Oh, Mom, Dad...look...look..." a little boy's peaceful voice spoke out of the ugly blanket. The mother of the man there would not pull her gaze again from her child.

Monty's heart turned to sad stone. His fury was flaming at the failure of words and the success of violence during this whole long trip. Especially this tragic morning. And now they were approaching the line of eleven law officers and FBI agents who would finally stop them.

*

The train moved slowly forward, this time without an engineer. People along the track began yelling again, warning others to watch out. Some of the earlier smart ones now desperately regretted their decision to hide from the shooting by ducking under the cars, behind the wheels. For the massive metal undercarriage was now rolling over them, as they huddled in small balls between the rails, or lay prostrate and terrified.

Panic has its way of drawing attention, and the police rushed to the aid of those in danger. A few people still standing on top of the cars further back had lost their footing, even though A.M. had masterfully inched the train ahead as he started. Two persons had fallen off, and were crying out in their pain. One young boy had his leg caught in the ladder on the end of Boxcar Three, and dangled helplessly over the passing rail. It was another nightmare in the middle of the day.

III was unconcerned with the problems of the intruding public. His attention was riveted to what was happening opposite the grain shed. The third and fourth grain cars were furiously dumping their grain through their opened bottom hatches, despite the agreements, and on top of his threats. He watched the first car pass him--the purchased grain, the mediated car-- now emptied.

Incredulous, he turned to see the fifth grain car reach the powerful demagnetizing bars, tripping the latches on the bottom covers and freeing one hundred more tons of wheat to the pull of gravity, creating more dust. Dust overwhelming enough to be a storm whirled madly, hiding him from being seen, or seeing anyone. He stumbled toward the dark outline of the grain shed. That control building would have the answers, and be able to stop this travesty. Why didn't someone stop the damn train yet?

The forward bystanders were trying to do just that. Several men familiar with train engines had run alongside the runaway, grabbed the ladder, and pulled themselves on board. Many more persons unfamiliar with locomotives had done the same thing, anxious to help, but clogging the catwalk. When the engineer-types finally did reach the locked cab door, they hollered down for crowbars, and for somebody to try the other side.

Back at the grain shed control room, III barged almost blindly inside.

"You've got to stop that grain from unloading!" he shouted at the man seated behind the desk.

"You don't say." The air was now cleanly filtered inside, so the foreman could see the dusty intruder plainly. But the EPA would have a heyday levying fines for the outside air problem.

"Where is the damn stuff going?" III demanded to know.

"Mister, I don't know your dusty hide from Adam. So not only ain't I gonna tell you nuthin', I'm callin' the cops on a trespasser!"

"You fool! I am the FBI! Which one of these buttons stops that grain?" He moved toward the electronic console, not bothering with ID.

The foreman stood, his short-sleeved shirt betraying lots of muscles. "Mr. Nobody, one of my jobs I like best is first to break both arms of any jerk touchin' that board. You catch my drift?"

"Well, damn it all, call d'Almeda! Tell him I'm here, ordering the unloading stopped--and the loading--and everything!" III raged.

"Then, you sit down over there where I can keep an eye on you. And who's you?"

III shouted "Ravenhead!" as he walked over to pace by the door, watching the hazy cars creep by outside. The foreman called a number, asked for Mr. d'Almeda, and waited. And waited some more.

After ten seconds, III walked back to the desk. "What are you waiting for?" he asked unpleasantly.

"Secretary says Mr. d'Almeda is in the bathroom, and she don't know when he'll be out."

III expelled a mammoth sigh. "Will you at least tell me where that grain is going?" as he thumbed toward the train.

"I never did see any identification."

In a great show of disdain, III pulled out his picture card. Unbelievably, the foreman hung up the receiver so he could take the little case. He studied it completely, front and back.

"Pretty high up, Washington and all?"

"High enough to have your damn job. Now where..."

"You wouldn't like my job, mister. Couldn't ever wear a suit like that to work in here. It'd get filthy, like it already has."

III glanced down in chagrin, and instinctively plucked off some of the larger chaff. "The grain...can you just tell me where the damn grain is going?"

"No need for all that cussin', feller. Lots of otherwise nice people make that same mistake."

"Grant me patience," III prayed, half seriously. "Where?"

"Why, straight into that ship out yonder at our dock. System's slick as a whistle, ain't it? And fast too."

"May I?" III started to reach for the phone. The foreman put his big hand down firmly on top of the set.

"I need to talk with d'Almeda."

"Nope. Mr. d'Almeda will be calling back. I get in real trouble if the line's busy."

"Got a private room where I can try my phone?"

"Sure. The john's right through that door."

*

The loping gait of a husky man accustomed to jogging was aimed to intersect with the fourth engine fifty yards before Engine 9039 hit the locked gate at the far north end. That would give him time to insert his key without fighting through the crowds, and apply the air brakes in sufficient power to override the 9039's thrust. Harrison Fruehauf had flown in to take back the train for his Mid-Western Pacific Railroad. But he would wait until the last minute, to make certain every grain car had a chance to be emptied.

*

"They can't stop the train! And they won't stop the grain!" III railed to his boss over his cellular in the water closet. "Yes, it's going into the ship, and the people know it. Hell, they can see it!"

He listened to his FBI director's question. "When I left the grounds to come in here, Peter and Monty were making a beeline for the ship. I radioed my agents to intercept and detain. There's no way anybody gets on that ship...No, I have no idea who shot Peter Wayman."

Then he listened to his boss describe the blanket procession he was watching on TV, and saying how much public support was switching with every passing minute.

"Well, then," III prodded, "so much for our good faith mediation agreements, eh?"

He listened attentively again, for his boss was saying what he wanted to hear: escalation. "Yes, sir, most assuredly," III responded. "Homeland Security is right to bring in the Coast Guard. They should move as quickly as possible, ideally while the terrorist *Sunrise* is still docked...No, one cutter vessel should be plenty. The freighter is too big, and getting too heavy, to maneuver out of this overblown bathtub." He looked around at his own surroundings in disgust as he finished. But he could still smile. For the would-be-king Peter was finally going to be checkmated.

III stepped back into the control room. He had come close to stopping this caper with his order to bring in the Montana group. And he would have serious criticisms to send indirectly back to them about their lack of expert firepower. But for now, he would see it finished, with back-up help from the military might of his tough nation.

"Hey, fella," the foreman hailed him on the way out. "Mr. d'Almeda did call back. Said your contract was only good on one car. The others he's loading the fastest way we have so, uh, so you can finish, since he knows you're in a hurry. He hopes he did the right thing. I think that's what he said."

III saved his message and cusswords for personal delivery, and stepped out into the swirling dust to tie up the loose ends on land: arresting farmers, the engineer, Peter, and his father--when he had the nerve to show himself.

*

Through a row of tall poplar trees they carried their blanket burden, onto a wide pier connecting Mannheim landside yards with the long dock.

Officers were there, but unorganized to stop the large group, which was never to have gotten this far. The towers of the tall steel superstructure supporting the grain conveyor belt forced the group apart momentarily to get around its legs, then they congealed again.

The conveyor which climbed high above them all the way along the pier entered a small blockhouse to drop its grain onto the next conveyor--this one stretching the length of the dock, a hundred feet in the air, supported by five more towers of steel.

The huge freighter took up more than the full length of the dock. Its stern was near the pier at the north end of the dock, with the bow proclaiming

Godavari Sunrise pointed south toward downtown Seattle.

Grain flowed freely down the five narrow tubes from the high conveyor, some of it blowing onto the decks and the water since the tips were lifted. The ship was low in the water, its decks floating twenty feet above dock level. A gangplank telescoped out to thirty feet long connected the tightly moored ship with the dock.

And there the authorities finally massed, refusing to let anyone step onto that narrow metal walkway with its rope banisters.

*

Tom Buchanan had climbed into a boxcar as it passed the waterfront, ridden into the plant, and had been on his way up to the engine just before the shooting. He watched the mayor as she was spirited away for protection, came close enough to the downed Peter to see he could not communicate, then hung back at the edge of the crowd.

Rumors and questions were flying: "Is his mother really here?...He's dead...He's only wounded in the arm...His dying wish was to go aboard... Monty told the doctors to shove it..." Tom looked at the downcast faces of Monty, then the women, and sensed the sad truth.

Tom waited for the official car to re-appear. He knew it would, for it was her city--her chaos to control. And when it did come to let the mayor out near the pier, he at once approached her. She ordered her bodyguards to permit a meeting with the remnant terrorist.

"Tom, I didn't do this to Peter."

"I had hoped you would say that," he admitted.

"Will you spare us a retaliatory bombing?"

He paused before answering, "What good would it do anyone now?"

And she thanked him.

"Is the grain surplus conference still on?" he asked as they walked onto the pier to catch up with the crowd. Several cameras were trained on her, and a furry boom mike floated over her, waiting for her response.

She had thought it all out in the equipment garage under duress, before calling the governor. She was prepared. "This shooting was not sanctioned by the State of Washington, for we gave our word to you and the National Peace Academy mediator for a non-violent resolution. We also agreed to hold an international conference--and that will be held!"

Tom realized he was part of an impromptu interview, which had served his purpose also, up to this point. "Mayor, alone for one minute?" he quietly asked. She debated his request, the appearance of impropriety, and the importance of the next fifteen minutes to her career, then agreed. She asked three of the group of police surrounding her to keep the media back, and walked to one supporting leg of the pier's steel tower canopied by the high conveyor chute.

"Mayor, Peter is probably dying in that blanket. Monty has refused medical assistance for him, and his mother has agreed."

"Peter's mother is here?" the mayor interrupted.

"Yes, high heels, brown suit," he gestured toward that spot in the crowd. "And his girlfriend Janet also."

The mayor was adjusting her thinking for the added emotion and pressures from family members. "His father?" she asked, anticipating more legal confrontations.

"I haven't seen him," Tom answered. "Will you let Peter and Monty board the ship?" The question of the hour, of her year.

"That's not up to me," was her first reaction.

"It can be--it must be," Tom contradicted. "The FBI will arrest them on the spot, and Peter will die on Seattle soil, your fault or not. If the wounds don't kill him, the disappointment will. Let him at least get on the ship with the grain, and leave port, whatever happens after that."

The mayor said nothing.

"We had negotiated for a fair trial," Tom continued pleading his case. "The bullets robbed us of that. So this must be his dying wish, to go with the grain he gave his life for. You can grant him that."

"I seriously doubt if the ship leaves, Tom. The Feds won't let it."

"Then all the more reason to let him go on board," Tom went on. "He won't get away, so you won't be accused of being soft. When he dies, then bring him back. Add his coffin to the others..." and his voice broke. "What a waste..." he tried to say, and couldn't finish.

"We'd better be getting on out there," the mayor said. She had seen III running from the grain shed. Seattle's Chief Executive didn't know what she was going to do, just that she had to decide very soon.

*

"Mrs. Wayman, I'm Judith Taulison, mayor of Seattle. I know this is a sad day for you." The two ladies stood beside the doubled blankets in which Peter lay, still held suspended by two dozen sympathetic hands.

Marion looked at the dry-eyed woman, and asked, "Was this stupidity your doing?" The mayor shook her head, denying it. "We had agreed on a peaceful ending."

"I'm Janet," said the young girl next to Marion. "I love him. He wants to go on the ship, with the grain."

"I know," the mayor shared. She had just made her decision looking at the torn body. "He's come this far. I'll let him go thirty feet more."

At the edge of the crowd, III arrived breathing hard, Switzer trailing right behind. "FBI!" he shouted out. "Have the arrests been made yet?"

At that outburst the crowd parted, mumbling, and he made his way in closer. "No, sir," one of the Seattle agents informed him quietly.

"Then the time has come, and I'm the man to do it!" His growing satisfaction showed in the smile, as he stepped up closer to the blanket and looked into it.

For a lingering moment there was total silence on the dock, with all eyes on III, who absorbed the attention. The number three man from the national Bureau office was totally in charge. "Is he still alive?" he finally asked loudly, of no one in particular.

"We don't know, sir," another agent answered.

"Then, Peter Wayman," III spoke out strongly, noting the many cameras focused on him, "alive or dead, I arrest you for high crimes against the United States of America..."

Without a word, Monty signaled with his good arm, twice in a forward motion, as if to say, *Come on, let's get going.* And those holding onto the blanket who saw that motion followed his slow shuffling lead, urging those ahead of them with gentle nudges.

"...you have the right to an attorney of your..." It took several seconds for III to see what was happening, and he stopped mid-sentence. "Where are you going?" he demanded, again singling out no one in particular for an answer. And none was given. "Put him down now!" They were steps away from being on the gangplank which four officers still blocked.

"I am arresting this mob for complicity!" III shouted. "Cuff them!!"

The agents under his command jumped to handle the impossible assignment, pulling on the arm of the nearest person to them, and snapping on one of their two pairs of handcuffs. But as they pulled one away from the blanket edge, another took that place. The blanket neither fell nor slowed. And somehow there was no loud protesting or violent resistance.

"Chief Simonet!" III hollered out to the head of the Seattle police forces, "order your men into this. They're doing nothing!"

"Which is exactly what they've been ordered to do by my boss!" the chief shouted back across the quiet crowd. Mayor Taulison stood tall, in fact on her tiptoes, to meet the poisonous glare thrown at her by III.

The FBI agents who had been part of the force blocking the gangplank had moved away to make arrests, and the Seattle police who had also been there shoulder to shoulder stood aside as the first few from the train stepped onto the narrow metal walkway.

Soon it was painfully obvious that the ship's plank would only accommodate two abreast. So there was no room for those on the sides of the blanket. Monty was one of the first two on the gangplank, straining to hold up the forward weight of his friend.

III pushed his way with difficulty through the unmoving extras in the crowd who didn't have a hold on the blanket edges.

Peter's body was halfway across the front edge of the gangplank when III grabbed at a free side of the blanket still over the dock.

"This damn hijacker isn't getting away!" he cursed. "Switzer, get hold of this with me!" The two men started pulling landward. "All the rest of you agents, come pull them back!" III yelled, puffing hard. "The rest of you people who are under arrest, let go--or you'll have the devil to pay. I'll see you charged with ten years!"

His threat had its effect. One by one even the brave hands let go which had held on all the way from the train. Marion and Janet screamed at them to stay, but the fear of jail was too great. The blanket began inching back toward the dock in the horrible tug of war.

Monty's body could no longer stand the strain with blood pumping out of his two wounds. He collapsed onto his knees, letting go of his hold of the blanket. One other man tried to hold it up, but could not. The best he could do was keeping Peter's head from hitting too hard onto the gangplank as the forward part of the blanket and body dropped with a soft thud. There was a gasp of protest and sympathy from the watching crowd. One agent suddenly grabbed the helper's arm and pulled him stumbling across Peter onto the dock.

The two women in Peter's life fought with all their might to push the agents away from the blanket edges.

"Shove the women aside, and pull that son-of-a-bitch back," III hissed slowly.

BAM!

A single rifle shot rang out, echoing off the grain elevators.

*   *   *

Chapter Twenty-Four

Everyone on the dock froze, looking around at the sound. It came from the ship, high up, on the top bridge. Captain Pradesh stood at the rail in his crisp whites, hat set straight on his head, with a rifle held in his right hand, barrel resting up on his shoulder, and a microphone in the other hand at his tense lips.

"All hands on deck to repel boarders!" At that instant, a dozen sailors stood erect at the edge of the deck's railing, on both sides of the gangplank entryway. Each had a rifle cradled in one arm, their other hand with a finger near the triggers.

The tugging on the blanket had stopped. And in the face of the immediate threat of force thirty feet away, those agents holding the blanket just naturally set it down gently. This not only reduced the tension a little, but also freed up their hands for the impending firefight.

The mighty engines of the ship had begun the propellers churning the waters astern, raising the noise level. So the freighter captain had the advantage with the ship's loudspeakers. Besides, III was at a momentary loss for words.

"There are two men on this ship's gangplank, which I consider neutral territory, no man's land." He carefully enunciated his words to be understood by everyone, including the media who were intent on capturing this speech.

"Any person from United States property who attempts to prevent those men from walking that plank and completing their boarding if they so desire, will be treated as an impending threat to our national security, and summarily shot."

Everyone inside the fence at the Mannheim grain elevators was assembling on the pier and out on the dock to watch the showdown. Nobody was pointing a gun actually at anyone, but almost everyone who had a gun now had a hand on it.

Cassie Cowdrey and Blackman had gotten separated, but Cassie was maneuvering her way tenaciously toward the gangplank area. Mediation of this bitterly tangled dispute was still her assigned goal.

Monty's mind was functioning well, even if his body wasn't. He had heard the captain buying them time with that shot and blatant declaration. Alone on the gangplank with Peter, he crawled onto the blanket and lay down with his head next to the bloody face.

"Peter, listen to me. You don't have to open your eyes," Monty said, seeing the dried blood caked over them, "just move your lips if you can hear me. Don't say anything, just move your lips so I know you're still with me, buddy. Come on, Peter...come on." The wait seemed an eternity before the foamy mouth parted just a little wider.

"Atta boy!" Monty said loudly, picking up energy from the mere fact of life. "Now here's what's coming down, farm boy." Monty was struggling up again to his knees, talking loudly. "We've got to get this grain to the kids, my friend. I know you're hurting, but you've got to get up on your feet to get the grain shipped. Try, Peter!"

The crowd of hundreds had quieted again, straining to hear Monty's pleas, watching to see any movement at all from the man who had started this journey.

Monty took hold of Peter's undamaged left arm with his own right arm, carrying the bullet, then braced himself on the ropes of the gangplank and pulled himself up with his good left arm. Both men screamed out in pain as Monty stood, bringing Peter up to his knees on the blanket. But Peter stayed upright on his knees with Monty's strength supporting him, except for his head which the neck wound kept bowed.

Many in the crowd choked at seeing the fresh red blood that totally covered Peter's right side, and others looked away. "Nobody can lose that much blood..." someone whispered, then stopped when Mayor Taulison turned with a scowl. Marion and Janet stood transfixed at the other end of the blanket on the dock. They so wanted to reach out to him, but massive violence was hanging by such a slender thread. One misstep...

Monty's voice carried out over the crowd. "Damn it, Peter, you may not be able to smile, but you've got to stand up and walk! I can't hold you much longer. Grab onto me and put one knee up, buddy. Come on now."

"You can do it, son." Marion's strained voice was the first to join Monty's encouragement. And into the awful silence Peter's muted voice cracked a small sound that perhaps only she heard.

"M..m..mom..?"

"Yes, m'boy," she answered softly. "Yes, it's Mom. Come on and take that first step for Mom--and for Dad." She didn't know why she thought of Frank then. Peter slowly was raising his left knee to brace his foot.

Monty leaned down to speak urgently to his struggling mate. "The world is watching you, Peter. Take these final steps."

"Come on, Peter," Janet choked out, unable to even see him through her storm of tears. "Be strong for all of us. We're counting on you."

And others picked up the call to find the strength. "Go, Peter! You can do it!" Agonizingly, Peter pushed up on his left leg as Monty pulled, and then in twisted torture he was standing. The crowd let out a huge cheer to see Peter again on his feet. The surge of emotion drove the last bit of adrenaline through his body, into his legs. He took one step toward the ship, and then another, before his legs began to buckle and he stumbled backward, pulling Monty with him toward the dock.

"Enough of this!" the mayor cried out, lunging forward at the same time Marion and Janet both did, trying to catch the two men as they were falling. The women worked desperately to keep their footing on the slimy blanket, and fell several times. But they managed to keep the two wounded men upright.

"There, you see," III shouted up at the Captain. "Those men cannot make it onto your cursed ship. They are rightfully mine!" As he drew his gun from his holster, his agents followed his lead.

"Those men clearly declared their intent!" the captain's voice blared back over the loudspeakers. "And my nation grants them the sanctuary they seek! Make no move against them, Mr. Ravenhead--on forfeiture of your own life!" The rifle in the Captain's hands was no longer on his shoulder, but came into deadly aim at the high-ranking FBI official. The armed sailors had also picked beads on their own individual targets on the dock.

Two sailors ran from the deck down the gangplank to take hold of Peter, one on each side. He slipped into unconsciousness. They moved sideways with him back up the ramp separating two countries. Two more came for Monty. Shooting was certain, and the people began scattering for cover.

Cassie then stepped squarely in front of III, facing him, blocking the captain's aim. "Oh, for heaven's sake, act your age, Terrence!" she scolded. "You'd just make a lot of widows for nothing. Besides, how many dozens of desperadoes worse than these will get away if you kick the bucket today?"

Her bravado mixed with such gravely tones had astonished the lines of gunners on both sides. She had put her life at risk for all of them. And it cooled things off. Monty had just been helped down onto the deck off the gangplank, and it was being withdrawn. Peter was on a stretcher being hurried to the ship's infirmary. The sailors were disappearing below deck, and the captain was inside at the helm.

"The sooner you retire, the better for your health," III said to Cassie. Then he turned to his agents who had congregated near him for his next instructions.

"Take all those in handcuffs to the buses. One of you ride downtown with them. Book them for failure to obey an officer. Arrest the girl and the mother as well."

Mayor Taulison was close enough to overhear, while trying to comfort a distressed Marion. "No," she spoke up, "that last order needs rescinding. Unless you want to arrest me, too, for we were all three there together. And if you even think about thinking about arresting me, you would have to be the dumbest Anglo-Saxon male of the species."

"Leave the women alone," he countermanded simply, "but go round up all the Colorado farmers--as we agreed!" he finished, shooting her the look that goes with having the final word.

Once the gangplank had been winched aboard, Captain Pradesh notified Mannheim that he was ready to leave port. The heavy three-inch diameter ropes were slacked by the ship's crew, and the Mannheim dockhands had routinely unlashed the two big forward hawsers holding the *Godavari Sunrise* close in. The hawsers were mechanically reeled back up to the deck, and two more amidships were also quickly loosened and hauled in, then securely battened down for the ocean voyage.

The dockhands moved through the crowd inconspicuously and began to untie the last two hawsers holding the stern in close to the dock. The long pipes that fed the grain into the holds were emptied and telescoping in. Departure was imminent.

"Hey, they're casting off!" someone shouted. III jerked his head toward the shout, in time to see one rope rising quickly up the freighter's side, and the other being loosed. He thought of reaching for his gun, then thought of Cassie, and yelled out his authority instead: "FBI! Hands off that rope!"

There is no doubting the intimidation of shouting that name. The workers stood up and looked, only to be shoved aside by agents with coats open, guns showing in their holsters. The low metal 'T' in the dock with its coiled rope was immediately surrounded and blocked. There would be no more heroics.

No verbal threats were issued from either side in the standoff. Without a very strong pull, the ship could not break its solitary hawser anchoring it to the dock. And that tug might ruin the whole shipboard housing for later emergency use. III had incapacitated the ship, knowing a Coast Guard Cutter was weaving its way through harbor traffic from its home dock, just three miles south in the Bay. His phone call to D.C. had triggered gratifying results.

But Captain Pradesh was not inclined to have his massive freighter held captive by the inertia of politics on a dock, or by a thick restraining bowstring. He studied the clear air over his ship's deck, and the secured covers over the grain holds. The breeze was still brisk. "Soak that hawser with diesel for a man's length, then torch it as it leaves the hull," he ordered his Second Mate Sheefah on the deck by radio.

His helmsman pointed toward the center of the bay, and the sleek gray craft a mile away converging on them. The captain raised his binoculars. Its deck superstructure, American flag, and forward gun identified it as one of the U.S. Coast Guard fleet.

"Engine room, all ahead full," Captain Pradesh ordered direct into the speaker, continuing to break his own protocol to save a few seconds, and prevent challenges. "Kasir, is the hawser burning?" he asked. His Third Mate looked down from the afterdeck cabin at the stern's rope housing. A sailor was just touching a lighter to the section of rope soaked with diesel fuel, still suspended over their deck. A puff of flame and black smoke jumped skyward.

"Yes, sir, it is torched."

"Play out the hawser," the captain ordered his deck officer, "for this ship is leaving port now. And keep the fire as high above the water as possible, at all costs." He returned his attention to the affairs of the bridge. "Kasir, radio the tug that we no longer require their services, and continue sounding the horn, to alert the small craft out of our way. Set our course due west for Puget Sound."

The ship's supply of the last anchored hawser continued running out smartly from the aft of the freighter, over the waters churning from engines cycling full. It was still burning in dirty flames.

Workers on the dock rushed for the chemical hoses, at d'Almeda's barked order, as he was proclaiming the captain a fool. "Which is the worse bomb? Wheat dust from loading high, or his diesel fuel on the water? He will never dock here again. Put out that fire!"

Captain Pradesh watched a long spray of white chemical piss from the dock hoses to engulf the rope fire. "Order the hawser anchored in housing," he radioed his deck master, "Have one man try to cut it quickly with an ax, but tell all other men on deck to take distant cover at once."

"Captain, the Coast Guard? He will soon be in our path."

Captain Pradesh watched the sleek silver craft maneuvering now at much slower speed through an incredible array of motorboats, yachts, and sailboats. They had formed a semi-circle of curiosity around his freighter at the Mannheim dock, and were now moving gingerly out of his way also. It reminded him of a fast-paced chess game he recently waged, with pawns scattering as the primary pieces advanced against each other. "We are by far the larger vessel. Nautical courtesy dictates that the Coast Guard give way." The ship's radio was still silent; no transmission had been received.

The hawser was tightening astern, then stretching out like a taut bowstring ready to let fly. The ax was bouncing off as if the rope was steel. For just a moment the engines struggled, slowing the forward momentum. Tensile strength was at maximum stress. Either the rope would snap, or the metal anchor on the dock or the deck housing would rip up its bolts.

That thought of what would happen to the taut rope ends if it broke hit the police chief and dockhands at the same time. "Everybody down!" shouted one. "Hit the deck!" said the other, and people began flattening themselves on the pier or on top of others who got down first.

SNAP! Two burned ends of rope hissed in opposite directions, seeking a target. That shorter piece anchored at the dock smacked a steel tower first, and dropped heavily but harmlessly onto clustered FBI personnel. The ship's end dropped like a shot snake into the Bay without flame.

"All right!" one onlooker on the Mannheim dock hollered out, and "Right on!" went rolling toward the back of the fleeing freighter. Fear and bewilderment and sadness seemed to be departing with the ship, replaced by a swell of cheering. Clapping erupted in spots, and soon became a thunder in hundreds of hands.

Someone had forced their way into the twice-bloodied cab of Engine 9039, and started long air horn blasts. Harrison Fruehauf joined in with his fourth engine's horn, having stopped the train. Their shrill tones met in mid-air with the heavy bleating of the freighter's low moan.

Tom had taken Janet's arm and moved her away from the crowd for an urgent talk. "Anyone who had a part in this train run will be restrained by the court from speaking about it for up to three years," he was saying. "Part of our mediated probation agreement. You are innocent. That makes you the logical choice for our spokesperson."

"Oh, there's no way," Janet resisted, barely focusing on what he was saying. "Peter will be back..."

"You know better than that, Janet. If...if he comes back, chances are he'll be imprisoned for life."

His bluntness shocked her. "We'll have to talk later. I just can't think now," she said, turning away from Tom to look at the tall stern of the freighter carrying Peter and Monty and the grain to a foreign shore.

"Mr. Buchanan, you are under arrest," III said with satisfaction, grabbing one of Tom's arms and forcing it roughly behind his back for the handcuffs. Janet turned back to watch the capturing of Peter's idealistic friend. The dream was ending.

*

"Madam Attorney General, thank you for accepting another Saturday morning call," Cassie spoke resolutely into the media van phone at Mannheim. "I have Mayor Taulison on with us again, and the chancellor of the National Peace Academy is also on the line." She was bringing in all the firepower she could quickly muster to urge non-violence.

"I'm glad I had planned this as a working day," the top U.S. attorney dourly greeted them. "It's dreary in D.C."

"It's getting drearier here in Seattle also, despite the sunshine," Cassie said. "Were you aware of the naval intervention in this Grain Train situation?"

"Yes. I agreed with the decision of Homeland Security. They thought the Coast Guard could keep the freighter docked, until we can legally sort out all issues."

Hopes dropped for Cassie and the mayor, who had been wishing their mediation partner might be reluctant.

"Well, that plan has gone awry. This could easily lead to more violence, due to the congested water environment now surrounding them, and the number of civilians involving themselves," the Academy executive started. He had more to say, but wasn't given the chance.

"My terms haven't changed," the A.G. said resolutely. "The fugitives must surrender themselves, and the stolen grain must be returned. At present they are merely escaping criminals with a hundred charges plus contraband merchandise, and will be treated as such."

"You make it sound simple," the mayor rejoined, "but I respectfully suggest that you are making a serious mistake. Part of the grain belongs to them already, I understand contributions are still pouring in, and there are the concert proceeds exceeding a million dollars. There may be enough to buy all the grain. As for your fugitives, take a look at TV! They are a dying boy and a wounded member of the AARP. What will you possibly gain?"

"What we are still all about, the rule of law," the A.G. answered bluntly. "How can a woman in your position not understand? The grain was initially obtained illegally."

"You've been more conciliatory recently," the male voice reminded.

"Times change," the D.C. lady threw back.

"As do people," Cassie interjected. "We have a crowd of hundreds out on the bay, and thousands are behind us here at the Mannheim fence. Do you really think that mob will tolerate yet another shooting to end this? I'm surprised they haven't lynched us already."

"Okay, people, here's how it sifts out," the A.G. concluded. "Because of laughable cooperation from your local authorities, that ship has been loaded with contraband and two prime suspects. It is not leaving U.S. jurisdiction, regardless of misguided pressure from the public, and from a handful of its officials. Our maritime codes of stop, search, and seizure appertain in this case. It's already gone too far, much too publicly, to have it end otherwise."

"Then understand clearly," the Academy Chancellor spoke into the silence of rejected requests. "The responsibility for the imminent damage which may occur to lives and property rests squarely on your shoulders."

"Which is precisely where it should be. Thank you for your efforts, however. Now I have more pressing matters requiring my attention."

"No, you don't!" Cassie protested, but her voice didn't get past the ending click of the D.C. line.

*

"I don't care how close the police chopper is, or what they are pointing at us, hold this position!" Donna Harrison yelled at the pilot. "These pictures are worth millions!" Then she clicked on the microphone switch to carry her broadcast live to Denver's TV-5 and its network affiliates around the country.

"No, it's not over yet, not by a long shot. The large freighter filling your screen is the *Godavari Sunrise*, registered out of India. The wheat from those fifty cars of the Grain Train has been transferred into its hold from the Mannheim Elevators. Peter Wayman and Monty Montropovich, the Robin Hoods or hijacker terrorists, call them what you will, are badly wounded but on board that large vessel.

"Now as your view of Elliott Bay gets wider, notice the next biggest ship up in the left corner. That's the Coast Guard Cutter *Rancor*, apparently sent to intercept the *Sunrise*. The smaller six or seven craft with the flashing red and blue lights are the Harbor Patrol, who for the past hour have been trying to break up the increasing congestion made by all the small private boats filling up the rest of your screen.

"The latest development, whether planned or accidental, is that as the little boats move out of the way of the freighter, which we clock at about ten miles per hour and picking up speed, they form a tight web of traffic, effectively blocking the progress of the *Rancor* and patrol boats."

*

On the dock, Janet and Marion walked slowly together, crushed in spirit, arm in arm toward the pier and land. They were planning a last look from the little office at the top of the tall headhouse building. For all they could see from water level was a fast disappearing freighter and many other boats. Marion also scoured the faces of the crowd for Frank. She needed him desperately.

Wafting wails of a dozen sirens from out in the Bay made talking difficult. And one strident voice began also intruding on their senses.

"Yes, he was one of the best," III was saying to a group of reporters, the object of several lights blaring even in the bright sunlight. "I'm not surprised that he and his crew took out two suspected assassins. I only wish...their assignment of reaching the third one...could have saved his son from injury."

The words were beginning to hold some strange significance for the two ladies walking by.

"...never condone the use of violent vigilante justice, even against subversive elements like these..." Some reporters began pointing and whispering, and III looked to see what had distracted them from him.

"Ah," he exclaimed, "there's a woman who may have more to add to this tragic story of an undercover officer dying in the line of duty--Frank Wayman's widow."

The reporters surged away from him and toward the shocked woman who had finally grasped what the vindictive supervisor was saying. That's why Frank hadn't been here when she needed him. And never would be again. Her world started spinning as she collapsed against Janet.

"Just give her air, she'll be all right," III interjected into the calls for a doctor. Persons from an ambulance rushed that direction.

"No, she won't!" Janet contradicted him. Bystanders were helping Janet lay the unconscious woman down.

"What do you mean, Miss Binghamton?" an alert reporter asked her.

A furious Janet stood up, staring straight into the hard tired eyes of the man she had learned to hate during this trip. "I said Marion Wayman will not be all right. Nobody involved in this will be all right again, not until this nation faces up to the obligation of sharing its food surpluses with starving people, wherever they are clinging to life on our small planet."

She had planned neither this speech, nor this step in the direction Tom had pleaded. But it was happening.

"Then you are championing Peter's cause?" several asked at once.

She instantly decided. "I'll be speaking to every college campus and service club and congressional committee that will have me."

III stared unblinking as his new protagonist was being born.

"There is quite a story to tell. Oh, and I'll be using very legal methods..." she explained, turning to confront him, "...to placate even the most insensitive legal asses." The bitterness between the two was not lost in filming the incident.

"I'll talk with any of you who want an interview, as soon as Mrs. Wayman is cared for," the young beauty offered, her hand on her friend's arm as the paramedics lifted the stretcher.

*

"Peter, we're getting ourselves into another mess," Monty said half to himself, half to the unhearing man on the stretcher--the man who would never again hear.

The ship's doctor had put aside his disdain for working on another country's criminal, and thickly bandaged the neck with its ruptured vessels and torn muscles, then stopped in futility. He had neither skills nor equipment nor blood plasma to keep the brutalized body functioning. He had notified the captain, who then yielded to Monty's request, ordering the body taken to the front rail of the forecastle where the train engineer had been standing alone. Peter had died.

"I'm not at the controls any more, Pete. Neither is A.M., nor Fork." He looked out at the jumble of boats around them in the Bay, those scurrying out of their path, and the trim gray one with the deck gun trying to get to them. "They're finally going to shut us down for sure."

The captain in his dress whites joined Monty at the most forward position on deck. "The Coast Guard has just radioed us to stand to, and prepare to be boarded," he apprised the older man in the stained shirt.

"To take us off?" Monty queried.

"That. And to inspect our cargo."

"You carrying drugs, Captain?" Monty managed a sick half-smile.

"No, not unless they can make an illegal substance from wheat. However, they might be able to tell one stolen kernel's State from another, under a microscope."

"What will you do?" Monty asked, staring out at the busy sea.

"When will you see our doctor about your wounds? And what will you do about Peter?" the captain countered.

Monty looked down at the body covered by a blanket, and pondered a long moment.

"Captain," Monty asked, "if you'll help me get my friend up to the rail, I can hold him then. He deserves to be part of these last moments. And there may be time later for the doc to take a look at me."

*

If the one biggest mistake could be identified that was made between 11:00 A.M. and noon this Saturday morning by U.S. authorities, it would be the literal interpretation placed on the tiny word 'now' by Commander Sandling of the U.S.C.G. Cutter *Rancor*.

His orders had been sent from very high sources, directing a stop and search mission against the *Godavari Sunrise*, "…now, before she reaches international waters."

Commander Sandling could have interpreted those directions to mean, "...now, off Port Townsend in the Juan de Fuca Strait, sixty miles away, before she reaches Canadian waters." Or he could have taken them to mean, "...now, once the freighter heads for Whidbey Island in the Sound, twenty miles out of sight of Seattle's harbor."

But III had said it must be stopped 'now,' and his director had recommended it the same way to Homeland Security, and they to the U.S. Attorney General and Joint Chiefs of Staff, and they to the Coast Guard Commandant as a 'NOW' kind of 'now,' much sooner rather than later.

And the young *Rancor* Commander was following his orders to the letter. "Clear away!" he said into his microphone, with speakers aimed in

all four directions. "Small craft, clear away! Give us right of way here!
Harbor Masters, sweep this area clean!" Commander Sandling sought total
immediate control on the waterway, as III had on the land.

*

On board the *Sunrise*, Captain Pradesh had a decision to make: succumb
to the vastly superior offensive weapon bearing down on him, surrender, and
be delayed indefinitely by the U.S. judicial system sorting out international
rights and wrongs. Or support the two men with him in the bow, who had
risked their lives and others for three days on a cause for humanity. He well
knew Peter as a man of principle--as also was he.

But his crew had divided opinions. And it was their lives on the line with
his in this foreign land.

However, this wasn't just any country. This was America. And not just
any town in America. This was Seattle: site of world fairs and Olympics,
peaceful host to all races and religions, intercultural in business and
neighborhoods, international in its concerns and T-shirts.

And this was the home of Greenpeace, known for its bravery in confronting
giants in pollution and whale slaughter and nuclear testing. And they did it
in little boats--rubber rafts and dinghies set against the brutality of men in
mammoth ships with law on their side. They might very well be bobbing
out there on the Bay right now alongside his ship.

"Never underestimate Seattle," the captain remembered Peter saying
during their last phone call.

Unencumbered by democratic traditions, Captain Pradesh quickly made
his own decision. He lifted his radio to his mouth: "Helmsman, come to
course bearing zero- degrees north, maintain half speed."

"Captain?" the voice crackled back over the radio.

The captain turned and pointed the full length of the ship back to the
steering cabin on the uppermost deck. "Aye, aye, sir," the voice now
radioed. The course just ordered would steer them broadside in front of the
guns of the *Rancor*, pushing forward on their left side from the west.

Captain Pradesh knelt and pulled back the blanket. The ship's doctor had
wiped the blood only from the gaunt young face. The ragged shirt had been
removed. Two areas of ripped flesh the size of coffee cups lay caked with
blood and tissue around the open wounds. The whiteness of his clean face
was shocking compared to the dark red covering his chest.

"It will never do for the people to see him like this," the captain said.

Monty was headed back into shock at the stark realization of such a pain-wracked death, remembering Peter struggling to climb the gangplank--at his friend's insistence.

The master of the ship removed his own starched white jacket. Monty watched him lift the limp form forward, pulling first one long white sleeve then the other over the arms drenched with dried blood. He lay Peter down again and buttoned the coat. "Are you still able to stand?" he looked up to ask Monty.

"Why are you doing...this?" Monty was barely able to ask.

"My son spent his senior year living with the Waymans. Peter saved his life, pulling him out of a burning car after an accident. I followed Peter's career, and together we watched the U.S. prosper as my nation starved along with others. His angry thoughts were my thoughts, his words urging change, my own."

But the linkages were lost in Monty's fog. "Let us stand him up, Monty. Let his spirit see success."

Monty obeyed the instruction, which followed his original request. The two men each reached under an arm and hefted Peter upright. Monty moved Peter's good left arm up over his own shoulders and around his neck to steady the body now wearing a white jacket and captain's bars against his own wounded side. He braced himself against the rail.

"Can you manage?" Captain Pradesh asked as he was leaving.

"As long as I need to," Monty answered in stronger tones. He raised his head and breathed in the brisk salty breeze to stop the spinning.

A most astonishing thing quickly started happening. From their boats, children and then adults began waving at the two men standing at the bow of the freighter. And people started pointing out the pair to others further back in the cluster of small boats. And motorboats began venturing in closer to the fast-moving grain hauler to get a better look.

They crisscrossed in front of the giant hull, like sporting dolphins leaping over waves. Then in feats of excellent seamanship, those with sufficient power and skill began forming a flying wedge, clearing the path with even greater urgency for the ship being pursued by the Coast Guard. They seemed to take on speed and purpose after seeing Peter with his head bowed, but standing out grandly in the white coat. Everyone in the Bay now knew it was he.

Suddenly, above all other sounds, the awesome ascending tone sounded loud and clear: the call of sailors to their battle stations on board the trim man-of-war. It was a sound most Seattle residents thought they would never hear except in movies, or maybe a drug chase. It signaled that the threat was no bluff to the bulky freighter gliding low in the water with its cumbersome load of grain.

Some of the smaller boats of citizens began scurrying out of the way of harm, and ticketing. But not all. For the seaport town was turning. It wasn't one alone, or someone acting first. It was the many riding by and looking up at the man called Peter, embodying the good and generous and frustrated in all of them. That's what made most of them stay defiantly in the sea-lane from which they were stridently being forced away. But it was their sea. It would be their say.

Despite the lingerers, Commander Sandling gave the order unhesitatingly: "Fire one shot across her bow! She will stop for us--now!"

The gunner was more deliberate. He could not see what was on the other side of the large hull, so he could not fire over her. And ships were everywhere in front of their craft, between them and the freighter. There was only the hundred feet of open water directly in front of the big ship's prow. He had entered course and speed of their two ships into the computer to calculate, then waited long seconds...for the flotilla to accidentally make a momentary gap...

BOOM! The five-inch diameter shell erupted from the mouth of the forward mounted deck cannon, sizzling on a straight-line trajectory directly into the immediate path of the *Godavari Sunrise.*

Ka-BOOM! The impact explosive hurled salt spray 150 feet into the sky, covering the freighter's forward deck, soaking Monty, and the man in the loaned white jacket. But Monty did not flinch away from the attack.

"Captain Pradesh?" Kasir asked of the man again fully attired to fit the rank. "Sir, shall we stop engines?"

"No, Kasir. We are bound for the Pacific Ocean. Second Mate Sheefah," he radioed down to the deck, "have six sailors report to the bow, each with rifles loaded for five shots."

The officer asked for the order to be clarified.

"We are honoring a leader who has died aboard our ship. And...lower our own flag to half-mast in respect."

"This seems quite irregular, sir," he responded.

"So is a shot off our bow. I'm trying to prevent a second one in our hull at water line. Do as I commanded."

In less than a minute, the sailors were in position, rifles aimed high.

*

"This has got to be one of the most bizarre moments in U.S. naval history," TV-5's Donna Harrison announced, "and perhaps one of the most tragic, when even the apparent winner will lose." Their helicopter hovered three hundred feet just behind the *Godavari Sunrise*, from where they filmed the warning shot. "It is a time for mourning, but there is no time. For more gunfire is imminent. When those grain sailors start shooting, they could kill or be killed, and the Cutter's next shell will surely tear steel apart.

"Wait, though, wait a moment. See, the freighter's sailors are standing in a formation...and pointing their rifles skyward. And their national flag on the ship is being lowered. Get a picture of that. This is shaping up to be something more like a military honor guard ceremony!" The chopper pilot maintained his speed constant with the fifteen knots the ship was traveling. Three different camera persons on board were depending on his skill to keep them steady, while avoiding the buzzing fly-bys of the Harbor Master's threatening copter.

"Three sailors have lined up on each side of the two train men forward, facing the railings. Their guns are poised in position...and there are the puffs of smoke from the first volley. Can the *Rancor* tell they are not being fired on? There's the second...the third. Can we get them a message? The fourth, we can tell by the smoke...the fifth.

"Now they are lowering their rifles...hah, would you look at that? One after the other...the sailors are walking to the rail, holding out their rifle, and very deliberately and carefully dropping it over the side into the bay...no danger of hitting anyone, for they look below first. It is quite clear that they are publicly disarming themselves...but this ship of peace is sure showing no signs of stopping either." Donna took a breath and kept reporting what her colleague was pointing out.

"We can see that the U.S. sailors who jumped to alert with their weapons on board the *Rancor* have relaxed, now that the shooting has ended. Our close-ups show some real perplexed looks after the rifle episode, and with a standing corpse, no offense meant.

"But both of the messages were clearly sent, and clearly received all across Elliott Bay, and the United States as well: Peter Wayman is dead, and the Coast Guard has ordered the ship bearing his body to halt.

"The repeated moan of the freighter's low horn is being joined now by dozens and dozens of the small craft. Can you hear it through the mike?" The pilot clicked on the directional microphone. The strange wail of different tones blended into a symphony of sorrow from the people.

"I'm hovering right over the *Sunrise*, watching a new and strange strategy taking place. Apparently it's coordinated only with hand signals from boat to boat. Let me try to describe it...no. *Herald* chopper, how high are you? A perspective picture from one or two thousand feet might really help us figure out what's going on at this point..."

The advice was taken. The *Herald*/KDNC Radio crew climbed vertically from their position a hundred yards in front of the freighter.

"Here's what we can see," Gene Valore began reporting. "The *Sunrise* is in the northern half of the bay, six miles or so from the grain dock. She sailed right past two major marinas to the north, and picked up possibly four hundred boats of all descriptions, scattered out around the freighter, let's say a hundred on each side, plus the same in front and even more behind.

"There are some spots," Gene continued, "where the boats are really clustered, like behind the ship, trying to catch up or keep up. And in front of her there are two ragged lines heading roughly northwest, as the Bay widens into Puget Sound. What did the Indians call it? Running the gauntlet. That's what it looks like the *Sunrise* is doing, except this is a gauntlet of nautical friends.

"As the ship passes boats along the line, the slower ones are falling in behind to join the increasing number there--as if she was a fishing trawler dragging a huge seine net. Those with outboard motors pull out, skirt around the busy Harbor Patrol and Coast Guard craft--ignoring them or slowing them--and join the left or right line ahead of the ship to deepen the layers of protective webbing. There's just no way the *Rancor* is going to get another clear shot at the *Sunrise*--if that ever was their serious intent-- without risking the shelling of five or ten civilian boats everywhere in her shadow."

"Don, a moment's interruption," Donna cut in. "This outpouring of public sentiment really reminds me of that whale in trouble inland from San Francisco, when everybody came out to try and save it. Except today, our military good guys are ending up on the wrong side..."

*

"Pete, I wish you could see." Monty made no movement of his own aching body, other than his lips, while still supporting Peter's arm and weight with his shoulders.

"The boats are lined up in front of us, as far as I can see," Monty described. "And here's twenty slick speedboats opening up the way just in front of us, like Navy motorcycles." Monty waved at a little boy on a sailboat who was waving up at them. The little guy was crying real hard.

"The gunship made a couple of runs at us, Pete, but I don't think they'll be back. Too many boats to go through, and God only knows where they came from, kind of sticking together like they were glued.

"Heck, Pete, they ain't even letting the ferry boats or other freighters through. Everything has to wait and go behind us after we pass...like a funeral. Just like when we were hammering down the mainline, Pete, with the people all clearing the tracks. Our Grain Train shipment is coming through, world!"

*

"This is Don Trujillo, of Denver's KDNC Radio, back with you from a helicopter high above the *Godavari Sunrise*. This freighter has made it fifteen miles from Seattle, picking up speed as she moves up the Puget Sound channel, still surrounded by its flotilla of supporters in every type of seaworthy craft. The Coast Guard Cutter *Rancor* is shadowing her, staying about two miles away on her port side, possibly waiting for an opening to attack.

"The large land mass you are seeing now on TV is Bainbridge Island, due west from Seattle across the Sound. Behind it you can see the body of water called Port Orchard, and on west of that is a spit of land with a place called Bangor on my map, with a notation 'U.S. Navy Submarine Base.' If we fly too close to it, the map says we will be shot down.

"This could be the source of the next governmental challenge to the cargo of wheat, which could be in Canadian waters within ninety minutes at this speed. And it would be the last challenge in this saga, for no freighter can withstand a belly shot by a torpedo. Stakes have mounted every mile that grain traveled across the country, and as every new politician and law officer got involved. Those stakes are now very grave indeed.

"Listen, folks, in my Denver radio job, I'm an ordinary workingman, with ordinary feelings. Now I guess a submarine could be ordered out of the pen down there, maybe already has been, by a lower level officer. Maybe that decision has gotten up to the top brass, maybe even the Secretary of the Navy is in on the act.

"But this is what I think--and what I call for. And that is that nobody less than the president himself, our President of all these United States, should make the final decision..." The picture had switched back to the freighter. "...on the fate of that grain in the hold of that ship."

There flashed up an amazing close-up of Monty's bleeding upper torso, and the sagging head and stained white coat on the body he held limp at his side.

Don looked, and went on. "When the heart of Peter Wayman stopped beating, Mr. President, it really didn't skip even a beat. For it is the same heart that beats there in his friend who supports him, and in the farmers who stayed with him all the way from Colorado. It is the heart of the people who climbed aboard in Utah, and Idaho, and Oregon, and Washington. It is the same heart beating in the women and men and kids who are now risking arrest and injury in these waters off Seattle." The picture was now scanning the whole flotilla, stretching all the way back to Elliott Bay and four miles ahead of the *Sunrise*.

"You and I know, Mr. President, that one torpedo, or even a thousand, will not still such a heart. For it has become the very heart of America pounding in the chests of patriots...who only want to give...to help others.

"So it should be only you, sir, as the head of our nation, who decides what happens today to America's heart."

*   *   *

The man in shirtsleeves leaned back in the tan leather chair. He was the latest in a line more than two centuries long to sit in that seat of immense power. His eyes moved from the television screen to the faces of the people standing almost at attention near the set. "Seems everyone else has had a hand in this…" and he left the phrase unsaid as he finished scribbling a hasty note. "It must indeed be my turn now."

He caught the eyes of the attractive lady in a dark suit, nearest his desk. "Join me in a trip to the wine cellar," he invited her. Then he reached over, picked up the phone receiver from the red console, and pushed a button.

"Are the Navy and Coast Guard Chiefs still down there? …Good. Tell them to stand down the Seattle action to a shadowing mission for a few minutes. The attorney general and I are on the way to the Situation Room to join them."

He hung up, stood, and moved from his large desk with the presidential seal on its front to open the door for his cabinet officer. He handed the note to his personal secretary with a nod as he passed her desk and left the office.

"Abe Lincoln had a lot on his plate also, so I've studied his thought process," he said on the way to the elevator. "Abe once said, 'We here hold the power and bear the responsibility. The dogmas of the quiet past are inadequate to the stormy present. The occasion is piled high with difficulties, and we must rise with the occasion.'"

Secret Service crowded onto the elevator with them, and as the door closed, he was finishing the old words remembered this afternoon. "'As our case is new, so we must think anew and act anew...and then we shall save our country.'"

fin

T.E.J.T.M.

Note to readers from the author:

This is where the manuscript originally ended. Thank you for your patience and interest in reading this story.

You may stop here, and draw your own conclusions as to the subsequent actions of the president. That is perfectly acceptable, for that is what I did for years, letting my mind ruminate on possibilities.

Or you may turn this page, and read the following epilogue chapter, in which I have included three additional pieces of concluding documentation that you may find interesting.

# # #

T.E.J.T.M.

EPILOGUE

Chapter Twenty-Five

The president had written a few notes during the telecast, and handed them with a nod to Mrs. Larson, his private secretary, on his way out with the attorney general. And now, at her desk just outside the Oval Office, Mrs. Kathryn Larson was calling down the list as tasked by the president. The note started with his nickname for her:

"Kat--pls call / ask these folks--standby for conf call in next hr re: grain train & freighter--may last awhile thx I'll call you to connect us

  1- Chancellor NPA for Cassie's ? ph # -- mediator in Seattle
  2- DC Ambass -- India
  3- Capt Pradesh -- Sunrise freighter -- leaving Puget Sound for Canada
  4- Monty Montropovich -- passenger on Sunrise
  5- DC Ambass -- Canada

  6-Janet ? -- Peter's girlfriend, Seattle dock w/Mayor Taulison? and call Ms. Wayman -- Peter's mother (and husband Frank killed) -- condolences only, no conf call

1st -- Ask Sec/St to join us in ~~war~~ crisis room "

*　　*　　*

Text of televised Presidential Address to the Nation on Sunday, August 14, 1:00 P.M. E.D.T.:

"Good afternoon. I wish to update you on the unusual and tragic series of events occurring in our western United States during the past four days. American citizens have a right to know the full truth, and the reasons for the actions that your government has undertaken.

A trainload of surplus grain was hijacked near Denver, Colorado, on Thursday, August 11. The internal terrorists responsible call themselves U.S.A.S., which stands for Unite Surplus and Starving. Their self-proclaimed mission was to force the United States to change its farm and export policies by the threat and use of deadly means. They initially bombed an oil refinery and public highway in Denver to insure that law enforcement agencies took their threats seriously. When it became apparent to them that your government would not be blackmailed, and would take action to stop the train, they ordered explosives detonated along their route--in Salt Lake City, Utah; Boise, Idaho; Portland, Oregon; and Seattle, Washington. Some of these explosions caused heavy damage to electrical and transportation infrastructure, and in some cases, resulted in death. America was under attack from within, originating with U.S. citizens. No foreign involvement has been uncovered.

Two of the hijackers were killed during this criminal spree. Several more were injured, some seriously. All have now been accounted for, tracked down, and are under arrest. Some law officials have been injured, with one killed, and some private citizens have also been injured, with two known fatalities.

To add to the tragedy of this situation, the stated end goal of the hijackers was admirable: to use surplus U.S. wheat to save starving children around the world. I agree with that end goal, and this Administration has often iterated that we are working to find a reasonable, efficient, and economical way to bring our plentiful food resources together with the urgent needs abroad.

But I vehemently disagree with the violent means chosen by these hijackers. America will guard its land and its people from all enemies, whether they be internal or from outside our borders. A terrorist is a terrorist. We will fight them using the fullest extent of the law, and we will stop them.

Through a bizarre series of incidents, the grain on the hijacked train was unloaded onto the grain freighter *Godavari Sunrise*, and left the port of

Seattle. This ship is owned by a foreign company, and registered out of the nation of India. I am in close communication with the prime minister of that country, and have outlined the necessity for my order for the U.S. Coast Guard to stop that ship, by the use of non-violent means. This is against the wishes of the ship's captain, but is being done to allow for the proven process of mediation to continue trying to resolve this conflict peacefully.

The National Peace Academy is the foremost mediation organization in our nation, and has been asked to facilitate this important dialogue. But let me make it clear to you that the hijacked grain is considered stolen property, and will not be permitted to be shipped abroad.

However, the U.S.A.S. group has brought an old value back to light, even though it cost some of them their lives to do so. America is a good country, and stands for doing the right thing. The hearts and minds of people and leaders in a democracy can be renewed by acts of bravery and self-sacrifice.

There was a mediated agreement in Seattle to hold an international conference on bridging the food gap between *have* and *have-not* nations to solve an urgent crisis. That conference will be convened in good faith by the United States in Seattle by October 1st.

I have commissioned a study to be made, with results to be published within fifteen days, calculating how much of our federal grain surplus in storage could be immediately replaced by available grain now being held in temporary facilities and grain cars. They will also study the immediate and long-term economic impact of releasing stored surplus into the world market.

Another group, a very unique group of leaders, will be asked to assess the humanitarian aspects of releasing that stored grain directly to proven agencies dealing daily with people who are starving, to insure that the grain flow is not interrupted with exorbitant charges and bureaucratic delays.

The conclusions of these commissions will be studied carefully and presented to you, the American public, and to the Congress, for quick response.

To those in America and around the world, who are looking into the face and heart of our nation, wondering what kind of country America has become to halt a life-saving shipment of grain: I pledge that at least fifty rail cars carrying loads of wheat will be unloaded into a freighter by this time tomorrow, and on its way to feed the starving. You will watch it happening. For it is the right thing to do, and the right time to do it, and very importantly, the right and legal process for doing it.

This nation remains resolute in defending our laws, which are the basis of our freedom, but we also remain humanitarian, valuing each life as precious.

Thank you. And may God continue to bless America."

End of complete text of the Presidential Address to the Nation, Sunday, August 14, 1:00 P.M. E.D.T.

*   *   *

Mediation conclusions reached by consensus of all parties, and publicized by the National Peace Academy as agreed by all parties, on Sunday, August 14, 8:00 P.M., E.D.T., four days after the hijacking of the Grain Train:

Participants in conference call:
U.S. Attorney General
Janet Binghamton, U.S.A.S. representative
Seattle Mayor Taulison
Washington Governor Archway
Antonio d'Almeda, Mannheim Grain Elevator administrator
Washington, D.C. Ambassador from India
Cassie Cowdrey, NPA mediator

1- *Godavari Sunrise* will return at once to Mannheim grain elevators and dock.

2- Ship's grain cargo will become the property of the U.S. Government, by right of eminent domain.

3- Ship's grain cargo will be unloaded fully, at Mannheim Elevator's expense, into a separate holding facility for easy identification.

4- The unloaded grain will be bought from the U.S. Government. This includes the full load, the lower portion previously loaded and the top portion from the fifty railroad grain cars. Purchase funds will come from the U.S.A.S. donation account.

5- The unloaded grain now belonging to U.S.A.S. will be donated by U.S.A.S. to the World Vision organization, in recognition of its ongoing successful efforts at reducing starvation worldwide. U.S.A.S. will pay for loading of this grain and shipment abroad, to become part of the World Vision food relief program.

6- The balance remaining in the various U.S.A.S. donation accounts will be added to the damage reimbursement fund, to be administered by a court of arbitration to handle all claims.

7- The unloaded *Godavari Sunrise* will be allowed to refuel, then released into the command of Captain Pradesh and his crew in international waters, carrying no cargo. The U.S. Navy will escort it to its home port, to be released there to the Indian authorities for local disposition.

8- No criminal charges will be made against the Mannheim Grain Elevator Company or its employees, nor will there be restitution for associated loss of revenue and added expenses from this incident.

9- Monty Montropovich will surrender himself to be arrested, will be treated for his wounds, and will be held without bail for trial.

10- The bodies of Peter Wayman, his father Frank Wayman, Fork Thompson, and Professor MacLeod will now be returned to their respective families and/or friends in Seattle for proper burial.

11- The shootings of Fork Thompson, Wilma Fletcher, Buck Bancroft, and the initial shooting of Peter Wayman will be fully investigated to determine all those responsible. Those apprehended will be given a fair trial. A reward of $50,000 will be offered by the FBI for information leading to the arrest of any additional conspirator.

12- The shooting of Monty Montropovich and the second shooting of Peter Wayman will be fully investigated to determine all those responsible. Those apprehended will be given a fair trial. Since these two men were under the protection of a formal U.S. mediation agreement, a reward of $100,000 will be offered by the FBI for information leading to the arrest of each conspirator.

13- The shooting of Frank Wayman will be fully investigated to determine all those responsible. Those apprehended will be given a fair trial. A reward of $150,000 will be offered by the FBI for information leading to the arrest of each conspirator.

14- Normal maritime laws will appertain to incidents resulting in damages to any water craft or person(s) aboard such craft directly related to the passage of the *Godavari Sunrise* out of Elliott Bay and beyond on August 13. The arrest and charges of those persons filmed participating in a protest action directly or indirectly resulting in the blocked passage of the U.S. Coast Guard Cutter *Rancor* will be given into the jurisdiction of court-mandated arbitration. This arbitration en masse will be conducted by representatives of the National Peace Academy.

15- All those agreements reached at the previous Seaticon mediation conference will be honored to the fullest extent still possible after intervening events during the last forty-eight hours.

16- Further matters pertaining, and unforeseen consequences of these decisions, will be dealt with in the reconvening of this same group for mediation of any disputes. The call to reconvene may be made by any party in this mediation group.

fin

T.E.J.T.M.
The End Justifies The Means

CHAPTER CONTENTS

(…presented here as a helpful reminder of that which has gone before,
for use only when returning to the story after an extended absence…)

WARNING: THIS WILL GIVE AWAY THE ENDING ! ! ! !

--Thursday, August 11 (cont.)

Chapter Four

(3:50 *a.m.*):   Train at Tabernash, CO 55

Denver train dispatcher Harran orders another train to CLEAR TRACK to avoid collision, and side railed engineers curse and take pictures of banners as 9039 passes. Frank as #2 in Denver FBI RESPONDS to oil fire, and radio announces USAS claim. Ruth sends second package with Wilma's message. *HERALD* newspaper office receives location and FREES ENGINEERS with help of KDNC radio, while filming rescue.

Chapter Five

(5:20 *a.m.*):   State Bridge, CO 76

Denver railroad boss Manchester takes charge of dispatch office, and gets full story. Ruth BOMBS small highway bridge to Denver International Airport. *Herald* discovers Wilma is missing, teams up with radio to cover story. Wilma makes visual/CB contact with TRUCKERS, and forms alliance. Manuel (SALT LAKE CITY), Jeremy (BOISE), Ardis (PORTLAND), Tom (SEATTLE) have placed bombs, receive hourly OKAY CALLS from Peter or detonate.

Chapter Six

(6:05 *a.m.*):   Dotsero, CO 94

III, third man from top in Washington, D.C. FBI office, calls for update, had warned of INTERNAL TERRORISTS everywhere. Ruth's fax promises no further violence if train gets green lights. NEWSPAPER, RADIO, TV ALLIANCE will cover story with leap-frogging helicopters. "Denver Under Siege!" headlines. Frank takes charge in dispatch office. FBI LINKS PETER with hijacking.

Chapter Seven

(7:00 *a.m.*):   Newcastle, CO 110

Second oil TANK EXPLODES, injuring officer in dispatch office. Monty demands Harran continue as dispatcher. FRANK TIES MONTY to hijacking, calls wife Marion to find their son Peter. III FLYING IN to take charge. NATIONAL PEACE ACADEMY getting involved, trying to prevent further violence. Chanto visits friend in Denver to track 9039's progress through CB network. FRANK AND PETER talk. Wilma reports to *Herald* for radio, argues with Peter.

Chapter Eight

Josephine and Matthew, Peter's grandparents, leave Wray farm with Monty's wife for Denver, and CARAVAN OF CONCERN joins them. Grain owners demand no damage. NPA CRISIS CENTER on full alert, with Monty as former student. TV copter makes contact with 9039, getting WILMA'S HOURLY BROADCAST to nation. FRANK REMOVED from case. Al of Brighton SERV-U.S. SUPPORTS Peter's actions. Debate with farm official at Wray barbeque remembered.

Chapter Nine

HOBO ATTACK repelled by boxcar farmers, with GUN FIRED by Peter and injured farmer airlifted, all filmed. III and Brody send Frank home, then go to DIA. TV interviews girlfriend Janet. TV NEWS SPECIAL shows forty cars in Wray caravan, interviews Dan in Wray on farm problems and equipment heading for protest, shows DIA restricted traffic, TV manager Tim spots III and alerts SLC TV, shows oil fires burning, and shows caravan now in traffic jam.

Chapter Ten

FBI AGENTS SEARCHING Frank's home when he arrives, and he warns wife Marion of bugging. NPA Crisis Center sharing info with reporters. 9039 REFUELS at Helper. From airplane, III orders agent to get 9039 moving. RESIDENTS JOIN boxcar farmers in support. National Serv-U.S. office POLLING clubs. SHOTS FIRED in Helper, and train rushes away.

Chapter Eleven

NPA campus tour. Crisis Center talks with Dave, a grad and Denver's regional director, and Intervention Team. Brody interrogates Waymans, places FRANK ON LEAVE without pay. LaGrande, OR, QUILTING CIRCLE debates grain train. NPA calls Peter, who remembers starving BOY DYING in his arms. III quizzed by media in SLC. NPA and Peter closer to agreement. NAMES OF SUSPECTED HIJACKERS given to III by his assistant Switzer.

Chapter Twelve

In Denver, RUTH IS IDENTIFIED by FBI. III orders gas attack in code. Dave asks Ruth for train's destination, and FBI BUGS her house and

--Thursday, August 11 (cont.)

Dave's car. Peter debates his philosophy and demands with NPA. Senator Frye tells media of new Congressional farm SURPLUS COMMITTEE. III BLACKMAILS railroad president Fruehauf into non-interference. 9039 crosses mountains. Dave warns Intervention Team of GAS THREAT.

Chapter Thirteen

TV NEWS SPECIAL--oil fire, SLC airport with III, farmers circling capitol in Denver, pictures of train engineers and riders and Wayman family, Senator Frye's press conference, NPA Intervention Team gearing up, stats of 300,000 hits on train's blog site. Train enters SLC depot, Peter waves to Harran in tower, DEMANDS CLEARANCE NORTH to Pocatello, ID. III prepares to get ahead, and goes to trackside to EXCHANGE LOOKS as train passes--looks that could kill.

Chapter Fourteen

FBI IDENTIFIES CHANTO. Intervention Team takes copter from Boise to check track then rendezvous with 9039. WAYMANS ARE BLOCKED at DIA from regular flights; Frank calls MOB BOSS for help. 9039 picks up expert regional engineer Andre (A.M.) and transfers Wilma to boxcar for night. Peter and Monty share memories. Farmer flirts with Wilma. Monty threatens A.M.. Train radio dead. Copter flies into GAS CLOUD, disables spray truck, but one escapes. Train picks up Blackman.

Friday, August 12

Chapter Fifteen

Wilma's HOURLY BROADCASTS build support nationwide. NPA Prof. MacLeod learns of rail blockade ordered AT EARLHAM by governor, and BOARDS JET. Ella and quilting ladies in LaGrande get food ready. Groups denounce U.S. farm surplus policy. HUNTERS Chet and Tim park pickup in trees near tracks, and load their rifles. FARMERS RALLY 5,000 in Denver protest, and stage benefit concert. Senator Frye defends legal stand. Tom and Seattle's MAYOR DEBATE. Fork and Wilma see wildflowers from window. Hunters sight, and SHOOT.

Chapter Sixteen

FORK IS KILLED, WILMA LOSES ARM, PETER IS HIT in the leg, one farmer is wounded. Peter calls order to detonate first bombs. Governor orders pickup stopped as truckers intervene. TRAIN STOPS to care for wounded, and TV coverage is live. III to Portland, with Astoria as presumed destination. Fork's body stays with train. BOISE EXPLOSION, and JEREMY ARRESTED. Ardis blows up transformers. RUTH IS ARRESTED. Train stops, LaGrande welcomes them sadly, and Ruth's grandma Ella heads CLEAN-UP CREW. Fork's CASKET placed in boxcar, as truckers block police. III demands that governor keep Earlham blockade despite Portland bombing.

Chapter Seventeen

Train drops off money for Pendleton HOSPITAL BILLS. Tom and Mayor Taulison prepare for Seattle train arrival. RADIO SPECIAL with nationwide reaction--$1.5 million for benefit concert, farm protest, a million hits on blog, attorney general and senators deplore train actions, 86 now on board, Serv-U.S. asking for clemency, Boise on emergency alert, Prof. MacLeod's poem, all interspersed with "America, the Beautiful." Blackman tries MEDIATION CALL with governor and Peter, which falters; Peter talks with FAMILY ON CELL PHONE, gives Janet Seattle as destination, and family leaves in loaned plane.

Chapter Eighteen

Blockade site past Earlham is decoy, with stack of railroad TIES ON TRACKS, but RAILS ARE LOOSENED earlier. Dave heads NPA Team, sends repair group, train 45 minutes away. Grain freighter *Godavari Sunrise* IN ELLIOTT BAY at Seattle headed for fuel dock. GOVERNOR'S ULTIMATUM--stop or be stopped. Train slows for half to leave, with Blackman. ARDIS BLOWS up Portland bridge as direct threat, and is ARRESTED. MANUEL IS ARRESTED in SLC. Governor orders RED ALERT, to evacuate downtown Portland. Tom refuses to detonate bomb, gives bomb location to keep mayor's support.

--Friday, August 12 (cont.)

Chapter Nineteen

{4:40 p.m.}   Earlham, OR 355

At two Earlham blockade sites, tracks are tightened, NPA Intervention Team works for non-violence, as TRAIN MAKES RUN for it. Prof. MacLeod and deputy die. Portland erupts into CHAOS. Mayor and attorney general agree on NPA mediation to avoid deaths. III indirectly ORDERS ASSASSINATION. Peter talks with riders as TV films, picks up professor's CASKET and Blackman. FUNERAL TRAIN turns NORTH into Washington under CEASE-FIRE, and supporters board by CANDLELIGHT. Mannheim grain elevator will receive. CONCERT rocking Denver. III en route, as Waymans and Janet arrive in Seattle.

Chapter Twenty

{10:00 p.m.}   mid-Washington State 376

MEDIATION CONVENES and struggles with anger and agreements at Seaticon in Seattle. FREIGHTER DOCKS at Mannheim. TV reports train full of supporters, and a DIVIDED NATION. Frank searches for shooters in park, and finds one.

Saturday, August 13

Chapter Twenty-One

{6:13 a.m.}   Seattle, WA 395

Frank KILLS SHOOTER, and moves search to residential area on hillside. Peter's mother Marion and Janet arrive at Mannheim, as do III and Switzer. Seaticon mediation ends with many agreements, to reconvene by phone at Mannheim. Train stops to allow departures for safety, then continues slowly with 193 aboard. MEDIA everywhere, and huge TRAFFIC PROBLEMS. Cassie and Peter MEDIATING as train nears end.

Chapter Twenty-Two

{9:00 a.m.}   Mannheim grain elevators in Seattle 410

Frank returns to park, where assassin is hiding. III AND CAPTAIN ARGUE threateningly on freighter. Frank starts PARK FIRE as distraction. TRAIN ENTERS MANNHEIM yards and stops, but no one gets off. MEDIATION CONTINUES in engine cab with Cassie. Attorney General secretly orders grain from first car unloading to be diverted from ship, so mediation reaches final agreements. FRANK KILLS SHOOTER #2, and IS KILLED.

Chapter Twenty-Three

(11:00 A.m.)   Mannheim 422
MEDIATION AGREEMENTS ARE REACHED, AND BREACHED. First grain car starts unloading, but GRAIN IS SECRETLY DIVERTED into the elevators. JANET EMBRACES PETER in engine, and as he prepares to leave, HE IS SHOT, and MONTY ALSO. Monty and Janet organize STRETCHER CARRY for Peter toward the ship. TRAIN STARTS moving slowly. Homeland Security calls for Coast Guard. Marion starts GRAIN UNLOADING again, visibly into the ship, and captain lowers gangplank. III tries to arrest Peter, while Monty tries to get him onto the ship. BLANKET TUG-OF-WAR between family, friends, and FBI on gangplank ends with A SHOT.

Chapter Twenty-Four

(noon)   Seattle 447
With shot, captain gives a chance for Monty and Peter to board ship on their own, but Peter is too weak. SAILORS BRING THEM ABOARD, and bloodshed is avoided with Cassie's help. COAST GUARD FIRES SHOT to threaten departing freighter, but FLOTILLA OF PRIVATE BOATS blocks its path. Train is stopped, Tom is arrested, III announces Frank's death, and Janet becomes spokesperson. PETER HAS DIED on board ship, but is held up in captain's white jacket by Monty at the ship's front bow, as CROWD CHEERS AND CRIES from surrounding boats. PRESIDENT MEETS with advisors and military on the crisis, quoting Lincoln on acting anew to save our country.

# # #

EPILOGUE

# # # # #

T.E.J.T.M.
Character Reminders

Name	Role	Chapter of 1st appearance
A.M. (Andre Maurantagne)	Local engineer joining train in Utah	14
ADMIRAL HILL	Residential area overlooking Mannheim elevators	20
AGRI-NET Co-Op	Owns some grain and grain hopper cars on train	8
AL Federson	Vice President, Brighton, CO Serv-U.S. service club	2
ANDERSON, Gov. Lee	Governor of Oregon	15
ARDIS Borgeba	Shakespeare Group, delivers bombs, Portland, Oregon bomber	1
ATTORNEY GENERAL	U.S. Attorney General	16
AURARIA	College in Denver	1
BARNEY O'Brien	National president, Serv-U.S. service clubs	10
BEN Cody	Leader of Wray farmers on train	2
BLACKMAN, Jerome	NPA Intervention Team mediator on train	11
BOYD Tangent	'Sky Spy', KCOL-8 TV copter reporter	9
BRIGHTON, Shorty	Sheriff of Earlham, OR	18
BRODY, Winston	Denver FBI Regional Director; Frank's boss and friend	4
BUCK Bancroft	Farmer from Wray on train	8

Name	Role	Chapter of 1st appearance
CANDICE Wayman	Peter's sister	1
CAPTAIN PRADESH	Captain on grain freighter from India	2
CARL Thompson	Farmer from Wray on train	8
CASSIE Cowdrey	NPA mediator sent to Seattle	20
CHANTO Kudjakta	Shakespeare Group, stays in Denver; diplomatic immunity; CB radio friend	3
CHET (Chetfield)	Hunter from Nevada	15
CILIANDO, Giuseppe	Local Mafia patriarch in Denver	14
CMDR. SANDLING	Commander, U.S. Coast Guard Cutter *Rancor* in Elliott Bay	24
COOKIE Gilchrist	*Herald* reporter, stays in Denver	4
D'ALMEDA, Antonio	Manager, Mannheim grain elevators	19
DAN Brown	Feed store owner in Wray; Serv-U.S.'er	9
DAVE Cranmer	Denver home, NPA grad; Ruth's friend; Intervention Team member	6
DAVIES, Mayor Jonathan	Mayor of Portland, OR	18
DIA	Denver International Airport	5
DOC Nevins	Retired Army medic joins train in Helper, UT	10
DON Thompson	Alias used by Tom Buchanan	5
DON Trujillo	KDNC radio newsman, shadows train by copter	4
DONNA Harrison	KTAD-5 television reporter, shadows train in copter	6
DREW Manchesky	Farmer from Wray on train	8
DUNLAP, Lt. Gov.	Lt. Governor of Washington	20
EARLHAM	Town with rail blockade in Oregon	15
ELLA Barnes	Wednesday Quilting Circle in LaGrande, OR; Ruth's grandmother	11

Name	Role	Chapter of 1st appearance
ELLIOTT BAY	Harbor port in Puget Sound at Seattle, WA	18
ENGINE 9039	Lead engine in hijacked GrainTrain	3
FASMA	*Herald* photographer, shadows train in copter	4
FELICIA Montropovich	Monty's wife	1
FORK Thompson	Back-up engineer, Monty's friend	2
FRANK Wayman	Peter's father; Deputy Director Denver FBI	1
FRUEHAUF, Harrison	CEO of Mid-Western Pacific Railroad	12
FRYE, Sen. Stuart	Senator from Colorado, office in Denver	1
FULTON Skinnard	Farmer from Wray on train	8
GENE Valore	*Herald* reporter, shadows train in copter	4
ARCHWAY, Gov.	Governor of Washington	19
GREGORY Smith	Farmer from Wray on train	8
HARGRAVE, Roger	*Herald*'s day editor	5
HARRAN Winfree	Rail yard train dispatcher in Denver for Mid-Western Pacific; Peter's friend	3
HARRY Blake	Farmer from Wray on train	8
HENDERSON	*Herald*'s farm bureau chief, Greeley, CO	8
HERALD	*Rocky Mountain Herald*, Denver newspaper where Wilma works	2
JANET Binghamton	Peter's girlfriend; Auraria student	1
JENNIFER Crussman	Day chief, NPA Crisis Center	7
JEREMY Downing	Shakespeare Group, Boise, Idaho bomb	1
JOE Donaldson	Harran's boss in rail dispatch office	4
JOSEPHINE Williamson	Peter's grandmother on Wray farm	8
KCOL-8	Denver TV station	9
KDNC	Denver radio station	4

Name	Role	Chapter of 1st appearance
KRISTINE Zowadsky	Night chief, NPA Crisis Center	7
KTAD-5	Denver television station	6
LaGRANDE, Oregon	Town with Wednesday Quilting Circle	11
LAKEY, "Bulldog"	*Herald*'s night editor	4
LARRY Shafner	Farmer from Wray on train	2
LAUREL, Oliver	Denver chief of Homeland Security	9
MANCHESTER, Sylvester	Railroad boss of Joe and Harran	4
MANNHEIM	Mannheim grain elevators in Seattle	18
MANUEL Gomez	Shakespeare Group, Salt Lake City, Utah bomb	1
MARION Wayman	Peter's mother	1
MATTHEW Williamson	Peter's grandfather on Wray farm	8
MONTY Montropovich	Engineer; Peter's good friend; prior NPA student	1
NPA	National Peace Academy, 3-year old higher education institution similar to military academies	1
PETER Wayman	Leader, Shakespeare Group; organizer of hijacking plan	1
PRESIDENT	President of the United States	24
PROFESSOR MacLeod	NPA professor; Oregon's poet laureate	15
QUEEN ANNE PARK	Park overlooking Mannheim grain elevators	20
RANCOR	U.S. Coast Guard Cutter in Elliott Bay	24
RAVENHEAD, Terrence III	National FBI Deputy Director "III"	6
RUTH Fitzwater	Shakespeare Group, stays in Denver; delivers messages, bombs highway; Dave's friend, Ella's granddaughter	2
SADRIEH	Chanto's friend, with CB radio at home	7

Name	Role	Chapter of 1st appearance
SCAR	Rider on spray truck of deadly gas, injured face in wreck; assassin	14
SEATICON	Conference center in Seattle hosting mediation	20
SHAKESPEARE GROUP	Cover name for student group at Auraria College in Denver; planners and perpetrators of hijacking	1
SHELLY Smith-Jones	Administrator, Serv-U.S. service clubs national office on east coast	10
SIMONET, Chief	Chief of Police in Seattle	20
SLIDER, Ron	KDNC radio manager	5
SMATHERS	FBI agent, Denver office	4
SWITZER	FBI agent, III's traveling assistant	9
III (Terrence Ravenhead III)	FBI's third-in-charge in Washington, D.C.; takes charge of stopping train and punishing internal terrorism	6
TAULISON, Mayor Judith	Mayor of Seattle, WA	15
TIM (Timothy)	Hunter from Nevada	15
TIMMERMAN, Tim	KTAD-5 television station manager	6
TOM Buchanan	Shakespeare Group, 2nd in charge; Seattle bomb, and liaison with mayor	1
U.S.A.S.	*Unite Surplus and Starving*, name of group claiming bombing responsibility	4
WILMA Fletcher	Reporter, *Rocky Mountain Herald* newspaper, on board train as U.S.A.S. voice	*2*
WRAY	Farm town in eastern Colorado	1

# # #

"About The Author"

Burton Mitchell wakes with the sun, and enjoys every new day in Highlands Ranch, beautiful Colorado near Denver.

Burton grew up (some would disagree) in Salt Lake City, Utah. Ed and Martha Lea were great parents, Jennet was a fun younger sister. Vacations back to the family home town of Shawnee, Oklahoma, were highlights of every year with swarming aunts, uncles, and cousins. Wonderful memories seem like yesterday -- fishing near the cabin at Shawnee Lake, roaming the chicken pen and garden, delicious food and overflowing love and fun.

Career choices were a struggle, for someone who felt they could accomplish almost anything. College was a hop-scotch: Whitworth in Spokane, U. of Oklahoma, U. of Utah, Mexico City College, U. of Denver, and finally, a B.A. degree in Social Sciences.

Burton and Kathryn married and started their family, then he returned for accounting classes and a better job as Sales & Use Tax Field Auditor for the City and County of Denver. Once more the hop-scotch to business offices at Stapleton International Airport, Theatres & Arenas, and Public Works, with a switch to Human Relations, then finishing in Parks & Recreation. That's a 33-year career in a packed nutshell, with a well-earned retirement in 2006. Kathryn retired from Denver Public Schools after 27 years, another captive of the security of government bureaucracy.

The ministry had been a dream of youth, but it didn't work out. Burton always wanted to help others, and is still working on that. Massage therapy presented itself as a healing tool during rehab from a minor car accident. He took classes to become certified, and is now building a massage business with people in the privacy of their own homes.

His thoughts have always seemed to form themselves into phrases wanting and needing to be written on paper. So observations and poems have just kept coming through all the experiences, filling file folders with no place to go. It may be time to be dusting those off now, giving them a chance to see the light of day with another novel, or bit of poetry. Kathryn also wants to collaborate with him to share her enlightening, rewarding, and frustrating experiences with children and not-so-grown-ups in the school system. They might include some fun stuff, with a bundle of dog and cat stories thrown in about the other family members. Oh, and the Mitchells love to travel, with even some Florida and Hawaii weeks and Caribbean cruises having helped realize and celebrate retirement.

Burton hopes to meet you at a signing party in your neighborhood bookstore soon, to find out a little about you and your writing dreams and projects.

Contact him online at www.burtonmitchell.com.

Reader's Notes to this first-time author

"Compliments:"

"Criticisms:"

"Suggestions to use in writing the second book:"

Please take a moment to send these ideas on for careful consideration, as sort of an honorary writer's group nationwide, to Burton's website:

www.burtonmitchell.com

Celebration Page

It is June 26, 2009, on the eve of the first printing. I let out a whoop from our computer office and my wife Kathryn came hurriedly in.

"What's all the excitement?" she asked.

"This!" I exclaimed, and pointed at the computer screen.

The headline of the article reads "First-Ever U.S. National Peace Academy Launched." Here are pictures of a room full of people seated at tables, two young people holding up a flip chart page of notes, a woman with a microphone gesturing, and a row of people standing and looking at a man with a microphone. Oh, my gosh, it is finally happening for real.

Sure enough, the article reports that on March 2-4, 2009, at Case Western Reserve University in Cleveland, Ohio, "over 170 academicians, business leaders, government officials, field practitioners, and community leaders from around the nation and 10 other countries gathered...to design and establish a National Peace Academy in the United States."

I couldn't believe it. I feel like I have just found the pot of gold at the end of my rainbow of dreams. I'm all smiles.

Here's a picture of the sweet and dynamic Elise Boulding, named honorary chair of the Advisory Board, who gave a video welcome to the participants in this Global Stakeholder Design Summit. Now there's a mover and shaker in the peace community: Quaker sociologist, author, researcher, Imaging Workshop leader. I remember that her husband Kenneth was one of those appointed by Congress to tour grass roots America as the Commission on Proposals for the National Academy of Peace and Conflict Resolution in 1978-79. I was fortunate to be at the right place and time to give a ride to several Commissioners after the meeting on the University of Colorado campus, up to the reception at the Boulding's home in Boulder. Oh, the dreams we peacemakers dreamed together.

Following that, back in 1984, Congress created and funded the U.S. Institute of Peace, based on Commission findings and recommendations. It continues a strong international mission today, and can be found on *www.usip. org*. The National Peace Foundation also grew out of those years, activists from the grass roots campaign continuing as a body of citizens interested in establishing foundations for peace through education, conflict resolution, and people to people exchanges, found on *www.nationalpeace.org*.

But it was even further back in 1976, our exciting bi-centennial year, that I was first given the powerful idea. I wrote to every U.S. senator and representative about the need for a National Peace Academy to rival our military academies. (The U.S. Air Force Academy is just over the hill in Colorado Springs, a model of how much can be done with imagination, resources, sense of purpose, and political will. Why not build one to help keep the peace--non-violently?) Some responses from Congress bore the good news: It's already happening in Senate Bill 1976! They were way ahead of me.

However, when all those efforts after ten years did not produce an actual academy, my enthusiasm in the real world shifted to an imaginary campus. I started a novel in 1986 to picture it already up and running. By 1995, I completed and copyrighted T.E.J.T.M., and no agent would touch it. After five more years, I got hopeful again and revised the time line, and still the literary agents were icy.

Seven years passed. I have now been working for a year on updating it once more, sent out the letters and got the good luck elsewhere responses. I may not have a bestseller book, but I know I have a bestseller idea that is worth self-publishing.

Then today, on June 26, it happened all over again when I found out that they were still way ahead of me. I stumbled on the web site listing today for *www.nationalpeaceacademy.us*, when I was looking for the National Peace Foundation. There they reported that inspired Congress persons had introduced bills in 2001, '03, '05, '07, and '09 to create a Department of Peace, with a Peace Academy. Déjà vu. The idea keeps going, and going, and going...

So it is with pride, pleasure, and humility that I bring these compelling pictures in my imagination to join hands with the visionaries and pragmatists in the real world. Let the sparks continue to fly in animated dialogue, rekindling one of humankind's brightest hopes and best challenges--living an honorable life of peace.

Happy Birthday, National Peace Academy! And many happy returns!

(P.S. To add even more candles to the celebration, this is the anniversary of my mom's birthday, June 26, 1911.)

#   #   #